John Katzenbach

IN THE HEAT
OF THE SUMMER

THE
SHADOW MAN

By the same author

Fiction
THE TRAVELLER
DAY OF RECKONING
JUST CAUSE
STATE OF MIND
HART'S WAR

Non-fiction
FIRST BORN: THE DEATH OF ARNOLD ZELEZNIK

John Katzenbach Omnibus

IN THE HEAT
OF THE SUMMER

THE
SHADOW MAN

JOHN
KATZENBACH

timewarner
paperbacks

A *Time Warner* Paperback

This omnibus edition first published in Great Britain by
Time Warner Paperbacks in 2003
John Katzenbach Omnibus Copyright © John Katzenbach 2003

Previously published separately:
In the Heat of the Summer first published in Great Britain in 1992 by
Michael Joseph
Published by Warner Books in 1996
Reprinted 1996, 1998, 1999, 2001
Copyright © John Katzenbach 1982

The Shadow Man first published in Great Britain in 1995 by
Little, Brown and Company
Published by Warner Books in 1996
Reprinted 1996 (three times), 2000
Copyright © John Katzenbach 1995

Excerpt from 'The Feel-Like-I'm-Fixin'-To-Die Rag' copyright © 1965 by
Joe MacDonald; Alcatraz Corner Music 1978. Used by permission

The moral right of the author has been asserted.

A CIP catalogue record for this book is
available from the British Library.

ISBN 0 7515 3509 5

Printed and bound in Great Britain by
Mackays of Chatham plc, Chatham, Kent

Time Warner Paperbacks
An imprint of
Time Warner Books UK
Brettenham House
Lancaster Place
London WC2E 7EN

www.TimeWarnerBooks.co.uk

IN THE HEAT
OF THE SUMMER

For Maddy

CHAPTER ONE

A runner found the first victim near the thirteenth green.

He was an ordinary man, middle-aged, worried about his heart and his paunch; a broker whose mind fixed on figures, stocks and options as he pounded out laps around the perimeter of the golf course. It was a private club in the midst of an exclusive section of the county, a place of manicured lawns, high pines and sweeping palms. The morning heat had risen fast and hard, and the runner traveled his route out of instinct and familiarity, not watching where his feet landed. He had circled the golf course three times, thinking more about the Dow and his work and what he would do with this holiday off than of what he was passing. As he cut by the edge of the green his hand came up reflexively to wipe the sweat from his eyes, and in the same quick clearing motion he noticed a streak of color in the ferns, ground palms and brush of the rough, a shape amidst the morning shadows.

The broker kept running, listening to the muffled sound of his feet hitting the fairway. He finished another long pass of the course, wondering what it was that had caught his eye.

And so, as he approached the thirteenth green

for the fourth and final swing, he slowed his pace gradually in order to get a longer look. He was aware then, suddenly, of the heat and the sun that seemed suspended over the golf course like a lamp. This time he saw flesh and a glimpse of blond hair. He stopped and sucked in his breath for a moment, then stepped through the scrub brush to the body. 'Oh my God,' he said out loud, though no one could hear him. He told me later that when he realized what it was that he was looking at, it took all the wind out of him like a hard sprint and that for a moment he had stood dizzily in the sun, locked in place, trying to catch his lost breath. He said he'd never seen a murdered person before; that he'd stared in mingled horror and fascination for a minute, maybe two, and then he'd run as fast as he was able, heart starting to pound so loud he thought he could hear it, for the nearest house and a telephone to call the police.

The victim was a teenage girl.

I did not realize then, at the beginning, that it would become the biggest story of my life. Nor did I have any precognition, any reporter's sixth-sense suspicion, that I would be drawn into the story, my usual detachment shattered and ultimately abandoned. The story took place during that year's hurricane season. It started in July at the time that the first big storms of summer begin to gather thousands of miles away across the Atlantic. It is the mean season in Miami; the tropical sun hits the city streets like a spotlight, eliminating all shadow and shade, leaving the air thick and still with an angry heat.

In its own way the story followed the same pattern

as a big storm, gathering momentum as it developed.
I remember that there was a big storm forming then, in
the Caribbean off the coast of Venezuela. It had blown
up in the waters off Africa, then ridden the air currents
across the expanse of ocean, a huge, misshapen force
of wind and rain. It was the first storm of the season
and the National Weather Service had dubbed it Amy,
which turned out to be the name of the first victim.

A large weather chart hung in the rear of the
newsroom which, during the storm season, was
marked with the locations and courses of all the
storms. Following the path on the map was a
part of all the cityside reporters' lives; daily we
would check the progress of the storm, check the
assignments, talk about the chances and point at
the satellite photos transmitted by the wire services.
The photo of that storm, I remember, showed a great
diffuse mass of swirling gray clouds, superimposed
over the map of the Caribbean. It seemed then that
the Florida peninsula was like some large beckoning
finger reaching down toward the storm. We would
watch the photos for the signs that this storm was
going to change, gather shape and consolidate into a
hurricane and come raging and screaming across the
waters toward the city.

On the wall next to the weather chart was a framed
old photograph, yellowed and creased, a reminder for
all of us who worked at the *Journal*. It was taken during
the 1939 storm, a Force Three blow. It showed a large
palm tree bent over so that the trunk was parallel to
the ground. In the background I could make out the
wave of water some twelve feet high that had swept

across Miami Beach and the Bay and finally spent itself on Biscayne Boulevard downtown.

Of course, the story was not about a hurricane, but in their own way, I thought afterwards, the killings seemed much the same; blowing up in some strange distant place, then breaking over the city like a wave, propelled by some great natural force. I remember that on the day of the first murder, the Fourth of July, a year before the Bicentennial, the year after the President resigned, we were all preoccupied with that first big storm off the Venezuelan coast, watching it suck up strength from the warm Caribbean waters. The newsroom was filled with talk about that storm; it seemed it would reach up and become a Force Five storm, the deadliest. The paper bannered speculative stories about the storm's murderous potential. We were long overdue for a major blow, the old hands in the office said, and there was a sense of foreboding that this particular gray mass of wind and rain some two thousand miles away was destined for us.

We were wrong, of course; it never did hit Miami but turned inland instead, rushing ashore in Central America where it killed many people and left many others homeless. That was a few weeks later, however. Then, in early July, it had all our attention, and, at least in my memory, serves as an excuse for why our eyes were elsewhere when the season's true storm broke in our midst.

I went into the office early on the Fourth; it was my first day back at work after my uncle's funeral. I didn't have to work that day, but I returned restless after the trip north, and I wanted something to take the scenes of family out of my head. I find now that my mind tends to run the two together, the teenager's murder and my uncle's suicide, as if they were part of the same play, though they took place a few days and hundreds of miles apart. There weren't many people in the newsroom, it being the holiday and early. I checked my mailbox, which was empty, and glanced over the first edition of the Miami *Post*, which was already out. I sat at my desk and thought of calling Christine to tell her I was home, but she was probably already at the hospital, handing over the sponges, clamps and scalpels in the theater, watching the doctors cut away another cancer. I'd call later, I thought, and we would be together for dinner. I opened the *Post*'s sports pages to check on the baseball scores, but my eyes fastened instead on Nolan, the city editor.

Nolan was a large man, well over six feet, with a sort of constant stoop that made him appear wider, slower than he was; but on a big story, he would straighten suddenly, as if shedding pounds and worries simultaneously, his mind focused on the details. He would lose his joking, playful tone, too, gaining instead a drill sergeant's swiftness and purpose. He was immensely popular in the newsroom, able to joke with reporters one instant, deal with management the next.

Now he was sitting in the center of the newsroom at a bank of desks talking animatedly on the phone. I saw him scribble a few notes, then hang up the phone with a sudden, satisfied motion, turning at the same time to look across the newsroom to see who was in. Our eyes met, and he got up and walked quickly to my desk. He pulled up a chair.

'I didn't expect to see you in,' he said. 'How'd it go?' He had a shock of dark hair, a child's cowlick that poked down between his eyes so that it bobbed as he spoke, as if underscoring his words.

'Pretty much like you'd think. Tears. A lot of talk about wasted lives. God's will, about going to a better place.'

'Sounds grim.'

'It was.'

'You OK?'

'I'm here, aren't I?' I smiled. 'Intact. One model 1970 journalist. High mileage but runs good.'

'OK, OK,' he said. 'Feel like a story, or do you want to take it easy for a couple of days?'

'A story, a story. My kingdom for a story. What there is of it, at least.'

'How about a murder?' he said.

'You want me to commit one?'

'Christ,' he said. 'What turned you into a comedian?'

'I'm sorry,' I said. 'I'm just trying to put it all behind me.'

Nolan's eyebrows rose, fixing me quizzically, cautiously. 'OK,' he said, 'whatever you want. A beer later if you feel like talking it out . . . A beer later, even if you don't.'

I laughed, and he grinned at me.

'But right now, a murder,' he said. 'Your basic blood and guts, cops and robbers, slow-news-day murder.'

'What kind?'

'A teenage girl. Probably from some wealthy family. Her body was discovered just a short time ago over at the Riviera Golf Club.'

6

'Sounds good so far,' I said. 'What else do you know?'

'Not much. You remember that homicide lieutenant who said he owed me a favor after we held off on the kidnapping story? Well, he just called me. He just dispatched a team out there and he didn't have too much information, only the location and the teenage girl. Could be good. I plan to keep that lieutenant paying off that debt for some time.'

'Was she raped?'

'I don't know. Why don't you take the photographer and go out and take a look? Call me on the radio when you get a handle.'

'OK,' I said. I got up, grabbed a notebook from the pile I kept on my desk and headed back toward the photography department.

'Hey,' Nolan called. 'Were you close to your uncle?'

'When I was small,' I said. 'In a small way.'

Andrew Porter liked to push the big car around corners, one hand on the wheel, the other gesturing at the early-morning traffic. Most of it seemed to be young people heading out to the beaches. A number of boats were being towed, and traffic was already backing up at the entrance to McArthur Causeway and Key Biscayne. We were hurrying in the opposite direction, moving along fast enough so that I could barely see the faces of the people in the waiting cars. The photographer's voice droned on, a story about another murder assignment, sometime in the past. The sound was low and mingled with the sound of the engine and the air conditioner blasting on high. At one point I watched him load his camera, one hand in his lap winding the film, the other resting loosely on the top of the steering wheel. 'Did this once at ninety-plus up on Route Four forty-one. High-speed chase, a couple of kids in a stolen car, a highway trooper and myself all screaming down the highway. Didn't have time to be scared.' He was laughing.

I thought how slowly the line of cars had moved from the church to the cemetery. I could see the hearse when it swung around a corner, and the long black Cadillac with my father and his brother's wife, right behind it. It had rained all morning, and the windshield wipers beat a kind of muffled drum dirge. My ears were still filled with the sound of the 'Marine Corps Hymn' that had cascaded from the organ through the church; a large, slow sound, the familiar cadence almost unrecognizable when played to celebrate the dead instead of the living. I remember how surprised I'd been when I saw the casket draped with the flag; the vivid colors seemed out of place, incongruous in that gray day and darkened church.

The priest had spoken first. 'Hear our prayer, Father, for the soul of Lewis Anderson, and grant him the peace in heaven that he sought here on earth . . .'

Peace, I had thought. The opposite of war.

My uncle had been a bear of a man, long arms that carried bunched muscles, a chest as broad as a knight's shield. His voice had always been deep and even in his laughter carried a menacing tone, a strained pitch that demanded attention. Then he

8

would fix me a look from his one good eye that would leave me cold and afraid.

He'd lost the right eye on Iwo Jima. Halfway up Suribachi, he said, just before the flag raising; he'd missed that moment, too drugged out on morphine and shock to understand what was taking place around him. He told me once that it was an odd sensation, losing the eye; he thought at first that he was dying, then that it was all happening to someone else.

He could feel the blood, he said, and the pain, like an explosion in his brain. But still, he was convinced, not him. Not then. Someone else entirely.

When I was young, he would give me things. Books about the Corps; a purple heart. A Rising Sun flag, a spoil from Tarawa. For Christmas once, he gave me a long, curved hunting knife in an expensive leather sheath. 'That'll come in handy,' he said. It stayed on my bureau for years. He told me: 'You ever need anything, anything at all, you know where you can get it.'

But I never asked.

Then the priest read from Ecclesiastes. The familiar section: to every time, there is a season. I remembered the popular song that had taken the words and set them to music. It sounded different, more sonorous, when read in a church, echoing through the rafters.

He and his wife would show up at holidays: Thanksgiving, Christmas, sometimes on birthdays . . . all the strained times. He had no children of his own, I never knew why.

On those evenings, he would drink too much. I

9

would watch him as he rendered himself pleasantly drunk, pouring and sipping, an endless chain; forgetful of most things, but humming the hymn to himself, his good eye dulled, his fake eye wide open, seeing nothing.

At night, sometimes, I would hear him call out in his sleep.

After the priest finished reading, there was silence, and then my father went up to the altar. The light seemed to reflect the colors of the flag; my father's face caught the light and he was bathed in a multicolored glow. 'In 1941 my brother went away to war,' he said. I listened closely. 'I am not sure that he ever came back . . .

I thought: We blame the war. Blame Iwo Jima. Say he left more there than his eye. I put my hand to my forehead, then covered my eyes. I could hear my father's voice rising and falling in the church.

On the telephone he'd been matter-of-fact. 'Your uncle has killed himself,' he said. 'I'm sorry to have to tell you.'

'How did it happen?' I asked. The journalist.

'There was nothing specific. In fact, he'd just been offered a new position by a university in the South. Fund raising, overseeing academic programs. The stuff he was good at.'

'Had he been drinking?'

'Your aunt says no. She said he was sober, but he'd been looking over his old scrapbooks, from when he was in the Marines. He didn't say anything to her, she said, just went upstairs and took a pistol from his study. A twenty-two, a target gun he kept. Then he went into the bathroom, closed the door and shot himself.'

'No note? No message?'

'Nothing.'

'I'm sorry for you,' I said.

'In a way, it's a relief. He'd been so unhappy for so long.'

'Why?'

'Who knows?'

But of course, I thought then, you know. Who else would know?

My father finished speaking, and the organist hit the first few chords of the hymn. From the shores of Montezuma – where? To here. A church, a funeral. There was an honor guard, and they carried the casket out to the hearse. *Semper Fi.* I followed them out. They slipped the casket into the back and stepped away. Their movements were economical, exaggerated. Precise military motion, I thought, it masks everything with pomp. My aunt was crying, but my father's eyes were dry. He seemed to be directing traffic, and we all slipped into the cars for the ride to the cemetery.

The service at the grave had been quicker than I thought it would be. The priest read again, traditional things: ashes to ashes, dust to dust. I didn't listen. I watched the faces of all the people who were there. I looked over at my own brother. If he were dead, I thought, how would I feel? I found myself listening to the rain striking the canopy over the grave. To the side the gravediggers waited next to a backhoe, patiently. I thought one must learn patience by working in a

11

graveyard. And then the service ended. We shook hands and murmured best wishes. I found my father.

'I have to go back,' I said.

'There's going to be food and drink at your aunt's. I'd like you to come.'

'I have to go back,' I repeated. 'There's a flight this afternoon. I can get a cab.'

'All right,' he said and turned away.

I thought of the storm off Venezuela. I tried to imagine the center, the winds racing in concentric circles, ever tighter. I had to get back.

'There it is,' Porter said excitedly.

I looked ahead and saw a half-dozen police cars, their lights gleaming in the sunlight, parked haphazardly by the side of the road. There was a knot of the curious standing a few feet away, on the lawn of a large, stately mansion. I saw the medical examiner's yellow car and a green and white panel truck that was used by the crime-scene technicians. We pulled in behind the first police cruiser. 'Hot damn, we beat everybody else. Not a television camera in sight.' Porter had already draped one camera around his neck and was adjusting another. 'Let's go,' he said, 'before they get everything covered up.' He bounded from the car and set out across the fairway in a rush. I followed him, a few feet behind, a half-trot, half-walk.

On the thirteenth green a uniformed officer stopped us with a barked 'Hold it!' He came up and said, 'That's close enough.'

'I can't get any shots from here,' Porter said. 'Just a

little closer. Don't worry, I won't shoot anything you don't want shot. '

The cop shook his head. I stepped in.

'Who's in charge?'

'Detective Martinez,' he said. 'Also Detective Wilson. You talk to them when they're finished. You wait here for now.' Then he turned his back on us.

'I'm going over there,' Porter said, pointing to the rough. 'Got to get a better angle.' He walked away, trying to keep out of the policeman's sight. I saw one of the detectives look my direction, and I waved. He walked over.

'How you doing, Martinez?' I said. 'What have you got?'

'Haven't seen you for a while,' he said. 'Not since that trial in March.' I remembered then that he'd been the chief witness in the trial of a teenage kid accused of murdering a tourist who'd asked for directions. The case had attracted lots of publicity, especially when the defense attorney had argued that the teenager had been rendered insane by daily life in the ghetto. A novel defense; the jury had been out for two hours before rejecting it. Everyone in the newsroom had thought it was pretty funny.

'There's just not enough quality crime, you know what I mean?'

Martinez laughed. 'Yeah, just the run-of-the-mill killings, rapes, robberies. None of the good stuff.'

'You got it,' I said. 'But tell me, maybe we've got something here?'

He looked at me. 'Bloody,' he said. 'Teenage girl, probably sixteen or seventeen, judging from her backside. Dr. Smith is here, but he hasn't turned her yet. It appears she was shot in the back of the head with a powerful handgun. A magnum three fifty-seven maybe. Possibly a forty-five or a forty-four special. Something big, though; most of the back of her head is gone.'

I had my notebook out and was taking notes. The detective looked at me for a moment, then continued. 'Christ, it makes you feel bad, seeing a kid like that get herself killed.'

I took down his words verbatim.

'One odd thing, though, but it's not for publication yet.'

'What's that?'

'Not for a story yet?' He pushed his question at me.

'OK, OK. What's the story?'

'Her hands were bound behind her. I haven't seen that kind of a shooting since' – he thought for a moment – ' that mobster, the gambler we found out in the Glades. You remember?'

'You mean what they call "execution-style"?'

He laughed. 'That's right. Now why would someone want to execute a teenager?'

'Was she raped?'

'Can't tell for certain, but all her clothes seem in place and intact. Can't figure that,' he said.

'What's she wearing?'

'Jeans. T-shirt. Sandals. The usual teenager outfit.' He paused and looked up. 'Oh boy,' he said, 'here come your brothers and sisters.' I looked back and saw that the television people had arrived.

They came in squads: a soundman, reporter and cameraman. 'Look,' Martinez said, 'catch me later. Talk to the doctor. Talk to that guy over there, with the shorts. He found the body. Talk to him. One other thing . . .'

'What's that?'

'Get the story from me. Wilson's got a teenage daughter himself. He appears pretty strung out about this already.'

'OK,' I said. 'Hey, any identification on her?'

'Later,' the detective said. He hurried back across the green.

With the arrival of the television cameras several of the uniformed officers who had been poking about in the underbrush came over to keep them back. They seemed happy to film from afar as the policemen went through the motions of searching the scene. I walked back to our car and called the city desk on the car radio. A secretary answered, and in a moment I heard Nolan's voice come scratching through the speaker. 'So,' he said, 'what've you got?'

'It's good,' I said. 'An abduction perhaps. I don't know. It seems like a real weird one. The girl's hands were tied behind her back. She was shot execution-style. That's not for publication yet, but it will be shortly.'

'Good art?'

'I think so. Andy Porter's off in the bushes with a long lens. Lots of cops searching the scene.'

'Sounds good. Better than the Glorious-Fourth-parade shot that we're planning on running.' I could hear him laughing.

15

'Listen, I need someone to start on something for me.'

'What? You name it.'

'Have someone call the missing persons bureau and the local desks for the cops. See if anyone called in last night or yesterday from the Gables with a missing kid report. Just a chance.'

'Good idea. I'll get somebody to start before the cops think of doing the same thing. See you later.'

I hung up the radio and stepped back outside. I could feel the sweat under my arm, sticky, unpleasant. The sky seemed to stretch infinitely high in an expanse of blue. There were no clouds, just the sun, the blue sky and the heat. I walked off to find the man who'd discovered the body.

He was standing by one of the cruisers. I introduced myself, and he told me that he read the *Journal* every day. He was a stocky man, short, with his hair cropped Republican-close.

'This kind of thing has never happened to me before. Even when I was in the Army, back in '54, I never saw anything like that.'

'Exactly how was it?' I asked. I took down his words in the notebook. He seemed upset enough and articulate enough to provide a sidebar to the main story.

'I remember looking at her arms. They were thin, a child's arms. They were pulled back, but not tightly, you know; more relaxed, as if the killer didn't want to hurt her. I mean, I would expect them to be pulled back tightly.' And he held his arms behind his back to demonstrate, thrusting his shoulder backward. 'Like

16

that. But that wasn't the case.' I continued taking notes as he talked.

'I could see her face. It was like she was resting, in a way, though I could see that most of the back of her head was gone.' He swallowed. 'That sounds cold, doesn't it? I don't really know what came over me. I was standing there, looking at her, my mind registering all the clinical perceptions: how she was lying, how her head was resting, the matted mess the blood had made of her hair. Blond hair.

'I went through it all with the detective, you know; simple, to the point, just the details. And then, you know what happened? I got sick, over there.' He pointed at some bushes. 'I guess you guys see bodies all the time. Murders.'

'Enough. Tell me, what do you do for a living?'

I half-listened as he went through his personal history. He told me about the running, and his route and the morning sun and that he must have run by her at least three times. 'My own kids are younger.'

'Can we get your picture?'

'I'd rather not,' he said, after thinking a moment. 'Do you have to use my name in the papers?'

'Oh, yes,' I said. 'No question about it.'

'Well, I wish you didn't have to. I don't suppose I'll sleep much until they catch the guy.'

'I wouldn't worry about that,' I said.

'Why not?'

'Well, it seems to me that some guy who gets off on tying up and killing teenage girls isn't going to want to take on an adult.' He nodded. 'But I'll tell

17

you one thing,' I said. 'I would try to steer clear
of the television guys; otherwise you'll be all over
the air.'

'Thanks,' he said. 'I'll keep that in mind.' When I
left him I saw him step back further into the shadows
alongside the road. I walked over to Porter who was
standing by the car, talking on the radio to the photo
studio.

'I got a shot of that guy you were talking to,' he
said. 'It's with a long lens, but I think it'll come out
all right. You think I can get a close-up?'

'No way. And it might point him out to the
television guys.'

'OK,' he said. 'Let's hang around until they bring
the body out. The desk always likes that shot, the body
bag on the stretcher. Just like in Vietnam, some black
bag with a zipper. Isn't technology marvelous?'

'You're a cynic.'

'Who isn't?'

We waited in the shade by the roadway, watching
the policemen work. After a short while they carried
out a stretcher. Porter said, 'Here comes my shot.'
There was a flurry of excitement as the television
cameramen ran alongside the rescue-squad men
when they brought the body out of the bushes. I
watched as they slipped the black bag into the rear
of their ambulance. I noticed that Porter had joined
the television people and was snapping off pictures
rapidly. At one point he looked up at me, smiled and
pointed at the body bag. I saw the medical examiner
making his way across the fairway, so I walked out
into the sun to talk with him. He was lighting a

pipe when I stopped him. 'What can you tell me?' I asked.

'Won't know too much until I get her cut open. Appears that it was a large-caliber handgun. Probably only one shot, judging from the extent of the damage. Appears to have been fired at close range, maybe a foot, eighteen inches.'

'How can you tell?'

'Stippling, the residue of powder around the wound. Really have a better estimate when I get it under a microscope. Just guessing now – but I'm a good guesser.'

'Any sign of sexual abuse?'

'Oddly, no. Makes one wonder, doesn't it? I mean, teenage girls aren't ordinarily murdered in that fashion.'

'What can you tell me about the way her hands were tied?'

'Not much. The crime-lab boys took the rope.'

'Are you sure she was killed here? Not just dumped here afterwards?'

'Oh, yes. I found some matter that was blown away in the explosion on some of the nearby palm fronds.'

'Got any theories? Any more good guesses?'

The doctor laughed. 'It'll turn out to be either a jealous boyfriend or a sex-crazed stepfather. Either way, it's OK for you people. Still a good story.'

I ignored his crack. The doctor puffed hard on his pipe, and I could smell the aroma of the tobacco mixing with the smell of the mown grass. 'Any idea who she is?'

'Ask the detectives,' he said. 'Why don't you call me later, after I've finished with the postmortem? She goes to the top of the list. I'll probably be finished by early afternoon.'

'All right,' I said. 'I'll talk to you then.' I saw Martinez and his partner, Wilson, standing by their unmarked car, dealing with a crowd of television reporters. I walked over to the scene to listen. Martinez seemed exasperated. It seemed that someone knew about the hands being tied. So much for it being off the record. Wilson was talking. He was an older man, probably in his mid-forties, on the elderly side for a homicide detective. He had a shock of black hair streaked with gray, a chin that was thrust forward in a constant state of defiance. He was wearing a conservative blue suit with a small American flag in the lapel, and his face was reddened by the sun and by the questions. As I stepped up, I heard him say, 'Listen! I'm not giving out any details. It just seems pathetic. I mean' – and he paused, looking out at the cameras – 'what's a kid like that ever done? I mean teenagers got the same right to grow up and get old like the rest of us. I just hate it when I see one like that. It really gets to you.' He was glaring now, angry. 'It really seems a shame,' he said. 'Lot you guys care.'

Martinez cut in. 'C'mon, Phil. That's enough. Let's go.' He looked across at me, and I saw him raise his eyebrows slightly. I wrote down what Wilson had said, shaking my head.

It's a job for them, I thought, it's a job for us. No difference.

'We'll catch this guy,' Wilson was saying. 'And I hope he rots away in prison. I wish we had the chair back.'

'C'mon, Phil. Enough.' Martinez had slipped behind the wheel of the car and started the engine. 'Let's go.'

Wilson looked down at him. 'All right,' he said. He looked back at the cameras. 'There'll be an official statement later.' Then he slid into the seat and slammed the door. The sound was like a shot at the start of a race. There was a quick surge of activity as the camera crews began to wrap up and head out. I found Porter waiting in the car. He had the air conditioner on.

'Hot day for a murder,' he said. 'Listen, I want to stop and get a parade shot before we go in, OK?'

'No problem.' He wheeled the car back onto the roadway, tires complaining.

'The glorious Fourth,' he said. 'Last year it was Watergate. The year before, the end of the war. Next year, the Bicentennial. A lot of people dressed up to look like George Washington. Transvestites, probably.' He laughed. 'I mean, who cares?' He paused and thought for a moment. 'I guess Boy Scouts care. I remember when I was a kid marching in the parade. It wasn't half bad; made me feel like it was really summer. Gotta say that for it.'

I thought of my uncle, in his uniform. My father kept the photo framed in his study. My uncle seemed young and strong. The blue and red dress outfit seemed stark, imposing; a blaze of color that meant more than clothing. When I was young I would look

21

at it with awe and fascination, as if it were possible to put on a uniform and wear bravery and strength and manhood at the same time. In the photo the colors were as vivid as emotions. My mind filled with the music at the funeral, and then I realized the window was rolled down and I could hear the strains of a marching band, the heavy thumping of bass drums and feet, a few blocks away. We parked the car.

'If we try to get much closer, we'll never get out,' Porter said. 'Come on. It's about three blocks away. Just a small parade down the main street. There's a bigger parade later, but I like to shoot the high school kids. They're fresher than some hotshot college marching band.'

I thought for an instant about the girl on the thirteenth green. She probably would have spent the day on the sidewalk watching. Or maybe she would have been a marcher. Blond hair, strutting her youth down the center of the street. I followed Porter toward the growing sound of music and recognized the strains of 'Stars and Stripes Forever.' What's a parade without Sousa?

The crowd was sparse but appreciative. There were lots of small children with balloons and children in strollers. The band was playing a hit song barely recognizable through the orchestration. The sun glinted-off the brass instruments and I heard the sound of feet in cadence. Porter melted through the people and slipped into the street. I had a view of him, ducking and swerving, running in front of the marchers, shooting pictures. As the music swelled and diminished, my eyes fixed on a group of baton twirlers floating down the center of the street, their silver sticks flailing in bursts of light around them. The girls wore gold uniforms that reflected the sun, making each, it seemed, gleam especially bright. I watched one girl, on the edge. Her baton seemed to move around her independently, catching the crowd's attention. She stepped back one instant and tossed the baton high into the air. The baton seemed to dance to the band music, twirling against the blue of the sky. Then it fell, tumbling, back toward the girl. Her hand reached out, timing the spin, and she grabbed for the baton.

For a second she seemed to have it, but the same life that she had given it when she tossed it up seemed to infuse it now in her hand, and it broke loose and spun to the ground. The girl broke her rhythm swiftly and swooped down to the baton. In a second it was back in her hand and dancing again, but her face was set, a frown that hid tears. Then she turned and danced out of my view. I thought of the girl on the thirteenth green again. Things were different at that age. A dropped baton brings tears. What else? A broken date, a harsh word, a failed test. No time for death, no tears for the dying.

I listened to the sound of the marching drums until Porter touched my shoulder. 'Back to the real world,' he said.

CHAPTER TWO

It was afternoon when we returned to the office. Porter went back to the photo studio to begin printing his shots, and I walked slowly toward my desk. I saw Nolan up at the city desk. When he spied me, he turned and came half-dancing across the room, his face open with a grin. 'Bingo,' he said.

'What bingo is that?'

'It appears that the dispatcher in the Gables logged at least a half-dozen calls last night from a Mr. and Mrs. Jerry Hooks. He's an executive with Eastern Airlines, top executive, big home in the southwest section, just past the Gables border. He's also got a sixteen-year-old daughter named Amy. She went out last night with friends to a party. Didn't come home again. Bingo.'

'Are you sure that's the one?'

'My police lieutenant just confirmed it, before you came in. He's already sent the two detectives out to the home. I suggest that you follow them.'

I remember thinking that this was the nastiest part of any crime story, especially a murder. Looking at the mangled body was nothing; a cold time of absorbing details. Visiting the victim's family was a different matter, however. I didn't know what to expect. In

25

the past I'd been threatened and embraced, cried on and shouted at. I thought: the dead are so easy to be with, the living so difficult. I collected Porter again – he had just begun his printing process – and we drove back through the city toward the bereaved family.

Martinez and Wilson were standing outside the door when we pulled up. Martinez was wearing reflecting sunglasses so that if you looked into his eyes you saw only yourself. Wilson was wiping his forehead with a white handkerchief. The white of the linen caught the heat somehow; it seemed to glow in his hand. Porter said, 'Welcome to reality, folks,' and we walked across the lawn.

Wilson spoke first. 'Christ, you guys are fast. Just can't wait, can you?'

I stared at him for a moment, then turned to Martinez. 'What's the situation inside?'

He looked at me from behind the sunglasses. 'They seem in shock. I had to tell them that one of them must make the positive identification at the morgue. We're waiting for the father now.'

'How did they take the news?'

'They didn't say anything. It was almost as if they were expecting the worst when the kid didn't come home last night. Apparently she was a regular type, never kept her parents worried, never stayed out late at all.'

'Boyfriend? Suspects?'

'Nobody regular. Nobody they knew who carried a grudge. Nobody she just broke up with, I mean.'

Wilson interrupted. 'She was just a good, straight kid. No drugs. No sex. She was a cheerleader over at

Sunset High. Good grades, all A's and B's. Wanted to be a veterinarian, to go to college. Christ, it makes me sick just thinking about it.' He looked at me, still wiping his forehead with the handkerchief. 'How you going to write this? Let me tell you, you cause this family any more grief and . . .'

'And what?' I said. 'What do you think we are? Christ.' I turned back to Martinez. 'So where do you go from here?'

'Well, we check out the party she went to. But from what the parents say, I doubt it'll be much. Just high school kids. Wait for the autopsy report. Start checking the sex offender file, but that seems like a dead end, too. I mean, this doesn't seem like a sex crime.'

I looked at Wilson. 'What do you think?' He paused, and I finished taking notes on Martinez, scribbling rapidly across the page of my small notebook.

'I think it's some kind of psycho. Who else? We just haven't got a handle yet. We will, though, I promise.' I saw Martinez turn away, as if in frustration over his partner's pledge.

'You know,' the younger detective said, 'most of the time when we get to a murder scene we already know who did it. Then you have the victim on the ground and the guy who killed him standing there with a smoking gun in his hand, crying. Or the wife gets tired of her old man punching her out after a tough day at work and so she blows him away. Or the father forgets to lock up the gun he keeps in the house to protect the family and then sees his five-year-old shoot himself with it. Then there's a

27

smaller percentage, the guy who gets wasted behind the register of his fast-food store in the ghetto. But we usually get them, too, because sooner or later somebody opens their big mouth and we shut it for them. Or drugs. People shoot up, people get shot. Like peanut butter and jelly, that's the way things work. Organized crime is tough. You know, professional killers cover their tracks. But at least we have some idea who did it, and who cares anyway, huh?

'But the smallest percentage are the random killings. Sex crimes fit into that category. The victim and the killer don't know each other. They may just meet that once. Just two lives that touch one instant. No clues, no witnesses, no leads. Real trouble for us. I think that's the kind of crime we've got here. Except for the sex angle; can't figure it.'

'What about the tied hands?' I asked.

'Who knows?' Martinez shrugged.

I looked at the two of them. 'You're holding back something,' I said. 'You give me this big "We got no leads" speech and you're going to make an arrest in the morning, right? On *Post* time. You're holding back. Listen, you don't have to tell me what it is you've got, but let me know what to expect.'

Martinez looked angry and Wilson turned away. 'I'll tell you nothing!' he said. 'A body, hands tied, in the bushes. That's it. Nothing magical. The killer didn't leave his prints on a nice white card with his name and address at the scene! You want an arrest fast? Well, you go make one. Christ.'

I didn't have time to reply because the front door of the house opened. The two detectives stepped back, leaving me a lane to the front. I tried to wipe the anger from my face, and I adopted my most solemn voice. It was a practiced tone I had for dealing with any bereaved family, whether victimized by crime, accident or act of God. I wanted to convey that I felt their tragedy but that at the same time I was insistent on getting my story. I introduced myself first to the man who emerged from the door, then to his wife, a half-step behind him. I could see that their eyes were red with tears.

'I realize that this is a difficult time,' I said. 'But it would be very helpful for me if one of you could take the time to tell me about your daughter, her hopes and dreams.'

The father nodded. He seemed in shock, my words barely registering. He looked toward the two detectives, who remained impassive. 'She's a lovely girl,' he said, his voice in the active tense. 'I mean, nearly perfect. Everyone loves her very much. We're very worried.'

Martinez took him by the arm. 'This will be difficult,' the detective said. 'It's better to get it over with now.' The man nodded, and Wilson and Martinez led him away from the porch to their car. I watched the three of them cross the lawn, the light seeming to accentuate each difficult step. I could hear the clicking and whirring of the camera behind me. I turned to the mother. 'Perhaps we could sit down and talk,' I said. 'They're likely to be some time.' She nodded, and I snaked into the house behind her, leaving the door open so that Porter could slip inside with me.

I watched the mother walk slowly through a

vestibule into a large living room. My eyes searched the room carefully, taking down details as accurately as in my notebook. I quickly asked, 'Do you think I could have a glass of water? It's terribly hot outside.'

She looked confused for a moment, then replied, 'Of course. Let me get you one.' Then she walked through a doorway into what I took to be the kitchen. I used the time to get my bearings, organize my thoughts. I examined one wall of the room which was filled with pictures of the family. I noted the careful placing of the furniture, modern, low-slung. Expensive, I thought. In one corner of the room there was a piano. I registered a question about that. There was a large stereo console and I noted the tides of records that were out; several rock, several classical. There was no television in the living room. I walked to the back of the room and looked out through sliding glass doors onto a rear patio – I could see a swimming pool, some trees and a lawn that appeared lush. In Florida, a green lawn tells you something about the dedication of the homeowners, to fight that battle against the sun. I heard the mother enter and turned to face her. 'I was just admiring your lawn. It reminds me of the North.'

She managed a short smile, as she handed me the glass with ice and water, and glanced at Porter, who was standing in the background, trying to take shots inconspicuously. She seemed almost resigned, gave a small shrug and slipped into a chair. For a moment she rested her head in her hands, and then she looked at me.

'You can't imagine the worry. How scared I am.' Her voice was even, but her eyes were filling with tears. She showed remarkable restraint. 'I didn't sleep last night. Neither did Jerry. Once he went out and just drove around the neighborhood. He said he knew he wouldn't see her but that he felt he had to be doing something. You see, she's never done this before, stayed out all night. None of our kids did.' (The present tense, too, like her husband. It hadn't hit her yet.)

'How many children do you have?' I asked. I was scribbling in my pad as fast as I could. Just keep her talking, I thought. The story will write itself.

'Three,' she said. 'Amy is the youngest. Jerry Junior is a sophomore at Stanford, and his older brother Stephen is in medical school in Boston.'

'Harvard?'

She smiled. 'I suppose he wishes it was. No, at Tufts.'

'Still,' I said, 'that's quite an accomplishment.'

She nodded. 'He was in the war, you see. As a medic with the Americal Division. I can't remember which number. But he saw a lot of action, and I guess it was there that he made up his mind. He came back and took summer-school courses in chemistry and I don't know what else and got accepted. He's in his second year now.'

'Tell me about your daughter,' I asked.

She caught her breath, as if surprised. 'They were all good children. I never had any real trouble. Stephen went to war over our objections, because, he said, he'd graduated from school and thought it was his duty

31

to go. He'd taken all the deferments and everything. Jerry Junior, well, he gave us some worries during high school, with marches and long hair and all that. But it seemed to have less passion for him. We worried mostly about drugs because it seemed everyone at his school was turning on, as they say. But he's done very well at school. He always did well at school, like his brother. I worry sometimes that Amy has had to live up to a great deal. Her brothers are very important to her; she always tried to do what they did, act like they did. I think sometimes it was confusing for her to be a girl and different. She was an outdoors type, and I guess that running and horsing around was more of her upbringing than dolls and – oh, what other things do little girls do? When we moved here – Jerry used to be with Northwest, and for years we lived in Minneapolis. We just came here – oh, two years ago, this October – I was glad because she could still be outside and enjoy herself. It wasn't as if we'd moved to New York City or anything. You know, where you have to worry all the time. And she's such a sensible girl.'

'A cheerleader?'

'That's right.' The mother laughed briefly, a short abrupt sound in the stillness of the living room. 'And vice-president of her class. She's going to be a senior at Sunset. She wants to go and become a veterinarian. I guess that's just a non-threatening approach to her older brother. I think she'll go to medical school, too . . .' And then she caught herself suddenly, like a diver stopped in mid-fall, suspended over the depth of waters. 'That is, of course . . . I don't know. Oh, my

God, what's happened?' And the tears that had been held back burst forth unchecked. The mother gave a low moan and seemed to slump in the chair. It was a moment of defeat, and she seemed to be lost and confused. It was a look I'd seen before. The room was silent except for the whirring of the camera. The mother put her face in her hands and leaned back and forth as if she were physically hurt. 'My God,' she said. 'My child.'

'Please, ma'am,' I said. 'Just another minute or two. Do you have a photo of Amy that we can take along? We'll be happy to send it back. Something recent?'

The mother took her hands away from her face and stared at me. 'A picture?'

'That's right. Yearbook, perhaps, or maybe a family shot?'

'I'll get you one.' She turned to Porter. 'Do you care for a glass of water also?'

Even I was impressed. I thought of fighters I'd seen, the type who could take a solid punch and then keep their wits about them. She stood as Porter nodded, and I watched her move. She was a tall woman, dressed in a simple, colorful dress, stylish, her light brown hair pulled back from her face. I noticed she wore little makeup. It would have run wet from the tears. She moved easily, gracefully. I looked over to Porter as the mother left the room, but he was looking at the photos on the wall. 'These are good,' he said. 'Somebody knows their way around a camera. Or they're professional. Good composition, lighting, the works.'

The mother walked in with a photo in one hand

and a glass in the other. 'Jerry Junior took most of them,' she said. She'd overheard his comments and reacted like any proud mother. 'He may try your profession when he finishes school.'

Porter said, 'Well, if you get a chance, tell him that I thought they were very good.'

She smiled. 'Thank you. It will mean a lot to him.'

She handed me the photo. 'Is that all right?' I looked at it closely. It was of a pretty blond teenager; wide smile, open face. She was wearing jeans and standing by the pool. There was a collie at her feet. 'That's Lady. I'm afraid we had to put her to sleep a few months ago. Amy was heartbroken. I think that's when she decided to become a vet. Jerry Junior took the photo.'

'It's perfect,' I said. It will break the readers' hearts, I thought. 'I'll send it back when we've finished.'

'That would be fine.' For a moment the three of us stood in the room. 'Do you suppose there's any chance, I mean, a possibility, that the police are wrong?' I could see the tears beginning to form again. 'They've been wrong before about these things, I believe. Did you, uh, see the . . .' She couldn't get out the next word.

I decided to lie. 'There are often mistakes. You should wait until you get word that's definite. I saw the remains, but' – I motioned to the picture – 'there's really no way of telling.'

'She was wearing blue jeans and a red-and-blue-striped shirt when she went out last night.'

I looked at Porter. The same mental image must

have passed through his mind at the same instant. He looked away. 'I'm sorry, I didn't get that close.'

But I had.

The mother sat back down. 'It all seems so unreal. It's like I don't know what's happening, but I know it's important. It's like it's happening to someone else. Not me. Like you're here for someone else. It's all a big mistake. Is this real? Oh, my God! I don't know what to feel, what to think.' She looked up at me. 'How can I make sense when the whole world seems suddenly out of whack?' I didn't know what to say.

And then the telephone rang. It was an angry, frightening sound.

The mother walked across the room and picked up the receiver. I listened. I knew what it was, although I could only hear her responses.

'Yes, dear,' she said. 'I'm OK.'

Her face seemed to pinch in suddenly, and her eyes went wide.

'Tell me!' she shouted. 'Tell me!'

I saw her close her eyes and grit her teeth. She sat down on a chair, her back rigid, her face thrust forward.

'I am sitting down! Tell me! Tell me! Tell me!'

And then her hand came up abruptly to her mouth, a single movement of horror.

'Oh, my God,' she said. 'My baby.'

She placed the receiver down carefully, gently, I thought, as if trying not to disturb anything. She looked at me.

'It's her,' she said. Her voice was flat. 'My child. My baby girl.'

35

'Ma'am,' I said. 'Is there someone we can get? A neighbor, perhaps?'

She didn't seem to hear me. 'My baby,' she repeated. Porter jerked his head toward the door. I nodded.

'We're going now, ma'am,' I said. 'We're sorry.'

Her voice remained cold and monotonal. 'Who could do this?' she said. 'What animal would do this? Oh, my God, what has happened? Who would want to kill my baby? Oh, my baby.' Finally the words seemed to break, as if they were crystalline, and she began to moan, rocking back and forth, holding her stomach. The telephone began to ring again, over and over, but she made no move toward it. After a second I stepped over and picked it up. It was her husband.

'Hello, hello, dear?' he was shouting.

'No,' I said. 'This is the reporter from the *Journal*. Listen, I think she needs someone to be with her. A neighbor, maybe?'

The husband seemed confused. There was a silence. Then he said, 'Yes. Next door. The Allens. To the right. I have to give a statement to the police. Tell her I'll be home as soon as possible. Thank you, uh, for helping.'

'We'll get the neighbors,' I said, and I hung up. Porter had handed her the remains of his glass of water and she was gulping it down. 'We're leaving now, ma'am. You'll be OK.' But she didn't seem to hear anything. She continued to moan.

When we stepped outside it seemed, if possible, that it was even hotter. 'Next door,' I said, 'the Allens.'

Porter nodded and ran across the yard. I saw him

step inside for a moment and then reappear, leading a man and a woman across the lawn. He let them into the house and then joined me.

'Did you warn them about the television people? They're sure to be here any minute.'

'I mentioned it,' he said. 'But I don't know if it registered. They'll figure it out, though, soon enough.'

'Let's go, then. Maybe we can catch the father at Police Headquarters. And we're beginning to run tight on time.'

Porter said little, then, and pulled away from the curb slowly. It must be getting to him, I thought, just a little bit, and I smiled. He grabbed the radio and called the photo department to let them know where we were heading. Nolan must have been listening in, because he came on the box next, asking to speak to me. 'So,' I heard him say, 'what's it look like?'

'Nolan,' I said. My voice was full and confident. 'Let me tell you this: I've got a hell of a story.'

The sun seemed to reflect off the road, washing the windshield with a blast of bright light. In silence but for the humming of the air conditioner and the tires on the road, we headed to the center of the city.

I saw the two detectives accompanying the father as they exited the Police Headquarters' side entrance. We were just pulling into the parking lot and I slid from the car before it had fully stopped. I managed to intercept the group a few feet before the police cruiser and placed myself between them and the car. I could hear Porter's steps behind me. 'Mr. Hooks,' I said, 'can I speak with you a moment?' The policemen looked annoyed and hesitated. I could see that the father didn't really place me. 'From the *Journal*,' I said. 'We talked on the phone just a little while ago. The neighbors are with your wife now.'

I could see recognition hit his face. He was reluctant. 'I really don't know what to say. I want to thank you for helping my wife, but I really don't have anything I want to say right now. I just hope they catch the person. I don't see how anyone could do that . . . but I really don't have anything to say. You understand?'

'Of course,' I said. But I didn't move from my position, blocking them from the car. 'Did you suspect anything like this last night?'

'How could I? How could anyone imagine this? Oh, I suppose I was worried. Who wouldn't be? I called all the emergency rooms in the city, to see if she'd been brought in. I thought she'd been in a car accident. That's what really scared me. A car accident. But I don't really want to say anything, all right?'

I continued taking down his words in my notebook. 'Would you like to see the man who killed your daughter punished?'

'God! Yes! I want him to suffer,' the father said, and I looked up because his voice was cracking, like thin ice beneath a skater's feet. 'I'd like him to feel what I'm going through now! I hope he can get just a taste of it.' And then the father stopped and looked at me. 'But I really can't say anything now,' he said.

'Of course,' I replied. 'I understand.' And then I stepped out of the way. Wilson glared at me as he got behind the wheel of the cruiser. I saw the father cover his eyes with his hands as the car pulled out of the lot. It was much the same motion the mother had used, as if they were trying to prevent their eyes from seeing some inner vision, some imprint on their imagination. I turned to Porter. 'Good stuff?'

'Yes,' he said. 'Top-notch.'

'Front page?'

'Can't miss.'

'Can't miss,' I agreed. The afternoon was late now, and I noted that the heat was beginning to diminish, as if hiding for the night. We turned and headed back to the newsroom.

Nolan was emerging from the last afternoon news conference when I walked in. He motioned to me and I walked up grinning. 'Good story?' he asked.

'I think so,' I said coyly.

'Fill me in while I get a cup of coffee.' He walked to a machine in the corner of the newsroom. I told him quickly, running down the main highlights of the story, skipping over some of the detail. I told him about the body next to the green and the runner who'd picked out the color in the rough. I told him about the mother and the photos on the wall and the telephone call and how she'd cracked then under the strain. Then I described the father and the detectives and read him a few of the quotes. Finally I paused, and he sipped on the coffee and thought for a moment. 'OK,' he said. 'I argued for the front page and got it. They knocked a feature back. Listen, here's what I want: about thirty inches for the mainbar and about fifteen for the sidebar. Incorporate the jogger into the main, using his quotes and color. Write a separate on the mother and the father. But save a quote or two from each for the main story. Lead with the body and the status of the police investigation, but work the color and the parents' reaction in very near the top. OK?'

'Sounds good, but I really would like to do a sidebar on the guy who discovered the body. And can I run long?'

'Tell you what,' he said, smiling. 'You run long, but only with color. I mean, I want people to really feel that girl. And just the one sidebar. On the parents. In a couple of days you can go back and talk with the guy who found the body and see if he's still running the same route. It'll make an interesting follow.'

I nodded. 'But I'm still going to work his stuff into the main.'

'Of course,' Nolan said. 'Don't hold anything out. This'll be the best-read story in the paper tomorrow by a long shot. And what about the art? Is it good?'

I handed him the photo the mother had given me. He stared at it for a second. 'Christ,' he said, 'she was pretty cute. This is really good. I'm going to go start negotiating for space with the newsdesk. You start writing now; I want to move all this stuff myself.'

'OK,' I said. 'Don't lose the photo. I promised I'd send it back.'

'Who took it?' Nolan asked.

'The brother. Jerry Hooks, Junior.'

'We'll give him a credit line then,' Nolan said. 'All right?'

'Good idea.'

*   *   *

I called Christine then, catching her as she was leaving the hospital. 'Are you OK?' she asked. 'How did the funeral go?'

'I survived,' I replied. 'Everyone survived.'

'When will I see you?'

'Not too early. I have a big story I have to finish.'

'You went to work?' She sounded surprised.

'I wanted to. Why sit around brooding? Work takes my mind off things, puts it somewhere else. It's a marvelous release.'

'You love it.' It was a small accusation.

'I must.' I laughed, and after a moment she joined me.

'Shall I get us something to eat?'

'How about a steak?'

'See you later,' she said. 'Sounds like you want to celebrate.'

'Just a good story,' I said. I hung up the phone and turned to the typewriter. Around me worked other reporters, and the sound of their voices on the telephones mingled with the staccato noise from the electric typewriters. The room seemed filled with the soft light of late afternoon; large windows on one side covered the whole wall. I could look out over downtown from where I sat. The buildings seemed to reach out and catch the evening shadows. I turned away and looked across the room at the old photo of the palm tree blowing in the storm. I could see that the big storm had moved slightly in its course, heading north by northeast, on a path with Miami. I closed my eyes for a moment and began to summon up images, like a conjuror with facts. I could see

41

the body, and the sunlight reflecting off her blond hair. I pictured the mother, then the father, each in their own state of panic. I slipped a sheet into the typewriter and began to punch out letters, forming words, shaping sentences and paragraphs. It was as if I were connected to the machine then; it was an instrument and I a musician.

I wrote:

A sixteen-year-old Sunset High School cheerleader . . . Discovered by an early-morning jogger . . . Her hands were bound and she had been shot 'execution-style . . .' Her mother's face was drawn and frightened . . . Her father's words were twisted and angry . . . Police are still seeking clues but have no suspects . . .

The pages slid through the machine swiftly, and slowly the other sounds in the newsroom slipped away from me; I was aware only that I was in my element, working with the thoughts and impressions of the day. I finished the main story and continued on with the sidebar on the parents. I hardly noticed when an assistant city editor picked the sheets off my desk and took them to the computer scanner to be fed into the newsroom system. I finished some fifteen minutes before deadline, with a quote from the mother: 'Who would want to do such a thing?'

I looked at it for a moment, and my mind filled with images of my uncle. I pictured him, highball in one hand, album in the other, poring over the moments of his past. I could see his face in my mind, his lips quivering with remembrances, his one good eye filling with tears. And I saw the abrupt, military movement of his hand as he snapped the album closed, closing his life at the same moment. His steps must have been measured, slow, like the pace of a funeral caisson. I could see him mount the stairs to his bathroom, his pistol, carefully cleaned and polished, in his hand. The crack of the gun must have seemed to him more like taps.

Nolan leaned over me. 'It's good,' he said. 'Are you finished?'

I handed him the final page. I followed his eyes as they scanned the words. 'OK,' he said. 'Come on up. I'll show you what changes I've made.' He dropped the last sheet with the computer clerk and then went to his desk. Next to it was a small television screen with a keyboard: the video display terminal. He punched a series of keys and my story appeared on the screen. 'Read it over.' There were a few minor changes, a few words slipped into different spots; a few paragraphs had changed location. Nothing major. Then he punched up the sidebar, and together we read through it. 'Not bad at all,' he said, smiling. 'Don't want to forget this.' And in quick succession he typed:

BY MALCOLM ANDERSON
Journal Staff Writer

at the top of each story.

He rolled through the two stories again and finally got to the mother's last quote. 'It's a really good quote to end on,' I said.

He agreed. 'Kinda says it all, doesn't it? Sums it right up.'

I nodded.

But, of course, we were both completely wrong.

CHAPTER THREE

The next morning, I didn't look at the front page right away. Christine rose first and retrieved the paper from the front doorstep. She made coffee and breakfast while I showered, and I heard her call through the bathroom door the same question as the mother: 'Jesus. Who would do such a thing?' I called back that it would probably turn out to be someone usual, an estranged boyfriend probably, someone that the parents didn't know about. Then I heard her shout, 'But that still wouldn't explain it.' I made no reply but continued rinsing the soap from my body, feeling the lukewarm water rush through my hair and onto my face. The bathroom window was open, and I could already feel the day's heat starting up, like an engine.

'It makes me sick,' she said, when I came out.

'What does?'

'That kind of crime. You know, your mind can envision a dozen explanations for the crime – passion, perversion, robbery, I don't know what else – but none of them really provide sufficient reason to rob that poor kid of her life. It makes me ill just to think about it. Didn't it bother you?'

'I don't think of it that way.'

'Well, then,' Christine asked, 'how do you think of it?'

She was spreading an English muffin with butter and marmalade. I saw the sunlight slip through the kitchen windows and glint off the knife handle as she put it down on the table. She had reddish-brown hair that was cut to frame her face and fell to her shoulders. The sunlight in the room brought out the red, and she seemed suddenly to be surrounded by color. 'Well?' she said.

'It's just a story,' I said. 'It's what I do. Look, the newspaper is mostly a chronicle of tragedy, OK? Yesterday was my turn to delve into a particular tragedy and then express it for all the other tragic people in the world, or at least in our circulation area, to shake their heads over. Your reaction was probably the breakfast-time norm for the Greater Miami area. But everyone who reads the story at least gets to say, "At least it didn't happen to me," and that's part of why it's there. Listen, it's probably the same in your business; when you perform surgery don't you feel a kind of divorce from the proceedings? As if you're glad to be unaffected?'

'No,' she said. 'Not exactly.'

I drank orange juice and picked up the sports section. The Yankees were widening their lead in the East, burying Baltimore and the Red Sox. The National League seemed to be all Cincinnati. I saw that Tom Seaver had pitched for the Mets. I liked to watch Seaver pitch; his body always seemed in complete commitment to the act of throwing the ball. He would rock back ever so slightly, then explode his arm and body toward the batter. His knee would dip down, scraping the mound, and his arm, like a shot, would race past his ear, releasing the ball at the proper moment. It seemed that there was no time at all between the release from his fingers and the appearance of the ball over the plate, as if Seaver were some wizard who made the ball's flight invisible. I liked to see him throw the hard stuff at ninety, ninety-five, so that when it detonated over the plate it was dipping and swerving, the ball no longer inanimate but infused with a life of its own.

When I walked into the newsroom I could see that most of the other reporters were standing around, drinking coffee and looking over the paper. There was always a stack of the day's papers by the entranceway. I picked one up, glancing at the front but not taking it in; I wanted to sit at my desk and savor the story. I also picked up the first edition of the afternoon *Post* to see how they had played the story. I couldn't remember seeing any *Post* reporters during the day, but that did not mean that they weren't there. As I walked to my desk a few of the other reporters called to me. One said, 'Good story,' and another joked, 'Encore, encore!' It was pretty much the same anytime anyone had a big assignment, a story that had jumped from the routine to the front page. I nodded my head in mock appreciation and settled into my desk.

The story had been played above the fold, skylined on top of the national lead for the day. TEENAGER FOUND MURDERED; POLICE SEEK 'EXECUTION' KILLER, the headline read. It was spread across all six columns, and I looked at the picture of the girl. Even in the fuzzy black and white reproduction of the paper she still seemed pristine, beautiful. The sidebar started on the front page also, indented in the major story. The headline there was smaller type: A PHONE CALL . . . AND TRAGEDY STRIKES, it read. I thought that it was perhaps a little overdone, but then, I considered, the newspaper is not in the business of subtlety. I scanned over the words of both stories with an inner satisfaction, a familiarity. It was as if the memories of the day before had slipped away and were replaced by the words of the newsprint, the real people replaced by the descriptions in the story. As I read, the telephone rang on my desk. It was Christine.

'I didn't want to have an argument,' she said.

'Did we?' I asked and laughed.

'No,' she said. 'I didn't want to accuse you of being cold.'

'I am. It goes, as they say, with the territory.'

'Well . . . you're not like that really.'

'But I am.' I laughed again.

'I don't believe so.' Her voice was exasperated.

'Where are you?'

'I'm at the hospital. I only have a few minutes. The doctors will be down to scrub in a moment and I have to check on things. I just wanted to call because, I don't know, you seem so unconcerned.'

'I am unconcerned. I'd go crazy if I let it all bother me. Anyone would. It's just my defense to the whole crazy show.'

'Well,' she said, 'I think you shouldn't be.'

'Look,' I replied, 'tell me this: who are you cutting into today?'

'A businessman. Or a lawyer, I forget right now. Middle-aged.'

'Family?'

'Of course.'

'Chances of survival?'

'I don't know. It's an exploratory, into the stomach. I don't really think they know what they'll find, but it won't be good, no matter what it is.'

'Have you talked with him, seen him with his family?'

'A little. I saw him yesterday, with a woman and a teenage son. They all looked so ill, especially the two who weren't.'

'And tell me, what went through your mind?'

'I don't know. Sadness. A kind of hopelessness. I wanted to walk up to them and tell them that they had nothing to worry about, that the surgeons were perfect and the disease in retreat. That they could relax and enjoy their time together because they had a future.'

'So why didn't you?'

'It would have been a lie.' There was a pause. I could hear voices in the background. 'I have to go,' she said.

'Well,' I said, 'in a way that's my point. I just can't stand thinking I'm lying.'

'Is it that simple for you?'

'Yes. I just watch and record. Sometimes I think of myself as a camera. My eyes are the shutter, the words are the print. Does that make any sense to you?'

'I have to go.'

'I'll see you tonight,' I said.

'Tonight.'

When I hung up the phone I had a picture of her in my mind, dressed in the baggy pale blue or green surgical outfit, her hair pulled back severely and hidden beneath the sanitary helmet, the mask she would wear dangling around her neck like jewelry. She was a slender woman; she could wear the loose shirt and slacks of the operating theater and still appear thin. With the mask pulled up all one could see would be her eyes.

I didn't think she was an overly pretty woman, but her eyes were exceptional; they jumped and shone and showed off her emotions. Her eyes sometimes seemed to speak before the words were out of her mouth. Often I watched them closely, to anticipate the swings of her mood. We had been together some time now, in essence living together, though she kept a one-room studio apartment near the hospital. She stayed there when I went out of town, on assignment or, as the day before, to my uncle's funeral.

She had questioned me about it when I saw her. I'd wanted to talk of the story instead, but she'd persisted in getting me to describe my family's responses.

'My father was the only interesting person,' I said.

'Why?'

'Because he was the one who was suffering the most and showing it the least.'

'How so? Was he close to his brother?'

'All brothers are close,' I said, 'regardless of the differences in their lives. Even if they hate each other, they have a kind of close hatred. One never equivocates on the subject of one's brother.'

She had nodded then and asked no more questions.

Christine and I had met a year earlier. I'd been filling in on the night cop beat while the regular was on vacation, and I had picked up the garbled transmission of a high-speed chase up on Route 95 that cut through the center of Miami. There wasn't much else doing, so I went out to see what happened when they caught up with the speeder.

It turned out to be the eighteen-year-old son of a county commissioner. And before he finished leading a dozen patrol cars through the city, he managed to run two other drivers off the road, wreck several of the cruisers pursuing him and finally wrap himself around a telephone pole. I latched onto the parade of angry and wounded at the downtown medical complex. I saw one uniformed officer, holding a bloody compress to his forehead, watch as the kid was carried in on a stretcher. 'I hope this little sucker buys it,' the cop said. I got his words down, thinking, 'There's my second graf,' when I was shoved out of the way by a nurse.

'Please,' she said, 'don't get in the way.'

'It's my job,' I said.

She looked at me oddly, then tried a small laugh. 'I guess it is.'

I measured her trim figure, the smooth manner she handled herself amidst all the broken and frightened people crowding into the emergency room. My eyes tracked her as she swept quickly from litter to bed, pausing to take vital signs, then moving on. I admired her efficiency at first, then her calm. She seemed such an island in a storm, I thought, then smiled at the cliché. She caught my look and smiled back. 'Humor?' she asked. 'Please share it.' It wasn't a reproach.

'I was watching you,' I said.

'Ah,' she said and smiled again. I remember how out of place the smile was in the room; it seemed to rise above all the sounds of hurt. 'It helps to keep one's sense of humor.'

'It does,' I agreed.

Then she turned away, back to one of the patients. I was closing in on a deadline; I needed to get to a phone, then a typewriter. But as I left, I stopped at the nurses' station and found her name written on a log. There was a home phone number. I took that down.

The next afternoon I called her.

My eyes turned back to the paper on my desk. I opened it to the jump on the inside page and saw that it had been laid out with photos of the man who'd discovered the girl's body, and of the parents, different poses. The father was captured slipping into the patrol car at police headquarters. His face was set and grim. The mother was pictured hanging up the telephone, a blank look on her face, caught in the moment of dissolution turning to distress. They were powerful photographs. I picked up the telephone on my desk and dialed the photo-studio number. I asked for Porter, and in a moment he came on the line. 'Really good shots,' I said.

'Thanks. I had a lot of good stuff. They never

did use the photo of the body in the bag like I said they would. They came close, though. They were going to use it until they saw the photo of the girl that the mother gave us. Still, all in all, they were good subjects for the camera. And for the typewriter.'

'True.'

'So,' he said, 'what's for an encore? Have you got some kind of follow?'

'I don't know yet. I'm going to talk with Nolan now.'

'Well, if you need photos, call me. I'd like to stick with this one, if possible.'

'I'll let you know,' I said and hung up.

I checked the *Post*'s coverage. They'd also played the story on the front page but didn't have many of the details that I had. They'd found one of the neighboring teenagers who'd seen the girl that evening. The kid had said he'd seen the girl walking alone through the neighborhood. It didn't really mean much, but the way they had written it implied that no one else had seen the girl later and that she'd been snatched during that evening walk. It was a skillful writing job, to create an illusion of knowledge where none really existed. I noticed also that they did not have a photo of the girl; they'd relied on the shot of the rescue personnel carrying her body off the thirteenth green in the body bag. They'd also been forced to interview the Allens, the neighbors we had summoned. I smiled and shut the paper, a sense of satisfaction running through my head. There is a kind of glow, a mixture of aggressiveness and pride that comes when one beats the competition in the newspaper business. Results are so immediate, so clear.

I picked up the phone again and started to work. It would be worthwhile to check with the detectives before I spoke with Nolan to give us at least some idea of what to do next. A voice answered, 'Homicide.'

'Martinez,' I said. 'This is Anderson at the *Journal*.'

I heard the clicking sounds of the call being transferred and then Martinez' voice. 'Big day in the news business,' he said. 'I can see the headline now: *Journal* reporter hits big time, gets job at *New York Times*.' He laughed.

'I'd never leave you guys,' I said. 'How would I get any stories if it weren't for you?'

'You'd make them up. You already do.' He laughed again.

'Touché.'

'So what can I do for you? Listen, I think you did OK. Even Wilson does, but he won't admit it. He's still pretty angry about the whole thing.'

'What's new?' I asked. 'I need a follow-up.'

'Well,' Martinez answered, 'we're going to get the autopsy report this morning, and ballistics says they can have a preliminary idea pretty soon, too. Other than that, all we've got planned is to canvas the neighborhood. Pretty routine stuff. Did anybody see her maybe get into a car or see anyone suspicious in the neighborhood? Talk to some of her friends. Drudgery. Not the exciting stuff your readers are waiting for.'

'How long are you going to be at it?'

'Probably all day. There's going to be a lot of pressure on Wilson and me to get this guy, but I doubt we will. That's not for publication, of course. We've got a few ideas, mostly that he's whacko. I don't want to talk too much about that.'

'All right,' I said. 'It's pretty early for me. I'll talk to you again this afternoon. OK?'

'Fine. The medical examiner will talk about the autopsy. I don't suspect there will be anything in it that needs to be confidential. He'll know, anyway.'

I hung up the telephone and looked down at the notes I'd taken of the conversation. Whacko, I thought. Maybe that's something we can follow up on. I picked up the sheaf of papers and walked over to the city desk. Nolan was on the telephone with another reporter, the courthouse man, arguing about the coverage of a trial. After a few minutes he turned to me. 'The bastard doesn't think that murder trial is worth much of a story. The irritating thing is he's probably right, because he knows an awful lot more about it than I do. So, good job yesterday, but that's water under the bridge. As they say, what have you done for me today?'

I smiled. 'We'll get the autopsy report and ballistics today. Martinez says he's going to be out canvassing the neighborhood. He doesn't expect too much.'

'Maybe we should do some of the same?'

I groaned. 'It's hot. If my mother wanted me to be a door-to-door salesman she'd have given me an encyclopedia.'

Nolan laughed. 'I took cruelty pills this morning. Along with my usual dosage of sadism and an injection of bilious bad temper. Before I do something rash, like send you out there, suggest something better.'

'Well,' I said, 'Martinez suggested that the killer might be some sort of crazy. A sex criminal, I suppose. I could interview some of the forensic psychiatrists over at the courthouse, see what they think.'

'A good idea, but I don't think we have enough information yet for them to go on. You might try calling a few and see if you can set up an appointment later in the week or tomorrow. We'll know a little more and things will be a little slower. Then head out into the neighborhood and knock on some doors. Get the people's reactions. See if they're buying attack dogs, that sort of thing.'

'Fear stalks,' I said.

Nolan laughed. 'That's right. Fear stalks quiet neighborhood in wake of teenager's murder. I realize it's standard newspaper fare, but it's still a good story, regardless of how often it's written. And it will keep the story on the front page for another day. Take a photographer.'

I waited outside for Porter to bring the car around. The *Journal* building was right on the bay, and I stood to the side, feeling the warm breeze that was lifting the slight chop on the waters. The bay seemed the same color as the sky, a pale blue, and for a moment I felt suspended between the two, the heat seeming to slip over me like fog. I heard the sound of a car horn, turned and saw the photographer. 'Back into the fray,' he said. I grunted as I slid into the seat, the sweat already slick on my forehead.

We drove by the murdered girl's home. It was closed, the window curtains drawn and the door pulled shut. I couldn't see any activity, but I noticed there were several cars in the driveway; friends, perhaps the girl's brothers, I thought, the gathering of death. We parked up the block. I saw a pair of teenage girls walking down the sidewalk and we rushed up to them.

'Are you a real reporter?' one asked. I smiled and showed her my police identification card. She looked at it and then at me. 'It's not a good picture,' she said. Her friend leaned over and looked at it wordlessly.

'Did you know the victim?' I asked.

'Oh, sure,' the first girl said as her friend nodded her head. 'Everyone in the neighborhood knew her. She was real popular.'

'Was she a classmate?'

'No, she was a grade ahead of us.' The second girl finally spoke. 'But we saw her all the time.'

'Tell me, are you scared? I mean, here you are walking around as if nothing happened. What do you think?'

The two girls looked at each other. They seemed to be twins in their cut-off blue jeans and T-shirts. They both had the same shoulder-length hair, too, and it seemed they could not speak without moving their hands or pouting or grinning, somehow punctuating their words with some motion or expression. 'My dad,' the first girl said, 'says I can't go out at night until the murderer is caught.'

'And you?' I asked the second girl.

'My mom gave me a lecture,' she said. 'My mom said I can't go anywhere, not even to the swim club, unless I walk with a friend. And I have to tell them where I'm gonna go at night. I don't think they'll let me go out, anyway.'

'When did they talk with you?'

'This morning. Right after the story came out in the papers. But we knew about it last night. Everyone was talking, everywhere. I still can't believe it.' It was the first girl speaking.

Her friend joined in. 'I mean, I never thought about anything like that before. And I wonder who's going to take her place as a cheerleader?'

Perfect, I thought. The teenage mind at work. 'Do you think everyone is scared?' I asked.

'Oh, yes,' both girls said quickly. 'All the grown-ups,' the second girl added.

'You're not scared?'

'Oh,' she said, 'maybe a little. It's daytime, and it's hard to be scared. Maybe tonight I'll be scared.'

I took down their words as they spoke, trying to add details of their expression. I noticed that a few other children, mostly between what I estimated to be the ages of nine and fourteen, had gathered to watch. It's the camera that does it, that always adds the element of fascination to the proceedings. I motioned some of the children over, and in a moment I was surrounded by perhaps ten of the neighborhood kids. I started to ask my questions as Porter swooped around the periphery, snapping shots of the children.

'I'm scared. I don't want it to happen to me,' said one boy.

'I think I'd punch the killer right where it hurts,' said one teenage girl, a child on the verge of adulthood.

Her response gained a ripple of embarrassed laughter from the group.

'I don't think the killer will come back,' said one small boy, perhaps nine, obviously upset by the situation. 'They never return to the scene of the crime. I read that.'

As they talked I wrote down their words, their names and their addresses. My notebook was filling with scribbling, hieroglyphics interpretable only by myself. Their voices came at me quickly, excitedly, their opinions probably reaching words for the first time. I thought of the discrepancy in time and place; in the sun, with the reporter and the photographer, the experience was novel. Alone in their rooms tonight, most of them will turn sleepless with dread. A child's imagination, I thought. Remarkable.

They grew quiet, and I looked up to see a woman standing a few feet away in the center of her front yard. We all looked at her. 'Who are you?'

'Anderson, *Journal*,' I said. 'Just asking the kids some questions.'

'Joey,' she said. 'Come here.'

The nine-year-old, the scared one, peeled away from the group. 'Go inside and play.' He marched across the lawn. 'I hope you know what you're doing,' the woman said to me.

'Ma'am?'

'You're probably scaring the daylights out of these children.' It was then that I first noticed the edge in her voice, the quaver of emotions.

'I don't think I follow, ma'am,' I said, walking over to her.

59

'This murder,' she said; 'you'll just scare everyone more by coming around here. Oh, my goodness, are you planning to run their names?'

'Probably just their first names, ma'am,' I lied. 'No one could figure anything out.'

She was shaking her head back and forth, as if trying to shake loose from some fearful thought. 'I can't believe what has happened. We're not freaks, you know. What gives you the right to poke around here, trespassing?'

'Take it easy,' I said.

'How can I?' Her voice was raised now and had the stretched quality of fear. 'How can anyone after what happened? I could hardly sleep last night after I heard. And then the papers, this morning. There's a fiend loose, I say, a madman. I just don't want him to come back again.' Then she turned and looked toward her house and yelled, 'Joey! I told you to stay inside!'

I remained busy scribbling in the notebook.

'I'm sorry,' the woman said suddenly, her voice gaining a more even tone. 'Everyone here is very upset over the Hooks child. Some of the parents were on the phone this morning, trying to organize people to patrol the streets. Nothing came of it, but people are upset. I'm upset.'

And then the woman paused. She looked at me and our eyes met. She seemed to be looking for some sort of answer.

I said, 'This is probably just a once-in-a-million-type thing, don't you think?'

'Oh,' she said. 'I know you're probably right. That's what my husband said, too. But I can't help but feel that it shows that we're all, I don't know, open to attack, vulnerable. And that's why I'm afraid. It's like an invasion of invisible enemies. You know that they're out there, but you can't see them to fight them, and that's what makes me so scared. I shouldn't yell at Joey, I know, because he's scared enough and it makes it worse for him to see me and his father so nervous, but how can you fight the feelings you have? And why should you? I'd rather have him safe indoors, if just until this blows over. I mean, this is the suburbs. We don't have this sort of inner-city crime here. Burglaries and robberies, but not this . . .' Her voice trailed off. Then she thought to ask me a question. 'You tell me,' she said, 'you're the professional. You've seen this type of thing before, I bet. What's going to happen; when will the police catch the guy?'

I thought for an instant, torn between reassuring the woman and frightening her more. It was as if I were considering the value of two responses, placed within the context of the story I was going to write.

'I think you're right to be concerned,' I said. 'But no one can really predict what this type of criminal will do. It's wrong to speculate.' I watched as her face grew unsettled.

'You think he might come back.' It was only a half-question. Her voice had grown flat with a fear I did not really grasp, that seemed half-acceptance.

I shrugged.

'I guess no one's safe. Really safe, anymore. Oh my God,' she said, 'that's a terrible, horrible thing.'

I nodded my head. I could feel the hot wind pushing on my back, sticking my shirt to my skin.

'Oh, God,' she said. 'What are we in for?'

Later, in the car, Porter said, 'That woman was perfect, wasn't she? The right mixture of pathos and fear, the rational and the irrational. She didn't know if it was more reasonable to panic or keep her head.'

'Yes,' I said. We discussed her as we drove, both young men slipping easily from what we saw. The car was shut tight, the heat and noise of the streets locked out by the droning air conditioner and the scratch and whine from the radios.

Back in the office, I settled into my desk and dialed the homicide number. After a moment Martinez came to the phone. I heard another extension being picked up and assumed that Wilson had joined in on the conversation. 'So,' I said, 'fill me in. What about the autopsy?'

'Call the medical examiner,' the detective said. 'It's weird. But this much I can tell you: she was killed with a single shot from a forty-five-caliber automatic, and she wasn't sexually molested. That's pretty much what we expected.'

'Well, what's so unusual?'

Martinez hesitated. 'Well, hell, I don't see why you can't know. The doctor says she wasn't killed until the early A.M. Probably around four-thirty or five in the morning. He figures it out by the rate of body-temperature loss. It's kind of interesting. '

'So why is that important?' I asked.

'Because,' Wilson cut in impatiently, 'she must have been snatched around ten the night before. Where was she all that time, and if this was an abduction, why not sex? Or a kidnapping that went wrong? She must have been somewhere, and it's going to be a bitch to find out.'

'Where was she killed?'

'You already know that,' Martinez said. 'Right where they found her. It was in your story.'

'Christ,' said Wilson, 'you ought to read what you write.'

I'd forgotten. Sometimes I asked questions to which I already knew the answers in order to get time to think up other questions. This wasn't one of those occasions. 'What about the murder weapon? I thought a forty-five would blow her head off at that range.'

'The bullet was fired at an angle,' Martinez said.

'Let me tell you something,' Wilson interjected again. 'This bastard really knows weapons. You can just sense it.'

'Maybe a professional, a kidnapping?' I asked.

'Let's just say we're trying to look at everything.' There was silence for a moment. 'Listen,' Martinez continued, 'we're trying to be helpful on this. We expect the same with you. You use your judgment writing this up. But let me tell you, we're going to look under every rock out there. We've got divers working the water hazard at the golf course, looking for the gun, and all the nearby waterways. It's just that we aren't sure yet what kind of crime it was. But something will shake loose, I promise you. It always does. We may not get anywhere, but something will happen.'

'Yeah,' said Wilson. 'Something.'

I was unable to reach the medical examiner and

left a message for him to call me. I talked briefly with Nolan about the follow-up story; he wanted me to blend the scene on the street with the status of the police investigation. I sat at the desk for a moment, staring at the paper in the typewriter. I always tried to pause before writing, even on the closest deadline, to construct the images in my mind. In quick order I pictured the house shut to the world, the children on the street. I heard their voices and saw their faces as they twisted with questions. Then I envisioned the mother who'd stepped out and added to the sensation of panic, an element of fear and confusion in her voice. I wrote:

> The house on Southwest 62nd Street is closed, curtains drawn, shutting out the curious; mute testimony to the tragedy that has struck the occupants.
>
> But outside on the sunlit streets of this exclusive residential area there is a new sense, a new mood. In a neighborhood usually filled with the suburban sounds of children playing, there is quiet.
>
> People are afraid.
>
> It is an atmosphere created by the murder early Tuesday of their 16-year-old neighbor, Amy Hooks. As police continue searching for clues in the still undefined crime, this neighborhood has drawn together in fear . . .

Nolan came over to my typewriter and watched the words as they appeared on the page. I stopped for a moment and he read silently. Then he nodded. 'Good, fine. Now work in a few quotes and then the police and the autopsy. Give the people some news, and then return to the scene on the street.' He walked away to talk with some of the other reporters working on stories, but I called after him.

'Hey, Nolan! Don't you live out there?'

'No,' he said, 'I live further out, towards the south in Kendall. Fear doesn't stalk my streets.' He laughed. 'At least, not yet.'

I returned to the story, thought of what Martinez said and looked down at my notes. I thought I would downplay the police inability to get a handle on the crime and emphasize instead that they were looking at several possibilities. I would work in a little speculation about the difficulty in solving the crime; the detectives would like that. It could make the killer relax, which was good, and take a little heat off them with the public. And, I thought, if they do catch the guy, it will make them look just that much better. I pictured the woman outside her house again, the look behind her eyes, the tone of her voice, the combination of fear and abandonment. I wondered how many others there were like her.

I looked back down at the page and my fingers hovered over the keyboard. The descriptions started to flow again, and within seconds I was back in the rhythm of the words and the story.

Nolan wanted to go out for a drink that evening. I called Christine to tell her I would be late. She was used to this particular type of delay and said little. 'I'll be here. I've got a book to read.'

'What's that?' I asked.

'Camus. *The Plague*. Some of the doctors were talking today, after the surgery, very upset. One of them started to complain that for all our knowledge and technology we were still as helpless sometimes as back in the fourteenth century, when the plague hit the cities. He said maybe we should go back to folk medicines . . . Then when I got here I happened to be looking over the bookshelf, and my eyes fell on the book, from school or whenever . . . You remember the opening? The doctor notices a dead rat on the landing of his apartment building, and then everyone starts to complain about the dead rats, coming out of every hole in the earth and the darkness to die in the sunshine. The city reminds me, the descriptions do, of Miami. And then the people start to die . . .'

'Why were the doctors so angry?'

'Because when we opened that businessman up, the one I told you about this morning, in the exploratory, it was no good. His whole stomach was falling apart. They kept trying to cut the cancer away, but it was everywhere. It looks black and red and ugly; unmistakable.' Her voice began to thicken.

'So,' I interrupted. 'What happened?'

'He died.'

'Oh,' I said. 'I'm sorry.'

'It's OK,' she replied. 'I cried earlier, after they told the family. I don't know why. Just sometimes it affects me and I want to be alone, so I went into one of the storage rooms and I wept a bit. I'm all right now.'

When I hung up the phone I felt a moment of guilt, a kind of relief that I didn't have to comfort her. Sometimes, I thought, she allows herself to feel too much. But then I shouldn't criticize her for her feelings, they were probably what made her a good nurse; that, plus efficiency. I looked up and saw Nolan by the door, waving his arm and pantomiming drinking motions. I grabbed my jacket and hurried to join him.

The bar was on Biscayne Boulevard, a place frequented both by reporters and by pressmen, who occupied different sides of the bar in an uneasy truce. The pressmen were union, the reporters were not. It seemed that conversation ended there. In the darkness inside the bar, we all seemed to melt into the atmosphere.

Nolan and I took our drinks to a booth and sat on red vinyl-covered seats. In a moment Porter joined us. 'So what do you two think?' Nolan asked. 'Where does all this go from here? What other stories can you guys work up?'

Porter shrugged. 'Maybe they'll make an arrest.'

'I managed to get the scene piece and the photos out front again today,' Nolan said. 'But after tomorrow's paper, unless we come up with something, the story will go back to the local pages. Then inside, and finally out of the paper altogether. What do you think?'

I considered for an instant. 'Maybe that's best,' I said. I looked at Porter, but he was drinking beer. 'I know that this has people bent out of shape, but then, so do most crimes, especially when they hit close to home. Maybe this is one of those that's bound to fade, unless they make an arrest.'

'Maybe,' Nolan said. 'I'm reluctant just to drop

it. Why don't you try tomorrow to talk with some doctors, see if we can't come up with some kind of seat-of-the-pants profile of the killer?'

'I don't know. The cops seemed to be backing off on the psycho angle today. You know, that family has to be pretty well off. Maybe this is some botched kidnapping.'

'I don't buy that,' Porter said. 'I could be wrong, but it just doesn't ring true for me. If that were the case, the kidnappers could just have easily dumped her out in the Everglades, and it would be weeks before she was ever found. Maybe even never, and then she would be considered another teenage runaway. Gone but not forgotten. And they probably would still try to extort the money from the family, especially if they'd already killed the girl. They would have nothing to lose.'

'That's a good point,' Nolan said. 'Let's go back to the psycho angle. It'll keep the story moving for another day, even if it lands off the front pages. Really push Martinez and Wilson for information. I know those guys. They're bound to be holding something back.'

Porter got up to get three more beers. I turned and watched him maneuver in the darkness, my ears filled with the soft sounds of people drinking; the cash register ringing. I heard laughter break out from one part of the bar.

'How are things?' Nolan asked.

'OK,' I replied. 'Oh, Christine said hello.'

'Say hello for me to her. I mean, what with the funeral and all, your family – that whole bit.' Nolan was leaning over the table, his eyes fixed on my own, as if he could somehow read behind them.

'It's good of you to be concerned,' I said. 'But there's really nothing to say.'

'All right,' he said. 'I'll drop it. I just wanted to be sure. You seemed distracted when you came back, and I didn't expect to see you in so soon.'

'I got a good story, didn't I?'

'That's right, a good story. A good story can go a long way to solving external ills and bumps.' He laughed. 'There are a lot of things that a good story can help cure.'

'A lot of pains,' I said. I lifted my glass.

Porter had returned and was settling into his seat. 'To pains,' he said.

'To all the ills in the world which keep us in business,' I said.

'To the good story,' Nolan added.

And then we all drank and laughed.

Late that night in bed, Christine said, 'I forgot to tell you, your father called. He said he'd call again tomorrow, maybe at your office. I told him you had a big story, but to go ahead and try.' We were naked in the darkness. I had the windows open and I could hear the night bugs humming. In the distance a siren wailed; it seemed far away, unconnected with the immediate night that covered us. Christine had shed the blanket, and in the faint moonlight I could see her breasts and her pubic hair. I reached over and stroked her and she turned toward me. 'I never know what to say when he calls,' she said. 'He seems pleasant

69

enough, but intimidating.' I felt her hand on my shoulder and her breath as she spoke.

'That's just his lawyer's mannerisms,' I said. 'I sometimes think he stepped full-grown, like Athena, from his own father's forehead. Spouting dicta and legalisms, precedents and torts, all the stuff of his life.' She laughed. 'He's always been a lawyer, sounded like one, acted like one. That's just the way it is in our house. There is the Law, and then there is the law. He defines both.' I pictured my father, tall, thickly built, working Sundays in his study, yellow legal pads filled with his scrawled notes, books split open around him like so many bodies on a battlefield. I could picture him that way, unchanged, for years, as if I were looking at him through a child's eyes, an adolescent's eyes and finally an adult's eyes.

'Why didn't you go to law school?' she asked.

'That was for my brother. We never talked about it, of course, but he was the eldest and it was just assumed. He did very well, too.'

'What did he want you to become?'

'Nothing.'

'I don't understand.'

'There is only the law,' I replied. 'After that, there is nothing. I wasn't a lawyer, my brother was. So there was nothing left, of any importance. Oh, I don't mean to say that he doesn't have a great deal of respect for the profession of journalism. It's just not the law.'

'It must be sad for you.' Her hand was kneading the muscles on my shoulder, and I turned toward her.

'I don't think about it anymore,' I lied.

And then she pulled me toward her, running her fingers down my back, scratching. I made a noise and she said: 'See how much nurses know about the body?'

Christine was gone in the morning. An early call, she wrote on the bathroom mirror in lipstick. I took my time, making coffee, some toast and bacon, reading the paper. The Red Sox had taken a twin bill from the Yankees the night before; Luis Tiant pitching a complete game, twisting and spinning and kicking in his own style, finally delivering to the plate unexpectedly sharp curves and dipping fastballs. I thought how much I liked to watch the pitchers, how the game revolved around the rhythm they created.

In my typewriter at the office were messages that the medical examiner had tried to reach me and that my father had called. I shuffled both aside for the moment. I picked up the phone and called the psychiatrist. He was an eminent man, a transplanted New Yorker who spent much of his time working with the criminal courts. He had served as an expert for me on other stories, and I thought he would enjoy the chance to speculate about this crime. He was with a patient, though, so I left a message with his service; then I sat back and read the *Post* before settling into the day's routine of calls and collecting information. They had already knocked the story back to an inside page, I noticed, and they had little new information. After being beaten initially, it looked as if they were throwing in the towel on the story. All the better, I thought.

As I was reading, the telephone on my desk rang.

I remember that I did not reach out and pick it right up, as I ordinarily did. I suppose I thought it was my father calling. Instead, I looked up first at the clock and noted that it was ten in the morning; then my eyes fastened on the hurricane map in the rear of the room. I could just make out how the storm's path had changed – it was heading now for Central America – and I could see the photo of the tree bent over in the wind. I picked up the ringing phone: 'Anderson. *Journal.*'

'Hello,' said a voice on the other end. 'I just wanted to say that I've been reading your stories about the murder. I've really enjoyed them.'

'Thank you,' I replied. The caller sounded young, unhurried. I fixed a mental picture of someone under thirty – close to my own age.

'I mean,' he continued, 'they seem very accurate. And descriptive.'

'Well, thanks again,' I said. Time to cut it off. 'Listen, I appreciate what you're saying, but I'm kind of busy right now . . .'

He interrupted my exit line, breaking in on the final words. His voice remained very even, calm, to the point.

'You see,' he said, 'I have a special interest in your stories.' The tone was friendly, unafraid. Usually, congratulatory calls are either angry or somewhat embarrassed. This caller seemed persistent, yet relaxed.

'What's that?' I asked. 'Why is this so special to you?'

There was a single second's hesitation.

'Because,' the caller said, 'I'm the guy who killed her.'

CHAPTER FOUR

I felt hot suddenly, as if the growing heat outside had abruptly burst through the walls of the building. My right hand shot out, reaching for paper and pencil to take notes, a reflex action.

Silence filled the line between us.

I used the moments to gather my confusion and scrawl across a sheet of gray notepaper the words: *I have a special interest in the stories because I'm the guy who killed her.*

I looked down at the words on the page, aware all the time of the quiet that dominated the telephone line. For a moment I was not sure that the voice was still there, almost as if it had never been there. I tried to force myself to think of questions to ask; thinking back, it seems odd that in those moments when my mind was racing with possibilities, the essentials of my profession seemed to slip away. It took me seconds before I could muster the simplest, most obvious questions, and it was moments more before my skepticism returned. Throughout the long pause he waited patiently.

'Who is this?' I finally asked.

He laughed, a short burst. 'You don't really expect me to answer that question, do you?'

'No,' I said. 'But you can give me some idea who I'm talking with.'

'All right,' he said. 'That seems fair.' Then he hesitated for an instant, as if ordering his response. 'I am an ordinary man. I come from ordinary people, heartland stock. I can blend in anywhere, everywhere; I am comfortable with anyone. I fit into the surroundings like a chameleon on a leaf of grass. I am your average American.'

'Average Americans,' I said, 'don't kill teenage girls.'

'Don't they?' he replied.

And then we were silent again for a few moments.

'Tell me why you did it?' I asked.

'That's a difficult question to answer.' He paused again, as if reviewing his thoughts before speaking. This was a cautious man. The voice was deep, yet clear. I imagined him in a room staring up at blank walls, doors shut tightly, windows closed against the heat, an air conditioner pushing and straining to keep the room cool. The caller had an unhurried style of talking, precise, literate. It was a voice that seemed unresponsive to stress, to emotion, as if the call and the thoughts that went behind it were among the normal, rather than the abnormal. I had my first feeling that I was dealing with an exceptional malevolence.

'I anticipated the question before calling you,' he resumed. 'I have spent some time speculating how I would respond. I could tell you that I did the murder for kicks, for thrills, and that would have an element of truth in it. I could say that it was the first act in an experiment in terror, a modern Leopold and Loeb, and that too would be truthful in part. I could tell you that she was randomly picked and randomly executed, and again I would be speaking the truth, but you will still lack the totality, the whole picture. I could go on to say that she was a victim of revenge, a personal vendetta, and other elements of the picture would fall into focus.

'It would be true, too, but you would be confused by the fact that I did not know her before that night, that I do not know her family and that I have nothing against them. Indeed, I was touched by your portrayal of their grief and my heart goes out to them; I have nothing but compassion for all victims. So you might think that she was killed as a symbol, and I might confirm that, and again we would have disclosed another fact that was accurate.

'Look at it this way: I could say any of these things, and they would all be signposts along the road to the truth. But you won't understand until you follow the whole path. And if I were to tell you now, here at the beginning, all of what I have in mind, then the excitement of discovery would disappear. You might doubt my sincerity also; after all, we hardly know each other, and I thought that the purpose of this phone call would be to find out something about you as much as it would be to let you know that I exist, and that I'm out here, and that this has all just begun.'

I got down snatches of his speech. He sounded like a man detached from the reality of what he'd done. It was as if he were discussing a book or politics, not a murder. I became skeptical then.

77

'Why should I believe you?' I said. 'Can you prove that you're really the killer?'

'Proof?'

'Yes,' I said. 'And I don't understand why you've called me. Or why you killed her, if indeed you did.'

'Ah.' Again the short bursting laugh, a cold sound without humor. 'The reporter as skeptic. I expected as much.'

'Right,' I said. 'Proof. How do I know that you're not some whacked-out crank? It happens all the time. People confess to crimes they didn't commit every day. Misguided guilt. Madness.'

He interrupted. 'I am not mad. Let's get that straight from the very beginning.' For the first time a real edge of anger had slipped into his voice. The words seemed more sharply cut off. 'Got that?'

I taunted him. 'Let's say I'm keeping an open mind for a while.' Again there was a silence.

'All right,' he said. His tone had changed abruptly. Now the anger was gone and in its place was the sound of resignation.

'I anticipated this response also. Let's say for the moment that I provided a means for you to know that I am who I am, who I say I am. We'll get to that in a moment. But as for my reasons for calling you and my reasons for the execution, they will become apparent shortly. You've already been given some of the reasons, but in abstract form. You'll just have to start to piece it all together. After all, that's what the *Journal* pays you for, to piece things together.'

'How do I know you're telling the truth?' I asked.

I was impatient; I didn't want to waste my time with a freak, no matter how well spoken he was. If he was who he said he was, then I would be onto a huge story, a terrific story. If he wasn't, well, I had wasted time before; this would be nothing new.

'All right,' he said. 'I assume your connections to the police investigators are pretty good. This clue is really simple. Ask them what she had in her right rear pocket. Got it?'

'Right rear pocket. What is it, some kind of note?'

'Just ask them. I'll call you back in thirty minutes, and then we can talk some more. You be at your phone. Someone else picks it up, and I'm gone.'

'Right rear pocket,' I repeated.

'Just be at your phone. Thirty minutes.'

'All right.'

'Good,' he replied, 'now we're getting somewhere.'

And then the line went dead. I heard a small click as he hung up the receiver, and for a moment I kept the phone to my ear, listening to the absence of sound. I replaced the receiver in slow motion, thinking of the girl's right rear pocket. I had a flash of memory, picturing in my mind's eye the sun and the green of the underbrush. I could see all the men circled around the body in the bushes. I could see the girl as she lay, and I focused, like a camera lens, on her legs and back. I remembered the jeans, faded to a light blue, and I tried in my mind to see the back pockets. I looked up then and stared across the newsroom. There were reporters working everywhere, and I became aware of the noise of typewriters and telephones, of voices moving loudly across the room. I looked at Nolan, working at the city desk amid papers and the gray lights of the video screens. I thought for a moment of telling him about the conversation, then as quickly discarded the idea. I knew I could answer the most important question by calling Martinez and Wilson. I picked up my phone again, thinking that I was somehow attached to the telephone, that it was an umbilical linking me to the world. I dialed the homicide number quickly from memory and waited for the detectives to get on the line. I heard Martinez' voice first, and I knew that Wilson was listening in also.

'Nothing new to report,' Martinez said, anticipating my first question. 'Wish we had something to tell you, like that we had the guy now and we were getting a signed statement. But no such luck. I think it's going to take us some time. Maybe you should go to work on another story.' He laughed. I decided to dispense with the preliminaries.

'You've been holding out on me,' I said.

'What the hell does that mean?' Wilson responded, voice rising.

'What have we been holding back?' It was Martinez, laughter gone.

'Right rear pocket,' I said.

They were quiet. I could picture them looking across the desk at each other. Again Martinez spoke first. I could hear the sudden injection of control into his voice, the studied calm that was part of his armor and his weaponry: 'What about the right rear pocket?'

'You tell me,' I said, my voice rising, too.

'Who told you about that?' It was Wilson, straining harder to control his tone. He was stretched tighter, more urgent.

'I'll answer your questions after you guys answer mine. Now, tell me about the pocket.'

'Shit,' Martinez said.

'Who told you?' Wilson went on. 'Listen, dammit, we're talking about a murder. First-fucking-degree murder and you're jacking us around. Now! Who told you about it!'

'What was in the pocket?' I persisted. I tried to keep my voice even, hard.

'Shit,' Martinez said again. 'Listen, Anderson, this isn't some game; we're not just screwing around over here. You talk to us, we'll talk to you. Always been that way, you know it . . .'

Wilson interrupted again, shouting. 'Who told you? How do you know?'

'Tell me what was in it first,' I said. 'That's the deal.'

'Wait a second,' Martinez said. The line went silent, and I guessed that he had clapped his hand over the mouthpiece while he was talking to Wilson. In a moment their voices returned. 'All right,' he said, 'we'll trade some information. But not for publication, OK?'

'I can't say that until I know what it is.'

'Shit,' Wilson said, 'what's the matter with you? You want to cause a panic? What's the matter? Christ!'

I said nothing in response. I could feel nervous

sweat running down from my armpits underneath my shirt. I hugged my arms close to my body while the line went silent again and the two detectives talked together. When they came back on, I could hear Wilson's breathing in the background, short angry gasps for breath.

'All right,' Martinez began. 'As you know, it's routine to search the area where any body was found and the body itself. That means the clothing and any orifices. Usually, that happens during the autopsy, back at the morgue. You want controlled circumstances, you know, with a photographer, so that any evidence can be preserved for trial. When we got the kid's body back the other day, we started to do just that. While the doc was starting to cut into her, we began going through the clothing. We found in her right rear pocket what we suspect is a message, although the meaning isn't clear.'

'What kind of message?' I was excited now, my nervousness dissipated. I was already beginning to think of the killer's return call.

'It was simple,' Martinez said. He hesitated. 'We're not really sure what it means, although on the surface it looks bad.'

'What is it?' My voice could hardly contain my excitement.

'It was written on a small white sheet of paper,' Martinez continued irritatingly. 'The type you can buy in any five-and-dime store. It was folded several times into a small square. There were two words written on the center of the paper in pencil. The words were written in block handwriting, with each character penciled in thickly several times. Makes any kind of comparison sample in the future virtually useless.'

'Jesus, Martinez, what did it say?'

He hesitated again. I could tell he was thinking like a cop, precise, detailed, his mind probably picturing the note, the moment that they first felt the wad in the girl's back pocket, the careful extraction with tweezers and the gentle way they pried it open, all under the harsh fluorescent lights of the morgue.

'It said *Number One*. That's all.'

'It was written out?'

'Right. Now, for Christ's sake don't go jumping to any conclusions. Especially the most obvious one.'

'Jesus,' I said. What a story.

'Listen,' Martinez continued. I could picture him, his tall frame bent over a desk, telephone stuck to his ear. The lights in the homicide office were bright, outlining the bleak rows of desks and file cabinets, casting shadows across the faces in the photographs pinned to the wall. He, like his partner and so many of the detectives, was a dapper man. I wondered if he was sweating, too. 'Look,' he went on, 'in a murder like this, that message could mean almost anything, if indeed it is a message at all. The lab still has the paper and is running it through tests, and it doesn't mean that there's necessarily going to be a number two or anything else. I mean, it could just as easily have been placed there to distract us as warn us. Got that?'

'Did you show it to the family? I mean . . .'

'You think we're stupid?' It was Wilson, interrupting. 'Of course we did. And of course they didn't recognize it or have any idea where she could have picked it up. Neither do her friends, for that matter. So it seems that it could have come from only one person, the killer. And we sure as hell didn't tell anyone about it, so now, dammit, how come you know about it!'

I thought then of lying, though I knew that the detectives would guess soon enough where I'd found out. And I knew that a lie like that would cost me Martinez and Wilson's cooperation. I added the equation swiftly in my mind, thinking all the time that I had to keep the detectives on my side, while at the same time not let on too much. If this story was going to be as big as I thought, I would need them. 'I got a call,' I said.

'What kind of call?' Wilson asked.

'On the telephone. A voice. I didn't recognize it.'

'What did he say? Exactly.'

'Well,' I lied, 'I didn't take notes.' I looked down at the sheets of paper covered with my scratches of sentences.

'What did he say?' Wilson was impatient.

'He said: "I'm the guy who killed her." Then he told me to ask about the right rear pocket. He said he'd been reading the stories in the paper. Then he hung up after rambling a bit. I didn't know what to make of it, so I called you guys.'

'Will he call again?' Wilson's tone was angry again.

'I don't know,' I lied. A small lie, I thought. I didn't really know for sure, even if the killer had promised.

'Christ,' Wilson said. 'Any ideas . . .'

'No,' I replied cutting him off. 'No idea who, or where he was calling from. His voice was soft, unpressed. He might have been changing it so that I wouldn't be able to recognize it again. Sorry, I know that doesn't help you guys much.'

'What else?' It was Martinez, and I could hear Wilson muttering obscenities.

'I told you, he rambled a bit. I'm still trying to make sense of it. That's all.'

'Try harder,' Martinez said. 'Whatever, anything; it might help us.'

'I know that,' I said. 'I'll try to reconstruct it in my mind and call you back.'

'Jesus Christ,' Wilson said. I hung up the phone and looked up at the wall clock. I had only a few minutes before the thirty-minute deadline passed and the killer called me back. I jumped from my desk and ran across the newsroom to the city desk. Nolan looked up at me from the sheets of copy paper that he was reading. For a moment I stared at the mass of printed words in front of him, and it was as if I couldn't read.

'Nolan,' I said, 'the killer called me.' The excitement in my voice spilled out swiftly, unchecked. I saw a few other heads, other reporters, editors, look up and stare. I was grinning, and my hands were waving back and forth as if by movement I could hurry the thoughts through my mind and out my mouth. 'He's going to call back in just a few minutes. I've got to get a tape recorder, one of those with the tapping attachments that fit onto the earpiece. I've got to get what this guy says down on tape without him knowing about it.' I watched as Nolan's face slipped from surprise to excitement. Then he cracked into a smile.

'You certain it's the killer?'

'Yes,' I replied. I told him I would explain later – the deadline was approaching. He nodded, and within seconds we had run to the library and were unlocking a recorder from a storage cabinet. We quick-marched back across the newsroom as I assembled the device. I plugged it together and slipped the attachment onto the phone as I tried to answer Nolan's questions. He still wanted to be certain it was the killer who had called me. I told him about the first conversation and showed him the scribbled notes that I'd managed to write down. He looked them over carefully, then raised his eyebrows quizzically. He wanted to know about the rear pocket. I told him what the killer had said, then told him about the shouting match with the two detectives. I kept staring up at the clock nervously, waiting for the minute hand to come to rest on the thirty-minute mark. I heard Nolan mutter more to himself than to me, 'Number One,' and shake his head.

The minute hand struck the mark.

The second hand swept by. Ten seconds. Twenty seconds.

The phone rang.

I looked at Nolan and he nodded. I pressed down on the recording device and picked up the receiver. 'Anderson,' I said softly.

'Hello,' said the killer. 'I suppose you were scared I wouldn't call back.'

'I wasn't certain,' I said.

He laughed. 'Certainty, I have learned, is something that is in short supply in the world.'

There was a moment of hesitation.

'Did you talk with the police?' he asked.

'Yes, right rear pocket.'

'And?'

'Why don't you tell me what they told me?'

'Ah! Caution,' he said. Again I heard the short laugh blow coldly over the telephone line. It was an awful sound, I thought. 'All right,' he continued. 'I can't say that I blame you for wanting to be sure. What the police found in the rear right-hand side pocket of the young lady's trousers was a folded white sheet of paper. Notepaper, ordinary. On the sheet were written two words. The words were *Number One.* Correct?'

'That's what they said,' I replied.

'Convinced now?'

'Yes.'

'Good. Now we can continue.'

'What is it you want?' I asked.

The voice seemed to catch; I heard a burst of air and breath. Again it seemed as if he were ordering his response. I looked over at Nolan, but he was staring at the recorder and I realized he couldn't hear the killer, anyway.

'I need you,' he said. 'I need the paper.'

'I don't get it,' I said.

'People have to understand.'

'Understand what?'

'Why there was a number one. Why there will be a number two. Why there will be a number three. Four. Five. Six. You can count for yourself.'

I grabbed a piece of notepaper and wrote: *He plans more killings.* I slipped the sheet to Nolan, who looked at it for an instant. Then he took the pencil and wrote Why? and underlined it three times.

'Tell me why?' I asked.

He paused again, considering, but after a moment began speaking in a low, even tone.

'When I was a small child we lived in Ohio, in farm country, a land I remember as filled with greens and browns. I can still picture the fields in the springtime, acres upon acres of deep brown earth turned up into furrows by the huge tractors and plows. Sometimes I would stop on my way home from school and watch the farmers astride the machines, driving in endless lines up and down the fields, every so often turning in their chairs, swiveling to see behind them, as if they could read the future in the tracks that they made.

'It was a sensual time then, during the planting; the trees were breaking into leaves, and the wintertime gray and black seemed lost in the growth. The air was warm and I watched, waiting for the planting to be finished. I can recall the distant rumbling sound that the machinery made throughout the day as it crisscrossed the fields.

'We lived in a small house, adjacent to a large farm.

The school bus would drop me off a mile or so away from the house and I would walk.

'There were just the three of us, my mother, my father and myself. He was a teacher and he taught in the school where I went, but he taught the older children. There were just two bedrooms in the house, and I can remember at night listening to the sound of the bathwater being drawn and trying to imagine whether it was my mother or my father who was slipping into the wet. He beat me most of the time, punishments for both the real and the imagined. He was a small man, wiry, muscled. He didn't look much like a teacher, though; more like one of the hands on the farms. In the evenings he would sit by the lamp in the living room and read. Almost always great works: Tolstoy, Dostoevski, Dickens, Melville. Occasionally he would stop and read a passage out loud.

'He was always stopping then, searching me out with his eyes, making me repeat the words that I'd heard, testing my memory. When he punished me, it would be in the kitchen. He had a board, an antique paddling board, left over from some earlier time in the school district. My mother would stand aside, often stirring the dinner slowly, watching, saying nothing. He would make me recite my transgression: staying out late, running around with banned friends, mischief, whatever; the stuff of small boys.

'He would always tell me in advance how many times he was going to hit me. I came to recognize what my own tolerances were, what I could attempt, regardless of the capture and punishment.

He would lay the blows on evenly, never adding or subtracting from the pressure and the strength that he used. He would have me count out the number as it fell. He was a hard man. His voice still has the same edge of disapproval in it constantly. When the blows fell I would look out the window in the kitchen, and I remember I was able to see up into a tree, through the branches and out into the sky. The punishment seemed to hurt less those times when I could let my imagination run away into the blue, gray, black, whatever color sky there was.

'The punishments were harshest in the summer that I turned thirteen, the number of blows rising, the tone of his voice harder, the force against my backside. I grew that summer, too much for him; I was taller suddenly and wider suddenly, and my voice went deeper like his own. Once he raised his paddle and looked down at me and our eyes met and I said, "No more," and he put the paddle down and nodded. I think then that he was afraid of me for the first time. I looked toward my mother then, and she smiled and said, "Good," in her small voice.

'I went to bed that night and listened for the sound of the bathwater being drawn, but it didn't come, and I slept fitfully in the night until just before dawn when I awakened, frightened by a nightmare. I remember it to this day: it was of my father paddling me, growing larger with each stroke, stronger and harder. In the dream I felt an absorbing fear, overwhelming, as if I couldn't breathe, that the new blows were knocking all the air from my lungs and that I was being smothered while my mother watched benignly.

'That afternoon I dawdled on the way home from a friend's house and I was late to dinner. My father yelled and swore and complained, but didn't reach for the paddle again. I remember a feeling of loss, as if I'd counted on the punishment, and oddly enough I felt regret then that I wasn't beaten. Over the next few days I tried a few other things, simple maneuvers that would ordinarily prompt his response.

'None succeeded. It was as if I left my childhood behind in those moments. I never slept well after that. Nights would run darkness into nightmare; I would wake up sweating, the sheets wet and cold around me. Sometimes I would lie awake, listening to the night, eyes wide open. Each sound seemed to me like a scream, no matter how small the noise was. Even when we moved to the city the restlessness remained. Sometimes I felt I could hear my body growing at night, and I tried to shut it away. I tried to shut away all the nightmares.

'Later they liked to put me in the perimeter listening post through the darkest time of the night, because the lieutenant knew I could hardly sleep anyway and knew my ears were sensitive to the smallest sound, and so, in a way, it helped to give the others more rest because they knew I would hear anything, sappers, whatever, coming through the wire.

'I would lie, feet out, back to the dirt wall of the hole, head cocked back, listening. My eyes would focus up into the sky most of the time; I remember that it seemed strange then that it looked the same there in that country as it did so many thousands of miles and years away in Ohio. Every so often I would slowly roll over in the foxhole the same way I would in my bed at home and stare out into the darkness of the perimeter. For some, the jungle always seemed to move, alive at night. But to me it was restful. I wasn't afraid. The others all were, but in a way I welcomed it and I would stroke the muzzle on my rifle sometimes while I waited.

'It was peaceful for me then. I suppose that was the essential paradox: that what terrified the others gave me a sense of rest. That's what I feel now. I remember later, during the real horror, that I thought I was part of a play, a dramatic exercise. That the horror my eyes saw wasn't real. I won't talk about that yet. But it was then that I decided something had to be done. You ask why? I'll tell you what this is. It's theater. It's a play. It's a chance for everyone, here in this well-lighted city, to know a little of night-time emptiness. Of nightmare.

'You want to know who I am? I'll tell you. I am the worst thing in the world.'

He stopped then.

His breathing was even, his tone had barely changed. For a moment I tried to think of a reply, a question; then I gave up, listening to the tape machine instead. I could see the capstans moving in slow circles.

'Why did you call?' I asked.

'You,' he said, voice still clear, even, harsh, 'are the method of expression. My words, your stories. The community's newspaper. Welcome' – he paused – 'to the parameters of nightmare.'

CHAPTER FIVE

Again, silence dominated the line. I could hear his breathing. Before I could say anything, he started speaking.

'Imagine for a moment what it was like for the first victim; the depth of feelings and emotions she went through during her last hours. We talked, she and I. At one point we cried together. There were moments when I wanted the night never to end.

'At the beginning I suppose she was just scared, but she kept herself together remarkably. She wanted to know where I was taking her, and she gasped when I said to a place where we could be alone. I guessed she thought she would be raped, so I told her that I wasn't going to touch her, that all I wanted to do was talk with her some. That seemed to calm her down and she grew quiet. She wanted me to loosen the bonds on her wrists, but I told her that I couldn't; that it was a matter of trust; later I might. She wanted to know if she was being kidnapped, and I said yes, because it was partially true and I thought she would remain quieter if she had some tangible idea to grasp hold of. I remember driving through the night; I had the windows up, but there was no air conditioning in the car and I could feel the heat at night, a darker kind of heat, seep through the windows. It seemed as if the streetlights were throwing grotesque shapes across the road; I had to fight the temptation to swerve to miss them.

'She asked me when we stopped – a lonely place, not far from the water so that she could smell the sea and it would comfort her – why I was doing this, and I told her that it was just the first act in what would be a longer-running show. She was having trouble understanding me; I suppose I kept speaking abstractly, and it was hard for her to grasp the ideas through the panic. But she remained persistent, asking questions, making me define my terms. My God, she was beautiful, lying against the side of the car, her face bent toward the sound of my voice, trying to hear, trying to feel the ocean.

'I felt a kind of inexorable calm then, and with it came tears. I wondered if all the victims would be so collected, so together. I began to cry, and she joined me, I think trying to comfort me some. I talked about the war, and she told me about her brother who was overseas at about the same time I was. I talked about growing up, and we had a laugh about that because she said that no matter how good your parents are, they still hassle you, and I had to agree. She was a remarkable young woman. For a moment I considered aborting my plan.

'But once started, I couldn't stop.'

Again, the voice was quiet, as if he were playing over in his mind the memories of that night. As he talked I thought of all the spots in the county, dark spots near the water, where he could have gone. There were thousands.

'You see, the same feelings that made me want to hold off, to stop myself from killing her, were the same ones that made me realize that she was the perfect selection. I had to shake my head at the thought; I remember I walked down to the edge of the water and ran my hand through it. It was warm, like a midnight bath. I could hear the waves breaking slowly on the shore, a light chop on the bay. The lights of the city and the lights from the sky, the stars and moon, reflected across the water. I went back and sat across from her, watching her in the darkness. I think she couldn't see me in the shadows; she struggled some against the rope.

'I waited until it was close to morning. In Nam that was always the time everyone was scared the most; we were daylight people. A false security, I suppose, but we couldn't wait for the morning. The Aussies – they had some troops there, did you know that? Anyway, they always had a complete alert right before dawn. Everybody up; weapons out, pointed, searching the perimeter. Ready.

'And they never got their asses overrun.'

He hesitated, remembering.

'We drove through the last darkness to the golf course. I think that confused her some, because she wanted to know why we were there. I think she had grown scared again about being raped, and I reassured her. When we got into the rough, there where they found her body, I put her down on her knees and turned her toward the east. I said to her then that I wanted her to watch the sun come up; it would be like an explosion of light, I told her. When she was ready, I moved the forty-five into position, so that the shot would deflect up and away; I didn't want to destroy the look on her face. I said to her, "See, the sun is rising," and as she craned forward to look, I fired.

'She didn't feel a thing. I'm positive. And she wasn't scared at the end.'

He paused. 'She might even have forgiven me, if she knew.'

There was another silence.

'When I read your story, about the family and who she was, I realized that I'd been extraordinarily lucky; that my first was the perfect choice by luck.'

I started to speak. 'How did you . . .'

'Easily,' he said. 'She was walking and I stopped, pretending to ask for directions. It was an easy matter to get into the car, get her tied up.'

My mind went blank. The words and images that had risen during the killer's speech disappeared into the silence on the telephone line. Finally, after a few seconds, I said, 'I still don't understand.'

'It would be difficult for anyone.' He thought again. 'There was a moment, a series of moments, when I was overseas. A time when reason suddenly was suspended. A time when I participated in a savagery. I can't describe it yet.

'But for years it has been there, festering in my mind, cancerous. One thinks of the ordinary emotions: guilt, anxiety, grief, whatever. None seemed to remove the images. They were like my nightmares as a child, only they were real and they dominated my waking time.

'And then this spring, the sensual time, I watched on the television as the world over there exploded. All I could see were the terrified kicking legs of men and women clutching to the metal runners of the choppers, trying to be dragged to safety. I watched the abandonment of the country. I thought then of all the horrors. I saw on the screen the faces, the fears.

'No one knows, I thought. No one really understands. It's just a television show, a newspaper headline, a grainy gray photograph in the paper.

'And I decided then that I would bring my own horror to them, all the complaisant ones, the ones who sent me there uselessly.

'And that's what this is all about.'

He laughed.

'Enough, I'll be in touch after Number Two.'

'Wait,' I said.

But he had hung up.

I replaced the telephone receiver and shut off the tape recorder. Most of the reporters in the newsroom had turned and were watching me. I pushed back in my chair, my mind a jumble of the killer's words.

Nolan eyed the tape and pointed to a conference room in the rear of the newsroom; no one said anything as we walked to the private office. For an instant my eyes caught the view through the newsroom windows. The sun was filling the city with tropical heat, the light reflecting off the white-washed downtown buildings, blinding, like so many small explosions. Behind me, the tempo and pace of the office returned, voices, telephones jangling, typewriters clattering.

I was aware of trying to hold my emotions in check. As Nolan listened, I paced in the back of the small office, already writing the words of the next day's story. Nolan let his chin sink down on his chest, scrunching up tighter within himself, drawing himself deeper into the words, letting the killer's voice melt into his memory. Occasionally he took a pencil and wrote a note on a pad in front of him. I was barely aware of the spoken words; they hardly penetrated my growing excitement. I champed, waiting for Nolan to respond. When the tape ended, there was a click, the sound of the telephone being hung up, followed by a humming noise.

'This,' said Nolan, unfolding in his chair, 'is a hell of a thing.'

He stretched, putting his hands behind his head, leaning back, balancing on the hind legs of his chair. He let his breath out slowly, the sound of his exhalation filling the small room. He lit a cigarette, then let the smoke rise, his eyes following the pattern.

'No easy decisions here,' he said.

I burst out, 'Decision! What decision? Jesus Christ! We've got to get this story into the paper. I mean, you heard that guy. Jesus, what a story he told. This town will rock when it reads what he had to say.'

'That's just it,' Nolan said.

'Jesus, how can we hold it?'

'I didn't say hold it.' An edge of irritation slipped

into his voice. 'Just try to curb your enthusiasm for an instant.'

'I . . .' but I cut myself off.

We waited for an instant. I watched his smoke climb to the ceiling; then I took a deep breath, trying to scour the excitement from my voice. 'I just think we ought to go ahead and write the story.'

'We're going to write it,' Nolan said. 'That's not the real issue. It's how.'

'Nolan,' I said, 'it's just a good story.'

'Right. A good story. That's going to change things.' He paused for another long second to think. Finally he shook his head. 'Well, I guess here we go. I wish it were as simple as you seem to think it is.'

But before I could reply, the telephone in the office rang. I started, but Nolan swept it out of the cradle and slapped it to the side of his head. He listened for a moment, then turned to me. 'Your friends Martinez and Wilson are here. They also have what's-his-name, the chief of detectives with them.' Then into the phone he said, 'Stall them. Tell them we're in conference and it'll be about ten, fifteen minutes before we can talk with them. Give them coffee, make them comfortable. Assure them we'll be there, but they're just going to have to wait a bit. Be friendly.'

Then he turned back to me. 'Things are moving fast now. I'm taking the tape in for the higher-ups to hear. You start work on the rough of a story. Type up the notes from the first conversation. I'm going to have a secretary transcribe this so there'll be no debate. My guess is we'll have to give it up.'

I had already finished putting the first conversation

down on paper when I saw two detectives and another stocky man walk across the back of the newsroom. Martinez gave a little wave; he was third in the line. They disappeared into the managing editor's office. A few seconds later I was summoned by an assistant city editor and told to join them.

The managing editor and Nolan met me outside the office. I could see the detectives sitting uncomfortably on the thick leather couch of the office. 'Come on,' Nolan said, and we followed the managing editor into an adjacent room. He shut the door. He was a short man, with thick gray hair pushed severely back from his forehead. His glasses rode down on the end of his nose, and when he was excited he peered over the tops, as if to tell you that he was putting you in a totally different perspective. Among the reporters he had a legendary reputation as a hard man on a story and a soft man with his personnel. He usually stopped by and congratulated reporters on stories; brief, almost embarrassing moments that ultimately meant a great deal to the staff.

He looked at me now and smiled. 'If I may be permitted a slight cliché,' he said, 'it seems we have a tiger by the tail.' Nolan laughed and I smiled with him. 'All right,' the managing editor said, 'a couple of quick questions: Did you ever promise the killer that you would try to protect his identity; that you wouldn't talk with the police; that your conversation with him was in any way off the record, or confidential in any manner?'

'No,' I said.

The editor looked relieved. 'There's one hurdle. Did

you ever promise him that you would write the story, or quote him in any particular way?'

'No. I hardly got a word in edgewise. I had the feeling he was making a calculated guess that we wouldn't pass up the exclusive character of the conversation.'

'Well,' the editor smiled, 'he's right on that score.'

Nolan spoke. 'Do you have any problem working with the police?'

I looked at him. 'Yeah,' I said. 'But it depends on the extent.'

Nolan nodded. 'So do I,' he added.

The managing editor shook his head. 'We need more time to make some decisions. But here's one that I'm going to make right now. We will turn over a copy of the tape under the proviso that it is not released in any way to any competitors. As for ourselves, we're going to write the story.' He turned to me. 'We need these cops, right?'

'They're running the show,' I said. 'If the killer does go on, we could get frozen out.'

'Right,' he said. 'That's what I thought. All right.' He clapped his hands together like a grade-school teacher. It was a mark of excitement. 'Let's go do some horse-trading. Don't open your mouth without checking with me first.'

I nodded to the two detectives and shook hands with the chief. There was a moment of strained silence, and then the managing editor asked precisely what it was they wanted.

'We want to take a statement from your man here,' the chief said. 'We also want to see all his notes. We'd like your cooperation; this is a murder investigation, after all, and I don't really see the need for us to go to the state attorney to get a subpoena.'

The managing editor stretched and nodded his head. 'I don't really see that need, either. But we can't turn over notes. Before you get angry, let me say this. We managed to tape-record a second conversation with the killer. We will provide a copy of that tape for your investigation, but only if you agree to certain conditions.'

'What conditions?'

'Just exclusivity,' the managing editor said. 'No release to other papers or television. Also, the ongoing agreement that we get first crack at developments in the case. After all, the killer may call again.'

For a moment the policeman was quiet. 'I think I can agree to that,' he said. He smiled.

'Good,' said the managing editor. He got up.

'We are, after all, members of the same community.'

'True enough,' said the managing editor.

'So's the killer,' said Martinez.

As I walked back to my desk, Wilson stopped me. He placed his hand on my shoulder, and I stared at it until he removed it. 'Listen,' he said, keeping his voice low, 'we still need to know about the first conversation. This is a two-way street, you know.'

'All right,' I said. 'I'll call you when I put my recollections down.' I stalled. The act of giving information, *my* information, disturbed me, felt alien.

The basic hypocrisy of newspaper work: we collect but don't give.

It was not long before one of the secretaries came up to my desk with a typed transcription of the tape. I looked down at the written words, trying to recall the tone of the voice that spoke them. Again, my mind tried to picture the circumstances of the call: the room, the telephone, probably the gun on the table in front of him.

Nolan walked by. 'You keep that thing attached to the telephone at all times. Keep fresh tape in it.'

For a moment I wondered how far it would all go, how far I could take the story; then I shook my head, looked down at the notes and the transcription, placed a sheet of paper in the typewriter and started to build the story:

> The killer of 16-year-old Amy Hooks has called the Miami *Journal* and pledged that the southwest section teenager's death is but the first in a series of murders he plans to commit.
>
> 'Welcome,' the killer said by telephone, 'to the parameters of nightmare.'

After writing the top, the story flowed easily. I relied mainly on the killer's words, laying out some of his own reasoning. I held back on the long story of his past he told, referring to it obliquely. I regretted the quotations describing the girl's final moments. I had a fleeting image of the mother and father standing in their living room, surrounded by pictures of their dead child. I wondered how they would react when they saw the story. I closed my eyes for an instant, thinking of this new pain I would bring; then, just as swiftly, the idea left me and I was back working with the killer's phrases and thoughts.

Nolan read carefully through the blocks of prose and quotation. The computer terminal made small electronic noises as he rolled the story on the screen before him. 'Jesus,' he said.

'What?'

'Look at this, the way he talks. His descriptions, his structure, his thoughts. No broken phrases. No hesitations. You ever know anybody who talked like that?'

'So he's smart,' I said. 'What does that mean?'

'I don't know,' Nolan said, turning to me. 'Just be careful, Malcolm, huh?'

'Sure,' I said thinking: careful of what?

Nolan turned back to the screen. 'I wonder,' he said, 'how this will all end.'

CHAPTER SIX

The story exploded across the top of the front page the following morning: KILLER PREDICTS 'NIGHTMARE'; PROMISES MORE MURDERS.

My telephone rang at 5:30 A.M., just as the main edition of the paper, with the story bannered just under the masthead, slipped from the presses to the delivery trucks. The first call was a reporter from the Miami office of the Associated Press. Christine tried to tell him that I was still asleep, but I rolled from bed and answered his questions groggily. I'd dreamed fitfully that night, a recurring picture of myself chasing after my uncle through the city. The shapes and shadows had been twisted and bizarre, as if seen through a curved mirror, Dali-esque.

As I talked, Christine sat drinking coffee and reading the paper spread out on the table before her, the early-morning light gently filling the room. Every few seconds she turned and looked at me, shaking her head. I fielded questions as best as possible; everyone wanted a copy of the tape. When the AP was finished, I had perhaps two minutes before the phone rang again. It was a reporter from the Miami *Post*, working on their first-edition story. He sounded angry that the killer had contacted me instead of himself. I got rid of him as quickly as I could. Another minute or two passed and the United Press International called. They had the same questions, the same requests. I kept telling them that the story was in the paper; that they could crib whatever they wanted from its pages. They wanted, instead, to interview me. UPI even wanted a photograph. I told them no. Then I took the phone off the hook. For a moment it made a half-beep, half-scream electronic sound; then it settled into quiet. Christine looked up from the paper and said, 'You know, this is just the beginning.'

I put my hands on her shoulders and kneaded her muscles for a moment, then slipped my hands under her bathrobe and cupped her breasts. I felt the nipples tighten under my touch, but she shrugged and pulled my hands away. 'I'm sorry,' she said, 'but reading this stuff just turns me off. I don't see how you can take it. I think I would have wanted to scream.' Then she thought for a moment. 'Did you ask the guy to give himself up?'

'No.' The thought took me by surprise. 'It didn't occur to me. His voice seemed too steady; he seemed too prepared, too involved in what he was doing and saying. He didn't sound like a man ready to give himself up.'

'Other times people have. To reporters, I mean. They surrender to the reporters because they think the police will hurt them. Or like at Attica, where they wanted observers.'

'Didn't do them any good, did it?'

'No,' she said, 'but you know what I mean.'

'I wish it had occurred to me. I wonder what his reaction would have been.'

'What do you think?'

'I think he would have laughed.'

Christine thought for a moment. She stood up then and walked to the window. The light framed her face suddenly, illuminating her cheekbones, making her eyes gleam. I tried to think of something to say to her to break the mood into which she was slipping. She shouldn't feel depressed; this was becoming the biggest story of my life. I was excited; I think that inwardly I didn't want the killer caught or surrendering – not yet, I thought. Her mind must have been on the same channel because she asked, 'Do you think he'll do it? I mean, go on with more killings?'

'I don't see why not,' I said.

She turned. 'Do you want him to?'

I shrugged.

'It's a better story if he does, isn't it?'

'Yes,' I answered. No denying that.

'A prizewinner?' she asked.

'Probably.'

'Maybe even the biggie, huh? The Pulitzer. Have you thought of that?'

'Oh, come on,' I said, 'don't get carried away.' But I had.

She laughed, but not in humor. I guessed she knew I was lying.

'Doesn't that kind of bother you?'

I shrugged again, but her questions continued, rapid-fire. 'Has it occurred to you that this creep may need the attention that he's getting in the newspapers and on the television? That without it he would feel ordinary and forgotten? That the attention he gets spurs him on to bigger and greater things?'

'Yes,' I said, 'those thoughts have struck me. But what am I supposed to do, ignore it? And who knows, he might continue with the killings regardless of what I write or anybody writes.'

'Doesn't it concern you?' she pressed.

'Not yet.'

I stopped in the *Journal* parking lot. The sky was a virulent pale blue – it seemed to have no end, no ceiling. Andrew Porter spotted me there and came up quickly. 'So they make the celebrities come to work, too,' he said, laughing.

'What do you mean?'

'You'll see soon enough.'

Outside the main entrance to the plant there were at least a half-dozen television camera crews. 'See you later,' he said. 'Remember, keep smiling.' Then he seemed to melt away through the crowd surrounding me. I kept pushing myself toward the doors, the day's heat abruptly doubled by the lights from the cameras. The first of the half-dozen microphones were shoved in front of me and I stopped. The questions came in waves, staccato, choppy. I barely answered one before another shot my way.

'What did he sound like?'

'Did he predict when the killings would begin?'

'Why do you think he called you?'

'Do you think he's crazy?'

'Do you think he'll call again?'

'Why is he doing this?'

Finally I held up my hand. 'I'm sorry,' I said, 'but I put just about everything I know in the story that ran in the *Journal* today. I can't add anything. I have no idea what's going to happen next.' And then I excused myself and headed into the building. A few more reporters were waiting by the doors, and they laughed and made the same joke Porter had made. I grinned. 'Hey, it's just my way of getting a raise.' I felt warm inside from the attention. I realized I had enjoyed the questions, enjoyed the focus of the cameras.

I passed the managing editor on the way to my desk. 'Terrific story,' he said. 'Keep at it.' He clapped me on the back.

Nolan smiled at me from across the room. He called out, 'Good job. Now you'll probably want a television contract,' and the rest of the office laughed with him.

I sat at my desk, glancing over the first edition of the *Post*. The killer's call was the lead story in their paper also, and I saw the byline of the reporter who'd called me earlier. Right after the killer's quotes, lifted from my story, were several quotes of my own. 'Anderson, 27, a *Journal* reporter for three years, said he was surprised by the killer's calm and singleness of purpose. "He seemed to be very confident and forthright," the reporter said today.' I read the story over and over.

The phone rang.

For a moment everything seemed to stop.

111

I put the paper down, feeling my heart accelerate. I punched the recording device and picked up the receiver. 'Anderson. *Journal*.'

And just as quickly, the excitement left me. I felt my system slow down and adjust. The call was from the main switchboard operator. 'Mr. Anderson,' she said as I shut off the recorder, 'what am I to do with all the calls?'

'What calls?'

'I have messages for you from reporters at a dozen newspapers,' she said. 'And besides that, people keep calling in on the main switchboard and asking for you. I think they're people who want to talk about the story today.' She had a pinched, tinny voice.

For the next hour I answered questions and fielded irate calls. It was almost noon when the ringing slacked off. Each time I hit the record button, each time I had to erase the tape. I took notes, though. I planned to write a a small story about the callers and their angers.

Nolan wanted a big reaction story. He sent several other reporters out to get man-in-the-street quotes. He put others on the phones, calling prominent Miamians for comment. I was to put the whole thing together; that was a decision, he said, made at the top. The stories were to carry my byline. It was for the killer's benefit, Nolan explained, to keep him thinking that I was the one connected to the story. He was afraid the killer would call the other paper or the wires or, worse yet, the television stations. 'We've got to keep this guy wrapped up,' Nolan said.

The day seemed to be streaking by.

I had scheduled an interview that afternoon with the psychiatrist. For a moment I felt uneasy about leaving the office. The thought went through my head that the killer might try to call in and get scared off when I didn't answer. After reflection, I realized there was nothing I could do to prevent it.

I tried to call Martinez and Wilson, but they were in the field.

I looked at the telephone on the desk. It was black, a simple, ordinary telephone. I had taken a ballpoint pen and inked in some of the numbers. It had a crack on one side, residue from an angry conversation with a politician when I'd slammed the phone down and it had tumbled to the floor. It seemed to me to be a live thing, breathing on the desk top, waiting as patiently as myself. I stared at it hard before leaving, as if I could tell it not to ring while I was out.

The psychiatrist was eating a sandwich when I walked into his office. 'You don't mind, do you?' he asked, gesturing. 'This is my lunch break.' I shook my head and looked around. His office was located in a medical building in the downtown area, a place of skyscrapers and glass that reflected the sun. From his desk I noticed he could see out over the bay toward Miami Beach and the ocean beyond.

It was a small office; a wall filled with diplomas, a portrait in pen and ink of Freud tucked in one corner. Another wall contained a bookshelf and several rows of books. There was a Picasso print, *The Musicians*, from the artist's first experiments with cubism. It hung on the wall above a leather couch. I took a seat across from the doctor's desk. He saw me looking around and asked, 'Does it make you nervous?' I laughed and didn't answer. He said, 'People have the strangest ideas of what a psychiatrist's office looks like. Oh, they know there will be a couch somewhere, but as to the rest . . .' His voice trailed off. 'I had a feeling you would be coming in,' he said. 'You want to know about your caller, I suppose?'

'Right,' I replied.

'Difficult,' he said. 'Very difficult.' He continued to eat the sandwich. He was a short man with wire-rimmed glasses and wore a dark blue suit which I imagined was very warm when he walked outside. His gray hair, still thick, was pushed back from his forehead, giving his face a childlike look, open and unassuming. We'd met before, usually in the courthouse where he did expert evaluations for several of the judges.

'Would it help to hear the tape?' I asked.

He smiled. 'What do you think?'

I produced the tape and a cassette recorder. The doctor slipped a pen from his pocket and placed a fresh sheet of paper in front of him. He nodded, and I started the machine.

'Certainty, I have learned, is something that is in short supply in the world . . .' the killer's voice said. In the room it sounded small but forceful; my own, I thought, sounded hesitant.

For the next few minutes all I could hear was the killer's voice mingling with the scratching sound the doctor's pen made across the white paper. He took notes throughout the tape, only occasionally lifting his eyes toward me; only once did his eyebrows shoot up in surprise at something the killer said. I turned and watched a big tanker slipping through the transparent blue of the bay; the colors of the Picasso on the wall were much the same as the water's. The tanker was heading toward the port of Miami, riding high in the water, empty. In the background the killer's voice went on, a cold passion attached to his words. When the tape ended, I looked back at the psychiatrist. He expelled air then, as if he'd been holding his breath throughout. It evoked an odd memory of driving with my father and brother in the family car. My father once told me that if you could hold your breath through the length of a tunnel you would get a wish granted. By whom he never specified – I supposed there was some tunnel genie or whatever – but for years, I remember, I automatically took a deep breath as the darkness jumped around the car and held it in, straining in silence as long as possible. Around New York it was particularly difficult; the Lincoln and Holland tunnels proved too long for my small lungs. There was always a moment of defeat with each sudden rush of breath from my body.

'Well,' the psychiatrist said hesitantly, 'this is a problem.'

'How so?'

'Let me say something off the record.' I nodded. 'I know that two of my colleagues have already been called in by the police to hear the tape. I talked with them late last night, knowing you were coming in today. You know, I have a habit of disagreeing with my peers.' He laughed and offered a small smile. 'But not on this occasion.'

115

'What's the verdict?' I said. 'I mean, what can you tell me about this guy? I don't want to sound overly simplistic, but my gut instincts tell me this man is serious. And he's dangerous.'

'Well,' the doctor started again, 'you're right on both those scores.' He looked down at his notes. 'I'm afraid I can't come up with an instant label that you can take to your readers. There's really not enough to go on, though the tape is remarkable.

'We often bandy about the terms psychotic, psychopath, sociopath. The last two mean just about the same thing. We talk about sexual deviations, aberrant behavior, paranoia, schizophrenia, all the twenty-five-cent terms with which you and many lay people are familiar. This killer seems to have several dominant features which would lend themselves to a number of psychiatric interpretations. I didn't see much paranoia in an obvious sense, but that doesn't mean it isn't there. In fact, some of the conversation that he relates about the victim would lend itself to that type of label. He is obviously very disturbed, near psychopathia . . .'

The doctor hesitated again and looked at me, his eyes intense. 'Let's try to cut through some of the gobbledygook, OK?'

I nodded.

'The psychiatric profession, as a rule, does not try to predict the relative dangerousness of various disorders. However, my belief is that this killer is highly dangerous. It is also my belief that he will kill again. And again.' He looked at his notes.

'People have to understand . . .' the doctor read.

116

'Well, it seems that he is expressing the need for recognition; that it is important to be justified in what he recognizes is behavior outside the norm.

'The killer then goes into a long description of growing up under stress on a farm in Ohio. That he is in contact with the history of abuse is unusual; usually, that would be blockaded by the mind. He speaks of the act of being punished irrationally. I suspect that the abuse he suffered was greater than he described and more arbitrarily applied than he lets on. Then there is a crisis: he challenges the father for control, and the crisis is exacerbated by the fact that he is successful. In that one moment his world was turned upside down; whatever feelings he had about guilt, punishment, right and wrong, they would be turned around, the apple cart upset. Note that he recalls the way his father made him call out the number of the blows; we see that repeated now in his numbering of the victim. She is Number One.

'I wonder about the mother, too. She seems to be a non-person; she just watches throughout. I doubt that was actually the case; I think she probably engaged in some aberrant behavior herself, but it's impossible to really speculate.

'Then there is a long period of restlessness; of lying awake at night. Psychiatrically, that time corresponds to the time of his sexual awakening. But by this point he is so confused – I wonder if he really heard the sounds of the bathwater being drawn, or if it was some other night sound involving his parents? But again, I'm only guessing.

'And then there is this remarkable section. Here,

see how I wrote this down: ". . . I tried to shut away all the nightmares. Later they liked to put me in the perimeter listening post . . ." You see, he segues from his childhood into the war. Vietnam. So there's the possibility of a type of battle fatigue. During the fifties, after Korea, I helped with some studies. We discovered psychotic symptoms arising under some types of stress and fatigue. OK. Generally, they were short-lived and dissipated when the subject was removed from the stress situation, but some of my friends who have worked with Vietnam veterans report the same syndrome, only to a greater extent; the symptoms do not reduce as swiftly. There are many theories about why that is, having to do with the nature of the war, the counterinsurgency, the savagery, the lack of defined enemies, the lack of a front, the shapelessness of it all, especially when combined with the contradictions of the war. I mean, here were men out in the field, performing routine tasks of terrible consequences: they feared they would step on a land mine, lose their legs or their genitals; that they would be lost in an alien environment; that they would suddenly find themselves in the midst of a firefight, unable to see or to fight the enemy, surrounded by death. And then, moments later, they would be on some hilltop and a helicopter would land, and everyone would drink a cold Coke or have a Schlitz, just as if they were back home, almost. This is incredibly disorienting. In effect, they did not know where they were.

'And in the midst of all this, our man finds peace. "But to me it was restful . . ." Extraordinary.

'But,' the doctor continued – 'and this is a big but – something happens. He talks for a second about "the real horror." And he sees it as some type of a play, a way of describing what we call a dissociative reaction, as if he were outside looking in at himself. And then he says he won't talk about that yet.

'That, I suppose, is the key. If I were a gambling man, I would put money on the guess that the course of murders he has seemingly embarked on is in some way, in his mind – which is a tangle, let me tell you – a duplication. He is, in effect, reenacting personal experience. It's like those sniper attacks you read about every once in a while: unconscious duplications of moments of war. The mind becomes confused; peace at home becomes the war. And the soldier reacts.

'I suspect that when you find out what the "horror" was, then we will have come a big step toward understanding the course of the killer's mind. But a word of caution. His mind can still make adjustments. He still appreciates symbolism. It won't necessarily be a one-to-one trade-off.'

The doctor swiveled in his chair and stood up abruptly. He walked to the picture window and looked out over the bay. His hands came up in a reflex motion and he pushed his hair back from his forehead. Still looking out, he began to speak again.

'I remember when I was in the Army, attached to the psychiatric facility outside of Vacaville in California. We must have treated thousands of cases of fatigue induced by battle conditions, residue from the Korean War. My God, it doesn't seem like a quarter century ago. Many of the cases remain fresh in my mind; they were like parts on an assembly line, put together with speed and efficiency, but with some inherent defect within, unseen, so that they couldn't function properly.

'On one ward we had to keep the lights burning throughout the night because the men had grown so afraid of the dark; strong men, who had seen terrible conditions and survived, but they suddenly couldn't control their fears when the lights went out. There was one case I remember particularly well; whether it's apropos of the present situation, I'm not certain. You be the judge.

'He came in shortly after the Chinese invasion, when the Chinese swarmed across the Yalu River and whole divisions were cut off before the command was centralized and the lines reformed. You probably don't remember it, and certainly few people in the States had any real idea of the suddenness and the frightening quality of that attack. Some of the racism that we found in the Vietnam War was prevalent then; the fear derived from propaganda about the yellow peril and the insensitive, animal-like Oriental. Much was left over from the Second World War, the jingoism and the anti-Oriental feeling. Then to be overrun by the hordes. Well, suffice it to say that it was a difficult time.

'Anyway, the disorientation and the subsequent reassignation of emotions that I see in the killer remind me of one of the cases I had then. He was a young man, blond, high cheekbones, the type of face that we would say then reflected breeding. And he was indeed the product of a good household: the mother was a New York socialite; the father, what one would call a captain of industry. The son had grown up, an only child, in New York; he had known private schools and chauffeurs and piano lessons and the opera. At the age of seventeen he entered Harvard, where he majored in history with a minor in political science. He was destined for the foreign service, at least at first; possibly law school, possibly a career in politics. A golden boy – right? – tremendous potential. He told me at length about the conversation he'd had with his father, discussing the future, and the thought they'd both had that a military experience would be helpful, even imperative; another step along the road to success.

'A short time after his graduation, the young man received a commission in the Army. He volunteered for the Korean action after much the same discussion with his family, the thought of a little combat, perhaps a medal or two, prominent in their minds. The father had done his service during peacetime, between the wars. The danger of the situation that the young man was entering was shrouded from them all. I cannot stress this naiveté enough; it surfaced again and again in our conversations. And so, when the Chinese poured over the Yalu, this young man was commanding a rifle company near the front lines.

'They were cut off, encircled by a superior force and slaughtered. The young man was with a platoon that was literally blown apart by heavy automatic-weapons fire. He was the only one of the group alive when the shooting hit a lull. He realized then that the Chinese were walking through the carnage, systematically checking the bodies.

'He decided, in a split second, that he would have to fake his own death to avoid being captured or shot. He dipped his fingers into the blood of his own men and soaked parts of his tunic with it. He told me that he worked swiftly, single-mindedly, really unaware of what he was doing. Finally, when his wounds appeared authentic, he pulled two bodies over him, so that he was beneath them. His last act was to take a handful of blood and brain matter from one body and smear it across his own forehead and scalp.

'Then he shut his eyes and waited, afraid that the cold air would illuminate his breath, feeling the dead weight of the men above him.

'There was a break in his perceptions, you see; he was limited to what he could hear and smell; he was like a blind man, every sound a note of terror, unfamiliar, frightening. He told me of hearing voices approach and of hearing the shuffling of feet. At one point he heard English spoken and guttural responses in Chinese. Then he heard shots, each one seemingly closer. He could feel the cold from the ground creeping into him like death itself, buried already under the bodies of his soldiers, the men he'd commanded, known just a few short hours earlier. His limbs were frozen with fear, he said, and each instant he expected to be plummeted into darkness more profound than that behind his squeezed eyelids. Finally he heard footsteps close by, and he could feel the weight of the bodies shifting on top of him, as if someone were poking them. Then the footsteps moved away, and he remained stiff and motionless for hours, waiting for another sound. He said it took more courage than he thought he had to open his eyes and look about him. He was alone, save for the dead.

'He was cut off for two days behind the lines. He wandered about, hiding mostly in scrub brush and trees. At night he sheltered himself with branches as best he could against the snow. He didn't eat; he couldn't find anything. On the third day he met up with a group of men who'd also been cut off but who had managed to establish radio contact. In another few hours he was safe back behind our own lines. He made a statement to superiors describing in detail the events, the loss of the men. He was able to name almost all, I believe, by memory. He was examined by a doctor, found to be in good health despite the ordeal and shortly thereafter was sent back to the States. The Army gave him the Distinguished Service Medal.

'His first night home he awoke screaming that he couldn't breathe, as if some weight were crushing his lungs. He began to shiver uncontrollably, regardless of the amount of heat in the room or how many blankets were piled onto his body. He became terrified of closing his eyes, afraid that he would not be able to open them. And then one moment, a few days after, sitting at the table with his mother and father and a few guests, enjoying a meal, he squeezed his eyes shut for a minute, perhaps two, and when he opened them he could not see. He was blind. Shortly thereafter he was sent to me at Vacaville.

'Hysteric reaction was the official diagnosis. A simple conversion from the event: blindness equals death.

And so he brought it upon himself, compensating for surviving that which had killed all his friends.

'We talked. We worked. He did not hide the events, but even when he came to appreciate the psychiatric basis for his loss of vision, it didn't return. I wondered then what deeper punishment he was doling out to himself.

'He was given a leave home, arrived at the New York apartment, kissed his mother, shook hands with his father, said he wanted to change – prophetic words, those – and walked into his bedroom. He put down the cane, found a revolver that he'd owned for years and shot himself. Right in the same spot that he'd smeared himself with gore from his companions.'

The doctor looked across at me. Outside, I could see the sun reflecting across the bay, and a flight of gulls swung by. They wheeled over the water.

'So,' the doctor continued, 'don't underestimate the strength of this kind of combination: battle-induced trauma on top of a more elemental mental illness.'

'Prognosis?'

'Very bad. Bad for the victims, bad for the killer. And one other thing . . .'

'What's that?'

'They can't catch him.'

'What do you mean?'

'This type of killer is the single most difficult to catch. The police uniformly have the greatest of problems with psychotic murderers. Look at Jack the Ripper. He was never caught. You see, they defy the usual methods of detection because of the essential irrationality of their acts. Their motive lies within their minds, not in greed or anger or any of the usual emotions that policemen are familiar with and which prompt homicides.'

I stared at the doctor. He turned and gazed out over the bay. 'Unless the killer makes a mistake, the same type that an ordinary criminal might make, he'll be almost impossible to capture. There is the chance that someone will spot him, or that some neighbor will detect his behavior, or that his weapon can be traced. That might lead to an arrest. But don't count on it.

'You see, one of the essential paradoxes of this type of killer and the situation he creates is that while he gains a satisfaction by taunting the police, by daring the community to find him – that's the underlying force behind the phone call to you – at the same time he wants unconsciously to be stopped. However, his conscious mind is one that deals in finite detail. He will think of almost everything to avoid capture. You tell me,' the doctor said, 'how the police can work with that?'

'I don't know,' I said. 'Do you suppose he'll slip up on the phone?'

'Maybe. Maybe not.' A buzzer went off under the psychiatrist's desk. He bent down, flipped a switch and looked back at me. 'A patient,' he said. I collected the tape recorder. He walked me to the door. 'You know,' he said, 'I surely hope I'm wrong. And don't assume that everything I've said is gospel. This is a severely disturbed individual; he is capable of almost anything. This may sound terrible, but suicide is a possibility. A person such as the one on the tape has a great deal of self-hatred. "I am," he said, "the worst thing in the world." We'll just have to see.'

'Thanks for your help.'

'It was my pleasure,' he said. As he shut the door I caught a final glimpse of the blue of the bay through the window.

Late that afternoon I began to put together the reaction story; other reporters dropped notes on my desk, usually typed quotations that came from officials or street people. Many seemed skeptical, almost challenging. It was as if people were going to make the killer put up or shut up, a kind of macabre dare. I blended the views of the psychiatrist into the reactions of the other people.

'This freak doesn't scare me . . .' a teenager, outside a playground.

'I think it's just some guy trying to get attention. I doubt that he'll do what he says . . .' a businessman stopped on the street.

'I trust the police will get this man quickly . . .' a housewife in the suburbs.

'All patrolmen have been briefed and will be on the lookout for unusual behavior. All unnecessary leaves have been canceled. Extra patrols will be added to certain high-risk areas . . .' a local police chief.

I tried to visualize the faces that went with the words, the expressions of anger or fear. I felt as if I were being squeezed between the words of the killer and the words of the community. I continued to type quickly, pausing only occasionally to grab a quote from the pages of notes. I did not look up until I heard the shouts from the rear of the newsroom. When I turned in the chair I saw a young man, I guessed in his early twenties, trying to free himself from the grip of one of the *Journal* security guards.

Everyone in the office turned to look at the disturbance, and the shouts suddenly became clear, like a picture that has slipped into focus. The young man was yelling: 'I want to talk to the guy who wrote this. Now, dammit, leave me alone!' The security guard gripped his arm, trying to hold him back. I knew that it was me he wanted to talk with. Out of the corner of my eye I saw Andrew Porter step from the photo lab to look at the commotion. I managed to catch his attention with my hands, making a motion as if mimicking taking a photo. He nodded and reappeared a moment later with his camera. He swiveled the lens and began to snap off shots as unobtrusively as possible. By this time the young man had calmed somewhat and was arguing with the security guard who still held him by the arm. I stepped across the room, and the two men turned and looked at me. 'I believe it's me you want to talk to,' I said as softly as possible.

The young man's eyes were rimmed with red. He had blond hair that fell over his ears, shaggy, unkempt. He looked at me for a moment and seemed to collapse, as if a string inside him had been sliced. His arms dropped to his sides and he ceased struggling. The security guard, a muscled Cuban with a thick mustache, looked at me. I nodded and he released the young man. He stayed close by, though, his muscles tensed.

'Are you Anderson?' the young man asked.

I nodded.

'I'm her brother,' he said.

'That's what I thought,' I replied.

'Why?'

I shrugged. 'Let's sit down.' The young man bent his head, and I motioned to an empty desk. He slid into the chair like a man exhausted.

'I don't understand,' he started. 'I've read this over and over, and I still don't understand. What did she do? Why should she have to pay for some – oh, I don't know – for something that happened somewhere else? I mean, why blame her?'

'You must have loved her very much,' I said.

He stared at me. 'She was very . . .' And then he hesitated. I could see him thinking, looking for words. 'I don't know. She was . . . she had a specialness about her. We all loved her. She was the baby in the family.' His eyes filled again.

'What can I tell you?' I asked.

'I don't know why I came,' he said. 'I guess that for a moment I thought you and he were the same. You know, you were the link; he called you, and I guess I thought that I should come down and talk to you as if you were him.' He paused. 'That doesn't make much sense, does it? I mean, I see now . . .' And he looked about the newsroom at the reporters and editors. 'Will he call again?'

'I think so,' I replied. 'It's hard to tell.'

'I wish I could get just five minutes alone with the guy. I don't care how much training he got, in the Army or wherever. I don't care what kind of a killer they turned him into. I promise I'd handle him! I'd just want one chance. Listen.' He looked at me. His voice had begun to pick up momentum, excitement. 'I'm going to write down my address. You give it to the killer, OK? If he really wants to start a string of murders, well, why doesn't he try to start with me, huh? Then we'll see who comes out on top.' The young man grabbed a piece of notepaper from the desk and a pencil and started to write furiously. 'Give this to him,' he said, handing me the paper.

I looked down at the address. It was the family's home in the southern section of the city. 'All right,' I said. I was lying.

The young man sat back in his chair, deflating again. 'Just five minutes,' he said. He looked at me. 'You tell me why. You've talked with this guy. You tell me why.'

I shook my head. 'He's crazy. Crazy people do crazy things. What can I say?' I shrugged my shoulders in an exaggerated fashion. Again, I knew I was lying.

'I don't care if he is sick,' the young man said. 'I want him dead. Just like he killed my sister.'

'I don't blame you.'

He wiped his eyes, rubbing his palms into the sockets hard for a long moment. 'It just doesn't seem fair. How could God do this? She never hurt anything in her life. She even went to a peace march when she was just ten years old. Can you believe that? She was marching along, skipping to keep up with the marchers, singing, "Peace now! No more war!" in her little girl's voice. She came home in tears because the policemen were so nasty. Can you believe that? Nasty, that's the word she used. And they were, that's exactly what they were. She wasn't afraid of anything. I bet she wasn't even afraid at the end.'

'You're probably right.'

The young man looked around. 'I'm keeping you from your story,' he said. 'I suppose there's going to be another story?'

'Yes,' I said. 'People's reactions. It'll be in the papers tomorrow.'

'Well,' he said, standing up, 'when that bastard calls you, you tell him that Jerry Hooks wants a piece of him. You make it a real challenge; tell him I'm waiting.' He made a fist and waved it in the air between us. 'I'll kill him with my bare hands.'

'I'll tell him,' I said. Maybe, I thought, maybe not.

'OK,' the young man said. He looked over at the security guard. 'I apologize.' The guard nodded, stone-faced. 'I'm sorry,' he said, turning back to me. 'To have disturbed you like this, I mean. I guess this whole thing has made me a little crazy.' He stuck out his hand and I shook it. 'I don't blame you,' he said.

And then he left, accompanied by the guard.

Nolan walked up then. 'Intense,' he said. I agreed. He looked at me. 'Write it. Word for word. Make that the lead of the reaction piece.'

I nodded my head. 'OK.'

'Terrific stuff,' Nolan said. 'Jesus, that poor kid must be really bent out of shape by this. Poor sucker.' He looked at me again. 'Capture it all: the look on his face, the way he wrote out that address. Get it all down. Phenomenal.'

I went back to my desk. But before I started writing I played over and over again the young man's final words. They stared at me from the page of my mind like an accusation.

And then I shook my head hard, as if to shake the image loose, and began to reconstruct the conversation. Minus the last words.

Christine was waiting for me when I arrived home. The evening sky had been a virulent purple-violet. The last light of the day illuminated huge thunderheads rising up to the west of the city above the Everglades. 'I saw you on the television,' she said. 'The national news. Cronkite and Brinkley and Chancellor, too. So did your father. He called just a few minutes ago.' She put her arms around my neck. 'I'm not sure whether to be proud or scared. I suppose a little of both.'

I went to the kitchen and opened a bottle of beer. She poured herself a glass of wine, and we sat and talked. She liked to run her fingers through her hair, pushing it back and up, as if to clear it from her ears. The beer was cold and seemed to spread through me, cooling. I loosened my tie and sat back, raising my glass. 'Here's to you,' I said. She clicked my glass with her own. 'So,' I said, 'tell me about your day.'

'It was an ordinary day. We had a child. No, not a child, a boy in that rough time when his voice won't stay low or high. You remember the time that just as soon as you get a crush on a girl a pimple breaks out in the center of your forehead.' She grinned and I laughed.

131

'And?'

'Oh, it was both sad and happy at the same time. I worry sometimes that I let myself get too affected by all the patients who come into the ward. You know, the administrator wanted to know if I'd shift to the terminal ward, to deal with those cases. Hope is all they have. Sometimes not even that. I refused. At least in my ward, the people have a chance. Slim to mediocre, but a chance.'

'The boy?'

'He had a big growth on his ankle. You can't tell, you know, before you get inside what it will be like. I mean, the X rays show you it's there, and they give you an idea of the size and everything, but it's not until you really see it, open to the air; in the theater under those bright lights that you really appreciate it. It has an ugliness, a malevolence all its own.

'Anyway,' she continued, 'the boy came in, and the tremendous thing about a kid that age is that they have an immortality about them; you can tell them the worst news in the world, tell them that they have days, hours, just minutes to live, and they still think that it's forever. They have this incredible confidence and trust in their own bodies. They aren't old enough to know the kind of betrayal that the body can perform.

'So the kid spends the night, jumping around the ward. The night nurse told me that even sedated, he was up and talking almost all night. She sat with him for a couple of hours. Baseball, she said; he wanted to talk about the Yankees and the Red Sox. I wish you'd been there. You could have told him a lot.

'Well, in the morning he's prepped and ready, and the orderly wheels him into the operating room, and he looks up at the doctor and says, "I trust you, but don't get carried away," and then he laughs and we all join him. I was standing behind his head to try and make certain he wasn't nervous, but the kid was cooler than I. He went out like a light when the Pentothal hit him. I remember when the section from the tumor was cut off for the biopsy I waited, praying that it would be negative.

'This job is turning me into a religious fanatic; I have conversations in my mind all the time, saying, "Look, God, this is a good kid. Give him a break, will ya?" Anyway, this time it worked. The growth was benign. The pathologist had a big smile when he came back into the theater with the news, and everyone grinned. Doctors look funny, smiling behind a mask; it seems to catch just the shape of the smile.

'But the bad news was that to get the whole thing out we had to break his leg. The surgeon worked for an hour to try and get it out before going with the bone cracker. He was swearing and bitching; he has a boy the same age.

'It was really hard for the kid to understand. When he woke up he seemed so disappointed; all he could talk about was his American Legion ball team and missing the season. He had this confused look on his face because he couldn't understand why everyone was so happy. It was because the tumor was benign and he didn't lose the whole damn leg. All he understood was that he had a broken leg, and he didn't even have a stolen base or a long slide home with the winning run to show for it.'

She drained off the last of her glass and poured it full again. She looked across the room to me. 'Can you remember what it was like to be that age? I can't picture you.'

I thought for a moment. Instead of a picture of myself, I saw a gangly youth on a dusty macadam road, walking in and out of the shadows on a late spring afternoon. I couldn't focus on the killer's face, but I could see a small room and a board and hear the gasping breath of the father as he labored to beat the son's backside bloody.

'Did you play ball?' Christine asked.

'Shortstop,' I said. 'My brother was a catcher.' I remembered a bright sun. Summer. I laughed out loud. 'Once we were in a close game, and one of the guys on the other team hit a screamer to my right, between me and third base. They had a guy, the tying run, on third. The kid on third broke for the plate. Two outs, you see, run on anything was the rule. I made this great leap, probably not such a great distance but at that age everything seems bigger and speeded up, and came up with the ball. More likely the ball accidentally jumped into my mitt. Anyway, at that age one's baseball instincts are nearly perfect. It only comes later with coaching that you get screwed up. I scrambled to my feet and whipped the ball to home. I couldn't make a more perfect throw today. It was waist high, with plenty on it. It beat the runner by almost ten feet. And my brother dropped it. I didn't talk to him for a week.'

I smiled, but Christine frowned. 'That seems cruel,' she said.

'Growing up is cruel.'

But I thought again of the killer. Not that cruel. The phone rang, and I went and picked it up.

'It's probably your father,' Christine said. She went into the kitchen and started to make me a sandwich.

'I saw you on the news,' my father said. He laughed. 'You looked exasperated at having the tables turned.'

'Well, I guess at first.'

'This must be something; did the killer call again?'

'Not yet,' I said, 'but I suspect he will.'

'It must be exciting. I wonder if there'll be something in the *Times* in the morning?'

'Well, one of their reporters called me.'

'So,' he asked, 'how do you like this sudden notoriety?'

Several answers ran through my mind. I thought of saying I was unaffected, that I remained the same objective reporter regardless of the story and the attention. Or that it was just another story and I didn't really think it would amount to much. That would be a transparent lie, though. So I told him that it was exciting and that I enjoyed being the focus of attention. 'It's not unlike what you go through,' I said, 'when you argue a high-visibility case. Suddenly you're projected into the center of the courtroom, and your words become the object of the exercise. I suppose there's an element of that here; for the first time, really, I can see what I've written having an effect. The killer said a couple of times that

135

he plans to create a theater; I guess I've become more than a bit player.'

'Ah,' my father said, 'you're enjoying it?'

'To be honest,' I replied, 'yes.'

He thought for a moment. 'In a way, it reminds me of a time when I was younger and with that big Wall Street firm; you remember, Clay, Michaels, Black. The firm routinely did pro bono work; usually class-action lawsuits and the like. This was back in the early fifties, the time old Joe McCarthy was grabbing all the headlines. Anyway, we were asked to represent a young man accused of murder, and I was assigned the case. He was an unemployed dockworker, a tough guy, a member of the Communist party. I remember him telling me about his older brother who'd died with the Lincoln Brigade in Spain. He was accused of killing another man in a fight. One punch to the jaw. The trouble was, the other man was the brother of a city cop, and there was some pressure on the prosecutors to bring a big conviction. No deals. I was tossed into the fray; the papers were making a lot of it, especially the tabs. We decided to argue self-defense. I remember my feelings in the courtroom. I was only a little older than you are now. The issues, the trial, the defense, all seemed secondary to the spotlight. It was electrifying, exciting. Like the feeling one gets after being with a beautiful woman.' He laughed at the memory.

'What happened?'

'Oh, winners and losers. The jury tossed out the murder charge but came back with a manslaughter conviction.'

136

'And?'

'It was sad.' My father's voice changed slightly. 'The judge bowed to all the pressure and sent the kid up. He was killed in a fight in the yard at Sing Sing about a year later.' He was quiet for a moment. 'I'll say one thing; I don't envy the prosecutor on the case or the defense attorney if they capture this guy. But then' – he paused – 'I don't suppose they'll catch him.'

'Why not?'

'He seems too crazy, too clever. A bad combination. You should exercise caution.'

Again, he paused for a moment. 'The notoriety is meaningless,' he said. 'I regretted it afterwards. So will you.'

'Maybe,' I said. But I wasn't sure. I could picture my father at his desk in his office at home. He would have a martini; there would be law books piled in front of him, sheets of paper covered with his notes and musings. He was a man devoted to the intricacies of the law. Like a surgeon who works with living tissue, that was his approach to statutes and regulations. It was a world I knew only obliquely; I would see the books and see his work; once I tried to read a brief of his. I was small, and I thought that if he wrote it, then surely it must be about himself and that I would be able to see a little better through his reserve. I struggled for days past each page, each citation, each footnote, searching the text for my father. In a way, I thought years later, I found him but didn't realize it. He was the reason I'd become a journalist; I'd slipped through school relying on my writing to sleep through courses. Finally, he said, what have you learned? Not much, I said. You can write, he said. True, I replied. Then, he said, do something that requires you to write a good deal. And a week later he came home from his office having stopped off at the local library and checked out a copy of *Editor and Publisher Yearbook*, which had full listings of papers and news executives throughout the nation.

'One other thing,' he said now. 'I'm not sure I buy all this Vietnam stuff.'

'How so?'

'It just seems too damn convenient. It seems everyone wants to blame everything on that damn war. The economy, recession, inflation. All because of Vietnam. Watergate, the damn president. Vietnam, they say. Now this guy thinks he can waltz around killing people and blaming it on the war. I just can't see it. Your uncle went through hard times in the war. Damn hard times. And he didn't come home and start killing people.'

'Except himself.' The words were out before I could hold them.

He hesitated. 'Yes, that may be true.'

I asked then after my mother, my brother and sister, and we chatted a few moments. Then he rang off with the advice, 'Don't get too dependent on this guy, and watch your step.' I understood what he meant in the second part of the message, but not the first.

That night in bed, Christine tried to apologize for not being responsive. She said the killer's proximity worried her and threw her off her rhythm. Then she slipped her hands onto my chest and began to stroke me slowly, expertly. Finally she reached over and pulled me across her and inside her in the same motion, doing all the work of the lovemaking. Afterwards she slept, but I was restless. I played over in my head the conversations with the psychiatrist, the victim's brother, my father. I went to the window and looked out. Past the trees I could see the street empty of traffic. In the distance I heard a siren, the wail drowning out the buzzing and clicking of the night bugs. The streetlights seemed dim, the light from the moon strong, shedding a pale color over everything. I thought of the city, lit up by the moon, wondered if the killer were awake, too.

I saw a man walk down the street slowly. I watched him, his shape an outline of darkness. He seemed to be looking for an address, and he paused near the front of my building. He looked up, but our eyes did not meet. Then he walked off slowly, still looking. I followed him until he turned the corner and disappeared through the wan yellow glow of a streetlight. I thought of the phone on my desk in the office and wondered when it would ring again.

And then I realized that I wanted the killer to call. I envisioned the string of bannered stories and the camera light in my eyes, microphones at my mouth. I laughed out loud at the novelty of it all.

Call, damn you, I thought.

Do what you have to, but call.

But he didn't.

For three days the telephone remained silent. I wrote two stories, one on the expanded police search, profiling Martinez and Wilson, the leaders. Then another reaction story from the street. Nolan came up on the third day and said: 'Christ, I think the killer may have felt the heat and taken the proverbial hike.' He looked down at the tape recorder still attached to my phone. 'We'll see,' he said.

The phone rang and I jumped.

For an instant I waited, letting the bell sound once, twice, then seized it in the midst of the third ring. 'Anderson, *Journal*.'

There was nothing.

I tensed, checking the tape recorder to make certain it was working properly. I drew in a deep breath and repeated myself. I could hear breathing on the other end. My pencil poised over a sheet of paper.

'Who is it?' I demanded.

And then laughter, high-pitched, giggling.

'Christine!'

'Good guess,' she said.

'Goddammit, what're you doing!' I punched off the recorder. 'What the hell do you mean by this!'

'Oh,' she said, 'try to relax just a little bit, OK?'

'Goddammit, Christine, this is serious business.' I was furious. My fist was clenched on the desk in front of me, punching the top to underscore my words.

'I know, I know,' she said. 'I'm sorry. It's just, well, you're so wrapped up in this. I just wanted you to – I don't know – not take it so *seriously*.'

'It is serious! Dammit, you've been telling me that for days now.'

'I know,' she said. 'But it's not everything, is it?'

'Well, damn close.'

'Don't say that,' she said. Her voice had grown subdued. 'Oh, Malcolm, it isn't the end of the world. It's just another story. You said that yourself.'

'Well, then I was wrong.'

'Hypocrite.' She wasn't angry. It was more a statement of fact.

I could feel the muscles in my neck and back relax. 'I am,' I said. 'You're right.'

'I'm sorry,' she said. 'I shouldn't have called like that. But it never seems to relent, not even for a moment.' There was sadness in each word.

'It's all right,' I said.

She rang off then, and I returned to my waiting. I found myself sweating, nervous. The phone rang other times. Each time I would reach out, like a drowning man for a rope. I could barely hide the disappointment in my voice. At home that night Christine watched as I fielded a phone call: one instant my body tensed; the next, frustrated, slamming the receiver down. 'I'm glad,' she said, 'no one is dead.'

She put some music on the stereo, country and western. She pulled me to my feet and started to step around me: 'Do, si, do,' she said. 'Step to your right, step to your left. Salute your partner. Wheel to the right, wheel to the left.' I stood in the center of the room while she seized my hand and spun around me. 'Oh, come on,' she pleaded, drawing out her words. 'Try to relax. Just a little bit.' She stopped and wrapped her arms around me. 'Stand by your man,' she sang, though the words didn't fit

141

the music. I laughed then, unable to hold back. Her face broke into a wide smile.

'See,' she said. 'People, look! The eighth wonder of the world! Right here in our living room! The great stone-faced reporter, just the facts, ma'am, just the facts, has actually smiled! Medical history made!' And we laughed together.

But that night, in bed with Christine asleep beside me, I could think of nothing but the killer. I tried to send a mental order: Call, dammit, even to say it's over. I reached out and stroked Christine's back, and she made a small noise in her sleep and shifted position. We are both, I thought, spurned lovers.

On the afternoon of the following day, late, while the sky was turning color and the heat was slowly dissipating, the phone rang again. It was the fourth successive call; two from cranks, one from a politician. I reached out, tired, angry. 'Anderson,' I said, clicking down on the recorder, keeping my finger on the button to shut it off again immediately.

'Tested your faith, didn't I?' came the voice. The words breathed a chill over the line.

'I didn't think you'd call,' I said.

'I told you this was just the beginning.'

He was silent for an instant.

'I saw you on the television,' he continued. 'Good. Really good. I decided it's just you and me now.'

'What do you mean?'

'Explanations later. Action first. Like the Army. Shoot first, ask questions later.'

'I don't get it,' I said.

'You will. Here's an address. Twenty-two ninety-five Nautilus Avenue on the Beach.'

'What about it?'

'Well,' he said, 'you don't have to do anything, really. I suppose the neighbors will get suspicious in a day or so. And then they'll walk right up and knock on the door. They'll probably catch the smell then. It's an extraordinary smell; it has a sweetness to it at the same time it reaches through your body and churns your insides. Once you smell it, you can never forget it. And the really odd thing is that when you smell it, you know exactly what it is without seeing; even if you don't know, you know.'

Another hesitation.

'We'll talk again soon,' he said. 'So long.'

And then the phone clicked, and I was left with an emptiness on the line.

CHAPTER SEVEN

The story turned then, with the discovery of the elderly couple's bodies. Their deaths also altered my own perception of the events of that summer. Much of the excitement and pleasure I had experienced in becoming the focus of so much attention – the object of interviews on television, seeing my own words quoted in the opposition newspaper and on the wires – seemed to slip away in the shadows on a quiet street in an older section of Miami Beach. Before, I suppose I had seen the killer as merely sick. Now his cruelty became apparent.

The death of the old couple had a singular effect upon the community, too; I began to see the first signs of stress and panic. I suppose I was like anyone in Miami; I thought that the killer was going to confine his murders to teenage girls, that at the root of the impulse to kill there was some sexual urge, misshapen, inexplicable. The old couple's death sent a shock through the community, not unlike an earth tremor that shakes the foundations and brings on nausea. It was as if everyone had the same sudden thought: My God, it could be me next.

When the phone rang on my desk the newsroom would quiet down inappropriately. I could feel the attention of the editors and the other reporters swinging over toward me, watching my face for a reaction. I felt increasingly isolated, as if I were alone with the killer.

After the call, I jumped up and paced across the newsroom to Nolan sitting at the city desk. He looked up and saw the mark on my face. 'Again?'

'On the Beach,' I said. 'I guess he's killed again. He gave me an address: Twenty-two ninety-five Nautilus Avenue.'

Nolan hesitated. 'Get Porter and get going. I'll call Homicide.' In a few moments he was speaking with Martinez and Wilson. I heard him tell them to meet me on the corner of Twenty-second and Nautilus. He did not tell them why, but I supposed there was little question in anyone's mind. He turned back toward me, waving his hand. 'Go, go, go,' he said.

Porter and I drove over the Venetian Causeway, cutting across the bay to the Beach. I looked out of the car windows at the water; a breeze was kicking up small whitecaps on the wavelets. In the middle of the causeway fishermen were casting lines out into the shallow water. I saw one old black woman leaning over the edge, twisting the handle on her spinning reel, the tip of the rod bending and jumping as the fish on the other end pulled against the hook. She was cackling and laughing, and her voice carried through the afternoon heat into the car.

We waited a few minutes for the two detectives to arrive. Porter adjusted his equipment; he had slung two cameras around his neck, one with a flash for indoor work, the other with fast film for outdoors.

He asked several questions, trying to find out what I knew about where we were going, trying to envision what we would see, what he would be shooting. 'I love the moment before something starts,' he said, 'the short time after the referee blows his whistle but before the kickoff. It's like when I shot that big storm down in the Caribbean. There were no phones, no communications. I had a beat-up Land Rover and I just drove from town to town. The storm had leveled everything. Trees snapped in half, houses collapsed, rooftops gone. There was always a moment coming around the last turn in the road before entering a town when I would feel this apprehension about what I would see; wondering how many bodies would be lying out in the street. They get swollen in the sun. That's how I feel now, as if I've just started to pull around that last corner.'

I said nothing and looked down at the paper in my hand. I had written down two names: Mr. Ira Stein, Mrs. Ruth Stein. They had come from a fast look into the city directory. It was a quiet street, typical of the Beach. The houses, mostly built in the 1930s, were white stucco and set back a few yards from the roadway. They were trim homes, Spanish design, with archways and fruit trees. I looked down the street and I could see no one. There were a few cars parked out front of the houses, but mostly there was silence. The wind caused a nearby palm to clatter its leaves together. 'There they are,' Porter said.

The two detectives got out of an unmarked cruiser. They had put a flashing light on the dashboard but hadn't used a siren. The crime-scene technicians remained in their vehicle.

'So,' Martinez said, 'what is it?'

'The killer called again. Gave me an address.' I pointed down the street. 'Down there.'

Wilson followed my finger. 'OK. Let's take a look.' He looked over at Porter. 'You can come in,' he said, 'but I want to know what you're shooting. I don't want to pick up the paper and see some piece of evidence on the front page.'

Porter nodded. 'No hassle.'

We got into our cars and drove slowly down the block. Twenty-two ninety-five was the last house on the left-hand side, and Porter pulled the car in front. I said, 'Let's move. I want to see,' and we stepped across a small green lawn, past some shrubs and up to the front door.

The killer was right. I could smell it. I paused, waiting for the detectives.

Wilson stood next to me for a moment, then turned to Martinez. 'Go call for a medical examiner,' he said. Then he waved to the technicians. The door was slightly ajar, and one of them took a penknife and swung it open. 'Don't touch anything,' Wilson said. 'Keep your hands in your pockets. If you have to get sick, make certain that you get outside.' He took out a handkerchief. 'Got one of these?' he asked. 'No? Here, use some Kleenex. Hold it tight over your nostrils, it might help. Ready?' Then he looked at Porter. 'Really glamorous stuff, huh?' He didn't wait for a reply.

Inside, the smell was overpowering, like a mask being cupped over my face. I had smelled bodies before, covering other crimes, but this was the worst. All the windows were closed; the air inside stifling and heavy. The killer was right; it was sweet. We walked into the living room.

I could not have been prepared for the sight. Not even in a nightmare.

There was blood streaked everywhere, on the walls, the floor, the couch, the rugs, the rest of the furniture. There was a huge mirror on one wall. On it, smeared in dark brown blood, were the numbers two and three. It looked for a moment like a child's fingerpainting.

The two old people were lying on the floor next to each other. They were naked. Around each of their heads was a pool of dried blood. I saw in a corner a common household sponge, barely recognizable, but the same color. The two bodies were swollen, stiff.

'Jesus,' Martinez said. He was standing behind me. I watched Porter bring his camera to his eye once, then let it slip down. He struggled for composure, then raised the camera again. This time the room was filled with the flash. I heard the motor on the camera wind the film, a quick whirring sound. Again the flash went off, then another and a fourth time. Wilson turned angrily. 'No more photos, no pictures,' he said. 'Jesus, look at this place.' He turned to me. 'Take a long look, then get out and let the technicians get to work. Not much of a game, is it?'

I didn't answer him. I made my mind focus on the details of the deaths. I registered the positions, the streaks of blood. Their hands were tied, just as the teenager's had been. I saw a painting on the wall, a bird caught in flight, a gull just above the waves.

149

I looked at the old furniture, the knickknacks and souvenirs of a lifetime. Then I turned and motioned to Porter. 'OK.'

Outside, I sucked in the clear air in great gulps, tasting the nearby ocean, shaking my head to lose the smell.

Porter started to bounce around, shooting the policemen as they swung in and out. I saw several old people step from their homes out to the street to watch. In the distance, I could hear sirens, probably the Beach police, ambulances, the medical examiner. Probably, too, the police higher-ups. I walked to the couple's mailbox. A letter was inside, sent from New York City. The names corresponded to the ones I'd found in the city directory.

'It's them,' I told Nolan on the car radio. There was some interference for a moment, then his voice came through: 'And?'

'Very dead. At least a couple of days. Maybe more. The smell was incredible. They were naked and there was blood everywhere. It was sickening.'

'Jesus.' I thought for a moment, how odd, everyone seemed to react the same, calling the same name. 'Talk to the neighbors; try to get some idea who they were, you know what I mean. We're going to be pushing deadline, so let me know as soon as possible.'

The radio went off, and I turned and saw the medical examiner on his way up. He caught my eye and waved. 'We've got to stop meeting like this,' he said, grinning. He entered the house. I took my notebook and began to interview the neighbors, watching their faces slip from surprise to shock to terror as they grasped what had happened behind the closed door of the house so close to them. I stayed at the scene until they brought the bodies out, the same zippered black bags like the one that the teenager had been slipped into. By then the television stations and the competition and the wires and all the others, freelancers and photographers, the whole bunch of us had collected outside. Most wanted to know from me if the killer had called. I said yes: he provided the address. A few times I felt the heat from the television lights as they played across the waiting journalists, searching me out. I did not tell anyone that I had been inside; only that I knew two were dead and it was bloody.

While we waited I watched one old woman who stood a bit to the side. I could see her eyes following the progress of the policemen, occasionally turning to look at the assembled members of the press. She wore a white housedress; it seemed to flow from her neck and shoulders down in great billowing folds. The wind would catch the dress and pull it back, outlining the bones and ridges of her aging body. I could see her lips moving, speaking a prayer. The kaddish, I supposed. She had gray wisps of hair that floated around her forehead in the wind. After the bodies were brought out, I saw her turn and leave slowly, walking down the street alone, her body swaying from side to side with the effort, her steps short, hesitant. I thought of the bodies in the bags; swollen, it had been difficult to estimate their frailty. But I supposed they were weak, no match for the killer's strength and anger. I pictured their bodies lying naked next to each other. I wondered how many times, in how much passion, they had sought comfort and pleasure in each other's nakedness.

The medical examiner had lost his humor when he came out. 'Wait for the autopsy,' he snapped at the sudden crowd of questioners. He looked at me, shook his head, but said nothing as he returned to his car.

Martinez and Wilson were surrounded just as quickly. I had an image of gulls on the beach, screeching around a piece of refuse. Martinez gave a brief synopsis to the crowd, swiftly describing the interior. He would not elaborate, waving his hand in front of him as if he could sweep the questions out of the air. He slipped into the passenger seat and drove off with Wilson. I watched their car travel down the street, then found Porter and left. He muttered and cursed throughout the whole drive. I watched the waves and the water as we crossed the causeway; it was closing fast onto night, and already city lights reflected on the surface of the bay.

The two detectives were waiting at the newsroom. 'We want to hear the tape,' Wilson said. 'We want to hear it right now.' I nodded and they followed me into the office.

Nolan saw us enter, and he jumped from the city desk and met us midway across the newsroom. The other reporters stopped their work and watched. 'You want the tape?' Nolan asked. Wilson nodded. 'I'll have a copy made,' Nolan said, his hand reaching down and extracting the cassette from the recorder.

'We want to cooperate.' He handed the tape to a copy boy, turned his back and gave instructions, while the two detectives slid into chairs at vacant desks. It was odd, I thought, how nervous their presence in the newsroom made everyone. We were so used to dealing with them, crime being such a staple of the newspaper, yet their presence on our territory was an intrusion, a small invasion. It was as if we wanted to protect the process of putting out the newspaper from their eyes, keep it mysterious. I watched as Wilson adjusted his sidearm; it was a short-barrelled .357 Magnum; its polished brown stock stuck up on his hip, ugly and foreboding.

Nolan sat down across from them. 'You wouldn't be thinking about a wiretap, would you?'

Wilson looked up, surprised. 'What for? We're getting the tapes.'

'I don't know,' Nolan replied. 'What about trying to trace the killer's phone calls?'

Both detectives laughed. Martinez sat back, smiling, but Wilson let out another short burst. 'You've been watching too much television,' he said. 'Trace the call, hah!'

'I don't get it,' Nolan said.

'Well,' Wilson started, his voice even, lecturing, as if he were dealing with a child. I saw Nolan begin to bristle. 'There are probably, what do you suppose, a couple of thousand lines into this building? Think of all the phones: circulation, advertising, up here in the newsroom. We would have to be able to find the specific wire that leads to this phone, this desk, the line that the killer calls in on.' He was gesturing with his hand. 'And then, assuming we could get the right type of tap on it, we would have to have people looking at all the various exchanges around the city, testing to see which one was connected to this line.

'It would be an impossible task. Even assuming the killer were to stay on the line for, say, six to eight hours and that we had a man on duty, it would still take that long to isolate the number, then find out where it was. And we have no indication that he's calling from a private line. We could, hypothetically, if everything went perfectly, trace the sucker to a phone booth. What good would that do us? Listen, even with computers and all the fancy electronics equipment developed in the war, it would still be better, we would stand a better chance of interrupting calls at random around the city to see if we happened to stumble upon the killer. So you don't really have to worry about being bugged. Except by the killer.'

The copy boy returned with the tape and Wilson pocketed it. They stood up to leave and I asked, 'Why were they naked?'

Martinez shrugged and turned away. Wilson looked at me and said, 'I think he's just a sadist. No sex, but he probably wanted to humiliate them. Just a guess, though.' I nodded.

The story came slowly. Nolan hovered about the typewriter for a few moments, gauging the progress, then went back to the city desk. I toyed with the lead, typing over and over again the same combination of words: elderly couple, bloody scene, execution murders, telephone call. All I could hear was the killer's voice as he gave me the address.

All I could see were the two bodies lying on the floor.

I wondered about the victims, Mr. and Mrs. Ira Stein. He was a haberdasher from Long Island and she was a housewife. They had two children, the son a doctor in New York City. They'd retired to the Beach a dozen years before, when the northeastern winter first blew ice into their bones. I thought about how ordinary they were, how frighteningly typical.

Andrew Porter emerged from the photo studio and walked to my desk. His face was set, frowning, an edge of anger in the eyes. He stood for a moment on the far side of my desk, looking down at the words that were resting in my typewriter. 'Here,' he said, 'these will help you set the scene.' He dropped a handful of prints onto my desk. Nolan came up, and within a few seconds the desk was surrounded by other reporters and editors. I looked at the photos; they were the ones that had been snapped inside. Black and white, which heightened their impact; had the photos been in color they would have been somehow surrealistic, unreal, but the unforgiving tones of gray that shaded the prints carried the horror.

There were a few exclamations, muffled obscenities, whistles of appreciation as the shots were passed around. There was a picture of the two bodies, a picture of the streaks of blood on the walls, another shot of the wounds in the back of the skulls of the old couple and one, taken at an angle to minimize the flash's explosion, of the numbers written in blood on the large mirror. Nolan held it up. 'We'll run this one,' he said. He looked at Porter. 'I assume you're developing some others, some shots we can put in the paper?' Porter nodded. 'All right,' Nolan said, 'we're beginning to push deadline.' He looked at me. 'Let's go.'

I turned back to the machine and slipped a clean sheet of paper into the roller. The crowd around my desk dissipated quickly, and for a moment I felt adrift, the words running through my head. Then it seemed as if they jumped into focus, and I began to race my hands across the keyboard, the words leaping onto the sheet of paper. I fought off thoughts of the couple's last minutes and replaced them with short bursts of sentences. It was as if by describing what I'd seen, what I'd smelled, what I'd heard, it became less real for me, placed inside the box of the news story; packaged for the frightened consumption of the hundreds of thousands of readers waiting in the growing nighttime darkness.

Writing again. Safe.

That night, before going home, I went to the bar with Nolan, Porter and some of the other staff. We commandeered a pair of tables in the corner, away from where a jukebox blurted country and western. A few of the pressmen and circulation drivers were sitting at the bar. I watched them throw curious glances in our direction, then return to the cans of beer in front of them, their eyes staring off into the darkness and the sound of music. The bar girl brought drinks to the table and shook off one editor's comment on her legs with a short smile and upturned eyebrows. There was laughter, and I leaned back in my chair, holding the beer bottle to my forehead, sensing the cool penetrate the skin. The liquid seemed to race down my throat, and the first gulp made me feel strangely high, released.

'Do you think that we're encouraging this guy?' I heard Nolan ask. 'That the more publicity we give him, the greater the incentive there is for him to kill?' Several voices answered at the same time. I closed my eyes, listening to the words, balancing in the chair.

'Of course not,' a voice said. 'We're just covering the story the way it should be covered.'

And another voice: 'I don't know. Are we covering it, or are we participating in it?'

'I'll say one thing' – it was Porter speaking – 'judging from the scene today, I'd have to say that this guy is just getting warmed up.'

'But what are you saying?' one of the voices complained. 'That we should ignore this thing to try to remove the incentive? Hell, I don't care if he murders a thousand people, we still have to respond as a newspaper. We're not the police, for Christ's sake.'

'But' – it was Nolan speaking – 'on a kidnapping, say, we always cooperate. We keep the facts from the paper until the drop has been made, or the person saved; or killed, for that matter. But we do work with them to make certain the situation isn't in jeopardy. Suppose we just stopped printing the story – continued all the research, all the interviews, but stopped putting it in the paper. Then, when the guy gets caught, write the whole thing up. What would be wrong with that?'

Several voices spoke at once. 'The competition, the television, the wires, everybody would be all over it. We would be alone.'

'I don't know,' Nolan said.

'And then the killer would probably call somewhere else,' someone said. 'And we'd be shut out.'

There was a quiet then, and I heard the sounds of music and the bar noise of clinking glasses. That, I thought, made sense to everyone. I opened my eyes. 'Lip service,' I said.

Nolan turned toward me. 'What?'

'Knee jerk, lip service, whatever cliché you want to find. None of them really matters. The bottom line – there's a good cliché – the final analysis will always be the same. No matter how many people this guy kills, no matter how sickening the crimes are, no matter how closely connected we are to the acts themselves, the paper will always pursue the story. We can't do anything else. We're not equipped to react like a responsible organization, like a bureaucracy or the police. Things happen, we write stories. For us, there will always be another story, bigger, more powerful, one that has the people in the street talking louder and more stridently. It may not happen for a month or a year, but it will happen. And then we'll all turn to that story, forgetting that this story ever took place. A year ago the *Post* in Washington broke the President's back, but now everyone is going around saying, "What have they done lately?" That's the nature of this business: what have you done lately? We're just lucky that crazy people like this killer come along every so often to help us do our job.'

I finished my speech and poured the last of the beer into my glass. I watched the suds boil up for an instant, then recede, leaving a white ring around the top of the glass. The voices of the others picked up, mostly in agreement. Nolan looked at me, though, over the edge of his own glass.

We walked out later, alone. 'Are you such a cynic?' he asked.

'Am I?'

'It seems that way. And you're a liar, too.'

'How so?' I said. I laughed. He didn't.

'I saw you this evening, staring at the pages. I knew what was in your mind. You were looking for the ladder, the gangway. When a cop goes to the scene of a murder, he jokes, laughs, makes sarcastic remarks – his way of creating an arbitrary mental barrier between himself and the scene, of saying, "I don't belong in that world." For us, it's easier. We do it with words. I remember once, when I worked for the *L.A. Times*, we had this old guy – you know the type, cigarette burns on his trousers, crumbs on his shirt – who worked rewrite. He used to say he didn't have to see the accident or the murder or the drowning, whatever, to describe it; that his mind created the right setting and pictures. He'd talk to a few people on the phone and then turn to his typewriter, and the most careful, accurate prose would emerge. He was totally removed, went from his small apartment downtown to the paper and returned every day, five days a week, year in, year out, and he wrote the best, most vivid prose in the paper. I think we all want to be that guy. That separate and distinct.'

He paused, thinking. The moon had risen early, and the pale light seemed to fuse with the fluorescence of the parking-lot lamps, turning the world a purplish blue.

'You're right, we'd never drop the story, never hide it, even if that killer calls you tomorrow and says the only thing keeping him at it is the publicity. I suppose that's the essential dilemma, the basic joke of this whole existence. Catch-Twenty-two.

'But I wonder, where are we when we start to justify our complicity by shrugging and saying, "That's the news biz"? And don't protest. I think we are accomplices. After all, it was us he sent to the scene, not the police, not the fire department, no one else.

'No matter what happens, though, it's still a hell of a story.'

We were silent for a minute or two. I watched the lights on the thruway cut through the evening. Nolan said, 'See you tomorrow. He'll probably call,' and wandered off to get his car. I waited, feeling the darkness, turning my face trying to catch some breeze. But there was none; all I could feel was the residue of daytime warmth floating up from the sidewalk, closing in on me like a wave.

Christine was in the living room in front of the television when I came in. 'Hurry,' she said, 'the news just came on.' I slumped into a chair and watched the television anchorman introduce the story. Christine was in her underwear, her white nurse's outfit tossed carelessly aside. I looked at her legs as the anchorman's voice droned. 'There you are,' she said excitedly.

I looked at the screen. I saw myself surrounded by microphones, bathed in the light of the cameras. The wind was blowing across my face, and I watched as I raised a hand and held my hair back. I watched myself tell about the latest phone call, and then the screen shifted suddenly to a shot of the two bodies being carried from the house. Again, the scene shifted, and there was a picture of Martinez making his way through the crowd of reporters toward the police cruiser. The television reporter on the scene ended with a stand-up, facing the camera, intoning the details of the latest murders and finishing with the cryptic statement, 'No one knows when it will stop.' I grunted and got up to turn the show off. Christine lifted her arms above her head and stretched. I looked at her body carefully, inspecting, my eyes playing over the legs, the stomach, the shoulders. 'God, it's hot tonight,' she said. 'I thought you looked good. Was it really terrible?'

'The television didn't really explain what went on inside,' I said.

'Well, they were shot like the girl, right?'

'Yes and no. Their hands were tied behind like the girl, they were shot in the back of the head like the girl, but the resemblance between the crimes stops there.'

'Why?'

'Blood, I suppose.'

Christine put her hand to her mouth. 'What happened?'

'The place was a mess. He'd streaked blood from the two victims everywhere. It looked like a slaughter-house. And the two were naked. It looked like he went

161

crazy after the killings. I'm surprised no one in the neighborhood heard anything.'

Christine had turned pale. 'Why?' she asked.

'That's what everyone wants to know.'

'But you should know. You've talked with him. What do you think?'

I snapped back, 'He talks, I listen! What else? He doesn't bother to fill me in on all the subtle details. How should I know? I'm no expert.'

'Maybe he will,' she said.

'I hope so, dammit, I hope so.' It was out before I really knew what I was saying.

'And?'

'And what?'

'And what will you do if he does tell you? Will you try to stop him?'

'That's not my job,' I said.

'That's disgusting.'

I grabbed her by the arm and she gave a little shriek as I shook her. 'What do you mean by that?'

She snatched her arm back, seized one of the pillows and put it on her lap, as if to cover part of her nakedness. 'I mean, this man is going around killing people. Killing, for God's sake. And you're the one person he's seen fit to contact about the whole thing. And your idea of community pride, of helping out, is to take notes and write stories which probably have the singular purpose of encouraging the madman to go out and do it again. What the hell's wrong with you?'

'There's nothing wrong with me.' My own voice was raised, near a shout. 'That's my job. I'm not a cop, I'm not a doctor. I can't do anything to make everyone well again. All I do is report on what I hear and see.'

'A robot.'

'No, dammit, people rely on me as much as they rely on you. They need information, knowledge. How else can they protect themselves?'

'Ah,' she said, 'you're the savior of the vigilantes?'

'You know, you don't make sense,' I said. She turned and picked a glass of wine off a side table. I had not noticed she was drinking. She took a long sip, then leaned her head back against the couch. I looked at her long throat, the muscles and shape of her gorge outlined. I felt suddenly passionate, sexual. I sat next to her. 'I'm sorry,' I said. 'I don't know what else to tell you.'

She looked at me and put her hand on my arm.

'What I don't understand,' she said, 'is why you think being a . . . watcher makes you immune.'

I thought about it. There really wasn't an answer. 'I think everyone in the business feels that it provides a kind of cloak. No one likes to think about the other. We hide from it. During the war a number of correspondents were killed. Some just took off one day and were never seen again. The actor's son, Sean Flynn. He was in Cambodia, a photographer. Heard there was some action a little way down the road and jumped on a motorbike. Another fellow accompanied him. They were never seen again. There's an old reporter at the *Journal* who covered the Dominican action; you remember, when the Marines were sent in? He got shot up pretty badly. The paper had a ceremony, but then, I think, they preferred to ship him out to pasture. The business doesn't like to have its damaged warriors around inhibiting the survivors on their next assignment. We all think the act of collecting and disseminating the news is a kind of protection. That because we're supposed to be objective, we don't have a vested interest in the outcome. So the bullets will just ignore us and seek out one of the real participants.'

'You're talking about wars,' she said. 'I'm talking about a madman.'

'But that's what he's doing,' I said, 'he's trying to make us all think we're at war.'

She was silent for a moment.

'Well,' she finally said, 'I think he's succeeding. I'm scared. I'm scared for you, I'm scared for me. I feel as if we're more vulnerable.'

'Why?'

'Because of you. How do you know he's only going to be satisfied by calling you up? He seems to want you to be involved in this thing. What makes you so certain he's not going to end this whole thing by coming for you? And suppose you write something he doesn't like? What do you think he'll do then?'

'I can't think about that. I couldn't write if I did.'

'Ah,' she said, 'your friend the psychiatrist would call that denial.'

'It's the nature of the business,' I replied.

'Some business,' she said. Then she laughed. 'Pour me some more wine.' But instead of handing me her glass, she wrapped her arms around me and put her head on my chest. I tried to look down at her, but all

I could see was the light catching her hair, bringing out its color. I could feel her breathing as she held close to me. Then she pulled back, handed me her glass and dropped the pillow to the floor.

But the lovemaking seemed jerky, uncoordinated, as if our bodies were out of synchronization. She lay back afterwards, looking out of the bedroom window. I sat on the side of the bed looking at her. She said nothing, but after a moment turned on her side and flicked off the lamp. I went and sat in a chair by the window, letting the night shapes grow around me. I thought about Mr. and Mrs. Ira Stein and my hesitation at the typewriter. I tried to picture them alive, walking the few blocks between their home and the beach, pausing every so often with that distinctive elderly abruptness, turning their faces up toward the sun. My mind kept picturing the two on the floor of their home. I wondered who'd been shot first, and what had gone through the mind of the survivor, during their final moments. Did they welcome the noise and shock and darkness of the explosion behind their heads? Or did they cling to the last seconds of life, even with their partner ripped away so terribly beside them? I thought, I will ask the killer when he calls. And then I pictured the bodies again, but this time I could see their hands flung out in front, reaching, as if for each other. Lovers.

CHAPTER EIGHT

The headline was a two-decker, 48-point Roman bold, strung across the six columns of the front page: 'NUMBERS' KILLER STRIKES AGAIN; ELDERLY BEACH COUPLE MURDERED. Underneath the headline was my name in bold print and a four-column photo, the shot of the mirror and the two numbers he'd inscribed in gore. Below that was another photo of the rescue personnel rushing from the front of the home with the body bags, heading toward the ambulances and the morgue.

The sidebar started out front, too: the story I'd written containing all the quotes from the neighbors, the same shock and disbelief that had accompanied the death of the teenager. The words were different, though; the language was the talk of the elderly, filled with the vulnerability of age. They were more afraid, I thought. Death was closer to them; they felt it more strongly. It was as if stealing life was that much greater from those with so little time left.

Both stories jumped inside, and more words and pictures filled a whole page inside the paper.

Christine was dressed in her whites. 'No surgery today,' she said. 'Thank God. After reading all this, I don't think I could handle it.' She drank coffee and looked over the paper.

I turned to the sports section and lost myself in the box scores. The Red Sox seemed to be getting stronger and had taken a 1–0 decision from Jim Palmer in Baltimore. He'd given up just three hits, but one of them was a long home run to Lynn, the Boston center fielder. Lynn was a rookie that year and was leading the league in everything, it seemed. I'd watched him play once in spring practice, before anyone had known who he was. He'd moved easily for the ball in center field, reaching up at the last second to pluck the dying shots from the air, like a magician, only in reverse. He'd always seemed to move at the same speed, regardless of the urgency of the play; had always arrived a split second before the ball, a note in the rhythm of the game.

'Oh,' Christine said, 'this is just horrible.'

For the first time that day, I could feel the pervasiveness of the killer's presence throughout the city. It filled the air like the wind before a late-afternoon thunderstorm suddenly blowing up and around, as if out of control, directionless. I did not spend much time in the office that day; Nolan took me aside early and said that I had to get outside to find out what people were thinking, how they were feeling. We both turned and looked down at the telephone on my desk, wondering if the killer would call, but Nolan said we couldn't wait on him. He tugged at the tie that hung loosely around his neck. He did that whenever he was anxious; by the time the paper went through its final deadline the tie would be more like a noose. He suggested that we take my phone off the hook so the killer, if he did call, would think it busy, not ignored.

168

I nodded but felt a kind of quickened guilt when I lifted the receiver from the hook. The phone made a beeping sound for a few seconds, then went silent, sitting dismembered on my desk. Porter joined me then and we walked from the building.

The day was filled with voices; the faces, the shapes of the people blended together, melding with the heat and the sun.

We rode a Metro bus, and the driver, a black man with curls of gray hair just above his ear, turned to me and said, 'Why should I fear that man? There's no reason, but I do. I look at the faces of the people who get on my bus and I wonder, are they next? Am I? And I think about the people who ride the bus, the strangers who board, dropping their money in the box. I look at the young men and think, maybe he's the one.' The driver had large, heavily muscled arms, and he spun the bus through the congested downtown streets easily, as if driving in a trance. He would turn the bus using just the palm of his right hand, the other resting on the edge of the wheel, his elbow out the window. 'The people,' he said, 'all the riders seem more nervous. You see the whole world on a city bus, just driving the route over the course of one day. People won't sit down next to each other. I noticed that, you know. People seem to want to keep to themselves.'

We walked through Little Havana, looking at the faces of the old men, their hair slicked back, the pockets of their Guayabara shirts filled with the elongated shapes of rolled cigars. The men stared out at us with the usual mixture of Latin distrust and curiosity. Some hesitated over their small glasses of thick black Cuban coffee. They had a way of peering over the edge of the glass as if drinking in the smell and the steam as it mingled with the heat of the day, at the same time assessing Porter and me.

We walked down Street Eight, the primary Cuban thoroughfare, reading the signs in Spanish, talking with the old men in the small restaurants playing dominoes in the shade. 'Death,' said one old man in his hesitant English, 'comes to everyone sooner or later. Why worry?' He lifted the edge of his shirt to display a reddish scar underneath his ribs. 'Playa Giron,' he said, 'La Brigada.' He spat onto the sidewalk, his spittle a dark mark on the white cement. 'I wish we could have this man go to Havana and do some of his work there.' Some other men laughed. The old man looked away, out across the buildings, his eyes up to the sky. 'It is not in us to be scared of such a man,' he said. 'But some of the children and the women are. They ask, "Will he come here?" As he did on the Beach with the old ones there. I say, "How can we say what such a man will do?" And many are worried, but they think that this man will stick to his own kind for whatever it is that he is seeking. Myself, I do not know, but I think that he will be killed soon, or that his grief will be too much for him and he will kill himself.' The old man shrugged his shoulders and stared back down at the table filled with dominoes in front of him. He took one from the pile and placed it on its end, balanced for an instant. Then the old man flicked it with his finger and it fell over. He moved it into place on the board, and the game went on.

We drove south that afternoon to a shopping center a few miles away from where the first victim's family lived. I had almost stopped thinking about them. For a moment I wondered what they felt now, if they realized they were caught up in something larger than the death of their child. But then I thought, what could be larger for them?

We went into a gun store, a shop called The Great Equalizer. There were a half-dozen people waiting to see the clerk, and he gestured over his shoulder toward the rear of the building when I asked for the manager. I found him in the back, at a table filled with rags and the pungent smell of cleaning fluid. A small-caliber automatic was disassembled on the table. He grinned when I introduced myself and explained my reason for visiting.

'This is the suburbs,' he said. 'And whenever there is something unexplained out there, the people get nervous. And whenever people get nervous, they go out and buy a gun. So to answer your question, since the news came out this morning I've been doing a steady business. I expect by tonight it will pick up even more. And tomorrow it will get even better. And if this guy goes out and kills someone else, well . . .' The manager paused and grinned. 'I know this sounds terrible, but I'll be doing land-office business.' He was a thin man, with a pair of muttonchop sideburns, hair that was combed sharply back, a refugee from the 1950s. 'Almost everyone complains about the three-day rule; you know, you buy your gun on a Monday, you got to wait until Wednesday to pick it up. A lot of people say, "But supposing that guy comes by tonight," and I tell 'em, "No, that isn't the way he works. You'll be OK." It seems to relieve them for the most part, reassure them, I guess, though why anyone would think that I know anything about it is beyond me.'

The gun dealer paused and looked out at the line of people. There was a steady clicking sound of metallic parts meeting as customers inspected the action on the weapons. He picked up the automatic from the tabletop and began to wipe the sides carefully with a streaked cloth. 'I saw a lot of strange things when I did my hitch, let me tell you. And I met a lot of guys who were on the verge; you know, just one step away from the funny farm. There was one guy, I remember, during basic, up at Fort Dix in Jersey. Damn, it was cold. All the damn time, I thought I'd never get warm again.

'Anyway, right at the start the drill sergeant starts shouting at us, "Call out! Call out! I want to hear your voice loud and clear!" And there was this one kid, about seventeen or eighteen, skinny, never been outdoors, I guess. And for the first week the sergeant just laid it on him. So the kid starts to raise his voice. Everything is shouted now, "Yes sir! Yes sir!" and louder and louder. And he starts it in the barracks, too. I mean, you can't talk to the kid; everything he says he says at the top of his lungs. Finally, after a couple of days, the drill sergeant caught on. By then the kid was marching around, eyes in front of him, but I don't think he could see a thing, calling out the cadence at the top of his voice. They took him away and I never did see him again. But I got to thinking about the kid the other day; you know, after the first murder. I thought, well, if you send a kid like that over to a place like Nam – you know, my younger brother, he went, said it was terrible – well, you don't know what's gonna happen, do you?'

The gun dealer paused, listening to the sound of weapons. 'So everyone wants to be protected. I'm just one way. I bet if you went to the pound you'd find that they've sold every big mean dog they got. Call up the Wackenhunts, those people. I'll bet they say the same thing. A gun isn't so bad. And let me tell you, the one that this guy's got is a helluva piece of work. Probably your standard Army-issue forty-five-caliber automatic. You know why that gun was invented? It was back in the early 1900s when we sent the Marines into the Philippines to deal with the native uprising there. Well, the soldiers used to carry rifles and bayonets, and when some wild man would leap from the bushes the guy could handle it OK; you know, jab and fire.

'But the officers all carried thirty-eights, the old Colts like the cowboys wore. Well, hell, half of them were getting killed because some native carrying a sword would jump out of the bushes and they'd put about three slugs in the guy's chest and the guy would be dead, see, but he wouldn't be stopped, and his momentum and that sword would just slice the officer up like cold cuts. So they had to develop real quick a handgun that would just stop a guy cold; you know, right in his tracks. And that was the Colt forty-five automatic. And damn, they still use that gun today in the Army. Never figured out anything better. Now a Magnum, a three fifty-seven or a forty-four, will do the same damn thing today, which is why you see the cops using them, but that automatic, it's something else. The cops will never trace that gun or that ammo. There must be thousands of those guns floating around. Hell, half the World War Two vets in the city probably have one sitting in some forgotten drawer.'

He looked at me and the words filling my notebook. 'You ever shot one?' I shook my head. 'Well,' he said grinning, 'here's your chance.' He took us through the back door to an adjacent shed. There was a sandbagged target there, and the walls had been soundproofed. He opened a locked chest. 'Here you go,' he said, handing me a pair of ear protectors. 'And here's the object of so much attention.'

He held up the automatic. For a second the fluorescent lights in the shed caught the dull sides of the weapon; then it turned back, black, ugly. He handed it to me and put his hands on my shoulders, positioning me in front of the target. It was a blacked-out profile of a human being, like some I'd seen policemen practice with. The gun felt extraordinarily heavy in my hand, and for a moment I wasn't sure that I could lift it. The gun dealer showed me how to stand, with both hands on the weapon. I practiced once, sighting down the short barrel. It seemed that my focus of vision narrowed then, tunneled into a single field: the target and myself. The dealer handed me the clip of bullets and grinned. I slid the clip in, feeling the weight grow, sensing the satisfying click as the clip was grabbed by the handle. 'All right,' I heard his voice at my elbow. 'Let fly. Just one gentle squeeze, OK?' I steadied myself and fired.

The noise of the report filled the room and the smell of cordite surrounded me. My hand felt as if someone had struck it with a hammer, the fingers tingling, electric. I dropped the gun to my side and peeled the ear protectors off.

'Not a bad shot for a beginner,' the gun dealer said. He took the weapon from my hand and slipped the clip from the handle. He replaced the weapon in the box and then gestured at the target. 'How about that?'

My shot had blown away the top of the target's head. I stared at it momentarily, then turned and followed the dealer back into the store. 'See what I mean?' he said. 'That's a serious weapon. Not like some of these little women's guns, like a twenty-five automatic or some cheap Saturday Night Special. A forty-five is good for one thing. Killing people very quickly and efficiently.'

The gun dealer escorted us partway out of his shop. He paused at the cash register to talk with a man in a business suit who was turning and hefting a large handgun. 'Now that, sir, is your Cadillac of handguns,' the shop manager said. 'A Colt Python, three fifty-seven Magnum, long-barrel. It is the height of accuracy, control and packs a wallop a lot stronger than a heavyweight's punch. Most of the policemen who come in here buy that gun, in the shorter-barrel version. Equip it with magnum load or with regular thirty-eight-caliber ammunition for target practice. I assume, sir, this gun is for yourself?'

The businessman shook his head. 'No,' he said. 'I was really looking for something for my wife.' He looked up at the dealer who had turned a cold glance onto the assistant behind the register.

'Well, then, sir, you need something that the little lady can handle. I assume that she is not particularly large?'

'That's right,' the man said, 'she's more petite. She's afraid, and I want her to have something that will make her feel more confident.' The businessman turned toward me and some of the other people waiting for assistance. 'I think she's worried about this fellow who's doing the killings.'

'She should be,' said a woman standing close by.

'All of us are,' said a man in a sport shirt.

'But it's not just this killer,' said the woman again. 'It seems there's so *much* lawlessness. And the police don't seem to be able to do anything about it. They just come and take a statement. That's what happened when I had my home burglarized.' She looked at me scribbling notes. 'You a reporter?'

'That's right.'

'Well, you can quote me, but I don't want my name in the paper.'

The businessman joined the conversation again. 'What worries me is that every punk who drifts down here looking for the sun and the easy life will see the stories in the paper and figure that here they get a free shot. I mean, what's to stop them from pulling some job and then trying to blame it on this killer? The police won't know what the hell to think.'

There was a chorus of agreement. The man in the

sport shirt lifted up a snub-nosed .38 special. 'Well,' he said, 'this might prove to be some deterrent. And I plan to keep it that way. You remember the Constitution. The right to keep and bear arms. Well, dammit, I'm not going to let some whacko murder my family without a fight.'

There was more agreement. The store manager interrupted to regain the businessman's attention. 'Perhaps, sir, I can show you something in a light-weight automatic?'

The businessman looked back at him. 'Yes, all right. But I'll take this Python thing, too. And some ammunition for it. And where can I go and practice with the thing? I haven't shot a gun since I was in the service.'

'Fine, sir.' The manager looked across at me. 'We have a range, and you can try it out there. I'll arrange for some time on a practice gallery also, if you like. Now' – and he reached inside of the locked glass showcase – 'here is something for your wife.' It was a nickelplated .9 millimeter. 'This is a bit heavier than I ordinarily recommend,' the manager said, maintaining his even, helpful tone. 'But then, these are special times. Perhaps you'd like to compare it with this?' And he held out a small .25-caliber automatic with a black finish, polished, gleaming.

'Good,' said the businessman. Then he turned back to the woman waiting in the line. 'Perhaps you could help me,' he said; 'my wife is just a bit smaller than you.'

'Glad to,' she said, stepping up and picking up the weapons.

*　　*　　*

I suppose the reactions in the gun shop were predictable. So, too, was the scene outside Morningside Park, near the swings where the children played. Their voices seemed to be swept up into the sky, carried by the breeze that filtered through the big banyan trees from the bay. There was a group of women there, just outside the sandboxes, sitting on benches. They seemed perched, ready, apprehensive. 'Children must play,' said one of them, peering past me at the group on the swings. 'They don't understand danger the same way we do. You can't keep them inside; it would only foster nightmares. You can't explain, because the killings are inexplicable, especially for a child. So,' she said, pausing and turning to the other women whose heads were nodding in agreement, 'we come here the same as on any summer day and watch the children play as if there were nothing wrong. But there is, and I can feel it.'

Another woman joined us, tugging at the sleeve of her shirt as if impatient, the words pressing hard on her imagination. 'What do you do if you've got older children? Eleven-, twelve-year-olds or teenagers. How do you keep them in? How do you protect them?' She brushed a strand of graying hair from her temple and looked for a moment out across the water, past the thick brown trunks of the trees and the dark shadows they cast on the lawn. 'I worry so much. I tell my boys they can't go anywhere alone. I tell them they have to be in before dark. I tell them if they're in doubt, to stop, to call home or the neighbors and if they see anything suspicious to call the police or for help or to do *something*. But you know all the advice and the orders and the protection in the world can't keep a child that age safe. They just don't know fear. My God, that poor girl getting into that man's car, walking alone at night. How do you teach them to be afraid?'

The first woman added, 'It's like it's a sickness. Like . . . all the wrongs that were wrapped up in the past ten years have suddenly come here to roost. And Miami, of all places. You would think Washington or Chicago or New York or San Francisco maybe – but Miami seems like such an innocent place.' She stared up into the sun.

'What makes a man do these things,' she said, 'and how many more will he do?'

Porter looked up from his cameras and lenses. 'Why should he stop?'

'I beg your pardon?' the first woman said.

He shook his head. 'He wants us all to be scared. He wants everyone to have nightmares. That's why he's doing it. As long as you and I and everyone else in this town react like normal people, with fear and apprehension, with . . . oh, damn, just scared, you know? That's what he's getting off on.'

Porter looked at me. 'And, boy, do we help him.'

In the car on the way back, I asked him what had changed his attitude. 'I thought this was just a story to you. What gives?'

'I'm becoming cynical,' he said. 'More than even I thought I could.'

'That's what Nolan called me,' I said. 'A cynic.'

'He's right. We all are. I just don't have to enjoy it.'

'You'll go mad,' I said.

He gripped the wheel and moved the car swiftly to the right, past another car, then accelerated and shifted back to the left-hand lane. We were running down Biscayne Boulevard, past the offices and trees of some of the exclusive housing developments. It was an area of contrasts; a block of busy offices with well-groomed men and women wearing designer clothes would give way to a block of motels advertising water beds and X-rated closed-circuit movies. I watched a black prostitute on one corner, the hair of her wig piled high on top of her head, but loosened, too, so that it cascaded like darkness around her shoulders. She wore a pink halter top that strained to hold in her breasts and red shorts that showed the flesh of her buttocks. She saw me looking at her as the light changed and smiled, a flash of white teeth, and lifted her finger in a beckoning motion. I shook my head and she pouted. Porter put his foot down heavily on the gas pedal, and we shot forward across the intersection.

'I suppose I will,' he said. 'Sometimes I can hardly stand the contrasts.' He hesitated, then looked quickly at me. 'You know what I was doing before your call came in to the photo lab and we went off to the Beach? I was developing my previous assignment. I shot a layout for the Living section; fashions for the hot summer days, I believe they called it. I was in one of the parks with the fashion writer and three models and a couple of PR types. The girls were dressed in bathing suits and wraparounds, flimsy, see-through stuff, and we were trying to pose them in a way that would be provocative yet not offensive for our "family newspaper." ' He said the last two words sarcastically. 'It made me laugh later to think that we were so careful about a bunch of beautiful young women, trying to make certain they weren't too sexy, and then I run off to the most disgusting murder scene I've seen. And that's OK; that's front-page stuff. I feel like a hypocrite. It made me feel dirty, shooting that old couple lying there on the floor. It made me feel as if I were the madman, focusing my camera, centering it on their bodies, robbing them of what little dignity they must have had. Sometimes I think I'm a parasite. We all are.'

'Listen,' I said slowly, 'if you want off this story I can talk to Nolan. He'll talk with the photo editor.'

'No.' His voice was suddenly free, easy. 'See, that's the really crazy thing. I wouldn't want to be off it. I couldn't stand not knowing, not being there.' He laughed. 'We're all going crazy. A story like this, it just does it to you. To everyone. You know, that guy buying the guns today? He'll probably end up shooting it out some night with his wife after a drunken argument. At least they'll be well armed. My God! Do you suppose the killer realizes all this?'

'Yes.'

'Yes,' Porter agreed. 'I bet he does.' And then he added, 'You see? No one has any real conscience.'

He swung the big car easily into the *Journal's* parking lot.

I watched Porter pack up his equipment and slam the car trunk shut. I could just see past the corner of the building, out over the bay waters. I thought of the sensation of being out on a boat, riding past the Beach through Government Cut, the channel where the big porpoises play, their gray backs rolling through the water. They like to jump in the wake of the sport-fishermen, the huge Chris Craft and Bertrams that go out after big-game fish. The porpoises roll up and suddenly shoot through the wake, twisting their sleek forms and landing with great splashes, then turning and dashing back through the wake to race again. The waters sometimes seem alive, rising up against the blue of the morning sky.

The last time I'd gone out was in late spring, the weekend Saigon fell, thousands of miles across the world. Nolan was there and a few others. We got into a school of big dolphin in the morning, a few minutes after we'd crossed the deep blue demarcation line that seems to course through the water, the mark of the Gulf Stream. We were sitting in the fighting chairs, talking about baseball and the war, drinking beer despite the early hour. The sun already hung above us, and the salt air seemed to stick to my skin, mingling with the sweat and the feel of the cold beer can.

The lines ran through two riggers and each made a pinging sound as it ripped free, a sound that rose above the constant churning of the twin diesels at trolling speed. The dolphin had come up and just smacked into the bait, and by the time the lines had come taut the fish were beginning their dance across the waves. They were beautiful fish, their stubby heads and long bodies, silver blue and green as they cut just below the waves and exploded from the surface in a burst of water and sunlight. We boated those two, and three others, before we lost the school; they were good-sized, fifteen to twenty pounds each, and we slapped each other on the back and drank more beer and picked up the conversation where it had been dropped. It was later when the big blue marlin hit the bait.

Nolan had finished holding forth on the coverage of Saigon's fall; it was an emotional discussion of photographs, a retelling of the powerful images of those few days. We'd run a front-page shot of people hanging from the runners of a helicopter as it surged from the roof of the American Embassy. One figure was holding on by just one arm, his legs kicking as if he were trying to swim through the air, the other arm waving to try to keep his grip. It seemed obvious the man would fall, but the moment for his decision to let go was upon him and one could sense the panic in the body twisting in the air. The picture had upset people; the phones had rung most of the day with readers wanting to complain or protest and some who had just wanted to talk.

I was listening to Nolan's voice as it mingled with the engine noise and watching the ballyhoo bait as it skipped on the surface, a small wake rising behind it, the silver sides catching the sun as it bounced and turned. It was hypnotic to watch the bait like that, feeling the beer grow heavy in my head. I did not at first realize what the shape behind the bait was; it just rose up darker and deeper than the water. I saw the long sword protrude from the surface, and then the captain up on a fighting tower began to shout, 'Billfish, billfish, Jesus Christ, a big marlin! Right rigger, right rigger, look alive!' The line snapped out of the rigger, and the voices continued. I began to freespool the line. 'That's it, drop it back, drop it back!' the captain continued to shout. 'Let him get it!' I flipped the reel to strike and put my finger on the line. I could feel the fish hit the bait again with the bill, and then the water exploded and the fish suddenly shot from the blue up against the sky, its belly gleaming. 'Good fish!' the captain shouted, and I rocked back hard, setting the hook. The marlin continued to jump, twisting, the sun reflecting off the water as it streamed from its sides.

And then, just as quickly, it sounded, went down.

The captain yelled to the mate, 'Where's it hooked?' and the mate turned to the bridge, shading his eyes, his voice sad. 'I couldn't see the feather. I think it's belly hooked,' and the captain said, 'Oh, shit,' in a voice that dropped the excitement and turned to the edge of anger.

'Oh, no,' I said, 'I hope not.' I could feel the fish on the end of the line, throwing his weight against the pressure of the boat, the yards of thin filament that held him. He pulled, twisting his head; I could feel the shakes through the rod. Five minutes went by, then another five. I saw the line begin to flatten out.

'He's coming up,' the mate said. 'Much too early. Damn.'

Nolan said, 'What do you mean, belly hooked?' and the mate explained quickly. 'It means that the fish managed to swallow the bait whole, and when he was struck the hooks ripped into his stomach, not into the flesh of his mouth. It means that even if he were to pull free he would bleed to death. And it means that the pain is too much; he's coming up, and there's still a lot of fight in a big fish. Damn.'

I continued to pump and reel the line in, and within seconds I could see the blue shape in the water. He must have measured over six feet, probably more than a hundred pounds.

'Shit,' the mate said, leaning over the transom, staring at the fish in the water. He walked to the side and grabbed a gaff. He looked up at the captain who shouted, 'Everybody move back! He's going to come in pretty lively!'

I pumped the fish in a little closer, and the boat swung around as the captain positioned the mate for the gaff. He was a thin man, with brown skin, shoulder-length blond hair and long muscles on his arms. 'When he comes over the side,' the mate said to me, 'get out of the chair fast.'

There was a second pause, and I said, 'Here comes the leader.' I could see the wire leader, just inches below the tip of the rod.

The mate grabbed the gaff handle, turning the sharp hook so that it caught the light. He reached out for the leader and said, 'Here goes nothing,' and swung the gaff suddenly, violently through the air toward the fish. There was a shower of water and the sound of the marlin's tail hitting the side of the boat. A huge splash shot over the side of the boat, drenching the deck and the mate. 'Shit! Shit! Shit!' he screamed. And as his voice raced across the swells, I jumped from the fighting chair and peered down into the green and blue of the Gulf Stream. I could just make out the sight of the marlin, streaming blood, descending into the coldness and dark. The mate held the broken leader in his hand. 'He'll go down there and die,' the mate said. 'A bad end for a beautiful fish. The sharks will feed on him, all the fish will.' Then he turned to the captain. 'He moved just at the last minute. I hit the leader with the gaff.' The captain nodded. 'Sorry,' the mate said to me. I shrugged.

It seemed unfair, not to me but to the fish. Hooked in the mouth, he'd have pulled, then twisted and leaped, shaking his head, and the odds would have been with him. A kink in the line, a slip on the reel, a little slack, and he would have been free, slipping back to the cool safety of the deep waters. I wondered if the fish knew that he was going to die, or if he sought the familiar darkness instinctively. I could see him there, in my mind, cutting through the waters, his bill pointed straight ahead, his small fish brain clouding with death.

The killer did not call that day or the next.

Christine had none of her previous optimism, though. She said he would call, that he was toying with us, that he liked to see the stories grow thin in the paper and then inject a new element to force them back to the front. She said the patients on the ward talked constantly about the killer; they felt safe because they knew he couldn't penetrate the white walls and clean corridors of the hospital.

In surgery the doctors, too, talked about the killer. The younger ones described gunshot wounds they had seen during tours with the Army in Vietnam, or during alternate service in the ghetto hospitals of the North. She said she had discovered a new type of fear, not the clenching, sudden panic when a car swerves toward you, but a dull apprehensiveness that made every small action throughout the day, even just washing her hands, seem larger and more important. Every breath she took seemed heavy with substance, the effort to draw in air a conscious choice. It was as if she were marking time, awaiting the moment when the drama took another step forward and the curtain rose on a new scene.

I had no more routine. When the telephone rang, I stiffened. When it did not ring, I sat tense. Sometimes I took the phone off the hook and walked through the city, a notebook in my pocket. When Porter accompanied me we did man-in-the-street interviews, the voices all rising into the vivid blue sky.

The city was a beast awakening from hibernation, its dulled senses slowly coming into focus, becoming alert.

We were talking about my family; about my father, his books, his laws. I said, 'There is no law anymore, not with a killer like this. One cannot write a statute that covers the situation.' And Christine agreed. I watched her stretch her arms wide, her fingers pointed out tautly. She threw her head back and asked, 'I wonder, do people draw closer together or pull farther apart in this kind of situation?' I got up from my chair and crossed the living room to her. She put her head down in my lap as I sat beside her. I stroked the length of her back, and for a moment she was silent.

And then the telephone rang.

'Don't answer it,' she said. 'This is our home.'

It rang again, the bell seeming to grow louder in my ears.

'Please,' she said. 'Leave it.'

But I stood up and crossed to the phone. I hesitated for a second, feeling the ring beneath my fingers. Then I picked it up. 'Hello?'

It was silent.

'Who's there?' I asked.

But I guessed.

'It's time again,' the killer said.

And I knew nothing had changed.

CHAPTER NINE

'I read your story, the one on the people's reactions,' he said. 'I particularly liked the sequence in the gun shop. I wonder how many of those people will manage to shoot themselves while trying to learn to handle a weapon? That was something I saw when I was overseas; sometimes the fear was so strong it overcame the natural aversion to self-inflicted pain. It would happen at a base camp, one of those dusty, hot, unpleasant places where we sat around waiting for the next trip into the jungle, a worse place by far. The camps were filled with slow time; it always seemed to take twice as long to do anything, the heat was so intense. Sweat just poured down the underside of my arms.

'Anyway, there was always a kind of military quiet about the camps; the noises were ordinary, choppers swinging in and out, voices raised in complaint. Periodically there would be a sound, sharper, more distinct, more familiar: A single shot from an M-sixteen. Then shouts for a medic with probably a few screams of pain mingled in. You always found the wounded grunt with a bullet hole in his left foot, or a toe blown off. He would be on his bunk, the area around him filled with clothes and

189

smelling of cleaning fluid. His first words would be, ''I was cleaning the fucking thing and it went off,'' and then the medevac would come and he'd be lifted out of there. Everyone knew, really, what had happened. No one really cared that much. At least, I didn't. I would shut my eyes and listen to the base sounds, the shouts and all, and sleep. I was never afraid like that.'

As he talked I motioned frantically to Christine to bring me paper and pen so I could take notes. I gestured wildly with my hands, making writing motions in the air. She nodded, her face set. In a second she returned to my side with a dozen sheets of white typing paper and a ballpoint pen. I wrote at the top of the first page:

THE KILLER

and then I underlined it three times and handed it to her. She put her hand to her mouth in a quick, reflexive motion, and I saw her eyes fill with tears. She sat down at the dining table, across from me, and watched me throughout the whole of the conversation, she told me later, because my attention had shifted to the telephone and to the pages of empty paper in front of me. I started to fill them as he continued to talk.

'Anyway, as I said, I read your story with interest. All those people thinking and worrying. Think of all the intellectual energy being expended over simple fear of the unknown, of the unmanageable. I suppose all the amateur shrinks and crime buffs think that it gives me a sense of power. Well,' he laughed, 'they're right. It does. I love it.' His voice gathered an edge of anger. 'They disgust me, all those people. Those smug suburban types buying the weapons – as if they would know how to use one, anyway – the people on the street with whom you talked, all their clichés of fear, their terror that their secure little lives are threatened. I wish I had a way to get to them all, to kill all of them. . . .' He hesitated. 'Well, just have to make do with what I can, right? But I want all of those safe people to feel it right in their stomachs, the worst kind of fear, the type that you know you can't do anything about. The perfect fear. I want them to think of me as a cancer in the gut of society, eating away at their lives.'

He took a deep breath.

'I hate them all. I can't even find the words to tell you.'

I could hear his breathing, like a runner's near the middle of a race, labored yet steady.

'You're the writer. You tell them.'

'And what if we stop?' I asked. 'What if the paper were to stop writing the stories, if I were to stop taking down what you say?'

Again he paused.

'Well,' he said, 'I'm certain that the television stations would love to put my voice over the air.' He laughed. 'I prefer to have more substance, to see one's thoughts and sayings down on paper in black and white. The daily paper just sits there all day staring out at you. Not like some television show that happens and is suddenly gone. So I prefer to have your cooperation. But it's not essential.

'And,' he said, 'I doubt that your paper or any paper could possibly voluntarily ignore a story like this,

191

regardless of their complicity in the whole matter. Regardless of how much they were used.'

I was aware of the darkness outside the kitchen window. The telephone was a wall model with a long cord. I walked to the sink, away from the paper and notes for a moment, trying to collect my thoughts. I could see the pale moon through the branches; the tree seemed to be filled with wan light.

The killer continued.

'I had another thought, an odd one, while I was reading your latest stories. I found myself thinking back to my own childhood, especially when you described those women and the children on their swings. When I was young my mother would take me to a playground; we lived in a small town then, and I remember the children took turns on the swings, moving their little legs back and forth as fast as possible. I was with them, pumping, and in my memory I could see myself, the parabola of the arc of my swing growing as I forced more and more momentum into my motion. I could see my hands, the fingers turning white, as I gripped the chains. When I reached the apogee of the arc I would thrust my head back, staring for one moment up into the sky, as if I were in flight; then as the swing began its downward flight I would tumble back to earth, my eyes shut. Almost like being weightless, or what I suppose weightlessness is like. I get that feeling sometimes with the forty-five, when it is pointing at the back of a person's head. I felt it first in Nam. Now here at home. The same sensation from childhood exactly, the delightful dizziness of being detached from the earth. Have you ever experienced anything similar?'

I was at a loss and said the first thing that leaped into my head.

'Perhaps with a woman, sometimes . . .'

He laughed, a burst of raucous noise.

'And why not?' he said. 'With a woman, yes. The feeling of letting go, of flying free. Not bad, not bad at all. Do you know, Anderson' – and his voice switched from a kind of jocularity to a deeper, more pressing anger – 'that I had my first woman when I was in the Army? Not until I was nineteen years old and a soldier, a trained killer, did I experience a woman. When I was young and we lived on the farm, I watched the animals mating with a kind of fascination, an envy at their lack of shame, the mere following of instinct. When I was very small there was a girl who lived next door to me, and often, you know, before one really knows one is doing wrong, she and I would play in the woods beside the houses. Not really woods, just a stand of trees and bushes that had grown up haphazardly, shielding the homes from the side.

'There wasn't much space in there; the underbrush was overgrown and pitched together like an obstacle course. It was a perfect place for kids; we could slide under and around the bushes and trees, unseen, private, hidden away from the eyes of our parents.

'She was an adopted child, I remember. She wore the circles under her eyes like makeup, and I thought that I loved her and that she and I would someday run away together. I was six, she was seven, and we played together in that stand of trees. At first we played simple child's games, hide-and-seek, whatever. Then she brought out her dolls; she had two homemade, floppy cloth dolls that she would cuddle. She said that they were our family and that we were in our home there. It became a make-believe house. In the summer we lay under the trees, hidden away, and talked about how we would run away together when we got just a little bit older.

'We didn't wear any clothes. I remember every inch of her body, her skin tanned and brown on her arms and legs, but a soft pink where her dress covered her from the sun. We lay together, sometimes embracing, and I remember the sensation of her body next to mine, comforting, warm, covered by the shade of the trees and bushes. I couldn't get enough of looking at her, all the secret places of her body. I would reach out my fingers and stroke her softly, not daring to push or pull or upset her in any way. It was like touching light, and I remember how I would shake, tremble really, with excitement, looking at her eyes closed. . . .'

He stopped and the line was silent.

'What happened?' I asked.

'We were discovered by my mother. I remember it like the stop-action frames of photographs. Sitting up suddenly at an unfamiliar sound in the bushes. Scrambling to grab my clothes. My mother shrieking with anger, her voice like a gunshot. The girl crying. I dove into the brambles, and when I returned home that night my mother made me strip off my clothes to show my father how I'd been scratched and cut trying to escape her.'

'And?'

'I was beaten.' His voice sounded like a shrug. 'She was beaten. The two families got together and cleared out the underbrush, cut down some of the trees. "Make good firewood," I can remember my father saying as he lifted the axe over his head and swung it at the base of a birch. They, the other family, moved away soon after. Why, I never could guess. Another job, another empty opportunity. Who knows?'

'You never found out?'

'I loved her,' he said. 'No, I never found out.'

There was silence then, and my mind raced ahead. I thought of the shifts that the killer manifested, the swings in his mood from a kind of joking friendliness to a darker evil, a virulent hatred. But when he talked of his family, of growing up, his voice seemed to slip into a hazy, soft-spoken tone. It was as if talking about the memories calmed his angers.

'You know, there was a time after that, soon after the girl and her family left, that my mother choked. It was a hot day, like the days we are having now, where the heat seems to blot out everything else, the sun smashing down like a round of high explosive. My father was out; at the schoolhouse probably. He usually took his lunch with him and didn't return until late in the afternoon, even during the summer session, which was mostly remedial lessons for the children who weren't going to be passed on to the next grade.

'So my mother and I were alone in the house, stifling in the heat. The windows were wide open, but there was no air. Nowhere. It was lunchtime, and I watched my mother get up from the divan where she had been resting. She was wearing one of those old-fashioned housecoats, the type that button up the front. It was a floral print with flowers on her chest.

'She had been lying on the divan, complaining about the heat, a glass of water at her side and a kerchief which she dipped into the glass spread over her eyes. In the distance I could hear the noon whistles from a train station a few miles away. The sound hung in the air, echoing. My mother had unbuttoned the front of the housedress. Her skin was red, with a rash, I suppose. She had pulled the housecoat back so that it just rested on the tops of her breasts. I watched her bosom as it swelled and fell with the effort to breathe the still air. I could see droplets of sweat that formed in the area between the breasts, running down her stomach. When she heard the noon whistle she swung her legs from the couch and sat for a second on the side, swaying slightly as if she were dizzy. She took the cloth and dipped it in the glass of water and then squeezed it out over herself, the water mingling with her own moisture, running down her front toward her lap.

'And then she got up, looked at me oddly and complained, "My God. I wish we lived someplace that the breeze would blow in. Like near a lake or in the mountains. I swear I'll never be cool again!" She tossed her head back a short way as if looking for some sign of the wind. I stayed in my chair and watched. Have you been a good boy? She wanted to know. And then, keeping up the same banter, a kind of childlike talk though she knew I was too old for that, she moved slowly into the kitchen. I'll fix us some lunch, she said, and I followed her in.

'It was just as warm there, and she sat down heavily at the kitchen table. "Come here," she said, "rub your mother's forehead." She closed her eyes and leaned her head back, and I began to stroke her forehead. She murmured and I saw her face crease into a smile. I watched her body relax. After a moment she opened her eyes and looked at me. "You are going to become a better boy," she said, "and then you will be mine forever." Forever. What a meaningless word.

'She rose and went to the small icebox. There was beef, left over from dinner the night before. She cut off two slices, one for herself and the other for me, and served it up cold on a plate. She cut off large chunks and slipped them into her mouth rapidly, jaws moving quickly.

'There was a moment, a pause in her eating, and I remember the change coming over her face; a sudden look of astonishment, surprise. She made a high-pitched sound, a half-gurgle, half-scream, and her face turned a whiteness that I'd never seen. Her breath came in short wheezing gasps, and I realized one of the pieces of meat had stuck in her throat. She bent her arms back like bird's wings, trying to pound on her back to dislodge the meat. She gestured for me to help her, trying to thrust her own hands down her throat. I sat rooted to my chair.

'Then, as I watched, she leaped up from the chair and tried to throw herself against the wall, frantic, choking. It was not until she fell to the floor that I got up and moved to her side. I aimed a blow with my fist at the center of her back, waited a second, then let fly. Her breath came shorter, and I hit her again. Then another time, and I kept it up until I realized she was gasping for air and the meat was unstuck. My eyes were closed. She rolled over on the floor, her housecoat undone, falling to her waist.

'I knelt by her, my eyes on her face but fighting not to look at her exposed body. She breathed in slowly, deeply. We stayed that way for a few moments. Then she opened her eyes and reached up and stroked my cheek. "Thank you," she said. I suppose she thought my pounding had worked, though I guess now that it hadn't. Who knows? She slipped her arms around me and pulled me very close in an enveloping embrace. I felt then as if it was suddenly I who was choking, who couldn't breathe. I could feel the sweat on her body, taste it against my lips. It was like being in a room in which the lights are turned off before you are ready for darkness. I closed my eyes and listened to her heartbeat. Sometimes when the artillery fired their defensive targets at night and it came whistling high overhead and exploded a thousand yards off, the earth gave great heaving shakes. The sound reminded me of my mother's heartbeat.'

I realized I was sweating, the telephone receiver sticking unpleasantly to my ear. 'Where are you calling from?' I asked.

He paused, then laughed. 'Just a phone,' he said. 'Do you know how many telephone booths there are in this city? Hundreds. Probably thousands. There are dozens of quiet places from which to call. Of course, I could be lying. I could be sitting in my own room, lying on my bed staring up at the familiar marks on the ceiling as I talk to you. See,' he said, pausing, 'how silent it is? No way for you to know.'

'Why did you call me here?'

'I just had the urge,' he said. 'I wanted you to know that I know where you are. That I was thinking about you. That these urges come over me at the oddest times.'

'What urges?'

'The two that concern you,' he said. 'The urge to kill and the urge to talk.'

I did not know what to say. I had the sensation that the words were not flowing over the phone but were being whispered hot into my ear.

'I was nineteen,' he said, 'when I had my first woman and I killed my first man. The woman was a prostitute; no, I think whore is a better word. The man was hardly a man, more a boy and probably no older than myself. She worked the strip, a section of bars and motels and sex flicks outside of Fort Bragg in whatever the name of that small North Carolina town was. That was where I did my basic, you see, and it wasn't until the very end that we were allowed to go into the town and partake of the pleasures there. Like everything in the Army, it was done in a defined manner; we were herded onto buses, excited like teenagers, which we were.

'There was a marvelous symbolism attached to the leave. I doubt the idiots in charge had any real idea, but what you had to do before they would grant you a pass was qualify with the M-sixteen on the rifle range. Learn to shoot one way before you got the chance to shoot another.'

I could sense his grin on the other end of the line.

'I remember the faces of those who were having trouble with their weapons; bearing down, cheek to the muzzle, eyes locked on the target, aiming down the long barrel, praying they would hit something. It wasn't a problem for me. When I was young and we lived on the farm, my father taught me to shoot. He had an old twenty-two, a Remington with a single-shot bolt action. On Saturdays we went next door and set up a target and spent an hour or two blasting away. Crouching on that firing range, waiting for the duty officer's command to start firing, I saw myself back on that farm, the target tacked to an old board, hanging against the horizon on the field. I have gray eyes. You know, they say that people with gray eyes are the best shots. Daniel Boone, I think. Sergeant Alvin York.'

I wrote that down quickly: gray eyes. For the police, I thought.

'It was odd: I saw the same thing on the qualifying range, and the same memory months later, in the country, when I sighted down the barrel at my first victim. He was running, perhaps thirty yards off, on the edge of a paddy, his black shirt outlined against the tree line. He must have been young, untrained; a real soldier wouldn't expose himself like that. I thought of the farm and the afternoons with my father, his voice harsh, demanding. "Squeeze! Dammit! Don't pull!" And so I squeezed the round off, one shot, and when I looked I saw the figure stumble and then fall, and all around me the rest of the patrol was shouting and yelling and hooting. I had no problem qualifying on the rifle range. They gave me a marksman's medal before I left the camp. So on a Friday night, just as it was gaining darkness, all of us dressed in laundered and pressed shirts and slacks, our hats pulled down in a jaunty fashion on our foreheads, we were loaded into olive green buses and launched into the town.

'There was a bar, the Friendly Spot, it was called. A Miller High Life sign in the window blinked in invitation, and there was a jukebox against the wall and a pool table in the back that had a long scar down the center where the felt had been ripped. There was only a cue ball on the table and I couldn't see any sticks. The juke played country music, with some rock and roll mixed in. Willie Nelson and the Rolling Stones. It was playing "Sympathy for the Devil" when I walked in. I had to blink because it was dark, and it took a few minutes for my eyes to adjust. There was a bartender, a big guy, the type who kept his pack of cigarettes rolled up in the sleeve of his T-shirt. He wore a beard. Didn't say much. The noise of the cash register was his language. The girls were sitting at the bar, and when we walked through the door they slipped from their seats and met us, taking us by the arms, leading us to the bar stools or to a few booths in the back. There were five of us, and we started to drink and laugh and joke. She was blond, I remember, and I looked for a long time at the way her skin seemed to rest in folds on her neck. Her breasts seemed worn, as if they had been pummeled by too many hands. She seemed old.'

Again he paused.

'And?'

He laughed. 'What do you think?' But his tone had shifted again, restored to an edge of anger.

'I don't know,' I said.

'Use your imagination.'

Silence again on the line.

'Why do you tell me these things?' I asked.

'I want you to know.'

'Why?'

'I want everyone to know what they're dealing with.'

'Aren't you afraid you'll say something and the police will trace you?'

'No.'

'No?'

'What's truth, what's fiction?' he said. 'How can anyone tell?'

'Suppose they catch you . . .'

'They won't.'

'Why not?'

'Because they're not smart enough.'

'Perhaps you underestimate them?'

'I doubt it. But if I do, then I suppose the joke's on me, isn't it?'

'Doesn't that worry you?'

'No.'

'Why not?'

'Because I'm already dead,' he said.

I scribbled that down verbatim on the page in front

of me. I looked up and saw Christine staring at me, at the telephone. I pushed the page across for her to read. Her eyes widened.

'How is that?' I asked.

'I feel like a wraith, a disease without substance. My insides are cold, blackened like from fire. There's no life left inside of me. Only hate. That's like death.'

'I don't get it,' I said.

'I don't expect you to,' he replied. 'At least, not yet. Maybe you'll come to understand later.'

I was exasperated. 'Listen, dammit, you keep toying with me, filling me in on memories of your past, talking of incidents in the war. What's the point? What are you trying to prove? Why do you do this?'

'I remember,' he said, his voice turning hard, 'a moment in the jungle. I was on a patrol, a few miles from camp with my platoon, a half-dozen of us, struggling through the underbrush. I was walking the point; I liked that, you know; everyone else hated it. That's because you were the first to attract fire from snipers – and you were the first to trip mines. Everyone was scared of the mines, more than any enemy. The earth beneath your feet couldn't be trusted. You never knew when the next step might be the one. The VC had one mine that just exploded when you touched it, blew off your foot. That wasn't so bad, but the one we really hated went off with a little pop! and then a roar. The mine, you see, had two charges; the first, when you triggered it, shot the main device out of the earth up to waist height. Then it would explode. Knees, thighs, balls, prick, stomach. All the truly horrible places to hurt a man. Sometimes it just cut the guy in two and he would be dead before we could reach him, but sometimes it just mangled the grunt, chopped him into hamburger, and you'd see him sitting on the jungle floor, staring down in disbelief at his crotch, watching the blood flow from where his genitals had been a moment earlier.

'But I liked to walk the point. Out there in front, testing the water. Living closer to the line. I knew I was safe the day I walked right over the trip wire, didn't even glance down and see it, just blundered right on past, my eyes looking up through the trees to the gray sky. The next guy wasn't so lucky, and I heard the pop! ka-boom! and even without turning I knew what it was.

'He was a young guy; he'd been in-country a week or two. Hardly long enough to lose the shine on his fatigues. He gave a little scream and then sat down, or was blown down. He looked like someone who'd spilled a plate of spaghetti with tomato sauce in his lap. The medic jumped up next to him and the radio man started to call for the dust-off, shouting into the radio we needed a jungle penetrator, the whole nine yards. The kid looked up, right at me, and said, "I'm hurt," and I nodded. Then he said, "I'm gonna die," and I nodded again. Then he screamed, and the medic cracked a needle and slipped morphine into him. I remember the sergeant shouting obscenities, over and over. The noise of the explosion made all the jungle birds rise up and tear away through the forest. I just sat and watched and waited, what, ten minutes? Maybe less. You could see the life slip from the kid. The more frantic the medic got, the worse the kid was, their motions in reverse proportion. After a while the kid died, just as the beating sound from the chopper's blades filled the air. The sounds of the jungle birds in flight and the chopper were not much different. The medic was screaming, too, pounding on the kid's chest, trying to revive the heart. It was an ordinary day, that day, just one of three hundred and sixty-five.'

He stopped. After a second, he continued.

'Let me tell you about the old couple. I suppose you want to know about them?'

'Yes,' I said.

'All right,' he said. 'It was a strange time.'

'Why them? What had they done to you?'

'You misunderstand,' he said, irritation in his voice. 'The point is that none of the victims have *done* anything to me. They are innocent. Is that what you want to hear? I know they're guiltless! That's the point.'

'Why the blood? It was everywhere.'

'To increase the horror.'

I took that down. 'Well,' I said, 'if they are symbolic, why don't you explain what they're symbolic of? I just don't catch the meaning.'

'You will,' he said. 'A teenage girl. An elderly couple. You should look at who the victims are. I told you, it's a duplication. There was a moment overseas, an incident. And that is what we're replaying here. You remember during the spring of 1971 when the Weathermen had their demonstrations in Washington? They ran through the streets throwing trash cans and litter, screaming imprecations, trying to disrupt the flow of society. They thought the American people were too complacent about the war, that they didn't understand what was happening over there. How could they identify with the disruption of Vietnamese society if they didn't know what it was like to experience it? The theme of the demonstrations was to "bring the war home," to heighten everyone's awareness through symbolic duplication. I was back from Vietnam, and I walked the streets with them, watching and listening. I saw it made no difference really. People saw it as a nuisance, not as a symbol. Well, the Weathermen lacked my resolve. People can't ignore what I'm doing.'

'But the war is over,' I said. 'Finished. Kaput. A mess that's ended. Everyone agrees on that.'

'It'll never be over for me.' His voice was slow and very deliberate. 'I see it every night during my sleep, every morning when I wake. Sometimes I look up into the sun and I think I'm back there, not here. It'll never be over for me.'

Another silence. 'And those old people?' I asked.

'You mean Mama-san and Papa-san?' He laughed.

'Listen,' I said, my eyes fastening on Christine's as she watched the conversation. 'You need help. There are programs, facilities for men damaged by the war. I can help you . . .'

It was feeble, and I expected his reaction.

'Shit! Shit! Shit! It's all shit! Have you seen any of those facilities, sat in on any of those programs? I doubt it. You know what a VA hospital looks like from the inside? I'll tell you. It is wall after wall of cold, pale green. Sometimes I thought I could see scars on the walls where the screams of all the men who'd passed down the hallway had left their mark. Row after row of beds and bedstands, cluttered with cigarettes and ashes and refuse and people discarded so easily. I was there; I know. And I won't ever go back. You think I'm crazy. I know you do. I read the story quoting the psychiatrists. They're real understanding. Sick, they say, disturbed. Reaching out. All the mindless words of their impotent profession. Well, I may be sick, I may be diseased, but I'm a damn sight more alive than any of them.' He drew in his breath in a long wheezing pull. 'And before I'm finished, a lot of people will wish they were safe from me. I'm not crazy. Goddammit! The whole world is crazy! People walk around acting like nothing is happening. They can't see beyond their own little world. Well, I did! I think I'm the only sane man left in the world,' he said, his voice slowly winding down. 'The only person who understands that for every action there is an opposite reaction. Well, society sent me there to be a killer, and now I'm back, the reaction, doing what I was taught best.'

Again he stopped to gather his breath. 'What about you?' he asked.

'What do you mean?'

'Did you go? We seem to be about the same age. So I know you had the same question. Did you go?'

'No,' I said. 'I didn't go.'

'Why not?'

I thought of a number of responses, of conversations with my father and with college students. I remembered growing my hair long and wearing jeans and peace signs and marching and singing. It all seemed so long ago. I thought, tell him about your student deferment; then tell him about the immorality of the war, that you were opposed, that you'd have fled to Canada instead. That's what he expects to hear.

But I said, 'Because I was afraid.'

'Of what?'

'I'm not sure,' I said. 'Of killing. Of being killed.'

'It was our war.' His voice was even.

'I know.' I thought of the portrait of my grandfather, dressed in his olive drab, tight military collar clasped at his neck. From the photograph he looked out quietly and at peace, a member of the American Expeditionary Force. He was a lieutenant, barely twenty-two, with the 77th Liberty Battalion. He saw action at Château-Thierry and then in the Argonne Forest. I could see him through small boy's eyes. He talked little about the war, and when he returned he went on to law school and then to become a judge of other men's failings from a seat on the bench. When I was eight years old he called me into his study. It was early fall, and he said the weather reminded him in a gray way of the overcast days of the Argonne. The sky before dawn would be a half-light, he said, as if a storm were breaking, and then the cannons would start, great booming sounds that shattered the night's exit. The sky would warm with dawn and the flashes of high explosives as they ripped across the no-man's-land toward the German lines. The whole earth would shake and heave with the movement of the guns. They created their own heat and wind, as if they were stronger than the weather. He looked across his desk at me and then handed me a present. It was his old steel helmet, so heavy I could barely hold it. He set it on my head and stood back and saluted. 'The war to end all wars, that's what we called it then,' he said. The helmet made my hair dirty, and I took it off and shook my head. 'That's French dirt,' he said. 'Been there for forty-odd years.'

There was another picture, too, in the house where I grew up; it occupied a spot on the shelf next to my grandfather's portrait. It was a grainy, slightly out-of-focus shot of a group of men kneeling on the tarmac surface of a runway. Behind them was the nose of a medium bomber, a Mitchell B-25. The men were slumped in relaxed poses; each had written his name in white ink underneath. Third from the left, right under the drawing of a scantily clad woman with a thunderbolt in each hand that adorned the nose of the plane, was my father. He was wearing a heavy sheepskin flight jacket and had his hat tilted back on his head. One arm was gently around the shoulders of another man wearing the same khaki and leather. Around my father's waist was a belt and pistol. It was probably the same .45 the killer was using.

'World War One, World War Two, even Korea, everything was clear-cut,' the killer said. 'But when they handed us our war, it wasn't that simple.'

'How could we know?' I said.

'You're right. How could any of us have guessed? I went. My old man went. His father before him went. It was just an accepted thing, I guess. God! How wrong they were.'

209

'Your father and your grandfather?' I asked, surprised.

'Yes,' he said. 'it wasn't that they were an Army family. It was just accepted. It was my turn.'

I pictured my father. He was speaking, pacing the room, trying to maintain his composure. 'Canada? Are you certain? Dammit, I know the war is wrong, but what will you be tossing away?'

'It was the same for me,' I said.

'But you didn't go?'

'No.'

'Did you demonstrate?'

'Yes. Everyone did. It was easy.'

'I suppose so,' he said.

We were silent for a moment. Then he added, 'You see, I bet we have more in common than you think.'

The flatness in his voice stopped my thoughts. I saw the old man and woman again.

'Tell me about the killings,' I said.

'It was easy,' he replied, mocking my own words. He laughed. 'They liked to take a walk in the evening, a constitutional. I watched them for a few days; they walked the same route at the same pace. Stopping at the same spots to pause for breath. They walked arm-in-arm. I liked that. Many people don't show their affection for each other the way they used to.'

'I don't understand . . .' But he cut me off,

'I simply followed them home that night. They didn't see me until I was right upon them, right in the doorway. There was no one else on the street, and they were too shocked and too scared to even call out. I said something cryptic and frightening, like, "One sound and you're dead," and I clapped my hand over the woman's mouth and kind of shoved the pair of them into their living room, slamming the front door shut behind me. It was that simple. Suddenly it was cool and quiet, as if the door slamming had cut the day away like a knife stroke and it was just me and them.

'I waved the gun under their noses for an instant. The old man was terrified. He stepped in front of his wife and said, "You take what you want, young man, but stop trying to scare us!" And then he thrust out what little was left of his chest. "I've seen tougher than you," he said. And I smiled at him and motioned them to the couch in the living room. There was another chair, which I plopped down in, and, holding the gun on them, I said, "Oh, yes? Where?" And the old guy gave a little shiver. "Auschwitz," he said, and he held up his arm and the sleeve dropped away from his scrawny wrist to reveal a tattooed number.

'I was, to put it mildly, nonplussed. I couldn't believe my luck. "Tell me about it," I said, and the old guy put his wife's hand in his – she hadn't said anything up to this point, just stared straight ahead, eyes glazed over – and he said, "So what is there to tell? You've seen the pictures?" It was a question and I nodded my head. "We all went in. Some came out. Not many. What's to say? Who likes to remember these things? But you cannot scare me, young man, not even with your big gun." I loved him then. Who wouldn't? After a minute he said, "So you going to rob us? Or what? You think we're rich? Not living here." I shook my head. "No robbery," he said. "What else is left? Murder? For what? Rape? We're too old. What's left?"

'But I didn't answer him. He was a proud old man; he sat with his back straight, his eyes right on me throughout. He kept one arm around his wife, the way a bird covers its young with a wing. He held her hand. I saw his eyes focus on the gun. Then he smiled. "A forty-five, perhaps?" he said and I nodded. "It makes some sense now," he said.

'Then he turned to his wife, and his voice was so soft I could barely hear him. "Ruth," he said, "you know that I have loved you all these years. Now it's going to end. This man is the man in the papers, the one who murdered that pretty young girl. He means to kill us, too." When he said that, she stiffened suddenly, and her eyes went wide and scared. She reminded me a little bit of animals, you know, a dog or a rabbit. But he swiftly shushed her and said, "We're old. What do we care? Is this something we should be afraid of?" His voice was marvelous – soft, reassuring, almost hypnotic. I watched the effect it had on his wife. She seemed to slow perceptibly and move even closer to him. She shut her eyes and nodded, and he turned back to me. "So," he said. "Do your worst."

'Tell me about your lives, I asked him. But he shrugged and said, "What's to say? We were born. We met, we loved. We survived. We lived. Now we are going to die." I shook my head. "Please," I said, "I want to know." His wife opened her eyes then. She gave him a small nudge in the ribs. "You tell him," she said. "I would like to hear it, too." So the old man looked at her with a kind of smile and started to tell me their life story. We must have sat for – oh, I don't know – an hour, two hours, three. You hear something like that, time just passes.

'Did you know that after the Second World War ended, the survivors of the death camps were kept in new concentration camps run by the British and the Americans? Relocation camps, they called them. That the United States – that's right, us, you and I, our fathers – had a quota, wouldn't allow many of the displaced people to enter the country? I heard all about that. The old man talked of coming here, one of the few allowed in. It was because he had a cousin already here, a man he hadn't seen since they were small children. The cousin sponsored him. He said he came into New York Harbor on a brutally cold day; there were icicles hanging from the docks. But he said he took off his coat and breathed in the air. He said he could taste it; it made him feel dizzy.

'I think they had a good life. Nothing exceptional. His sons did better than he, which gave him great pleasure. He had seen his grandchildren grow up, if not into adulthood, at least past adolescence. He said he'd worked hard and enjoyed most every minute of it. Making and selling clothing, an honorable profession. Clothing the people, he called it. Good clothes, he said, sturdy, utilitarian designs of good quality. When people bought a suit from him, they knew it was a garment that would last. Then he turned to his wife and said, "Like us. We've lasted." She just tucked her head down onto his shoulder and smiled, closing her eyes. You know, I could tell they were still in love, probably as much that moment as any during their decades together. "How did the two of you meet?" I asked him, but the woman looked up. "The old-fashioned way," she said, "through a matchmaker." She talked awhile, telling about their courtship, their marriage. They were separated in the camps, but afterward they found each other. It took six months, but she found him. She said she knew all the time he hadn't died, that there was too much life in the two of them. She was smiling throughout her story, every so often leaning over and touching her husband. And then she looked at me and said, "You must be a very sad young man to be doing these terrible things." You know something – I agreed with her. I nodded my head and I could feel tears in my eyes. "It hurts," I told them, and the two of them nodded sagely. They wanted to know about my mother, my father, and I told them about growing up. Just a little, you know, to keep them interested. I talked about the farm, and then the city and the differences.

'Isn't it remarkable? Each second, each minute that passed, brought them closer to death, and in the same time we grew closer as people, moving from meeting to acquaintanceship to friendship. It was the same with the girl. I feel I can only know people, really know them, in death. All the masks, all the bullshit, just drops away. It's a pure thing, pristine. Perfect.

'The three of us had a little cry then. I finally wiped my eyes and thanked them for the memories that they had shared with me. I saw the fear enter the old woman's face. She had white hair pulled back from her face, and a strand had come free. She shook her head to get it out of her eyes. "Are you still . . ." she asked and I shushed her. "Nothing changes," I said. "Don't be afraid." I saw her give a little shiver and shrink closer to her husband. He looked at me. "Are you going to tie us? Or what?" And I produced the rope from my pocket.'

I interrupted him: 'How did they get naked?'

'Simple,' he replied. 'I simply told them it was going to be like going to sleep. And I told them to get ready for bed.

'She had to help the old man off with his shirt. She turned to me and said, "Arthritis," and grimaced. He dropped his pants to the floor, then his underwear, and stood naked.

'He made no attempt to cover himself. I have to admit the old man moved with grace throughout. He helped the old woman off with her shirt, then her skirt. She hesitated for an instant in her slip, then pulled it slowly over her head. Stockings, lace underwear; everything lay in a heap on the floor. She looked down at the piles of clothes for a minute; then she reached over and picked them up and arranged them neatly on the couch. I suppose old habits die hard. The old man watched her with a half-smile on his face. I'd never seen two elderly people naked before. I stared at them. The old man's penis had shrunk, shriveled. His hair was gray. So was hers and her breasts deflated, the nipples a dark brown. Her chest and his were both sunken. Yet he filled his with air and stared at me. "Would you hurry now?" he said. I motioned them to the center of the room, and in a second they were kneeling, side by side.

'I tied their hands swiftly; I doubt that I needed

to, but I was concerned that one might panic in the seconds between the shots. They were composed, though I could see the old woman's shoulders start to shake, palsied. "I'll go first," the old man said, "but send us together." I felt as if I were in the midst of a dream; they were cooperating, their voices so calm. It was as if I were merely an instrument and this was their suicide. "All right," I said, "say what you will to each other." They put their heads together, kissed lightly on the lips and smiled. "We have no more words," the old man said.

'I saw them close their eyes. I grabbed a pillow from an armchair. It was as if I were outside myself, watching myself perform the act of execution. I placed the pillow against the old man's head and looked for a moment at the forty-five. I could see my finger squeezing the trigger. Each minute space, each micrometer of the pull, took seconds, minutes. Then there was a roar and the familiar jolt running from my palm up through my arm. I could feel my fingers tingling, numb. The old man pitched forward. I saw the old woman grit her teeth. She was saying a prayer, I suppose; her lips moved. I was behind her almost before the old man had finished twitching on the floor. This time the movements seemed speeded up, like a movie picture being run at the wrong speed. The pillow was on her neck, the gun barrel poised, and then the shock of the explosion and she spilled forward, too.

'I think I went berserk then, playing in the blood. I went to the kitchen and found a sponge which I dipped in the mess on the floor and used to write the numbers. I do not know how long I was there. Five minutes. Maybe an hour. I danced around the bodies until darkness filled the room and I could barely see. Then I left the house, door ajar. I walked down the street toward my car, the streaks of blood on my clothes gleaming. I was invisible. No one walked from their house, no one was on the street, no car drove by. I carried the forty-five in my hand, and the night stood still as I made my escape.'

He hesitated.

'They were perfect innocents,' he said.

I felt a complete exhaustion and let the silence on the line grow until it filled the room. My eyes refused to focus on the pages of notes and quotations that I'd hastily scribbled. My own handwriting was unfamiliar, alien.

'I feel,' the killer said, 'like a thirsty man after the first long taste of cold water. I'll call again soon. Maybe here, maybe at your office. Depends. It just depends.'

And then he hung up the phone.

CHAPTER TEN

Christine started to dance then.

She said it was her method of dealing with the release of energy created by her fear. I would find her in the mornings on the floor of the living room, curled around a pillow, sleeping. On the stereo turntable was soft jazz; she preferred Miles Davis and Keith Jarrett. Sometimes, however, she used classical string quartets, the volume turned down so low that only the barest of rhythms could be discerned. She danced naked, dropping her bathrobe to the wood floor, arching her body back in salute to the sound. I think she felt the music mingle with the nighttime sounds of cicadas and distant traffic. She would dance until exhaustion brought her to the floor, and then curl up and sleep soundly until morning.

Her eyes showed no sign of the nocturnal activities, her voice was clear in the mornings. Her work at the hospital continued unchanged, too: three days a week in surgery, her hands seizing the instruments and dealing them to the doctors with the confidence of a Las Vegas blackjack dealer; two days on the ward, checking the progress of the diseases, all the varieties of cancer that peeked out from under the coverlets at her as she swept past, resplendent in her white uniform. She passed cancers of the blood, cancers of the organs, cancers in retreat and cancers charging unchecked. She talked often of the diseases that lived on the ward, the stages they went through, the prognosis for this one, the projection for that. Of the killer she said little but to point out that if he knew our phone number, then he knew where we lived. When the police came to install the recording device on my home phone, she watched with a kind of detached fear, her face registering the same look of concern I suspected she adopted when she walked past the bed of a patient on her ward and in the morning light saw the appearance of some new manifestation of the disease.

As for myself, I began to stare at people in the street.

I divided each passerby into one of two categories: a potential victim or the potential killer. I began to wonder about everyone I passed, who are you? What are you thinking? Are you the next? Are you him? Often I stopped people randomly, slipping my notebook from my pocket as I introduced myself and began to interview them. Most people refused to give their names, as if afraid the killer would single them out and punish them for expressing their fears. They averted their faces when Porter was with me, and he would drop the camera to his waist in frustration. The comments and quotes that I collected all began to sound alike, variations of the same themes of fear, anger and bewilderment. More and more, people criticized the police for not catching the killer. There was a new wariness in voices, and I discovered that people turned away from my stare rapidly.

At night, I took to driving through the city after dark, trying to determine what was different and what was the same. In the suburbs and the residential enclaves of the city, there was a hesitancy: houses seemed to gather the darkness around them in retreat. There were fewer children in the summertime streets; as we entered the dog days of August, the sounds of laughter and play were seldom heard. There was a shutting up, a closing down; people talked of staying inside.

There were exceptions, of course. The winos and bums who proliferate in Miami's downtown were still on the streets, guarding their few possessions, scraping together their pennies toward their next drink. I talked to a few who seemed unaware, or unconcerned. One old man, whiskered and streaked with dirt, looked up at me and said, 'Why should he kill one of us? What the hell would that prove? We're all dying, anyway.' The other men around him, seeing me scribble the words in my notebook, called out and wheezed congratulations. I wrote a story that night about the derelicts and the lack of fear they felt. Porter had taken fine art and Nolan loved the story. 'Terrific, terrific,' he said. 'More like it.'

The next day I found a teenage couple in a McDonald's, eating hamburgers and drinking milk shakes; it caused Porter to laugh and say, 'Cliché, cliché. Can you believe that?' The couple, after gentle prodding, told me that the previous Saturday night they'd gone to a 'numbers killer party.' There'd been booze and dancing, and they'd all played a game; one of the partygoers was designated the killer, and he had a list of all the kids and numbers assigned to them. Over the course of the party he symbolically killed them all, catching them alone and taking a red pen and marking their foreheads. The teenagers warmed to the story, telling how two of their number were designated the police and had to try to figure out who was the killer. It had been fun, they said, because the killer had managed to dispense with about a dozen of the guests before he was uncovered amidst much laughter and more liquor. 'I just hope we weren't being prophetic,' the girl said. I wrote that story, too, describing the party and talking to the teen who'd played the killer. 'It was easy,' he told me. 'No one suspected me because I shouted the loudest that we had to find the killer. It was fun.' I asked him if he was scared, but he said no. Later, his father called me, begging me not to print the kid's name. I talked it over with Nolan, and we agreed to use just his initials. Nolan loved that story, too.

I had not been able to get the story of the killer's latest phone call into the next day's paper; when he'd hung up and I'd looked across the table at Christine, it had been close to one A.M., too late for that day's editions. The main run was already winding off the presses, bundles of newsprint tied together heading on metal runners toward the loading docks in the basement of the *Journal* building. By the time I was able to get through to Nolan, awakening him at his house, the press run was in top gear, huge Goss Metro printing machines spitting papers out at a rate of close to one a second. When the presses were running it could be felt throughout the whole building. The floor of the newsroom trembled and shook, and my ears could just pick out a distant rumble.

Sometimes, when I was in the building late at night working on a story, I got up from my desk and went to watch the start of the press run. The huge, cavernous room would be filled with blue-shirted pressmen wearing the traditional paper hats to protect their heads from flying ink. There was a lot less of that now with the new high-speed printing machines, computerized and sophisticated, but the pressmen clung tenaciously to the forms of their jobs and wore the small skullcaps with élan. There were clocks on all the walls, and an insistent clanging bell signaled the start of the run.

I would stand to the side as the men fed the huge rolls of paper into the machines, switched on the presses and stood back. A great whirring and shaking began then, gathering momentum until finally the machines were at full speed and the papers rolled from the presses in great streams, like water. A few stories had stopped the presses; it was still an extraordinary moment. The bell clanged three short bursts followed by a loud long peal; the pressmen, glancing at each other for a second, stepped to the machines, and the room slowly came to a halt, suspended, as if arrested by some giant hand. It was like the moment in an operating theater when the patient's heart stops – a second of nightmare – then starts up again, renewed, reinvigorated.

'We'll sit on the story,' Nolan said, his voice clearing

quickly from sleep. 'We'll hold it for tomorrow's paper, so we can do it right, OK?' I agreed. 'Now, the important thing is that the wires and the *Post* and the television stations don't catch wind of this.' He hesitated. 'We have to go to the cops. That was our part of the bargain. But you make certain that they understand their half. No leaks. This is our story.' Then he paused for a moment. 'Did you get extensive notes?' I described the pages of paper filled with scrawled quotes. 'Good,' Nolan said. 'Don't turn those notes over. You allow them to question you, take a statement, whatever. But keep the notes. What did the guy say, anyway?'

'He said he gets the urge to kill and he gets the urge to talk.'

'Unbelievable. That sounds like the lead to me. What else?'

'There was a lot about his life, anecdotes really. I'm not sure why he tells me. And then he described how he killed the old couple.'

'In detail?'

'In great detail.'

'My God,' Nolan said. 'What a story.'

Christine wanted to come with me to Police Headquarters. She said she could not stand to be alone, that she had the sensation the killer was somehow close by. I told her she would just be bored and that she had to work in the morning. I waited as she prepared herself for bed, watching as she slipped out of her clothes and left them on the floor. I thought of her nakedness, and for an instant the picture of the old couple slipped into my mind. Then, just as quickly I dismissed it and put my hands on her breasts, pulling back the thin sheet under which we slept. She closed her eyes and rolled onto her side, facing me. I rubbed her neck, then reached over and switched off the light. 'I wish you could come to bed,' she said, 'and just hold me. I don't know if I'll be able to sleep.'

'Don't be foolish,' I replied in the darkness. I would bolt the door securely and see her in the morning. In the weak light filtering in from the street through the window I could see the outline of her body. I wondered why I was not more aroused and then let the thought pass as I stepped from the bedroom back into the living room, closing the door gently behind me. My eyes swept the room, looking for my notes.

Martinez was waiting in the lobby of the headquarters building that night. He was wearing a suit but no tie, and his shirt was opened, exposing the hair on his chest. He grinned at me when I entered. 'A stewardess,' he said.

'What?' I replied, shaking his hand.

'Blond. National Airlines. About twenty-three years old. She was teaching me how to fly.' He grinned again.

'Sorry,' I said.

He shrugged. 'Business before pleasure. Anyway, I should never have given her number to Wilson. I bet he's glad to crawl out of bed in the middle of the night.'

We got on the elevator with a pair of uniformed officers. They stared at me for a moment, then turned away. I listened to them talk about a fight they'd broken up earlier in the evening; one man was complaining that he'd pulled a back muscle. The other wasn't sympathetic. 'This way,' Martinez said when the doors opened to the third floor. For an instant the lights filled my eyes and I blinked back the glare. The homicide office was a large room divided into dozens of smaller areas by partitions that did not reach to the ceiling. Inside each was a pair of desks, back to back, chairs and telephones. The desks were old, gray metal and scarred by cigarettes.

The detectives watched Martinez and me walk through the aisles as they stood in the doorways, their suits and ties somehow incongruous in the bleak world around them. I saw a black man, his hands cuffed behind his back, sitting in one of the small offices. He was leaning back in a chair, listening to a detective speak. The black man's face was set in a sneer, and periodically he shook his head. I turned away and looked at the walls. They were institutional green and reflected the fluorescent lights. There were photographs on the walls, mug shots and wanted posters, a duty roster and a large handwritten sign that said: Those Assigned to Numbers Killer Squad *Must* Check Daily with Sgt. Wilson or Duty Officer. I continued to follow Martinez through the room, pausing once to glance in at a desk.

There were dozens of glossy color photographs strewn about the tabletop, and as I passed by I realized the shots were of a murder scene. I could see a body, covered in blood, twisted into the rear of an automobile trunk. Martinez stopped when he saw me looking. He stepped into the room and pulled a photo off the desk. 'Ever seen what a twelve-gauge shotgun does to someone at close range? Not too pretty huh? This is a gangland thing. Barely made the local section of the *Journal*. You see, crime doesn't stop when there's a psycho loose. We still have to get the rest of it done.'

I looked at the photo. The victim's face, streaked with blood, was frozen in shock, mouth open, eyes rolled back. His chest had absorbed the blast; it was a mess of entrails and blood. I closed my eyes and handed it back. I was dizzy for a second. 'Did you make an arrest?' I asked.

'Just a matter of time. We've got a guy in a holding cell now who is making his mind up to talk. Drove the getaway car. I don't think he's too anxious to take the fall for the triggermen.'

We continued toward the rear of the room amid the hum of voices and the ringing of telephones. A dozen conversations were going on at once; the noise seemed a backdrop to the activity, like in the newsroom. Detectives swept in and out of the room, some carrying sheaves of paper, others strapping on their weapons. I could hear sirens outside, penetrating through the walls, and the hum of the air conditioning.

We passed by an office with a closed door but a small window. Martinez peered in. 'Ah,' he said, 'confession time.' I looked in the window and saw another black man, smoking a cigarette. Two detectives were in the room, one with paper and pencil taking notes. In the corner sat a man at a stenographic machine.

His fingers moved above the keyboard, taking down words. 'Killed his wife,' Martinez said. 'She'd been chipping on him. They got into it at their home, and he decided to show her who was boss. Beat her to a pulp.' We walked further, and I saw Wilson waiting outside an office.

'Thanks for calling,' he said. 'You ever been up here before?'

'No.'

'Not too fancy, is it?'

I shook my head.

'Listen, what I'd like is for you to go over what the killer said with us, and then, when the steno's finished down the hall, we'll bring him in and you can run through it again. Sometimes you remember something the second time around. Did you take notes?'

I hesitated. 'Yes. But I need them for my story.'

Wilson looked at me. 'How about a copy?'

I shrugged. 'Why not? It's the same as a tape.' I envisioned Christine and what she had been saying. I was a citizen, too. And I hadn't promised the killer that I wouldn't cooperate with the police. 'But you've got to remember the agreement,' I said. 'No leaks to anybody. I don't want to have to start fielding phone calls from the rest of the media before I get the story into my own paper.'

'Agreed,' Wilson said. 'I understand.' He looked angry. 'Everyone's got to get their money's worth out of this.'

'What do you expect?' I replied.

He turned away. 'Who cares?' We walked into the

office and sat in silence. My eyes drifted around the room to a blackboard with names on it. Wilson followed my glance. 'You know how many guys are working this full-time now? Thirty detectives. More than a third of the staff.' He got up and walked to the board. 'You haven't seen this,' he said. 'It comes out, it's my ass.' Martinez got up and shut the door. 'I don't know why I'm helping you,' Wilson said. He rubbed a hand through his cropped hair.

There were four lists of names on the board, detectives divided into four squads: ARMY-VIETNAM, MENTAL HOSPITALS, SEX DETAIL, STREET. There was another listing in a different part of the blackboard with more names under the headings: BALLISTICS, HANDWRITING, VOICE. On the wall above the blackboard were blown-up photos of the bullet fragments taken from the bodies. Points of comparison were listed by numbers in red pencil.

'You see,' Wilson said. 'We're checking into all this stuff. Each team, around-the-clock coverage, works on a specific section. For example, we're running down all the mental cases in hospitals in Ohio, Chicago and Florida. We figure that the city the killer moved to was Chicago; it's just a guess. We're going through draft records, schools, you name it, trying to get a handle.'

'Are you getting anywhere?'

Wilson turned away. 'It's an either-or thing. We know the weapon; we're checking all the dealers for ammunition, that kind of thing. We compile lists, ideas, you name it. But nothing really amounts to anything until we get a good subject.

And we don't have anybody yet. No name, no identity.'

I looked at my own notes. 'He says he has gray eyes.'

Wilson's face changed quickly. It gathered a kind of intensity, and he peered across the room at me. Martinez slipped a notebook from his pocket. 'He told you that?' Wilson asked.

'He said he was a good shot. Gray eyes. Like Daniel Boone.'

Wilson nodded. 'That's helpful. Especially with army records.'

I looked across my pages again. 'He said he was out of the army by 1971. He said he'd been in a VA hospital.'

'He told you that?' Wilson repeated excitedly. 'All right, all right.'

'This helps,' Martinez said, grinning the same smile as when he had mentioned the stewardess.

I handed him the sheaf of papers. 'Run those off and we'll go through it line by line. We'll see how much I remember. The guy was talking fast; we'll just have to see.'

Wilson put his hand on my shoulder. 'Don't worry,' he said. 'You have my word there won't be any leaks to the other papers.'

I thought of the killer's voice; his memories, his arrogance. I felt I was shifting the balance between him and the police, somehow lending weight to their side.

I should have felt exhilarated. Instead, I felt queasy. I wasn't sure why.

* * *

The story, of course, dominated the next day's paper.

It was morning when I left Police Headquarters. Martinez walked me out. 'You keep this sucker talking,' he said, 'maybe we'll have a chance.' He shook my hand. I looked up into the front of the building; the windows stared down at me like the vacant eyes in the photo of the murdered man. Martinez turned and waved as I walked down the street toward my car. I felt a light-headedness, which I attributed to the night without sleep. The morning sun was beginning to gather momentum, and I could feel the first of the day's heat around me.

I closed my eyes when I slid into my chair at my own desk. It was a sensual familiarity, like slipping into bed next to a familiar body; the curves, the pressures on my own flesh, were all safe, known. I fingered the keyboard of the typewriter, not pressing down but just touching the letters.

Nolan walked up to me. 'How did it go with the cops?'

'They say I'm a big help,' I replied. 'He said several things which might contribute to his identification.'

'How do you feel?'

'OK, I guess,' I said. 'I feel as if I'm doing something that I shouldn't, though.'

'Why?' Nolan persisted. 'We trade information with the cops all the time. And what makes us different from the rest of the citizens of this town? If you or I witnessed a crime, wouldn't we be just as obligated to bring the criminal to justice? What makes us any different?'

'I don't know,' I said. 'It just makes me feel strange.'

Nolan laughed. 'You're just like any reporter,' he said. 'Can't stand to part with information except in a news story.' He reached over and picked up my notes. 'He must have talked for some time.' I nodded. 'OK,' Nolan said, 'write it up, and then go home and get some sleep. If there are any problems I'll call you this evening.'

It was not difficult to write the story. For the most part I used the killer's voice. At the top I used the most sensational parts, quoting him on his urges and his description of the murders of the old couple. I said his voice was steady, even enthusiastic throughout the conversation, but I did not describe the mood swings, the sudden anger, and I excised most of his personal history, paraphrasing and condensing it into a narrative instead of using his own words. It crossed my mind that I was somehow protecting his memories, trying not to lay them raw on the page, as if they should remain private.

Nolan looked over the pages I handed to him. The story was long, but I knew it would be all right. I watched his red pen flick through the sentences, adjusting a phrase here, editing a word there. 'OK,' Nolan said, 'this ought to open the eyes of some of the people out there. Talk to me after you get some sleep.'

But later we had little to say. The story was dummied, edited and set in type. Once again the headline ran all six columns, stretched across the front page, bannered just below the mast-head: 'NUMBERS' KILLER CALLS AGAIN: 'I GET URGES,' HE SAYS.

I looked at my name underneath the headline, and then at the words:

The man dubbed the 'Numbers' killer by local police has once again telephoned this *Journal* reporter to recount the grisly details of the recent murders of an elderly Miami Beach couple.

Ira and Ruth Stein, the killer said in a voice devoid of emotion, 'were perfect innocents.' And once again the killer pledged to continue his string of murders, a reenactment, he said, of an as-yet unspecified act of violence in Vietnam during the conflict there.

Police, meanwhile, have renewed their efforts to identify and apprehend the killer.

My eyes glazed over the rest of the text; the words seemed to melt into a great gray mass on the page in front of me. I was aware of a pleasurable warmth, the satisfaction of seeing the story so prominently in print. Just him and me, I thought. That's what he said. Together, putting the story out slowly but surely. I wondered if I was starting to need him as much as he needed me.

In the days following the phone call and the subsequent story, I returned to the psychiatrist to see if he had any advice. He seemed glad to see me, held out his hand and shook my own warmly. He gestured for me to take the chair across from his desk and then took a moment to light a pipe, swinging back in his own chair, balancing behind his desk as on a high wire. It was late afternoon and the sunlight filtered through the window. 'I read all the stories with great interest,' he said. 'Let me compliment you. I think they are very well done.'

I nodded thanks.

'So,' he continued, 'what brings you back? Oh, you don't have to answer, I know. More instant insight needed.' He laughed.

'I just wanted to ask you your impressions,' I said. 'Perhaps something has occurred to you. Maybe you can think of something that I can ask the killer, something that will trigger more information about himself.'

'Well,' the doctor said, smoke slipping from between his lips, 'I don't think that there is any single question you could ask that would cause him to explode. That's the stuff of fiction, really. The great sudden breakthrough. The revelation. Honesty suddenly plucked from a world of lies.' He shook his head. 'I wish things worked like that. Hollywood. We should all move to Hollywood, perhaps. No' – and he dragged in deeply on his pipe again – 'even when there are revelations, sudden catharsis, they're usually accompanied by setbacks, denial, and the mind compensating for the admission it has made. It's always a slow process. There are victories, don't get me wrong, and days of great progress, but it isn't quite so quick as one would like.' He paused again.

'Anyway, from reading the stories, particularly the one the other day where he described the second murders, it seems you're getting more information about this fellow than you can use.'

'I don't get it,' I said. 'He ricochets back and forth between some incident during the war, his family, growing up. It comes across as a jumble.'

'You would prefer someone totally calm, rational and explicitly helpful? People like that seldom commit series of random murders. And they certainly don't sit on the telephone giving clues to the press, the police and the public at large.'

'All right,' I said, laughing. The doctor smiled with me. 'You add it up for me.'

The doctor thought for a moment, swiveling in his chair, then stopped abruptly and turned toward me. 'I don't think the situation has changed much from the first time we talked. The killer sees himself as invulnerable, yet at the same time he gives up clues to his identity. A part of him wants to be caught; a part of him loves the act of toying with the whole world. He mingles the two courses of his life in the conversations with you because they're confused in his mind. The reasons he enjoys killing today are for the most part rooted in his childhood. A seductive mother, perhaps worse; a father who alternated between demands and beatings. A sense of isolation, alienation. He grows up, his anger unchecked. Then he goes to the Army – or says he does – and learns to kill. He says, I'm already a good shot, or, translated, I'm already a killer. I wonder, though: this is an intelligent man. Did he really go to Vietnam? Or is he using the collective national guilt to obscure the feelings he already had, the course he was already set upon?'

I interrupted. 'His descriptions are explicit. His knowledge seems very real, very familiar. . . .'

'Almost too much so, I would think,' the doctor remarked.

'I don't buy that.'

'Just a theory, mind you. Just a possibility. As much evidence that I'm wrong as that I'm right. So much of this is guesswork, really. Psychiatry is not designed to anticipate, to predict.'

'What is past is prologue,' I said.

The doctor laughed. 'Touché.' He thought for an instant. 'Let's assume that he's telling the truth, there was an overseas incident – and I caution you, be wary, because what is truth for a psychotic is not necessarily truth for a journalist. This incident overseas, I would suspect, would tie in with some experiences that he had here, as a child.' He waved his hand. 'I know, I know, journalism doesn't want to hear about latency and anal phases and all the preadolescent stuff that is the cornerstone of my profession. But you look for it, and it will help.'

Again he paused, swiveling to look out the window.

'It's all a game to him, I think. I still don't think he'll be caught, no matter how much information he imparts.'

'Still pessimistic,' I said.

He laughed. 'It still goes with the territory.'

I asked him about the reactions I'd observed on the street: the concern, fear, even challenges.

'I think people will continue to fear this man. Whether we see any hysterical symptoms . . . who knows? A colleague of mine told me he has a patient who can talk of nothing else, hour after hour. That, I suspect, is the exception rather than the rule. And don't underestimate the ability of people to ignore that which stares them in the face. You've read Poe?'

I nodded.

' "The Masque of the Red Death." Very appropriate, dancing as death enters the ballroom.' He got up and walked to the window. 'Miami is a city that is spared so much,' he said. 'We have the sun, the water, boating, tennis, outdoors, the beach. It's a community that thrives on escape. There are no winters here. When was the last really big storm? Nineteen thirty-seven or thereabouts. No one even remembers. It's harder here to feel those old people's deaths, to believe that underneath the sun and in the warm air there is something inherently evil stalking us. Oh, don't get me wrong, you'll see fear everywhere you go. You take out your notebook and you remind people. But can we really understand what's out there? I don't know.'

His voice trailed off. He turned and looked at me.

'I must be getting old. I ramble on. I spend so much time listening that when I get the chance to talk it just pours out. Forgive me.' We shook hands a second time. 'I find it all very interesting,' he said. 'Anytime I can be of assistance.'

I did not hear from the killer for nearly two weeks.

The time seemed to pass interminably from second

to second. I'd had the impression so firmly that he would act again swiftly that each moment seemed elongated unnaturally. Miami crept through August, the pace of the city dictated by the heat; slow, irritating. A man was shot during an argument over a fender bender, the assailant standing in tears by the dented automobiles, waiting for the police while the victim choked in his own blood. There was a series of convenience-store robberies, two of which ended in the shotgunning of the teenage bandits by a police stakeout squad. There was a scandal in the local government; an accountant uncovered a significant loss of money from a petty-cash fund, and the prosecutor's office subpoenaed records from the mayor and two commissioners. I worked on none of the stories; Nolan kept me in the office most of the time.

I wrote one long piece detailing the police activities, describing how one team was working with army records at Fort Bragg in North Carolina and the Pentagon in Washington. There were other items as well. One night I rode in a police cruiser through the section where the first murder had taken place and talked with a pair of officers about their beat. They told me it had changed in subtle ways; first there had been fewer people out in the evenings, then fewer teenagers. The neighborhoods were a lot quieter. The officers spoke angrily about the killer, vicious talk about getting him alone for a few minutes, about the chance to shoot it out. They were both young men and had served in Vietnam. Sure, one of them said, it was bad over there, but we're home now and it's over.

He repeated himself, saying 'over' again and again. His partner agreed, grunting as he swung the patrol car down darkened streets, past homes that seemed closed, shut away.

During those two weeks I spoke with Wilson and Martinez every day, sometimes twice a day, trying to develop stories out of their leads. They were both open and circumspect in their dealings with me; they showed me some areas of investigation, the ballistic exams, the canvassing of ammunition dealers trying to find who had purchased .45-caliber bullets in recent months. About the probes into Army records, they were more reluctant. I suspected that they had developed some ideas, perhaps even gained a few names, but wouldn't tell me. I went to Nolan with my thoughts and he put pressure on his source, the homicide lieutenant, to find out, but the source related only that there had been some progress but nothing concrete. My suspicions remained.

Nolan decided then that we shouldn't rely on the police as much and put me to working up a profile of the killer based on the tapes and the notes of the conversations. Near the end of the second week, as I was completing the profile, the managing editor called me in to ask if I thought perhaps the killer had departed. He stood up from his desk and walked to the window in his office that overlooked the newsroom, his eyes scanning the activity in the huge room.

He was worried, he said, that the paper might be prolonging the atmosphere of fear by daily stories about the killer and the progress of the police. Let's hold off, he told me, until we're sure this guy is out there. He spoke his words into the window, and I had to strain to catch them. He was a dapper man who wore well-tailored suits. His sleeves were forever rolled up, though, and his hands were often darkened with the stains of newsprint.

Nolan was there listening to him speak, and I saw his head nod in agreement. The trouble is, I heard Nolan say, that he was torn. One could argue that perhaps we were preventing more murders by continuing the stories; that the killer seemed to respond to the lack of news more violently than to the constant flow of stories. Every time the flow slackened, he acted, or that's what he said. The managing editor agreed that this put the paper in a difficult situation, but that we couldn't let our decisions be made by a madman. All right, Nolan said, let's see what happens.

As for myself, I didn't think the killer had disappeared. I could sense him just outside my reach.

The profile was in the form of notes, not intended for publication; only, as Nolan said, something for us to measure him by. I wrote:

Only child.
Beaten.
Humiliated.
Seduced?

I went to the library just off the newsroom and took out an almanac and an encyclopedia. I looked up the state of Ohio. It stared out at me from the pages of thick books, square, solid, like a Midwesterner's unwavering gaze. My eyes tracked the roads that crisscrossed the state, stopping at the small dots that corresponded to the small towns. I saw the serpentine shape of the Ohio River, and I tried to imagine flat fields stretching from its banks inland, crops reaching up under the August sky to the sun.

Porter happened by and stopped to peer over my shoulder at the map. 'Ever been there?' he asked. I shook my head. 'Cold in the winter. Hot in the summer. Conservative. I was at Kent State when the guardsmen shot the students. It was a clear day, sun out, bright. I remember the whole thing seemed more like an exercise; the crowd swept over the hill, slogans, shouts, the usual. There was this one wretched moment after the volley was fired; I didn't know what had taken place, but I was stunned nonetheless. It was as if the knowledge that they'd fired into the crowd was inside my head, fighting to get into my conscious thought, like the last few minutes of sleep in the morning. There was a scream, more like a wail – it reminded me of the Arab women in *The Battle of Algiers* – and I knew then, without seeing what had occurred. Of course, I ran. Everyone did. I ran right past one of the bodies. I still remember the blood against the black macadam of the pathway. You know, there's a sculpture in the center of the campus, a sharply defined piece filled with angles and lines. It's made from a kind of steel that looks bronze. There's a bullet hole through it, right through one of the corners, a small round circle. You know, the

241

type that you simply have to put your finger through and feel? Perfectly round.'

I returned to my desk and wrote:

The City.
The Army.
The War.
The Incident.

What was the incident? In the office of my college newspaper, we had framed the famous photo from Mylai 4. It was an oversized poster, a great mass of yellow and green and in the center a tangle of bodies streaked with the red of their own blood. I thought of other photos, too: the girl running naked toward the camera from the explosions of napalm, her mouth open in a great terrified circle; the blank look of death on the face of the VC in the microsecond his head began to blow apart from the force of the police chief's bullet. What was the incident? What had the killer done?

I wrote:

Age: twenty-five to thirty.
Time in VA Hospital.
Gray eyes.

I wondered if he was telling the truth. What's fact, what's fiction. Those were his last words.

The telephone rang as I was stepping from the shower. I heard Christine answer it, and I hurriedly grabbed at a towel and began to dry my body. There was a knock on the bathroom door, a small sound that seemed to hide in the steam. She pushed the door open and her eyes were wide. 'It's him,' she said. 'I'm sure of it. He hesitated a moment when I picked up the telephone, then asked for you by name. He's waiting.'

I slipped a bathrobe around my shoulders and sponged my head swiftly, I could still feel the moisture on my back when I picked up the receiver.

'That must be your girl friend,' the voice said. 'She sounds very nice.'

'Where have you been? It's been nearly two weeks.'

'Here and there,' he said. 'Uptown, downtown, all around the town.' I waited for something else, but he had stopped. After a pause he started again. 'Tell the police to keep checking those records, they're sure to come up with something. They've got the gray eyes, what else? Oh, marksmanship. I got a medal. Tell them to check into that, it should narrow the field some. Diligence has its rewards; you tell them that.'

And then he hesitated again.

'But it won't do them any good.'

A pause.

'They'll never catch me. No matter how much help I give them.'

Another silence.

'You must be anxious to get to work,' the killer said. 'Well, here's something to work on: Number Four.'

'Where?'

'Out to the west, off Krome Avenue, where it

cuts close in to the start of the Everglades. That's a marvelous area, quiet, deserted. A person can really think out there, no sounds except for the animals and an occasional jet passing overhead. Go three miles down Krome from where you get on after the expressway. You'll see a dirt road to the left. Take it for six-tenths of a mile. Stop and walk about a hundred yards through the underbrush. There'll be a clearing. Better hurry, because there's a surprise.'

And then he hung up.

It was barely eight in the morning. I heard a chair scrape behind me and knew Christine had sat down at the kitchen table. 'He's killed again,' I said. She made no reply. 'You were right, it was him.' I looked back at the telephone. I had better hurry, that's what the killer had said.

Wilson took little time in reaching the phone. I pictured him on the other end, his face already beginning to twist with anger, reddening up toward the roots of his salt-and-pepper crew cut. 'Again?' he asked, prescient, as he picked up the telephone.

'Out Krome Avenue, toward the Glades,' I said. 'He said there was a surprise. As well as Number Four.'

'What do you mean, surprise?'

'How the hell do I know? He plays with me as much as he plays with you.'

'That's a big area,' Wilson started, but I interrupted him.

'Here, listen for yourself.' I took the recorder the police had placed on my phone and rewound it. Then, holding the receiver down to the speaker, I played the conversation to Wilson. The killer's words filled

244

the room, and I turned to Christine. She sat shaking her head.

It was over in what seemed a second. I stopped the tape and put the phone back to my ear. 'Did you get that?' I asked Wilson.

'Son of a bitch,' he replied.

I waited.

'Fucking son of a bitch. I'm going to get him. I'm going to get him myself.' His voice changed. 'Thanks for calling. I'll see you out there.'

After I hung up the telephone I walked over behind Christine, put my hand on her shoulder and squeezed, trying to convey a sense of support. She reached up and touched my hand with her fingers but said nothing, just continued to shake her head. But my mind was already back to the conversation, and I was trying to imagine what it was that was waiting out on Krome Avenue. I went to the bedroom and began to dress.

It was several minutes before I realized that I had neglected to call Nolan and tell the city desk. The thought came over me suddenly, and I felt a type of panic, like a child in a classroom who's been caught by a question from the teacher when he hasn't been paying attention.

And so, tucking in my shirt, I dialed the city desk. As I waited for Nolan to come on the line, the image filled my mind of the pressroom chief, hesitating for a last second, his eyes scanning the big room and the waiting presses, and then hitting the button that started the machines rolling and filling the air with noise.

CHAPTER ELEVEN

The killer's 'surprise' was cruelty.

It stirred an almost universal rage throughout the city at the same time it increased the tenor of the fear that had become so commonplace. For the first time people began to meet in groups, civic organizations held rallies, community patrols were initiated. The publicity redoubled, also: *Time and Newsweek* devoted considerable space to the killer and his series of murders and telephone calls. My photo ran in each magazine, and I was quoted in both. I was also interviewed by television newsmen, but that had become almost routine. The *New York Times* and the *Washington Post* sent stringers over to talk with me and then ran lengthy pieces. The *Chicago Tribune* sent a feature writer down to Miami. She stayed at one of the hotels on the Beach, and I took her around to the spots where the bodies had been discovered. They ran the story stripped across the bottom of their front page; she sent me a copy a few days later. I began to clip the stories myself – my own and the ones that I saw in the national press – and kept them on my desk in a file which thickened daily.

I had dodged through the city traffic as quickly as I could, heading toward the expressway. The morning rush hour was in the other direction, downtown toward the bay and the center of Miami, and so I pushed the car past the speed limit easily, the window down and hot air sucking through the car. The sun glistened off the road, and I held one hand on the wheel as the other slipped my sunglasses from their case. Within a few seconds I saw a car come up fast behind me; it was Porter, far above the speed limit, swinging the big sedan from lane to lane, oblivious to obstacles. He waved as he went past and I accelerated to keep pace.

We were both doing close to ninety. The Krome Avenue exit came up fast, and as we swung down onto the two-lane road I saw a green and white police car roar past us. It was then that I caught the first sound of sirens and knew that we were part of a wave of vehicles descending onto the Everglades. As I swung the car onto the road, I saw a flight of white herons swing out of the swamp up into the sky, a half-dozen birds, their feathers reflecting the sun, wheeling against the blue sky and disappearing. A rescue-squad ambulance came up behind us, its lights blinking red and yellow, its siren filling the air with harsh urgency. We slowed to let it pass, then accelerated to keep up. I knew it was not far away, and within seconds I saw a dozen cars and unmarked cruisers pulled haphazardly to the side of the road, lights flashing in an uncoordinated symphony of sight. The ambulance pushed as far through the mass as it could, then stopped, tires throwing off gravel and dirt. Three yellow-jump-suited rescue personnel leaped from the ambulance, pushing a stretcher. One carried a black doctor's bag and had a stethoscope hanging from his neck. I stopped and followed, watching the uniformed officers as they guided the rescue squad through the swamp. Porter shouted at me, 'Let's go, let's go!' as he turned and rushed through the scrub brush and sickle weeds, down a path that had already been trampled by the hurrying policemen. As I followed him, two television trucks and a car from the *Post* pulled in.

The ground underfoot was marshy and soft, and we slid as we ran. The brush seemed to reach out and trip us as we swept past. On either side of the small pathway leading from the road was dense swamp; we were running on the only hump of dry land. I saw a small island ahead, a patch of solid ground covered with saw grass and weeds. It was there the policemen were gathered. And it was from that scene that I heard the first cry.

It was a high-pitched, wordless sound of despair and loneliness. I did not recognize it for what it was; I think Porter did, for he turned momentarily and stared back at me. We scrambled up a small embankment, and several of the uniformed officers saw us and halted us from going any closer. Porter was already snapping pictures through a long lens, the camera whirring and clicking. 'There,' he said, pointing the camera. I followed the lens and saw a body pitched forward, obscured by the foliage. A single officer stood over it, as if guarding it. But the policeman's eyes were locked on the crowd of rescue personnel and other officers a few feet away. I could make out a rough, makeshift lean-to that seemed to be propped up in the midst of the crowd. And then I heard the cry again, wailing, piercing the morning heat. 'My God,' Porter said, putting down the long lens for an instant, 'it's a kid.'

As I watched, the policemen seemed to pull back, and I saw them slapping each other on the back and two uniformed officers' hands being pumped. The three rescue-squad personnel turned and, half-jogging, headed toward the pathway crowded with reporters and cameramen as the policemen cleared a trail.

The man in front had the child in his arms, wrapped in a rough blue blanket pressed tightly against his yellow jump suit. He was smiling and talking to the child as he went past, shielding the baby from the cameras and lights. 'How old?' I asked as he swept past.

'A year, maybe,' he answered, 'eighteen months.'

'Is he hurt?' I called.

'It's a she, and nothing except a. little exposure, I think.' He continued down the gauntlet of press toward the ambulance, speaking in a soft voice to the child.

'Jesus Christ,' I heard Porter say. 'Can you believe that?'

The police would not let us out into the scene of the fourth murder for close to two hours. By that time the sun was high overhead and the morning had dissolved under the probing heat. As usual I was questioned by the other reporters, and I confirmed that the killer had called and provided directions to the location. After about an hour, word came in over a television-truck shortwave that the baby girl seemed to be fine and was in the pediatric-care ward of a big downtown hospital. I told the other reporters that the killer had promised a 'surprise,' and it was my guess the child was what he had had in mind. The questioning dropped away and we waited. I sat by the side of the path on the damp ground, watching the crime-laboratory personnel combing the area and the assistant medical examiner attending to the body. Porter complained about the lack of shots and jumped to his feet when the body was brought out; I remember thinking it was the fourth black bag I'd seen that summer and wondered if it was one of the same bags that had been used to carry any of the other victims.

Wilson and Martinez finally came and briefed the press, myself included. They said that it appeared the child and the victim – a white woman in her late twenties – and the killer had stayed in the clearing for a day or so. There was debris, they said, indicating they'd had several meals. They would not give us the woman's name. Martinez nodded when asked about the cause of death and the style; the same hands bound behind and wound to the back of the head. Wilson said the same knots that had been used to bind the hands had been used in the construction of the little lean-to. It was obviously shelter from the sun for the child. He said there would be no further comment. I caught his eye for an instant, but his return glance told me nothing.

Single-file, the reporters and cameramen were led

through the scene. We were told not to touch anything, and for the most part the tour was conducted in silence. I could see the bloodstains on the saw grass where the woman had lain. A pile of items was being tagged and registered by a technician; I could see empty hamburger boxes from a fast-food chain, several disposable bottles, some diapers, and a few crumpled packs of cigarettes. I paused by the little lean-to. The walls were constructed of scrap wood and boards, and the top was a thatch of grass and palms. A few strands of rope held it together, and I had the impression a strong breeze would blow it apart.

En masse the press interviewed the two officers – patrolmen riding their regular shift out in the countryside – who had found the scene and the child. They had been told to secure the area for the detectives, but one of them had heard what he thought was a cry, and they had blundered through the brush toward the lean-to and the child. There was a combination of pride and anger in their faces; they were pleased with saving the child, but confused and angry over the circumstances. 'What kind of guy,' one of them said, a young man, blond-haired with a thick mustache, 'would leave a little child behind like that after murdering her mother?'

And that, of course, was the question everyone had.

My father called after the articles in the newsweeklies appeared. I answered the telephone hesitantly, with a tentativeness brought about by my lack of contact with the killer. I had adjusted, but only in part, to my dependence upon the telephone. When it rang I still felt a rush of excitement, thinking it could be him, and, when it proved otherwise, disappointment mingled with relief. I had not realized up to then how often the telephone rang or how closely it had become entwined with my life. 'I saw your picture,' he said. 'This seems to be turning you into a celebrity.' I made no reply, and he added, 'It seems a terrible way to become known. Do you suppose the police are any closer to capturing this guy?'

I told him I didn't know. The killer seemed to be toying with the police, with his partial descriptions of himself, but no one was certain he was telling the truth.

We continued to talk, small talk about my brother's law practice, my sister still in college, my mother. She had taken up social work at a local hospital, my father said, a psychiatric ward, interesting stuff. He said she was worried about me, in particular the closeness that had come to exist between the killer and myself.

'What closeness?' I asked. 'I'm on the end of his rope. He tugs, I respond. He calls, I write. The distance remains infinite. '

'No,' my father said, and I realized suddenly that the fear was as much his own as my mother's. 'You're wrong. In each call, each conversation, he brings you closer. The distance, I think, diminishes.'

'I'm not afraid.'

'You should be.'

Distance, I thought, has always been important in my family.

253

His mind must have been working on the same thought. He continued, after a moment: 'When you were young and growing, you were always the silent one. Your brother, your sister, both threw themselves into things more readily. You always hesitated. I suppose I always thought you would become a journalist. You spent so much time watching.'

'I'll be all right,' I said, but my voice was like an echo in a canyon.

The story dominated all other thoughts.

For days the woman and child remained unidentified. All the reporters in Miami working the story chafed under the mystery, unable to give the murdered woman a past, a sense of being. As each day passed, speculation grew. We wondered where she came from, whether she had some special connection to the killer, what her role was in the symbolic drama. A lover, some thought; a woman who knew his identity; a sister, perhaps. We struggled with the possibilities, making her death larger than her life.

I wrote, over and over again, every particle of the story that I could discover. The meeting with the managing editor and Nolan was forgotten; the story gained its own momentum, The headlines developed a manic sense; the words 'Massive Manhunt' and 'Unrelenting Around-the-Clock Investigation' crept into the prose. All the clichés of a big-city crime were there. We shifted, calling him sometimes the 'Numbers Killer' and sometimes the 'Telephone Killer.' Regardless, everyone knew who we were talking about.

A local movie house brought in a double feature: *Dial M For Murder* and *Wait Until Dark*. It played to packed houses, and I spent an evening talking with the people lined up outside the theater waiting for the next show. 'It's incredible,' one girl told me. She had blond hair, and she clutched her boyfriend's arm in mock fear. 'It seems so Hollywood, and yet it's really happening, isn't it?'

I used her quote to lead a story.

There were many others. I spent another night riding through the southern section of the city, row upon row of trim, single-story, white-washed middle-income homes. This time I was not with the police but with a group of neighborhood homeowners. They had formed an 'association,' and part of the association's duties was to patrol the area. They had foiled a burglary on their first night, the driver said. The other man in the car, a big man with thick arms and sideburns that curled down the side of his head, turned to me then and whispered, 'The cops say we shouldn't carry weapons, but . . .' and pulled up the corner of his sweat shirt to display the pearl handle of a short-barreled Colt .32 stuck in his pants. He laughed, his voice filling the inside of the car and spilling through the windows into the dark outside.

He, too, became a story.

I went to a civic-group meeting and listened to speaker after speaker rise to question the police efforts at finding the killer. The meeting was held in a high school gymnasium, and I looked up through the lights to the ceiling where a huge banner, a championship season, hung. The words all seemed the same that night, the same as those of the people on the street, of the men in the car, the same as the words heard everywhere. A woman rose and looked over the crowd. I could see her face twist as she struggled with her thoughts. Finally she opened her mouth. 'What can we do?' she asked, and I thought: nothing. Nothing can be done. I scribbled her words into my notebook and kept my pessimism out of the story.

The local politicians, too, had their say. There was an almost endless series of press conferences and publicity stunts; they rode with the police, they wore weapons to meetings at City Hall. They, too, became part of the canvas.

And then there was my own role.

At a similar meeting there was another woman; small, barely five feet, but with a high-pitched voice that projected far beyond her size. Her face was pinched, and the wrinkles on her forehead seemed like lines drawn with a pen. She stared at me, open-mouthed, when I asked her a question, as she sorted through her memory. Finally, she said, 'You've talked with him!' and I nodded, and she continued, 'You're the one he calls!' and I nodded again. Her voice rose against the auditorium noise; a crowd swiftly gathered, and I felt a sudden rush of heat as the bodies pressed around me. Porter was close by; I could hear the sound of his camera. 'Why don't you tell him to stop!' the woman went on. 'Why don't you make him stop!' Her voice had become a shriek, but one that bore the sympathy of the others gathered around her.

'I've tried,' I said.

'Try again!' she screamed. 'Keep trying!'

'How?' I asked.

But she had turned her head, shaking in anger and tears.

A man, thickset, shook his fist. 'Tell him we're waiting for him! Tell him we're not afraid!'

I thought how simple it all was. Fear engenders such basic reactions: the man threatened responds aggressively, posturing; the woman, realistic in her way, responds in anguish.

Porter punctuated my thoughts. 'Just once,' he said, smiling, 'I'd like to see some guy standing around wringing his hands, tears running down his face, shouting, "What can I do, what can I do?" and have his wife walk up and gruffly shake her fist in our faces and say, "Dammit, I'm ready for the sucker. Let him show." ' He laughed and continued to take shots of the meeting.

That night I sat at the typewriter thinking of the woman's words. Try again, keep trying. But how do I do that? I put it out of my head and began to write the next day's story.

Wilson called one night just as I was preparing to leave the office. 'I've got something you probably want to see,' he said. I walked out into the Miami evening. The black seemed to gleam, alive with small breaths of wind. I felt I could reach out and touch the night, grasp huge handfuls out of the air. I drove through the downtown, the headlights mingling with the lights on the street, cutting a brightness out of the dark sky. Wilson met me at the entrance to Police Headquarters.

'Come on,' he said. 'Have your horizons broadened.' He laughed at his cliché and led me through the entrance. The high-intensity fluorescent lights hurt my eyes for a moment, and I blinked as we walked to an elevator. The eyes of the policemen followed me across the lobby.

We got off on the homicide department's floor, but instead of entering the main workroom, Wilson took me down a side corridor. The walls were painted white and there were no signs, no posters, nothing to say where it led. I followed the detective's back, keeping pace as he marched down the center of the hallway, leaving not enough room for me to walk beside him. Finally he paused outside of an unmarked brown door. 'All right,' he said. 'Don't say anything until it's over. Don't make any fast movements, don't light any cigarettes. Just watch, got it? Listen and learn.' He swung the door open quickly, and the two of us entered a small darkened room. There was only one light, and that was shaded severely so that only the shadows of the men in the room could be made out. I saw a table with a flat reel-to-reel tape recorder. A man sat behind it, watching the reels turn, but my attention went quickest to the window. It was about two feet by four feet, and through it I could see into an adjacent room, one where the lights were turned high. 'One-way glass,' Wilson muttered. I stood next to him, peering into the second room.

A young man sat at a table. He had long brown, nearly red hair and a meager beard. His eyes were rimmed and dark, and he kept wiping at his nose throughout the conversation. He used the back of his hand, drawing it in a slow, unthinking motion across his face. His head jerked about as he spoke, trying to follow the glance of the two detectives in the room. One of them was Martinez, his tie loosened and the top button of his shirt undone. His vest was open, and I could see his empty holster. The other detective, also in his shirt-sleeves, sat on a chair, leaning back, arms folded, looking skeptical and angry.

'All right,' Martinez said, 'run through it again for us, will ya, Joey?' He paced about the room, walking behind the man and pausing, then moving on, varying his speed, moving his eyes to the ceiling, to the floor, then suddenly boring in on the man at the table.

'What is it you guys want?' the man said. 'I did it. Each one. What more do you need?' His voice was choppy, anxious and sounded tinny through the speaker built into the ceiling. 'First the girl, then the old couple, now the woman and the kid. I'm tired of it now.'

'That's why you turned yourself in?' Martinez asked.

'Yeah.'

'Where's the gun?'

'I threw it into a canal.'

'Which canal?'

'I don't know. How should I remember?'

'When?'

'Before I came here.'

'And you don't remember? Come on, Joey.'

'I tell you I just don't remember.'

'How'd you get here?'

'I walked.'

'What route?'

'From uptown.'

'No canals there.'

'Yes, there was.' The voice was whining, pleading.

'OK, Joey, tell me about the girl.'

'What's to say? I killed her.'

'Got to do better than that.'

'OK,' the man said, after a moment. 'I raped her, too.'

Martinez shook his head. 'Why did you call the paper, Joey?'

'I wanted to tell them about it. I wanted everyone to know.'

'Why?'

'So they would know I was important.'

'Killing makes you feel important, Joey?'

'That's right.'

'You feel important now?'

The man hesitated, wiping his nose vigorously. 'You bet,' he said. He smiled at the detectives. I saw Martinez nod at the other detective. He uncoiled explosively, his arm suddenly up above his head, then his open palm smashing down on the table a few inches from the confessor's own hands. The noise resounded in the small room.

'Liar!' the detective shouted. 'Fucking jerk-off liar! Wasting our time!'

The man recoiled, throwing himself back in the chair, his hands springing up to shield his face.

'No!' he shouted. 'The truth. I swear.'

'Liar!' the detective repeated. Martinez had slipped to the rear of the room and was leaning against the wall lighting a cigarette, as if oblivious to what was going on. The other detective jumped to his feet and circled around, standing over the confessor. He bent over and I saw the man shrink in fear. 'You come in and tell us this bullshit! That's what it is! Bullshit!' The detective raised his hand. 'I ought to knock you . . .' Then he paused. There was silence in the room, save for the worried scratching of the confessor. The detective moved behind him, and the confessor kept shifting in his seat, trying to keep him in sight. Suddenly the detective leaned forward, his mouth only inches from the confessor's ear. 'Fucking liar!' he screamed. The man quivered, as if hit. The detective grabbed the back of the seat and shook it hard for a moment, and the man almost tumbled to the floor. I saw Martinez take a long drag of his cigarette and give a small hand signal to the other detective. The detective nodded, leaned down once again, shouted, 'Fucking liar!' into the confessor's ear, then backed off, out of the man's sight.

'Now, Joey,' Martinez said slowly, 'why don't we try again?'

The man started to cry, and Martinez waited patiently for the sniffling to stop.

'I'm sorry,' the confessor said. 'I didn't mean nothing.'

Martinez stood up, stretching. He took out another cigarette, lit it and passed it to the man.

'Can I still spend the night in jail?' the confessor asked, puffing gratefully on the smoke. Martinez started to laugh, and after a second the other detective joined in. Finally the confessor did, too, but his laugh was hesitant, and he kept turning nervously, looking for the detective.

Wilson touched my sleeve. 'Let's go.'

We met Martinez in the hallway. 'Quite a show,' I said. He grinned.

'Easy. No challenge left. But getting to be a real pain in the ass. That's the fifth off the street this week. People come in saying they're the man, wanting to unburden themselves. Sometimes it takes an hour, two, three . . . before we get the guy to change, and all the time we know he isn't the guy. They just don't have the right information, the right personality. And mainly, they don't have the evidence. Like no gun.'

The detectives walked me outside. After the confines of the small room it was a relief to look up into the dark sky. I asked them how the records check was going. 'No computers,' Martinez said. 'They have to check by hand, each file. A big slow pain.'

Wilson looked at me. 'Hasn't called again?'

'Not yet,' I said. 'How much more do you need?'

'How about the dates of service, the rank he reached? It would be a big help.'

'I'll try,' I said. I seemed to be promising that a lot. The two detectives walked back into the building, and I went back to the office. My description of the phony confession became yet another story. Nolan liked it, as did the news desk. It ran in a corner of the front page.

Christine would only make love with the telephone off the hook. She said she could not stand the thought that the killer might call while we were, as she put it, engaged. I shrugged and went along with her wishes, but afterward I would rise from the bed and replace the receiver, wondering if I had missed any moment of contact in the interim. 'Is it all you can think of?' she asked.

'You don't understand,' I replied. 'A story like this is everything. It won't stop now – it can't stop. It's not just me. Any reporter would be the same.'

She shook her head. 'I don't believe that,' she said.

I walked to a window and stared out. An image rose in my mind: myself at age eleven, staring from the second-story window of my home. I could see the others, my father, mother, brother and sister in the yard, sitting close to a picnic table. I saw my brother and father get up and begin to toss a ball back and forth while my sister moved closer on the bench to my mother. One instant I was staring through the glass, and then things moved in stages. My hand tightened as I balled it into a fist; I heard the noise, a splintering crack, like an alarm. Blood was streaming down the back of my hand, and shattered pieces of glass lay on the window frame. I turned, with a small boy's cry, and ran to the bathroom where I immersed my hand in water, watching the rim of the sink turn pink, then red with blood. After a moment the pain seemed to diminish, and I wrapped my hand in a towel. In another few moments the bleeding subsided, and I looked down at a ragged cut across my knuckles and a deeper cut in my index finger. I kept the towel wrapped tightly and returned to my room. I did not look out to see if they had heard the sound of the window breaking, nor did I look up an hour later when my father poked his head through the door, glanced at the window and then sat on the side of my bed. I remembered the sensation of his hand resting on my forehead, cooling, like an ice pack.

Christine saw my expression, rose from the bed and slipped her arms around me. She rested her head on my shoulder, and I could feel her hand reaching up for the back of my neck in caress, almost as if I were that small child again.

It was early evening, a week after the fourth murder, that Wilson called me. I could hear voices in the background and the sound of a cash register. 'This is Wilson,' he announced. 'We know who she is.'

'Who?' I reached for note pad and pencil.

'You want to know, meet me here. Otherwise, wait for the general press release later tonight.'

He was in a bar called The Alibi in a hotel across from the county's large criminal courthouse. It was a place I'd been inside before, dark like most bars, little decoration save for the liquor bottles stacked up behind a fake mahogany counter. There were booths where conversations could be held quietly, served by women in short skirts and black mesh stockings. It was frequented by detectives, defense attorneys and prosecutors, a place where the rules of court did not apply, where deals were struck and insults traded. It was always full and always loud.

I discovered Wilson in a booth in a corner. Martinez was with him, his head stretched back and feet out, relaxed. 'What are you drinking?' he asked. I ordered a beer. I looked at the two detectives, waiting.

'Shit,' Martinez said, straightening himself in the chair. 'Here you go.' I saw Wilson's eyes follow the younger detective's hand as he reached inside his jacket pocket and pulled out a sheet of white paper. He handed it across the table to me, and then the two men's eyes fixed on me as I read the words.

At the top of the page were the words 'PRESS RELEASE' and the county seal. In the center were the words:

> The fourth victim in the 'Numbers Killer' case has been identified as: Susan Kemp, 29, a resident of Building 6, number 110, in the Fontainebleau Park apartment complex. The child has been identified as her daughter Jennifer, age 21 months. The child remains in stable condition at Jackson Memorial Hospital. The investigation continues.

'It doesn't tell me much,' I said. 'Like how you made the identification and how she was selected and picked up.'

'We were hoping,' Martinez said slowly, 'that by now you would have provided that information.'

'Why won't the fucker call?' Wilson said. He took a long drink from his glass.

I shrugged. Martinez glanced over at Wilson, then continued. 'We don't know why she was selected, or how. Obviously they used a car to get out to the Glades. And obviously, from the debris that remained behind, they were there for some time, possibly overnight. But motive; Christ, who knows?'

'How did you identify her?'

Again Martinez looked over at Wilson. He nodded

and took another drink. 'She had no ID on her, no name tag, driver's license, nothing. Neither did the kid. This morning, though, this woman calls up the office. Says she lives out in the development. Says her next-door neighbor fits the description of the woman in the papers; she hasn't seen her for days, and she's worried. We went out to check it; routine, you've got to do that sort of thing. The manager lets us into the apartment; seems he was kind of worried, too. We walk through the door, and there on the wall is a nice photo of the woman and kid. Probably taken about a month ago. No doubt about it.'

'Who is she?'

Martinez leaned back, holding his glass against his forehead. 'No one special,' he said. 'Just divorced. A schoolteacher taking the summer off before returning to class. She taught the fourth grade.'

'Husband?'

'Businessman from Tampa. Flew in this afternoon, ID'ed the body. Gonna take the kid, too, when he gets over the shock.'

'Where is he?'

Wilson put out his hand and Martinez cut off his reply in midbreath, before he could get started. 'Give us a break,' the detective said. He shook his head. 'Don't you think the guy has had enough of a rough time for one day?'

'Maybe he wants to say something,' I said. 'Usually, they do.'

Wilson put his head against the back of the booth and closed his eyes. 'Tell you what,' he said, 'I'll ask him. Give him your number. Leave it up to him.'

I agreed. He was probably upstairs in the hotel, anyway. It would be no problem to check.

'Still no idea how the killer managed to pick her?'

'None,' Martinez said. 'No one in the apartment complex saw or noticed anything unusual. No strangers hanging about street corners. No nothing.'

'How about the records check? The Army?'

'We've taken the years 1963 to 1973. At a minimum we're talking about several thousand names – and those who have to be cross-checked for unusual eye color. And then we have to come up with addresses. It's gonna take forever.' His voice was flat, depressed. 'We stand a better chance of somebody seeing something here. Unless we get more out of the guy.'

'The psychiatrist I talked with thinks he'll continue to give information out. Teasing, just daring you to catch him.'

Wilson closed his eyes. 'That's what really fucks me up,' he said. His eyes blinked open and he stared across the table at me, through the bar darkness. 'You know, today I decided to send my wife and kids away to visit their grandparents. In fucking Minnesota, for Christ's sake. Maybe that's far enough away.' He laughed, a short snorting sound. 'Martinez doesn't have to worry. All those girl friends, hell, he wouldn't even miss one or two.'

Martinez smiled but did not laugh.

Wilson continued talking, pausing only to wave for another drink. 'We go out, you know, cruising the streets, talking with informants. Anybody who might have a line. I've twisted more arms in the last three weeks than I have in years. Nobody knows nothing.

Hell, the junkies in Liberty City are just as scared as the mothers in Kendall.'

Martinez spoke. 'We get calls, you know, every day, sometimes every hour, especially after the first edition of the *Journal* comes out. This guy wants to report on his neighbor, acting suspicious. Another guy thinks he saw a forty-five-caliber pistol in his brother-in-law's house. We take the information and then out we go, check it out. We check everything out. Every little detail, every little tip, no matter. And we're no fucking closer now than we were at the start.'

'Something will break,' I said.

'Yeah,' Martinez said. 'Like maybe the fuck will dump the next body off on our doorstep. At least then we'd know about it before the rest of the world.'

Wilson looked up, across the room. His eyes fixed on a man carrying a drink, heading in our direction. 'Oh, shit,' he said.

The man approached and seemed to hover for an instant on the edge of the darkness. He stared at the two policemen, ignoring me. I watched as he slowly raised his glass to his lips and, eyes still focused on the policemen, drained off the glass. His voice, when he spoke, was unsteady. 'So,' he said. 'Off duty, huh? No need to hunt murderers when you can have a drink, huh?'

Martinez stood up and, reaching over to an adjacent table, seized a chair. 'Mr. Kemp,' he said, 'please sit down.'

I pulled out my notebook again.

'I don't want to sit with you,' he said, but he slid into the chair.

'Mr. Kemp,' Martinez said, 'this is Malcolm Anderson. He's a reporter with the *Journal*.' Martinez motioned at me. I nodded.

'You're the one who talks to this guy, right?'

'That's right. It was your wife?'

'That's right.' He was wearing a conservative blue suit, but it seemed to hang from his body, as if he had shrunk in size over the course of the day.

'I'm sorry,' I said.

He looked at me. 'No, you're not. They aren't, either . . .' I started to protest, but he moved his hand up in a half-drunken wave. 'Don't let it bother you,' he said. 'I mean, why should you care? Why should anyone care?' I saw tears forming at the corners of his eyes. 'You know, the stupid thing is, two months ago, when we were going through the divorce, we were yelling at each other all the time. Real bitter over the baby, the home, the car, all the little things. I must have wished her dead a dozen times, a hundred times. And now she is.'

He looked at me for an instant, his eyes watery; then he slowly shifted his gaze to the two policemen. 'Just another dead body. I bet you see hundreds of them, huh?'

'Mr. Kemp,' Martinez started in, but the same hand motion cut him off. 'Oh, don't let my attitude make you angry,' the man said, shaking his head uncoordinatedly. 'She was nothing special. Nothing to get upset about. Just another murder. Hey, you get some free time, maybe you'll find this guy. I know you've got better things to do.' He stood up sharply, and the chair behind him turned over with a crash that quieted the bar and turned all eyes our way. 'No, don't get up!' he shouted as Martinez started to stand. 'Don't put yourselves out. Do your little investigations, write your little stories. . . .' He looked at me. 'It doesn't mean anything. Nothing means anything.' And he turned sharply, unsteadily, and looked across at the men in the room staring at him. 'Fuck you all, every one of you.' No one moved. His words hung in the air for a second. He balled his hand into a fist and made punching motions in front of him. Then he stopped, suddenly looked about him, and with his head abruptly sinking into his hands, he ran from the room.

In the darkness, I hurried to scribble the words and the motions, to capture it all in my notebook. Wilson watched me. 'Get it all?' he asked, sarcastic.

I looked at him and paused before answering. 'That's what it's all about,' I said.

I got up to leave and Wilson's eyes followed me. For a moment our glance locked, and I watched as he seemed to be turning something over in his mind. Finally he spoke: 'Set him up,' he said.

Martinez also stared at me. 'Do it,' he said; 'set him up.'

'I'll think about it,' I replied. I turned and left them in the bar. I walked out into the beginning of the night, a blue-black sky naked of clouds. I breathed in deeply, the leftover daytime heat filling my lungs, replacing the stale air-conditioned air of the bar. I felt a sudden dizziness as I replayed the detectives' words in my mind. They mingled with my father's and Christine's. I saw the murdered woman's husband, lurching in grief, striking out at the emptiness in the bar, confusing that for the helplessness in his mind.

CHAPTER TWELVE

I returned late that night to the office. I could feel the vibration from the presses coursing up through the floor as I walked into the newsroom, the early-edition run streaming through the catacomb network of sorting and assembling machines. It was as if the steady shaking rose through my legs and into my body, that as I sat at the typewriter to write I was a part of a huge machine.

Earlier, Porter had met me at the murdered woman's apartment. We started in, knocking on doors, talking with the neighbors. They seemed resigned, a glumness marking their faces and voices; they had seen the police officers earlier in the day; they had talked with the detectives who'd probed them with many of the same questions I asked. They knew the woman was the killer's victim, and they were trying to ignore the fear that had stepped up so close to them.

A sweet, gentle woman, they said. She managed a smile throughout the day, always quick with a greeting. A woman, though, who kept mostly to herself and her child; she had no close friends that I could find in the complex. Visitors, I asked? None, said the next-door neighbor, a middle-aged woman, hair pulled sharply back from her head in a red bandanna. Her husband leaned over her shoulder, the two of them crowded into the doorway, unwilling to step into the hall as if refusing to be lured out from sanctuary. She was quiet, the man said; kept to herself mostly.

I took down his words, knowing they would find their way to the top of the story. I felt as if I were taking part in an ornate dance, an Elizabethan set piece filled with dips, bows and flourishes. I knocked on the doors, took down the words. I knew what the neighbors would say; I could have guessed the quotations beforehand. Yet it was an intrinsic part of the ritual of newspaper death. Reporters always ask the neighbors, and the neighbors always say the victims were quiet and kept to themselves. And then the reporters put that in their stories.

Behind me Porter snapped pictures, cursing the light, his flash a sudden burst behind me, another entry in the dance. It did not take us long to find the apartment building's resident manager. An older man, he walked slowly, deliberately, running his hand across his head, brushing gray hair away from his eyes. He told me the woman had paid her rent on time, rarely complained; he'd fixed a stopped toilet once inside her place and she had shown him pictures of her family, away on the west coast. He, too, had never seen any boyfriends or men hanging around.

At first he refused to let us into the apartment – private property, he said – but I persisted, cajoling and finally discovering that a twenty-dollar bill would turn the trick. 'For five minutes, only. At the most,' he said, slipping the money into the pocket of a work shirt. 'Just to take a quick look, that's all. And don't touch nothing.'

He opened the door after looking to be sure all the neighbors had cleared the hallway. We were like thieves, seeking to steal a few details, some substance, so the woman would come alive in the columns of newsprint in the morning. We were barely inside before I heard the click of Porter's camera. On one wall was a row of photos; the woman and her child, posed professionally, standing on a green lawn underneath a tree. There were others, smaller: candid shots of the child, naked, crawling on all fours; the mother rocking the baby in her arms. There was a family shot; I recognized the husband and what I assumed were relatives. They all stared out at the camera, smiling. I turned away and surveyed the apartment. There were two small bedrooms, each immaculate, frilly with lace and colors. A woman's place, I thought.

A mobile of small plastic animals, smiling lions and elephants, hung over the child's crib. A paperback bestseller, a book on self-improvement, lay cracked open beside the woman's bed. I wrote down the title, picked up the book and read the admonition: Treat every day as if it were a new challenge. I took that down, too.

The old man was getting nervous and anxious to close up. I wandered into the kitchen. Baby food and frozen dinners, cottage cheese in the refrigerator. A diet schedule had been posted on the door of the refrigerator. In the living room there was a stereo, tapes and records. I looked them over quickly; they dated to the late sixties. California sound, rock and roll. Everything was trim, in its place. The furniture was modern but not striking, the type one buys at discount warehouses, knockoffs of designs. There were two posters on the walls, framed in steel: a Sister Corita that carried the message, Do Unto Others; and the famous Ben Shahn of Sacco and Vanzetti. I wondered if she knew who they were.

The manager was standing by the doorway, gesturing with his hand, trying to wave us out of the apartment. I nodded at him and stepped back outside.

Porter was right behind him. 'Hard to shoot,' he said. 'But I got pictures of the wall of pictures and the kid's room and hers, too. Should be OK.' The manager asked us if there was anything else. He seemed angry. I told him his night was just beginning, that the press release would soon be issued and the place would probably be crawling with television people trying to beat their 11 P.M. deadline to get something on the late news. As I spoke I saw the first of the television trucks rolling into the parking lot.

We left. Before we got our cars, though, Porter turned to me, shaking his head. 'Do you notice,' he said, 'that all the victims are so ordinary, so . . . unexceptional? Except for those who know them, I guess.' He bent his head and slipped behind the wheel. The car door slammed shut, cutting off his thought like a knife.

I knew then why the killer had waited so long to call. It was a test. He was waiting to see how long it took for the police to identify the woman.

When I returned to the office that night it was close to deadline; there was no time to polish words. I put sheet after sheet of empty paper in the typewriter and tore the filled pages out. Nolan was still there, waiting on the story, treating each segment as it slipped from the roller into the computers. He said little, other than exhortations to hurry:

The most recent victim of the man called the 'Numbers Killer' has been identified by police as a 29-year-old divorcee who lived in a western-section apartment complex.

Friends and neighbors of Susan Kemp described her as a friendly, outgoing young woman who kept mostly to herself at the apartment complex. She was, they said, devoted to the upbringing of her 21-month-old child, Jennifer.

The victim's ex-husband, Tampa businessman Martin Kemp, arrived in Miami yesterday to take custody of the child and to identify the mother's body.

Police are still searching for the means the killer used to snatch Mrs. Kemp and whatever motive may lie behind the crime. The killer has, as yet, failed to telephone with his explanation as he has done on each previous murder.

The story went on, racing into a description of the apartment, the photos on the wall. There were jumbled-together quotes from the neighbors and the husband. His anguish was described in one or two paragraphs in the middle of the story. The police efforts and their frustration were recounted. I quoted Wilson, but not by name, removing the expletives from his feelings.

As the kicker to the story, the final paragraph, I described the posters on the wall of the murdered woman's apartment, the flash of color flowing against the white background of the Sister Corita, and the hard, black-ink eyes of the two martyred workmen staring blankly out from the Ben Shahn. I let that description flow into the message from the book open by her bedside.

I saw Nolan's eyes as he scanned the final take, the last page that had raced through the typewriter. I knew he was on the final words and I saw his head move slowly, a nod, an approval. I watched his fingers slide to the keyboard, make a simple adjustment, then punch the keys that would send the story electronically to the copy desk for layout and headline. He held up his hand, made a small saluting motion and smiled. I followed his eyes to the wall clock. 'We make most of the run,' he said. 'Maybe all the Final and all of the Home. The Street has gone already, but – ' And he shrugged.

Nolan walked me over to my desk and put his hand on my shoulder. 'Why don't you go home, get some rest?' he said.

I thought of my father, when I was young, no more

than ten or eleven. He would sometimes come out and play tennis with me. I was learning; he was an expert. His thick legs hid remarkable speed; his hands were quick. He would rally effortlessly, racing me back and forth across the court until I made an inevitable error. He would call, teasing, 'Need a breather?'

I looked up at Nolan. I shook my head. 'He'll call now. Tomorrow probably. Maybe the next day. After he sees the story.'

'Here or at your house?'

'I don't know. What's the difference?'

'None, really,' Nolan said. 'Still, you should get some rest.'

We walked out together, but we did not speak again that night.

I was wrong. It did make a difference.

I did not know then that Martinez and Wilson had gone before a friendly judge, a one-time police officer himself, and obtained a wiretap for my home telephone line; nor did I know that the phone company had developed a slow yet accurate capacity to trace the incoming calls through a computer system at their central switchboard. These facts were explained to me afterwards by Martinez, when he told me of some of the events that had taken place outside of my presence. I had foolishly assumed when the detectives told me they couldn't trace calls coming in on my office line that the same was automatically true for my home telephone. I didn't see the detective, dressed in work clothes, khaki pants and denim work shirt, who slipped into the door of the apartment building behind me and walked down to the cellar where the telephone terminals were located. I met him later, a bookish man, a technician with glasses. He was the listener, two wires wrapped onto the terminal for my phone, another that connected him with Police Headquarters. Another man was waiting at Southern Bell's offices; he was the computer man who would start feeding possible exchanges into the system until he arrived at the right one. Then it was merely a matter of making the computer system race through all the open lines in the given exchange until the right connection was found. At a trial run, Martinez told me, it took slightly under ten minutes.

Christine would no longer answer the telephone when we were home together during the night. She did not want the killer to know she was there, she told me; she did not want him to know anything. It was all she could do to tolerate the telephone at all; on several occasions I found she had taken it off the hook.

On the night after the latest story appeared, the killer called. I did not even look at Christine who sat as before at the kitchen table watching and listening to my half of the conversation, filling in my long silences with her imagination. It was close to midnight when the telephone rang, the insistence of the bell seeming to signal the identity of the caller. I flipped on the tape recorder, then picked the telephone from the hook. 'Be careful,' Christine said, as I lifted the receiver.

'Yes?' I said.

'It's me,' he said. 'I suppose you've been waiting?'

'I knew you would call.'

'Yes.' His voice seemed distant, hazy for an instant, as if he were thinking as he spoke. 'I guess you did. So, she was divorced. She told me that her husband was coming home soon, that she had to be there to meet him. She was hysterical much of the time, and it was only when the child started crying that she regained her senses.'

In the basement the detective stiffened. For a moment he felt a rush of heat. He listened just a few seconds before dialing the headquarters' number. He was a young man, excitable. He misdialed and cursed, then dialed again on the small hand-held telephone-tapping device. He reported later he could feel the basement darkness harder than the night. At the second ring a headquarters' detective answered. 'It's him,' the man in the basement whispered, 'calling now!' And he listened as the killer gathered himself and continued to speak.

'She was the hardest to snatch, you know.' His voice was calm and deliberate. There was none of his usual teasing and jocularity this time. I wrote notes as quickly as possible.

'I had to watch her for several days to understand her routine. She seemed a person of habits, of cleanliness, neat; the type that would walk the same route every day. In the midafternoon she would take the child for a walk. They would exit the apartment and turn to the right, heading toward the tennis courts. That's where I was waiting. I pretended to be working on my car, just off the walkway. I had the hood up and the trunk open. I remember it was so bright, I thought the sun was like a spotlight on a stage, tracking me, illuminating everything, every small little movement. She approached. I looked around and saw no one. I readied the automatic. She stepped closer. I could feel the tension in my mouth, my breath catching fear with every second. I had never really worked in broad daylight, you see. She was next to me then, looking over, smiling a little, friendly.'

He hesitated, but I did not fill the silence with a question.

At the telephone exchange the detective supervised the computer check of exchanges. He fed in the first three numerals of all the different areas of Miami. He, too, was sweating, watching as the system digested, then rejected each three numbers and he typed in a new series. Wilson and Martinez waited, too, in the parking lot of Police Headquarters. The engine in the cruiser was turning over silently, and they had the air conditioner on full blast. They were waiting for the radio to speak to them, to give them an address.

'She did not cry out when she saw the automatic. She put her hand to her mouth as if to cover a scream, but she remained calm. I said for her to take the baby and get into the car. She seemed to be dazed and I had to repeat myself. But I did not have to touch her, that was the oddest thing. In a second she began to cooperate, lifting the child from the stroller and slipping into the car. I folded the stroller and threw it into the back seat with the supplies I'd gathered. I kept the automatic in my hand where she could see it, and then the three of us just drove away as easy as could be.'

Another pause. 'Why her?' I asked.

'A mother and child,' he said. 'I wanted a mother and child.'

He waited another long moment, and I closed my eyes.

'There was a famous photograph,' he continued. 'Taken at the start of the Second World War. In Hong Kong, I think. No, it was Shanghai. When the Japanese bombed the city. In the center of the photo there is a baby, covered with dirt, its mouth open wide in tears and fear and screaming for its mother. In the background all you can see is burning refuse, debris; the upheaval caused by bombs. I remember looking at the photo and wondering, where was the mother? And wondering what would happen to the child. I suppose they both died. I suppose the children always die.

'You see, this woman, Mrs. Kemp – you know, I didn't even know her name? – wasn't the first mother that I killed. There was another, carrying a small child the same way; protective, frightened. In Vietnam. I told you, there was this incident, and she was a big part of it.'

He sucked in his breath then, a quick, harsh noise.

At the telephone station the detective was swearing to himself. It was taking longer than the trial run. 'Where are we?' he shouted to a technician sitting at a bank of television screens filled with electronic numbers of computers.

'Key Biscayne,' the technician replied. 'Seven sixty-five exchanges.' His fingers were typing in numbers. Then suddenly he leaned back in his chair and turned to the detective. 'Got it!' he said. 'He's out on the key.'

The detective turned to the telephone and spoke to headquarters.

'We did not talk,' the killer said. 'She was too upset. She kept asking, "What are you going to do to us? Are you going to kill us?" I think she thought I would rape her. I tried to tell her, but she wouldn't listen, and finally the sun went down. I made her eat then, and feed the child and change its diapers. I had built the little shelter for the child, and after a while it went to sleep. But the woman just stared at me through the night. The moonlight caught her face, seemed to make it swell with fear. After a long time I gave up trying to talk with her. It made no difference. Her hands were tied, she could go nowhere. I told her she should try to sleep and made her move away from the child, out to the spot where you found her. She was restless, but fear exhausts most people and finally, toward morning, she fell asleep. I waited until I knew she could feel nothing. You know, the shot didn't even awaken the child. She slept right through. The birds around, though, rose up suddenly, crying and shrieking. They were egrets mostly and gulls; I could see their white feathers.'

He paused. 'That's all,' he said. 'I'm tired.'

'Don't go!' I raised my voice.

'What?' he said. 'I'll call again. Later.'

'I want to meet,' I said. 'Face to face.'

Silence. I heard Christine's sudden intake of breath and heard her whisper, 'No!'

'Don't be ridiculous,' the killer said. He laughed briefly and hung up. I turned to Christine, but she was already crying and turned away. I wanted to explain, to tell her this was the only chance. But I could not find the words, so I simply sat across from her at the table feeling the distance between us grow.

In the basement the detective glanced at his watch. 'Shit!' he said. 'Eight minutes.'

Martinez and Wilson were driving fast through the darkness. They cut through downtown, running the red lights. Martinez was behind the wheel; later he told me how excited he was. This was where it was all going to end, he thought. Wilson checked the action on his revolver as they drove, the older detective barely aware of the centrifugal force as the cruiser bent around corners. The engine sound grew as they headed through the toll booth and over the causeway. The moonlight reflected off the bay waters on either side, and behind them the lights from the tall apartment buildings on the shoreline were like beacons. Martinez pushed the car up to eighty, then ninety, the wheels screaming as they flew over the bridge past the empty beaches.

At the telephone station the detective wiped sweat from his face. 'He's off,' he said. 'Where was he?'

The technician bent over the screen, watching the

computer make its final sortings. He made a small sound of exultation and clenched his fist. 'Got it!' he shouted. He punched the numbers into the keyboard and watched as the computer screen blinked, then typed an address. 'The pay phone at the tourist booth!'

The detective shouted the address into the open telephone line, then slumped back into his chair. 'They got him,' he said.

The radio voice was thin, disembodied. It repeated the location to the two detectives and then put out an all-cars call for the whole key. Martinez swore and slammed the car into a 360-degree turn, tires squealing, the steering wheel shimmying in his hand. 'Damn!' Wilson said, 'we passed it.' The detectives raced back, heading in the wrong direction on the four-lane roadway.

The tourist booth is a small building, one room with a window for a person to ask directions. It is open only during the winter season. Behind it is a pay phone, set off the road some thirty yards, surrounded by palms and ferns. It is a lonely place.

By this time there were sirens wailing all over the area. The two detectives arrived first, skidding in, their cruiser turning sideways under the braking pressure. Martinez said that his weapon was already out when he slipped from the door, crouching in the darkness. Wilson was running, weapon extended, for the booth.

It was empty.

'Dammit, the bridge,' Wilson shouted. He ran to the car, to the radio, and told the dispatcher to have the span raised, trapping cars on the key. By now there were a half-dozen police cars at the booth, their lights throwing shadows over the brush and palms, cutting red and blue streaks into the darkness.

The policemen returned to their vehicles and headed in a convoy toward the bridge, some three miles away. Martinez could see the raised span when they emerged from beneath the trees, back out into the wan moonlight. Four cars were stopped by the barrier, waiting. He and Wilson stepped from their car, weapons out, and began to walk the line slowly, peering through the darkness at the people inside the cars.

There was a family inside the first, a station wagon, a man, a woman and two sleeping children in the back seat beneath a blanket. The man rolled down his window. 'What's wrong?' he asked. 'We've been to visit friends.' But neither detective replied, continuing to walk toward the front, Martinez on the driver's side, Wilson on the passenger side.

There were two teenagers in the next car, a Volks-wagen. They stared out at the policemen's weapons silently, frightened. Martinez heard the sound of doors opening and shutting behind him as the other officers removed the people from the vehicles. He was peripherally aware of Wilson's presence moving as if in step, in time.

The third car contained a pair of older people, and the detectives swept past, ignoring them. The woman in the car gasped when she saw the weapons. Martinez told me afterwards the adrenaline in his ears was like the ocean, constant, pulsating. He felt heat under his collar, a moment of almost shattering excitement.

There was only one head in the final car in line, behind the driver's wheel. It looked straight forward. Martinez felt the muscles in his hand tighten, knotting almost in a cramp on the handle of his service revolver. He thought wildly about the small automatic that he kept as a backup fastened to his calf under his pants leg. He wondered if he had taken the safety off. He could not remember. He and Wilson continued forward, moving slowly, deliberately, still in tandem, each step unsteady as if moving on ice. A few feet from the door he stopped. 'You!' he shouted. 'In the car! Police! Step out! Hands out front!'

There was a moment then when Martinez held his breath. He watched as the figure began to move slowly from the car; the detective could feel the pressure of his partner's weapon tracking the back of the driver's head. Martinez watched, his own weapon up, pointing, as the door opened and first a leg, then a torso, emerged. His eyes strained against the moonlight and the city lights across the bay. Sweat ran into his eyes, and he blinked furiously to clear them. He clutched a flashlight in his left hand, and when the figure turned toward him, the detective shouted, 'Freeze!' and switched it on, the powerful beam cutting the darkness between them, smashing into the driver's face like a blow. He saw the driver's hand come up to his eyes. Then he heard Wilson's voice, hard and angry. 'Fucked. Fucked. Fucked. Dammit!'

The driver was a woman, the light from the beam

shining off her blond hair. Martinez turned away, hearing Wilson's voice begin the explanation, and walked to the side of the bridge. He told me later that he'd looked out over the water, dizzy, still queasy from the tension, listening to the sound of the light bay-water chop as it tapped against the pilings. The noise was like laughter, he said, the cackling of the escaped killer, adrift, free in the city night.

CHAPTER THIRTEEN

Nolan listened to the latest tape intently. He was bent over slightly from the waist, his elbows on the table. He tracked the turning spindles on the recorder; twice he scratched notes in pencil on a plain sheet of copy paper. When the tape finished, he straightened and looked across the room at me, holding my gaze for a moment before speaking: 'Well, you tried.'

'I guess.' I shrugged. 'Perhaps.'

'I'm concerned about the tone,' Nolan said. 'The changes in this past conversation. He seems hurried, different. He didn't take his time. He didn't mix his feelings with descriptions like he has in the past. Why was he so uptight about this murder? I'd like to know.'

He rewound the tape, and for a second time the killer's voice filled the small room. 'Listen,' Nolan said, 'he sounds nervous. Where's his confidence?'

'. . . I had to watch her for several days . . .'

'He stalked her,' Nolan said. 'This wasn't spontaneous.'

'. . . I thought the sun was like a spotlight on a stage . . .'

'So, he was afraid. Afraid he would be seen.'

'. . . In the center of the photo there is a baby . . .'

'Right there,' Nolan said. 'He connects with one memory.'

'. . . this incident, and she was a big part of it.'

'See, he remembers the photo and then his own memory.'

'. . . Don't be ridiculous.' The phone clicked off.

Nolan walked about the room impatiently, rubbing his hand against his head. Occasionally he paused and looked up at the copies of the stories I had written on the killer that were pinned to the wall. 'I think he's undergoing a change,' Nolan said. 'Nothing positive, it's just a feeling. He may have had enough killing. Suppose we're dealing with some kind of split personality? Perhaps one of the other characters is beginning to take over. Did you ask your psychiatrist friend about that?'

I shook my head. 'I don't think he saw any evidence of a split in the tapes that I played for him. But how would he know? I mean, as long as the personality he heard was consistent. Psychopathic, he said. Born killer.' Nolan looked at me, an editor's look. 'All right,' I said. 'I'll call him and ask him.'

That afternoon I played the tape over the telephone for the psychiatrist. As always, he paused to think before he spoke. 'Interesting,' he said. 'Imagine the conflict that must be functioning in the killer's mind; killing the woman, leaving the baby. I wonder if he was symbolically killing his own mother.'

'Nolan says he thinks the killer is a split personality and that another personality is beginning to infringe on the one that kills people. What do you think?'

Again, the doctor hesitated. I imagined the smoke from his pipe curling up around his head.

'Not impossible,' he said. 'We don't know much about that particular illness.'

'Probable?' I asked.

'No. But not improbable, either. Actually, it's not a bad idea. But there would be no way to tell unless the killer began to demonstrate different personalities under a clinically controlled situation. I suppose it is conceivable. I do not offhand remember a case in the literature of one personality being homicidal while another was not, but it could happen. One personality psychopathic, another suicidal, another homicidal and yet another, oh, say a librarian. All struggling together. One would think it would cause an explosion . . . but these things are remarkably complicated. Tell your editor that it's a good theory but as of this time impossible to prove.'

'What about the tape?' I asked. 'Doesn't he seem different?'

'No, no different. Perhaps a bit disappointed. The killing was less of a success than the others. His selection seems to have been less propitious; there seems to have been less interaction between him and the victim. That must have been a disappointment to him.'

'Predictions?'

He laughed. 'Out of what, my crystal ball?' His voice turned serious. 'Well, you know one thing. That this incident in the war, the one he says he's recreating, contained a mother and child. Those are potent psychological bombs. And another thing . . . I would be very careful suggesting any meeting.'

'You think he would hurt me?'

'Why not?'

But I didn't believe him.

I went to the hospital one day, to go up to the pediatric ward and see the child. I was tempted to stop and see Christine first but realized she was probably in surgery. I had never visited her in the hospital and thought it best I didn't: let her tell me of her impressions rather than forming my own. The nurse at the station was reluctant at first, but she recognized my name from my press card and decided it would do no harm to look through the glass window into the ward. I followed her down a white corridor, listening to the proper clicking of her heels against the polished tile floor. The world inside the hospital seemed blank, bright, like the moment the sun glints off the water and fills your eyes. The nurse took me up to a window and pointed. 'There, second bed in.' I peered through the glass at a room filled with cribs. 'She's off critical. Should be ready to leave in a day or so.' I watched the child for an instant. She was sleeping on her side, tucked over, sucking on a pacifier. I did not know what I was searching for or what I expected to see. Perhaps some look of fear, some memory of the sun, the swamp and the afternoon heat. I turned away, thanking the nurse.

'Not much to see,' she said. 'You look at her and you can't tell anything. She looks just like the other children, cries the same, everything. I wonder, how will she be different?' She paused and then asked as we walked back, 'Why? I mean, what possible reason could there be?'

I shook my head. 'Outrage, I think. Vulnerability. Heartlessness. I don't know, either.' She was a young woman, dark hair pulled back unfairly from her face by the nurse's cap. She smiled at me as I left, the elevator door closing on the ward with an abrupt metallic sound.

I thought about what I'd said. Trying to find a rationale for the murders was absurd. They existed in a different plane, a different time; they were senseless, that was the point. They were savage, that was the point. They were inconceivable, that was the point.

I wondered, too, why it was I could not bring myself to hate the killer, like so many of the people that I'd seen and interviewed, whose words had ridden my fingers into the columns of the newspaper.

In the afternoon Porter stopped by my desk. He was holding the body of a camera in one hand and fitting it with an assortment of lenses from a strap around his neck. After he fixed each one to the body, he lifted the camera and peered through it, sighting across the expanse of the newsroom. 'You know what I did yesterday night?' he started in, barely pausing for the shake of my head. 'I went to the scene of what the cops like to call "a domestic." It was up in Carol City, in the working-class section; you know, mostly black, guys who bring home a weekly paycheck from the county for working on a garbage crew. When I got there, oh, there must have been four or five cop cars parked on the lawn and the street.

'It seems that some guy stopped off at the pool hall after work, managed to lose a good deal of his paycheck. Rent's due at the end of the month; utility bills, grocery bills, no more credit at the supermarket, that sort of thing. So, as you might expect, they get to shouting at each other, man and wife, loud enough so the neighbors can hear just about everything. After a while the woman hauls off and slaps the old man hard on the side of the face. He doesn't like this too much, so he lets her have it, too, right in the chops.

'He likes it, you know, and so he decides to let her have it again. Takes another swing at her. She starts to back up, finds herself up against the kitchen sink.

'The old guy's coming hard for her now, going to really lay one on her. So she grabs the first thing that hits her hand. Turns out to be a big carving knife, and she slashes out with it. Catches the husband on the side of the neck, severs the jugular. He goes right down in a pile at her feet.

'She stands there crying and screaming until the neighbors come and call the police. The guy must have bled to death in a couple of seconds. Anyway, the cops come, take pictures, take her confession right there and charge her with murder. And off she goes to the Women's Detention Center. I got a good shot of the police leading the woman away from her house; she has this confused and crushed look on her face. As they put her in the back of the patrol car, she called out for help. You know who she called for? Her husband, the man she just killed.'

He looked across the desk at me, took out a corner of his shirt and wiped one of the lenses, then twisted and peered through it. After a second he continued, 'I asked one of the policemen how many murders they'd had lately, not counting, of course, our boy. He looked at me and said, "Oh, same as usual. Somebody usually gets killed every night. No end of business for us." And the thought hit me: it makes no difference. No difference at all. They don't have to catch the killer.'

He stopped and I said, 'I don't follow.'

'Suppose,' he replied, 'that we just ignored the killer. Let him continue doing what he's doing. It wouldn't change the totals at the end of the year, you know. I mean, there'll be just as many murders in the city regardless of what the killer does. In reality, he's just another statistic. Another angry act amidst hundreds of the same. That woman's husband is just as dead as any of the killer's victims. So was the guy who got killed the night before, so will the people who get killed tonight. He's no different from anyone else; he's just more consistent.'

Porter straightened up and laughed. 'You see,' he said, 'how jaded we become.'

But I didn't join in his humor.

His story did give me an idea, though. I rode that night with a homicide team to the location of another killing, a murder in a bar in the downtown ghetto. The dead man was sprawled on his back, the blade of a flick knife deep in his chest. The blinking lights from a beer sign in the window reflected off the blood smearing the barroom floor. In the back I heard the sound of a pool cue striking a ball; two patrons oblivious to the routine of death before them.

In another corner I took in the look of compressed rage on the face of a prostitute as she watched the detectives and the medical examiner work swiftly, efficiently around the corpse. The suspect was already in cuffs in the rear of a cruiser, staring from the window at the half-interested crowd that had gathered.

I wrote all that and numbered the murders that had occurred in the city since the first of the killer's slayings. It ran front page under the headline: THE ROUTINE OF VIOLENCE: 'ORDINARY' KILLINGS CONTINUE. It was a slow news day and I was allowed plenty of space, three legs of copy running outside, then the rest jumping to a display page inside the paper.

I saw Porter after the story appeared. He smiled across the room at me and held his thumb up in the universal salute. The managing editor sent me a note through the interoffice mail: Good story, puts it all in perspective, it said.

I wondered, though, had it been the killer who'd stepped into the bar and shot the man dead with his .45 whether the pool game would have stopped in fear.

Porter found the photo that the killer had described. I sat at my desk staring at it through the course of one afternoon, my imagination running wildly, as if I could hear and feel the explosions from the bombs. I thought, too, of my father; I wondered how many children had wailed in the wake of his own raids. I could see my father hunched over in the nose of the B-25, peering down through the bombsight at – what? A city? A railroad? A factory? They would be shapes without substance, like drawings upon a sheet of paper. He would read the coordinates off from an attack plan, sight down through the nose of the plane and at the proper moment, or as close to it as he could, release the load. The plane would be buffeted by flak exploding close by and would surge forward, lightened by the release of the racks of bombs, accelerating away from the fury and smoke, up into sky and clouds.

He flew most of his missions out of North Africa, from a strip cut from dirt and dusty hills, out across the Mediterranean toward Italy and Sicily. I imagined he felt suspended between the blue of the sea and the ceilingless blue of the air. I supposed there were moments of terror, too, when it seemed as if the earth were reaching up angrily for him, shaking the space with explosions. He never talked much about the war itself. He talked instead of the return, the cheers and parades, the flush of victory before the return to routine. It was a heady time, he said once, a time of spirited drunkenness and excitement. He marveled in the mere knowledge that he was intact, that his organs and extremities all seemed to function. It was as if he could feel the blood in his body traversing the network of veins. He went then to visit his brother, still in the medical facility, adjusting to the loss of his eye.

At my desk I raised my hand and held it over my right eye. I looked about the newsroom, surveying the activity. I twisted my head to take it all in: reporters working the telephones, editors at the banks of computer terminals. I thought of the way

299

my uncle must have turned his head at the sound of the hospital-room door swinging open, rotating in his bed toward my father.

For an instant the noise of telephones and voices faded away, and I tried to imagine the two men staring across the room at each other.

What did they say? One intact, one damaged. Going different directions.

When I was young, caught in age between my brother and sister, my father would settle our disputes in mock court. Each would get a moment or two to explain his side; my brother speaking quickly, excitedly, amassing facts, impressions and desires in a linear way, the words thrusting out from his mouth, falling quickly and persuasively. Or my sister, halting, her tears overcoming her voice, finally relying on the most persuasive argument of all, tumbling across the room in a run to be swept up in my father's arms. And myself: anger flooding my brain, standing in the way of the words I wanted, blocking all the reasons, the arguments. I stuttered and stumbled – and I lost. My father, leaning back at his desk, a pencil in his right hand, thumping on a pad of paper unconsciously, would issue his decisions, render his opinions. He was not a harsh man, nor unfair. He was a man of codes and rules. To me it seemed as if his decisions came down from on high, inviolable, precise – as explosive as the bombs he had unleashed from the bombardier's position in the nose of the plane, suspended above the horror in a thin plexiglass booth.

My own voice such a failure, I took to writing other people's voices . . .

And then the telephone rang.

The newsroom noises seemed to increase, like the volume on a radio, then to settle back into the constant familiar hum. I reached across the desk and punched on the recording device, my hand functioning independently as if it belonged to someone else. I felt the cool plastic of the receiver under my palm, and I slowly lifted the telephone to my ear. I waited for the voice.

He spoke coldly, unhurried. He began with no note of familiarity or introduction. One moment there was silence on the line, and the next he was speaking in a flat, expressionless tone.

'I've been thinking about you,' he said.

'And?'

He said nothing, instead letting the silence hang on the line.

'When I was overseas, I remember a moment. I used to volunteer for what the Army called LURPS, which was an acronym for Long-Range Reconnaissance Patrols. There'd be myself, a radioman and another rifleman, alone in the jungle, moving through the bush at that infuriatingly slow pace that the jungle demands. The humidity would be so thick, so high, that I'd feel as if the air were creating friction against the skin of my arms as I swung a machete at the vines and weeds that were everywhere. It was as if I could feel the heat steaming around me; we would be soaked by our sweat. Almost like it had rained.

'I loved the sensation of being alone – almost alone. The radio was really the only link back to safety, and it was, of course, unreliable. I think there's nothing as exhilarating, as sensual, as walking abroad in an alien and dangerous land. I could feel the fear and excitement right through my body. I would think, "I'll die out here, and no one will ever find me. It will be as if I'd disappeared, simply faded away from life," but that never happened. Close, though, many times.

'There was once . . . we were cutting our way through the growth, moving so slowly sometimes I thought the jungle would have the time to grow behind us. A VC patrol must have been cutting through from the other direction, their minds the same as ours, concentrating on the weeds and vines and just trying to free themselves for another step forward. The two groups bumped directly into each other.

'I was out on the point and suddenly became aware of the sounds of hacking and pushing coming toward us. I stopped at precisely the same instant that the VC point man must have hesitated. There was a long second, and then I lifted up my rifle and let loose on full automatic in their direction. The radioman and the other rifleman joined with me. At the same moment precisely the jungle around us started to rip apart with the fire from their automatics, AK-47s, I remember, because of the distinctive sound, like a sheet of paper ripping. Everyone must have panicked simultaneously; one instant there was silence, the next the jungle was being ripped apart by fire.

'And then there was this remarkable instant. Everything stopped. Sudden, total silence.

'Everyone's weapon had been on full auto, and in the same instant all the ammunition was expended.

302

Then out of the silence came this perverse clicking. I looked down and realized it was coming from me as well as the others. Everyone was changing the clips in their rifles as quickly as possible. Click, click, out came a clip. Click, click, in went a new clip. I started to laugh at it all. So much fear exhausted in one swift second, so much murderous intent. My voice rose above the silence through the jungle. The other two looked at me, and I made a hand motion. We slipped back down the path we'd cut, moving away, disengaging. I suppose the VC did the same, the social inappropriateness of our meeting hitting them, too. I had to laugh.

'I feel much is the same now. It would be a cliché to tell you that the city is the same as the jungle to me, but it is. I think of myself cutting a swath through the city as I did the jungle: out on patrol, searching, destroying, abroad in a dangerous, strange land. I walk the streets the same as you, staring at the people, locking onto their eyes, watching their glance turn.

'One night I went to a neighborhood meeting. You know the type; you've been to some yourself, I've read the stories. I've read every word you've written. Anyway, I went one early evening to a school auditorium – the type of place that all these meetings are held. There is something about the fluorescent lights, the bright school colors, pennants and plaques that is reassuring and familiar. A stream of people headed inside, mostly in groups of two or four. I simply followed them into the building and sat in the midst of the crowd, another concerned face, worried and frightened.

'There was a man sitting next to me, alongside his wife. She was plump and flushed with the exertion of squeezing into a seat designed for a child. He was angry, a frown set on his face, staring up at the podium. I watched his hands clench into fists and then retreat, relax for an instant, then tighten again. He turned to me at one point: "Dammit," he said, "this has just about gone on too long. What the hell's the matter with the police?" I nodded sagely and replied, "I just don't think they're doing everything they should." And the fellow's head went up and down sharply in assent. "Damn right," he said. "You're damn right," and he mumbled that several times more.

'The auditorium was nearly filled by then, and as I watched, a man got up on the stage. He blinked in the lights for an instant and then introduced himself. A politician. He thanked everyone for turning out and made a few remarks about the police. He trusted them. He was sure they were doing all they could. Then he introduced an officer in uniform, the type of ranking officer I knew in the Army, who is privy to information yet doesn't understand a word of it.

'He stood at the podium, rocking back and forth slightly, eyes surveying the crowd. He made a small speech, outlining all the man hours and detectives they have working on the case – just the stuff that's been in your stories. My neighbor kept saying over and over, "Bullshit. Bullshit. Get to the point." But the cop never did. He just stopped, saying, "I know it's hard to be reassured, but the police are following up every lead, no matter how small. Every piece of evidence is being scrutinized. We have teams going through Army records at the Pentagon."

'He offered to answer questions from the floor, though he cautioned that he wouldn't be able to go into specifics. I watched as people shifted in their seats for an instant or two. And then, one after another, the people got up and started to ask questions. Did they expect to make an arrest? How far through the records were the investigators? Why was it that the police seemed helpless to act until I had already found a victim? I think you would have been pleased; the questions were good ones, tough. The cop squirmed under the lights, shading his eyes so as to be able to see the questioners.

'He had few answers, and the less he was able to say, the angrier people got. It was infectious, the spirit of outrage amidst all those secure, middle-class mothers and fathers, husbands and wives. As the cop continued to dodge their verbal bullets, they grew more and more unruly. Questioners started to shout from their seats, no longer standing up and speaking politely. A few obscenities rolled through the auditorium. They exploded among the crowd like grenades, increasing the fervor.

'I saw my neighbor's face contorting, and he, too, shouted out, "Why aren't there extra patrols out at night?" And when the cop started to talk about manpower shortages, they shouted him down. I finally couldn't hold back anymore, I had to join in. It was as if I heard my own voice speaking from some other place, a recording, perhaps. "What we want to know," I yelled above the crowd, "is one thing. How is it that one man can hold an entire city, in effect, hostage? And the police, for all our hundreds of thousands of tax dollars, can't do a damn thing?"

'Everyone grew quiet. My neighbor clapped me on the knee and said, "That's damn right. That's the whole ball of wax." He grinned at me and I smiled back at him. On the stage, the policeman turned my way. "All I can say," he said, "is that we're doing our best job." The rest of his response was lost in angry shouts and cries.

'The meeting broke up then, and we all stood and filed out. I lost track of my neighbor. I remember how different it seemed outside; it was no cooler than the auditorium, but the air seemed less oppressive. I felt a breeze as if the darkness were cleansing me of the crowd and I was alone again. I was walking, toward my car when I spotted the two policemen. They were standing next to their cruiser, watching the crowd filter out and away through the parking lot. For a moment I thought of running in the other direction as fast as I could, but it was as if I were outside of myself, watching my actions from apart. It was like walking the point in Vietnam; I had the sensation of being ahead, exposed, vulnerable. And so I walked past. Their eyes were elsewhere. I don't suppose they even noticed me. I knew then that I was free. Invisible.'

A hesitation; then he continued.

'When I got into my car, I could hardly contain myself. I laughed and laughed. I rolled the windows tightly shut so they couldn't hear me. There were tears coming down my cheeks, and after a few moments I was gasping for breath.'

Again he paused.

'They'll never catch me,' he said. 'Not unless I want them to.'

I interrupted. 'How long do you intend to keep this up?'

'The killings? Oh, a bit longer.'

'How long is that?'

'Not too long. Don't be so impatient.'

'And what then?'

He thought for an instant. 'Perhaps another city. Another identity. A new life. Or maybe,' he said, pausing between the words to add emphasis, 'a continuation of the same.'

'Murders.'

'You can call it that,' he said. 'Or reminders. Memory lessons from the past.'

'They'll catch you,' I said.

'No. And if they do, what of it? What a trial that would be. That would be best for you, I suppose.' Again his voice slipped away, and he seemed to be thinking. 'But I doubt that will come to pass. I think instead that I'll just fade away in confusion. I will become like those men declared missing in action; a body decomposing somewhere out of sight, out of smell. But not out of mind.'

He laughed. 'Gone but not forgotten.'

I sucked in my breath, listening to his joyless laughter as it strained over the telephone wires. 'Why do we have to talk this way?' I asked. 'Why don't we meet face to face?'

Abruptly the laughter ceased.

'What for?' he asked. 'So you can lead the police to me?'

'No, I wouldn't,' I lied. 'It would be just the two of us.'

'No, it wouldn't,' he said. 'It couldn't.'

We were both silent. After a moment he continued, again in the same singular tone.

'What makes you think we haven't met already?'

I coughed. I couldn't answer.

'On the street, perhaps. In a crowd somewhere? On an elevator. Haven't you ever stopped and looked at the person next to you and wondered, "Is that him?" Haven't you ever been at a stoplight in your car and swiveled in your seat when you felt the sensation of being watched and discovered the eyes of the driver next to you peering at you? A moment of contact, almost physical. Then the light changes, and the two of you head off intact, alone. Think about it. One of those times, it might have been me. Think of all the little signals that I might have made, the look in my eyes, the nod of my head, the wave of my hand. Anything small, private, between the two of us, something so that you would know: it's him. And yet you never knew. We are so close, you and I, and yet you cannot recognize me. You are blind, stumbling, your hands outstretched seeking the wall. And I'm there beside you.'

He breathed in, hissing.

'I don't believe you,' I said.

I could hear his shrug over the line.

'Believe what you will. Remember: truth and lies

are often the same . . . fact and fiction divided by such a thin line.'

Another quiet. I was aware of the sounds of the newsroom around me taking precedence, as if the killer's voice was fading out and the world around me coming back to life.

'I am most ordinary-looking,' the killer said. 'Just under six feet tall, about one hundred and sixty-five pounds. Brown hair. Like yours. Tell that to the police. Perhaps it will help them.'

'What makes you think I tell the police?'

'Don't lie to me,' he replied. 'They tap the phone. They get the recordings that you make. They follow you. You talk with them and then they talk with you. It's a partnership of sorts. You should be more independent.' He stopped and inhaled before continuing. 'You see how much I know. I could be anywhere. I could be anyone. So don't lie to me.'

'Why are you doing this?' I asked. They were the only words I could think of. He didn't respond.

'Good-bye, Anderson. We'll talk again soon.'

And the phone clicked off.

CHAPTER FOURTEEN

There were big storms throughout the Caribbean during late August of that year, blowing in on the islands haphazardly, spending themselves in great ripping gusts of wind and rain. The city, though, seemed immune, protected; the storms that threatened the mainland spun off into the Atlantic to die out of sight in the reaches of the ocean. In the city the heat was like a mask, covering every feature.

The killer's latest conversation spawned renewed anger; the thought that he walked abroad so easily seemed to cause the city dwellers to withdraw further. Eyes on the street met and turned away; distances were maintained; to be aloof became routine. There was a jumpiness, too, as if contact were somehow dangerous. I saw a woman accidentally brush up against a young man while they waited for the streetlight to change. At the same instant they sprang apart, scowling, staring at each other for an instant in fury. Then they each set out across the street, on the same path but ignoring each other.

There was no end of stories to write. I wrote that the police had come up with a list of 250 possible names from Army records and that they were slogging through the list, trying to find the killer among them. Martinez laughed when he told me about it. 'As if he'd be here under his own name,' he said. 'He's not a fool.'

The evening paper, the *Post*, actually brought in a famous psychic from New York to try to find the killer. He went to the locations of the murders, poked around meaningfully, sniffed the air and pronounced the vibrations to be very strong. He then predicted that the killer would never be found but would die in a bizarre accident. This, I suspected, was not what the *Post* wanted. Nolan ripped the story out and put it on the office bulletin board. He scribbled a note on it: 'Why can't we have more enterprise reporting?' The office got a great kick out of it. There were many kidding suggestions: divining rod, seances and the like. Christine found none of it amusing. She reminded me instead that the killer was between killings and that his pattern was now to kill again.

'What will you do next?' she asked.

'I don't know,' I said. 'Just wait, like everybody.'

She frowned. 'I hate the waiting.'

'That's what it's like. It's the nature of the business.'

'I still hate it,' she said. 'And I think the killer means to change all that.'

I made a negative sound, a snorted denial. We did not talk about it again, but, of course, she turned out to be right.

Martinez called one evening, and Nolan and I walked from the newspaper to a downtown bar to have a talk with him. He was sitting at the counter, an empty glass in front of him. He gave a little wave toward the seats on either side and motioned to the bartender, rubbed his eyes hard for a moment, then pushed his fingers back through his black hair. His voice was tired and low, mingling with the sounds of glasses, liquid and the other soft voices in the room. I wondered where Wilson was. 'We've got to get more out of this guy,' he said. 'We need something else to work on.' He drained off part of a scotch the bartender had set down in front of him. 'I think we're no better off than when we started.'

Nolan looked at him, his editor's eyes cautious over the rim of a glass of beer. 'What about the list of names from the Army?' he asked.

'He won't be on it,' the detective replied. 'He enjoys the game too much, this guy. He feeds information that probably misleads us, not helps us.'

'But the doctor said . . .' I interjected.

Martinez cut me off. 'They don't know everything. In fact, sometimes they know very little. Listen, he's just guessing, the same as everyone. Let me give you an example. We've spent weeks going through army records, at the Pentagon, Fort Bragg. We've even sent people through the Ohio draft board records, trying to come up with something. And all along I've thought it was bullshit. You know why? Because of the weapon. This guy really knows how to handle that forty-five. I mean, he knows how bullets can deflect, how to control the shot so it doesn't blow his victim's head off. So I figure he's been trained with it. That means he was an officer in the Army or, more likely, a military policeman, because they got training in handguns.

The regular grunt got a rifle. But on the other hand, the forty-five was standard issue to Marines. And they learned how to work one, had to qualify. You see what I'm getting at? If he saw the combat he described, and at the same time gained access to and learned how to use that forty-five, well, then he was probably in a different branch of the service than the one we've been looking at. Just a theory, mind you. But it makes me think. It's all lies, half-truths and made-up stuff. Maybe a little true experience mixed in.'

Nolan interrupted. 'So what you're saying is that you're really nowhere with this thing.'

'Right,' Martinez replied. 'My opinion.' He hesitated for a moment, then continued. 'Look, I didn't call you up expecting to see a story tomorrow about how we're a bunch of screw-ups. I just wanted you guys to know the whole picture.'

'All right,' Nolan said. 'For now.'

'It's fucking depressing,' Martinez said. He finished his drink and motioned to the bartender for another. 'Tomorrow I'm going to Ohio with Wilson, just for the day. Gonna check out some names. Be back tomorrow night – empty-handed.'

'What does Wilson think?' I asked.

Martinez smiled, looking down into his drink. 'Now, he's a piece of work, isn't he? You know, when I first started to work with him, I figured we'd last together, oh, maybe forty-eight hours at best. It's been close to six months now. He's crazy, you know. They always say that a cop isn't supposed to take his work home with him. That's a crock. You never forget. Hell, they don't let you. Always supposed to have a gun on you, anyway. How can you forget with a gun strapped to your leg? Wilson, let me tell you, he's dying, he wants this guy so bad. First off, the first victim was just like his daughter. Second, he can't stand the way the guy calls you. Being a cop is being in the know. I mean, that's why I went into homicide, the same as Wilson. Because you like to find things out, like to put things together.

'And here we're always waiting for this guy to call you. Nothing much we can do about it, but it gnaws away at us. Wilson especially. Did you know he lost his nephew in the war? Kid was nineteen. Wanted to be a cop like his uncle. Wilson's brother died a long time ago – heart, I think – and Wilson was the kid's father, kind of. Kid gets drafted coming out of high school, gets blown away overseas. By a mine, I think he said. Just walking around. I don't know, but it makes him a little crazy sometimes. I think he's going to kill this sucker if we get the chance. He hardly leaves the office now. Just catches a few hours on a cot in the corner. Showers, shaves over at the jail. Not me. Sometimes I just got to get out, go back to the apartment, listen to some music. Forget it for a while. Wilson never forgets.'

'So what do you think will happen?' Nolan asked.

Martinez laughed. 'Maybe we get lucky. Maybe he decides to quit. One or the other. Like the way he snatched Mrs. Kemp – anybody could have been looking from their apartment, noticed a plate number or the car. Something like that.'

'We had this conversation weeks ago,' I said. 'You said the same thing.'

'See,' Martinez said. 'That should tell you how close we are to catching the guy.'

We stepped from the bar into the night. Nolan and I walked together a few steps, leaving the smell, the sound of glasses clinking and the detective behind us. After a minute, Nolan stopped and asked me what I thought.

I shrugged. 'Who knows what to believe now?'

He nodded and we walked on a few more steps. 'Should we write the story?' I asked.

'Which?' he queried.

'Martinez,' I said. 'That they're really no closer to a solution than when they started. It's a helluva piece.'

'I know,' he said, but he waited before answering. We walked a half-block in silence. 'No, let's hold off.'

'Why?'

'What do you think the effect would be on the people in the city?'

'Bad,' I conceded. 'More vigilante patrols. More homeowners buying guns. More of the craziness.'

'That's what I think. Let's hold off until they've gone through this list of names, at least. And let's try to find some way of softening the blow when it happens, some extra perspective.'

We walked again in quiet.

And then he added: 'You've got to remember. We're the ones who count. No one gives a damn what the television stations say; or the *Post*, for that matter. The killer calls us. He calls you. We're the ones with our heads in the middle of this thing, so what we say is a hundred times more important. If we say that the cops are fuckups, everyone will believe it. If we say they're doing the best they can, well, everyone will believe that. We are – God, it sounds funny – the paper of record for this murderer. If we tell everyone to panic, then, dammit, that's what they'll do. You know that Circulation reports subscriptions have increased by ten percent, and we thought we were already at saturation level? And on days when you have a story above the fold on page one, the street sales go up some fifteen thousand copies? They did a survey; most of the people buying the Street already get the paper delivered. They just can't wait until the morning to read the next story.' He grinned. 'Sometimes I think the killer is someone down in the circulation department. They're going crazy. They love this guy.

'So we've got to watch what we say. Everyone is looking at us – at you. Circulation did another study. You know, nobody reads bylines? Well, they started asking subscribers who you were. A helluva lot of people recognized your name and associated it with the stories. Fame may be fleeting, but at the moment, you've got it.'

He hesitated for another instant while we walked. I heard a siren in the background, and I stared up at the massive *Journal* building, standing square on the bay, the lights in the offices still bright.

'So you see the situation. We've got to be damn sure of what we write. Oh, I know, we're always careful. But people are counting on us. More than I think you or I realize.'

We stopped in the parking lot. 'Helluva way to become famous,' I said.

He smiled. 'You love it,' he said. 'We all love it. A story is like a live thing, isn't it? Slippery, beating with life, hard to catch, hard to hold. But we love it.'

And the two of us shook hands in agreement.

The following morning I received the letter.

It was typed haphazardly through a bare ribbon, the letters making a faded imprint on the single sheet of white paper. I fingered the cheap dime-store envelope for a moment before opening it; it had arrived in the morning delivery at the office with the usual press releases and political statements. There was no return address; only my name, the *Journal's* address and a stamp. I opened it and read:

DEAR MR. ANDERSON:
I have followed your many stories concerning the recent wave of killings in Miami with great interest.

But it was only after the latest murder that I realized that the pattern the killer professes to be following duplicates an incident that I witnessed while serving in the U.S. Army in Vietnam. The killing of the mother and the abandoning of the child was what convinced me that I saw the incident that the killer has said he wishes to recreate.

I am willing to talk with you only. No police, no cameras, nobody else. If I see anyone else, I will deny everything.

I will be at my apartment at 671 NW 13th Avenue at 1 P.M. on the date you received this letter. Apartment Number 5.

The letter was not signed.

I drove through the downtown ghetto, a system of decrepit woodframe houses and battered two-story apartment buildings constructed from cinder block. On the sidewalks was a mix of the displaced and the disadvantaged: tired black men, the lines in their faces like scars of age; drifters and hoboes, Miami's regulars, grizzled with time and tattered clothing. They leaned against the whitewashed brick of the buildings, eyes vacant. The sun sliced down through the heat of the day; the sky was the same rich, living pale blue that hung above the luxury yachts and speedboats moving across the bay. It was a stark world, illuminated by the unforgiving light. I sensed the stares from the sidewalk following me as I passed. In the background I heard the deep muffled sound of construction work. It mingled with the noise of children who skipped among the derelicts and the sidewalk domino games, oblivious.

A sign hung outside the address I was hunting: Furnished Rooms. Daily, Weekly, Monthly. Inquire Within. It was a typical downtown building, but painted a faded red in contrast with the ubiquitous white of the other buildings. It rose up three stories, just higher than the others on the block. A single outside stairway, black steel, steeply pitched, led to the upper floors. There were two apartments on each floor and a small cement courtyard crisscrossed with clotheslines flapping a few sheets and shirts in the light breeze. I hesitated at the bottom of the steps, catching my breath against the heat, struggling against the gazes of the neighbors who had stepped out onto the street to watch me. I suppose they thought I was a bill collector or a detective. None of them made a sound. I climbed the stairs slowly.

I found Apartment Five at the top of the stairway. There was no nameplate, no mailbox, just a painted number on an old wooden door. The door showed signs of abuse, a deep gouge near the lock; probably the result of a failed break-in. I knocked once, then four more times. The sharp sounds hung in the hot air around me, reverberating.

The door opened a crack. I could not see inside, but I could feel the occupant's eyes moving over me, checking, inspecting. A muffled voice asked, 'Alone?' and I replied that I was.

It was a moment before I could inspect the premises, my eyes blinded from the transition from light to dark. I blinked hurriedly, trying to hasten the adjustment. 'I'm glad you came,' the person said. 'I'm not certain what I would have done if you hadn't come.' I looked down and saw the voice was coming from a man in a wheelchair.

I nodded, and he turned sharply in the chair, spinning in place for a moment, then heading deeper into the apartment. The dim light filtering through one small window threw shadows across the room and glinted on the spokes of the wheels and the polished steel of the frame. 'Come on,' he said, motioning with one hand and pointing toward a seat at a kitchen table.

There was little furniture in the apartment: a lumpy couch, a plastic-coated table next to a stove and small refrigerator, a few odd chairs spread about. On all the flat surfaces there were cigarette butts in ashtrays. A few magazines – *Time, Newsweek, Playboy* – were tossed about. There was also a stack of newspapers on the floor. My latest story was on top. I could see huge red circles drawn around different paragraphs. I sat down and pulled out my notebook and tape recorder. The man in the wheelchair looked at them.

He wore large, aviator-style glasses, tinted yellow, and his blond-streaked hair was brushed severely back from his forehead and hung down over his ears. He seemed halfway between a shave and a beard, the hair on his face seeming to be darker beneath the yellow of the glasses. His arms were long, with bunched muscles. He wore a gray T-shirt and jeans but kept a white sheet over his legs. The side of his face seemed swollen; he saw my eyes on his cheek and said, 'Don't worry. Just an abscessed tooth. Go down to the VA hospital tomorrow, get it out. They take care of me pretty good.' His eyes returned to the tape recorder. 'You gonna use that thing?' His voice was thick from the swelling.

'If you let me,' I replied.

He shrugged. 'Hell, why not?' He grew quiet. After a moment he said, 'You know, I spent so much time wondering whether you would show up, now I don't know what to say.'

'Why don't we start with your name?' I said, pushing the record button.

'I don't know about that quite yet,' he said. 'You gotta promise not to use it.'

'Why?'

''Cause I know this guy, the killer, and I don't think he'd wait one instant before coming over and wasting me.' He laughed. 'I'm half-wasted already,' he said, pointing to his legs. 'I got to try to hang on to what little I got left.'

I thought for a moment. What harm? I'd get the story first, then the name. 'OK. I'll give you anonymity, but I know the cops'll want to talk with you.'

'Let me think about it,' he said. 'First let me tell you what I know.' He hesitated again. 'I don't suppose there's any money in this; you know, for expenses, maybe?' I shook my head. 'Didn't think so. Just thought I'd try, you know. The payments from Uncle only go so far, you see. It's not like this is a real fine place to live, you know.'

I nodded again. 'What happened?' I asked. 'I mean, if you don't mind.'

He shook his head vigorously. 'Don't bother me much now.' He put his hand to his face and rubbed at his beard. I could hear the crackling sound under his fingers.

And then he spoke, his words at first exaggerated, thrust toward the tape recorder. 'My name is Mike Hilson. Former Spec-Four in the U.S. Army. I caught a piece of shrapnel from a mortar round in January 1971 near some little dink village I don't even remember the name of. Batangan Peninsula. A real shithole. You know the real bummer? I was really short at the time. Done nine months in-country and was just about ready to pack it in, get a transfer out of a combat platoon, go back to Saigon or Da Nang or someplace and file shit for a while, work regular hours, you know. Anyway, all of a sudden this one night there's all sorts of shit coming down, and I wake up and all I can hear is everybody yelling, "Incoming! Incoming!" and the whump! sound the mortars make, and everybody is scrambling for cover. Except me.

'I'm lying there flat on my stomach, wondering why I can't move and whatever the hell is this numbness in my back, you know. And then it all gets kind of dizzy and goes around and around, the way you get when maybe you've had too much to drink and that last second before you wipe out. And that's it. They took a hunk of metal out at the base hospital and then shipped me back home to the States. Only hassle was I couldn't use my legs no more. Couldn't get it up, either. I did about three years in the VA hospital, and then I had to get out.' He looked around the room, his eyes glazing over empty, pocked walls and unraveling furniture. 'Not much of a home, huh? Let me tell you, it's a damn sight better than the para wards. I got a nurse, comes here in the afternoons, helps me out some. I get about, you know; the hospital ain't too far away. I get over there just about every other day. Groceries, the works, you name it.'

His hand swept around the room in a broad gesture. 'Do you come from here?'

'Folks did. Died a year ago. Car accident up north. Wiped 'em both right out. I've got a sister, lives in Orlando. That's it.'

'So tell me,' I said. 'Tell me about the killer.'

323

He laughed. 'I don't know his real name. That was one of the things about the war. Everybody seemed to have a nickname. They called me Slick because I wore my hair in a ducktail like, you know, from high school. In the platoon everybody had a different name. It was almost like you didn't want to make the name you was born with dirty, you know, over there in the war, killing.'

He reached down and drummed his fingers against the wheel of his chair. He started to speak about the war, about the platoon. When he grew excited he rapped his fingers against the chair to underscore the strength of his memories. Sometimes he rocked back in the chair, raising the wheels in front from the ground, spinning them underneath his legs, as if to rearrange his thoughts.

'I mean, there was a nigger from Arkansas we called Big Black and another kid from the Bronx in New York we called Streets. Another guy, drafted out of some fancy school in Boston, he became College. You see what I mean. In the Army they make you wear this little name thing on your shirt, even your fatigues. Hilson, mine said. I don't think anybody 'cept maybe some of the officers ever called me by that name. And if some dude didn't know enough to call me Slick, then he would find some cuss word and shout it at me, and that would work just about as well.'

He lit a cigarette from an open pack in front of him.

'I mean, you gotta understand this was a very strange place in 1970. I still ain't got most of it figured out, and that's what I do most of the time.

Sit and think. The Army helped me with that.' He waved his hand at the chair. 'You bet your ass.'

He blew smoke rings, and I followed the circles through the still air of the apartment.

'Did you do any time there?' he asked.

My mind filled with images of those years: high school, college, graduate school. I had a fleeting memory of the conversation between my father and myself. To run or not to run, that had been the question. I recalled the letter from the draft board requesting I show up for a physical examination. I had been reclassified 1-A. My father had been angry, his face a deep red, complaining. I had neglected to fill out the proper forms at the college, forms that would guarantee the continuation of my student deferment. 'Damn,' he'd said, 'how could you forget?' I hadn't answered. I hadn't forgotten. I'd remembered the forms; all I'd had to do was write in my name, classification number, course load, address and that was it. Drop it in the mail to the registrar's office; they took care of the rest. But the forms had stayed on my desk for months. Occasionally I'd picked them up and looked at them in wonderment, trying to figure out why I would not fill them out. It was as if I were daring the real world outside of the college: come and get me. And they tried.

I took care of it easily enough, though. The local draft-counseling service, which had offices on campus, got me out; I transferred my physical from location to location throughout the course of the dangerous semester. Once, when scheduled to go, I simply slept through the meeting time.

Eventually my deferment was restored. It was that simple.

Sitting in that small apartment, I thought of all the aspects of the war that had filled my life. I read the latest on the front page every day; I stared at the grainy black and white photos of the faceless men in helmets and flak jackets walking through the strange country. I marched; I handed out leaflets; I raised my voice at dozens of protests, my fist in salute to a hundred different speakers. But I really did not know what I was doing.

My last year in college my next-door neighbor in the dormitory was a returned vet, a tall man with black curly hair that grew wildly from the top of his head and fell in great folds over his ears and neck. He walked with a limp and a cane, the reminder of a foot wound. On the wall of his room he kept a photo of himself, taken by a *Life* magazine photographer; full color. He was set back in the center of the shot, his face contorted, his hands reaching down toward the ground and a mass of blood welling from his shoe. The photographer had captured the scene as a still life: a medic vaulting over some sandbags, another reaching out his hand. There was an explosion in the rear of the photo, kicking dirt and mud up in the air. Everyone seemed streaked with the same filth and terror.

My neighbor did not go to marches, nor did he attend the rallies or speeches. He refused to talk about the war and slammed the door to his room in the face of the campus activists who sought to enlist him. 'You don't understand,' he would say, then shut the door. I asked him why once, but he simply shook his head.

One morning, not long after graduation, I spied his picture in the paper. There had been a march on Congress by a veterans' group; a ragged line of soldiers in their old fatigues, marching out of step down the boulevards of the Capitol toward the Hill. They were returning their medals. The photo, transmitted by the AP, showed my neighbor standing at a fence, flinging his award onto the steps of Congress. The caption said he was giving back a Silver Star, the nation's second highest medal for bravery. I wondered what he had done to deserve the honor. It was as if for him, and for the others, there were two lives: home, normalcy, cheeseburgers and fast cars; then the war. I never saw my neighbor again but read in the college alumni magazine that he had graduated from medical school.

'No,' I said, 'I missed it.'

'Student, huh? Got a deferment, I bet,' the man in the wheelchair said.

'That's right.'

He laughed, his voice ending in a cough, and grinned at me. 'Ah, you should have been there. I mean, it was really something.'

'I know.'

He shook his head. 'No. No you don't. You had to be there. That's the problem. Nobody understands unless they were there.'

'You tell me about it,' I said. The phrase I live by.

He coughed again. 'OK,' he said. 'Sit back and relax. Have I got a war story for you.'

I heard voices from the hallway outside, footsteps against the cement of the landing. The man in the wheelchair turned sharply toward the sound, his hands grasping the armrests, his knuckles turning white with sudden effort. A voice called out, 'In yo' face, mother!' and there was the sound of running feet. The man in the wheelchair relaxed, visibly relieved. He stroked the sheet over his legs smooth. 'Sometimes the neighborhood kids try to break in. Little fuckers. I ought to get a gun and shoot one or two. Maybe then they'd stop. This may not be the best neighborhood, but it suits me OK.'

His eyes followed my pen scratching on the pad, then shifted to the tape recorder. 'OK,' he said, 'like I told you, we knew everybody by nicknames, and the guy I think is doing these murders was called Night Eyes, because, man, the dude never seemed to want to sleep at night. You'd be out on the perimeter catching your shift, trying to keep your eyes open, so fucking scared of the dark – and this guy would come sliding along, eyes wide awake, looking out over the wire into the jungle as if he could see plain as day. He'd catch a few hours in the evening, waiting for the sun to go down, then in the morning when it started to get light, he'd crawl into his hole, pull his poncho liner around him and sleep. He just seemed to need less than everybody else.

'Anyway, he was there the same time I was. Longer, in fact, though I heard he got flaky – I mean flakier – after I caught the shrapnel. I heard they shipped him off Section Eight to a psycho ward somewhere. I believe it, man; look what he's doing now. I don't think I ever saw the dude stoned, or drunk, or anything. All he did was play soldier. He liked to kill, you could see that. Never talked much to anybody. Liked to walk point, so's to be away from everybody else. I mean, he was one very quiet, very strange guy. I don't think the platoon would have put up with him too long if it hadn't been that everybody was a bit spaced out over there. There was a lot of weird heads.'

'You didn't know his real name?'

'No, I told you that already.'

'Well, what was the outfit? The commanding officer?'

'The CO was a lieutenant named O'Shaughnessy. First name, Peter. I couldn't forget a name like that one. Red hair, just like you'd expect. Able company three hundred fifty-second field infantry, American Division.'

'And where – '

'I told you that, man. Batangan Peninsula.'

'That's right,' I said. 'Just trying to keep everything straight.'

He smiled and started to drum his fingers against the steel again. 'That's cool,' he said. 'I want everything to be right.'

'Do you remember any other names from the outfit?'

'No. Like I said, just the nicknames. Strange, huh?'

I shrugged. 'Where'd this guy learn how to use a handgun?'

He exhaled sharply. 'Man, I don't know. But I

remember he had one over there. A big mother forty-five just like he's using over here. Probably got it in Saigon on the black market. You see, we were doing what they liked to call Search and Destroy. Everybody was always looking for an edge, you know, something that might help them out of a tough spot. This guy carried a forty-five. I knew a couple other guys that did, too. Sometimes in the afternoon he sat on the edge of the perimeter, you know, when we weren't out in the fucking swamp or jungle, and he plunked away with that thing. Shot at coconuts, birds, anything.'

'Anybody ask him about it?'

'No, like I said, he was strange. Wigged out. Everyone, even the CO, left him alone. Why not? Wasn't doing any harm. And the dude would volunteer for all sorts of shit, like lurps out into the country. Not me, man. I wanted to keep what little ass I had left intact. So as long as he did that, and as long as he took the dog shift at night, man, everybody just left him alone. And let him think whatever was in his head.'

'And you don't know what happened to him?'

'Just rumors. Flipped out, screaming and shooting. Somebody said he shot some peasants and just started laughing and laughing until they came for him. Hushed up, I guess. You know, the Army didn't mind publicizing heros like me who get their ass shot off while they're asleep, but the guys who went over the deep end, well, mostly they just got shipped home and shipped out, if you catch my drift.'

I nodded. The man in the wheelchair was shaking

his head, repeating under his breath, 'Weird, man, very strange.'

'So,' I said, 'tell me about the incident.'

Another long exhale as he thought.

'It was so damn hot; that I remember as clear as anything. Like right now, you know, the heat just hangs around. No air at all. As I said, we were doing Search and Destroy, which was the pits, man, the absolute worst.' He laughed. 'Number ten. That's what the grunts used to say. We'd get picked up by the choppers in the morning and flown into the target area for sweeps. You should get the chance to ride in one of those things sometime. The pilots were just as scared as we were; one second you're hanging up in the air a couple of thousand feet, the next second the slick's screaming down into the landing zone. The engine's wailing and the door gunner's shouting and swearing and firing-off the fifty-caliber as fast as he can, chopping up the jungle. You know one of the really strange things about Vietnam? We was always shooting at things that weren't really there. I mean, when we went into a landing zone, everybody was emptying their weapons at an imaginary enemy hiding in the bush. At night the artillery would fire over our heads, to get the coordinates right in case we was attacked during the dark. And there was never anybody there. Well, hardly ever.

'On this one day we were put into a cold LZ; there was no return fire, which made the chopper jockeys happy and they split right quick. We were supposed to make two separate sweeping actions, meeting up at some village that was on the map. There we were supposed to move through some paddies and chase anything we came up with toward another company that was heading toward us, in a block. It was the kind of damn-fool idea that looked real good on the paper back at the division HQ but which didn't work worth a shit once we got into the field. Anyway, I remember the CO, O'Shaughnessy. Christ, he was as big a mick as you could find. And big, man, the dude was at least six feet five and about two hundred and forty pounds. I mean, when he said to do something, it got done. Big, bad temper, too. I was always surprised nobody ever blew him away in a firefight. As far as I know, nobody did. And got to give the guy credit: when I got hit he was screaming at that chopper jock and told him he'd shoot him hisself if he didn't pick my ass out of there. So I guess I got no complaints, really.

'So like I was saying, we was all tossed into the middle of this paddy, collected around O'Shaughnessy, and the choppers were tailing away into the sun. I remember the feeling of being alone; even though you were surrounded by other men and weapons and you had the radio to call in help, I never could shake the sensation of being abandoned, just like I was adrift at sea; you know, like some Robinson Crusoe. It was so damn hot; in just a few seconds we were all dripping wet. The sweat used to run down between my eyes under my helmet. I couldn't stand it, you know; I wanted to scream. But there's no way to wipe it out when you've got your weapon and maybe you need to steady yourself with your other hand. I saw guys go crazy in the heat, start yelling, refuse to move, up to their ass in mud and water and leeches in the paddies. The sun was as bad as anything the VC did sometimes.

'He split us into two squads. He took one, and the first sergeant took the other. We were supposed to maintain a common distance, like a quarter mile or so between us, but, hell, that never worked over there. I mean, one squad would get bogged down in some shit, and the other would get ahead, then slow down. then speed up. I think it was all crazy, man, every bit of it. Being out in the field was no different. So we took off, about a dozen of us. And pretty soon we're slogging through the shit, just like always. I remember that morning like it was a blur, you know. It was just like so many other fucking mornings in Nam. It wasn't until we got close to the village that things started in different.'

He paused, taking the moment to light another cigarette. His eyes, behind the glasses, followed the smoke as it rose from the ashtray.

'We got there first, a good ways ahead of the other squad. We camped down on the edge and started to wait. It wasn't so bad; I mean, we all needed a blow. Well, the dude I was telling you about, the guy doing these killings, he was out on the point as usual. And when we halted, he was off sitting a little ways away, just as usual. And while we're sitting there, he's staring through the brush into the village. Then suddenly he stands up and turns to the rest of the squad.

' "I saw something," he says. "Looked like a chick with an a-kay." Well, everybody grabs their weapons and straightens out real fast. You got to remember, this guy had eyes that could pick a shape out of the middle of the night, so we always trusted him. And I remember what he said, because he was standing right there, with his back to the sun, and I remember having to shade my eyes so I could see his face.

'Well, there was a lot of discussion as to what to do. Most everybody wanted to wait for the lieutenant and the other squad to show, but the sergeant, he was a lifer, and I guess he was looking for some kind of promotion or medal or some such shit, because he says, "No way," and the next thing I know we're all spread out and humping very carefully into the village. Moving from hut to hut, just like in the movies. Only scared, man, truly scared.

'There must be, oh, I guess maybe five, six pathetic little huts in this whole town. I mean, it hardly qualified as a village at all. Just a little bump on the ass of the world. So it doesn't take us long to move through it, even if we are being real careful 'cause of what the guy said he saw.'

Hilson rubbed his hand through his hair and pulled at the cigarette. Then he started drumming his fingers again against the side of the chair, as if to increase the tempo of the words as they flowed out into the still of the apartment.

'I never told nobody this story,' he said. 'I'm not looking to get put on trial like that dude Calley.'

I nodded at him. 'I understand. This is confidential.'

'You got it.' Then he started in again.

'At the end of the village we stop and collect ourselves. The sergeant puts men out on the perimeter and sends a couple of guys back to wait for the other squad. I was jumpy, man; we all were. Something about the heat, you know. And we'd been told the VC were real strong in the sector. We were told we'd probably have contact, that anyone we saw was probably VC. So I guess it was to be expected.

'I mean, that's what *they* told us! Trust nobody! Not even the oldest, dumbest dink in the world. He'll blow your ass off as soon as you turn your back. Cut your balls off if you smile at him. Or her. We just had no way of knowing, man! No way. Not even when they sent those VC deserters or ARVN guys with us. They'd just as soon tell you to kill somebody as question them. They were no fucking help at all. And we didn't even have one of them with us on that day.

'So we lined up all the people in the village. There were nine of them. Old men and women, kids. No young men. There was this one old guy, spoke some American. He was the one that got questioned. I remember he just sat there bobbing his head up and down. "No VC here," he says. "No VC." And the sergeant is yelling, "Bullshit! Bullshit" and the dude, Night Eyes is saying, I know what I saw. He's standing there, fingering the forty-five. He used to wear it in a breakaway holster in his armpit, up under his flak jacket. But he had the fucking thing out, and he was clicking the safety on and off, fiddling with it.

'So the sergeant yells at the rest of us to start checking inside the hooches, and pretty soon we're tearing the places apart, pretty angry 'cause it's hot and we're scared. And sure as shit, one of the guys finds a rifle stashed up in the rafters, in the brush alongside the ceiling. And then we are really scared and pissed.

'The sergeant is still yelling at the old guy, but he just keeps saying, "No VC here," even when we shake the a-kay under his nose. The rest of the people are looking very frightened. There are a couple of small kids crying and a baby wailing. I remember turning to the guy and saying, "I guess you was right," and he just nodded, kind of, and grinned. The sergeant was just about to give up when the guy says, "I'll take care of it, sergeant," and the sergeant just shrugs and says, "Do what you like."

'So the guy walks over to a teenage chick, who's sitting on the ground just about ready to piss in her pants, and he grabs her real hard by the arm and pulls her over in front of the old guy. He clicks back the hammer on his forty-five and says, "Where VC?" And when the old guy shakes his head, the guy pulls the trigger.

'Damn! I can still remember the click as the hammer came down on the empty chamber and the second click as the automatic thrust up. I mean, no one knew whether he'd emptied it purposely or not. And he just smiled at the old guy and said, "Where VC?" And the old guy just shook his head.

'And the next thing I remember is the explosion from that big fucking forty-five. It was loaded, after all. And the kid just pitched forward, half her head gone, landing at the feet of the head man. I remember it like it was a picture. He got some of the blood and brains spattered on him. I saw his face just twist then;

all sorts of things must have been going through his head – fear, I guess, mostly – but he just stayed right there shaking his head, repeating over and over, like some fucking record that gets stuck, "No VC. No VC here." The first sergeant is looking at Night Eyes like he's crazy, which I guess is right. But the dude hasn't barely budged, and his face is still set, cold and looking the old guy dead in the eyes. He walks nice and slow over to the group of people and pulls an old couple out. He looks over at the head man. The head man says, "No VC," and then that fucking forty-five explodes, Boom! Boom! and the old couple are in a pile on the ground. I remember the blood mixing with the dust. And everybody else is just standing around. I mean, we were just frozen, watching what was going on. I don't think I ever thought of trying to stop the dude. He seemed to be the only person who was *doing* anything. It was like it was all happening in some weird nightmare, man.

'Hey! I ain't proud of it. Shit, no. But you got to understand, we was all a little crazy that day. The sun, maybe. The fucking jungle, the fucking paddies. I don't know. I remember the sun most when I think about Nam. We were all off the end for that little bit.

'So I guess that's why no one stopped him.'

There was a moment of silence. I watched the eyes behind the yellow glasses. They were raised now, looking up at the white ceiling.

'The next person he grabbed was some mama-san with her kid. Nobody moved. Boom! went the forty-five. And then I heard the dude laugh a little. Like he wasn't getting mad at the head man at all. He just wanted it all to keep going. Like it was some game. "Where VC?" he asked, and he laughed again.

'But the guy didn't answer, because we found out.

'Suddenly out on the perimeter there was that sound. Man, once you hear the sound of small-arms fire, you never forget. And behind us there was a whump! and an explosion as a mortar round disintegrated one of the hooches behind us. I remember the guy just laughed. He picked up his M-sixteen and everybody was yelling to take cover. We were all running back towards the direction we knew the lieutenant was coming. Shit! There were mortars coming in all over the place, and the air was full of shit and shooting. I was cutting loose, too, to the front, I don't know at what. I do remember one thing, though. When I turned around I saw the whole pile of villagers in a heap, all of them gunned down. Except the little kid, the mama-san's baby. The kid was bawling and screaming. I could hear it for a minute, maybe just a second. And then there was too much noise.

'We all collected back at the rear of the clearing. I remember the radioman screaming for the lieutenant. And the lieutenant coming on and telling us to withdraw towards him. Then he said he was calling in an air strike. It was all simple, you see. That's how we did things over there. The bunch of us, still firing a bit, you know, at nothing except fear, headed away from the village. And in a few minutes I heard that sound, you know, the real high-pitched sound of a

Phantom when the jock cuts it down to a couple of hundred feet and he comes winding in. There were four of them in the flight. I could see them come through the sun. It reflected off the wings, just like they were lights. They dropped those canisters and just blew the hell out of that village and whoever was anywhere near it.

'And if there was any evidence of what that dude did, then it went up in smoke, man, because that place was scorched.'

He took another long pause, thinking, I imagined, of what he had seen.

'We made a report. O'Shaughnessy called all of us in, asked us what we'd seen, what we'd done. Even called in the dude. You know the really weird thing, man? Nobody lied. Nobody told the CO anything different than what happened. And you know who he told? That's right. Nobody. I remember he came out and I overheard him tell the sergeant, "Fuck it. Who cares?" And the sergeant nodded. And a week later he got his transfer back to Saigon. And I got my ass in this sling. And that was all there was to it.'

We were quiet for an instant.

'No investigation?' I asked.

He shook his head.

'No records?'

Again he shook his head.

'And the CO?'

'Killed, I heard. Fragged, I bet. Who knows?'

My imagination raced with the details: The girl. The old couple. The woman with the child. They were all there.

'Let me get this straight,' I said. 'When you turned around, the whole group of villagers, they were all dead, right?'

He nodded, his eyes fastened on my own.

'How did they die?'

'What d'you mean?'

'Well, did this guy mow them down, or were they caught in the cross fire, or were they killed by the mortars?'

'Is it important? I mean, man, they were dead.'

'Yes,' I replied. 'Oh, yes, it is very important.' My mind jumped ahead, dizzy with the possibilities. If Hilson were right, either the killer was finished – or he was just beginning. And I was the only one who'd know. I could feel the excitement rising up in me.

He hesitated, his hand rubbing his beard.

'I just don't know, man. I think I see what you're asking. I mean, what's this dude going to pull next, huh? I don't think I can help. All I remember is hitting the deck when the first explosions came in, and then getting up and hightailing it out of there. You know, you don't do a lot of sightseeing under those circumstances.'

He paused again.

'Still, I remember the bodies, all in the same general area. Just like somebody'd opened up on them with an automatic. But I couldn't say for certain who did it, 'cause, shit, there was firing all over. You know what I mean? Anything could have happened.'

Disappointment flooded me, but still, I thought, he'd given me many answers. If the major question remained, it was still a great deal closer to an end. I

340

tried to picture the cluster of villagers, streaked with dirt, blood and their own gore, but I couldn't. At least not the way this man had seen it.

'So,' he said, 'you gonna figure it out from here?' He grinned, showing a row of even white teeth. 'It's good, huh?'

'Yeah,' I replied. I peered down through the smoky offlight of the room at my notes. Here it is, I thought, in a way the beginning and the end. I was getting closer to the edge of the killings. My imagination started in, blocking out the paragraphs. I pictured the headline, the front-page play. I sucked in a deep breath and stood to leave.

The man in the wheelchair led me to the door. We shook hands; his was slick with sweat. I stood in the doorway, looking out at the late afternoon. I paused, turning back to him. He was fiddling with the dead-bolt lock on the door, nervously sliding it closed, then open. 'I've been a big help, huh?'

'Yes,' I said. 'No doubt.'

'That's good.'

I raised my hand, then remembered the key question, one I'd foolishly let slip past. 'Listen, just one more thing. I need to know who can confirm the story.'

He shrugged. 'Maybe God. But I think He didn't care much what went on in Nam.'

Then he shut the door, and I heard the dead-bolt lock slide into place.

CHAPTER FIFTEEN

It was, of course, the lead story.

They'd stripped the morning headlines across the top of the front page beneath the *Journal* masthead, the same position where so many of the stories had run: EYEWITNESS RECALLS KILLER'S 'INCIDENT.' I lingered in my bathrobe at the kitchen table, drinking coffee, racing my eyes over the page of newsprint, feeling a quickening excitement as I read. I felt I had managed to shake a tree, and now I merely had to wait for the vibration to work its way up the trunk and out through the branches before the fruit came tumbling down from the sky.

I was alone; Christine had left early, sliding naked from the bed in the half-light of the summertime dawn. She had early-morning surgery scheduled. She had placed the paper, still folded in the newsboy's delivery fashion, unread on the table. She had been waiting up the night before when I came in after deadline.

I had paced through the apartment describing it all to her, while she sat, hands clasped, listening patiently. She said little; instead I paused, asked myself questions, interrupted myself with comments. It was as if I were acting in her stead, trying to anticipate the questions she might have forming in her own mind.

I told her, too, about the struggle in the newsroom to get the story into the paper. Nolan had listened to the first few minutes of the tape recording, then to my reconstruction of the conversation from my notes. He, too, had been excited, but he'd stumbled on the issue of confirmation. I hurriedly placed a late-afternoon call to the office of public information at the Pentagon, but it was too late to confirm if either Hilson or O'Shaughnessy had been overseas at the relevant time.

Nolan had hesitated. 'What happens if we hold off for a day? What do we lose?'

I had shaken my head. 'An edge. This guy could go to the cops, could go to the television stations. Or he could disappear. I want to go with it.'

Nolan had nodded and we'd struck a compromise: I would withhold the informant's identity, describe the unit that was involved in the operation and include the commanding officer's name. I would also omit anything that indicated the officer knew about the incident, so as to leave the question of an army cover-up untouched.

'But keep at it,' Nolan had said. 'We'll break that later.'

I'd sat at the typewriter, convinced the story would flush the killer from his camouflage in the city. The story would break the rhythm of the murders; we would move ahead of the killer. He'd want to know from *us*, not the other way around.

Christine had shaken her head, though. 'It'll just

344

speed him up, make him realize his time is limited,' she'd said. When we went to bed later she was hesitant, unresponsive, but I exploded inside her and then slipped from her body. Within seconds I was asleep as she turned on her side away from me.

It was mid-morning when Martinez called. 'We're coming over,' he said. 'Right away.' It was a call I'd been expecting.

I expected to hear from the killer, too. The morning had passed quickly as I accepted congratulations from the other reporters and the editors at the paper. I placed a call to the Pentagon's public-information office, and they promised a quick response to the two names and the unit number. It was mostly a matter of waiting.

Nolan came over, expecting the detectives at the receptionist's desk. The night before he had raised his hands and shaken his head when I'd started to talk about the man in the wheelchair. 'I don't want to know,' he'd said. 'The cops may have a subpoena, and I don't want to be put in that position. He's your source, and you're going to protect him. The paper stands behind you. It is that simple. I hope.' We'd laughed.

A copy of the paper lay on my desk now, and he picked it up. He read out loud: 'On a blisteringly hot day some five years ago, nine men, women and children in a Viet Cong-controlled village in South Vietnam were executed by U.S. troops in the "incident" that has prompted the recent wave

345

of murders in Miami, according to a now-disabled veteran who was an eyewitness.'

'Eyewitness,' he said. 'God, what a great word to have in the beginning of a news story. It's as if the veracity of what follows is no longer in question.'

He skipped over several paragraphs and then started to read again. ' "I'm scared," the witness said, as he started his description of the atrocity that he believes is the basis for the recent Miami killings. The witness, whose name is being withheld by the *Journal*, was able to recount the incident in extraordinary detail. "Hell, I'm not proud of what we did," he said.' Nolan stopped and looked at me. 'I bet the cops just about croaked when they saw this.' I nodded. 'Well,' he said, 'they should be here soon.' He left me for a moment to answer the telephones at the city desk.

I had little doubt about what would happen with the man in the wheelchair. Now that the story was out, I would go back to him, and he would agree to be interviewed by the police. It always worked that way. Once the story was told it could be repeated a hundred times, a thousand times. It was as if it had become safe, no longer a memory banging angrily in the interior of the imagination.

From Hilson's memory would come the names and addresses of the men in the unit. For the first time I felt as if the story had almost run its course. It was only the proverbial matter of time. The man's memory would squeeze the killer from his hiding place, out into the sunlight. And, I thought, I had done it. I felt as if I were shaking my fist at all the fears of my life:

my family, Christine. I could not help breaking into a smile.

Nolan's voice interrupted my reverie. 'They're here.'

We stepped away from the desk, and the telephone rang.

I looked at it for a moment, wondering, then looked at Nolan, and he shrugged. 'I'll go ahead,' he said. So I reached out and picked up the receiver, clicking on the recorder simultaneously. I watched Nolan step away as I brought the receiver to my ear.

I think back. I try to remember, but my recollection is more a blur than an etching. I wonder when it was that I lost what little control I had, and I suppose it was then, at that first call, that I began to realize the walls of the room that held me, to sense the suction at the bottom of the pool grasping at my legs, pulling me under the surface.

The call was from the public-information officer at the Pentagon. He spoke in a clipped, military manner, his voice filled with the jargon of the Army. 'Sir!' he said. 'I have personally checked those records you requested.'

'And?'

'Negative, sir.'

'What do you mean?' I felt a sudden heat on my forehead.

'Well, we keep all records of men and units. I have determined that the outfit you cited was in fact performing search-and-destroy missions in that sector of the combat theater. But I was unable to find any record of any PFC Hilson or any Lieutenant Peter O'Shaughnessy operating with that unit.'

'Not with that unit?'

'That is correct. I further checked the list of men wounded in action during that time period. Again, negative on those names.'

I stumbled. 'Perhaps at a different time?'

'Possibly, sir. But I checked thoroughly for surrounding months, also. It is possible, if the year is incorrect, that I may be mistaken. But in a different year I doubt that you'll find that unit operating in that area. Units were shifted about with some frequency, sir, as you will recall.'

'All right,' I said. My mind was fighting with the information. I could think of nothing further to ask.

'May I ask a question?' the officer said.

'Go ahead.'

'Does this have anything to do with the murders down there?'

'Yes,' I said. 'It has a good deal to do with the murders.'

'Well,' he continued, 'I wish I could be more help. If you want other dates and names checked, just call me, sir. I'm afraid we haven't been much help. Especially to the police. But it is not difficult to check specific references such as you provided.'

'Thank you,' I said.

'Anytime,' he replied, hanging up the phone.

I looked at the newspaper on my desk. A lie, I thought, it was all a lie. I took a deep breath, fighting a sensation of nausea. I got up from the desk and looked back to the conference room. Through the glass windows I could see the detectives waiting for me.

I sat next to Nolan, slipping him the note: 'Pentagon says negative on Hilson, O'Shaughnessy.' I underlined 'negative' three times. Nolan's eyes widened, and he looked at me as he comprehended the sudden shift. But he had no time to make a response, to get us out of the room, before Wilson thwacked the table with his open palm. 'We've played fair with you!' he was shouting. 'And now you get a break, a huge break, and you shut us out! I ought to arrest the two of you for obstructing justice.'

'Listen,' I said, 'there's a problem – '

'You bet there's a problem! There's a fucking murderer out there, and you guys have the key to finding his ass, and you won't even give us the courtesy of a fucking telephone call! Christ! What a bunch of fucking hypocrites!' He slammed back in his chair. 'I want to know,' he said. 'I want to know everything! Don't hold back anything! Goddammit, we can get this guy now! Today! You tell me where this "disabled veteran" is. I want to talk to his ass! Now!'

Martinez broke in, his voice also strained but under more control. 'We feel this guy is a material witness. If we have to, we can come back in about thirty minutes with a subpoena. But we shouldn't have to do that. We've been up front with you,' he said, looking first at me, then fixing his eyes on Nolan. 'And I think it's your turn to be up front with us.'

349

'There's a problem,' Nolan said.

'What fucking problem?' said Wilson, leaning toward me. Nolan looked at me, too. 'Tell them.'

I hesitated, looking for words. 'We checked the Pentagon this morning. They have no record of the informant's name. They also don't have any record of the man whom he said was the company commander.'

Wilson slumped back in his chair. 'Christ!' he spat.

'Explain,' Martinez said.

'The guy gave me a phony name. A couple of phony names. I don't know what else was phony in the story he told.'

Martinez nodded. 'You mean you didn't bother to check beforehand?'

'I tried.'

'Good try.'

For a moment there was silence in the room.

Nolan broke it after a few seconds. 'That means his confidentiality no longer has to be protected. I mean, if he lied, we don't have to protect him.' He nodded at me.

'Tell us,' Martinez said, pulling a pad out. Wilson leaned forward on the table, staring at me.

I began to retell the story from the beginning. I described driving across the city into the downtown ghetto. Then I described climbing to meet the man in the apartment.

'Stop there!' Wilson said. I held in mid-sentence. Martinez turned and looked at his partner, as if wondering what he was thinking.

Wilson spoke. 'The man was in a wheelchair, right? Spinal cord severed, right?'

I nodded.

'How many flights up?'

'Three.'

'And he says he gets out every day to the hospital?'

'He said that, yes,' I replied.

And then things happened very swiftly.

Wilson slumped back in his chair for an instant, his eyes locked onto mine, and put his hands to his face. Then suddenly, without warning, he shot his body out of the chair, stretching it across the table, his hands seizing me by the shirt. I could feel the strength in his arms, and he jolted me out from the chair, pulling me across the table to meet his face, contorting with rage. 'You dumb fuck!' he screamed. 'You stupid, stupid idiot fuck!' I could feel the spittle in my face. 'You damn fool!'

'Let me go!' I shouted. Both Martinez and Nolan had pushed out of their chairs and were trying to separate us. For a second all four of us were twisted in the middle.

And then, as swiftly, Wilson dropped his hands. I fell back into my chair as he slid into his. His eyes seemed glazed over. He was simply repeating, 'Fuck, fuck,' over and over again.

Martinez started to shake him, and Nolan turned to me. 'OK?' His face was concerned. I reached up, straightened my tie and shirt. I nodded. We both looked at the detective.

'Don't you see?' Wilson asked. His voice was empty.

And then we did see.

Nolan let out his breath and sat down hard in the chair.

Martinez put his hand to his eyes and shook his head.

I felt ill, as if I were going to be sick to my stomach.

It was him, I thought. A meeting, just as I had requested.

Andrew Porter swung the big car hard through the lunchtime congestion. At the intersection in front of us the stoplight changed from green to yellow. He put his foot down hard on the accelerator and we shot through, people on the sidewalk stepping back quickly. I heard Nolan muffle an obscenity from the back seat. Porter glanced into the rearview mirror. 'Stayed right with us,' he said. I turned and saw that Martinez and Wilson in their unmarked cruiser were only a few feet back. Porter slid the car around a corner, and suddenly we were leaving the boulevard behind and cutting through the tall downtown buildings. I saw the sun gleam off the white roof of a city police car as it braked at a side street and then swung into line behind the two detectives.

'Coming out in force,' Porter said. 'But for what?' He laughed. 'I don't know, but I tend to doubt he'll be waiting for us. It would be too much like Jimmy Cagney in *White Heat*. "Come and get me, coppers!" No, I don't see it.'

Nolan swore.

A block from the apartment we stopped, pulling sharply to the curb. I could hear the tires complain as the police cars came to rest next to us. Wilson was out of the car before it quit quivering. 'Let's go,' he said. We headed down the block. Halfway there, he turned to Nolan. 'Stay back.' He motioned at Porter. 'You, too.' I could see the other police taking positions around the perimeter of the building, out of sight of the landing. I watched the men working their way into locations, weapons out. I saw shotguns and pistols gleaming in the noon sun. It was like a battlefield, and any second the order to attack would sweep me along, out of control. 'Come on,' Wilson said. 'It's just you, me and Martinez.' We started across the courtyard. I felt the heat rebounding from the cement floor, curling like smoke around my feet and ankles. I couldn't see any of the people who'd populated the courtyard before; they had sensed trouble and faded into the shadows, invisible.

We climbed the stairs slowly, each step taking more effort.

'Now, you're really in it,' Wilson whispered. 'How does it feel?'

I didn't reply. Martinez looked at me carefully. 'You certain you want to do this?' he asked. I nodded, despite myself. The two detectives paused at the landing, checking their weapons.

'All right,' Wilson said. 'It's time.'

I tried to keep in mind what they had told me. I stepped out onto the landing and walked the few feet to the doorway. I saw the same deep gouge as before. Standing to the side, I knocked on the door loudly.

There was no sound.

I knocked again.

Still no response.

I glanced back at the detectives. Martinez made a motion with his left hand, turning his wrist as if opening the door. I put my hand on the handle and tried it.

It opened easily.

I pushed the door open fully. I could see the sunlight cutting into the darkness of the cavernlike apartment. For a moment I thought I saw movement inside and jumped back against the wall, my mouth dry. But there was no sound.

I called out.

No reply.

Slowly I peered around the corner, moving my head as carefully as possible, so slowly I thought each micrometer took seconds, minutes.

And then I saw the sunlight glint off an object in the center of the room. It took a moment to realize what it was, but when I knew, I turned back and pressed myself against the wall again, breathing in and out heavily, feeling the hot air fill my lungs, like a drowning man suddenly brought to the surface.

It was the wheelchair. Empty.

The two detectives pushed by me, swinging themselves, weapons extended, into the apartment. I knew they would find no one. I had seen the message left behind. I heard Wilson muttering obscenities. He came to the door. 'Is that it?' he asked, and I nodded my head. 'Well,' the detective said, 'that's all he left behind.'

But he was wrong.

Martinez called out suddenly. I followed the detectives inside. 'See that?' he said. He was pointing to the center of the wheelchair. There was a small cassette tape in the middle of the seat.

Wilson looked at it for a minute. 'Have you got your machine?'

I pulled the portable recorder from my jacket pocket.

'All right,' Wilson said, 'let's see what the fucker has to say.' Using the end of a pencil, he picked the tape off the seat and, without touching it, slipped it into the machine. I pushed the play button, and for a moment all we heard was hissing.

And then laughter.

It continued unabated, growing in volume for perhaps thirty seconds, a minute, then ended abruptly, leaving the room suddenly empty. The tape spun quietly and I stopped the machine. I stepped out onto the landing and looked up into the sky, picking out the white trail of a high-flying military jet against the light blue. Around me the landing filled with policemen and technicians. I heard Nolan's voice and Porter's camera as he stood by the doorway taking pictures of the abandoned wheelchair. But around me the sounds of voices faded, and all I could hear was hypnotic laughter.

Nolan sat at the computer screen, his hands playing on the keyboard, his face twisted into a frown as he surveyed the words blinking white against the gray background. 'Damn,' he said. He rearranged a sentence, words disappearing when he pushed buttons, other words jumping into their places. 'Damn,' he repeated. He pushed himself back from the screen. 'I just don't have any fucking idea how we're going to say this.' His eyes swept across the newsroom to the managing editor's office. Again he frowned and turned back to the screen.

I had written a description of the police raid and what they had discovered. In clipped, proper journalese, I had written that the man in the wheelchair had, in all likelihood, been the killer himself. We had hedged on that point, trying to write around the obvious, trying to obscure my own foolishness. It was that section with which Nolan was struggling. 'The problem is, we just don't know how much of it was the truth. I mean, how can we write that he told a whole series of lies, when we don't know that? Suppose the only lies were the names? Like O'Shaughnessy, for example. Suppose he merely changed it slightly; the real commander was an O'Hara or a Malone or some other Irish name. It wouldn't be past him. Shit.' He looked back at the screen, changed a few other words around.

'They're still waiting,' I said. Martinez and Wilson were in the back of the newsroom, sitting at a vacant desk, their eyes fixed on us. The detectives had arrived after finishing with the management of the apartment building and canvassing the neighbors. No one, it seemed, knew much. A man came in. Paid cash for a week. Wasn't seen again. Wore a hat, dark sunglasses. Didn't say much. It was the type of apartment building where few questions were asked, especially with cash up front.

'I know,' Nolan said. 'You might as well go with them. And bring the sketch back, so we can run it with the story. I'll work on this while you're gone.'

I nodded and watched as he continued to play with the story. I felt a kind of loss, watching him maneuver my words. It was the first story since the first murder that had undergone such severe editing. I could feel the story slipping away from me. I started to speak as I watched a change made but turned away. I motioned to the two detectives and reached for my jacket, draped over the chair at my desk.

And the phone rang.

My first thought was, 'Not again.' The continued ringing was a summons, a seduction. I looked back at the two detectives. They stared at me. I punched the recorder and picked up the receiver. 'Hello,' I said softly.

All I could hear was laughter.

'You!' I said. It was loud enough so that motion seemed to stop in the room. Martinez and Wilson started toward me; Nolan, at the city desk, stopped his work.

'So,' the killer said, the laughter ceasing abruptly. 'You wanted to meet. You wanted a war story. You got one.'

'Why?' I asked.

He did not answer my question.

'You see,' he continued, 'you're not immune, are you?'

'Dammit, why?' I shouted. 'What are you doing?'

'No one is safe,' he said. 'You thought you were. In school. Studying. Marching. Drinking beer, getting laid. And now it turns out there are no deferments.'

'What do you mean?' I was furious.

His voice went soft, very cold and calm.

'I study, too,' he said. 'Habits, routines, schedules. It is surprising how organized, how regular our lives really are.'

'What are you talking about?' I asked, slowing my voice.

'One merely has to wear a white jacket. Perhaps a stethoscope folded and hanging from a pocket. One becomes invisible, capable of checking any schedule, especially one posted so prominently.'

Christine, I thought suddenly.

'So, imagine one wants to meet a particular person, a nurse, say. He would know when she leaves the hospital, when she walks through the big parking lot to the assigned spaces. And suppose her car wouldn't start. How would she know that the battery cable had been sliced? And, you think about it, would she turn down the offer for help from a young man, so obviously an intern, or maybe a resident, who happens by at that moment? An offer of a ride to a service station? An offer that turns out to be something altogether different.'

'Leave her alone!' I yelled. 'She's done nothing!'

'Look at the time,' the killer said. 'It's already done.'

Abruptly he hung up. The line was dead.

I turned toward the clock on the wall. It was

five minutes before four P.M. The time she would be leaving the hospital.

'Well? What did he say?' It was Nolan. Wilson was next to him, rewinding the tape.

I grabbed the telephone, dialing the number of the nurses' station. I misdialed and, cursing, dialed again. 'Christine!' I shouted at the voice that answered.

'I think she's gone for the day,' came the reply.

'No!'

'I'm sorry,' went the voice on the other end. 'She's gone.'

'No! Goddammit, stop her!'

'Who is this?' Suddenly suspicious.

'Have her paged!' I screamed. 'She's in danger!'

'I'm sorry,' continued the voice, cool, the collected tone of a nurse not swayed by demands. 'I must know who this is.'

'For Christ's sake, it's Anderson! Her boyfriend. Now stop her, please!'

'Oh, Mr. Anderson, I didn't recognize your voice. Hold on while I page her.'

I held the telephone in my hand, squeezing it. I was fighting the pictures in my mind: the parking lot, her car disabled, the sudden offer of assistance. Around me I could hear Wilson, Martinez and Nolan trying to ask me what was going on. Then the nurse came back on the line.

'I'm sorry, Mr. Anderson, but she doesn't answer. She's probably out of the building.'

I slammed the phone down.

I could think of nothing except speed.

The afternoon traffic seemed to reach out and stop

me. I twisted the car through the streets, running the lights, leaning mercilessly on the horn, ignoring the shouts and curses from pedestrians and other drivers. I swerved to avoid one collision and forced another car to careen into the curb, but I was barely aware of them. They were like slides in a show. I knew the two detectives were following behind me, but I paid no attention to their progress. I remember the afternoon sun filling the windshield. blinding me, and I held my hand up against it, as if I could block out all the terror within me.

The car pitched wildly as I slammed into the hospital parking lot. Another car jolted to a halt, tires squealing, blocking my path. The man inside shook his fist at me, but I ignored him, jumping from the car, running across the lot. I could hear the soles of my shoes slapping against the black macadam, like an angry drummer's beat. The heat seemed to surround me, pushing me down. I pumped my arms, running as hard as I could, sprinting toward the rear where I knew she parked her car. I heard the caterwauling sound of sirens as the police began to descend on the lot; the noise filled my ears and mind, adding to my fears. I could hear other feet behind me running; the detectives, I guessed, but I pressed on without turning.

And then nothing.

I stopped sharply, stumbling, steadying myself against a car. I looked through the lot, my eyes racing as madly as my feet had just a second earlier.

No sign of her.

No sign of the car.

'Christine!' I yelled. My cry flew up and away, useless.

'Where?' went a voice beside me. It was Martinez, breathing hard.

'Here,' I said.

His weapon was out. His eyes followed the same path as my own.

'She's not here,' I said. My voice wavered.

Martinez turned to Wilson. The older man was gasping for breath, leaning up against a car. 'She's not here. She's gone. No car?' He turned to me.

'No car,' I said. I inhaled sharply. Another thought formed slowly, then burst forth explosively. 'Oh, my God!' I said. 'He was lying. About the parking lot. He's waiting at home!'

For a moment Martinez looked wildly at me, his eyes blinking wide. 'Shit!' he said. Wilson seized a portable radio from a jacket pocket and began talking into it.

I raced back to the lot entrance for my car, but it was blocked by a police cruiser. 'Move it! Move it!' I screamed. 'Move the fucking thing!' A policeman looked oddly at me, then saw Martinez behind me, waving his arms wildly. He jumped into the seat next to me, and I floored the accelerator and the car shot backward. The gears complained loudly as I shifted, and we shot forward, fishtailing, barely under control, heading down the street.

We sped through the expressway toll booth without pausing. I headed through the traffic, cutting back and forth, leaving a braking, swearing mass behind me. Martinez had gripped hold of the door but was urging

361

me on. 'Hit it! Hit it!' he kept saying. I aimed the car between two others and shot through. 'The shoulder,' he yelled above the noise of the air pouring madly through the windows. I slid the car onto the roadway shoulder, and we raced up past the traffic. 'Lean on the horn!' he shouted, and I complied, the sound rising and trailing off behind us like a boat's wake.

We cut through quiet suburban streets, through stoplights and stop signs. I was no longer aware of what was taking place behind me, my mind centered on what was waiting. 'Hurry!' the detective urged. 'Keep it up!' The car swerved wildly as I turned toward the small apartment building where I lived. It was on a quiet street, and the noise of the tires broke the air around us. I stopped the car and thrust myself out, stumbling, catching myself and then running hard, my mind filling with noise and fear. I could hear Martinez laboring a few steps behind me. 'There!' I shouted.

It was her car.

'Oh, no!' I said, stopping suddenly, staring ahead. The hood was up.

'Christine!' I shouted. My stomach was clenched tight with tension. 'We're too late,' I said. 'He's taken her.' Martinez pulled up beside me. He, too, was staring at the car.

'Shit,' he said. 'You sure?'

But another thought cut through me, and I jumped for the door to the apartment. My mind filled with a picture of her body, twisted, misshapen in death, on the floor of our home. 'Upstairs,' I cried, my voice passing back over my shoulder. I took the stairs two, three at a time, my feet crashing against the wooden steps, the stairwell echoing with noise. I threw myself against the apartment door, my shoulder meeting the wood with a crash just as I twisted the doorknob with my hand. I felt myself slipping, falling into the living room, my balance suddenly evaporated. The floor rose up to meet me, and I held out my hands to brace my fall. Martinez was behind me, leaping through the open door, sweeping inside, half-crouched, gun extended in both hands, his voice near a scream. 'Freeze!' he shouted, before knowing whether anyone was inside or not.

And then we both stopped as if our frame was indeed frozen.

She was standing in the center of the room. I saw her face contort in abrupt fear and confusion. A magazine fell to the floor, pages fluttering. Outside, the sound of sirens filled the superheated air, growing in tempo and volume as they approached.

She gasped, choking, and put her hand to her mouth.

'Oh, my God!' she cried. 'What is it?'

For a long moment I felt suspended, unable to respond. Martinez turned, his face marked with the struggle to comprehend. He shook his head slowly, in disbelief; his hand fell limply to his side, quivering slightly, the gun pointing downward. I rolled over onto my back listening to the sounds increase: footsteps on the stairs, car doors being slammed, sirens winding down, voices raised in mistaken urgency. I heard Christine's voice, too, struggling against thickening tears, trying to ask her question again. I breathed in great draughts of air, trying to contain my racing heart, and then all the other noises slipped away into the background, and all I could hear repeated over and over again were the killer's words:

There are no deferments.

CHAPTER SIXTEEN

Christine left the following morning.

I watched her from the bed as she packed her things into a large plaid suitcase. Her hands moved swiftly, seizing items from her bureau and the closet. I envisioned her in the operating theater moving with the same studied efficiency, the same quick, steady motions. She said little, except to wonder out loud where she might have misplaced an article. Throughout the packing she averted her eyes from mine. When she finished, she squeezed the lid of the suitcase down hard, leaning her body's weight against it. It snapped shut with two resounding clicks that filled the space between us. Then she straightened, lifted the case from the corner of the bed and set it down firmly on the floor. 'It's heavy,' she said, finally looking toward me. She managed a small smile just at the corners of her mouth, a slight turn and shape upward. She shook her head, as if to loosen the smile. 'I've got to go,' she said. 'I just can't stay now. Even the detectives said that.'

I nodded but said nothing.

She looked at her watch. 'Will you drive me to the airport?'

'Of course,' I replied. I kept my voice flat.

* * *

In my memory, the time seems to melt together. It was as if a starter's gun had fired at the first stroke of the killer's phone call and extended through a long race, first to the hospital, then to the apartment, through the rest of the night, into the dawn, directly to the moment I waved as she stepped through the gate to her waiting plane.

It had all been confusion in the apartment as the room jammed with policemen and detectives. Christine's exterior calm had shattered, and within minutes, even before she knew what had happened, she was sobbing, repeating to herself, to me, 'I knew something would happen. I just knew it.' It was minutes before I was able to explain. I sat next to her, my arm wrapped around her shoulders, trying to help her pull her emotions under control. She touched hysteria for an instant, turning to me savagely and saying, 'I told you! I told you! I knew what would happen.' I recoiled at her sudden anger, but within a moment she had slipped her head back onto my shoulder. I wondered why I was not able to comfort her better. Each minute retrieved some of her reserve, however, some of her control; and finally she relaxed and said, 'Explain carefully for me so that I know what's happened. So I understand what I'm up against. '

'What we're up against,' I corrected.

But she shook her head.

I told her about the killer's phone call and the seeming kidnap plot he'd outlined to me, then about the race across town and the second sprint to the apartment. She made me go back over the conversation, particularly the description he'd given of himself in the guise of a doctor by her disabled car.

'But he was there!' she said abruptly.

Martinez and Wilson, standing to the side, turned their heads sharply. At the same time she turned from me to the two detectives. 'I saw him. Just like he said.'

Martinez sat down next to her, notepad out. 'Carefully,' he said, 'try to remember what you saw.'

Christine took a deep breath, nodding her head. She smiled at me for an instant, then shuddered. 'My car was disabled out in the parking lot. I left work a little early, maybe a quarter to four. When I got behind the wheel, it wouldn't start. It was just dead.'

'Like he said,' I interrupted.

The detective glared at me, and Christine continued. 'I was sitting behind the wheel, swearing, cranking the engine over, pleading, the way, you know, I talk to my car when I want it to go. Then all of a sudden there was this shape by the window, and a face bent over, peering in.'

'Do you recall what he looked like?' Martinez asked. Wilson was close by, too.

She hesitated. 'Not precisely.'

'Just describe what you remember, as many details as you can recall.'

'He seemed tall, perhaps a little over six feet. Brown hair, a little long, like over the collar. But he was wearing those big mirror sunglasses, with really large lenses. He was standing with his back to the sun, too. I remember I had to hold my hand up to shield my eyes from the glare. It seemed to flow right over his shoulders. And when I could see, all I could see was myself in the reflection of the glasses.'

'What did he say?'

'He just asked me what the trouble was. He was dressed just like he told you he would be. White coat, dark slacks, a stethoscope. I thought he was someone on the staff.'

'Go on.'

For a moment she gathered her thoughts. I felt suddenly excluded. I wanted to interrupt, interject a comment, something.

'I popped the hood and started to get out of the car, but he said for me to stay behind the wheel. Then he said, "I can see the problem." I could just make out that he was fiddling with something, and then he shouted, "Try it now." I turned the ignition key and the engine started. I remember he slammed down the hood and stepped to the side all in one motion.'

'What did he say?' I blurted. The detective nodded at Christine.

'He said, "All fixed. Nice seeing you." And that was it.' She paused. 'No, he said one thing. He said, "Life is filled with mystery, isn't it?" And then he just faded away behind me.'

'Did you see a car, or where he was heading?'

'No,' she said, tossing her head back and forth. 'He just seemed to disappear into the sunlight.'

Martinez scratched a few more notes. I listened to the sound of his pencil moving against the page, irritating, like a screech of chalk against a blackboard.

'What had he done?' she asked.

'Probably the battery cable, just like he said,' the detective replied. Christine shuddered again, a long, involuntary motion up in her shoulder blades. She reached out and squeezed my hand. I wondered why the killer had passed her up. The phone call. It had been five of four when I'd looked up at the clock, listening to his voice. It's already done, he had said. He was right.

'But why was the hood of the car up when we arrived here?' the detective asked.

She looked back at him. 'It overheated in traffic. It's been doing that lately.' She turned to me. 'Remember, I asked you to fix it the other day?'

But I had not remembered.

I telephoned Nolan from Police Headquarters to fill him in on what had occurred. He was already revamping the story, incorporating the latest tape and the threats to Christine. 'It's a mess,' he said, 'and we're getting behind.' I told him what had actually taken place. 'Jesus,' he said, 'that was close.'

'I don't know,' I said.

'I don't get it.'

'Was it close? Who knows? I mean, what was he trying? Did he mean to take her and stop, or did he see something which caused him to give up, or did he just mean to scare me? He's succeeded, let me tell you.'

'I know,' Nolan said. 'How's Christine?'

'Home to the folks.'

'Where's that?'

'Madison, Wisconsin. Far enough away, I guess.'

'I hope so,' he said.

I could hear the clicking noise of the computer as Nolan took down the notes I dictated. I felt odd, a sense of violation, as I quoted Christine, knowing her words would be in the story. He kept asking for description. I was reluctant, and he had to push me before I gave in and fully detailed what I had seen.

'All right,' he said finally. 'I'll get it all in. It'll be a hodgepodge, but it's the best we can do. I'll see you in the morning. And take your phone off the hook when you get home.' Before I hung up he added, 'Oh, the byline will be yours. As usual.'

I shook my head but said nothing. I could not bring myself to say that I didn't want it, that I wanted to be divorced from the story and the killer. I didn't say it because I couldn't. It wouldn't have been true.

The police artist finally completed his sketch late that night. The two detectives sat by quietly as Christine and I talked with the artist and he put together his composite of the killer. She kept shaking her head, saying, 'It's just not quite right,' but as the shape of the cheeks, the eyebrows and the chin took form on the sketch pad, I felt the likeness was growing close. The artist drew in thick aviator glasses, which helped the effect. Christine shrugged. 'I didn't really see him. I can't really tell.'

Martinez looked over at me. I nodded.

'It's a start,' the detective said. Wilson stared at the composite for a minute before moving his hand in a fist and shaking it at the blank eyes staring out from the white sheet of paper.

I took a copy of the sketch to the office that night, late. Nolan was gone, but the night city editor was there. He looked over at Christine for an instant, admiring and studying her at the same time; then he took the sketch and went to the copy desk. They pulled a photo from the final edition and ran the picture adjacent to the story with the cutline in bold, thick, black type: HAVE YOU SEEN THIS MAN? There was an earlier edition in the newsroom, and I could see my name beneath another striking headline, but my eyes glazed over the words. They were no longer mine.

We drove home together silently. The streets had emptied of most people by now and been taken over by Miami's derelict population: drifters, old men, young men, some in on buses, some hitchhiking, others who simply materialized on the streets. Many lived underneath the thruway ramps, making huts out of discarded cardboard boxes, scraping together a few filthy possessions. They were older men covered with sores who moved silently through the darkness, looking, for the most part, toward their next drink and their next drunk. They mingled freely with the younger men, the runaways who moved south down Interstate 95, that great wide roadway that ended in the middle of Miami, all the way from Maine.

At night the two groups came out on the street. We waited at a stoplight and watched a pair of teenagers tease an old man; they had stolen a baseball hat from his head and were tossing it back and forth, just beyond his outstretched fingers, making the old man twist and pirouette trying to capture his property. 'Why do they do that?' Christine asked. I did not know. As we watched, the old man finally stumbled and fell to the ground. I could see his chest moving up and down, heaving with the exertion and probably with emphysema. The two young men looked down for a moment, then tossed the hat back to him. He did not reach out for it but remained in a heap on the sidewalk.

I saw a car stop and a window roll down. The two young men went up to it, and, after a few words, one went to the other side and disappeared through an open door. The remaining teenager stared after the disappearing lights, then wandered off into his own darkness. Our stoplight changed, and I accelerated up a ramp to the freeway.

'What was that?' Christine asked.

'A pickup,' I said. 'A chicken hawk; that's what the cops call them. An elderly homosexual picking up his date for the night.' She made a sound of distaste, and then we were silent.

At the airport they announced her flight over the loudspeaker, and she raised her hand and stroked her fingers across my cheek. 'You must be tired,' she said. 'I'm sorry it has to be like this.'

I shrugged.

'We haven't touched very much, you know,' she said.

I nodded.

'Will you call?' I asked.

'Of course.'

'Will you come back?'

She hesitated. 'I don't know.' There was a moment of quiet between us. 'Suppose he tries for you?' she said. 'Are you scared?'

'I don't think so,' I replied.

She frowned. 'No. That's the trouble. You see everything. And yet you're totally blind to what's really happening.' Tears formed at the corners of her eyes. 'I'm so sorry,' she said. She turned, seized her pocketbook, a parcel of magazines and a paperback copy of Hemingway's short stories, and firmly, quickly, walked across the gateway to the entrance to the plane. I waved, a short lift of my hand, but then thought better and stopped. She didn't turn back, anyway.

And then my thoughts returned to the killer.

At my desk that afternoon I took out all the sheets of notes I'd kept on the killer. I went through them, culling a list of traits, clues, all the efforts to try to sort out the identity of the man. I made a separate list of all those items and then stared at it.

Only Child was at the top.

Youth in Ohio. Adolescence in city.

Father, vindictive, weak. Mother, seductive, strong. Army.

Cruelty. Others followed, through the most recent conversation. I wrote at the bottom: No Deferments.

Then, one after the other, I drew lines through each entry. All the stories, all the words and sentences that had filled the columns of the newspaper, meant nothing. No more existence, no more substance. I looked down and saw I had drawn a large question mark on the page. I smiled. Appropriate, I said, but quietly so that none of the other reporters would hear me. Out of all that had happened, all that had been said, I really knew nothing. I stared at the police artist's sketch and thought back through the conversations with the killer. I remembered something he'd said early on in the killings: it was just him and me, he'd said. I understood that now.

The manager of the gun shop looked up as I walked through the door. The store was empty except for a pair of men looking at shotguns displayed in a locked glass case. The manager smiled, and I saw he was reading the *Journal*. He held out his hand. 'You know, I was just reading your latest story. I kinda had the feeling we'd see you in here. Got to be ready if he tries again, huh?'

'Right,' I said.

He rubbed his hands together. 'Don't get too many young types like you in here,' he went on. 'I mean, we get plenty of young guys, but they're not like you. Educated, is what I'm saying, whitecollar jobs. No, most of the customers your age, they're mainly construction workers, cops, an occasional fireman who likes to do some shooting. Duck hunting or maybe deer, out in the Glades. Of course, since this killer hit town, we get all types. But not like you.'

I said nothing in reply, so he continued. 'I think it's got something to do with the war, you know what I'm saying. They don't go in much for weapons. Handguns, rifles, hell, not even a good slingshot.

Just a theory, mind you, an observation. You see a lot of life from a gun shop.

'So,' he said. 'No story this time, huh? Not looking for quotes, I guess. What'll it be? How about a Magnum three fifty-seven. I think I showed you one of those before, didn't I? No? Well, should be what you're looking for.'

I shook my head.

'How about one of these?' he said, slipping an automatic from a display shelf. 'Nine-millimeter automatic. Takes a thirteen-shot clip, ejects the cartridges. This is a particularly smooth model. Never jams, or so they tell me.'

Again I shook my head. 'I want what he's got,' I said.

The gun dealer smiled. 'I should have guessed. Fight fire with fire. Make things equal, huh? Figure then, little bit of brains, little bit of luck, you can gain an edge. Good thinking.' He stooped down and pulled out a gray metal .45 from the case. 'Here it is. The basic model. This ought to stop that sucker at the door. Nothing fancy, no frills at all, just the essential weapon. Why go with something more than you need, huh? I mean, this weapon has a limited and specific purpose, right?'

'Right,' I said.

'A judge of human nature, that's what I am. You get that way when you sell guns. Got to be able to anticipate the customer's needs. What he's got in his mind. A gun is like that, you see. An extension.'

'I'll take it.'

'Whoa,' he said. 'You know about the seventy-two hours. The cooling-off time?'

'Come again?'

'You're a reporter, you ought to know. Not supposed to let anyone just buy a handgun and walk out with it. County ordinance. Show your license, pay your money and come back in seventy-two hours to get the gun. Designed to prevent you having an argument with your next-door neighbor or your wife or your brother-in-law and coming down here and buying something to blow them away. Legislature figures that in a couple of days you'll figure out another way.'

'That's a problem,' I said.

He looked across the counter, his eyes locked onto my own. 'That's what I'm thinking, too.' He leaned across and brought his head close to mine. 'Tell you what I'll do. You give me your word it never leaves here, and I'll back-date the sales slip. And you can have the weapon. I never done it before, but I figure one time I won't get caught. And I'd sure feel guilty to find out that sucker came and wasted you during the cooling-off time. Call it sympathy, huh?'

'You've got my word.' I didn't recognize my own voice.

As he rang up the sale I hefted the automatic in my hand. It seemed to fill my fist, covering every pore in the skin. It was a satisfying weight, shape, cool to the touch. I looked down at it, feeling a sense of excitement sweep out of my hand, up my arm and into my body. The killer, too, must have felt much the same thing at some time.

*   *   *

'We are responsible people,' Nolan said.

I watched as his eyes tracked across the pages and headlines, boring in on the photographs. He was sitting at a desk, looking up at our coverage of the slayings pinned to the wall of a small office.

'I simply can't see it,' he said. He leaned back in his chair, rubbing his eyes with his fingers. 'We've handled ourselves in a completely ethical fashion. Look at the stories – no screaming frontpage editorials calling for vengeance, no hate mongering, no panic inspiring. I'm trying to think where we've gone wrong. How have we instructed this guy? How have we encouraged him? Hell, the *Journal*'s been careful. Aggressive, sure, but *careful*, right up to the last stories. Would the *Times* or the *Washington Post* have handled it any differently? I don't think so. Oh, they might have made the decision to gang-bang it, sure, with a half-dozen reporters on the story, but I'd still defend the decision to stay with you alone. It kept a focus, a center. And hell, he was calling you, not the whole staff.'

He paused, thinking. 'I suppose if we'd been a Hearst paper it might have been different . . . or one of the British papers, a Fleet Street type. We could have brought in psychics and written open letters to the killer. We could have shouted *Murder*! in the headlines every day, built it up into some journalistic frenzy, like promoting a holy war. We could have run the goriest photos in full color.

'But we didn't do any of that. We remained calm – aggressive, like I said, but circumspect. We acted with all the respectability and . . . *responsibility* one would expect from this city's paper of record. No one can accuse us of leading this guy on.'

Again Nolan rubbed his eyes with his fingers. He was less talking to me than to the stories on the wall.

'You know, I even had the library pull all the paper's editorials on the Vietnam War. Just to check, to see where we were. Moderate, from the start. Initial support that faded in the late sixties to a call to bring all the troops home immediately in 1971. Also to end support of the puppet regimes. I guess we weren't first, but we sure as hell weren't last, either.'

He let out a long sigh. 'I'm getting old,' he said. 'I think this has all started to get to me.' He looked at me. 'You know, I sent my wife and kids off to visit my brother and sister-in-law, all the way to California. Two weeks ago.'

'Why?'

He frowned. 'Are you kidding? Because I was afraid. I'm in the phone book. He could decide to go after me just as easily as after Christine or anyone else.

'I suppose,' he said after a momentary pause, 'we are all vulnerable.'

And so I began to wait.

At home and at the office I stared at the telephone, willing it to ring, trying to bring the killer into grasp. I don't think I was scared; not like Wilson or Nolan, who'd sent their families away; not like Martinez, who needed to lose himself in a drink or a different girl to wrestle his thoughts away from the killer. I concentrated, trying to focus my thoughts. I fantasized a meeting, alone, some lonely place. I could see the two identical weapons jump into our hands and hear the twin explosions. In my imagination, he was always that small second slower. I saw him twist, fall, shatter under the impact. Sometimes I thought of myself as bait, bouncing along the surface of the water, hook hidden deep inside but deadly. Already dead myself.

And as the wait lengthened, I took to playing the tapes of the killer's calls, filling the air with the sound of his cold voice. Just him and me, alone.

There were no stories to write. Simply a wait.

Then the call came from O'Shaughnessy.

The ringing, as always, was like a church bell's sudden peal, and as always, I thought first of the killer, snapped on the recorder and lifted the phone with the thought: here it is; now is when it begins to end. It was as if I had only to remove him to restore myself to the world. I said nothing until I heard the voice on the other end of the phone.

'Hello? Hello?' it said. My hands loosened their grip.

'Yes,' I said. 'This is Anderson.'

'Mr. Anderson,' said the voice. 'My name is Peter O'Shaughnessy. Formerly a lieutenant in the U.S. Army.'

For a second I was unable to speak. I had assumed, after talking with the Pentagon, that the names were all lies.

'My God,' I said, 'you exist.'

He laughed. 'I should hope so. I did this morning when I woke up, and I assume I still do.'

'But I don't understand. The Pentagon told me there was no O'Shaughnessy.'

He interrupted. 'Oh, I'm not sure I'm the man you want. But the similarity in names, well, I figured I just had to call you to find out.'

'Where are you?'

'Memphis, Tennessee. I'm a lawyer. A friend of mine who lives down in Miami sent me a copy of your story, the one with my name in it. I've been sitting around for a couple of days trying to figure out whether to give you a call or not. Curious, I guess. The coincidence was just too great, and anyway, I'm not too certain there were any other O'Shaughnessys in the service when I was. It really isn't that common a name.'

'Where did you see combat?' I asked.

'Well,' he said, 'that's the really odd thing. I never did see any real shooting. Not like what this fellow describes. You see, I was in control of a section of clerks, back on the air base near Da Nang. The only combat I ever saw was an occasional rocket or mortar round that came into the compound. Sometimes you'd see the type of stuff the VC pulled on the roads – land mines, mostly – but combat, the way some of the grunts saw it? No way. I pushed paper, forms, all the stuff the Army always needs in triplicate.'

'Clerks?' I said.

'You got it. Oh, I don't know how many, probably fifty to a hundred different guys during the eighteen months I was there. All different sorts, but everybody had one thing in common.'

'Which was?'

'They were there because they wanted to avoid getting their ass shot off.'

'I don't get it,' I said.

'Well,' he replied, 'the Army would offer you a deal right before you were shipped off to some fire base in-country. Re-up – that's re-enlist for an extra year or two – and they'd send you back to division and a job with a typewriter and a filing cabinet and clean uniforms.'

'So – '

'So we were all the cowards, I guess. Scared and safe.'

He and I talked for almost an hour. His physical description, he conceded, matched the one the killer had provided. He talked about the military, about life within the barbed-wire limits of the compounds, where every so often you stared out at the streams of refugees as if the wire were a barrier that stopped your feelings just as surely as it stopped sappers. He said he never could tell whether the soldiers were trapped inside or the civilians were trapped out. I took notes rapidly, for the first time in days. His voice seemed to rejuvenate me. I felt a malevolent glee, and the thought kept going through my brain: now I've got you.

O'Shaughnessy spoke, too, of riding into the city and walking the crowded streets, shoulder to shoulder with other Americans towering over the locals.

He talked of dark bars, where the sun outside was shut away and red light reflecting off the naked skin of a nameless nude dancer was the only glow in the room. There were many stories there, he said, stories of killings, atrocities, murders, all wrapped in the guise of war; thick voices, clouded by beer or cheap scotch, speaking horrors in the gloom. 'We all heard them, you couldn't avoid it. The soldiers from the field used to drink to forget, but it's a slow process, you know? Moves in stages. And there's one point where these nightmares loosen up and tumble out, you know, like a confession. Like telling it would make it go away.'

I could see the killer there, listening to other voices, the words flitting in and taking hold in his imagination.

'You know what the damndest thing was?' O'Shaughnessy asked.

'Tell me.'

'You heard so much, and yet we were so divorced. It was so unreal. Kind of like when you wake up and you can remember the dream you just had. It's real, but then, it's not. Sometimes now I'll be sitting around, and someone will say something – a word, a tone of voice, perhaps – and some remembered conversation will come back. It's almost like feeling a ghost inside of yourself.' I could sense he was shaking his head on the other end of the line, trying to free his thoughts from his memories.

'Why do you think it affected you so much?' I asked.

He paused. 'I didn't tell you what my section of clerks was in charge of.'

'Well?'

'We processed our own dead. Names. Identifications. Making certain that the right effects accompanied the right casket. Our offices were just off a morgue, you see. Bodies on slabs, some recognizable; others, well, just all chewed up. That's why there was so much turnover in the section. It was just too macabre, too bizarre, working all day right next to all the stiffs. It was air-conditioned, you know, but I still wake up sometimes smelling death. Get sick to my stomach. Not much I can do about it; the doctors say it's all in my head, anyway. You know, that was the trouble with the war. It was always in our heads too much.'

I couldn't think of anything to say. I pictured the killer at a desk breathing in and out, slowly, all day. Getting the stench in his nostrils with every living breath.

'Have I helped?' O'Shaughnessy asked.

'More than you know,' I said.

CHAPTER SEVENTEEN

Now I've got you, you bastard.

I didn't tell anyone at first about my conversation with the Tennessee lawyer. Instead, I let my imagination whirl and dance. Visions of capture formed in my head; I felt I had suddenly jumped the huge gap between the killer and myself, that his lies would all evaporate now. I stayed at my desk, rocking back and forth in my chair. Who's the hunter now, I thought, and who's the game? I clenched my fists in exultation. Nolan saw it and wandered over from his seat at the city desk. 'Something new?' he asked. 'Something good for a change?'

I nodded and he grimaced slightly, then faded it into a smile. 'Please, for my sake, not something like the meeting fiasco. And not something dangerous.'

I shook my head. 'We've got him,' I said.

Nolan smiled and held up his hand. 'Please, not the conclusion, just the evidence.'

So I played him the conversation. He listened silently, his hand to his chin, rocking slightly forward. Then he leaned back in his chair. 'You may be right,' he said. Then he laughed, a great burst that filled the small conference room. 'Damn! This could be it.'

'It's almost over,' I said.

'Right. Call the Pentagon.'

'They'll have the names . . .'

'And we'll have the killer.' We looked at each other. 'Maybe. Suppose he's using an alias?'

'You think so?' I replied. 'You think that's his style?'

Nolan shook his head. 'No. No, it isn't.'

We stared across the table at each other, the tape recorder between us. On the walls the stories stared down, marking our days, our lives, the highs and lows.

'Let's get the son of a bitch,' he said. 'You get him, goddammit. You get him.'

The public-information officer at the Pentagon snapped his responses like so many salutes. 'Yes, sir. A list of names, sir. Can do.' I heard his pencil scratching as he took down the information. I let my voice trail off. 'Yes, sir,' he said again. 'That will be sufficient. Let me just get this straight, now. You want an accounting of the names and possible addresses of the clerks who did part of their tour of duty in Da Nang.'

'That's right.' I gave him the section and unit numbers again, just as O'Shaughnessy had provided them. I also asked the public-information officer to check out O'Shaughnessy for me.

'Roger,' he replied. 'When will you be needing this information, sir?'

'As soon as possible.'

'Take about twenty-four hours,' he said. 'But I will see to it personally, then get back to you.'

'Fine,' I said. Suddenly I felt relaxed, as if I had

all the time I needed. I'm after you now, I thought, closing in. I wanted the killer to call me so I could tell him, obliquely, make him sweat. Closing in.

In the afternoon I went to see Martinez and Wilson in the homicide offices. I followed them through the maze of desks and cubicles unchanged from previous visits. It seemed as if the same interviews were going on, the same tired voices replaying the same information. Sunlight penetrated the room awkwardly, throwing shadows into the corners and across the floor. The voices rose up through the smoky air, mingling with the strained humming of the air-conditioning system. We talked in the room set aside for the investigation of the killer. Now, in addition to the list of names, places and dates, the walls were littered with copies of the police sketch.

'Has he called you?' Wilson asked.

'Not yet,' I replied.

'He will,' Martinez said. 'He always has. Once a killer establishes a pattern like this, it's very difficult for him to break it. It's true of the worst psycho – like this guy – or the coolest contract killer. They get accustomed real fast to the system they create, their own way of doing things. They've got to stick with it, or they get no satisfaction. It's like a signature, you know; sometimes it wavers just a bit, seems a little different, but the whole thing stays pretty much the same. And this guy's pattern is to call you.'

'You don't think that last call may have been his last?'

'No. Just a guess, but I think he's beginning to wind

387

down. Maybe one of the detectives out working the street got close, you know, just asking around; maybe he's scared. But I don't think he will be able to resist talking with you again. Or killing, for that matter. He's made it too important for himself. I don't think he can go on without it; too much ego. That's why we'll catch him.'

I thought of telling them about my conversation with O'Shaughnessy. Wait, I told myself.

'You think I'm in danger?' I asked.

'Hard to say,' said Wilson. 'He may have done what he wants to do to you, what with the scare and everything. On the other hand, it could be just the start. We have to assume you're in danger.'

'That's not logical,' I said.

'Logic. Who gives a flying fuck? Certainly not this guy.' Wilson turned away and looked at the walls.

'He could have killed me a hundred times,' I said.

'Sure,' said Martinez. 'That doesn't mean there won't be a hundred-and-first.'

I shook my head. He's not after me now, I thought. I'm after him.

'You got to realize,' Martinez continued, 'that he likes to establish a personal relationship with his victims. That's why he was so frustrated by the woman and the kid, out in the Glades. She wouldn't talk. But of all the people, he's developed most of a relationship with you. Why wouldn't he kill you? And think of the headlines that murder would get.'

'I still think he needs me, that he won't try for me. Just a gut feeling.'

Wilson swore. 'A feeling that could kill you. Don't be so dumb. And don't think you can shoot it out with this freak. This isn't the Old West. That guy knows his weapons and he knows that gun.'

'Don't try to fuck with him,' Martinez cautioned. 'He'll drop you certain.'

'What makes you think . . .'

'Oh, shit,' Wilson interrupted. 'You must think we're really stupid.'

'We know about the forty-five you purchased the other day,' Martinez said. 'Get rid of it before you shoot yourself or blow your damned foot off.'

I said nothing.

'Don't even think about it,' Martinez said.

'What's next for you guys?' I asked, deflecting the subject. 'Where do you go from here?'

'Back to the streets,' Martinez said. 'With the sketches and the flyers. Something will turn up soon. A suspicious neighbor, a bartender who stares at faces, someone will recognize the picture. And then we'll start to move in. It'll happen. Take a few days, but it'll happen. Just a matter of waiting.'

'That's it?'

'That's all we're saying.'

I envisioned the final story. I could see the words materialize before me. First the hard news: the killer's identity, the capture, perhaps the shoot-out. That would segue into the path taken to the killer's door, the information provided by the Pentagon and by

O'Shaughnessy. Then it would return to the active, to a description of the final confrontation, the cornering, the running to ground.

I thought of T. S. Eliot. No whimper here, I thought. A bang all the way.

The last story. No more lies, no more half-truths, no more misstatements or misleading information. The real truth: names, places, facts, identities.

It will set everything right, I thought.

The truth.

I called Christine at her parents' home in Madison. Her mother answered the telephone, pausing when I identified myself. 'She may not be ready to speak to you,' she said, 'but I'll ask her.'

I heard voices in the background, noises, no discernible language. In another moment Christine came on the line.

'How are you?' she said.

'Good,' I replied. 'Will you come back?'

Silence. I could hear her breathing.

'Why?'

'It can be the same again.'

'And the killer?'

'It's almost over.'

'How do you know?'

'I have a lead. I know this is it.'

'And if it is, what makes you think that things will be different?'

'Christine, this is the end. I feel it.'

'Maybe for this story,' she said. 'But there'll be others.'

'Why, yes, sure, of course there will be. I mean, it's what I do – '

'It's all you do,' she said. 'They squeeze everything else out of your life. There's no room for anything else. Especially me.'

'I want you. I'll make room.'

She gasped, and I could hear her lose control, tears creeping into her voice.

'It's just not true,' she said. 'Malcolm, you know it's not. Let me ask you this: would you rather have me or break the story on the killer?'

'That's not fair.'

'Nothing is fair,' she said. 'Would you take a plane tomorrow to come get me?'

'Of course.'

'Then why don't you do it?'

'I – ' I was silent.

'See.'

'I *will*,' I broke in. 'I just can't believe you'd ask me.'

I sensed her shaking her head. 'No, don't. I'm not asking. I don't know if it would do any good. You'd just be miserable. You care more for the story than for me. You always did.'

'That's not true. You just name what you want. I'll do anything you ask. I just want you back.'

She caught her breath and laughed a little. 'I wish I could believe you. It sounds so nice.'

'Try me,' I said. I was praying she wouldn't ask.

There was a second of tension. I could feel the plastic of the telephone wet with sweat under my palm.

'No,' she said finally. 'Call me again. When it ends.'

'All right,' I said. 'When it ends.'

'If it ever does,' she added. Then she hung up.

It was late the next day when the officer at the Pentagon called back. 'Sir! I have compiled the list you requested.'

I felt an instant rush of excitement. 'How long?'

'Approximately one hundred and seventy-five names, sir. That's one-seven-five.'

'Addresses?'

'Yes, sir. But I cannot guarantee their complete accuracy. The addresses were gathered at the time of the men's service. Many factors could have altered their situation since that time. Veterans move about and often fail to notify the VA. So I cannot guarantee their authenticity, sir.'

'But the names . . .'

'Oh, that's different, sir. We kept very good records of those particular clerking sections. Had to. Didn't want any foul-ups there, if you follow my meaning, sir. Everyone who worked those details is on the list.'

'And O'Shaughnessy?'

'Lieutenant Peter O'Shaughnessy, serial number DR one-seven-one-four-three-oh-seven. His records correspond with the dates and times you gave me. Honorable discharge, 1972, March. Present address, Memphis, Tennessee.'

I felt suddenly drained. It is over, I thought. This time it really is over.

'Thank you,' I said.

'Our pleasure, sir. The list will be sent down by overnight courier.'

The list arrived in the morning. It came inside a thick manila envelope; I could see it protruding from my mail slot from several feet away. I hefted it in my hand, feeling the bulk, feeling the excitement. He's here, I thought, in the palm of my hand. I knew he hadn't bothered to change his name, that he had laughed at the idea of taking that rudimentary precaution. Why choose a new identity when he had so carefully obscured the old? And yet, left doors open. I remembered what the psychiatrist had said: he wants to be caught. Well, so be it. He set his own rules, he played by them – as I, too, had done. I tore the envelope open and without looking inside walked toward Nolan at the city desk.

He stared up from his computer terminal, frowning. For a moment his eyes met mine, questioning; then he saw the yellow envelope in my hand. He smiled.

'That's it?'

'This is it.'

I went to my desk and stared at the names on the page. At the top was Adams, Andrew S., serial number AD2985734, hometown, Lexington, Kentucky. I flipped over the sheets of paper to the last page. Zywicki, Richard, serial number CH1596483, hometown, Chester, Pennsylvania. I looked over at the corner of my desk, at the large telephone book resting there. It can't be that simple, I thought, reaching out for it.

But it was.

I stared at the name in front of me, my finger

resting, trembling slightly on a page in the Miami phone book.

It was name number forty-seven.

Dolour, Alan, serial number M131269854, hometown, Hardwick, Ohio.

And there on the phone-book page: A. Dolour. Two Twenty-four NE Seventy-eighth Street.

It's him, I thought. No doubt about it. I waved at Nolan, and he walked swiftly to my desk. Without saying anything, I pointed at the two names. His eyes went wide for a moment, and then he nodded. No smiles now, I thought, serious.

And the phone rang.

I knew it would be him. The coincidence of timing was too great for it not to be. There was something new in his voice, a tone of urgency, as if his breath were short, his chest tightened and his lungs laboring.

I punched down on the recorder and nodded at Nolan. I frantically pointed at the phone number next to the name in the telephone book. Nolan nodded and stepped to an adjacent phone.

'It's me,' he said. 'I suppose you've been waiting for my call.'

'That's right,' I said.

'What have you learned?' he asked suddenly. I thought for an instant he was talking about the list before me. 'Have you begun to understand?' he said, and I realized he was still back in the war he'd created.

'What should I have learned?'

He did not answer. I looked over at Nolan. He was

staring down at the receiver in his hand. While I watched he pulled a sheet of paper from the desk and hurriedly scrawled a note: *busy*.

'We were all caught up,' the killer said. 'We were all guilty. You. Me. Everyone.'

'And what's left?' I asked.

'Nothing. Just darkness. Evil. Death. Destruction.'

'You're going on?'

He ignored me. 'We're all sick. Diseased.'

'Are you going to kill again?' I shouted into the phone.

'I will never stop,' he said.

I gambled. 'I know who you are.'

He stopped, and I heard his breath sweep in suddenly.

'Good-bye, Anderson. Good-bye for good.'

'I know!' I said. 'Dammit, I know!'

He laughed again.

'Missing In Action. Gone, but not accounted for.'

I started to say his name, but the line went dead.

I stared at the receiver, holding it just away in front of me as if uncomprehending. Then everything happened around me all at once. Nolan was talking to Martinez and Wilson on the phone, explaining quickly, efficiently. Andrew Porter was running from the photo studio, throwing cameras over his neck, his musette bag of film and lenses swinging wildly in his wake. 'This is it! This is it!' he shouted. 'Let's go, let's go!'

Then I was on my feet, Nolan pushing alongside me, the two of us a step behind Porter, heading for the elevator bank. 'Go! Go!' he repeated. He screamed ahead, 'Hold the elevator. Goddammit, hold it!' I was swept along, as if caught in the morning riptide off the beach. 'I'm not missing this,' Nolan said as we piled into the elevator. 'Move!' he shouted at the machine, and we were plunging down, descending from our sanctuary.

The heat was like a wall outside. 'Come on! Come on!' Nolan and Porter called in unison, and again I was swept along.

The car thrust forward, engine and tires screaming angrily under Porter's abuse. We headed north on the Boulevard, cutting in and out of the afternoon flow, horn blaring.

I heard sirens in the distance.

'Boy! Adrenaline is pumping,' Porter said.

I saw the faces on the street staring at us, so many frames per second in the window as we tore northward on the Boulevard. People stopped to see what the commotion was; I saw faces turn in curiosity, in fear, in excitement. And still we raced on. Flashing blue lights appeared in the distance; the police, I thought, moving in.

'There, there!' Nolan shouted.

I saw a modest apartment building, surrounded by police cruisers and unmarked cars. As I watched, the special-weapons-and-tactics truck screeched to a halt on the opposite end of the street, quickly disgorging a squad of flak-jacketed men wearing blue jump suits and baseball caps. I recognized their automatic weapons. They were carrying M-16s, just like the ordinary foot soldier in Vietnam. 'Christ,' Nolan said. 'It looks like they're ready for World War Three.'

Porter was already out of the car, running forward, snapping off pictures the way an infantryman snaps off bursts of fire. It was a small building, perhaps four or five apartments spread over two stories. I noticed a crack in one wall and a long streak of dirt running down under the red tile roof. No lawn, just the city street and dirt. A dozen policemen and plainsclothesmen were in the entranceway, weapons out. As I watched, the SWAT team penetrated the door, weapons held ready. Time seemed to wait, holding still underneath the sun.

And then it was over.

I sensed a relaxing. The guns were being bolstered, the detectives turning and talking angrily to each other.

I walked forward with Nolan toward the crowd. Martinez was in the center. He waved me over.

'Gone,' he said.

'Where?' I asked.

'He's close,' the detective said. 'We'll get him now.'

Wilson came down the stairs and joined us. He turned to Nolan. 'Thanks for the call. But what scared him?'

For a moment I was quiet; then I said, 'It was me.' The two detectives looked at me. 'I told him I knew who he was.'

Martinez groaned and Wilson turned away.

'We could have had him easy,' Martinez said. 'You know that?'

I didn't reply.

'Well,' he continued, 'I suppose you still deserve

397

a look.' He turned and led the three of us into the building. It seemed cooler inside, and for a moment I had trouble seeing through the sudden darkness. 'Cheap,' Martinez said. 'Not much different from that place downtown.' We went up to the second floor. A SWAT member was smoking a cigarette outside the open door to one of the apartments. Martinez nodded at him and said, 'Lab crew will be here in a minute.' Then he turned to us. 'Same rules. Don't touch. Just look.' He looked over at Porter. 'Use your judgment,' he said, 'but don't fuck us up.' We stepped inside.

The apartment was small, cramped for space. In one corner there was a small stove and refrigerator, in another corner a bed with a single dirty sheet. There were clothes strewn about and a musty, unused smell. The telephone had been ripped from the wall and lay on the floor, its wires twisted and exposed. My eyes fastened on the wall.

He'd built himself a montage. In the center was the huge yellow, green and red photo-poster of the massacre at MyLai. Mushrooming out from it were dozens of other images in different sizes and shapes: Jane Fonda, General Westmoreland, Robert MacNamara, the Chicago Seven, LBJ, Daniel Ellsberg, Ho Chi Minh. Pages torn from old *Life* magazines showed soldiers slithering through swamps and paddies under fire; children, their eyes blank with despair, staring from behind barbed wire in a refugee camp. On some he'd done creative surgery: Nixon and Agnew, arms raised in victory, cradled a dead Vietnamese child. Henry Kissinger, in black tie, escorted an evening-gowned figure wearing a forlorn Vietnamese woman's head.

From ceiling to floor, the images marched, adding to the eeriness of the apartment.

I turned away and saw a tape recorder left on a small table next to the apartment's only window. Beyond that was a mirror on the wall next to the bathroom. The mirror was shattered, its center a black, gaping hole. Shards of glass were scattered about the floor.

I looked back at the table. A paperback, its spine worn and cracked, lay open next to the recorder. I looked closer. *Man's Fate* by Malraux.

Martinez saw them, too. Gingerly he picked up the paperback, after wrapping his hand with a cloth. He read for an instant, then held it out so I could see. A passage was underlined on a page close to the end.

'. . . He had seen much of death . . .' the killer had picked out. '. . . He had always thought that it is fine to die by one's own hand, a death that resembles one's life. And to die is passivity, but to kill oneself is action . . .'

Martinez and I looked at each other. We said nothing.

Wilson came over to where we were standing, and Martinez placed the book back in the space it occupied by the recorder. 'Let's see what the sucker has to say,' Wilson said. He punched the play button on the tape machine.

At first there was quiet.

Then his usual short laugh.

Then a voice: 'Hello, Anderson. Hello, detectives.'

Again the same laugh.

'You'll never catch me.'

There was a hissing and Wilson moved to shut it

off, but another sound interrupted. It was the killer humming. I recognized the tune instantly, a memory from college rallies.

He began to sing in a high-pitched, strained voice:

. . . And it's one, two, three
What are we fighting for?
. . . Don't ask me, I don't give a damn
Next stop is Vietnam.
. . . And it's five, six, seven
Open up those pearly gates.
. . . Ain't no use to wonder why
Whoopee, we're all going to . . .

But the last word was drowned by the explosion of the .45 and the shattering of the mirror's glass.

'Jesus,' Martinez said. We had all jumped at the sound of the explosion on the tape.

'That's it,' said Wilson. 'We've got an APB out on Dolour with a description. A neighbor gave us his car. White Plymouth. We should pick him up today, tonight at the latest. Where can he hide?'

I looked down and saw the capstans of the tape recorder turning in circles, continuing to run. Martinez reached out to shut the deck off, but as his hand hovered over the button, the killer's voice, even, hard, almost taunting, returned:

'Anderson . . .' He drew my name out, accenting each syllable. 'Just for you, Anderson. One more. Got it? One more.'

Martinez looked at me suddenly. 'What the hell does that mean?' said Nolan. Porter's camera swung toward me, the lens like the barrel of a pistol, shooting my reaction.

'Now, don't worry.' Martinez was calm, reassuring. 'He could mean almost anything.'

'You think he means me?' I asked.

Martinez shrugged. Wilson replied, 'So what? We've got this sucker now. We'll nail him this afternoon. You've got nothing to worry about.' Then he looked at me closely, his eyes searching my own. 'I love it,' he said. 'Seems a whole lot more real when it's you on the line, huh?'

'Look, don't worry,' Martinez said. 'We've got him. No problem.'

But he was wrong.

CHAPTER EIGHTEEN

The headline filled two decks in forty-eight-point Roman bold type:

'NUMBERS KILLER' IDENTIFIED;
POLICE MANHUNT UNDERWAY

I led the story with the hard news – the name, the address, the race through the city to the killer's apartment – and went from that to a description of the wall and the apartment. The news desk set the opening paragraphs in fourteen-pica type, spread over two columns, dominating the front page. Above the fold, next to my story, was the police sketch of the killer and a photograph, years old, transmitted by the Associated Press from Washington. The photo had been obtained by the Pentagon. I described the raid on the apartment, the tentacles of the police search, the telephone call from O'Shaughnessy, the list of names from the Pentagon. The main story jumped inside the paper to a display page with more photos: a four-column shot Porter had taken with a wide-angle lens, capturing the whole of the interior of the killer's room. The figures in the killer's mural were distinct in the background, like so many ghosts.

Nolan had paced by the side of the desk, peering over my shoulder, urging me on like a cheerleader at a football game. 'Get it all. Get it all. Don't worry about length, just get it all down. More. More.'

I did. When I pulled the last page from the typewriter platen, setting the roller spinning, I felt a burst of exultation, almost sexual excitement. My mind raced momentarily to Christine, but I hurriedly pushed the thought away.

Nolan stared at the final take.

'Dammit, there it is,' he said. 'There it all is . . . except for one thing.'

I heard the killer's voice in my head: one more.

'Should I – '

Nolan cut me off. 'No, no, we don't know, do we? What's he mean? You're the expert, I guess. What do you think?'

I shrugged.

'That's right,' Nolan said. 'Why add more fear when we don't know?' He turned away, the final page clutched in his hand.

But my stomach clenched involuntarily, cramping suddenly, as if someone had grabbed hold of the muscles and twisted them violently. I sucked in breath and rocked in my chair, feeling the color flow from my face. Dizzy, I bent over, head between my knees.

I do know, I thought.

It's me.

Nolan walked me to my car after the story had been edited and set in type. The city sounds of traffic blended with the darkness. 'You going to be OK?' he asked. 'Look, they'll get him tonight. Bet on it.'

I drove home, circling my block several times to examine the neighborhood. All seemed quiet, normal, in place. I sat in the car watching, waiting for my eyes to adjust to the nighttime. Night eyes, I thought.

I did not switch on the lights as I entered the apartment; I slipped inside the door, waiting, holding my breath, trying to feel any other presence or shape in the dark rooms. I exhaled suddenly, the small noise filling the apartment, startling me. Still in darkness, I went to the bedroom dresser and pulled the .45 from the top drawer. I slid a clip of bullets into place and snatched back the automatic's action, chambering a round. Then I slowly made my way through the apartment, checking each closet, each closed door; each an adventure, a moment of panic, a wave of relief, then a slow buildup to the next. Finally, satisfied, I turned on a few lights, barely creasing the darkness, and sat facing the front door – waiting.

I jumped when the phone rang.

Heart beating, I stood by the receiver. Once, twice, three times. I let it ring. Five. Seven. Nine. I counted until thirteen. It stopped.

Just you and me, I thought.

I did not sleep that night.

When I went into the office, Nolan was pacing the newsroom, his hands clenching into fists, then relaxing. 'Idiots,' he said. '*Idiots*.' He turned to me. 'Nothing. No sign of him. Every cop in town looking.

405

They've got a fucking photo, for Christ's sake, a description, the car, everything. What do they need, an introduction?'

'No sign?'

'Nothing.'

I felt sick again.

That morning I called a Mr. and Mrs. Raymond Dolour in Hardwick, Ohio. The first three times I rang the number, the line was busy. On the fourth try a gruff voice answered. I introduced myself carefully: 'Mr. Dolour, I'd like to talk with you about your son.'

'I have no son,' he replied. The phone crashed as he slammed it down.

Nolan was torn; we had to send someone; he wanted to know if I wanted to go knock on their door. 'It's your story,' he said. 'But we haven't written the ending here.'

For a moment I thought of going. It would be safe, I thought. No fear there. I felt the tension within me: personal safety versus what? I couldn't put a word to it. 'No,' I told him, 'I'll stay here.' Another reporter was dispatched.

I couldn't bring myself to read her story.

That afternoon, the city police chief went on all three local stations to make a plea to the killer to give himself up. The chief said it was only a matter of time before he was spotted. 'If you're out there watching,' he said, staring into the television camera, unblinking, frowning, 'give yourself up. Save yourself. Let's try to avoid any further bloodshed.'

Nolan roared with laughter, and I joined him. We had a bank of televisions in the newsroom, and the chief came across like so many mirrored images. 'I love a good cliché,' Nolan said. 'Just like some crime-busters show from the fifties.'

Still, there was no sign of the killer.

MANHUNT FOR KILLER CONTINUES; POLICE NOOSE TIGHT AROUND CITY. 'Where the hell is he?' Nolan asked. I can't believe they can't find this guy.' He continued to stomp around the newsroom, his attention focused solely on the police search, delegating all responsibility for other stories to subeditors. I waited for him, my own apprehension taking shape.

I rode with Martinez and Wilson, sitting in the rear of their unmarked cruiser, the three of us leaning forward, staring out through the windows at the faces on the street, absorbing them, then rejecting them quickly. I wrote that story; the details of the search, the locations checked and discarded, the suspects interviewed, examined and released.

On the third day a security guard at the University of Miami found the white Plymouth. The plates had been changed; a quick check showed they were stolen. A list of all the reported stolen cars during the three days of the killer's disappearance was circulated to detectives. They staked out the bus station, the airport, the train station. Extra personnel were brought in; overtime mounted. I documented all of it in the following day's story.

The city seemed to fill with rumors: he'd grabbed a private plane or boat and headed out of town undetected. He was spotted in Key West one instant, in Fort Lauderdale the next. Some people thought he'd taken a family hostage and was waiting in suburban quiet for the attention to fade, and then would slip through the city, walk calmly away.

On the fifth day I collected all the rumors into another story. It ran on page one under the headline: WHERE IS HE?

'That's right,' Nolan said. 'Just where the hell is he?'

In the cruiser one afternoon, Wilson turned to me. 'You still got that illegal forty-five?'

I nodded.

'Good,' he said.

'Why?' I felt my stomach tighten again.

'I don't know. I got a bad feeling about this.'

'Shut the fuck up,' Martinez said. 'Pay no attention,' he said to me, accelerating the car down the street. 'He's out there trying to keep his own ass safe. No way he's worrying about yours. It'd be ridiculous to think he was looking for you. No matter what he said.' Martinez glared at Wilson, but his partner just snorted and said nothing. Ridiculous, I thought. I remembered when I had heard that word before.

I slept fitfully, if at all, the .45 next to the bed.

More often, I would fall asleep in the living room in a chair facing the door. The night noises seemed to penetrate even my sleep; I would awaken, startled, eyes suddenly wide open, at the smallest sound. I could feel my heart straining, muscles stretched and bursting. I waited.

The detectives grew surly and morose with the failure; their tempers shortened with each passing hour. Nolan, too, took the delay personally, as if it were an affront. I spent as much time as possible with the detectives, watching Wilson idly polish the blue metal of his service revolver as Martinez chauffeured the cruiser down another empty street. 'I'm not going to call in the SWAT boys,' Wilson said under his breath. 'This sucker's mine. I'm going to take him out myself.'

Martinez kept quiet. Once, he turned to me: 'You shouldn't have told him. It could have been easy.'

I shrugged. I kept my own weapon in the car whenever I drove anywhere. When I went home I entered the apartment, gun held out in front of me. Safety off.

On the seventh day after the killer's disappearance, he called.

The phone rang; I followed my routine, snapping on the recorder, seizing pencil and notepaper. Still, I was taken aback when I heard his familiar voice. He was laughing.

'I told you,' he said. No introduction.

I fought off the urge to hang up, to hide.

'Where – '

He interrupted. 'Not so fast.'

'You can't get away,' I said. 'Why don't you give yourself up?'

He laughed again.

'It's time, Anderson.'

I choked out the word: 'No!'

His laughter seemed an echo across the line.

'Anderson,' he said slowly, 'good luck.'

'What?' But I was talking to an empty line.

Emotions wrapped around my throat. I did not know what to do. I shut off the tape and peered across the newsroom to Nolan. I thought of the detectives. I pictured: NEWSMAN GETS KILLER'S PHONE CALL. But what had he said? What did it mean? The two of us. Luck? In the back of my mind I realized a panic was trying to break through; I fought to deny it. No, he wasn't going to come for me. And if he did? The two of us. It had to be the two of us. I swallowed hard, took the tape out of the machine and dropped it into the top drawer of my desk.

'Anything new?' Nolan asked later.

I shook my head.

'He's got to be somewhere,' he said.

'He's out there,' I replied.

That night the heat in the apartment seemed heavy, uncontrollable. I sat in the chair, fingering the gun. The phone rang once; Christine? My hand reached out for the receiver, then pulled back. I couldn't be sure. At midnight I dozed, half-awake. The sound on the steps outside the apartment penetrated through the demi-sleep; for a moment I struggled, trying to pull myself to alertness. The sound increased; a scraping, footsteps. I was awake. My eyes fixed straight ahead.

The sound hesitated outside the apartment.

It's him, I thought.

There was silence. No motion, no noise.

I breathed in quietly. Held it in.

Still no sound.

Get ready, I thought.

I brought the automatic up to eye height. I leveled it at the door. My ears were electric, alive for sound.

I heard a hand close on the door handle.

I fired.

The roar of the .45 seemed immense; the force of the thrust threw me back against the chair. My nostrils filled with cordite and smoke. For a second it was as if I had been knocked out; my reactions seemed slowed, awkward. Then the noise faded, my ears no longer rang. I jumped across the room, my eyes fastened on the black, shattered hole in the door. I seized the handle and swung the door open quickly, crouching at the same time, the .45 ready to fire again.

And nothing.

For an instant I was confused. Where? I thought. Where's the body? Where is he? I saw a bullet hole in the plaster across from the door. But someone was there, I said out loud. I heard him. He was there. I spun and ran down the stairs, out into the night. The street was empty. 'I know you're here!' I shouted.

A voice behind me said, 'Where?'

I spun, rocketing the .45 up into position. But I did not pull the trigger.

'Jesus Christ, man! Watch what you're doing!' It was one of the neighbors, in pajamas, hold-ing a baseball bat. He stared at me. I was aware of lights clicking on, of other voices coming into my hearing. 'Are you OK?' he asked. 'Was he there?'

'I'm OK,' I said. But I didn't believe it.

CHAPTER NINETEEN

The letter arrived the next day, the eighth day after the killer disappeared.

It was the same common notepaper, the envelope without a return address. When I picked it up, I knew there was only a single sheet inside. I looked at the postmark, Miami, but the rest was blurred. My name was printed carefully on the outside, in large black letters. I waited until I was back at my desk to open it. Nolan was on the phone, his back to me. I tore it open carefully. The lettering inside was the same.

ANDERSON:

Here's a quote for you.

Sometimes it is as reasonable to represent one kind of imprisonment by another, as it is to represent anything that really exists by that which exists not.

Think about it. And here's a message for you.

Don't believe everything you see.

Got that? And here's the most important thing.

I'm alive.

It was not signed.

I do not know why I did not show the letter to Nolan or to the police; it went into the top drawer

413

of my desk, locked, with the last tape recording. I know it seems odd; I could have built a story around the letter the same as around the tape. It would have underscored, for all to see, the relationship between the killer and me; it would have been another detail, crucial, perhaps, for the readers to note, another brushstroke in the portrait painted over the course of that summer. I sat, thinking there were dozens of reasons to show the letter, to publicize it. But I did not.

I'm alive.

What is it I'm not to believe?

The answer was five days off.

I had fallen back on writing updates on the police search – eight to ten paragraphs reporting that there was nothing new to report. I went out and talked with the psychiatrist again. I tried to call the victims' families, but none would speak to me. I did the man-in-the-street interviews. The reactions were pretty much the same: a quickened tension waiting for an arrest, coupled with relief that the killer had a name, a picture and a past. One woman said, 'It's only a matter of time.' She smiled at me. 'But I think he's gone, long gone. To California, probably.' I didn't ask her why that particular state.

Some information began to come in about the killer. His Army record: unexceptional. Attendance at state schools in Illinois and Ohio. He never stood out; his teachers could remember nothing. I tried to find someone who knew him. No success. The same with the neighbors of the apartment house where

414

he'd lived. He kept to himself, they said. I could have guessed their words. But even the lack of information was part of the story – people able to say they didn't know the killer were as quotable as someone who did. The desk liked that story. They stripped it across the bottom of page one, below the fold.

Nolan took the call at the city desk.

He swiveled in his chair, raising his arm above his head, gathering my attention and waving for me to join him.

It was September then, August melting away; more heat, more storms out in the Caribbean blowing up hard and taking wild runs at the islands. The hurricane season still had more than a month to go; some of the newsroom elders talked about the late storms that seemed to bide their time through the oppressive summer and then, as the weather gave signs of shifting, formed and charged across the waters. Still, the heat dominated, the city shuddering under the scorched air. I slept little; since the night I'd heard the hand on my door I'd taken to lying awake until early morning. The gun remained close; I could not make up my mind what I'd heard on the steps outside. Martinez and Wilson had stared at the shattered door and shaken their heads in unison. 'It's close,' Wilson had said to me. 'It's real close in here, isn't it?' I hadn't understood what he was driving at.

I punched Nolan's line on the telephone and picked it up, Nolan gestured frantically: I was to speak. 'Yes?' I said.

'This Anderson? The reporter?' The voice was tinged with a southern accent.

'Right.

'I got a letter for you,' the man said. 'Found it this morning in one of my boats. Right on the seat, mind you, in plain sight. Shit, I'd been looking for that damn boat for nearly three days. Finally catch up wi' it, and there's this damn letter. You want me to open it?'

'Yes.' I looked over at Nolan and shrugged. He was bent over the desk, hanging on the words.

'Shit,' said the man. 'Don't say much.'

'What?'

'It says, lemme see, just this: "I'm out here waiting." That's it. No signature, nothing else. Seems pretty strange to me.'

I stared over at Nolan. His eyes had widened and they locked in on my own. He pushed back in his chair, his face alight with excitement, and shot a hand up in the air, as if in victory. 'This is it!' Nolan said, 'Goddammit, this is it!'

Nolan's clenched fist waved in the air.

The city slipped behind us in a haze of heat and sunlight. Porter drove; Nolan sat in the back seat, staring out the window, a small smile on his face. I watched the highway unfold through the scrub brush and weeds toward the west as we cut through the great Everglades expanse of swamp and water. 'You know, he could hide out here for months if he wanted to,' Porter said. 'I used to go bass fishing out here. Got lost once. I remember night was dropping awfully fast and the sky was all purple. I could see gators in the water and some water moccasins. I thought I was going to die; there was nobody. I was so alone, I had this crazy thought that there was no more civilization, that I was abandoned. The rangers found me around midnight. It wasn't cold, but I was shaking. If he's been out here, no wonder no one's found him.'

'We still haven't found him,' Nolan said. 'You think he plans to shoot it out?'

I didn't answer. Porter shrugged. 'Maybe,' he said. 'Look!' He bent down and pointed through the windshield. A police helicopter plowed through the air above us, the rotors filling the car with noise, shaking us. Porter accelerated, pushing the car faster.

An hour out we turned off the expressway and started down a two-lane side road, the big car rocking on the bumps and potholes. The huge cypress trees and palms reached out over the highway; we cut between the mottled colors and shadows. I could see the pale blue of the sky high above the treetops, vanishing, it seemed, in an expanse of white light. My eye caught a hawk circling slowly in the distance. He floated above the earth, turning with the small wind, as if suspended invisibly like a mobile. Then, just before we passed out of sight, the bird rose suddenly, its wings shooting up over its body, and plunged downward toward some sighted prey. I imagined its shriek of murder as it fell from the clear sky into the shadows.

We pushed on.

Up ahead I saw a clearing, a few shacks strung out against the edge of the swamp, adorned with crude hand-painted signs advertising beer, bait and boats for hire. Behind the shacks I could see a few fishing skiffs pulled up on the shore and a pair of airboats idled, high and dry. 'That's got to be it!' Nolan said.

On the far edge, closing quickly as Porter mashed down on the accelerator again, were the familiar flashing blue lights of police cruisers. Another helicopter passed overhead, the pressure from the blades seeming to drive us down into the ground. I ducked involuntarily.

'Christ,' Porter exclaimed under his breath, 'they've got a fucking army.'

Squads of jump-suited SWAT members from two huge blue buses milled about outside. Most of them were checking their weapons and ammunition. Off to the side I saw the medical examiner's truck. They're expecting bodies, I thought. A roadblock had been set up, and the car jammed to a halt outside it. Porter was loading quickly, grabbing his cameras and bag. Nolan leaped out of the car, and I followed quickly behind. The heat wrapped my body like a noose.

Another chopper swept overhead, kicking up dust. I shielded my face and saw Martinez and Wilson down by the boats, talking with a weathered old man. The postman, I thought.

The two detectives waved us through. Martinez thrust a piece of paper at me. I saw the block printing, the same as the other. 'Look familiar?' he asked.

'That's it.'

'Stay close,' the detective said. 'It's going to get exciting.'

We waited with the old man in one of the shacks. A tired air conditioner stirred the air feebly, making a tortured beating sound. He said he'd discovered one of his boats missing several days back; gone out looking for it, without success. It had turned up a few days later with the letter on the seat in a protective plastic bag. 'Damndest thing,' he said. 'I was certain I'd looked in that spot before. Damn if I can figure it out.'

He's gone back to the jungle, I thought. The jungle he was scared to fight in before.

'Can he last in there?' Nolan asked.

'Shit, if he wants to,' the man replied. 'It ain't nice, though.'

I waited. My mind filled with images from the war: mud, sun, blood and death. This is it, I thought. Nolan spoke the same words out loud: 'This is what I expected. This is it.'

One hour passed. Two. We continued to wait. The policemen went out in teams; I heard their radios crackling with static as they coordinated their positions with the circling and buzzing helicopters.

Another thirty minutes. The old man said, 'Shit, they ain't never gonna get this buck.'

A sudden shift: I heard a cop yell back at a resting SWAT squad, 'It's him!' Men leaped up, slapping at weapons. Porter was swearing hard and fast. 'I've got to get out there; damn, I've got to get my shot.' Nolan grabbed hold of my arm, not to hold me back but to steady himself.

And then, just as at the killer's apartment, a relaxing.

'What's going on?' Nolan asked. There was no response.

I tried to ask some of the cops, but they shook their heads. Martinez and Wilson were gone. So was the medical examiner. We waited again, by the swamp's edge. Another thirty minutes. Time seemed stretched like leather, cracking, not elastic.

I saw a boat with two uniformed officers head into the shoreline. Their jump suits were blackened with sweat and mud. One of them looked at us and steered the small outboard toward us. 'You Anderson?' he shouted from a few feet away.

I nodded.

'Get in. The detectives want you out there. The body is about a half-mile in.'

'Body?' Nolan asked.

The policeman didn't respond. He restarted the engine. The three of us crowded into the front; the metal seats were scalding.

'I can't figure it out,' the cop said as he turned the boat. 'He couldn't have swum from where he put the boat to where he is now.' He maneuvered the skiff past a mass of weeds and logs. A flight of egrets rose up to my right. I remembered the killer's description of his fourth victim, the woman at the edge of the Glades. We were much farther in, much more hidden. 'You see,' the cop continued, 'you can't really swim through this shit. Weeds grab you, drown you. Snakes can kill you. Alligators, hey, look there!' I swiveled and caught sight of a six-foot gator sliding through the brush. 'How'd you like to tangle with that sucker in the dark, huh? Not likely.' Porter snapped off pictures.

We rounded a corner in the small channel, and I

saw a humpbacked rise in the water, a slight island of mud and bushes. A few more uniformed policemen stood on the edge, but in the center were Martinez and Wilson bending over alongside the medical examiner. I could not see what they were focused on. 'Chopper spotted it,' the cop said. 'You'd never see anything from the water, not even if you was next to it.' The boat grounded itself on the mud. 'End of the line.' I stepped out and sank down more than an inch into the marsh. Martinez waved us over.

I was unaware of the stench until we were almost on top of the body; a small turn in the breeze brought the smell sweeping over us. For a second I thought I would gag; then the feeling passed, and we were left with the horrid sweet stench of death. I thought for an instant of the house on Miami Beach. Wilson saw the effect of the smell on my face and said something to the medical examiner. The two of them laughed. I did not catch the joke.

Martinez spoke first. 'Take a look,' he said.

The medical examiner was lighting his pipe, eyes following my movements.

'Look at what?'

'Right here,' Wilson said. He pointed down at his feet. 'Not pretty.'

I stepped over to the three men and stared down at the shape on the ground.

At first it was hard to tell that it had been a man. The flesh had grown pasty, white, like fish left in an oven hours too long. The eyes were open, but the sockets were empty, the eyeballs gone. The skin seemed pulled tight, cracked and fidged, and burned brown at the edges by the sun. The lower half of the man's face was gone; a few jagged white bones protruded where the jaw should have been. The top of the skull had been blown out. I turned away, nauseous.

'Keep looking,' Wilson said.

I took a deep breath and looked down again. The body was wearing Army jungle boots of canvas and rubber. His jeans had faded like his life under the hard sun. There were rivulets of dried blood on his chest, streaking a white T-shirt. 'What am I supposed to see?' I asked.

Martinez pointed, and I saw the gun. The gray metal .45 caught the sun for an instant, and the light refracted, spinning, into the brown and green undergrowth. The automatic rested a few inches from an outreached hand, as if half-dropped, half-tossed in the moment of death.

'So,' Wilson said. 'Seen enough?'

I nodded.

'Then,' he said, suddenly quiet, 'who is it?'

For a moment I was confused. I shook my head. 'You know,' I said.

'You tell me,' Wilson replied.

But I remained silent. I looked down again at the features ravaged by the gunshot and the sun. Who is it? I thought to myself.

Martinez stepped beside me and motioned to Nolan to join us. 'We need an identification,' he said, 'to make it official. To be certain.'

Nolan spoke before I had a chance. 'What the hell do you mean?' His voice was angry. It carried over the stillness of the Glades. 'There's the gun. Hair color. Physical size. It's all right there. Check his fingerprints, for Christ's sake. What about teeth? The Army must have dental records, you know?'

The medical examiner joined the conversation, pulling on his pipe stem, releasing clouds of smoke into the breeze to be carried across the marshes. 'No good,' he said.

'Explain "no good" to me,' Nolan said.

'All right.' His voice was steady, a lecture suited better to a classroom. 'Number one: too much decomposition of the skin for fingerprints. Impossible with all the stretching and loss of tissue consistency and integrity to get an accurate print, so that method's out right away. Number two: eye color. It would be a help to check against Army records, but the local birds have taken care of that for us. Let's move on to another method: teeth impressions. Great. Records available from the Army almost instantly. Only trouble is this guy must have been anticipating that, or else he was just lucky. He put the gun against his chin and pulled the trigger. Blew the mouth all to hell but left a bunch of the face intact. Other identifying marks or scars? That would be the next step sure, but the Army records say the killer had none. So we're down to one last method of identification: personal observation. Oh, the gun will turn out to be the killer's, of course, but that doesn't prove anything. Is it him? He's been out here a number of days. Hard to tell precisely. At least three, more likely five, possibly a week. Wouldn't even count on his mother recognizing him now.'

The medical examiner held up his hand to cut off the obvious question.

'Yes, she's been contacted. Refuses. Hasn't seen her boy since the war. But that was in your paper already.'

He paused, looking at me. 'See the dilemma?'

I thought of the letter in the top drawer of my desk. How close, I wondered?

'So many factors aid in the decomposition of a body,' the medical examiner went on. 'Sun alternates with rain. Humidity. You know, out here, it can rain like the dickens a half-mile away, but this area stays dry. Just no scientific way to determine absolutely the length of time. There was a body once we knew positively had been dumped out here, not too far away. Contract killing. We got the shooter. By the time we got to the body, it was virtually a skeleton, picked clean. One week. Lots of factors.'

I'm alive, I thought. Don't believe everything you see.

Wilson interrupted. 'You see, we got to be positive. You got the best look at him, in that apartment. Is this the man you met there, the man in the wheelchair?'

I hesitated. 'I don't know.'

Wilson exploded. 'Look, goddammit! Look! Look at the face! The cheeks, the nose, the ears, the eyebrows! Is it him? We have to know. Not later; right now! Is it him?'

I stared again at the features, breathing in hard and holding it. Nolan grasped my arm, turning me toward him, but I kept my eyes on the torn face. 'It's important,' he said. 'They're right. It's important. Look,' he whispered into my ear, 'this has been our story from the very start. No one else's. We have to write the end to it. If we don't write that it's him, then no one will ever know, no one will ever be certain. It's not just an identification, it's the whole city, the whole mood. We can't waffle. We can't be unsure. It doesn't matter one damn bit what anyone else says, just what we say. We're the only paper anyone will believe on this.' I could feel his own eyes marking me, measuring me. 'Look again,' he said. 'We have to be sure. Is it him?'

'Is it him?' That was Wilson. He was standing over the body, shaking his fist first at me, then down at the inert form slowly melting into the earth and air. 'Is it him?'

I looked over at Wilson, then to Martinez and the medical examiner. I saw the ME slip a photo from his pocket and bend over the corpse. He stared hard for a moment, shook his head, shrugged and turned to me. Nolan, too, was watching me. Porter hung to the side, his camera whirring. Then he, too, stopped, waiting for my answer.

'Is it him?' Nolan asked again.

I forced myself to stare into the sightless eye sockets.

The sunlight seemed to spiral down, freezing everyone in a blast of heat and brightness. I felt the warmth on my scalp, boring into my brain. Images jostled and elbowed for space in my mind. I saw the killer's grin as he peered through the smoke and shadows of the darkened apartment, his fingers drumming against his wheelchair prop. I imagined him leaning over the window, staring at Christine. I saw the victims as if in array: the teenage child, the elderly couple,

425

the young woman and her crying child. I searched around me, my eyes sliding over the surrounding marsh and trees. I thought of the war; the morgue by the runway. The killer's words came back again: the two of us, him and me. I thought of the letter in the drawer. Is it him? Don't believe everything you see. But what was I seeing?

My mind produced an instant's scenario: a picture from the night he'd played his charade of murder with Christine. I imagined the young men on Miami's ill-lit downtown streets, aimless, nameless, abandoned. The casual pickup, I thought. How easy it would have been for him to cruise the streets, looking for a surrogate, searching for the proper height, build, the same common brown hair. A stop, a quick hand motion, perhaps the flash of money, and his victim would be seated in a car, unknowing, unafraid. Drive west, deep into the Glades. Steal a boat. Out to the rise. Place the gun against the victim's chin and pull the trigger. Toss it down by his hand; the apparent suicide. I remember the lost boat, the carefully prepared note to summon me, the cop who drove me to the rise. He didn't swim out here, he said. Perhaps two came out and one went back, melting away into the darkness, searching for another city, another identity.

I looked at the corpse on the ground. Was it him? I looked closer. Was it an imposter? Was this another lie, another fiction? Possible. Everything was possible. I looked at the body.

No, I thought, it's him.

I looked again.

No, it isn't. It's someone else.

No. Yes.

Who is it?

Nolan was at my side, his voice soft, yet insistent: 'We have to know for certain. No doubts, no maybes. The city has to know, has to be freed once and for all. That means it's up to you. It has been from the start. Is it him?'

Wilson burst out, anger flowing from the air: 'Stop jacking around,' he yelled. 'Come on! Is it him?'

I thought of Christine, of my father, of my uncle and his flag-draped casket. The sun seemed like a pendulum, swinging in the wind, moving inexorably closer to me.

'Is it him?' I heard the voice but did not know who spoke.

And so I lied.

'Yes,' I said. 'It's him.'

CHAPTER TWENTY

My lie expanded, took root and flowered. The morning headline jumped at the city:

'NUMBERS KILLER' A SUICIDE;
CORPSE FOUND IN GLADES.

One of the news-desk editors told me it was the largest type they'd used since the President's resignation and, before that, the walk on the moon.

It was the last story, a rushing forth of all the other stories. I'd worked the telephones the evening before, following the long drive back from the rise in the swamp. This time the victims' families had talked; I'd collected quotes and reactions to blend into a description of their feelings. Nolan had pulled the best quotes out of the story and had them set in a bold, black-lined box which ran in the center of the inside jump page. 'It's a relief,' one person said, 'to know it's over.'

But was it?

As I strung all the impressions of the day, all the assembled voices and facts together into the mainbar and sidebars, I came to believe that my doubt was unfounded. As I talked and as I bent over the typewriter keyboard, I searched the ravaged features in my mind, measuring, contrasting, matching the ears, eyebrows, nose and cheeks with the shadowy figure I'd seen in the dirty apartment. In my mind's eye I overlaid the features against the sketch the police artist had drawn, then against the photo provided by the Army. I clenched my teeth; dammit, it's him.

I'm alive.

Don't believe.

When no one was looking, I reached into the top drawer and slipped out the letter. I stared down hard at the words, trying to force them into clarity. A final lie? After so many conversations, so many twists of his imagination, turns of his plot, I still did not know what the truth was. Nolan had been ecstatic, reading the story as it marched through the typewriter. 'This is it!' he'd said, waving a sheet of copy covered with words. 'This is the story. It's all right here.' He'd fed the pages into the computer scanning equipment himself, shaking off the copy aides and assistant editors. He's wrong, I thought. It's never all there. But that thought hadn't stopped me from continuing, from massaging the lie into the story, making it beat like a drum inside every paragraph, sentence, word and phrase. For an instant, as I wrapped the end tight – a final description of the murder weapon catching the sunlight – I imagined the killer reading the story. I could see him smile, then fade into whatever oblivion he had selected for himself: officially declared dead and forgotten on the front page of the *Journal*.

I shook my head to clear the image. No, I thought, the body I saw was the killer.

Nolan was hunched over the video screens, absorbed. For the moment I was ignored. I looked again at the letter.

No. He went out there alone, to die alone, never discovered, a final gesture of mystery and confusion. That would be like him. Enigmatic, especially at the end.

But.

The word hung in my consciousness. I fought the rush of possibilities. I took a page of copy paper and listed the factors:

It's time, he had said. Time for what?

I'm alive. Well, he had been, when he wrote it.

Everything you see. But had he counted on me seeing his body?

The note on the boat. *I'm waiting.* And there he was. Dead.

Or was he? How did the boat get back to shore, away from the body's location? Did he put it there?

I wanted to scream: I just don't know.

And then I shuddered hard.

I would never know.

My eye caught the telephone on the corner of the desk. The wires running to the tape machine were tangled around the receiver. I thought: ring, dammit. Tell me the truth. Whatever it is.

But it remained inert. Suddenly, after so many weeks, silent, dead.

Christine wrote: 'I am not coming back to Miami. What we had is lost. It sounds trite and corny, doesn't

431

it? I wish I could express myself better, but if I had been able to, maybe this wouldn't have happened. I'm sorry it has to end this way. Or any way, for that matter. But it has to.'

I packed some things she had left behind and sent them to her home in Wisconsin.

Nolan wanted to get drunk after the story had been sent to the composing room. He called back to the photo department to collect Porter and escorted us to a nearby bar. He said we would get pleasantly drunk, then go back and catch the edition as it came off the presses. The voices in the dark bar flooded over me as I walked through the door. Most were from the paper; most were talking about the story. A few turned and nodded, waved or clapped me on the back. They wanted to buy me drinks in celebration. I took a glass of beer from one offered hand, feeling the release in the room. I raised my glass and there were cheers. Nolan swallowed a scotch and added a quick beer. He maneuvered the three of us into a corner booth, waved for more drinks and leaned back against the seat. 'What a story,' he said. 'Jesus H. Christ. What a story. Can you believe it?'

Porter sipped on his drink and lowered his head toward the table. A small smile slid across his face, and he shook his head slowly. 'I've been thinking,' he said. 'What was it, really?'

Nolan looked quizzically at him.

'I mean,' Porter continued, 'a man kills four people

and calls the paper to tell us about it. Is that such a helluva story?'

'I don't follow,' Nolan said.

Porter went on. 'There've been so many other killers a whole lot worse. Speck in Chicago . . . the guy in the tower in Texas . . . what about Leopold and Loeb? The crime of the century, they called it. And the Lindbergh kidnapping – that was the crime of the century for a while, too.' He took a cautious amount from his glass.

'What are you driving at?' Nolan asked.

'It was just a story. There'll be another tomorrow.'

Nolan thought for a moment. 'That's true, but it's always been that way. It doesn't diminish the moment. That's what journalism is – a celebration of the instant. No past, no future, no history, no vision. Now is what's important.' Nolan threw back his head and laughed. Some of the others at the bar turned to look, then turned back to their drinks. He pointed a finger at Porter. 'Still, it was a helluva story.'

And Porter joined in, laughing long and hard himself.

'I agree,' he said, raising his glass in mock toast, 'even if it means contradicting myself.'

The next day Nolan told me to take a vacation. I deserved it, he said. He told me to fly to Wisconsin and bring Christine back. I shook my head. 'Another story,' I said, 'just another story.'

He was slow to respond, his eyes searching my own. 'Only if you really want it.'

'I really do.'

433

'All right. Up in the Panhandle. There's been a resurgence of Klan activity up there. They've been burning crosses, holding marches, generally making life a pain. How about a piece on the new nightriders, that sort of thing?'

'I'll go Monday,' I said.

'Suit yourself,' he replied, turning toward the city desk.

I went back to my desk and once again pulled out the letter from the killer.

One more, he'd said.

I'd thought it was me. Was it him?

Missing in Action.

My mind swirled with possibilities again. Then, making certain no one saw me, I tore the letter into small pieces and tossed it into the wastebasket.

At noontime I left the office to walk the streets. Big thunderheads were forming over the west out over the Glades, and I felt a steady breeze hitting the city from that direction. I figured an hour or two at the most before the storm hit the city, sheets of rain riding the air currents. I looked at people's faces, trying to discern some difference, but I was unable to detect any emotion, any memory. All that had seemed so obvious so recently had slipped away. Had I imagined everything? All the fears? What had happened?

That weekend I flew to New Jersey to see my uncle's grave. It was beginning to turn from Indian summer to real fall. The change in seasons showed on the edge of the leaves, rolling up, browning slowly with age.

I rolled the window down as my father drove me toward the cemetery and felt the wind in my face. It was cool, unfamiliar, intoxicating.

At the gravesite there were flowers, freshly picked. I wondered where they had come from. My father stood next to me, looking down. After a moment he spoke matter-of-factly. 'I tried to tell him, years ago. The war is over, I said to him; let's get on with it. But he never really adjusted. Sometimes events are simply too powerful for the mind to comprehend, sort out and put away. Most of us adjust and grow old with indifference, but for some the memories just won't let go. Some people get choked by their memories. Like your uncle.'

He caught my eye. 'And you?'

'I should have gone,' I said.

'What? To war? To that godforsaken little country to get killed for no reason other than stupidity?' He was angry. 'You would have been worse than him. Crippled more than by any bullet.'

He was silent for a minute.

'There are two types of wounds,' he said, finality tinging his voice. 'Some heal. Some never do. You make your own choice which you'll have.'

We drove home without speaking.

I have not heard from the killer again.

Sometimes, when things in the newsroom are slow, I go back to the morgue and pull the file marked NUMBERS KILLER, July–September 1975. I spread the mass of words that mark the biggest story of my life on the desk before me, my eyes searching through the columns of newsprint for the clue, the statement, the forgotten phrase that will answer the question that persists in my mind. But it remains a mystery. Nolan likes to point out, after a few drinks, that it was all luck that broke the case; that the hours we spent and the police spent, and all the fears and frustrations of the people of the city, were all useless in cracking the killer's game. I wonder, though, if that wasn't how the killer meant it to play.

Sometimes I see the story of another murderer or of an inexplicable killing in another city or another state, and it causes me to pause and wonder. Sometimes faces leap out at me; I find my imagination comparing the features in front of me with those I saw decomposing under the harsh sun. Often when the telephone on my desk rings, I hesitate before reaching out, wondering whether this will be the time the familiar voice blows cold through the earpiece. I think, too, that it was my lie that set the city free from the same fears, the same doubts.

And for that, I suppose, I take some comfort.

THE
SHADOW MAN

No novel ever gets finished without some assistance. Sometimes this help is technical, as in the readers who review early drafts of the manuscript and point out all the mistakes one has made. Sometimes it is less tangible, but equally important. (The children who leave you alone when they'd much rather you came out and shot baskets with them.) To complete this book, I was greatly aided by my friends Jack Rosenthal, David Kaplan and Janet Rifkin, Harley and Sherry Tropin, all of whom contributed comments that improved the final version.

There are many extraordinary books about the Holocaust, each more heart-breaking, more frustrating, more astonishing than the next. I do not intend to list all that I examined, but there is one work that I think worth mentioning. When I first started to nurture the seeds of ideas that ultimately became this novel, the late Howard Simons at Harvard University gave me his copy of a remarkable work of nonfiction: *The Last Jews In Berlin* by Leonard Gross. Those interested in learning about true resourcefulness and bravery would be wise to examine it.

As always, my greatest debt is to my family, so it is to Justine, Nick, and Maddy that this book is dedicated.

History, Stephen said, is a nightmare
from which I'm trying to awake . . .

James Joyce, *Ulysses*

CHAPTER ONE
An Interrupted Death

Early in the evening on what promised to be an oppressively hot midsummer night on Miami Beach, Simon Winter, an old man who had spent years in the profession of death, decided it was time to kill himself. Regretting for an instant that he would be creating a messy job of work for others, he walked slowly to a closet in his bedroom and removed a scarred short-barreled .38 caliber detective's special from a faded and sweat-stained brown leather holster. He cracked the cylinder open and removed five of the six bullets, which he slipped into his pocket; this act, he believed, would help remove anyone's doubts as to what his intentions had been.

Carrying the pistol in his hand, he started to search for paper and pen to write a suicide note. This took several frustrating minutes, and it was not until he shoved aside some white, pressed handkerchiefs, tie bars, and cuff links in a bureau drawer, that he was able to discover a single clean sheet of blue-lined notepaper and a cheap ballpoint pen. Well, he told himself, whatever you're going to say, you'll have to keep it short.

He tried to think if there was anything else he needed, as he paused momentarily by the mirror to inspect his appearance. Not too bad. His checked sports shirt was clean, as were his khaki trousers, socks and underwear. He considered shaving, rubbing the back of the hand that held the gun across his cheek, feeling the day's stubble, but decided that it was unnecessary. He needed a haircut, but shrugged as he hastily combed his fingers through his shock of white hair. No time, he told himself. He suddenly remembered being told when he was young that people's hair continued to grow after death. Hair and fingernails. He wished it were true. This was the sort of information that was whispered from one child to another with absolute authority and invariably led to ghost stories told in darkened rooms in hushed tones. Part of the problem with growing up and getting old, Simon Winter thought, was having the myths of childhood erased.

Turning away from the mirror, he took a quick glance around the bedroom – the bed was made, there were no piles of dirty clothes in the corner; his midnight reading, paperback crime novels and adventure stories, was stacked by the bedside table – and he thought, if not precisely neat, it was at least presentable, which was more or less the same as his own appearance. Certainly no mess that wasn't understandable for an old bachelor, or, for that matter, a young child, which was an observation that momentarily interested him and gave him an abrupt sense of completeness.

He stuck his head into the bathroom, saw a vial of sleeping pills, briefly considered using them instead of his old service revolver, but decided that would be a cowardly way of murdering himself. He spoke inwardly: You should be brave enough to look down the barrel of your gun, not merely pop a handful of pills and ooze gently into a fatal sleep. He moved into the kitchen. There were a day's worth of dirty dishes in the sink. As he stared at them, a large bronze palmetto bug crawled up on the edge of a plate and paused, as if waiting to see what Simon Winter would do.

'Disgusting beasts,' he said out loud. 'Glorified cockroach.' He raised the pistol and took aim at the bug. 'Bang,' he said. 'One shot. Did you know, bug, I never received less than an expert rating?'

This made him sigh deeply and smile as he put his gun and paper down on the cheap, white linoleum countertop, grabbed some dishwashing soap and quickly started scrubbing the dishes. He talked out loud: 'Let's hope that cleanliness *is* next to godliness.' He supposed that it was slightly ridiculous to do the dishes as one of his final acts on earth, but then, if he didn't, he knew someone else would have to take care of them. This, he understood, was a part of his nature. He did not leave things undone for other people to finish.

The palmetto bug seemed to catch a whiff of the soap, recognized it was in mortal danger, and fled across the counter, as Simon Winter took a halfhearted swipe at it with a sponge.

'That's right. You can run, but you can't hide.'

He reached beneath the sink and found a can of insect poison, which he shook hard and then sprayed in the general area where the bug had disappeared.

'I guess we'll go together, bug,' he said. He remembered that ancient Vikings used to kill a dog and place it at the feet of a man about to be buried, the thought being that the warrior would want companionship on the road to Valhalla, and what better comrade than a faithful dog, who presumably would ignore the fact that its own life had been cut short by barbaric custom. So, Simon Winter thought, if I had a dog, I could shoot him first, but I don't and I wouldn't do that anyway, so my companion on the road to wherever will have to be a palmetto bug.

He laughed at himself, wondering what he and the palmetto bug would talk about and guessing that in an odd way, their lives hadn't been that different, poking around in the unpleasant remains of day-to-day life. He swiped the sink clean with a flourish, put the sponge down on the corner, and, taking up the paper and pistol, went back into the modest living room of his small apartment. He sat down on a threadbare couch and placed his revolver on a coffee table in front of him. Then he took the notepaper and pen and, after a moment's thought, wrote:

> To Whom It May Concern:
>   I did this to myself.
>   I am old and tired and lonely and haven't done anything useful in years. I don't think the world will miss me much.

Well, he said to himself, that's all true, but the world seems to get along pretty well regardless of who it is that dies, so you haven't really said anything. He placed the tip of the ballpoint pen against his teeth and tapped it once or twice. Say what you mean, Simon Winter insisted, like an elementary school teacher frustrated with her students' compositions. He scribbled quickly:

> I feel like a guest that has overstayed his welcome.

That's better, he thought. He smiled. Now, get on to business.

> I have slightly more than $5,000 in a savings account at First Federal, part of which should be used to pay to fry up these old bones. If someone would be kind enough to take my ashes and throw them in the waters

off Government Cut on an outgoing tide, I would appreciate it.

Simon Winter paused, and thought: It would be nice if they did this when the big schools of tarpon that live in the cut start to roll on the surface, grunting, gulping air, and picking up speed as they get ready to feed on the pinfish and small mackerel. They are beautiful animals, huge silver scales like armor on their flanks making them seem like medieval knights-errant of the sea, with great, powerful, scythe-like tails that thrust them through the water. They are an ancient tribe, untouched by any evolutionary change in centuries, and some of them are probably as old as I am. He wondered for a moment whether a tarpon ever grew tired of swimming, and if it did, what it did then. Perhaps it just slows, and doesn't run as hard when a big hammerhead stalks the school. He thought: It wouldn't be half bad to come back as a tarpon. Then he continued writing:

> Any money left over should go to the Miami Beach Police Department's widows' fund, or whatever it's called nowadays. No relatives to call. I had a brother, but he died, and I haven't heard from his kids in years.
> I have enjoyed life and managed to do a few good things. If anyone's interested, there's a scrapbook with some clippings about my old cases in the bedroom.

He decided to allow himself a small conceit and an apology:

> Once, I was as good as they came.
> Sorry to be such a bother.

He paused, examining the note, then he signed it with a flourish:

Simon Winter. Detective. Retired.

He took a deep breath and raised his hand up to his eyes. It was steady. He glanced down at the handwriting in front of him. Not a waver there, he thought. All right. You've faced far tougher things. There's no reason to wait anymore.

He gripped the gun, placing his finger on the trigger. He could feel every part of every action, as if, suddenly, each motion took on a specialness of its own. The tension in his finger around the trigger tightened the tendon in the back of his hand. He could feel his arm muscle working as he lifted the pistol, strengthening his wrist to hold the weapon still. His heartbeat accelerated. His imagination flooded with memories. He ordered his eyes shut, trying to squeeze out any residual doubt. All right, he said to himself. All right. It's time.

Simon Winter placed the barrel of his revolver against the roof of his mouth, and wondered whether he would feel the shot that killed him. And in that short hesitation, that single, momentary delay, the silence he'd created around him was abruptly shattered by a loud and insistent knock at the front door of his apartment.

The sound crashed through his suicidal determination, startling him.

In that same instant, he became aware of dozens of small sensations, as if the world had abruptly demanded he acknowledge its presence. The pressure in his finger on the trigger seemed to threaten to slice his skin; where he had expected a quick sheet of scorching oblivion, now he tasted the metallic harshness of the revolver barrel and choked on the oily, pungent smell of the cleaning fluids that he had used on the weapon. His tongue slid up against the smooth icy steel of the trigger guard and he could hear the wheeze of his breath.

Farther in the distance the diesel engine of a bus droned past. He wondered if it was the A-30, heading to Ocean Drive, or the A-42, on its way to Collins Avenue. A trapped housefly buzzed frantically at a window, and he remembered an unfixed tear in one of the window screens. He opened his eyes and lowered the pistol.

There was a second knocking at the door, more demanding.

The noise had an urgency that overcame his resolve. He put the revolver down on the coffee table, on top of his note, and rose.

He heard a voice saying: 'Please, Mr Winter . . .'

It was high-pitched and frightened and seemed familiar.

It's after dark, he told himself. No one has knocked on my door after the sun's gone down in twenty years. Moving swiftly, forgetting for a moment the hesitation that age forced onto his limbs, he hurried to the sound. He called out, 'I'm here, I'm here . . .' and he opened the door, not knowing precisely what it was that he was opening to, but vaguely hoping in some distant spot within him that he was allowing something of importance to enter.

Fear like a halo of light seemed to illuminate the elderly woman standing outside. Her face was rigid, pale, drawn tight like a knot, and she looked up at Simon Winter with such helplessness that for a moment he stepped back, as if struck by a sudden strong gust of wind, and it took an instant for him to recognize his neighbor of almost ten years.

'Mrs Millstein, what is the matter?'

The woman reached out her hand, grasping at Simon Winter's arm, shaking her head, as if to say that she could not force words past fright.

'Are you all right?'

'Mr Winter,' the woman said slowly, the words creaking past lips squeezed together, 'thank goodness you were home. I'm so alone, and I didn't know what to do . . .'

'Come inside, come inside. Please, what is the matter?'

Sophie Millstein stepped forward shakily. Her fingernails sliced into the flesh of Simon Winter's arm, her grip like a climber threatened with a fall down some sheer precipice.

'I didn't believe, Mr Winter,' Sophie Millstein started softly. But then her words picked up speed, following in a torrent of anxiety. 'I don't think any of us really believed. It seemed so distant. So impossible. How could he be here? Here? No, it just seemed too crazy, so none of us believed. Not the rabbi or Mr Silver or Frieda Kroner. But we were wrong, Mr Winter. He is here. I saw him, today. Tonight. Right outside the ice cream store on the Lincoln Road Mall. I stepped out, and there he was. He just looked at me, Mr Winter, and I knew right then. He has eyes like razors, Mr Winter. I didn't know what to do. Leo would have known. He would have said, "Sophie. We must call someone," and he would have had the number right there, ready. But Leo's gone and I'm all alone and he's here.'

She looked helplessly at Simon Winter.

'He will kill me, too,' she said, gasping.

Simon Winter steered Sophie Millstein into his living room, depositing her on the sagging couch.

'No one's going to kill anyone, Mrs Millstein. Now, let me get you a drink of something cold and then you can explain what has you so frightened.'

She looked wildly at him: 'I must warn the others!'

'Yes, yes. I'll help you, but please, have a drink and then tell me what is the matter.'

She opened her mouth to reply, but then seemed to lose her grip on the words, so no sound came out. She put a hand to her forehead, as if taking her temperature, and said, 'Yes, Yes, please, iced tea if you have it. It's so hot. Sometimes, in the summer, it seems as if the air is just burning up.'

Simon Winter swept up his suicide letter and pistol from the coffee table in front of Sophie Millstein and hurried into the kitchen. He found a clean glass into which he poured water, ice cubes, and instant tea mix. He left his letter on the counter, but before taking the glass back into Sophie Millstein, paused and reloaded his weapon with the five bullets in his pocket. He looked up and saw the old woman staring blankly in front of her, as if watching some memory. He felt an odd excitement, coupled with a sense of urgency. Sophie Millstein's fear seemed thick and choking, filling the room like smoke. He breathed hard and hurried to her side.

'Now, drink this,' he said in the same tones one would use to a fevered child. 'And then take your time and explain what has happened.'

Sophie Millstein nodded, seizing the glass with both hands, gulping at the frothy brown liquid. She swallowed hard, then put the glass to her forehead. Simon Winter saw her eyes fill with tears.

'He will kill me,' she said again. 'I don't want to die.'

'Mrs Millstein, please,' Simon Winter said. 'Who?'

Sophie Millstein shuddered, and whispered in German: 'Der Schattenmann.'

'Who? Is that someone's name?'

She looked wildly at him. 'No one knew his name, Mr

Winter. At least, no one who lived.'

'But who—'

'He was a ghost.'

'I don't understand . . .'

'A devil.'

'Who?'

'He was evil, Mr Winter. More evil than anyone could think. And now he's here. We didn't believe, Mr Winter, but we were wrong. Mr Stein warned us, but we didn't know him, so how could we believe?'

Sophie Millstein shuddered hard.

'I'm old,' she whispered. 'I'm old, but I don't want to die.'

Simon Winter held up his hand. 'Please, Mrs Millstein, you must explain yourself. Take your time and tell me who this person is and why you're so frightened.'

She took another long pull at the iced tea and set the glass down in front of her. She nodded slowly, trying to regain some composure. She lifted her hand to her forehead, her fingers stroking her eyebrows gently, as if trying to loosen a hard memory, and then she wiped away the tears that were gathering in her eyes. She took a deep breath and looked up at him. He saw her hand drop to her throat, where, for just an instant, she fingered the necklace she wore. It was distinctive; a thin gold chain that held a stamped replica of her first name. But what separated this necklace from the same type worn seemingly by teenagers everywhere was the presence of a pair of small diamonds at either end of the S in Sophie. Simon Winter knew her late husband had dipped into his modest pension funds and given her the necklace the birthday before his heart failed, and like the wedding ring on her finger, she did not remove it.

'It is such a difficult story, Mr Winter. It happened so

long ago, sometimes now, it seems like a dream. But it was no dream, Mr Winter. More a nightmare. Fifty years ago.'

'Go on, Mrs Millstein.'

'In 1943, Mr Winter, my family – Mama, Papa, my brother Hansi – we were still in Berlin. Hiding out . . .'

'Go on.'

'It was such a terrible life, Mr Winter. There was never a moment, not one second, not even the time between heartbeats, Mr Winter, when we thought we were safe. There wasn't much to eat, and we were always cold, and we thought every morning when we awakened that that would be our last night together. Every second, it seemed, the risk grew. A neighbor might grow curious. A policeman might demand your papers. Would you step on the trolley car and spot someone who recognized you from before the war, before the yellow stars? Maybe you would say something, any little thing, Mr Winter. A gesture, a tone, some slight nervousness, something that would betray you. There are no more suspicious people in the world than the Germans, Mr Winter. I should know. I was one of them once. That would be all it took, just a tiny hesitation, maybe a frightened look, anything that indicated you were out of place. And then it would be over. By 1943 we knew, Mr Winter. I mean, perhaps we didn't know it all, but we knew. Capture was death. It was that simple. Sometimes at night, I used to lie in bed, unable to sleep, praying that some British bomber would drop their load short, Mr Winter, right on top of all of us, and so we could all go together and end all the fear. I would be shivering, praying for death, and my brother Hansi would come over and hold my hand until I fell asleep. He was so strong. And resourceful, Mr Winter. When we had nothing to eat, he could find some potatoes. When we had no place to stay, he would find us a new flat, or a basement somewhere, where there weren't any questions and we could spend a week, or maybe more, still together, still surviving.'

'What happened to—'

'He died. They all died.'

Sophie Millstein took a deep breath.

'I told you. He killed them. He found us and they died.'

Simon Winter started to interject another question, but she held up a quivering hand.

'Let me just finish this, Mr Winter, while I still have the strength. There were so many things to be frightened of, but I suppose the worst were the catchers.'

'The catchers?'

'Jews like us, Mr Winter. Jews that worked for the Gestapo. There was a building on Iranische Strasse. One of those awful gray stone buildings the Germans love so much. The Jewish Bureau of Investigation was what they called it. That was where he worked, where all of them worked. Their own freedom depended on their hunting us down.'

'And this man you think you saw today . . .'

'Some were famous, Mr Winter. Rolf Isaaksohn, he was young and arrogant, and the beautiful Stella Kubler. She was blond and pretty and looked like one of their Nordic maidens. She turned in her own husband. There were others, too. They took off their stars and moved about the city, just looking, like birds of prey.'

'The man today . . .'

'Der Schattenmann. He was in all our nightmares. It was said that he could pick you from a crowd of people, just as if he alone could see some glow to your skin, some look in your eyes. Maybe it was the way you walked, or some smell you had. We didn't know. All we knew was if he found you, death would come knocking at your door. People said that he would be there in the darkness when they came for you, and he would be there when they shipped you out in the morning gloom on the transport train for Auschwitz. But you wouldn't know, you see, because no one saw his face and no one knew his name. If you saw his face, they said you would be taken to the basement at the Alexanderplatz prison, where it was always night and everyone knew that no one came out of the basement, not ever, Mr Winter. And he would be there, to see you die, so that the last eyes you saw on this earth would be his, Mr Winter. He was the worst. The worst by far, because it was said that he enjoyed what he was doing, and because he was so good at it . . .'

'And today.'

'Here. Here on Miami Beach. This cannot be so, Mr Winter. This must be impossible, yet, I believe. I truly believe I saw him today.'

'But—'

'Just for a few seconds. There was a door left open and they were moving us through the offices because there was paperwork. Paperwork! The Germans even had paperwork when they were going to kill you. And so the Gestapo clerk finished with us, and stamped his documents and we were being taken down to the cells to wait for transport and I happened to look in for only the tiniest time, Mr Winter, but he was there, between two officers wearing those horrid black uniforms. They were all laughing over some joke and I knew it was him. His hat was tipped back on his head and he looked up and shouted something and they slammed the door closed and I thought it was the basement for me, for sure, but instead I was put on a train that day. I suppose he thought I would die in the camp. I was so small, I was sixteen, but hardly bigger than a child, but I surprised them all, Mr Winter, because I lived.'

She stopped, catching her breath in a rush.

'I didn't want to die. Not then. Not now. Not yet.'

Sophie Millstein was a tiny woman, barely five feet tall, even with the lifts that she wore in her orthopedic shoes, and slightly overweight. She was dwarfed by Simon Winter, who, even with age, still stood nearly six and a half feet tall. She wore her white hair teased into a bun, to further add to her height, an effect that usually seemed to touch the ridiculous, especially when she emerged from her apartment in brightly colored polyester pedal pushers and flowered shirts, dragging a two-wheeled cart behind her on the way to the grocery. Simon Winter knew her mostly to nod hello and dodge any lengthy conversation, which invariably centered around some complaint or another, about the city, about the heat, about teenagers and loud music, about her son who didn't call frequently enough, about growing old, about outliving her husband, all of which he preferred to avoid. But if his usual opinion of his neighbor up to this moment was one of distance and studied politeness with little shared concerns, the fear she wore in her eyes on this occasion slid him away from the usual and into a different place altogether.

He did not know precisely what to believe, feeling the detective's hesitation within him; nothing was true until he himself confirmed it.

And, he realized, the only thing he could confirm was Sophie Millstein's fear.

As he looked at her, he saw a shudder crease her body. She turned toward him with a questioning look.

'Fifty years. And I just saw him for that moment. Could I be wrong, Mr Winter?'

He decided not to answer this question, because, in his experience, the likelihood of Sophie Millstein being correct was nearly nonexistent. He thought: This person – this Schattenmann – must have been young, no older than his early twenties fifty years ago. And now he would be an old man. His hair would have changed; the tone of his skin, the shape of his face would have sagged and loosened with age. His walk would be different, as would his voice. Nothing would be the same.

'Today, did this man say anything to you?'

'No. He just stared. Our eyes met, it was late afternoon and then the sun seemed to glow right behind him and he was gone, just like that, as if he'd disappeared into the glare – and I ran, Mr Winter, I ran. Well, not like I could run once, but it felt the same, Mr Winter, I was so glad to see the lights on in your apartment, because I was so afraid of being alone.'

'He said nothing?'

'No.'

'Did he threaten you, or make any gesture?'

'No. He just looked at me. Eyes like razors, I told you.'

'And what did he look like?'

'He was tall – but not as tall as you, Mr Winter, but thickset, strong. A young man's arms and shoulders.'

Simon Winter nodded. His skepticism was gaining momentum within him. To recognize a man you saw only for seconds after fifty years was not within what he used to call the homicide detective's realms of possibility, even though these realms were very far-reaching. What he guessed was this: Sophie Millstein, whose loose grip on the ways of the world had been eroded further by her husband's death, had been walking beneath a sun that was too strong on a day that was too hot, lost in memories that were too painful, when some person had caught her eye in the midst of one of those recollections and she had become disorientated and frightened because she was old and because she was lonely. And he thought too, ruefully: Would I be that different?

But instead of saying this, he stated firmly: 'I think, Mrs Millstein, that you're going to be okay. What you need is to get some rest.'

'I must warn the others,' she said quickly, her voice racing ahead. 'They must be told. Mr Stein was right. Oh, Mr Winter, we should have believed him, but what's to do? We are old. We didn't know. Who would you call? Who would you tell? I wish Leo were here.'

'What others? And who is Mr Stein?'

'He saw him too. And now he's dead.'

Simon Winter instantly checked his doubts when he heard these words. He spoke slowly: 'I do not understand this, Mrs Millstein. Please explain.'

Instead, she looked wildly at him. 'Is that your gun? Is it loaded?'

'Yes.'

'Thank goodness. All those years as a policeman, same gun?'

'Yes.'

'You should keep it close, Mr Winter. My Leo, he wanted to get a gun, because he said the Negroes – actually, he used a different word, he wasn't prejudiced, but he was scared and that made him use that terrible word – he said they liked to come over to the Beach and rob all the old Jews that are here, and that's what we were, just old Jews, and I suppose, if I was a criminal, that's what I would be thinking too. But I wouldn't let him get one, because I was too scared to have a gun around the house, because Leo, he wasn't a careful man. He was a good man, but he was, I don't know, what? Careless, sometimes. And that's not a wise thing to be around guns, and I thought he might hurt himself with it, so I wouldn't let him have a gun and now I wish I had because I would have it, and I could protect myself. I mustn't hesitate any longer, Mr Winter.

I must call the others and tell them he's here and that we must decide what to do.'

'Mrs Millstein, please, calm down. Who is Mr Stein?'

'I must call.'

'There will be time for that in a moment.'

She did not reply.

Sophie Millstein was now sitting rigidly, eyes straight ahead, staring intently into the space in front of her. He remembered suddenly a shoot-out he'd been a part of, years earlier, a bank robbery that had erupted into a tangled flurry of bullets, over in thirty seconds. It had not been his own shot that had stopped the robber, but he had been the first to reach the man, kicking his pistol away from an outstretched hand, then looking down and seeing the man's eyes widen as he felt his life's blood bubbling through the hole in his chest. He was a young man, in his early twenties, and Simon Winter had not been much older, and he had looked at the detective and wrapped within that look were a cascade of desperate questions, ending, of course, with the one that mattered: Will I live? And before Simon Winter could respond, he'd seen the man's eyes roll back, and he'd died. It was that moment of losing grasp that Simon Winter thought he saw in Sophie Millstein's face, and he could not prevent some of her panic rushing through his own veins.

'He will kill me,' she said blankly, her voice filled with resignation. 'I must warn the others.' There was a dryness, like leather stretched to cracking, in her words.

'Mrs Millstein, please, no one is going to kill you. I won't let them.'

Sophie Millstein seemed to have locked her gaze straight forward, as if Simon Winter was no longer in the room. After a moment, her body quivered, almost as if she was physically struck by some memory. She turned slowly toward the old detective and nodded.

'I was so young and I was so scared. We all were, I suppose. It was such an unlucky time, Mr Winter. We were all in hiding and no one thought they would live much beyond the next minute or so. It's a terrible thing, Mr Winter, when you're young and everywhere you hide, death seems to track you.'

Simon Winter nodded. He needed her to keep talking, thinking that eventually she would steer herself back to the present. 'Please, continue.'

'A year ago,' Sophie Millstein said slowly, 'a man named Herman Stein who lived in Surfside killed himself.' Her voice had flattened once again. 'At least, that is what we were told by the police, because he shot himself with a gun . . .'

Winter thought: like I planned to do. 'Yes?'

'After he died, after the police came and the funeral home and his relatives sat shiva and all those things took place, a letter arrived at Rabbi Rubinstein's home. Do you know the rabbi, Mr Winter?'

'No.'

'He is old, like me. Retired. And he got a letter from a dead man, mailed a few days before. And this, Mr Herman Stein, who I didn't know, I mean, why should I? He lived up in Surfside, which is how many blocks away, Mr Winter? Seventy? Eighty? Like another world. He sends a letter to the rabbi, whom he knows just ever so little, because once he learns that the rabbi, he too once comes from Berlin, like this man, and he too lives through the camps, which is almost impossible and this man I don't know named Mr Stein says in his letter: I have seen Der Schattenmann. And the rabbi, of course, he knows this name, and so he finds me, and a few others, Mrs Kroner and Mr Silver, who also were once Berliners, and that's all

he can find, because we are all growing so old now, Mr
Winter, there are so few of us left, and there were so few
of us to survive in the first place, and he brings us together,
and we read the letter, but who knows what to do? There
is no police to call. There is no one to help us, and of
course we don't know what to believe anyways. Who
would think he would be here, Mr Winter? Of all places.
Here. And so, months pass and every so often I go to the
rabbi's house and we all sit together and talk, but this is not
the things that people like to remember so much, Mr
Winter. Until today, because, just like this poor Mr
Herman Stein from Surfside who I did not know, who is
now dead, I too see him here, and now he will kill me too.'

Sophie Millstein's cheeks were laced with tears, and her
voice was whispered fear.

'Where's Leo?' the old woman said. 'I wish Leo were
here.'

'This man, this Mr Herman Stein, he committed
suicide?'

'Yes. No. That is what the police said, Mr Winter. But
now, tonight, right now I am thinking something different.'

'And the others, the rabbi . . .'

'I need to call them.'

Sophie Millstein suddenly looked about wildly.

'My book. My little book with all my numbers. It's in my
apartment . . .'

'I'll go with you. It will be all right.'

Sophie Millstein nodded and gulped the remains of her
iced tea down.

'Could I be wrong, Mr Winter? You were a policeman.
It's been fifty years, and I just saw him for that tiny little
moment before they slammed the door closed. Fifty years
and people change so much. Could I be wrong?'

She shook her head.

'I want to be wrong, Mr Winter. I am praying I am wrong.'

He did not know what to say, so he remained silent. He thought: She is probably mistaken. But the story she'd told was unsettling, and he was unsure what to make of Mr Herman Stein's suicide. Why would an old man kill himself after posting a letter? Maybe he was simply old and feeling useless, like I was. Maybe he was crazy. Maybe he was sick. Maybe he was tired of life. Maybe a hundred reasons; when one is filled to overflow with sorrow, they don't shed only a single tear. He did not know, but he suddenly wanted to learn. Winter felt within him a sensation that he'd thought had disappeared, erased by retirement and the steady passage of time. It was a quickening in his core, where his neighbor's words and the panicky look in her eyes became factors in an equation, and he felt compelled, like some electronic calculator being fed information, to come up with an answer.

'Mrs Millstein, whether you're right or wrong is not important. What's important is that you've received a scare and you need to speak with your friends. Then you need to get a good night's sleep, and in the morning, when everyone is refreshed, we should get to the bottom of all this.'

'You will help me?'

'Of course. That is what neighbors are for.'

Sophie Millstein nodded gratefully and reached out her arm, placing her hand on Winter's wrist. He glanced down and, for the first time in all the years he'd known her, noticed the fading blue tattoo on her forearm. A-1742. The seven was in Germanic style, serpentine, with a cross mark.

*

Night had closed with determination.

Simon Winter and Sophie Millstein walked across the courtyard, enveloped by the relentless dark. Heat like ribbons of silk wrapped around the two of them. In the center of the courtyard there was a statue of a half-naked cherub playing a trumpet. The cherub had once graced a small water fountain, but this had been dry for years. The apartment complex was small, a pair of identical tan stucco two-story buildings that faced each other. They had been built in the Miami Beach boom time of the 1920s, and there were certain Art Deco touches – an arched entranceway, rounded windows, an almost sensuous curve to the facade – that gave the buildings a femininity, like the soft shape of a longtime lover's embrace.

Age and unrelenting sun had treated the apartments roughly; some paint flaked from the walls, air conditioners rattled rather than hummed, doors creaked and stuck, their jambs swollen by the cycles of tropical humidity. Outside by the street was a faded sign: THE SUNSHINE ARMS. Simon Winter had always appreciated the wondrously fractured metaphor, and he had been comfortable in the familiar decrepitude of the buildings.

Sophie Millstein paused outside the door.

'You will go first?' she asked.

Winter took the key from her hand and slipped it into the dead-bolt lock.

'Shouldn't you take out your gun?'

He shook his head. She had insisted he bring his weapon, which he had, but he felt brandishing it was slightly foolish, and he had enough experience to know that Sophie Millstein's fear had made him jumpy and nervous as well. Put the gun in his hand, and he would be likely to shoot Mr and Mrs Kadosh or old Harry Finkel, her upstairs neighbors.

'No,' he said. He unlocked the door and stepped inside.

'The light switch is on the wall,' she said, which he knew, because the layout of her apartment was a mirror of his own. He reached out with his hand and flicked on the lights.

'Jesus!' Simon Winter screeched in sudden surprise.

A gray-white shape raced through his legs.

'What the hell . . .'

'Oh, Mr Boots, you naughty thing!'

Simon Winter turned and saw Sophie Millstein admonishing a large, fat cat, which was, in turn, rubbing against the old woman's leg. 'I'm sorry if he startled you, Mr Winter.'

She lifted the cat up into her arms. The animal eyed Winter with irritating feline complacency.

'No. It's fine,' he said, feeling his heart thump away within his chest.

Sophie Millstein hung in the doorway, caressing the cat in her arms while Simon Winter inspected the apartment. A quick glance told him that they were alone, save for a parakeet in a cage in a corner of the living room, which made an irritating scratching sound as he passed by. He called out: 'Everything's okay, Mrs Millstein!'

'Did you check the closet? Under the bed?' she responded from the hallway.

Simon Winter sighed and said: 'I'll do that now.' He went into her small bedroom and surveyed the scene. He felt an odd embarrassment, being in the room that Sophie Millstein had shared with her husband. He saw that she was a woman of organization; an off-white nightdress and robe were arranged at the foot of the bed. Her bureau top was clean. He saw a picture of Leo Millstein framed in black, and another photograph of what he immediately took to be Mrs Millstein's son and his family. It was a studio shot, everyone wearing jackets, ties, Sunday best frilly dresses. He noted a small jewelry box on the bureau, a finely wrought brass container that some artisan had spent time over. A family heirloom? He suspected so.

Winter went to the closet and opened the door, revealing no intruder, but seeing that Sophie Millstein had kept Leo's supply of stolid dark brown and navy-blue suits, each one like the next, hanging next to what seemed to be a stockpile of flower-print dresses. There was also a silky brown mink coat hanging in the corner, which Simon Winter thought was not the sort of item that gets a helluva lot of wear on Miami Beach, but which probably was worth its weight in memories. He saw that Sophie Millstein's shoes were carefully lined up on the floor, next to her late husband's.

Simon Winter turned away, looked once toward the picture of Leo Millstein, apologized under his breath, 'Sorry, Leo. Don't mean to intrude, but she asked . . .' quickly bent down on one arthritic knee that immediately complained, and saw that no one was lurking beneath the bed. He noted, as well, that there were no little dust balls or ancient magazines shoved out of the way, as he might have found in his own apartment. Sophie Millstein, he considered, probably greeted a speck of dust or a smudge of dirt with the same scorn as a commanding general inspecting a slovenly soldier.

He called out again: 'Everything's okay, Mrs Millstein . . .' and walked into the kitchen area. There was a sliding glass door just opposite the sink, which led to a small tile patio in the back. The patio was perhaps ten yards from a fence, and a back alley, where the garbage cans were located. He rattled the doors to make sure they were locked, and then walked to the living room.

Sophie Millstein met him there, still carrying the cat.

The color had returned to her face, and relief covered her words.

'Mr Winter, I can't say how much I appreciate this.'

'Think nothing of it, Mrs Millstein.'

'I should call the others now.'

'I think that would be wise.'

He watched the old woman move across the living room, and thought that amongst her own knickknacks and photographs, with her cat and frilly pillows on a sofa, her own furniture and furnishings, probably the feeling of threat that had overtaken her was eroding quickly.

'I always keep my telephone numbers right here,' she said as she slid into a large easy chair. There was a yellow telephone on a small side table, next to the chair. She opened the single drawer in the table and produced a cheap red leather-bound address book.

He felt, abruptly, as if he were intruding.

'Would you like me to leave?' Simon Winter asked. 'While you make your calls.'

She shook her head as she dialed the first number. She paused, then grimaced. 'It's the rabbi's answering machine,' she whispered. Then, a second later, she said in a loud, firm voice: 'Rabbi? It's Sophie. Please call me back. As soon as you can.'

The words themselves seemed to restore some of her urgency. She was breathing hard when she hung up the telephone. She turned and looked up at Simon Winter, who continued to stand awkwardly by her side.

'Where could he be? It's dark. He should be at home.'

'Perhaps he went out for a bite to eat.'

'Yes. That must be it.'

'Or a movie.'

'Possibly. Or a meeting at the synagogue. Sometimes he still goes to the fund drives.'

'There you have it.'

The innocence of these explanations did not seem to relieve her anxiety.

'Are you going to call the others?' Simon Winter asked.

'I have to wait,' Sophie Millstein responded nervously. 'It's Tuesday. On Tuesdays, Mr Silver takes Mrs Kroner to the bridge club over at the senior citizen center. He does this ever since we started our meetings with the rabbi.'

'Perhaps you want to make another call?'

'To who?'

'Your son? Maybe speaking with him would help you feel a bit better.'

'You're very thoughtful, Mr Winter. I will do that in just a moment.'

'Do you have something to help you sleep? You've had quite a fright, and it might be difficult . . .'

'Oh, yes, I have some little pills. Not to worry.'

'How about something to eat. Are you all set?'

'Mr Winter, you're too polite. Yes. I will be fine. I feel much better now that I'm home and safe.'

'I thought you might.'

'And tomorrow, you will help me? And the others. To . . .'

'. . . get to the bottom of all this. Of course.'

'What will you do?'

This was a good question, and he wasn't precisely certain of the answer. 'Well, Mrs Millstein, I think the least I can do is check out the circumstances surrounding Mr Stein's death. At the same time, perhaps, we can all consider what it is exactly you want to do. Perhaps your friends and I can get together and we can map something out.'

This prospect seemed to cheer Sophie Millstein. She nodded rapidly.

'Leo,' she said, 'Leo was like you. He made decisions. Of course, he was a haberdasher, not a detective, so what would he know about solving this mystery, right, Mr Winter?'

'I'll leave you, then. Make sure you lock the door after I go out. And don't hesitate to call if you're still frightened. But I think a good night's sleep would be best. Then a fresh start in the morning.'

'Mr Winter, you are a complete gentleman. I will take a pill as soon as you leave.'

She rose and walked with him to the door. He saw the cat leap up into her chair, curling down into the spot made warm by her body.

'Lock the door,' he said.

'I could be wrong,' she said hesitantly. 'It's possible. I could have been wrong, correct?'

'Anything is possible, Mrs Millstein. The point is, we will sort it all out.'

'Until tomorrow, then,' she replied, nodding gratefully.

He stepped into the hallway and turned back just long enough to catch his neighbor's wan smile as she closed the door behind him. He waited until he heard the sound of the dead-bolt lock clicking shut.

Simon Winter walked out into the courtyard of the Sunshine Arms and let the sticky night air cover him. A weak street lamp from beyond the apartment's entrance threw a thin shaft of light onto the statue of the cherub, making it glisten as if wet. The darkness surrounding him seemed rich, thick as coffee. He had an odd, droll thought: Well, if you're not going to kill yourself, you might as well get something to eat. Will it be death or chicken tonight?

He did not think himself particularly amusing, and decided to head out, rapidly considering potential places to get some food. He took a step forward, then another, then he paused. He turned and looked back at Sophie Millstein's apartment. The curtains were drawn. He could hear the sound of a television playing loudly coming from another apartment. This mingled with some laughing voices coming from down the street. He could hear a motorcycle accelerate in high-pitched whine from several blocks away. Everything was, he insisted, as it should be. Not perfect, but familiar. It is a night like any other. It is hot. There is a breeze that cools nothing. The tropical sky blinks with stars.

He insisted to himself that there was nothing unusual in the world at all except for an old woman's memories of nightmare. But we all have those, he thought. He tried to reassure himself with the ordinariness of the world around him, but was only partly successful. He found himself peering into the shadows, looking for shapes, listening for telltale noises, behaving like a man suddenly afraid he was being watched, worried that he was being pursued. He shook his head to dislodge the sensation of dread that overcame him, chastised himself for showing the uncertainty of age and strode determinedly past the cherub in the dry fountain. He was overcome suddenly with the desire to walk, to try and put distance between him and his neighbor's fears.

He stepped forward quickly, wondering, for just an instant, if death, when it arrived, was like the night.

CHAPTER TWO

Sleep

Sophie Millstein peeked around the edge of the curtain, watching Simon Winter disappear into the darkness of the courtyard. Then she turned away and slumped down into her easy chair. Almost immediately the large gray and white cat leapt into her lap.

'Mr Boots, did you miss me?'

She stroked the soft fur on the nape of the cat's neck as it settled in.

'You shouldn't get too comfy,' she warned. 'I've still got things to do.'

The cat, as cats will, ignored this and merely began purring.

Sophie Millstein rested her hand on the cat's fur and suddenly thought herself exhausted. She told herself that it would be all right for her to just shut her eyes for an instant, but when she did, she found herself enmeshed in a tangle of nervousness, as if closing her eyes reawakened fear, instead of bringing comfort. She put her hand to her forehead and wondered if she were perhaps coming down with something. She thought she felt hot, and she cleared her throat several times harshly, as if checking for telltale signs of congestion.

She took a deep breath.

'You've had an easy life, Mr Boots,' she said to the cat. 'Someone has always taken care of you. Warm and dry home. Plenty of food. Entertainment. Affection. Anything a cat could want.'

She abruptly slid her hand beneath the cat and pushed him from her lap. She forced herself to rise.

She looked down at the cat, which despite its abrupt ejection, rubbed itself up against her leg.

'I saved you,' she said bitterly, surprising herself with her own anger. 'That man put you and all the rest of the litter into that bag and was going to throw you into the water. He didn't want kittens. No one wanted kittens. There were too many kittens and everyone in the world hated kittens and no home would have any of you and so he was going to kill all of you, but I stopped him and took just you out of the bag. I could have chosen one of the others. I had my hand around one of the others, but I let it go because it scratched me. So it was you I grabbed, and so you've had an easy life, and all the others, they went into the bag and the bag went into the water and they drowned.'

She pushed Mr Boots away with her foot.

'Lucky cat,' she hissed sharply. 'Luckiest cat in the world.'

Sophie Millstein walked into her kitchen and began to straighten the shelves, making certain that every label on every can was face forward, lined up by size, ordered by group, so that a tin of olives wouldn't be next to a can of tomato soup. When those goods were properly placed, she did the same to the perishables, imposing military precision on the refrigerator. The final item she inspected was a flounder fillet which she had earlier intended to broil for her own dinner, but she was no longer hungry. For a moment she hesitated, fearful that the fish would not keep.

She decided that she could cook the fish in the morning and have it for the next day's lunch.

The cat had followed her and meowed. The noise irritated her.

'All right. All right. Coming.'

She opened a can of cat food. Manipulating the opener was difficult for her, and her hand stung with sudden soreness. She told herself to march down to the discount hardware store in the morning and purchase an electric opener. She set the food out for the cat and left it eating.

In her bedroom, she stared at the picture of her late husband.

'You should be here,' she said, reproaching him. 'You had no right to leave me alone.'

Sophie Millstein marched back into the small living room and sat down again. She felt abruptly as if she were caught out on the street in the moments before a thunderstorm crashed down, when impetuous, sharp surgical gusts of wind sliced through the humid stillness, assaulting her from all sides.

'I'm tired,' she said out loud. 'I should take a pill and go to bed.'

But instead she rose, tramped into the kitchen, seized the telephone and dialed her son's number on Long Island. She let the phone ring once before hanging it up, instantly deciding that she didn't want to speak with her only child. He will just insist again that I move out into some old people's home where I don't know a soul, she told herself. This is my home.

Sophie Millstein went to the tap, filled a glass with water and took a long drink. It tasted brackish, metallic. She made a face. 'Miami Beach special,' she said. She wished she'd remembered to purchase some bottled water at the store. She poured some back in the sink, then took the remainder in and filled up the water container in the bird cage. The parakeet chirped once or twice. She wondered briefly why she'd never bothered to name the bird, as she had her cat. She wondered if this was somehow unfair, then doubted it, and returned to the kitchen to rinse out her glass and place it on the drying rack. There was a small window above the sink, and she glanced out into the night. She told herself that she was familiar with every shape and shadow that she could see; everything was in exactly the same spot that it had been the night before and the night before that and every night for more than ten years. Still, she continued to examine the darkness, watching each corner of the backyard for movement, like a sentry on patrol.

She turned off the faucet and listened.

There were a few distant sounds of traffic. Upstairs, Finkel was shuffling about. A television was on too loud; that would be the Kadoshes, she thought, because they are too stubborn to turn up their hearing aids.

She continued to look out the window. She let her eyes read each shaft of light, study each dark spot. For a moment she was astonished at the number of places she thought someone could hide without being seen: the corner where the orange tree lurked next to the old chain-link fence; the shadow where the garbage cans were placed.

No, she told herself, it is all as it always is.

Nothing different.

Nothing out of place.

She breathed in hard and went back to the living room. Television, she told herself. She flicked on her set and settled into a chair. A situation comedy was on, and for a few minutes she tried to follow the jokes, and forced herself to laugh at the same moments that the canned laughter did. She let her head drift down into her hands, and as the program continued in front of her, she shivered, as if cold, but she knew that wasn't the reason.

He's dead, she said to herself. He's not here.

She wondered, for a moment, whether he had ever really existed. Who was that I saw? she asked herself. It could have been anybody, especially with that hat pulled down over his forehead and the dark overcoat. And they shut the door so quickly after he yelled, I hardly had a chance to see.

But she knew this was untrue. It was him.

She felt herself fill with bitter anger. It was always him. Day after day. Hour after hour. He had been there, even when they had thought they were relatively safe. But they weren't. He'd stalked them like some particularly patient and coldhearted hunter, waiting, biding his time, until the right moment. And then he'd taken their money first, then their freedom, and with it, their lives.

Sophie Millstein felt hatred reverberate within her. She spoke out loud:

'I should have killed him then. If I had known . . .'

Then she stopped and realized she'd had no chance. She told herself: You were only a child – what did you know of killing?

She answered her own question harshly: not much then. But you learned soon enough, didn't you?

On the television, an advertisement for a beer came on the screen, and for an instant she watched muscular young men and nubile young women cavort around a pool. No one really looks like that, she thought. She realized when she was the same age as the models in the advertisement, she weighed less than seventy pounds and resembled someone that had already died.

But I didn't die, she reminded herself.

He must have thought we would all die, but I didn't.

She put her head down in her hands once again.

Why didn't *he* die too? she wondered.

How could he have lived through the war? Who would save him? Not the Germans he worked for. When he was no longer useful, they would have shipped him off to Auschwitz as well. Not the Allies or the Russians, who would have prosecuted him as a war criminal. Certainly not the Jews whom he so eagerly helped along the road to death. How could he have lived?

She shook her head at the impossible thoughts that filled her.

He had to die. They all did, and he died right alongside the rest of them. It had to be that way.

She repeated this to herself: He had to die. He had to die. Then she shortened it, mentally, simply to: He's dead. He's dead. He cannot be alive. Not here. Not on Miami Beach. Not surrounded by the few people who managed to survive.

For an instant she thought she might become ill.

Sophie Millstein, filled with an old and misshapen fear, stood up. The characters in the television show were all laughing and the audience was laughing at them.

'Leo,' she said out loud. She walked to the telephone and swiftly dialed the rabbi's number. When she heard the voice on the answering machine respond, she hung up. She looked down at her wristwatch and thought: still too early for Mr Silver and Frieda Kroner. They won't be back until after midnight. Her finger hesitated above the dial, and then she punched in Simon Winter's number. She expected he would pick the phone up immediately, and she tried to think what she could say beyond the fact that she was still frightened, but all she could think of was Simon Winter's pistol and how it might protect her.

The phone continued to ring, unanswered. After a second an answering machine clicked on: 'You've reached Simon Winter. Leave a message at the beep.'

She waited, and after hearing the electronic signal, said:

'Mr Winter? It's Sophie Millstein. I just wanted . . . Oh, it's just . . . well, Mr Winter, I just wanted to thank you again. I will speak with you tomorrow.'

She hung up, slightly relieved. He will have some good advice, she thought. He is a very nice man, with a level head and plenty of smarts. Maybe not as much as Leo, but he will know what to do.

She wondered where he'd disappeared to. He probably just went out to get a bite to eat, she explained to herself. He'll be back shortly. He's out just the same as Rabbi Rubinstein. Everything tonight is normal. Just like any other night.

Sophie Millstein wondered abruptly: Mr Herman Stein, who were you? Why did you write that letter? Who did you see?

She took a deep breath, only to have it repair her nervousness.

She thought in sudden panic: I'm all alone.

Then, just as swiftly, she insisted to herself that she was mistaken. The Kadoshes, old Finkel upstairs, and before too long Simon Winter, would be back from his meal; they would all be surrounding her, and she would be fine.

She nodded to herself as if insisting on the safety of her observation. She took a step back toward the television. The comedy had been replaced by a darker drama.

Who else could it have been? she suddenly demanded.

The question made her breathe in sharply again. It stung her imagination, and she swiftly tried to anesthetize her feelings with complacencies.

Why, it could have been anyone. Another old man on

Miami Beach – why, the place is positively thick with them.
And they all look alike too. And maybe he thought you
were someone he knew, because of the way you stared, and
that's why he looked back so carefully. And when he
realized you weren't familiar, why, to save you the embarrassment, he just walked away. Happens all the time. Go
through life meeting hundreds of folks, and so it's not
unreasonable to get mixed up every once in a while.

But she did not feel mixed up.

Why here? she asked.

I don't know.

Why would he come here?

I don't know.

What will he do?

I don't know.

Who is he?

She knew the answer to this question, but she would not
articulate it to herself.

She tried to take charge of her emotions as they
catapulted about the small apartment. She decided that in
the morning, she would go over to the Holocaust Center
and speak with the people there. They were always so kind,
even the young ones, and so interested in everything she
had to say, she was sure they would listen to her once
again. They would know what to do.

She felt immediately better.

That's a good plan, she told herself.

Sophie Millstein picked up the telephone and dialed the
Holocaust Center number. She waited until the taped
answering machine had completed its recitation of operating hours, and then, after hearing the signal beep, said into
the phone: 'Esther? This is Sophie Millstein. I need to talk
to you, please. I will come by today, in the morning, and
talk a bit about how I was arrested. Something has

happened. I was reminded . . .'

She stopped, not knowing how much she could explain. In her hesitation, the tape machine ran to its end, beeping and disconnecting her. She held the phone out, considering calling and adding to her message, then deciding not to.

She hung up, feeling better.

She went to the front window and just slid a corner of the curtain back, peeking out once again, as she had earlier when she'd watched Simon Winter depart. She saw the lights were off in his apartment. For a moment she watched the courtyard, straining her eyes to see past to the street. A car went by rapidly. She caught a glimpse of a couple walking swiftly down the sidewalk.

She abandoned the front, then walked to the rear patio door, checking, just as Simon Winter had, to make sure it was locked. She gave the sliding door a little shake. Lamenting the flimsy lock, she decided another thing she could do in the morning was to call Mr Gonzalez, the owner of the Sunshine Arms. I'm old, she thought. We're all old here, and he really should install better locks and maybe one of those fancy alarm systems like the one my friend Rhea has over at the Belle Vue. All she has to do is push a button and the police are called, just like magic. We should have something like that, she thought. Something modern.

She glanced outside again, but saw nothing save darkness.

Mr Boots was at her feet.

'See, kitty. Nothing for you to worry about.'

The cat did not respond.

She felt exhaustion battling with fear within her. For a moment she allowed herself to think that perhaps the elderly complex her son was trying to persuade her to move into wouldn't be such an awful idea.

But like everything else, she decided it could wait until the next day. She reassured herself with a mental list of the things she would have to do in the morning: call Mr Gonzalez; purchase a new can opener, an electric one; call her son; visit the Holocaust Center; talk to the rabbi and Mr Silver and Mrs Kroner; and meet with Simon Winter and make a decision. A busy day, she thought. She stepped into the small bathroom and opened her medicine cabinet. Lined up at attention were a number of medications. Something for her heart. Something for her digestion. Something for her aches and pains. In a small container near the end of the shelf was what she was searching for: something to help her sleep. She poured a single white pill into her hand and swallowed it without using any water.

'There,' she said to her reflection in the mirror. 'Now, maybe ten minutes and you'll be out like a light.'

She hurried into the bedroom and slipped out of her clothes, taking the time to carefully hang her dress in the closet and drop her undergarments in a white wicker hamper. She slipped on a rayon nightgown, adjusting the frilly part near her neck. She remembered it was one of Leo's favorites, and that he'd teased her and called her sexy when she wore it. She missed this. She had never thought herself sexy, but she'd liked it when he'd teased her, because it made her feel desired, which was pleasurable. She glanced at her husband's picture one last time, then slid under the thin covers. She could feel a warm, dizzying sensation moving through her body as the sleeping pill took effect.

The cat jumped up on the bed next to her.

She reached out and stroked it.

'I was mean to you,' she said. 'I'm sorry Mr Boots. I just need to sleep.' He curled next to her.

She closed her eyes. It was all she wanted in the entire world, she thought: a single, restful evening of comforting, dreamless sleep.

Night like a box closed around Sophie Millstein. She did not even stir several hours later, when Mr Boots suddenly rose up, back arched, spitting and hissing in hasty cat-fear at the harsh and heartless sounds of intrusion.

CHAPTER THREE

The Accountant for the Dead

It was already nine minutes after midnight and Miami Beach 911 operator Number 3 was irritated that her shift replacement was delayed for the third time that week. She knew Number 17's toddler had been ill with bronchitis, but still, nine minutes was nine minutes, and she wanted to get home so that she would not be completely exhausted when her own son awakened her as he did almost every morning by banging his way around the small bathroom and kitchen of her home in Carol City. One of the advantages, she knew, of teenage, was a certain obliviousness to racket. So she counted the minutes, adding Number 17's tardiness to the drive across the beach, over the causeway, past downtown and up onto the expressway, skirting Liberty City, until finally reaching the small house she owned in a dusty part of the county that was neither city nor suburban, a lower-middle-class enclave that offered modest safety and slightly less heartbreak than the world barely a mile or two away. The trip would take her just under an hour in her eight-year-old Chevy.

To her right and left, numbers 11 and 14 had already settled into the nightly routine. Number 11 was moving a hook and ladder company to a third-story apartment fire just off Collins Avenue, and Number 14 was patching a state trooper through to wants and warrants as he chased a big BMW across the Julia Tuttle Causeway. It had been a tiring night: a convenience store robbery, a reported rape, a fight outside a nightclub. Plenty for her to do, nothing she thought that would make the papers in the morning. Number 3 looked up, craning her neck away from the bank of phone lines, looking for Number 17.

She was still looking when the light on the board in front of her blinked red, and without thinking, she punched the connection and spoke, sounding machinelike and well-drilled.

'Miami Beach Fire, Police and Rescue.'

As she heard the first words, she knew it was an old person's voice:

'Ohmigod, please send the police right away! Somebody's killed her! Oh, poor Mrs Millstein! An ambulance! Send help! Please!'

Cutting through hysteria was her job.

'Yes, ma'am. Right away. Give me an address.'

'Yes, yes, oh, the Sunshine Arms, 1290 Thirteenth Court. Hurry, please . . .'

'Ma'am, what sort of assistance do you need? What has happened?' Number 3 remained perfectly even-toned in her questions.

'We heard a noise, my Henry and I, and he went down to check it out and Mr Finkel went too and she was dead! Oh my goodness, what's the world coming to? Send the police. Please. Someone's killed her. Oh my lord, what are we coming to?'

'Hold the line please . . .' Number 3 left the woman on an open line while she punched another button: 'Any officer. Possible ten-thirty, 1290 Thirteenth Court. Code is Three. People on scene. Patrol sergeant, please respond . . .' She punched a second button, connecting herself to an ambulance crew. 'We have a ten-thirty at 1290 Thirteenth Court, but there are elderly people involved. Drive by. See if any need assistance.' This wasn't precisely procedure, but Number 3 had been a 911 operator on the Beach for over a decade, and she knew that more than once the sound of sirens and excitement strained fragile heart muscles.

Number 3 then calmly reconnected herself to the frantic woman on the open line.

'Ma'am, help is on the way. An officer should be right there. And I've notified Rescue as well.'

'He saw him, my Henry did, running out the back. A black man and Henry chased him to the alley, he did, but then he got away and I called. Oh, poor Mrs Millstein!'

'Ma'am, is the perpetrator still on the scene?'

'What? The who? No, he ran away down the alley.'

'Ma'am, hold on. I will need your name and address.'

Again she left the caller on the open line, as she dialed another number.

'Beach Homicide. This is Detective Robinson.'

'Detective? This is Operator Three down in 911. I do believe your slow night is about to pick up. We just got a call, possible ten-thirty at an apartment complex called the Sunshine Arms in South Beach. Uniforms are en route, but maybe you want to send someone over there before they make a mess of things.'

Walter Robinson recognized the voice. 'Lucy,' he said, 'my night wouldn't be complete without a call from you.'

Number 3 smiled, wished for an instant that she were younger and sexier, and that her husband wasn't at home snoring in the big double bed they owned, then replied: 'Well, Detective, it's complete now. I've got a hysterical old woman on the open line, saying the perpetrator just fled the scene. Maybe you can hurry and get lucky.'

'Luck,' Robinson answered, 'is something in short supply in this world.'

Number 3 nodded. She looked up and saw Number 17 entering the phone room, looking sheepish and apologetic for being late.

'Well, Detective, if you don't need luck . . .'

'I didn't say I didn't need it, Lucy. I just said there wasn't much of it available. Especially late at night in the city.'

'Amen,' said Number 3 as she disconnected the detective and heard a distant siren come over the open line, its insistent wail rising above the teary sobs of the elderly woman.

Walter Robinson put the phone back on its cradle and wrote down the address on a piece of scratch paper, thinking to himself that it was hot outside, a nasty, thick, clutching oily heat that threatened to rob his lungs of air. He knew already what he would find when he exited the cool, sterile interior of the homicide offices. A world compacted by stifling humidity, weighing on his chest like a tight jacket. He took a deep breath and shoved the legal textbooks he'd been studying into a drawer, then reached for a portable radio phone resting in an electric charging device on the corner of his desk. He said to himself: this is an awful night for anyone to have to die.

Robinson, aged less by years than a steady dosage of street cynicism, twenty credits shy of a law degree which he thought was his ticket out of police work, drove fast through the pale yellow sodium vapor lights that gave the city its otherworldly nighttime glow. Although he did not think of himself as a native Miamian – that was a category reserved for slow-drawling crackers and rednecks from the southern part of Dade County – he had been born and raised in Coconut Grove, the son of an elementary school teacher.

His middle name was Birmingham, though he never used it. It was too difficult to explain to the primarily white and Hispanic membership of the Beach force why he had been named, at least in part, after a city. His mother was a distant cousin to one of the children killed in the Birmingham church bombing in 1963, so, when he was born shortly thereafter, she had vented some of her frustration by naming him after the Alabama city, giving him a reminder, she often informed him, so that he would not forget where he had come from.

Forgetting where he had come from, however, did not seem such a terrible thing to Walter Robinson. He had never been to his namesake in Alabama, and didn't particularly like returning to the part of the city where he'd grown up. The Grove is a curious section of Miami. By accident of time and development, one of the city's worst slums butted directly up against one of its most affluent areas, creating a constant ebb and flow of fear, anger, and envy. Robinson had lived with all those sensations, and didn't particularly enjoy reminding himself of them.

And, despite eight years in the Miami Beach department, first in uniform and then three with a gold shield, he didn't consider that home either. He thought his rootlessness unusual, was slightly bothered by it and generally tried to ignore it.

He pulled down Thirteenth Court and spotted the cruisers parked outside the Sunshine Arms. He was pleased to discover that uniformed officers had already stripped ubiquitous yellow police-line tape around much of the area. He got out of his unmarked car and walked past a small group of elderly people gathered into a corner of the courtyard. A patrol sergeant greeted him by name as he approached the apartment building, and he nodded his response:

'So, what have we got?'

'Elderly victim, in the bedroom. Signs of forced entry in back. A patio door, you know one of those sliding ones that my six-year-old could break in . . .'

'I know the type. Signs of struggle?'

'Not too much. But looks like the perp grabbed everything he could before the neighbors got there. He must have run when he heard them come poking around. One of them, a Mr Henry Kadosh, upstairs apartment, chased the perp out to the alley, got a pretty fair look. His wife called 911.'

'And?'

'Black male. Late teenage to mid-twenties. Five feet ten to six feet. Slight build, maybe 175 pounds. Wearing high-top sneakers and a dark T-shirt.'

'Sounds like me,' Walter Robinson said. 'I know somebody's gonna say "But they all look so much alike" before I clear this scene.' He imitated an elderly person's voice as he spoke.

The patrol sergeant grinned. 'When you walk over there, someone's gonna yell: "There he is!"'

Robinson laughed. 'Probably. Wouldn't be the first time.'

The patrol sergeant continued. 'I put out a BOLO. Maybe we'll get lucky.'

'You're the second person to say that to me in the last half hour. I don't feel lucky tonight.'

The patrol sergeant shrugged. 'I guess she didn't either.' He jerked his head in the direction of the apartment.

'You think the witness could work with an Identikit technician?'

'He said he got a good look. Maybe. But, hey, after he

said that, his wife handed him his eyeglasses.'

'Great. They over in that bunch?' Robinson pointed at the collection of elderly people.

'Right in front.'

'All right, let me take a look inside first.'

'I've already called forensics. And the medical examiner. They're on their way over.'

'Good going. Thanks.'

The detective stepped up to the front of the building. He hesitated for a moment, and then walked slowly into Sophie Millstein's apartment. With each step he shed a bit of the easygoing camaraderie that he'd employed outside, replacing it with an attention to detail. Another uniformed officer was standing in the living room, next to a covered bird cage, writing in a notebook. He nodded and pointed toward the back, needlessly, because Walter Robinson was already headed in that direction. He was glad that he'd arrived before the forensic team, heartened, as well, that the first police on the scene were not milling about the body, as they tended to do. He preferred to have a moment alone with every victim; it was a time when he could let his imagination play out the dead's final seconds. If there was a moment when he could hear the murdered person's voice speaking to him, it would be then. In the sturdy, fact-driven world of the homicide detective, this he knew was romance. But it helped him along the path of under-standing, and he had long ago recognized that anything that spurred the steady progression of comprehension was useful.

As he quietly sidled into the bedroom, moving like a parent careful not to awaken a sleeping child, he thought, as he always did, that he hated being a homicide detective. It was an endless succession of hot nights, dead bodies, and paperwork. Heat, stench, and drudgery. Although he was still a young man, he had long before given up the fanciful notion that he was somehow linked with Sherlock Holmes or Hercule Poirot, nor did he see himself, as some of the more experienced men in his office did, as society's surrogate avenger, dedicated to righting the seemingly never-ending succession of wrongs that people committed against each other. He had come to see himself as an accountant for the dead. It was his job to tidy up and organize their last, awful moments and present the truth of those seconds to a subsequent authority, be it grand jury or court of law.

The body was spread-eagled on the bed, twisted about unnaturally, tangled in a knot of torn bedclothes. He thought: She must have kicked hard against the weight holding her down, killing her.

He believed he performed his job in a routine, dogged fashion, preferring not to focus on the moments of electric recognition and surging imagination when he centered on a killer. He preferred to consider the excitement he felt as the inevitable result of mere tenacity, where others, who watched him work, would have spoken about artistry. Regardless, his style created results. He cleared as many cases as any other detective on the force, and was held in high regard by his shift commander, a man who cared little for how crimes were solved, but who valued the power of statistics, and thus Walter Robinson was considered a man of potential by the hierarchy of the Beach department.

He, on the other hand, ignored labels, thought potential something similar to a disease, and preferred to work alone.

Robinson approached the victim slowly, taking care with where he put his feet, keeping his hands close to his body. He made a quick notation of the strident red marks on her throat, and saw that her eyes were open wide in death; there was an old myth that a murdered person's eyes would print a vision of the killer as death snatched them. He had more than once seen a victim's eyes ripped from their skull postmortem by superstitious killers. He wished the myth were true. Make things a lot easier, he thought.

He wanted to ask: Who killed you? But all he saw was terror. This did not surprise him; what awakened her was the pressure around her windpipe. If the noise of the break-in had aroused her, then the killing would have taken place somewhere else. He glanced around, looking for sleeping tablets. Check the bathroom, he told himself, knowing that he would find them on a shelf.

Robinson let his own eyes move from the body, surveying the room like an appraiser in the moments before an auction. Drawers were torn open, their contents dumped out. A bedside lamp was smashed to the floor. At first he thought: struggle. But then he appended this idea. No, he told himself. The struggle was on the bed, in the knot of sheets and ripped nightgown, and it was over quickly. This was hurry. Someone who knew he didn't have much time, and so he ransacked the room as fast as possible. He saw that a pillow was lying on the floor, without a case. An old woman sleeping on freshly laundered sheets without a matching pillowcase? No, that's what he grabbed to hold what he was stealing. He made a mental note, memorizing the floral pattern of the sheets. Are you smart enough to throw that away? I doubt it.

The detective gave a long sigh, slowly letting his breath slide from his body. It was hot in the room; the warm air from the broken patio door, and from the front door left open for the medical examiner and the forensic teams, was overcoming the air-conditioning. He could feel a line of sweat starting to form on his forehead, unpleasant stickiness beneath his arms.

He shook his head slowly.

It was all so terribly, horribly familiar, he thought.

An elderly woman. Alone. A garden apartment without a good lock on a patio door. A neighborhood filled with shadows and alleys, and old folks who cashed social security checks. Just enough jewelry and twenty dollar bills to hold out the promise of a quick and easy score, not nearly affluent enough to warrant alarm systems, security guards, and Dobermans. The fringe world, he thought.

Typical urban routine nightmare, he said to himself.

It happened somewhere, every night. Little variations on a common theme. You're old and vulnerable and trying to hold on to what little you have left of this world, and there's someone younger, stronger, and more desperate who's going to come and take it from you. If you're lucky, he just knocks you down, or hits you in the head. You survive with a concussion, a fractured arm, a broken hip. If you're unlucky, you die. He tried to imagine how many cases like this one he'd seen. A dozen? A hundred? Did she have any idea when she went to bed that she was prey?

He spoke softly, out loud, addressing the killer:

'So, you broke in, that wasn't too hard, and then you caught her in her bed asleep, and you strangled her, but killing her made too much noise, and so you jumped up and grabbed what you could and then ran, but not fast enough, you bastard, because somebody saw you.'

He heard voices coming from the living room, and realized that the processors of violent death had arrived. He heard a police photographer's voice call out, 'Hey! Walter, where you at?' and he answered: 'In here.'

He glanced at the body again. Something struck him as out of place, and he couldn't quite identify it.

Still vaguely bothered, he moved to meet the men

coming into the bedroom. He immediately retreated into the forced jocularity that protects all the people who are charged with sorting out violent death.

'Hey, Walter,' said a diminutive technician, lugging a huge, leather case. 'What's shaking?'

'Not much. She lived alone, Ted. Should be prints. Make sure you get those drawers good. Bobby, you shoot everything, including all the stuff in piles where the perp threw it. And then get shots of the forced entry. Is Doctor Death here yet?'

'He was just pulling up. Actually, it was one of the assistants. The chief must be sleeping in tonight.'

'Nah, he's probably working that triple over in Liberty City,' the photographer interrupted as he adjusted his light meter and flash bar. 'Little problem at a crack house, so I heard on the scanner driving over. You know: "That's my pipe!" "No it ain't!" Bang, bang, bang. That's what's gonna grab headlines tomorrow. That's where he'll be.'

Robinson knew that the county's chief medical examiner liked to attend the deaths that would preoccupy the *Herald* and the local television stations. But he shook his head. 'He may start out over there, but you watch. He'll get here before we're finished. And so will the papers and the TV stations. So he'll be here, probably right about the same time they show. I'd like to say he's working himself to death, but that doesn't sound quite right.'

The other policemen crowding into the room laughed. There was a popping sound as the photographer started taking his shots. It mingled with the activity that immediately enveloped the room as technicians working fibers, fingerprints, and searching for other evidence began doing their jobs.

He decided he would go outside and speak with the people who'd chased the killer away. They're old, he thought, and it's late, and pretty soon the hour will catch up with them. Get their story while it's still fresh.

From the doorway, Robinson scanned the room again, trying to discover why he felt unsettled. He glanced over at the body another time. He still did not form her name in his mind; that, he knew, would come soon enough. For the moment, she was just another item to be catalogued.

CHAPTER FOUR

Hope

When he saw the flashing strobe lights of the police
vehicles from the end of the block, Simon Winter stopped
short, his feet suddenly rooted to the pavement, his jaw
dropping open in abrupt astonishment.

He took a single step toward the lights, his imagination
racing through a series of nightmares. He told himself:
There's been a fire. A break-in. A heart attack. An
accident. With each possibility, his pace picked up, so that
by the time he reached the yellow police tape, he was
running hard, his shoes slapping a cadence of worry
against the cement. He would not allow himself to form the
words he feared most in his head: There's been a killing.

He stopped at the entrance to the Sunshine Arms,
breathing hard. There were at least a half-dozen cruisers
pulled up on the narrow street; their lights bathed the area
in strident blues and reds. There were a pair of television
station vans, and he saw camera crews jawing by the
sidewalk. He noticed a station wagon marked with the
county medical examiner's shield, and saw several
uniformed officers standing next to the empty fountain
in the courtyard. He realized immediately that there was
no urgency in anyone's actions, and this made him inhale
sharply. People work fast when there's a heartbeat. They

take their time when there isn't.

He swallowed once, his throat abruptly dry, and ducked beneath the yellow tape. This motion caught the eye of one of the officers, who waved at him.

'Hey, pops! No entry here.'

'I live here,' Winter replied. 'What's happened?'

'What's your name?' the policeman asked, approaching him. He was a young man, with the artificial bulk of a bulletproof vest making him seem larger than he truly was.

'Winter. I live in 103, right there. What's happened?'

'You live alone, Mr Winter?'

'That's right. What happened?'

'There was a break-in. Old lady got killed.'

Simon Winter choked on the name. 'Sophie Millstein?'

'That's right. You know her?'

'Yes.' He stumbled over the word. 'Just tonight. I saw her tonight. Helped her lock herself in . . .'

'You saw her tonight?'

Winter nodded. He felt his stomach clench with pain. 'I want to talk with the detective in charge,' he said.

'You know something, Mr Winter? Or you curious?'

'I want to talk to the detective in charge.' He fixed the young patrolman with a long look, one that covered up the turmoil he felt ricocheting about within him.

The patrolman hesitated, then said, 'I'll take you to him.'

He started to steer Simon Winter across the courtyard, when the old man saw the other members of the complex standing in their nightclothes in a knot to the side of the fountain. Mrs Kadosh instantly began waving at him.

'Mr Winter! Mr Winter! My God, is terrible!' Mrs Kadosh burst out. Simon Winter walked quickly toward them. Mr Kadosh was shaking his head back and forth.

'Terrible is right,' he said, echoing his wife.

'But what happened?' Winter asked. 'I went out to eat, and then I took a walk, and I only just returned and—'

Mrs Kadosh interrupted swiftly. She was a plump woman wearing her frosted blond hair beneath a hair net large enough to trap most species of fish, and sporting a bright red quilted bathrobe that had a huge flower embossed on the breast and surely was sweltering to wear on this humid night.

'Is almost midnight, and Henry is readying for bed after watching just a few minutes of Jay Leno, just the jokes part, not so much the talk, talk, talk, and I am sitting up waiting, when I am hearing a scream, maybe, more like a shout of fear, just sudden, coming from where I do not know, but after I think about it, I am thinking it is poor Mrs Millstein, and think maybe this is nightmare because she no longer sleeps so good, and sometimes I hear her calling for Leo, may he rest in peace. So, I am not paying too much attention, but my Henry, he comes in and saying "You hear that?" and of course I say "Yes." And he says right away maybe we better need checking on Mrs Millstein.'

'Is right,' Henry Kadosh muttered. 'Need checking, Mrs Millstein.'

Simon Winter wanted to urge them to hurry their story, but he knew the Kadoshes were Hungarian – Henry had once been Henrik – and between their age and their fractured use of language, hurry was not something they ever really managed. So he simply nodded.

'So, my Henry, he goes and finds his slippers, and then he finds his robe and goes to the kitchen and finds the flashlight and then he goes next door and knocks hard for old Finkel to come too . . .'

Mr Finkel nodded his head in agreement. 'This is true,' he said.

Mrs Kadosh shot him a quick glance, as if to say that she

was accustomed to interruption by her husband, but that her neighbor should wait his turn. Then she continued:

'So, Finkel, of course, he has his hearing aid out, and so he doesn't know from nothing, but he gets his robe too, and the two men, they go downstairs and knock on Mrs Millstein's door. Knock, knock. But there is no answer. "Mrs Millstein, Mrs Millstein, are you okay?" But nothing. So Henry and Mr Finkel, they trudge back upstairs and he says to me, "What should we do? There is no answer." I tell them to go around the back and look in the patio door, and so, back they go, to do that. And you know what?'

'Patio door is broken in. Pulled right off,' Henry Kadosh answered.

'So,' Mrs Kadosh continued, 'Henry and Mr Finkel come rushing back to the front, where it is I am waiting, and saying, "Maria, Maria, calling police, 911 dialing. Right away!" And, as he is saying this, we are hearing another noise, right from the back. This noise, it comes from the patio. Around we all run, and Henry, he sees quick—'

'Is not cats or dogs in garbage. Is nigger running out of Mrs Millstein's apartment!'

Mrs Kadosh shook her head. 'Henry, he chases man to alley. And old Finkel and I, we stick our heads in the door. And inside, is poor Mrs Millstein. Murdered dead.'

Winter's head reeled and he felt a rush of heat rise through his gorge, flooding him with a disorienting dizziness. The young patrolman touched his back, and Winter turned toward him.

'Come on, old-timer. Now you know what happened. You still wanna talk to a detective?'

'Yes,' Winter replied. 'The victim . . .' He stumbled and stopped, thinking to himself: The victim *what*?

His mind raced with a blistering equation. An old woman arrives at your door, afraid that she is going to be killed. And then she is killed, but by someone totally unexpected?

He thought he needed time to think, but then realized that he was walking across the courtyard, following the young patrolman, heading toward the entrance to Sophie Millstein's apartment. He walked past the trumpeting cherub. The figurine was hit every few seconds with a shaft of red light, so that it appeared to be bathed in blood. He paused at the doorway, staring inside at the activity that seemed to energize the interior. He saw a man with a fingerprint case working the kitchen. Another was taking carpet samples. The young patrolman walked up to a wiry black man who was loosening his tie against the building, thick humidity of the room, gesturing toward Simon Winter. The old detective paused, waiting for the younger man to approach him. He studied the activity within the apartment. He clamped down hard on emotions that seemed to dash about headlessly within him, trying to concentrate, steadying himself with memory. *You have been here many times before*, he told himself. *Process the scene. It will tell you everything, if only you take your time and let it converse in its own way, in its own voice, speaking in the ancient language of violent death.*

For a moment he watched Simon Winter, and saw the way his eyes scoured the room. He mistook this attentiveness for nervousness. Walter Robinson turned to the uniformed officer who'd escorted the old man into the apartment.

'So, what's the geezer's story?' he asked.

'Name is Winter, lives across the courtyard. Says he saw the deceased this evening. Probably the last person to see her before the break-in. Heard her lock herself into the place. Thought you might want a statement.'

'Uh-huh,' Robinson replied. 'Yeah. You take it.'

The patrolman nodded. 'Maybe he could do the ID for us?'

Robinson considered this, and thought: why not?

'Good idea.' Making a short gesture, he and the patrolman walked over to Simon Winter. Walter Robinson quickly introduced himself as the detective in charge.

'We'd like this patrolman to take your statement,' he said to the old man. 'And, if you're willing, we'd like to have you make a tentative identification for us. If you're up for it, of course. Just for paperwork, you know. And we like to be completely certain before we call the next of kin. But only if you're willing. It's not pretty . . .'

Simon Winter kept his eyes darting about, then finally turned and fixed them on the detective.

'I've seen it all before,' he said quietly.

'What?'

'I've seen it. Twenty-two years with the City of Miami Police Department. The last fifteen in homicide.'

'You were a cop?'

'That's right. Retired. It's been a while since I was at a crime scene. At least a dozen years.'

'You're not missing much,' Robinson said.

'That's right,' Winter said quietly. 'I don't miss much.'

Robinson ignored the double entendre, extended a hand, and they shook. The younger man did this out of a professional courtesy. 'Things must have been different back then,' he said.

'No,' Winter replied. 'People die in much the same fashion. What was different was the science. We didn't have a lot of the stuff you young guys have today. Scientific profiles. DNA testing. Computers. We didn't have computers. Are you good with computers, Detective?'

'Yes, I am.'

'Think they can solve this crime?'

Robinson shrugged. 'Maybe.' Then, after thinking for an instant, he added, 'More than likely.'

For a moment he watched Winter, whose eyes had once again started to sweep the crime scene, absorbing what he saw there. The young detective had two quick thoughts. First, that he wasn't sure he liked Simon Winter, and second, that he was sure he didn't want to end up an abrasive old man, retired to the Beach, existing on memories of years on the force. Dozens of killings, rapes, and assaults remembered in advanced age as the good old days. His mind abruptly wandered to a torts law problem discussed in a class two nights earlier. He had written a mock brief on the issue, and it had been his effort that the professor singled out for praise.

Walter Robinson was determined not to simply trade in his badge and revolver for a briefcase and a slightly more expensive suit and work the other side of the criminal street, as had many of the other policemen he'd known who went on to law school and became criminal defense attorneys or prosecutors. He told himself that he would land in some corporate firm, shaking hands with executives and businessmen, and soon enough would forget about crime scenes and the helplessness of sudden death.

'Okay,' he said, shaking the pleasant images of the future out of his awareness, 'let's make the ID, then you can tell your story to the patrolman.'

Simon Winter followed the young detective through the apartment, remembering that he had taken the same path earlier that evening. But the small space was crowded with technicians and policemen, every light was turned on, and strobe patterns from the assembled squad cars outdoors marked the walls, disorienting Winter, almost as if the apartment he'd entered while Sophie Millstein waited at her door was someplace different and distant, like a memory from childhood. The angles, the colors, the smells, all seemed alien to him. He looked about for the cat, but it had disappeared. He followed the detective into the bedroom.

Sophie Millstein lay on her back on the bed.

Her nightclothes were torn from her struggle, the flaccid curve of her breast exposed. Her hair had come unpinned, and fanned out haphazardly from her head, as if she was underwater. Her nose had been bloodied and her upper lip was stained brown where the blood had dried. One knee was thrust over the other, almost coyly, and the flesh of her hip was bared. The sheets on the bed were tangled around her feet. He had an urge to reach out and pull the off-white nightgown over Sophie Millstein's alabaster skin.

Simon Winter glanced quickly around. He saw a photographer taking a picture of her purse, which had been ripped open and discarded on the floor. Another was dusting the bureau for fingerprints. The drawers had been torn open and clothes were strewn about. Winter remembered the small jewelry box next to the picture of Leo on the bureau top. But the picture was now in a corner, glass shattered, and the jewelry box missing.

He turned to Walter Robinson.

'She had a box, you know, a little metal thing. It was sort of reddish brass with a little design carved on the top. She kept her rings and earrings and stuff in it. Right up there.'

He pointed, and the detective took notes.

'It's gone,' Winter said redundantly.

'You would recognize it?' Robinson asked.

'I think so,' Winter replied.

He turned back to Sophie Millstein.

A second fingerprint technician was working on her

neck, carefully dusting her skin.

'Bodyprint?' Winter asked.

'Yeah,' Robinson replied. 'Shot in the dark, really. Maybe lift a usable print about one time out of a hundred. Still, worth trying.'

'We used to try, occasionally. But it never worked for us.'

'We've got new paper. And the lifting tape is much better. Sometimes use an ultraviolet technique as well. And, you know, they're developing this laser that reads the print ridges. Still . . .' He shrugged.

The technician bent over Sophie Millstein, obscuring her from Simon Winter's view. He had a small piece of tape in his hand, which he pressed to the old woman's skin, then lifted carefully. He placed the tape against a sheet of special white paper, depositing the print. 'Maybe,' the technician muttered. 'Looks okay.'

The technician stepped back, moving aside.

'You want to do the ID now?' Walter Robinson said.

Winter stepped forward and looked down at Sophie Millstein.

Strangled, he thought immediately. He fixed the red and blue-black bruise marks on the old woman's neck in his memory. The skin by her windpipe was crushed, deformed by the force that had encircled her. Mentally, he measured the distance between the marks.

Large hands, he thought. Strong hands.

'Is that Mrs Sophie Millstein?' Robinson asked.

Simon Winter continued to stare. The woman's eyes were still wide open, staring sightlessly up toward the ceiling. Winter saw the fear in his neighbor's face. She must have known, if only briefly, that she was dying then and there. He wondered if he'd worn the same look earlier in the evening, when he lifted his own pistol to his mouth.

He wondered if she'd managed to think of Leo in her last panicked moments.

He looked at Sophie Millstein's eyes again. No, he thought. All they saw was terror.

Winter took note of a scratch, really a long frayed slice of skin on her neck, oddly unaccompanied by blood. He remembered the gold necklace she wore. It was gone. Ripped from her postmortem, he thought. That's why the cut to the skin didn't bleed.

'Mr Winter?' Walter Robinson's voice was questioning.

Simon Winter quickly glanced down at his neighbor's fingers. Did she fight back? Did she scratch and flail away and try to win her remaining years back from the man who sought to steal them? Her killer's flesh should be beneath the fingernails. But he saw Sophie Millstein kept hers cut close.

His eyes moved up to Sophie Millstein's right forearm. He could just make out the number tattooed there in faded blue.

Winter felt something touch his sleeve, turned and looked hard at the young detective.

'Of course,' he said slowly. 'It's Sophie Millstein. Her necklace is missing. A single strand, gold chain, but it had her name stamped in a charm at the center. The same kind that kids like to wear, but hers was distinctive. There were two diamonds, not big ones, at either end of the *S*. Her husband gave that to her about eighteen months ago, and she never took it off.'

He took a deep breath, watching Walter Robinson make a notation in his book. 'You'd recognize the necklace?' the younger man asked.

'Yes.' He continued, 'You might try taking samples from beneath her fingernails . . .'

'They do that at the morgue,' Robinson replied. 'Standard procedure. Do you know her next of kin?'

'Yes. She has a son named Murray Millstein, who's an attorney on Long Island. She has an address book in a drawer in the living room. The little table that holds the phone. A little leather address book. That's where she said she always kept it.'

'In the living room?'

'That's right. I'll show you.'

Robinson started to lead Winter from the room. 'Thank you for your help on this, Mr Winter. We really appreciate it . . .'

'She was scared,' Simon Winter said abruptly, under his voice, to the detective. 'That's why she came to me.'

'Scared?'

'Yes. She'd had a fright. Today. She saw someone. She was scared and threatened.'

'You think this person that scared her had anything to do with the crime?'

'I don't know. It was unusual. She was very frightened.'

'It was unusual for her to be frightened?'

'No,' Winter replied, slightly exasperated. 'She was old and alone. She was always frightened.'

'That's what I would have thought. Well, just give your statement to the patrolman. Tell him what happened.'

'This person was someone—'

'He'll take your statement. I need to secure this scene and contact the family.'

'But the person—'

'Mr Winter, you were a detective. What do you think happened here?'

Simon Winter didn't look around. Instead he eyed Walter Robinson. 'I'd say someone broke in, killed her, robbed her, and ran when he heard the neighbors. That's the obvious explanation, isn't it?'

'That's right. And we even have several witnesses who saw the perpetrator fleeing. Mr and Mrs Kadosh and Mr Finkel. Your neighbors. So what is obvious is also true. Now, let the patrolman take your statement. Tell him who she was scared of.'

He didn't finish his thought out loud, which was: *Whoever it was, it was the wrong damn person.*

The two men paused in the center of the living room. Simon Winter wanted to get angry, but felt himself searching instead for a grip on the events. He cursed his age and indecision inwardly.

'Now, where's that address book?'

'In the drawer.'

Winter pointed, and Walter Robinson stepped across the small room and opened the drawer beneath the phone.

'It's not here.'

'I saw it there earlier. That's where she always kept it.'

'Not here now. What did it look like?'

'Red leather. Not expensive. About four by five. Gold-embossed "Addresses" in script on the front. The sort of thing you'd get in a drug store.'

'We'll look for it. Not the sort of thing a junkie looking for cash is likely to grab. It'll show up.'

Winter nodded. 'She had it out, tonight, when I left her.'

'Well, give your statement to the patrolman, Mr Winter. And don't hesitate to call if you can think of anything else.'

Robinson handed Simon Winter a business card. The old detective put it in his pocket. Then the younger man turned away, leaving Winter to be led outside by the patrolman. Winter started to say something, but stopped, and keeping the surge of thoughts to himself, reluctantly followed the patrolman, leaving Sophie Millstein behind. He glanced back over his shoulder once, back into the bedroom, and saw that her last moments were being documented by a police photographer's camera. The photographer dipped and swayed, dancelike, around Sophie Millstein, his camera popping with each flash of light, taking another series of shots while the morgue team waited patiently in a corner, talking quietly amongst themselves. One man idly worked the large brass zipper on the shiny black rubberized body bag, making a small tearing sound.

Walter Robinson looked on the floor in the bedroom for the address book, but could not find it. He made a note of this as well. Then he went back to the telephone in the living room and dialed directory assistance on Long Island. Sophie Millstein's son's number was listed in Great Neck. But before calling the victim's son, he dialed the twenty-four-hour service for the Dade County State Attorney's Office and received the number for the assistant with homicide duty that night.

He dialed and waited through a half-dozen rings before a sleepy voice staggered across the line:

'Yes?'

'Is this Assistant State Attorney Esperanza Martinez?' he asked.

'Yes.'

'This is Detective Robinson. Beach homicide. We haven't met . . .'

'But we're going to meet now, right?' the sleepy voice replied.

'That's right, Miss Martinez. I've got an elderly victim, killed by an unknown assailant inside her apartment, twelve hundred block of South Thirteenth Terrace. Crime could fit the profile of a series of break-ins we've had out here, except this time the perp strangled the old woman.

We have a witness who got a look at the suspect. Tentative description: black, late teenage to early twenties, slight stature, about five-ten, maybe 175 pounds, and moving fast.'

'You think I need to be there?' the prosecutor asked. 'Is there some legal issue you need advice on?'

The young woman's voice had gathered an edge of irritation. Robinson ignored it.

'Well, no. No legal issue that I can see. The crime itself is pretty cut and dried. But what we have is an elderly white, Jewish victim and a young black perpetrator, and it's my guess this will be high-profile real quick, what with this being an election year for your boss and there being at least a half-dozen reporters and cameramen outside who are gonna be damned after waiting around all damn night if they don't make this into something that lands 'em on the front page, or maybe the top of the newscast. . . . You hear what I'm saying?'

'You think—'

'I think you've got race and murder, and that's a cocktail that don't mix too good in this county, Miss Martinez.'

This was standard police procedure in Dade County: invoke the riots of the 1980s, and instantly obtain people's attention. There was a momentary silence on the line before the woman's voice, considerably more alert, answered:

'I hear you loud and clear, Detective. I'll be right over and we can wave the flag together.'

'Sounds like fun.'

He hung up the phone, grinning. Occasionally waking up hotshot young prosecutors was one of the homicide detectives' job perquisites. He figured at least a half hour before she arrived and got tossed in front of the press. He decided he could wait while inspecting the progress of the

search team working the alley behind the Sunshine Arms.
Maybe they've found something, he thought. The jewelry
box. It had to be close by. The perp probably threw it in
the first trash can he could, after conveniently covering it
with fingerprints and the unmistakable scent of panic.

Esperanza Martinez went by the nickname of Espy to her
friends, which were few. She dressed swiftly in the
semidarkness of her bedroom, first pulling on jeans, then
discarding them in favor of a more fashionable loose-
fitting dress, when she considered she might have to face
a camera crew. Although she was alone in her apartment,
she was careful to be quiet; she lived in a duplex, half of
which was occupied by her parents, and her mother was
uncannily sensitive to her daughter's movements, and was
probably, despite the wallboard, wooden frame, and insu-
lation material that separated them, lying awake in bed,
listening.

She double-checked her appearance in a small mirror
that hung next to a crucifix by the front door. She made
certain that she had her State Attorney's Office badge and
a small .25 caliber automatic pistol in her pocketbook, and
exited into the sticky nighttime. When she started the
engine on the modest, nondescript compact car, she
glanced up and saw the light flick on in her parents' half of
the house. She put the car in gear and maneuvered quickly
out into the street.

Late at night in Miami in the summer, it seems as if the
day's heat leaves a residual glow, like the musty warmth
that rises from a recently extinguished fire. The huge
office towers and skyscrapers that dominate the downtown
remain lit, shedding darkness like it was so many droplets
of black. But for all its tropical smoothness, the city has an
unsettling pulse, as if, when one slides down from the

brightly illuminated highways that crisscross the county, one descends into a basement. Or perhaps a crypt.

Espy Martinez feared the night.

She drove rapidly, slipping from quiet suburban streets onto Bird Road, then up Dixie Highway, heading fast toward Miami Beach. There was little traffic, but just as she maneuvered onto the four lanes of Route 95, a red Porsche with ink-black tinted windows flew past her, screaming by in excess of a hundred miles per hour. The velocity of the sports car seemed to suck her along, as if she'd been buffeted from behind by a sudden strong gust of wind. 'Jesus Christ!' she swore out loud – and felt fear sear through her for just one nasty instant, then flee as she watched the car rapidly disappear, momentarily glistening in the yellow-tinted sodium vapor lights of the highway before being enveloped by the night. A quick glance into the rearview mirror warned her of the state trooper's car coming up equally fast behind her. The trooper was traveling without lights or siren, trying to close on his quarry before the speeder knew he was there. She understood this went against established procedure, and she guessed the trooper would lie about it in a court hearing, if he got asked. But she also knew it was the only way he could hope to catch the Porsche, which was faster and more maneuverable, so, mentally, she forgave him as he roared past her.

'Good luck,' she said. 'You'll need it.' She hoped the driver of the Porsche would turn out to be some middle-aged doctor or lawyer or developer trying to impress a date who was half his age, and not a twenty-one-year-old coked-up drug smuggler, brain-fried from narcotics and machismo, who kept a machine pistol on the seat beside him.

The night, she thought, was dangerous. Anger hid so

successfully after dark, lurking, obscured by the warmth and the rich black air. Espy Martinez pushed her hair away from her face nervously and kept driving.

She spotted the flashing lights and the haphazardly parked television trucks from a block away, and quickly turned into a parking spot. She hurried down the sidewalk, ducking under the yellow crime scene tape before she was spotted by the dozen reporters and cameramen milling about, waiting for someone to come talk to them.

A patrolman started to wave at her, but she swiftly produced her badge.

'I'm looking for Detective Robinson,' she said.

The patrolman inspected the badge. 'Sorry, Miss Martinez. But I made you for one of those television reporters. Robinson's inside.'

He pointed, and she stepped across the courtyard without noticing the cherub. She paused, almost as if she were abruptly out of breath.

This was only the third homicide scene she'd been required to visit. The other two had been anonymous narcotics assassinations; in each instance, young Hispanic men lacking identification, probably illegal immigrants from Colombia or Nicaragua. Each had a single gunshot wound to the back of the head, administered by a small handgun. Murder at its neatest and cleanest. Almost delicate. Their bodies had been discarded with little ceremony in vacant lots – gold jewelry, wallets stuffed with cash, expensive clothing – all intact. In many jurisdictions the similarities would have had press and public buzzing, questioning whether these were the work of a serial killer.

Not in Miami. Prosecutors in the Dade State Attorney's Office termed such homicides *felony littering*. There was a macabre theory among prosecutors and police that the closer to the center of the city each body was found, the less important the particular victim was. The truly significant narcotistas ended up dead, decomposing beneath the swampy muck of the Everglades or sinking chained to a cinder block in a thousand fathoms of Gulf Stream waters. So, these two men that Espy Martinez had merely glanced at were nobodies who amounted to nothing. Their deaths probably resulted from a single unfortunate flight of ambition, wherein they crossed some invisible but uniquely deadly line. Murder as organizational housekeeping. Even their assassins couldn't be bothered with the lengthy, messy, and bothersome effort required to dispose of their corpses where they wouldn't be discovered. No arrests were expected. No trials. Just a pair of numbers tallied on an unfortunate set of statistics.

Espy Martinez hadn't even had to approach either body. Her attendance had been requested only by homicide detectives eager to make sure the state attorney understood the inevitability of the failure attached to the investigation of those crimes.

This case, she knew, was different.

A real person, with a name. A history. Connections. Not someone who simply dropped in and out of life.

She hung in the doorway of the apartment, collecting her fears. A crime scene analyst pushed past her carrying an armful of scrapings and other samples. He muttered 'Coming through' as he passed her, and to avoid standing in his way, Espy Martinez stepped into the apartment. Another policeman glanced at her, and she took the time to fasten her badge to her pocketbook. When she looked up, she saw the policeman jerk his finger toward the bedroom. Taking a deep breath, she walked through the apartment, trying to see nothing and everything at the same time.

She lingered for a second on the edge of the activity in the bedroom.

Her view was blocked by several men standing at the foot of the bed. One moved slightly, and she saw Sophie Millstein's foot. The toenails were painted with a confident red. She bit her lip at the sight. Espy Martinez took another deep breath, and despite fearing the croaking sounds she thought would emerge, tried her voice:

'Detective Robinson?'

The wiry young black man turned, nodding. 'You must be Miss Martinez?'

'That's right. Can you fill me in?'

She thought her voice wavered, and she thrust her shoulders back hard, her eyes meeting the detective's.

'Sure,' he said. He pointed down at the body: 'This is Sophie Millstein, white female, sixty-eight years. Widow. Lived alone. Apparently strangled. Here, look at these marks.'

Detective Robinson gestured, and Espy Martinez stepped forward. She narrowed her gaze, as if by looking at parts of the victim – her throat, her hands, her legs – not all of her at once, she could minimize the fear she felt.

'Best as I can tell, he pinned her down, like one knee to the chest, and simply throttled her. Couple of bruises on the forehead, here and here, like he hit her a couple of times. But he must have got his fingers round the windpipe real quick, this is probably where he had his thumb, because it's all pushed in and crushed, and the neighbors only heard one little scream.'

Walter Robinson saw the color drain from Espy Martinez's face. He stepped swiftly into her line of sight. 'Come on, let me show you where the perp made his entry.'

He grabbed the young prosecutor's arm and turned her out of the bedroom.

'Wanna glass of water?' he asked.

'Yes,' she replied. 'And some fresh air.'

He pointed at the patio door ripped from its moorings. 'Wait right out there. I'll get you a drink.'

When Walter Robinson found Espy Martinez, after rinsing a glass and filling it with tap water, she was breathing deeply outside, as if she could swallow the night air. She took the water from his hands and gulped it down. Then she let out a long sigh and shook her head.

'I'm sorry, Detective. It's kind of a cliché, isn't it? The young woman upset at the sight of violent death. Let me get a grip, and then we'll go back inside and you can finish.'

'It's all right. There's no need, really. I can fill you in here.'

'No,' Espy Martinez replied. 'One more look. It's my job too.'

'It's not necessary . . .'

'Yes it is.'

Without waiting for the detective, she reentered the apartment and stepped through the living room, into the bedroom. She tried to blank her mind of all thoughts, but this was impossible. Questions, fears, angers all ricocheted about within her, a racket of passions. She told herself: *This is why you became a prosecutor – this woman, right here.* The two morgue technicians were getting ready to lift Sophie Millstein from her bed.

'Just a second,' Espy Martinez said. She approached the corpse and looked down into Sophie Millstein's eyes. What an awful way to meet someone, she thought. Who were you? She continued to stare at the murdered woman, and saw the same fear that Simon Winter did, and this infuriated her. *Coward,* she said to herself, as if addressing the killer. *Punk coward.* Steal an old woman's life just like it was a pocketbook that you ripped from her shoulder. I'm going to see you go to Hell. She held her gaze still for a moment, then nodded.

The two men from the morgue glanced at each other. What was special to Espy Martinez was the stuff of daily drudgery to them. Still, they lifted Sophie Millstein slowly and carefully.

'Jesus!' one of the morgue men shouted. He almost dropped the body back on the bed.

'Holy shit!' his companion said brusquely.

Espy Martinez gasped and had the presence of mind to slap a hand over her mouth to keep from crying out.

'Goddamn, look at that!' the other morgue man whispered. 'Hey, Detective! You might wanna picture of this!'

Walter Robinson had darted to the side of the bed. He looked down at what had been uncovered. He held his gaze for a moment, then gestured to the police photographer, who was setting up for yet another series of pictures. Then he turned to Espy Martinez. She had taken a step back, but held her position.

Their eyes met. He shrugged.

'I'm sorry. I didn't know,' he said.

She nodded, not eager to try her voice for an instant or two.

Walter Robinson looked down at the bed again. He stared at the small white fangs bared in terror.

'I've never seen a strangled cat before,' he said quietly.

'Neither have I,' Espy Martinez said grimly.

Simon Winter stood outside next to the young patrolman, but his eyes caught the sight of Detective Robinson and Espy Martinez, heads together in discussion, standing in Sophie Millstein's living room.

'Who's that?' he asked.

'That's the assistant state attorney. Martinez, I think.'

'What's she doing here?'

'Policy, you know. There's an ASA assigned to every recorded homicide, but the reality is, they're only called in on the ten percent or so that the detectives think are gonna make the evening newscasts or land on the local front of the *Herald*.'

'Sophie Millstein?'

'Yeah, more'n likely. News for a day or so, at least until something else happens.'

'I guess so. You're probably right.'

'So,' said the patrolman, 'I bet you want to head in and get some sleep. Right, Old-Timer? Me, I've got four more hours on this shift. Tell me your story.'

'What do you mean?'

'You saw the victim tonight, right?'

'You want my statement?'

The patrolman had a small pad and pencil in his hand. He looked exasperated. 'Yeah. That's right.'

Winter organized his thoughts and spoke rapidly. 'Early this evening, perhaps seven P.M., Mrs Millstein knocked on my apartment door. Number 103, right over there. She had been frightened after doing some shopping, and she wanted me to accompany her through her place, to make certain it was safe.'

'So you did?'

'That's right. The apartment was empty, and I checked the doors and windows and they were all securely locked. But what frightened her—'

'You didn't see anyone hanging around. Especially anyone who fits the suspect's description?'

'No.'

'Like out back, when you checked the patio door? Nobody hanging back there?'

'I told you, no. There was no one that I saw. There was

nobody there when I was in the apartment. But she described this person she saw earlier.'

'Okay, tell me about that.'

'She said it was someone she had seen during the war . . .'

'What war?'

'World War Two. In Berlin. In 1943.'

'Berlin?'

'Germany.'

'Oh. Okay. So, this someone she saw, he wasn't a young black male was he?'

Simon Winter stared at the patrolman as if he had just asked the stupidest question he'd ever heard, which was undoubtedly true.

'No,' Winter said carefully. 'He wasn't a young black male. He was an elderly man, but she described him as singularly intense. She called him Der Schattenmann.'

'Someone shot a man?'

'No. It's German. Der Schattenmann. It's a title, not a name.'

'A title? Like what? Mayor? Or County Commissioner?'

'I'm not sure what it means.'

He saw the young patrolman's pencil pause above his notepad, then scribble down something swiftly.

'She didn't know the guy's name?'

'No. He was someone connected to her arrest and subsequent deportation. To Auschwitz. He was someone—'

'Yeah, a lot of the old folks here on the Beach got busted back then and did time.'

'Auschwitz wasn't doing time. It wasn't a prison. It was an extermination camp.'

'Right. Right. I know that. So this guy she recognized . . .'

'She wasn't sure.'

'She wasn't sure she recognized him?'

'Correct,' Simon Winter said. 'Fifty years had passed.'

'Okay, so she was frightened by this Shotinmin guy. If it was the guy, after all. You're not sure, and neither was she. Okay. You think it had anything to do with her murder tonight?'

'No. I don't know. It's just unusual. Maybe coincidence.'

'Was Mrs Millstein ever scared? I mean, like other days?'

'Sure. She was old and alone. She was frequently nervous. She changed her schedule so she wouldn't be out at night.'

'Okay. But, like, you didn't see anything strange or different tonight. And her behavior wasn't *that* different, correct?'

Winter froze the patrolman with a stare. 'Yes. That is correct.'

The younger man flipped his notebook closed. 'Okay. I think I got it. You remember anything else, you call Detective Robinson, okay?'

Winter swallowed several nasty retorts and nodded. The patrolman smiled.

'Okay, you can head on home now, Mr Winter. This crew will be wrapping up shortly. Might be some attention around here for a couple of days. News guys might bug you, but just tell 'em to go to hell if you want. Usually works. I'll make sure the detective gets a report of everything you said.'

Then the young patrolman turned and headed back toward the street, leaving Simon Winter alone, his face bathed by flashing police strobes.

*

In the kitchen, Espy Martinez watched as Walter Robinson picked up the telephone and carefully, double-checking each digit, dialed a number.

He finished and cupped a hand over the mouthpiece. 'Middle of the night, phone rings. Your mother's murdered. What a nightmare.' Then he shrugged, as if to distance himself from the pain he was preparing to deliver.

Espy Martinez watched, slightly ashamed with herself for her own fascination, the same commonplace guilt one feels when one turns and gawks at the accident that has left the highway bejeweled with broken glass and stained with blood.

Robinson mouthed the word 'ringing,' and then straightened slightly when he heard the telephone receiver lifted.

'Yes?'

'Murray Millstein, please.'

'This is he. What—'

'Mr Millstein, this is Detective Walter Robinson of the Miami Beach police, down in Florida. I'm sorry, but I have some bad news.'

'What? What?'

'Mr Millstein, your mother, Mrs Sophie Millstein, died earlier tonight. She was the victim of a robber who broke into her apartment shortly before midnight and apparently killed her before looting her valuables.'

'Oh my God! What? My mother what?'

'I'm sorry Mr Millstein.'

'What are you saying? My mother what? I don't—'

'I'm sorry, Mr Millstein. Your mother was killed earlier tonight. That's what I'm saying.'

Robinson hesitated, while the voice on the telephone seemed to gather itself. He could hear another voice in the background, penetrating the night, shrill questions, edgy panic. The attorney's wife, Robinson thought. She's sitting up in bed and she's turned on the lamp on the table where she keeps her alarm clock and a picture of her children, and now she's reached out and grabbed her husband's arm, pinching it tightly, and she's demanding to know why he's swung his feet out of bed and is sitting there, frozen in place, pale, rigid, terrified.

'Detective, uh ...'

'Robinson. Do you have a paper and pencil, Mr Millstein? I want to give you a telephone number.'

'Yes, yes, but—'

'This is the number of my office at police head-quarters.'

'But what happened? My mother—'

'We do not have a suspect in custody yet, Mr Millstein. But we have a description and a significant amount of physical evidence gathered from your mother's apartment. We are really just initiating our investigation, but we have complete cooperation from the state attorney and other forces in Dade County, and I'm hopeful we'll make an arrest.'

'But my mother, how, she always locked—'

'The perpetrator apparently forced a patio door open.'

'But then, I don't understand. . .'

'Preliminary investigation suggests she was strangled. But final determination rests with the medical examiner.'

'She's . . .'

'Yes. Her remains will be transported to the county morgue. But after their examination, you will need to contact a local funeral home. If you call the morgue in the afternoon, a secretary there will give you some numbers.'

'Oh my God.'

'Mr Millstein, I'm sorry to have to deliver this news. I

have to warn you, you might hear from the local media. I'm sure you'll want more details, and I'll provide these as best as I can, but right now I have work to do. Please telephone me at your convenience at the number I gave you. I should be there by eight this morning. You could call me then.'

The attorney seemed to answer with a half sob and grunt, and Robinson hung up the telephone.

Espy Martinez was watching him closely. She felt, in part, like some voyeur, fascinated and repulsed, everything happening in front of her in some oddly slowed-down time. She saw a look of helpless discouragement pass across the detective's eyes, stopping for just a moment, just long enough to play a single note, before it disappeared, echo fading. She abruptly thought: We are both very young.

But what she said, quietly, was: 'That must be hard to do.'

Robinson shrugged, with a small, wry look on his face, and shook his head.

'Well, you get used to it,' he replied in a tone of voice that helped her recognize he was not anywhere near to telling the truth. And that he knew this.

The detective and the prosecutor walked outside. Espy Martinez thought the darkness seemed to have thinned, and she glanced down at her wristwatch and saw that morning was closing fast. She spotted a clutch of elderly people standing to one side of the small courtyard, but before she could ask, Walter Robinson anticipated her question.

'Those are the folks that live here. Kadosh is the name of the old guy who got a look at the perp running away down the alley. His wife called 911. The tall guy is Winter.

He walked Mrs Millstein home earlier, and double-checked her locks. Apartment owner is a Gonzalez, but he's not here yet. On his way. You know the damnedest thing? One of the neighbors told me he'd already put in new locks on half the apartments and was scheduled to come back this weekend to do Mrs Millstein's place. I don't think it would have made much difference, but you never know. That's what's gonna be in all the papers tomorrow.'

Walter Robinson gestured toward the group of reporters and cameramen. He gave them a quick wave, to let them know he was on his way over. Then he lowered his voice and said to Espy Martinez, 'Okay, what we're gonna hold back is anything about that gold chain with her name on it, and we're not gonna talk about the print the tech lifted from her neck, at least until we see if we can make a match with it.'

Robinson lifted his eyes and saw a pair of detectives and several patrolmen coming around the corner of the Sunshine Arms, from the back.

One of the detectives waved and approached the pair. From about five feet away he said: 'Hey Walter, you called that shot.'

Robinson introduced the detective to Espy Martinez and then said, 'Down the alley?'

'That's right. In a trash container. We took pictures and then the lab guy bagged it. We might be really lucky; I think I saw a little bit of blood on one corner.'

'What is it?' Espy Martinez asked.

'A brass jewelry box,' Robinson said. 'We're not gonna mention it to the press either. Okay?'

'No problem. I'd rather you did the talking anyway.'

Robinson nodded. 'All right. Let's go.' He smiled again and made a joke: 'Hey, no worse than going to the dentist.'

He touched her elbow for just an instant, and then the two of them together walked into the sudden glare of the television minicam lights.

CHAPTER FIVE
Hunters and Hunted

Simon Winter sat in his apartment, one finger hesitating over the push buttons on his telephone. Although midday sunlight filled the air, he had the sensation that he was about to step into a darkened room without knowing where the light switch was. What little sleep he'd managed had been fitful and nightmarish. Exhaustion mocked his movements. He took a final look outside his window, across the courtyard, where a slight breeze riffled the yellow police tape. Along with a red CRIME SCENE DO NOT ENTER sign posted on Sophie Millstein's door, it was the only outward, remaining indication of what had taken place the night before.

He did not know whether he was beginning something or ending it, but he thought himself obliged to make the call. He felt dizzy, almost as if he were sick, but then dragged himself to attention as the telephone started ringing on the other end.

It was answered by a distant 'Hello?'

'Is this Rabbi Chaim Rubinstein?' Winter asked.

'Yes. Rabbi once, but now retired. And who is this?'

'My name is Simon Winter, I'm a . . .' He paused, trying to think precisely what he was, and then answered, '. . . a friend of Sophie Millstein.'

'Sophie is dead.' The rabbi's voice was singularly cold. 'She was killed. Last night. By some intruder. A man searching for money for drugs. That is what the paper said.'

'I know. I'm her neighbor.'

'So. You know more than I. You know more than was in the papers. What is it you want?'

'She came to me yesterday. Only hours before her death. She was frightened, and she felt she had to tell you something. You and two friends. A Mr Silver and a Mrs Kroner. She didn't speak with you last night?'

'No. No, I did not speak to her. Tell us? Tell us what?' The rabbi's voice had risen slightly, pushed by stress and sudden fear.

'That she had seen—' He stopped, correcting himself, '. . . that she believed she had seen a man she called—'

The rabbi interrupted: 'Der Schattenmann.'

'That's right.'

Silence gripped the phone line.

'Rabbi?' Winter asked.

There was another hesitation before the rabbi spoke ice words.

'He will kill us all.'

Rabbi Chaim Rubinstein lived in a modest high-rise condominium on the wrong side of Ocean Drive, its view of the sea mostly blocked by two larger, more imposing buildings. From the best apartments, Winter saw, there would be just a sliver of pallid blue available to the eye. Otherwise, there was nothing to distinguish the old building from dozens like it up and down Miami Beach, stretching into Fort Lauderdale, Delray, up to the Palm Beaches, save its name: The Royal Palm. There was, of course, nothing royal about the building, nor did he see any palms, except for a single, unassuming potted tree drooping in the lobby.

Winter rode the elevator up to the sixth floor and stepped into the hallway. A blandly irritating Muzak played through tinny speakers in the ceiling. The corridor itself employed a depressing uniformity: a beige carpet, flower-print wallpaper, a seemingly endless series of white doors, notable only for the gold-plated numerals in the center of each.

He knocked at number 602 and waited. He could hear locks being disengaged, and the door opened partway, still secured by a chain.

'Mr Winter?'

'Rabbi?'

'Could you show me some identification? With a picture on it?'

Simon Winter nodded, reached into his wallet and produced his driver's license. He held this up for the rabbi to inspect.

'Thank you,' the man said after a moment. He closed the door to release the chain, and then opened it wide. 'Please come in. Thank you for coming.'

The two men shook hands. Rabbi Rubinstein was a short, thin man, but without the bony, cadaverous look of an aesthete. He sported a shaggy, curly mane of gray hair that toppled over his ears, and black-rimmed eyeglasses that were perched at the end of his nose. Through these he examined Simon Winter for an instant, then, with a wave, he directed Winter into the living room.

Winter saw the elderly couple sitting on a white couch, behind a glass coffee table, waiting for him. They rose as he entered.

'This is Mr Irving Silver and Mrs Frieda Kroner,' the rabbi said. Winter stepped forward and shook hands. Mrs

Kroner, thickset, wearing white slacks and a bulky sweater that made her seem twice the rabbi's size, immediately sat back down and poured him a cup of coffee. Mr Silver was a small, round man, nearly bald, who nervously drummed his fingers against his knee when he returned to his seat on the couch. Winter glanced around for an instant. He saw a bookcase and quickly read titles. There were some works on Judaica, a great number of histories of various aspects of the Holocaust, and a smattering of contemporary thrillers and horror novels. The rabbi caught his eye and said:

'So, most of the time I study and learn, Mr Winter. I try to understand these events that I was a small part of. It is what I have devoted my retirement to. But sometimes I, too, like to read something by Stephen King. This is not terrible. All the supernatural monsters and evil things he writes about, they cannot truly exist, can they? They are not real, and yet, he makes it seem as if they do, and that is most interesting, isn't it? We all like a good scare once in a while, do we not? It's entertaining.'

'I suppose so,' Winter answered.

'It is much easier, some nights, Mr Winter, to read of terrors that jump from a man's imagination, that are fantasy, than to study horrors that truly happened.' He pointed at a row of books examining the Holocaust.

The detective nodded.

'. . . Or are still happening,' the rabbi added.

The rabbi swept him into a chair with a gesture. Mrs Kroner handed him the cup of black coffee. She did not ask whether he cared for sugar or cream. He saw Irving Silver shift in his seat, leaning forward. His hands shook slightly as he rattled his cup into the saucer on the table in front of him. Winter saw a pale restraint in Irving Silver's face as he looked toward the rabbi with nervous need. The rabbi nodded, and then asked:

'So, tell us, Mr Winter. Tell us about what Sophie told you.'

The rabbi had an odd voice, one that started with a gravelly, deep tone, and then rose sharply with each word, so that at the end of his question, it was high-pitched and insistent.

'I can only repeat what I told you on the phone, Rabbi. She came to me in a panic. She believed that she had seen this man that she remembered from fifty years ago. She felt it was her responsibility to warn the three of you. And then later last night, she was killed—'

'Yes. Yes. The junkie,' Mr Silver interrupted. His voice was shrill. 'Isn't that what they still call some addict? We read about that in the paper. It was on the noon news too. He broke in and then he killed her and stole some things! The police are searching for him now! There was no mention of Der Schattenmann!'

Rabbi Rubinstein glared at Irving Silver, and asked Winter: 'So, how sure was Sophie, may she rest in peace, of the man she saw?'

Winter hesitated before replying, looking at the frightened eagerness in the three faces in front of him. He had the feeling that he was entering in the midst of an argument that had been going on for weeks, which he suspected was precisely the case.

'At first, when she knocked on my door, she seemed afraid enough to be certain. As she calmed down, she seemed less sure.'

He stopped abruptly.

'See?' Irving Silver insisted sharply. 'She didn't know for sure! None of us know for sure!'

The rabbi shook his head slowly. 'Irving, please. Let Mr Winter finish. Bear with us, Mr Winter. We do not want to believe this man is here. Now. Today.'

'He should be dead!' Mr Silver interjected swiftly. 'How could he not be dead? And why here? Why now? No, he must be dead! He could not have survived!'

Frieda Kroner frowned at Mr Silver. Then she spoke for the first time. Traces of German hid in her accent.

'He is here, you old fool! And where else would he be?'

'But we are the people he once . . .'

'That is correct,' she said coldly. 'He killed many of us once. And now, he is doing it again. This is to be expected. Why are you so surprised? Does a man who hates so much ever really stop? Poor Sophie. When he saw her, she didn't have a chance. Nobody ever did.'

A large tear dropped down her round cheek. She sat back hard, folding her arms across her ample bosom, making no effort to wipe it away.

Simon Winter held up a hand.

'Mrs Kroner . . . there's no indication that someone other than the suspect the police are searching for is involved in Sophie's death . . .'

'If he saw her, he wouldn't hesitate. He would act swiftly. And she would die. And this is what happened.'

The woman spoke with a bitter finality, forcing Winter to hesitate, his mind racing with questions, as he told himself to move slowly.

'There was a letter. Sophie told me about a Herman Stein who killed himself. He allegedly saw this man as well?'

Again there was a small silence in the room.

Rabbi Rubinstein nodded his head gently.

'We talked, but we could not agree. It is hard to believe.'

'You have the letter?'

'Yes.' The rabbi reached down and picked up a copy of Raul Hilberg's *The Destruction of the European Jews*, which was resting next to the coffee service. The letter was inside the book. He handed it to Simon Winter, who swiftly read:

Rabbi:

I know of you through Rabbi Samuelson at Temple Beth-el, who gave me your name and told me that you were once a Berliner, as I was, many, many years ago.

You, perhaps, will remember a man we knew in those sad times only as Der Schattenmann. This was the person who found my family, when we hid out in the city, in 1942. He saw to our deportation to Auschwitz.

I hoped that this man was dead, along with all the others. But it is not so! Two days ago I attended a large meeting of the Surfside Condominiums Association and accidentally saw him in the audience, sitting two rows behind me! He is here. I am certain of it.

Rabbi, who am I to call?

What am I to do?

It is wrong that this man still lives and I feel I must do something. My mind is black with questions, clouded with fears. Can you help me?

The letter was signed by Herman Stein, who also gave his address and telephone number.

Simon Winter looked up from the single sheet of paper and the handwritten message.

'The letter arrived?'

'Three days after Mr Stein's death. All the way from Surfside, this is not far, it is not Alaska or the South Pole, but the postal service does not deliver the letter until three days after it was written. Such a thing.'

The rabbi's lip quivered slightly.

'I was too late to help this poor Mr Stein.'

'And?'

'I contacted the police. And I called Mr Silver and Mrs Kroner and of course your neighbor.'

'What did the police say?'

'I spoke with a detective who made a copy of the letter, but who told me that Mr Stein, whom I didn't know, had lived alone for many years and all his neighbors had been worried for him of late, because he seemed so sad. Moping about. Talking to himself—'

'Acting crazy just as if death was standing beside him,' Frieda Kroner interjected.

The rabbi nodded. 'The detective told me Mr Stein had written a suicide note before he shot himself and that was that, he could not help me further. He was a nice man, this detective, but I think he was busy with many other things and not so interested in my problems. He showed me Mr Stein's suicide note.'

'Do you remember—'

'Of course. How can you forget such a thing? I can still see the words, right in my memory. It was one sentence only: "I am tired of life, and miss my beloved Hanna and so I go to join her now." That was all. He shot himself. The detective told me. One time, right in the forehead.'

'The forehead?'

'That is what the policeman said.' The rabbi tapped the space just above his eyebrows as he spoke.

'You're sure? Did you read the detective's crime scene notes? Did they show you any of the crime scene photographs? Did you see the autopsy protocol?'

The rabbi arched a single eyebrow upward at the quick array of questions.

'No. He just told me this. He showed me nothing. A protocol?'

Simon Winter started to ask another question, then stopped. He thought: *the forehead*. Not the temple. Not the mouth, as he had selected for himself in what seemed years beforehand. In his mind's eye he tried to envision holding a pistol in that position. Awkward. Not impossible. Not even improbable. But awkward and why would anyone make their own suicide awkward? His immediate answer to this question was that the rabbi had misunderstood the detective.

The rabbi looked over at him sharply. 'You know of such things, Mr Winter?'

'Yes. For two decades I was a policeman for the City of Miami. I retired to the Beach a number of years ago. So, yes, it has been a long time, but I still know of such things, Rabbi.'

'You were a policeman?' Mr Silver asked hurriedly. 'And now?'

'And now I'm just another old person on the Beach, Mr Silver.'

Rabbi Rubinstein snorted. 'This is why Sophie went to you.'

'Yes. I suppose so. She was afraid, and she knew I had a gun.' Winter took a deep breath. 'She thought I could help her.'

'I am going to get a gun too,' Irving Silver said defiantly. 'And I think we should all go get one and be able to defend ourselves!'

'What do I know of guns?' Frieda Kroner interrupted. 'And what do you know, you old fool? More than likely, you will shoot yourself, or your neighbor, or the delivery boy who brings your heart medicine from the pharmacy.'

'Yes, but maybe I will shoot *him* first, when he comes for me!'

This statement brought a silence crashing into the room.

Simon Winter looked at the three faces in front of him.

The rabbi seemed exhausted by fear and sadness; Mrs Kroner's eyes captured a combination of despair and defiance; while Mr Silver covered the terror he felt with anger. The rabbi spoke first.

'You must forgive us, Mr Winter. Sophie was our friend and we are in mourning. But we are also upset, and now, I think, we are afraid as well.'

'There's no need to apologize, Rabbi. But why is it that you are so convinced that she was killed by this man? The police have a witness, another neighbor, who saw the perpetrator fleeing the murder scene. A young black man.'

'You believe this?' Irving Silver demanded.

'An eyewitness,' Winter replied sharply. 'He chased the man into an alley.'

The rabbi shook his head. 'I am confused, Mr Winter. And confusion only seems to make me more uncertain and afraid. Mr Stein says he sees Der Schattenmann and then he dies. A suicide. Sophie says she sees Der Schattenmann and then she dies, killed by some unknown black man. This is a mystery to me, Mr Winter. You are the detective. Tell us: can such odd coincidences occur?'

Simon Winter paused before replying. 'Rabbi, for many years I was a homicide detective—'

'Yes, yes, but answer the question!' Irving Silver interrupted. He opened his mouth again, but Frieda Kroner snapped an elbow into his ribs.

'Let the man speak!' she whispered harshly.

Winter let quiet fill the room while he considered his response. 'Let me say this. Coincidences do occur. Fantastic, unbelievable coincidences. All detectives remember remarkable events, things that no one could have anticipated in a million years. In homicide work, these things are, if not commonplace, at least familiar. But, that said, you should understand that the vast majority of deaths are perfectly routine and straightforward. It is important to always search for the simple answer first, because in almost every case, that is the truth of the death.'

'So what you're saying is—' Irving Silver broke in.

'Let him finish!' Frieda Kroner said, exasperated. Again she jabbed at Irving Silver's ribs. 'You rude old man!' she chastened him.

'Thank you, Mrs Kroner, but I have.'

The rabbi was nodding his head. 'You're saying yes – it could be exactly what it seems. A suicide. A murder by some animal off the street.'

'Correct.'

Again silence occupied a chair.

'Do you have an opinion, Mr Winter?' Frieda Kroner asked.

'I have questions, Mrs Kroner,' Simon Winter replied. 'And, I think, it is wise to remove doubts where there are so many. Regardless of how Sophie and Mr Stein died, I think it will be difficult for the three of you to go about your business if every second you think you are being stalked by this fellow. If he exists.'

She nodded, as did the rabbi.

'I still want a gun,' Irving Silver muttered.

They all remained silent. Winter watched tears form in the corner of Irving Silver's eyes, and the man started to shake his head, slowly, almost imperceptibly, as if trying to loosen and discard all the thoughts that had emerged.

The rabbi leaned forward, pushing the fingers of each hand through his tangled mass of hair. He puffed out his cheeks and let his wind slowly seep through pursed lips. Then he looked up at Simon Winter.

'You will help us, Mr Winter?'

Winter felt a rigid toughness within him. He looked at

the three faces of the elderly people in the room, and he remembered the shaky hand his neighbor placed on his own, as he'd interrupted his own death to let her enter his apartment. He took a quick glance and saw a similar blue tattoo on the rabbi's forearm, and suspected that beneath Mrs Kroner's bulky white sweater and Mr Silver's loose, checked shirt, he would find the same. He thought: I promised to help her, and then I didn't. He realized that promise was still lingering about within him, and so he replied:

'I will try, Rabbi. I'm not certain what I can do . . .'

'You know things we do not. Many things.'

'It has been a long time.'

'Does one ever forget these things? These techniques?'

'No.'

'Then, you will be able to help.'

'I hope so.'

The three elderly people took quick glances at each other.

'I think we are in need of help,' Mrs Kroner said. 'Maybe even more than we even want to say out loud, Mr Winter.'

'I still want a gun,' Irving Silver muttered. 'If we'd had guns back then—'

'Then the Nazis would have shot us on the spot!'

'Maybe that would have been better!'

'How can you say that, you old fool! We lived! And now the world does not forget!'

'Maybe it doesn't forget, but what has the world learned?'

Irving Silver and Frieda Kroner glared at each other. The rabbi sighed.

'They are frequently like this,' he said to Winter. 'We were all once, when we were so young, caught up in these immense events, and now we argue. Even the scholars argue. But we were there, and we were a part of something that is maybe more than just history.'

'So was he . . .' Irving Silver grunted.

The rabbi stopped speaking, and looked at the others.

'That is true. He was as much a part of it as any of those who either died or survived.'

'And he hasn't forgotten either,' Irving Silver added.

'No. I think not.'

Frieda Kroner started to dab a napkin at the corners of her eyes. 'If he is here . . .'

'And he finds us . . .' Silver joined in.

'I think he will kill us.'

Simon Winter held up a hand. 'But why? And why would he kill or want to kill Sophie and this Mr Stein? You haven't explained this.'

As soon as he asked this question, Winter realized he had entered a realm ruled by history and memory, dark at the edges, pitch-black at its core.

'Because,' the rabbi started after a moment's silence, 'because we are the only people who can rise up and point him out.'

'Bring him to justice,' whispered Frieda Kroner.

'If he's here! I don't believe it! I don't believe any of it!' Irving Silver slapped his palm against his knee. The others looked at him sharply, but it was Winter who spoke first.

'But if he is here, you would recognize him?'

It took Irving Silver several seconds to answer. The old detective saw his chest heave with deep breaths as he struggled with the question.

'Yes,' Silver said. 'I saw his face too. For just a few seconds. He took money from my brother and I.'

'It was my father,' the rabbi said quietly. 'It was my father that he recognized, when we were riding on the trolley. My father turned my face away, but I saw too. I was so young.'

Frieda Kroner shook her head. 'I was young too. Like the rabbi and Sophie, little more than a child. He caught us in the park. It was spring, and the city was filled with rubble and death, but still, it was spring and I remember so many people were outside, enjoying the fine day, and so my mother and I, we went out too, because it was so important to behave like all the others. Before the war they called it Führer weather, as if Hitler himself could rule the heavens!'

Again a silence creased the room.

'It is difficult to speak of these things,' the rabbi said.

Simon Winter nodded. 'Yes,' he said slowly. 'But I think I will need to know more if I am to help you.'

'That is not unreasonable.'

'And, there is something I do not understand.'

'What is that, Mr Winter?'

'Why would he kill you? Why not simply hide? It would not be difficult. He would not face a risk. Why not simply disappear?'

'I can answer that,' Frieda Kroner said quickly.

Winter turned toward her.

'Because he is a lover of death, Mr Winter.'

The two others nodded in agreement.

'You see, Mr Winter, what made him different from the others, why we were all so frightened of him, was that we knew he did what he did not because he believed some Nazi lie that by helping he could stay alive! He didn't do it to protect his family – that was another excuse we heard. He did it because he enjoyed it.'

She shuddered hard.

'And because he was better at it than anyone else.'

'Iranische Strasse,' Rabbi Rubinstein added. This time

his voice did not rise, but remained low and harsh. 'The Jewish Bureau of Investigation. That was where the Gestapo watched the catchers, who then watched for us.'

'They took off their stars,' Irving Silver said. 'And then they hunted us down.'

'Berlin, you see, it was Himmler himself who came on the radio and promised that the city would be *Judenfrei*!' The rabbi added, his voice gathering momentum. 'But it wasn't! It never was! When the Russians came, there were still fifteen hundred of us hiding in the rubble! Fifteen hundred out of 150,000! But we were still there when the tanks thundered in and all the Nazis were swept up in their own fire! Never was Berlin *Judenfrei*! Never. If there had been only one of us left, it was never *Judenfrei*!'

Simon Winter nodded. 'But this man—'

Frieda Kroner spoke quickly. 'Der Schattenmann covered his tracks better than any other catcher. It was said that if you saw him, then you died. If you heard his voice, then you died. If he touched you, then you died . . .'

She hesitated, then added: 'In the basement at Plotzensee Prison. A terrible place, Mr Winter. A place where horrible death was the norm, and the Nazis created even worse. Racks and meat hooks and guillotines and garottes, Mr Winter.'

'We were told that his would be the last living eyes you saw,' Irving Silver said flatly. 'His breath on your cheek would be your last memory.'

'How did you know?'

'A word here, a conversation there,' Frieda Kroner said. 'It got around. People would talk. A shopkeeper to a customer. A policeman to a landlord. An idle word overheard at a park or on a trolley. And then mothers told their daughters, as mine did. Fathers told their sons. That was how we knew of Der Schattenmann.' She breathed out deeply, as if the very words were painful.

'But the three of you. And Mr Stein. And Sophie. You all survived . . .'

'Luck,' said the rabbi. 'Accident? Mistake? The Nazis were so efficient, Mr Winter, sometimes now, in history, we think of them as superhuman. But so many of them were bureaucrats and clerks and little men pushing pencils! And so, instead of the basement, some of us rode the trains to our deaths.'

At that moment Irving Silver burst out in a sob.

They turned toward him and saw his eyes had reddened and he had clapped a hand over his mouth, as if to prevent the words he spoke from tumbling out. He was breathing hard again, battling with his breath.

'My brother,' he choked out, behind a clenched fist held to his lips, 'he went to the basement.'

The others were silent.

'Oh, poor Martin,' Irving Silver moaned. 'My poor brother Martin.'

After a moment, his eyes swept around to the others.

'I'm sorry,' he said. 'It is hard to remember, but remember we must.'

Irving Silver took a deep breath.

'This is all remembrance,' he continued. 'We remember. And so does Der Schattenmann. He must have thought he had killed us once, and now he will try again. We were all just slightly more than children, then, Mr Winter, and this must have been what saved us from him. My older brother, he was a threat, so . . .'

'My father,' murmured the rabbi.

'And my mother,' Frieda Kroner added.

'Surely, Mr Winter, this cannot be so surprising,' the rabbi said. 'Just as Frieda says. If we know no peace because of what lives on in our memories, why would he be any different?'

Irving Silver reached out and squeezed Frieda Kroner's hand. She nodded.

Simon Winter felt as if he were suddenly caught in a strong current, pulling him into a deepening sea, dragging him away from the shoreline. He thought: All detectives work from memory; one crime resembles another. A third is reminiscent of a fourth. Even within the most exceptional, there are common threads: a motive, such as greed; a weapon, like a gun or knife; evidence – fingerprints, bloodwork, fiber or hair samples, whatever. And all those threads strive toward a commonality of crime. But this, what the three old people in front of him were speaking of, was a sort of crime that defied characterization.

He paused before replying. Silence swept the air.

'I think I will need to know more about this man. Who was he? Surely someone knew his name, where he came from, something about his family . . .?'

There was another momentary silence before Frieda Kroner replied: 'No one knew anything for sure. He was different from the others.'

'He was different,' Rabbi Rubinstein added quietly, 'because he was like a knife in the dark. The others, people knew, you see. If the catcher knew you, then you might know the catcher too. Maybe from the synagogue, or the apartment building, or the doctor's office or the school-yard, from somewhere before the race laws were put in effect. So, if you were alert, you could perhaps stay . . . what? One jump ahead? You might be able to hide. Or run. Or bribe them. They were traitors, but some, even near the end, some still had some feelings . . .'

The rabbi breathed out slowly.

'. . . But no one knew who he was. It was like the Nazis

just invented this golem. A wraith.'

'Can you describe him?'

'He was tall, like you—' Frieda Kroner started, but Irving Silver shook his head and waved his hand.

'No, Frieda, no. He was a tiny man, like a ferret. And older. More mature . . .'

'No,' the rabbi interrupted angrily. 'He had to be young in order to survive. Young and strong and smart and ambitious.'

They looked at each other and fell into quiet.

'We were little more than children,' the rabbi started. 'Our memories . . .'

'I was small, like Sophie,' Frieda Kroner said. 'All men looked large to me.'

'My poor brother Martin was still strong and tall, and so I thought everyone not like him was short . . .'

'You see, Mr Winter?' the rabbi said. 'Der Schatten-mann was better than any Gestapo. He was like a ghost. Wherever he walked, there was darkness, even in the daytime. Just like a . . . what is it, Irving?'

'A will-o'-the-wisp.'

'And we all knew,' the rabbi said coldly, 'that if he found you, then you could not hide.'

'But couldn't he be bribed?'

'Yes and no,' Irving Silver said. 'Perhaps you would hear a voice in some dark alleyway, and you would promise your money and you might deliver it all to him. But then the Gestapo would come anyway, and the person Der Schattenmann had touched would be taken to the base-ment and the rest of his family put on the next train for the camps. He covered his tracks. If he found you, then it was like the world had never seen you.'

Frieda Kroner gasped at a sudden memory. She shuddered hard, but held up her hand and did not speak when the others turned toward her.

'But Sophie. The three of you. Mr Stein. You're suggesting . . .'

'Mistakes. Mistakes,' the rabbi said. 'No one was ever supposed to live, but sometimes we did. This was a mistake. And now, fifty years later, are those mistakes not being erased from the board?' Irving Silver shivered and Frieda Kroner dabbed her eyes.

Simon Winter nodded. He was having trouble understanding the fear he saw before him, but knew that it filled the room. He looked around for a moment at all the simple, ordinary things that filled the rabbi's apartment. A large brass menorah. Photographs of friends and family. A finely embroidered tablecloth. But it was as if all these items were obscured by smoky memory, and that the air was filled with a noxious smell.

Rabbi Rubinstein leaned back heavily. 'It is hard now, to be old and to be remembering these things,' he said. 'It is like discovering a new pain.' He sighed. 'I had forgotten what it was like to be hunted.'

The others nodded in agreement.

Simon Winter wanted to reach out and touch the man, but could not. Instead, he said: 'I do not understand something. Why would this man be here? On Miami Beach, where there is a great concentration of survivors. Wouldn't this be the place where he would most likely be recognized? Why wouldn't he be in Argentina or Romania or someplace safer?'

Irving Silver shook his head. 'This is where he'd be safest.'

'But how?'

'You do not understand, Detective Winter,' Rabbi Rubinstein said, starting slowly but rapidly accelerating his words as he spoke. 'Der Schattenmann was not a Nazi! He wasn't Gestapo! He wasn't S.S.! He was a Jew, like all of us! There was no Odessa organization or Iron Cross group to help him find freedom and safety after the war! There was just himself!'

'But certainly there were organizations. The Red Cross. Groups that helped displaced persons . . .'

'Of course! That was how I arrived here—'

'And me, too,' said Frieda Kroner.

'Not me. I had distant relatives who helped,' Irving Silver said. 'But who would help Der Schattenmann? Not the Russians. They would have shot him. Bang! No trial. So who!'

'Tell me,' Simon Winter asked.

'His own people. The same people he'd betrayed,' Silver said.

'But not if they knew who he was, right?'

'Of course. Were not the Kapos in the camps turned over to authorities?' Silver replied. Rabbi Rubinstein nodded in agreement.

'But *he* would have known of that danger,' the rabbi added.

'So what are you saying he would do?'

The three old people turned and looked at each other. For a moment Winter could hear them all breathing. It was as if they were conversing, arguing, debating, assessing this question, but without words, without gestures. Simply letting their imaginations blend together and come up with a single conclusion.

The rabbi wiped a hand slowly across his face. 'He would need to become one of us. A survivor.'

Frieda Kroner nodded her head. 'Of course. How else?'

'But how could he fake that?'

Irving Silver frowned. 'He was Der Schattenmann! He could do what he wanted!'

'But . . .' Winter hesitated, '. . . surely there were others like him. And they were caught?'

'Really? Not like him. I do not think so.'

'But why here?'

'Because we are his people!'

'No one knew us better than him? That was how he was so successful. Why would he be frightened of us?'

Rabbi Rubinstein rose, but as he did, he lifted the volume of *The Destruction of the European Jews* from the table. Stein's letter fluttered to the floor, but no one moved for it. The heavy book swayed in his hands. He did not open it, and Winter realized the old rabbi could recall what was in the book by memory.

'If you remember the times,' he started, 'remember the times. Confusion and depravity. The Holocaust, Detective, it was like a great machine devoted to the murder of the Jews. But for the Nazis to accomplish this task – they kept talking, over and over, in all their speeches and propaganda and writings of the "monumental" task – they had to have help. All sorts of help, from all sides . . .'

'From the Pope, who did not condemn them . . .' Irving Silver said.

'From the Allies, who did not bomb the camps or the rail routes into Dachau and Auschwitz . . .' Frieda Kroner added.

'From the non-Jewish people, the Poles and Czechs and Rumanians and Italians and French and Germans who watched. Really, from the whole world, Detective; in one way or another, everyone helped. Including some of the very people they were trying to destroy.'

Simon Winter sat quietly, listening.

'So, consider Auschwitz, Detective. After the Nazis did the selecting, someone had to close the doors on the gas chambers and someone had to remove the bodies afterward. Someone had to stoke the fires of the ovens and someone had to keep the whole thing working smoothly. And oftentimes those someones were ourselves.'

The rabbi sat down heavily, the book in his lap.

'We helped, you see. Just by living, by doing whatever it took to stay alive, it helped perversely, to keep it all going . . .'

He looked at Mrs Kroner and Mr Silver.

'Could it have been more right, more moral, just to die in the face of all that evil, detective? These are questions that haunt philosophers. I am just an old rabbi.'

He stopped, shaking his head, breathing in hard before continuing.

'It is crazy, all of it you see, Detective. Look at the world we live in today. Some days you think this is all so far away and back in the past that it cannot really have happened, but others, well, then you know that it is right there, still alive today, just as evil and terrible and waiting to rise up again.'

'Der Schattenmann, he was the worst of all of us,' the rabbi continued. 'He was worse than the Nazis. Worse even than those strange evil things that Mr King likes to write about.'

'And now, he's here, right amongst us,' Irving Silver said bitterly. 'Like an infection.'

'Is there not always someone like Der Schattenmann amongst us?' the rabbi asked quietly. This question went unanswered.

'Can you find him, Detective?' Frieda Kroner asked quietly.

'I do not know.'

'Will you try?'

'If he's here. If what you suggest is true . . .'

'Will you search for him, Mr Winter?'

Simon Winter felt a vast echoing sadness within himself. The answer seemed to well up through that personal darkness.

'Yes, I will try.'

'Good,' Frieda Kroner said. 'Then I will help you, Mr Winter.'

'I, too. I will help,' said Irving Silver.

'Of course, I will join in as well,' said Rabbi Rubinstein. 'We will do whatever we can.'

Frieda Kroner nodded, then reached forward and poured herself another cup of coffee. Simon Winter watched as she took a long pull at the dark cup, letting the bitter taste cascade through her. She smiled, but coldly.

'Good. And when you find him, Detective, with our help, then you will kill him.'

'Frieda!' Rabbi Rubinstein interjected. 'Think of what you say! Our religion speaks of forgiveness and understanding. That has always been our way!'

'Maybe so, rabbi. But my heart speaks for all those he betrayed and who died. Think first of them, rabbi, then talk to me of forgiveness.'

She turned to Simon Winter.

'I would rather speak of justice,' she said. 'Find him and kill him.'

Irving Silver leaned forward. 'I will help. I will do whatever I can. We all will. But Frieda is right. Find him and kill him, Mr Winter.' He took a deep breath, then added: 'For my dear brother Martin. And my parents and all my cousins . . .'

Frieda Kroner joined in softly, '. . . And my sister and her husband and my two little nieces and grandparents and my mother who tried so hard to save me and all the others . . .'

Simon Winter didn't reply. He stared over at the rabbi,

who was looking at the other two. He saw Rabbi Rubin-stein's hand seem to quiver as it tightened around the book on his lap.

Irving Silver spoke bluntly: 'Kill him, Detective. And then there will be one less nightmare in the world. Kill him.'

And then the rabbi, too, nodded.

CHAPTER SIX

Prayers for the Dead

Simon Winter shifted about uncomfortably on a gray steel folding chair while a young rabbi spoke at the gravesite. Although the gathering was collected beneath a dark green canopy provided by the funeral home, the insistent heat of midday forced its way unbidden and unwelcome, amidst the mourners. They were mostly older people, and the dark woolen suits they wore seemed to steam under the noontime sun. Simon Winter urgently wished he could loosen his tie, snugged tightly beneath the starched white collar of the sole remaining dress shirt he owned. As he looked about, he thought: we all look like we're ready to join Sophie Millstein in her coffin. He was slightly ashamed at the irreverence of his opinion, but forgave himself with the wry notation that it would not be too long before it was himself dressed out in some box or stuffed in some urn, with someone else whom he didn't know and didn't care about droning on above his head.

The rabbi, a short, rotund man, battling hard against the sweat collecting at his tight collar, raised his voice:

'This woman, Sophie Millstein, was thrust into the inferno only to rise and through goodness and devotion, like a phoenix, become the beloved wife of Leo and the adored mother of a brilliant son, Murray...'

The young priest's voice was high-pitched, needlelike. The words seemed to prick the still air. Winter's eyes swept up into the expanse of eggshell-blue sky, searching the horizon for gathering clouds that might carry the promise of an afternoon thundershower and the momentary relief of a steady downpour. But he saw none, and he inhaled sharply, breathing in air as hot and thick as smoke.

As he sat alone, near the rear of the gathering, he berated himself for allowing the heat to distract him.

He could be here, he insisted.

Over there, just beyond your eyesight, obscured by those trees. Or sitting, head down, in a row to the side, acting like a professional mourner. If he's hunting, this would be the first place he'd look, right amidst Sophie's old friends.

What he doesn't know, Winter thought, is that someone is looking for him.

Then he stopped, and let some doubt creep into his thoughts: if *he* exists at all.

To his side, Mr Finkel and the Kadoshes paid rapt attention to the rabbi's words. Mrs Kadosh clutched a white linen handkerchief in her hand, which she alternately dabbed at the corners of her eyes and then used to wipe the heat from her forehead. Her husband held a printed program in his hands, rolling it tightly, then spreading it out, smoothing the pages. He occasionally, surreptitiously, fanned the paper in front of him, trying without success to move some of the warmth away.

The other residents of the Sunshine Arms were spread about the gathering. Winter saw that Mr Gonzalez, the landlord, kept his head bowed throughout the rabbi's eulogy. His daughter had accompanied her father to the service. She was as tall as her father, and wore a slim, black dress that Simon Winter thought would have served her equally well at an opera's opening night as it did at a funeral.

Simon Winter sighed. For six months Mr Gonzalez's daughter had occupied the empty apartment next to Sophie Millstein. She had enthusiastically and energetically entertained a number of boyfriends there, usually failing to close the curtains in the living room, permitting Winter to watch her. He thought she had been aware that he watched, thought, too, that she left the curtains open as an unspoken favor. He shook his head. When she had moved to fancier digs on Brickell Avenue, she had taken much of the energy out of the Sunshine Arms.

Before taking her seat next to her father, she had glanced back over her shoulder, and her eyes had met his, for just an instant, just long enough for her to pass along a small, sad smile, coupled with a slight nod, as if to remind him of what he missed in her; and this, despite the solemnity of the occasion and his troubled thoughts about his murdered neighbor, managed to bring a somewhat distracting, but altogether pleasurable, internal laugh to Simon Winter's heart.

'And so today we all feel the loss of this woman . . .' The rabbi's speech continued predictably.

He pulled his eyes off of Mr Gonzalez's daughter's back and once again swept them across the seated mourners. If *he*'s here, he'll be looking hard, Winter thought. He'll be searching the faces, as he ransacks his own memory.

Winter centered on one man, off to his right. The man was staring hard at the rabbi. The old detective felt a quick surge within him. Why are you so curious? he wondered.

But then, just as swiftly, he saw the man turn and whisper something to an elderly woman at his side. The woman touched his arm.

No, Winter thought. You'll be alone. Aren't you always alone?

If you exist.

Winter inclined his head slightly, dropping his chin toward his chest in thought. He had told Irving Silver, Frieda Kroner, and Rabbi Rubinstein not to attend the service. He did not want to give the man they feared the advantage of seeing them before he had had time to consider his own course of action. They had objected. He had insisted.

He surveyed the crowd again, looking for faces that he didn't recognize, but there were too many. Sophie Millstein had belonged to too many women's groups, bridge clubs, synagogue assemblies. There were nearly a hundred old people shifting about on the steel chairs.

The rabbi's words seemed to shimmer in the heat.

'To go through so much, only to be robbed of life near the end, is a tragedy almost too great for the heart to bear . . .'

Winter glanced about, trying to spot Detective Robinson or the young woman from the State Attorney's Office, but he did not see them. He suspected that there was someone from the Miami Beach police mingled in amidst the mourners; this had been procedure on any homicide specified as nonsubject, when he was a detective – even when the prime suspect was a different age and different race. There was still no telling who might show up, curious. He suspected that Robinson had sent a subordinate; his own skin color would have made it impossible for him to remain hidden, watching the people beneath the canopy.

Of course, whomever the detective had sent might be searching for the wrong person altogether.

Simon Winter breathed out slowly, and wrapped his fist

around the printed program. He felt an unruly anger, a frustration pounding around within him.

I don't know anything, he said to himself.

All I have are some odd coincidences and a trio of frightened old folks and a nightmare from a different era.

He looked up into the sky again. He felt his anger slide away into guilt. Can you really remember how to do it? How to take some suspicions and turn them into something hard and cold and true?

He gritted his teeth.

Start acting like what you once were, he demanded.

You want them to call you Detective again? Then behave like one. Ask some questions. Find some answers.

In the front row, next to the grave, a young child of four or five fidgeted nervously, trying to speak over the rabbi's words, only to be swiftly shushed by his mother. The rabbi paused, smiled at the child, then continued:

'So who was this woman, this Sophie Millstein, who gave so much of herself, who achieved so much in her life? I feel I should learn more about this remarkable woman, so that the lessons of her life can teach me, as they have taught her son and her daughter-in-law and her beloved grandchildren . . .'

Simon Winter could only see the back of Murray Millstein. But as the rabbi spoke, he saw the attorney slide his arm around his wife's shoulders and reach all the way to his son, where his hand remained. The rabbi continued, finally switching effortlessly into Hebrew, speaking the kaddish over the coffin, but Winter no longer heard the words, and no longer felt the oppressive heat. All he saw was the hand of the young father, lingering on his son's shoulder, and the son gently leaning his head toward the hand, resting his cheek there, reassured, all the terrifying child fears of death and dying destroyed in that instant by his father's firm touch.

Winter hung near the end of the reception line, following the service, waiting for a moment when he would have more than a second, because he wanted to do more than simply murmur a few words of solace and head off. As the gathering thinned and he saw the young attorney start to search for his wife and children, he stepped forward.

'Mr Millstein, I'm Simon Winter. I was one of your mother's neighbors . . .'

'Of course, Mr Winter. My mother spoke of you often.'

'I am sorry for your loss . . .'

'Thank you.'

'But I was wondering, have the police—'

'They say they're making progress, and that they'll keep me informed. You were once a policeman, true? I seem to remember my mother—'

'Yes. Here in Miami. I was a detective.'

'My mother spoke highly of you. She spoke highly of all her neighbors. What was your specialty?'

'Homicide.'

Murray Millstein paused, as if measuring the weight of Simon Winter's one word response. He was a short man, slight, but with a wiry appearance, like a distance runner, and an alertness that seemed to speak of attention to detail. The old detective thought that whatever tears Murray Millstein was destined to shed over his mother's murder would be dispensed in private. He eyed Winter carefully before responding quietly.

'The Miami Beach police seem quite capable. Is that your impression?'

'Yes. I'm sure they are. It's just, well, is there somewhere

I could ask you a few questions? Somewhere away from this?'

Winter gestured, and as he did, he saw the rabbi and the funeral director moving toward the two of them.

'We plan to sit shiva back in Long Island. We're supposed to fly out tonight. Is there something specific you wanted to ask about?'

'No, I just, it was something your mother said to me, shortly before her death.'

'Something she said?'

'Yes.'

'Which you think has some connection . . .'

'I'm not sure. It bothered me. Maybe I'm simply old, with an overwrought imagination. It probably wasn't anything important. You should trust the Miami Beach police. I'm certain your mother's death will be a high priority case.'

Murray Millstein hesitated, then responded quickly.

'This afternoon, I'm meeting some movers at my mother's apartment. Four P.M. Why don't we speak then?'

Winter nodded, and the younger man turned away from him in order to address the approaching pair.

Simon Winter was waiting by the cherub in the courtyard of the Sunshine Arms when Murray Millstein, accompanied by a man wearing an ill-fitting tan suit, arrived. The murdered woman's son took a quick glance around before walking to the apartment door. There was a large red printed sign posted there: CRIME SCENE NO UNAUTHORIZED ENTRY. Winter saw the younger man stop, with a key poised in the air. The attorney turned to the man in the suit and said: 'I don't want to go in. Just walk through the place quickly, and remember not to touch anything. Then we can talk.'

The man in the suit nodded, and Murray Millstein unlocked the door. Then he turned toward Winter and sat down heavily on the front steps.

'I wanted her to move into a retirement home. You know, one of those places up in Fort Lauderdale that specialize in elderly people. Especially ones that are alone. A planned community. Twenty-four hour security. Bingo games. A recreation center.'

'She mentioned that once.'

'She wouldn't do it. She liked it here.'

'Sometimes, when you get older, change is more frightening than whatever threat is out there.'

'That's probably true. But it's only relevant if all those things that are out there don't show up one night and murder you in your sleep.' Murray Millstein's voice was heavy with bitter guilt. 'Are you the same, Mr Winter?'

'Yes. No. Who knows? I wouldn't want to move into one of those developments either. Of course, when I finally got there, I'd probably like it . . .'

'That's the problem, isn't it?'

'I guess so.'

Winter sat down on the steps next to Murray Millstein.

'I can't go in,' the younger man said. 'I thought I could. I thought I needed to. You know, see where it happened. But I don't want to.' He took a deep breath. 'Is there blood?'

Simon Winter shook his head. 'No. Not really. It's a bit of a mess. All crime scenes are. Fingerprint dust on the furniture. Signs of people tramping in and out. Your mother would have been embarrassed. She kept a clean home.'

Murray Millstein smiled. 'She would have been mortified to think that she died in disarray.' Sadness rode every word, despite the upturn at the corners of his mouth.

'True enough.'

The younger man exhaled slowly. 'It's unbelievably hard,' he said quietly. 'You have this relationship that's filled with all the mundane and difficult parts of life. Trying to get your mother to do something she doesn't want to do. Complaining to your wife. Then having her defeat all that irritation by sending presents to her grandkids. I knew she was getting old. I suppose I knew there wouldn't be a lot of time left. And there were so many things I needed to say. When my father died, I saw it, you know. I saw how terrible it was to want to say things and then not have the chance. So I was determined to make sure I told my mother everything I wanted to. But one thing, then another, and I was so busy and time slips away so quickly, Mr Winter. It just races away, no matter what you do. And then it gets cut short because some fucking animal needs ten bucks or twenty bucks so that he can buy himself another pipe of fucking crack or whatever and he thinks it's worth my mother's life to get that . . .'

Murray Millstein's voice had risen, like a river of anguish flooded by storm waters, until his words were reverberating about the courtyard.

'Some fucking junkie. An addict. That's what they think. Shoots my mother's life into his fucking arm or smokes her future in some fucking pipe. I hope when they catch the fucking beast they'll let me tear his heart out.'

He paused for a breath of air.

'Fucking animal . . .' he added caustically.

Then he stopped, as if he was uncomfortable letting his emotions fly about the courtyard with such unbridled intensity. He stared out straight ahead for a moment, before turning to Winter and asking:

'Do you think they'll catch the bastard?'

'I don't know. Their techniques have improved. Maybe.'

'But maybe not, right?'

'Maybe not. Most of the homicides that get solved are ones where you know right away who did it. A husband. A wife. A business partner. Another drug dealer. Whomever. When two lives just touch randomly . . .'

'It's harder.'

'That's correct.'

'Did you talk to the detective? The black guy?'

'Yes. He seemed quite competent.'

'I hope so. We'll see.'

'Keep the pressure on,' Winter said.

'What?'

'Don't stop with the phone calls. Letters to the state attorney. Write the damn newspaper, the television stations. Keep reminding them. It will help. It will keep the case at the top of someone's file cabinet, instead of getting buried under all the other crap that starts to build up.'

'You know about that? Cases that just slip away?'

'Every detective does. Keep them thinking about this case. Maybe you'll get some results.'

'That's good advice.'

They were both silent for a moment, and then Murray Millstein swept his arm in front of them in a wide gesture.

'I'm thirty-nine years old and I want to get the hell out of here and never come back. I want this goddamn moving man to finish his estimate and I want to get on a plane and go back to my home . . .'

He half turned toward Winter.

'So, ask me your questions.'

'On the day that she was killed, your mother came to me. She had been scared. She saw someone from her past. Berlin, 1943.'

'Really?'

'Does the phrase *Der Schattenmann* mean anything to you?'

Murray Millstein paused, then replied: 'No. Not that I recall.' He said the name, as if by repeating it he might clarify it: 'Der Schattenmann? No. It doesn't ring a bell.'

'Did your mother talk about her wartime experiences much?'

Murray Millstein shook his head. 'Do you know much about the relationships between Holocaust survivors and their children, Mr Winter?'

'No.'

'They are, uh, problematical.' He placed a hand over his forehead, as if wiping away some difficult thought, before continuing.

'She would not talk about the camps. Or her life before the camps. Or her life up until the time she met my father. When he bought her to the U.S., she used to say that was when her life started. Do you know she couldn't speak English when she came here? Not only did she learn the language, but she was equally determined to erase – just totally and completely eradicate – any trace of her German accent. My father said she would stay up late at night, practicing in front of a mirror.'

Simon Winter shrugged. 'I see,' he said.

'No, you don't,' Murray Millstein replied, as if irritated. 'No German cars. No German products, No German anything. If a story came on the goddamn television about Germany, she shut it off. You've got to understand that even if it was never spoken about, her survival dominated our house. Everything my father did. Everything I did, as a child, growing up, right up to the day she was murdered, had some connection, unspoken, unsaid, shit, I don't know, with what happened to her. It was always there. Always.'

Murray Millstein shook his head.

'I grew up with ghosts,' he said flatly. 'Six million ghosts.'

'But she didn't speak of her experiences . . .'

'Not to me. But she made a videotape. Last year. For the Holocaust Center library here on the Beach. I haven't seen it, but she made it.'

'How did—'

'I found out because they sent me a solicitation. Fund-raising. They wanted a contribution. I sent them money. I called her up and said I wanted to see the tape, and we argued. Probably the only real argument we'd had in years. She forbade me – until after she was gone.'

'Will you go see it now?'

'No. Yes. I don't know.'

Murray Millstein stood up. The man in the tan suit emerged from the apartment. 'How much?' the young lawyer asked.

'To Long Island. Total contents? Twenty-two hundred, packed up and marked. That's our special move service,' the suit replied.

'Fine,' Murray Millstein said. 'I'm sure it's very special.' He handed the man the key. 'It may be a couple of weeks before the police release the apartment . . .'

'Don't worry, Mr Millstein. You just call, and we'll come right over. I'll send you a contract.'

The young man nodded, then looked down at his watch. 'I'm leaving now,' he said to Winter. 'You go.'

'What?'

'You go see the tape, Mr Winter. Then let me know about it.'

Murray Millstein turned and took a couple of steps into the courtyard before stopping and looking back over his shoulder at Simon Winter. 'I took German, you know.'

'I'm sorry?'

'I studied German. In high school. We had a language requirement and I took German. She hated that. Hardly spoke to me for an entire academic year. She wouldn't even allow a German dictionary into the house. I had to do all my studying at school. I got an A.'

Winter didn't know what to reply. He thought that sometimes the world seemed to accumulate an awful array of pain and hurt and deliver it unfairly, unequally, right on the heart of the unlucky.

Murray Millstein appeared to be thinking hard, for just an instant, before adding: 'Do you know what it means?'

'What?' Simon Winter looked up, almost startled, as if all his thoughts had been suddenly carried into the vortex of a strong wind and he was only brought back to earth by the sound of the younger man's voice.

'Der Schattenmann,' Murray Millstein said, shrugging his shoulders. 'Do you know what it means?'

Simon Winter shook his head. He had not thought to translate the phrase.

'It means the Shadow Man.' He paused, then said: 'I wonder what she meant by that?'

But Murray Millstein did not wait for a reply. Simon Winter watched the young attorney turn and walk quickly through the courtyard, past the trumpeting cherub, whose music, the old detective imagined, was on this occasion a dirge.

CHAPTER SEVEN
Urgency

When Espy Martinez arrived at the Dade State Attorney's Office the morning after Sophie Millstein's funeral, there were a pair of messages waiting for her: one from Walter Robinson, and the other a summons to meet with the chief assistant in the felony division. She knew instantly that he would want to know what progress was being made on the case, so, despite the fact that he'd marked his note with a red ink IMMEDIATELY she hurried through the warren of prosecutors' cubicles to her own and swiftly dialed the number for the homicide department at the Beach police.

Walter Robinson came on the line after a moment's delay.

'Miss Martinez,' he said, 'glad you phoned.'

'Detective, I'm about to be called in front of the chief assistant and asked to give a status report on the Millstein killing. What can you tell me?'

'Well, the first thing I'd say is to not worry that much about Abe Lasser. He may look like Dracula, but he's not really all that terrifying. Especially during the daytime.'

Espy Martinez wanted to smile at the detective's description of her boss, but instead imposed a rigidity on her words to mask her own nervousness. 'He's going to

want to know where we stand. Where do we stand,
Detective?'

Robinson started to say one thing, then paused, and
asked: 'Are you getting some heat on this case?'

'No,' she replied. 'Not yet. But I think I'm about to.'

Robinson nodded, though she couldn't see his head
moving. 'I thought you might. Well, I got the preliminary
autopsy and crime scene reports this morning. Here's
what we have. Death was by manual strangulation. Bruis-
ing to the larynx and carotid artery areas suggests that the
distance between the killer's thumb and index finger is five
point seven inches. There was no sign of sexual assault.
Preliminary blood toxicology showed traces of Dolmane.
That's a commonly prescribed sleeping agent. There were
some signs that she was beaten about a bit, but I think that
happened only in the first seconds. The sleeping pills must
have had her pretty knocked out, so much that probably
the first thing she was aware of was the guy choking her to
death. Not much time to fight back. There weren't any
significant defensive wounds on her hands or arms . . .'

Robinson traveled through the minutiae of Sophie
Millstein's final seconds of life with a practiced, routine
tone. Espy Martinez listened, trying to attach the words of
the clipped, official reports to the real-life terror that
engendered them, but found, after a few moments, that
she could not.

'Actually, that sort of bothers me,' Robinson said
quietly.

'What?'

'Well, guy breaks in, murders a sleeping woman, then
ransacks the place as fast as he can and splits. You see the
glitch?'

'No.'

'Why kill a sleeping woman? Why not just take what you

want real quiet-like and get the hell out?'

'She woke up.'

'Yeah. Probably. But wouldn't she have really screamed? Or fought hard?'

'The neighbors said they heard a noise.'

'Yeah, but not a real scream. More like a shout. And what about the cat? Mr Boots? Why kill the damn cat?'

'Maybe the cat was making noise?'

'A cat? Maybe Fluffy or Fido or some silly little barking toy poodle or something, but a cat? Come on. The stupid thing would just hightail it right out the patio door and never be seen again.'

'So, what are you saying?' she asked impatiently.

'Nothing. It just bothered me.'

Espy Martinez remembered the stiff body of the cat, its eyes bulged out, teeth bared, frozen in death. She shuddered. It bothered me too, she thought, but what does it have to do with anything? She ignored this and spoke out with a false bravado:

'Okay. So?'

'So, nothing,' the detective said.

'Keep going, then.'

Robinson sighed, and turned his attention back to the sheaf of reports on his desk. He thought sometimes that he was spending the majority of his adult life either reading reports or preparing them.

'Okay, let's see. Oh, there was one postmortem cut on the victim's neck.'

'Yes. And?'

'Well, there have been a number of break-ins throughout Sophie's neighborhood in the past couple weeks. Robbery is sending over case summaries. Maybe I can tie the perp into them.'

'Makes sense. What else?'

'What else?'

Espy Martinez glanced at the clock, and knew that the chief assistant would be looking for her. 'Detective ...'

'Actually, you can call me Walter. Most of the prosecutors in your office do.'

'I've got to talk to Lasser.'

'You want to know if I'm optimistic. Well, the answer is no. I'm never optimistic about this sort of case, Miss Martinez. Statistically, well, nationally we solve maybe one in three. Locally, we might be a bit worse. But I'm trying. Lasser knows the score. Don't let him muscle you.'

'Okay, Walter, I'll try...' She laughed, just a small amount. '... but it's the blood dripping from his fangs that gets me disconcerted. So, please tell me something that's gonna help put the guy who killed Sophie Millstein on Death Row.'

'You want to know how we're going to convict her killer, huh?'

'Yes.' Espy Martinez couldn't hide the remaining nervousness in her voice.

'Well, more bad news is this: no gun to trace. That makes things more difficult. Guns are great. They make noise, leave a mess, they're easy to match up in a laboratory, and people aren't generally smart enough to dispose of them where we can't find them. No knife either. Did you know that strangulation is a remarkably efficient way of murdering someone? It generally leaves little connective tissue between killer and victim. But on the plus side, forensics came up with two prints from her dresser, and a third from the jewelry box we found down the alleyway. They also managed to lift a partial thumbprint – just a small fragment, can't really tell if it's usable or not – from the victim's neck. That's a rarity, Miss Martinez. But if we can get a match, well, even the most incompetent prosecutor will nail the son of a bitch.'

'I'm not incompetent, Detective.'

'That's not what I meant . . .'

There was a momentary silence between the two. Walter Robinson thought it would have been hard for him to say something stupider to Espy Martinez.

'Okay, Detective. So, now I see how we get a conviction. Great. One problem, though: How are you going to go about catching the killer?'

'Well, first we're going to check the best of the prints we've got against those obtained at the other break-ins and robberies around the Beach in the last few months, see if we can't pick up the bastard's pattern. Then I'm gonna work some of the pawnshops and fences, see if we can't find some of that jewelry. Sophie's son gave me a pretty good description of some of the pieces stolen. I've already sent out a flyer to some places. Gonna look hard for that necklace with Sophie's name on it.'

Espy Martinez was going to remark on the offhand way the detective referred to the victim by her first name, but stopped herself. 'And then what?'

'And then hope we get lucky. We'll run the print through the county's Gotcha Computer, but I don't know—'

'The what?'

'The Gotcha Computer. The fancy one they got last year with all that federal money. Supposed to be able to match crime scene prints with prints stored in the computer's memory.'

'Will it work?'

'It has before. But only if our bad guy has been arrested and printed in the last year or so. We'll see.'

Espy Martinez stood up at the side of her desk. 'Is there anything else you can tell me, before I talk to Lasser?'

'How about, I've got six other open cases.'

'How about, this one stays at the top of the list,' she replied before hanging up.

Walter Robinson cradled the telephone against his ear, listening to the dial tone. He wondered what Espy Martinez was like when she wasn't frightened, and then he wondered whether she was ever not frightened.

Abraham Lasser was a thickset man with a drooping mustache and a wiry mane of gray-streaked black hair that seemed to explode from his scalp in an uncontrolled wildness. This was contradicted by his penchant for wearing sleek, Italian double-breasted suits and shoes always polished to a reflective sheen. Stalking through the maze of offices on the sixth floor of the Metropolitan Justice Building, he seemed like some fashion designer's nightmare. When he made an appearance in one of the fourth-floor courtrooms, he showed a snarling, sarcastic side that was routinely mocked and just as routinely feared by criminal defense attorneys. He was a man who placed great value on intimidation, both of his opponents and the people who worked for him.

Espy Martinez had been assigned to his felony division for eight weeks. In that time she had met with him only a half-dozen or so times, and on each occasion it was merely to get his authorization for a plea bargain. This was standard procedure in the office, and had been since one unfortunate assistant had agreed to an unauthorized plea in a weak case of spouse against spouse assault, and the accused had walked directly from the courtroom to the automatic rifle he kept in his car, which he turned on himself, after gunning down his ex-wife and her two sisters outside the Justice Building. The wags in the office suggested it would have been better for the assistant who offered the plea bargain if he'd been assassinated as well, death preferable to facing Abe Lasser's volcanic anger.

She took a deep breath outside his office and knocked and entered.

Lasser's secretary looked up at her and smiled. 'Go on in. He's been waiting for you.'

Then she pointedly glanced at her wristwatch.

'I needed to speak with a homicide detective,' Espy Martinez said.

'Go right on in, dear,' the secretary said.

Espy Martinez marched into the office. Lasser was behind his desk, on the telephone. He waved her into a seat and continued talking. She let her eyes wander about the room. There were several framed diplomas and Bar Association memberships. There were also the obligatory photographs of Lasser and various county and state politicians, including an enlarged color snapshot of the chief assistant and the governor, tanned, grinning, in T-shirts and shorts, standing on the edge of a dock, each holding up a large dead fish.

Separated a short distance from these photos were seven other pictures, each carefully matted and framed in glossy black steel. No politicians in these photos, they were full-face and right and left profile mug shots taken at the county jail. Espy Martinez stared at the faces that looked sullenly out at her. Four of the seven were of black men, two apparently Hispanic, one with a tear-drop tattoo beneath one eye and the other sporting a scar running through the hair of his eyebrow. There was one white man, who stared out with an unsettling malevolent insouciance. She looked at this face, then over at one of the black men. He had a sleepy, almost nonchalant appearance, eyes partly closed, as if being photographed in jail were the stuff of daily routine for him.

Abe Lasser suddenly started speaking loudly:

'Look! Goddammit! If you print that before I get into court, the bastards will walk. Walk, understand? You want that on your conscience?'

He cupped a hand over the receiver, smiled at Espy Martinez and whispered: '. . . The fucking *Herald* got hold of the grand jury testimony in the Abella beating.'

Espy Martinez nodded. Enrique Abella was a drunken motorist who took a half-dozen policemen on a high-speed chase and then, when finally cornered, surrendered loudly and abusively and arrived at the county lockup some forty-five minutes later with three fractured ribs, multiple contusions, a broken jaw and six missing teeth, a second-degree concussion, and an eye that might not regain its sight.

He swiveled rapidly in his seat.

'No, damn it, you listen. You hold off until after the indictments are handed down – they're gonna be sealed, I promise. I'll make sure you – and only you – know when those bastards are gonna turn themselves in for prints and mugs. You'll have the only camera there, got it? That's the deal.'

He paused, listening, before shouting a response:

'No, you fucking don't have to talk to any goddamn editor! We've known each other for ten years! And if after all that you can't make a deal where you end up getting two fucking exclusives just by holding off . . .'

Abe Lasser started to nod. He was smiling. His voice instantly went smooth.

'Of course I trust you. And you trust me. Everyone trusts each other. And you get something and I get something and everyone's happy, right?'

He suddenly leaned forward and spoke quietly, without bombast, but cool and menacing.

'But screw me on this and you won't see another story

out of this office for the next hundred years. And neither will the new asshole the *Herald* replaces you with. Or his replacement. And you'll all end up in Opa-Locka covering all-night meetings at the zoning board of adjustment.'

There was a momentary pause, then Abe Lasser leaned back abruptly, bursting into laughter.

'Well, hell, you're probably right about that. Point well taken.'

He cupped his hand over the phone again and said: 'The sonofabitch says I'll be lucky if I end up prosecuting jaywalking and litterbug cases in what's left of Homestead.'

He turned back to his conversation.

'So we have a deal? Good. Wanna have lunch sometime? My treat? Hell, maybe it ought to be your treat. Call my secretary.'

He hung up the telephone.

'Can you do that?' Espy Martinez asked. 'I mean, promise him that he'll be the only reporter around when those cops turn themselves in . . .'

'Of course not,' Abe Lasser replied.

Lasser smiled and shifted some papers about on his desk. For a moment he swiveled away from her, looking out his window, which had a view of Miami's inner city, stretching out beyond the stolid, squat architecture of the county jail.

'So, Espy, do you know where I live?'

The question took her by surprise. 'No, sir. I don't believe I do. . . .'

'We've got a real nice house right on the La Gorce Country Club golf course right in the middle of Miami Beach. Old, built in the Twenties. You know the type: high ceilings, Cuban tile floors, art deco window frames. My

wife spends most of her time fixing it up because something breaks every damn week. Plumbing. Roof leaks. Air-
conditioning. The A.C. went out yesterday morning. You
know how fucking hot it was last night?'

'Yes. But—'

'So, I'm sitting there Espy, worrying mainly about how
I'm gonna put the slam to these four cops and thinking
how lucky I am that Enrique fucking Abella isn't black so
we're not having a riot, but also thinking that maybe
because he's Cuban those bastards are gonna make all
sorts of political trouble over the case, and it's ten million
degrees in the house and it's gonna cost me three grand to
fix the damn central air unit and there's sweat dripping off
my forehead onto the sports section I'm trying to read and
guess who calls me on the telephone?'

Espy Martinez didn't reply. She didn't think she was
supposed to interrupt her boss's soliloquy with anything so
mundane as a question.

Abe Lasser leaned forward, smiling, but without pleasure. 'My fucking rabbi calls me.'

'I beg your pardon?'

'My rabbi. Rabbi Lev Samuelson, Temple Beth-El. This
guy that I don't talk to except once a year when he's raising
money for State of Israel bonds. But last night he's not
selling bonds. You know what he wants to know?'

'When we're going to arrest Sophie Millstein's killer.'

'Precisely. Apparently his fellow rabbi, from some other
temple, one down in South Beach, called him, because
somehow he's figured out that Rabbi Samuelson knows
me, and guess what?'

Abe Lasser slammed a hand down on the desk.

'And I couldn't tell him. So you tell me: When are we
going to make an arrest? Who's the detective on this
anyhow?'

'Walter Robinson.'

Abe Lasser smiled. 'Good. At least he has some idea about what he's doing and he's not a complete and total fuck-up. And he says?'

'He's working on it.'

Lasser shook his head.

'Do better than that.'

'The forensic and autopsy reports suggest that—'

'I don't care. You just find me her killer. Then I can go to my rabbi and tell him that the Dade State Attorney's Office follows the same principle established in Exodus, 21:12. You know that passage, Espy?'

'No, sir.'

'Look it up.'

Lasser stood and gestured toward the door. 'First real case, right?'

'Well, I handled the Williams prosecution, sir, the home invasions. That was in the papers ...'

'I know. That's what got you assigned to my division.'

Lasser moved out from behind the desk and walked to the wall where the seven photographs of prisoners were hung. 'You were looking at these. You know who they are?'

'No, sir.'

'These are the seven men, I've personally put on Death Row. Now I ought to take this guy down, because he was executed last year. A gentleman named Blair Sullivan, who killed so many people I've lost count. Twenty-two-hundred volts courtesy of the State of Florida and yours truly. Went to meet his Maker cursing, foul-mouthed and unrepentant, not an approach I particularly recommend. Anyway, I keep him up there with his compatriots for sentimental reasons.'

Espy Martinez couldn't imagine what those reasons

might be, but she was certain that the one thing they weren't was sentimental.

'You find Sophie Millstein's killer and then you can put a mug shot on the wall of your office and I can call my rabbi and everyone will be happy. Except for the killer, of course. And Sophie Millstein.'

He looked at Espy Martinez.

'Exodus, 21:12. I'll want another report by the end of the week. And make sure there's some progress, okay? Jump on Walter Robinson, and jump on him today. And for Christ's sake don't listen to him complain about all the other fucking cases he's got. Tell him he's only got one case. My rabbi's case.'

Then, with a chopping wave of his hand, the chief assistant dismissed her, returning to the paperwork on his desk.

Espy Martinez quickly exited the office, but after closing the door behind her, she turned to Abe Lasser's secretary.

'Do you keep a Bible handy?' she asked.

The woman nodded, reached into a drawer and produced a leather-bound copy of the Bible, handing it to Espy Martinez.

'Page seventeen,' the secretary said, turning back to her work.

Espy Martinez flipped the thin, crinkly pages quickly. It wasn't hard to find the proper passage. It had been marked with a yellow highlighting pen:

He that smiteth a man, so that he die,
shall be surely put to death . . .

Walter Robinson ignored the thick pressure of the evening humidity as he stood in the alleyway behind the Sunshine Arms adjacent to the trash canister where Sophie

Millstein's jewelry box had been discovered.

He spoke steadily and quietly to himself as he dissected the crime, occasionally pausing to make a small notation on a pad of paper. He walked back to the spot where Kadosh, the neighbor, stood and saw the perpetrator. He thought: Kadosh must have seen him as he turned and discarded the box. Eye to eye for just a second. Face lit up by that streetlight over there. Then he ran. Did he know he'd been seen? Yes. So: panic. No thinking. No nothing. Just gotta get outta here panic.

Walter Robinson moved from the end of the alley to a side street.

Well, my man, your blood pressure must have been soaring, ripping a hole in your chest, adrenaline hammering away inside your ears. Breathing short and shallow, just excited, afraid and juiced all at once, didn't even have time yet to think about the bag of crack you'd be able to buy. You wanted to just get the hell out of there, didn't you? You were scared as hell, and you just wanted to make tracks. Get safe.

So, what did you do?

His eyes swept down the block toward Jefferson Avenue.

Did you have a car? Possibly. Something old and nondescript. But maybe you sold it a few weeks ago, because you needed the money, didn't you? So maybe it was something you borrowed? Who would lend a junkie a car? Did you get a friend to drive you? Another crackhead looking for an easy score? Maybe. But I doubt it. Crackheads don't make for lasting partnerships.

In the distance the diesel whine of a bus coming down the avenue filled the air. Walter Robinson listened carefully, still thinking hard.

Did you ride our nice, safe public transportation system

here and then home again? Did you take the J-50? That would have carried you to Forty-second Street. And then you could transfer to the G-75. That would take you right across the Julia Tuttle Causeway, right back into the heart of Liberty City, and you'd be home and feeling safe.

Walter Robinson felt the night starting to gnaw away at the remains of the day.

Is that what you did, my man? he asked himself. Did you use a goddamn bus to escape from a murder?

If Sophie Millstein's killing was simply an afterthought to robbery, then yes, absolutely, Robinson told himself.

He slowly walked back to where he'd parked his car. He felt there was something terribly wrong in a world where killers rode public transportation. And then he thought how crazy that idea was. Murder is as routine as anything else, he told himself, as ordinary as a bus stop. He got behind the wheel and, after checking his watch, put the unmarked car in gear and headed to the Beach's bus terminal.

Exhaust fumes seemed to blend with the remains of the day's heat, creating a thick, sticky, noxious concoction. Walter Robinson felt as if he was walking into a basement or attic, fighting through a tangle of cobwebs. He wondered how anyone could breathe inside the terminal, even though it was constructed like a covered parking area, with huge gaps where walls should have been, ostensibly to let the air breeze through, though Robinson thought that no self-respecting gust of wind would ever volunteer to enter the poisonous space.

Inside a small office the night dispatcher turned through the pages of a logbook. She was a gruff, middle-aged woman, with carrot-red hair teased into a helmet upon her head, who talked interchangeably to herself and to him. As she searched for the proper log page, Robinson spied a pin-up calendar on the wall. August was illustrated by a not particularly pretty bleached blonde, slightly overweight, with pendulous breasts that were offered toward the camera and a slightly dopey expression on her face. The detective wondered why the dispatcher allowed August to stay on the wall, almost mocking her.

'Here it is. Jesus, why can't those dumb drivers ever fill this stuff out right? I've got what you need, Detective.'

He leaned toward the logbook, and the dispatcher continued speaking.

'These are the routes closest to your homicide. Christ, what's the world coming to, anyway, little old lady, Jesus, I saw it in the papers, Christ, and we were running a single shift on that night, but there was one trainee too, riding in the number six. Ahhh, no one reports any incidents, except one guy, right here, says he kicked a pair of teenagers off near Jefferson, because they were playing a boom box too loud. I hate that kinda music, what do they see in it anyway? Country and western for me. Not this rap shit. That's surprising . . .'

'Why is that?' Walter Robinson asked.

The dispatcher looked up at him as if he were crazy. 'Two teenagers. Boom box. You know the kinda weaponry those kids mighta been carrying? I'm gonna stop my bus and kick them off and maybe get a bullet in my chest from some angry punk? No thank you, Detective. Just gonna let 'em ride, and listen to that crap loud as they like . . .'

'But nothing else?'

'Nah. Not that night. But you know, these damn incident forms take damn forever to fill out, why'd they ever come up with them, triplicate for Christ's sake, I dunno. So, maybe somebody remembers something, maybe helps you out. Bus drivers see a lot, you know. We see a lot.'

He nodded, and the dispatcher pointed him toward a grimy driver's lounge, which sported a soda machine, a cigarette machine, and a candy machine, all with hand-written OUT OF ORDER signs taped to their fronts. A couple of drivers were sitting on a beaten, fake leather couch, waiting for their shift to begin. They looked up as Walter Robinson entered and identified himself.

An older man, bald, with a short ring of gray hair, nodded when he explained what he was searching for.

'That was me and the kid driving that route,' the bus driver said.

'Th-th-that's right,' a considerably younger man, wearing a much fresher and cleaner blue uniform, stuttered in agreement.

'You recall that night?' Robinson asked.

'All the nights are pretty much the same. Up and down. Up and down. Late at night, mostly tired people. Drunk people. I don't know if I remember anything special.'

'A young black man. Nervous. In a hurry . . .'

'No—'

'S-s-s-sure, there was, remember? You hadda yell at the g-g-g-guy to s-s-s-siddown . . .' the younger driver interrupted. He looked eagerly at the older man, who rolled his eyes back in frustration.

'I don't like to make trouble,' the driver said, in a halfhearted apology. 'Ain't my business. I just drive.'

'Tell me,' Robinson demanded.

'Not much to say. Guy gets on. Slams some change in the box. Bus is nearly empty, but he stands there, looking out, acting nervous, just like you said, and telling me to get going, get going, put a move on it. Like he was in some big fucking hurry. I yelled for him to siddown and he told me to fuck myself, and I told him I'd rip his fucking head off and that kept up for a minute or two, you know, fuck me, fuck you, so a couple of stops up, I told him to either siddown or get off. He sat down. Not that big a deal, Detective. Happens all the time.'

'Where did he get off?'

'Godfrey Road. Transfer to a city bus. Don't know where he was heading, but I can guess.'

Walter Robinson nodded. 'Recognize the guy again?'

'Maybe. Yeah, probably.'

'S-S-Sure,' said the younger driver.

'See him, call me. I'll be back in touch. May want you to look at some mug shots.'

'I'll be here.'

Robinson left the bus terminal. He drove a few blocks over to Collins Avenue, parked and walked through to the boardwalk that the Army Corps of Engineers had constructed for the old folks to walk up and down the beach. He stood, leaning up against the wooden railing, staring out toward the waves. There was small surf running, just the mere insinuation of ocean power, rebuking the sand and rough coral stone beach. He let the hot salt air clear his lungs, and he talked to himself with some astonishment: You were right, goddamn it. He rode the damn bus. And now, maybe, you've got a chance.

He inhaled long and hard and thought: screw the statistics.

Walter Robinson spoke to the night sky and expanse of dark sea and the man he believed had killed Sophie Millstein. *You thought you could just come over here and rob and kill a little old lady. Well, you were goddamn wrong.*

I'm going to find you.

CHAPTER EIGHT

The Woman Who Told a Lie

The young woman closed a shade, making the room seem gray. There was a moment's delay while she fiddled with the videotape machine, then an electronic interference bar scarred the television picture. A second later Simon Winter saw Sophie Millstein on the screen.

He leaned forward in his chair, listening carefully. The young woman sat down next to him.

Sophie Millstein wore an expression that mingled a small amount of anxiety with discomfort. Winter noted she was wearing one of her finer, go-to-services dresses and realized that she had fixed her hair carefully. She wore white gloves on her hands and she clutched a matching pocketbook. For an instant he wondered how he had failed to take notice of her appearance on a day when she had left the Sunshine Arms dressed up, as if ready for a wedding.

'Do I look okay?' she asked nervously.

A voice off camera replied: 'You look fine.'

'I was worried,' Sophie Millstein said. 'I've never been on television, and I wanted to look nice. This dress . . .'

Her voice trailed off, its tone a question mark.

'You look just fine,' repeated the off-camera answer. Simon Winter recognized the voice of the young woman who sat quietly beside him.

'I don't know what I'm supposed to do,' Sophie Millstein said.

'Just relax and don't worry about the camera,' the young
woman's voice reassured.

Sophie Millstein shifted about in her seat. 'I'm not so
sure this is a good idea,' she said hesitantly.

'Just ignore the camera, Sophie. You'll get used to it in
no time. Just about everyone is nervous at first.'

'Really? Everyone?'

'Everyone.'

'Well, that makes me feel better. But I don't know what
it is I'm supposed to say.'

'What do you want to say?'

'I don't really have much to say. Not at all.'

'But you came here,' the young woman said. Her voice
was soft. 'Something told you to come here and tell us
something. What was that?'

Sophie Millstein hesitated again, and Simon Winter
could see her eyes narrow with concentration.

'They should all know,' she replied.

'Who should know?'

'All the people too young to remember.'

'What should they know?' the young woman prompted
off camera.

'What happened. The truth. Because it really happened.'

Sophie Millstein's jaw clamped shut and she folded her
arms across her chest.

After a brief quiet, the voice of the young woman,
soothing, coaxing, asked: 'Why don't you just tell me
what happened to you? That's a good enough place to
start.'

Sophie Millstein opened her mouth once, then closed it
tightly again. Winter could see her lower lip quivering ever

so slightly. She remained like this for almost a minute, the videotape machine recording her silence faithfully.

Then, finally, Sophie Millstein gasped, as if she'd been holding her breath. A few words trickled out: 'These are things I wanted to forget so I do not talk about. Not for many years, not even with Leo. I wish he were here now, because he would help me . . .'

'But he's not here, and you've got to do it alone.'

Sophie Millstein nodded. Tears forced their way into her eyes and she struggled with her composure. Again silence crept onto the tape, save for a rasping noise that the old woman made as she fought for air.

'Alone,' she said finally. She looked across at the camera, and then Simon Winter saw his neighbor on the television screen seem to gather herself. She bit down on her quivering lip, straightened her shoulders and looked out, directly at the camera, shedding discomfort and the terror tyranny of memory, and began speaking, a torrent of words and images bursting through, a maelstrom of recollection. Like a wave, it broke upon Simon Winter, and he gripped the edge of his chair to keep his own balance.

'. . . We were three days on the train. Jammed down together, like animals, in our own filth and dirt. People died around us, one lady, I never knew her name, she died and for eight hours I could feel her weight pressed up against my back, and I couldn't do anything about it until the old man she was next to, he died too, and I could push her backwards so that the dead fell against the dead, and I remember how still she was, and white, like someone had carved her out of stone. I kept thinking afterwards that I should have found out her name, I wanted to know her name, so that I could tell someone. But I didn't. The air, I can still taste the air in that train. Every morning, still. I

remember it. Maybe that's why I came down here to
Florida, because the air is so clean, and I wouldn't have to
remember it the way it was those three days. It was like
compressed together evil, just thick and harsh, like a
disease covering us. Hansi held me, that was my brother
Hans, he was fourteen, two years younger than me, but he
was strong. He was always so strong. I was short, but he
was tall and he held me so I wouldn't try to help Mama or
Papa, who was coughing and grew so weak, I thought he
would die, but he kept waving to me and saying, I'm fine,
I'm fine, don't worry about me. Everything will be all
right, but of course it wasn't, though, I knew we would die
when we got to the place, Auschwitz, but still, when they
opened the door and the fresh air came in, I thought it
would be all right to die, because just once I could breathe
fresh air again, but even that wasn't to be, because even in
the cold, the stench from the dying was so great, I couldn't
breathe, and they were yelling *Raus! Raus!* and everyone
had to pile out of the train, and we were clutching each
other, trying to stay together but I couldn't hold Hansi
anymore, because they made us get into lines, women on
one side and men on the other, and I saw him holding my
father and I didn't know where my mother was, and they
kept yelling, forcing us in line, the dogs were barking and
snarling and I didn't even see anyone try to run, we were
all so weak and stumbling toward a table. The S.S. man
just looked and asked a question or two and then pointed
one way or the other, but of course, you know all about
that. That's been told over and over, but it happened. It
happened to me. He sat there, with his gray greatcoat and
his hat, the one with the death's head insignia, I remember
that. And he wore gloves, so that it was just this black
leather hand pointing one way or the other, it was so quick.
And I saw, just for a second as my line stepped forward, I

saw Hansi and my father, and my father was coughing and Hansi was holding him, and the S.S. man pointed to the left for my father, and to the right for Hansi, but Hansi shook his head and helped my father over to the left and that was it, oh my God, he wouldn't leave him, so he went to his death. Hansi was so strong, he might have lived. He might have, that's what I always thought. He was wiry and strong, with muscles that grew even when we had nothing to eat for days. And he always smiled, did you know? He just lived so well, fourteen, and always happy and smiling, even when everything was awful and everything was all death and dying and he looked over toward me in that little instant, and I knew that he knew he should let Papa go to the left but he wouldn't, he held his arm and helped him be strong too. He was just a boy, but he knew. He smiled at me. Oh my God, he smiled at me, just like he was saying it's all right to die even though I haven't lived yet. Fourteen, but he was the strongest. So he went to help our father and so he died and I was alone forever. Oh Hansi, why didn't you go to the right?'

Tears were streaming down Sophie Millstein's cheeks, and Simon Winter thought: How many tears can you store up in fifty years?

On the tape, the young woman's voice asked: 'Do you need to take a break?'

'Yes,' Sophie Millstein said. Then she added: 'No.'

She stared at the camera.

'I lied,' she said, suddenly forceful.

'What lie?' asked the young woman.

'When I reached the table and the S.S. man, he was a doctor! A doctor! How could a doctor do what he did? He asked me how old I was and I said sixteen and he was thinking and then he started to lift his hand, and I thought he might point to the left, and I said very fast, but I am an electrician. And he looked at me and I said my father, really, was an electrician, and I was his assistant, but that he taught me everything, and so the S.S. man would think I could be useful, and he pointed to the right.'

'Did you know . . .'

'Nothing. Not really. I lied and I lived.'

Sophie Millstein grew quiet. Then she added: 'It always bothered me, did you know? I mean, of course, there was nothing wrong, but my mama and my papa – he was really a professor of linguistics at the university – they had always taught us that a lie was like a sin and that it was like a little dark spot on your soul that you could never quite clean away and that it was always, always, always better to tell the truth than to put that little mark there next to your heart. And I hated that, you see, that S.S. man, he made me lie to save myself. And everything else that happened to me, it all seemed like a part of that lie. And I hated them and I guess I hated me for that.'

'If you'd told the truth . . .'

'I would have died.'

'So, you became an electrician?'

For an instant Sophie Millstein paused, and Simon Winter saw her eyes narrow again with remembered hatred. She struggled with the words, but after a moment they leaked out.

'No . . .' she said slowly. 'No. That's what I told Leo. That's what I told anyone who asked. But that was a lie too. They shaved my head. They shaved my entire body. And I became a whore.'

She took a deep breath. Her words seemed to shiver with cold.

'And that's how I lived. A whore.'

Sophie Millstein reached down, and Winter saw her retrieve a lace handkerchief from her pocketbook at her feet. She dabbed her eyes and then looked at the young lady, off camera.

'I guess I was wrong,' she said bitterly. 'I have lots to say.'

Sophie Millstein gazed toward the camera, her eyes still glistening with tears. Again she breathed slowly, deeply.

'It has been very hard for me to forgive myself,' she said softly. 'I feel all these years like I did something terrible and wrong. And I cannot just blow that feeling away into air like it was dust or fluff.'

Again there was a silence on the tape, until the young woman's voice said:

'Sophie, you lived. That was what was important. Not how or why or what you had to do. You lived, and you shouldn't feel guilty.'

'Yes. That is true. I have told myself that over and over all these years.'

Sophie Millstein hesitated again. Tears now flowed freely down her cheeks, smudging the makeup she'd carefully applied.

'I guess all this time I thought it was wrong. Living when so many others died.'

Again she paused.

'Can I have a little glass of something?' she asked with a small, delicate smile, like a child who has realized they've just read their first word all by themselves. 'Perhaps a little iced tea?'

Sophie Millstein on the tape abruptly disappeared, replaced by gray bands of electronic interference followed by a blue title board with her name, the date, and a document number on it.

Esther Weiss rose and flicked off the television. Then she went to the window. The flat blinds being raised made a rattling sound. Light streamed into the room, and Simon

Winter blinked sharply. He saw the young woman hesitate by the window, as if gathering herself.

She turned toward him. She was casually dressed, in jeans and a loose-fitting cotton shirt. Her mane of curly hair fell down to her shoulders and seemed to frame her face with intensity.

'Did you know how remarkable a woman Sophie was, Mr Winter?'

Simon Winter felt a catch in his own throat and shook his head.

'An extraordinary woman. You cannot quantify bravery, toughness, dedication, will to live – all those things that are just words, Mr Winter. Words that describe concepts that seem unbelievably distant and lost in society today. All the survivors had them to some degree, but Sophie, Sophie was a bit special even among special people, Mr Winter. Did you know that about your neighbor, Mr Winter?'

He shook his head again.

Weiss continued: 'It's all oddly deceptive. She looked like just a little old lady. A little dizzy, perhaps. A little crazy, maybe.'

She looked at Simon Winter.

'Everyone's typical Jewish grandmother. Chicken soup and kvetching about this or that. Right?'

Winter didn't answer.

'That's what you thought, right?'

He nodded slowly.

'Well,' she said slowly, 'you were damn wrong.' The woman looked hard at him. 'Just completely goddamn wrong.'

The young woman rubbed what were the start of her own tears away from her eyes. Winter saw her take a deep breath.

'That was just the first, you know, getting started.

Breaking the ice, so to speak. We had high hopes. But your neighbor was only able to make one additional tape before she was—'

She stopped abruptly.

'Damn,' she said. 'Murdered, goddamn it.'

Simon Winter remained silent.

'Unfair. What sort of world is this, Mr Winter? Isn't there any justice at all?'

Winter didn't reply. He understood: What is there to say? She's right.

'Did she talk much about her time in Berlin, before her deportation?'

The young woman looked down at some notes on a page. When she looked up, Simon Winter saw her eyes glance toward his forearm. He realized she was looking for a tattoo.

'Why exactly? You're not a survivor, are you, Mr Winter?'

'No,' he said rapidly, thinking instantly that that was somehow an inaccurate response. 'I was once a police-man.'

'Why Sophie's story, now?'

'It was something she said. Right before her murder. About the man who turned her in.'

'U-boats,' Weiss said.

'I beg your pardon.'

'U-boats. That was one of the nicknames the people who tried to hide out in the cities used. Because they were beneath the surface. It was a very difficult life. I will give you some books about what they tried to accomplish. Remarkable, really. Hiding in the midst of a police state dedicated to your very destruction. I think, in history, there are few people who were able to show the sort of creativity, resourcefulness, bravery, oh I don't know.

These were extraordinary people, and so few survived the war to tell their stories. That's why we were all so excited when Sophie came to us and started making tapes. I don't really think we can understand today the sort of courage those people had without their firsthand testimonies. And the life? Starvation. Fear. Always fear. They could never stay more than a few days in any location. They had to move about, frequenting spots where they wouldn't stand out. When they could, they bribed people. Jewelry usually. If they had gold coins, so much the better. Sometimes they could even bribe the catchers and maybe gain a few days extra suffering, before being caught and sent off to die.'

'That's what I've learned.'

'Who have you been speaking with?'

'Rabbi Chaim Rubinstein. A Mrs Kroner and a Mr Silver.'

'I know these people. They were U-boats, like Sophie.'

The young woman hesitated, then shook her head. 'Jewish people employed by the Gestapo to hunt down other Jews. In a society that seemed to breed irony and betrayal in equal amounts, they were maybe the most ... I don't know – what? Morally unique?'

She paused while Winter inhaled sharply. He saw her glance toward the window, her eyes tracking the shaft of light that speared the room.

'Do you suppose someone like that would go to a special ring in Hell, Mr Winter?'

He did not answer that question, though he thought it a good one. Instead, he started to ask: 'Did she describe—'

'It's an incredibly important subject, Mr Winter. A sort of moral cannibalism. Betraying your own people to monsters in order to save your own life. Over the years, we have had several important scholars visiting the center to study the tapes.'

Esther Weiss glanced at Simon Winter.

'She made one other tape. I'll get that.'

The young woman went to a bookcase and started rummaging through shelves of tapes. She double-checked one against a master list, then turned to Winter.

'Here it is. You want me to get the shade?'

He shook his head. He felt somehow that the nightmares contained on all the tapes were safer in the bright daylight. She nodded and fed the tape into the video machine.

Sophie Millstein appeared on the television screen again. This time she was wearing a less formal dress, one of the many flower prints that Winter recognized. Two electronic interference bars marred the screen and every little motion Sophie Millstein made was jerked by the tape's speed as the young woman fast-forwarded to the point the conversation started.

'Right about here, I think . . .' Weiss said. She punched a button and Sophie Millstein's voice returned to the room.

The disembodied voice spoke first.

'Sophie, how was it that you happened to be caught?'

Sophie Millstein put her hand to her mouth, as if to prevent the words from tumbling out. Then she sat forward rigidly, like an eyewitness in court, and spoke:

'I remember it was the only time I saw Hansi scared, because he came home that day saying he might have been seen by someone. He wasn't sure, you know, everyone changed so much in those years. You could stare right at someone you'd known for years and not recognize them. The war did that. And starvation and allied bombs all the time. But Hansi was upset. Still, the next day he went out to look for some work. We needed to eat and there was no choice and it was possible that Herr Guttman at the print shop would give him some bread for a day's work and bread was too important. So he went, and he didn't come back that night at all, until late, long after dark, slipping past the night curfew guards, which was something he never did, because if he'd been caught without papers it would be all over, and even if they believed his papers it might be all over anyway. He came home and I saw him speaking closely, frightened again, with Papa, who refused to let Mama or me hear what they were saying. But I saw Papa go to the coat that had all our money sewed into it, and he came back and gave Hansi a ring. A gold ring. Papa's wedding ring. Hansi took it and went back out, through the trapdoor, out of the basement. He returned a few minutes later and I remember him saying to Papa everything will be all right now, but maybe only for a few days, and so they talked about moving us. I didn't want to move. The basement was warm and as safe as anything when the bombing raids came over. Maybe that was why we didn't move as fast as we should have. They came two days later. Gestapo knocking at the door. They took us out. I remember poor Frau Wattner standing, watching, with two soldiers on either side of her. She looked so scared. She was saying, but I didn't know, I didn't know, I thought they were just *bombengeschädigte*! She turned to Papa and spat in his face! *Schweinejude*! she said, but we all knew she had to say that, still, the word hurt. We were put in the car by the Gestapo man and I looked back once and I saw soldiers throw poor Frau Wattner up against the side of the house. Papa made me turn my head, but I heard the submachine gun and when I looked back, I could not see her anymore . . .'

On the tape Sophie Millstein was once again fighting tears. She held up her hand.

'I'm sorry Esther,' Sophie Millstein said. 'Poor Frau Wattner. She brought us soup when we had none. I do not think I can speak of that day right now.'

'Sophie,' the young woman's voice coaxed from off camera. 'These things are important.'

Sophie Millstein nodded toward the camera.

'Hansi, wouldn't say much. Not that night. After Mama and Papa were asleep, I crawled over to where he was lying underneath his greatcoat, we had no blankets, really. I asked him: "Hansi, what is it? Who is it?" and at first he wouldn't answer, but I poked him hard and he held his hand up so that just a little light that came in from the only little window we had threw a shadow on the wall, and then I knew...'

'Knew what?' the young woman's voice prompted.

'I knew he was out there. And I knew he would sell us to the Gestapo before too long. I knew that. I must have stiffened or gasped or something, because right away Hansi says, "No, don't worry. I've paid him something and he will leave us alone..." But I didn't believe that and I don't think Hansi did either.'

'That man. The one he met...'

'The one who turned us in.'

'Yes. How did—'

'From the academy, I think. Not a classmate of Hansi's, but perhaps someone a few years older. That must have been it, because my brother cursed, which he never did, and I remember him saying it would have been better never to have learned to read or write at all.'

Sophie Millstein paused, then added coldly: 'He knew. That night in all that dark. You know, I remember the bombing was going on, off at Templehof, again, like so many times, and we could hear it in the distance, growing closer, and usually that scared me, but not that night. That night I remember praying that perhaps one of the British bombers would get hit and drop its load short and have it all come down on us just quickly and painlessly and it could all be over.'

She continued quietly: 'Hansi knew, and I knew and I suppose Mama and Papa knew that we were all dead already. We were dead at the very moment that *he'd* first spotted Hansi. Dead each moment that he'd followed my brother around the city, every stop on the streetcar, every step on the sidewalk. Dead every second that he'd watched and waited for his opportunity. Dead when he'd trapped my brother in a corner in some alleyway and hissed at him "Jew! I know you!" in some snake's voice. We were dead when Hansi pleaded with him. We were dead when he forced Hansi to take him to Frau Wattner's basement and dead when he demanded a bribe. He was killing us when Hansi handed him the ring and whatever money we had and heard him promise that great lie. No, we were all dead, even though he promised us life.'

Sophie Millstein paused. She was breathing hard on the tape, her face flushed with rage.

'But you lived, Sophie,' Esther Weiss interjected softly. Sophie Millstein's eyes narrowed and her voice rasped in reply:

'I lived? You think anyone who went through that lived? Ach, you don't know anything! We all died, right inside! Maybe the body went on. Maybe we could still breathe. Maybe we still woke up every morning and saw the light of day, but we were dead inside! Dead!'

'Sophie, that's not true,' the young woman argued gently. 'You lived. Others lived. There was a reason for that. It was important that you lived.'

Sophie Millstein started to reply, then stopped. Her eyes filled once again with tears. 'I'm sorry, Hansi,' she said slowly. 'I'm sorry Mama and Papa. I'm sorry to everyone who died.'

She took a deep breath and nodded.

'Esther, I have loved living, that's true. Maybe it wasn't a perfect life, maybe I shouldn't have done some things I did, or said some things I said, but I have and there's no going back, is there?'

'No, there isn't.'

Sophie Millstein started to say something, then stopped. She seemed to think hard, then she whispered, 'And to think . . . he was one of us.' She shook her head. 'I need to take a break,' she said.

'Sophie, this is important. What about the man who turned you in? We need to know about him.'

'I know, I'm sorry. Perhaps tomorrow. Or next week. But I need to think of happier things, Esther, because sometimes these memories just make my heart want to stop.'

There was a momentary pause, then the young woman's voice replied: 'That's fine, Sophie. We have plenty of time. All the time you need.'

Then there was another blue slate, with a date and document number, before the screen went blank again.

Esther Weiss turned off the television and shook her head. 'I was wrong,' she said. 'She didn't have time. Damn.' She sighed and eyed Simon Winter. 'So, there was just that. Her brother paid the catcher – maybe a former schoolmate, teacher, who knows? It wasn't like the majority of good Germans were hiding Jews – a bribe. But it didn't work. They got denounced anyway. Denounced and shipped off to die. Does that help you?'

'Perhaps.' He was thinking hard, trying to measure what he'd heard. He summoned Sophie Millstein's words spoken in his apartment on the day of her death: '*I only saw him that once, and for such a little time* . . .' Would you ever forget that face? he demanded of himself suddenly. Would you recognize that face, no matter how few seconds you saw it that day fifty years ago, no matter how the years had aged it? Would you ever forget?

He answered that question instantly: no.

Then he turned the equation around in his head. Would the owner of that face ever forget what he'd done?

No.

The young woman hesitated. Winter saw a frown pass her eyes before she added: 'You know what's odd? That was what she wanted to talk about the night she was killed.'

'What?'

'She left a phone message on the Holocaust Center's tape recorder. It was after hours and no one was here. She just said she was going to come in and she wanted to talk about her arrest.'

'What exactly did she say?'

'Just that. It was very brief.'

'Did you tell—'

'I called the police. They didn't seem very interested.'

Winter nodded. 'They believe she was killed by a narcotics addict, or someone similar. Someone who's done a bunch of robberies near Sophie's apartment,' he explained.

'That's what they told me,' she said. 'But you seem troubled Mr Winter. You don't believe them?'

He paused. He was struck by the German words that had rolled from Sophie Millstein's tongue. I never realized, he thought. All those years, watching her coming and going, living right across from her in the Sunshine Arms, and I never knew. Some detective you were, he reproached himself.

'Of course I believe them,' Winter said slowly.

'So, why are you here, Mr Winter?' the young woman asked.

He thought how stupid he was. All those years as a policeman, day in and day out, living daily with all of death's caresses, in every manner of murder. And Death had walked right into the Sunshine Arms and been right there when he'd reached for his pistol to take his own life, and for some evil reason had taken the wrong person. Not him, but his neighbor.

'I'm here,' he said with a hard-edged tone, 'because someone murdered a person close to me.'

He glanced quickly toward the window, as if the bright sunlight streaming through could help remove the dampness of his heart. He guarded his words carefully, doling them out with a cold precision: 'On the night she died, when she called here ... did she use the phrase *Der Schattenmann*?'

Weiss shook her head. 'No. I don't believe so. The Shadow Man? No, I would have remembered that.'

Simon Winter gritted his teeth. 'Does it mean anything to you?'

'I don't recall it. But ...'

'He might have been the catcher.'

'That would be reasonable. They all went under pseudonyms and nicknames. And she describes her brother's hand ...'

'Did any survive the war?'

'Maybe one or two. One, a woman, was tried by the Russians, did some time and now lives quietly in Germany.'

'The others?'

'They disappeared into the camps. Or into the rubble. Who knows?'

That's right, Simon Winter thought. That's the question.

CHAPTER NINE
The Helping Hand

Walter Robinson followed the G-75 bus as it accelerated across the Julia Tuttle causeway, leaving the beach as it headed toward the core of Miami. It was midday; he saw a belch of smoky exhaust absorbed by the spongelike heat as the bus churned up the three-lane highway.

Miami has a linear quality to it. The city stretches north and south along the coastline, clinging to Biscayne Bay with an urban tenacity, taking not only the image that it wants to show the world, but also a sort of internal bearing from the glistening, azure waters. In recent years it has begun to flex to the west toward the soggy expanse of the Everglades, growing housing developments and shopping malls like so many boils on an infected man's back. But these are the inevitable eruptions of shifting population trends. In attitude and essence, Miami remains a coastal city, oriented toward the ever-changing fields of blue-green ocean.

Walter Robinson, however, hated the water.

It was not that he didn't enjoy looking out over the ocean, a view he frequently sought out, especially when considering a case in hand. He had long since discovered that the sea's rhythms had a subtle, encouraging sense and that the monotonal sounds of the waves against the shore helped to filter out extraneous details and focus his thoughts, and so he appreciated the great expanses of ocean and bay as tools which aided him. His hatred, however, was a more political one.

He thought the water was something that belonged to the wealthy. There are dozens of docks and marinas and boat ramps in Miami and none abut areas where blacks live in any numbers. He had become aware of this at a young age, when he would walk from the poverty of what is known as the Black Grove, through increasing affluence, down to the water, where he could watch the well-heeled and influential mount sailboats, speedboats, or large cabin cruisers and idle past the shore, heading out through the bay. In his solitude, watching, he was aware that his color made him different from virtually everyone heading toward the water. He had complained of this once to his mother, the elementary school teacher, and her response had been to insist that he learn to swim, if he was going to frequent the watery areas of Dade County. It was only as an adult that he'd realized that many of his schoolmates had never bothered to acquire this skill, so ingrown was the prejudice that the water belonged to others, not them.

So Walter Robinson had forced himself to become a powerful swimmer – fast, strong, and confident even when the ocean currents pulled and tugged with dangerous desires.

As he drove across the causeway, speeding to keep pace with the hurrying bus, he glanced at the bay, which shimmered on either side of him. He was always unsettled by the trip between the beach and Liberty City; the bay seemed to mock the blight that rose up a half mile inland from the shoreline. Six blocks, perhaps nine, and any memory of the water dissipated in a rigid, unforgiving dusty heat. He kept close to the G-75 bus as it downshifted on an exit ramp, sending another cloud of dirty gray smoke into the air, and descended into the inner city.

The G-75, he knew, in unspoken truth, existed for a single purpose. It made the loop between a half-dozen stops in Liberty City and a similar number on Miami Beach so that the cleaning women, dishwashers, lawn men, and the occasional private nurse who lived in the city could get up early and ride through the heat to their difficult and low-paying jobs, without complaint or hope, and then make the return trip at night, swaying with noise and speed as the bus hurtled across the causeway.

He kept a street map on the seat beside him, and as the bus maneuvered down Twenty-second Avenue, he noted the location of every pawnshop and check-cashing store. There was a depressing frequency to these businesses, at least one per block.

The pawnshops, in particular, interested him.

Which one? he wondered to himself. Which one would open for you in the middle of the night? Which one did you slip right into, trying to shake off the last droplets of panic? Which one gave you the quick and easy, no questions deal?

This was just an educated guess on his part. He knew that a sophisticated burglar would have a regular fencing operation that he would frequent. Some fringe person who could be trusted. A fence, as well, would be able to handle more expensive pieces of jewelry, and give a higher return.

But a professional fence would also have more sense than to deal with some strung-out crack-bedeviled low-life, Robinson thought. So, he guessed, his quarry didn't have a regular bank where he could take his stolen goods and make what in Liberty City passed for a regular deposit. He drove along, speaking to himself:

'No, my man. You were all strung out, weren't you? And

you'd want to get rid of almost all this stuff real fast, so a pawnshop would be right. One that you knew keeps two sets of books. One that would simply fork over some tens and twenties and not ask any questions. Enough to keep you from getting rich, but not enough to keep you from getting high, right, my man?'

There were seven such shops along the G-75 route.

Walter Robinson parked and smiled to himself.

'You wouldn't want to walk far, would you? You'd just want to get rid of the stuff nice and quick and get some cash and forget about that big step you just took. You know what step I'm talking about, my man? The one where you went from punk and burglar to the big time. The step that's gonna put you on Death Row in Raiford Prison wondering what it is about life that's so sweet because it's gonna be taken away from you.'

Robinson stepped out of the car and felt a blast of heat rise from the sidewalk, enveloping him. He locked the unmarked car and hummed a snatch of a song to himself.

He breathed in deeply and thought: No, my man, you don't know how close I am, but I'm close. Real close. And gonna be closer still, before you know I'm right there beside you.

He paused and let his eyes sweep into a low-slung housing development across the street from where he stood. Three small children were playing with a garish pink-colored plastic scooter bike on a dusty brown spot between cement walkways. Behind them were two two-story-high rectangular apartment buildings. Graffiti marred the fading white paint on the walls. Most of the doors and windows were open to the oppressive humidity; if there were air conditioners, they either didn't work or were too expensive to operate. Occasionally a loud voice, raised in some sudden anger, flung an expletive or two through the hot air over the heads of the children, who played on, oblivious to the sound. Robinson knew that as the day dwindled into nighttime, the same voices would be accompanied by the inevitable sound of liquor bottles smashing and an occasional, but hardly infrequent, gunshot.

He hesitated, and two of the playing children stopped and looked up toward him. They pointed, and he realized how he stood out, in his tan suit, button-down shirt and tie, polished shoes. The children stared at him, put their heads together momentarily, then returned to their game, ignoring his presence.

He shook his head and thought: seven years old and already they make the cop. In ten years will some policeman come looking for them with his pistol drawn? He did not have to answer that question.

He looked around to see if he could spot someone keeping an eye on the children as they played, but saw no one. At least, when I was growing up, my mother watched me, he thought. The memory filled him with a sense of isolated sadness, and he turned away quickly, back to his task.

A breeze swirled some dust around his feet, but brought no relief to his temple, and he set off down the block toward the first of the pawnshops. He stood outside, pausing before pushing his way inside. As he reached out his hand for the door, he heard a car pull to the curb behind him, and he turned quickly.

It was a white City of Miami police cruiser. The sunlight hitting the car's hood almost blinded him. A window rolled down and he heard a familiar voice:

'So, it's the famous Beach detective, here to make trouble.'

Walter Robinson shaded his eyes from the glare and quickly replied: 'Well, only because you deadbeats and do-nothings let all your bad guys come make trouble in my town.'

He heard laughter from the passenger seat, and as he stepped to the side of the cruiser, another voice said:

'Well, better there than here, that's for sure.'

The cruiser's door swung open and a large black man, wearing the navy-blue uniform of the city police, with a sergeant's stripes on the shoulder, stepped out. There was a quick handshake and a 'Hey, Walter, my man, how yah doin'?'

'Fine, Lionel, just fine.'

The police sergeant was joined by a thin, considerably smaller hispanic officer, who also shook hands. 'Hey Walt, amigo, *como está?*'

'What's that foreign tongue you're talking, John?' Walter Robinson grinned and accentuated the man's name.

'It's Juan, not John, and don't you forget it, you big old black gringo. You're as bad as my partner. And anyway, it's gonna be the national language any day now, and we're gonna force you guys to speak it.'

The three men laughed together.

'So big guy, you on a case?' the police sergeant asked. His name was Lionel Anderson, and Walter Robinson knew that on the street he was called *Lion-man* at least in part for his regal bearing, but also because of his no-compromise attitudes. He had been a classmate of Robinson's at the academy, as had Juan Rodriguez, the other sergeant at his side.

'Why else would I want to visit this particular locale?' Robinson replied.

'Maybe because you miss the ambiance, the sense of community spirit and attitudes?'

'I think it's the cooking, partner. The detective cannot get proper black cuisine out on the Beach. He's tired of chicken soup and matzoh balls. He needs a fix of collard greens and ham hocks.'

'Well, perhaps,' Lionel Anderson answered. 'Sure taste a whole lot better than those fried banana things you're always wolfing down and forcing me to eat. Disgusting.'

'Plaintains are good for you. Help you learn a new language and understand a whole culture.'

Robinson shook his head and said: 'Hell, Juan, the Lion-man can't even understand the one he's got, and you want him to understand another? A new one?'

'Well, Walt, amigo, I admit you gotta point there....'

The three men started laughing again.

'So,' Anderson asked again, 'whatcha doing over here in scenic Liberty City?'

'You know about that killing we had the other night?'

'Little old lady?'

'Right.'

'We had a flyer. Stolen jewelry. Came out of your office.'

'That's the case. I think maybe the perp rode the G-75 over and back.'

'You think he took a bus to kill somebody?'

'I don't know he meant to kill anyone. He'd been having some luck over the past coupla weeks just doing B and E's.'

'That weren't no routine breaking and entering the other night.'

'No, you're right about that. But I figure he still had to get back, and only this time all the hot stuff he's used to carrying is a mite hotter. Maybe like burning a hole in his pocket ...'

'... And so,' Rodriguez said, 'you think he just jumped off the bus and wanted to dump it quick and he'd take whatever he could, right?'

'You got it, Juan.'

'Makes sense. I mean, none of it makes sense to any reasonable person. But in this world, sure. Makes sense.'

'So,' Robinson continued, 'I'm looking for someplace that maybe hasn't been keeping regular hours, you know? Someplace maybe that's open in the middle of the night . . .'

Lionel Anderson and Juan Rodriguez looked at each other momentarily, then almost in unison they said: 'The Helping Hand.'

'What?'

'The Helping Hand Pawnshop. Three blocks up . . .'

'Great name, huh?' Rodriguez said.

Anderson shook his head. 'Maybe three, four times, guys on my shift have been complaining about the dude that runs the place. They say that place is open at the oddest times, day and night and they ain't dumb, they know what that means. Anyway, the owner's name's Reginald Johnson. Got a gal working with him named Yolanda, says she's his niece down from Georgia, but I don't buy that and neither does nobody else around here. Ain't *nobody's* niece look like Yolanda. She's one of those girl-women. I mean, she's the entire package. Tits that go north. Butt that heads south. Long legs and something real special waiting at the top of them, you can bet. We're talking sweeter than your ordinary sugar, that's Yolanda. Anyway, word is, he's trying to expand his operation a bit. Got a couple of receiving stolen property busts, but they always fizzle, you know? Walks in, pays a bit of cash to some lawyer, gets it all continued to the next century, shifts it from court to court, finally pleads it out to misdemeanor possession of stolen goods, pays a fine and he's back in business thinking he's a whole lot smarter than the cops, the state attorney, and the rest of the world. I hear he's moved into a new house and filled it with new furniture, because Yolanda, she wants a real home. I was told he has his eye on a new Buick for Yolanda too. A nice red one. Now, Walter, you know I wish *I* had a niece do what she does . . .'

The policeman laughed and his partner joined in, grinning, slapping a hand against his leg, nodding his head.

'Now, you just know he's gonna be looking to keep her happy, and *you know* that the way things are going, well, little old Yolanda, she may not be the brightest light around, but it ain't gonna be too hard for her to figure out who's who and what's what and she's gonna get a quick taste for the nicer things and the finer things.'

'Ain't life sweet,' Juan Rodriguez added.

'And you know, those things cost money . . .' Lionel Anderson rolled his eyes and opened his palms skyward, as if exhorting the heavens to rain down some cash.

'I think I get the picture.'

Rodriguez smiled. 'I would just *love* to see you screw up this nice little side business he's got going. And, if your perp came from here, why, the Helping Hand is sure where he'd run first and fastest. Only one problem . . .'

'What's that?'

'I think old Reginald has figured out that he can't be leaving that stolen shit around his store too long, because even us dumb old cops gonna come looking for it. I don't know where he connects, but I think he's dumping that stuff fast.'

Lionel Anderson nodded. 'You may be too late to find that stuff in the store. And you ain't gonna get no warrant on a hunch.'

The big man smiled over at his partner.

'Still, it wouldn't do no harm to help this brother

detective out and watch old Reg squirm a bit. Likely even he understands the difference between receiving stolen property and accessory to first-degree murder. Perhaps we can enlighten him further.'

Walter Robinson let some of the amusement the two uniformed officers were sharing linger on his face, but inwardly he felt a narrowing, a harshness, and allowed himself the hope that he was riding the right path.

'Lead the way,' he said quietly.

The Helping Hand was a narrow storefront, its windows set behind thick black bars. The door itself was reinforced with steel plates and several dead-bolt locks, giving the entrance to the pawnshop all the welcoming appearance of some particularly dark, medieval fortress. Walter Robinson saw that a series of mirrors prevented anyone arriving inside the Helping Hand from discovering any shadow in which to hide. A video camera mounted adjacent to the front door switched on as the door opened, a detail that Juan Rodriguez immediately pointed out.

'Hey, Reginald, my man,' the wiry policeman called out in accented language. 'This is very fancy shit. Very high-tech. I like it. I do. *Muy bueno.*'

'I got to protect my stuff,' came a sullen voice from behind a counter.

Reginald Johnson was a short, thickset man, scowling, close-eyed, with bodybuilder's arms that pressed hard against the cloth of his sport shirt. He wore a holstered nine-millimeter pistol on his right hip to discourage any customers from debate, and Robinson suspected that a twelve-gauge was lying on a counter shelf just out of sight, within easy reach.

'Whatcha doing here?' Johnson asked. 'You need a warrant to search the place.'

'Why Reggie, we're just inspecting the merchandise. We like to see what the local merchants have to offer. Just our way of helping to promote good police and community relations,' Juan Rodriguez said, his voice filled with mockery. 'Like this showcase filled with guns, Reg. Now, I just know that you can produce the paper on each and every one of them, am I not right?'

Rodriguez drummed his finger on a glass countertop.

'Sheeit,' the pawnshop owner muttered.

'Reg, you want me to get the gun file from the safe?' This question floated from the darkened rear of the pawnshop.

'That sweet voice would be Yolanda,' Lionel Anderson whispered to Robinson. 'Hey! Sugar. Come on out here and say hello to my partner and me!'

'Yolanda!' Reginald Johnson admonished quickly, but not quickly enough.

'Is that Sergeant Lion-man?' she asked as she stepped beneath the fluorescent lights that illuminated the interior of the pawnshop. Walter Robinson quickly realized that his old friend had not exaggerated Yolanda's considerable attributes. She had cocoa skin and a sweep of night-black hair that cascaded down across her shoulders. She wore a tight, white vee-necked T-shirt that forced one's eyes directly into her cleavage, and she grinned at Lionel Anderson whose attention was riveted on her barely contained breasts. 'Why, Sergeant, how come we don't never see you no more?' she asked. 'I've been missing you.'

Anderson rolled his eyes back, looking up toward the ceiling for assistance in answering the question.

'Why, sweetness, if I knew you wanted to pass the time of day with this old cop, why don't you know you'd get the best police protection that this city has to offer? I mean, round-the-clock, twenty-four-hour police protection. . . .'

Yolanda laughed and shook her head. Walter Robinson wondered if she was fourteen or twenty-four. Either was a strong possibility.

'Yolanda! Go get those papers from the safe!' Reginald Johnson almost shouted.

The young woman turned at him, frowning. 'I already asked you if'n that's what you wanted,' she retorted.

'Go get them so we can clear these cops out of here.'

'I'm going.'

'Well, get a move on, gal.'

'I said I was going.' Yolanda turned toward Lionel Anderson. 'I'll be right back Sergeant Lion-Man.' Then she glanced over at Robinson. 'I didn't know you and your little partner were gonna bring a handsome friend along on this visit,' she added.

'I'm Walter Robinson, Miami Beach P.D.,' he said.

'Miami Beach,' Yolanda said wistfully, as if she were talking about some faraway, exotic location. 'Reggie ain't never taken me over there to look at the waves. I bet it's right beautiful, ain't it Mr Detective?'

'It has its attractions,' Robinson replied.

'See, Reggie, I told you so,' Yolanda said, turning and pouting.

'Yolanda!' Johnson yelled again, without effect.

'Little partner! Little! Yolanda, you break my heart!' Juan Rodriguez interrupted, grinning. 'I may not be some big old lunk like him, but you got no idea. You ever heard of Latin lovers, Yolanda? They're the best. *Muy perfecto!*'

'I never heard that.' The young woman smiled at Rodriguez. 'I'll bet you'd like to prove it too.'

Rodriguez clasped both hands over his heart, as if smitten, and Yolanda laughed.

'Yolanda, go get those papers,' Reginald Johnson

muttered. He stomped across the store, grasped her by the arm and steered her to the back office area, behind a wire-mesh gate, and triple locks.

'I ain't done nothing wrong,' the pawnshop owner insisted. 'And you stop screwing around with Yolanda.'

'Your niece,' Anderson reminded him.

Johnson scowled again.

Walter Robinson started to move throughout the small store, inspecting the items in various display cases, a dizzying collection of weapons, cameras, toaster ovens, tape recorders, cutlery, a waffle iron, several guitars and saxophones, and occasional pots and pans. The access-ories of life, the detective thought. He moved quickly over to a display case containing an assortment of jewelry and began examining each earring, necklace, and bracelet. He pulled out the flyer he'd prepared and began checking the descriptions of items stolen from Sophie Millstein's apart-ment against what he saw arrayed on the shelves in front of him.

Reginald Johnson approached Robinson, leaning over the countertop toward him, his voice low and iron. 'I got paper on all this shit too, Detective. You ain't gonna find whatever it is you looking for.'

'Is that right?' Robinson replied softly, very coldly.

'That's right.'

'I'm told you keep pretty late hours.'

'Sometimes in this neighborhood, people got a need to make a transaction at night. I got plenty of competition, or maybe you ain't noticed. Just trying to serve the clientele, Detective.'

'I'll bet. How about Tuesday last?'

'What about Tuesday?'

'You open late?'

'Maybe. Probably.'

'Anyone come in late? Maybe midnight.'

'I don't know if I recall nobody.'

'Try harder.'

'I'm trying real hard, and I don't just recollect nobody.'

'You lying to me?'

Johnson scowled. 'You finished hassling me, or do I got to call my lawyer?'

The two men continued to stare at each other, before Walter Robinson said: 'Fifteen to life, Reg. That's for starters.'

'What you talking about fifteen years?'

'I'm talking accessory to first-degree murder, Reg. Maybe you want to think about that a bit before you try to recall last Tuesday and who may or may not have been in your store here late that night.'

'Don't scare me. Don't know nothing about no murder. I think maybe I'm calling my attorney right now. Maybe he'll be looking to file a harassment suit.'

Reginald Johnson seemed inordinately proud of the word *harassment*. He repeated it two or three times for Walter Robinson's benefit.

The detective glanced down into the shelf of jewelry again and wished he had pictures of the stolen items, rather than simple descriptions. Every piece looked more or less the same to him, and he thought this was the inevitable result of being single, and not paying much attention to the subtleties that attracted women's eyes. He tried not to let discouragement show in his face.

'I think maybe you'd better be showing up here with a warrant, you want to look closer,' Johnson said confidently.

As he spoke, Yolanda emerged from the office area, buzzing herself through the locked steel grating, carrying a sheaf of papers.

'I got all that stuff for the guns, you want to see it,' she said. She approached Reginald Johnson. The two uniformed sergeants came over to where the pawnshop owner was standing.

Yolanda spread the papers out on the counter. 'We got it all,' she said. 'Ain't no illegal guns in there, Sergeant.' Her voice seemed to combine pleasure and disappointment simultaneously. 'Like that big old thirty-eight right there,' she said, leaning over the countertop. 'We got the license and registration right here.'

None of the policemen looked at the weapon that had Yolanda's attention. Instead, each had occupied his eyes with a generous inspection of her breasts as she bent over the glass display.

'I do believe you on that one, honey,' Lionel Anderson said quietly, appreciatively.

'Yolanda!' Johnson blurted out once again, still angry.

The young woman stood up, straightening coquettishly. She smiled at the police sergeant, then over at Walter Robinson.

Robinson, however, was no longer watching the young woman's cleavage, his eyes centered instead on the light brown skin of her throat. The fluorescent lights of the pawnshop made the single gold strand she wore flash brightly.

Robinson turned to Reginald Johnson. He leaned forward, narrowing his eyes, letting harsh, barely controlled fury slide into his voice, so that each word carried a promise of ferocity.

'Your niece sure has a pretty name,' he said.

Johnson didn't reply.

Yolanda looked around suddenly, as if the detective's tone had frightened her.

'Why, thank you,' she said hesitantly.

'A very pretty name,' Robinson repeated.

The room grew quiet. Lionel Anderson and Juan Rodriguez moved to either side of him, and he heard both men unsnap the leather flaps that held their service weapons in their holsters. At the same moment, Robinson abruptly jackknifed his body across the countertop, seizing Johnson's arms and pulling them forward, throwing the burly pawnshop owner off balance. His chest slammed against the countertop with a thudding sound and he cried out 'Hey!' in surprise.

Robinson grabbed Johnson's neck with one hand and forced the man's head down while he twisted his arm. He realized that Rodriguez had seized the pawnshop owner's free hand and was pinning it to the case.

'I want my attorney!' the man cried out. 'What you be doing? I ain't done nothing! Let me be!'

'No, you ain't done nothing,' Walter Robinson whispered.

He was breathing hard and he placed his face right down next to the pawnshop owner's.

'Yolanda's such a pretty name,' he continued harshly, softly. 'So, you tell me, you low-life scumbag motherfucker, why she's wearing a gold necklace with the name Sophie on it?'

Robinson lifted his eyes toward the young woman, who gasped and put her hand to her throat in sudden memory. She looked over at Lionel Anderson and protested, 'But it was real pretty . . .'

Reginald Johnson groaned, and Robinson heard Juan Rodriguez reach for his handcuffs, which made a wondrously satisfying, musical, jangling sound.

CHAPTER TEN
The Way It All Works

Espy Martinez flashed her identification to the desk sergeant, who directed her toward the bank of elevators with a cryptic, 'Third floor. They're expecting you....' before turning back to a paperback novel resting on top of a stack of paperwork. The book sported a voluptuous, barely clothed woman wielding an antique pistol on the jacket, and instantly gathered the desk sergeant's total attention. She hurried past him, her shoes making a flat, eager sound against the polished linoleum floor.

The elevator rose silently through the center of the building. She stepped out as the doors rattled open, looking for Walter Robinson, but spotted instead a detective from the robbery division who had been her lead witness in a case several months back. He looked up from a notepad and smiled. 'Hey, Espy! Moving up into the big time, huh?' She shrugged her reply, and he added: 'The show's down there. Squeeze time.'

It wasn't hard for her to guess what he meant by that, and she grinned in anticipation. She followed the detective's finger down a narrow corridor, beneath fluorescent lights, into the core of the police headquarters, giving her the impression that she was somehow being sealed away from the unforgiving heat and sunlight outside. The air-conditioning ducts poured ice air into the small space, and she shivered involuntarily. She realized her footsteps had disappeared into an industrial gray carpet; all she could hear was the rasp of her own breathing. For a moment she felt completely alone, and she realized this was precisely the sensation that suspects were supposed to have as well.

Midway down the hallway there were a pair of doors facing across from each other. A small plastic sign on each said: INTERROGATION 1 and INTERROGATION 2. There were windows in the corridor, so that a person could stand in the hallway and stare in at the subjects in each room. Espy Martinez realized this was one-way glass; that she could see in, but the people inside could not see out. She noticed a small intercom system next to the window.

She hesitated and saw Walter Robinson sitting in one room, across from a young, strikingly attractive black woman, who had obviously been crying. She turned and saw a stocky black man sitting at a table in the opposite room. He was drumming his fingers against the plastic surface, glaring at a pair of uniformed City of Miami policemen, who studiously ignored him. She watched the man light a cigarette, angrily tossing the spent match into an ashtray filled with discarded butts. The man swiveled about in his seat impatiently, a movement that caused both policemen to raise their eyes momentarily and stare pointedly at him until he settled back into his chair. Then they went back to ignoring him. She saw his mouth form an obscenity, which she suspected he spat into the stale room air. It had no effect on the policemen.

She turned and entered the room where Robinson sat.

As she came through the door, he quickly rose. 'Ah, Miss Martinez, glad you could make it.'

'Detective,' she replied, with a false formality.

Walter Robinson, smiling, but not particularly pleasantly,

turned to the young black woman. 'Yolanda, take a long look at this woman here.'

The young woman raised her reddened eyes toward Espy Martinez.

'You see the nice suit, Yolanda? Take a look at those shoes, Yolanda. Check out the heels. Pretty sharp, huh? See the briefcase? That's real leather. Nothing cheap. You see all that, Yolanda?'

'I see,' Yolanda replied sullenly.

'You can tell right away that she ain't a cop, right, Yolanda? You can see that, can't you?'

'She don't look like no police.'

'That's right, Yolanda. This is Assistant State Attorney Esperanza Martinez. Miss Martinez, Yolanda Wilson.'

Espy Martinez nodded at the young woman, whose eyes reflected nothing but fear.

'Yolanda,' Robinson continued, in a low voice that contained equal parts threat and seduction, 'you try to make a real good impression. You try to make the best impression you can, because Miss Martinez, well, Yolanda, you know what she does for a living? You know what she does each and every day? Every hour that the sun is up, Yolanda? You know what she does?'

'No,' the young woman replied, looking toward Espy Martinez then back at the detective. She dabbed at her eyes with a ragged piece of tissue paper.

'She puts people like you in jail,' Robinson said harshly. He rose and gestured to Espy Martinez. 'Think about that, Yolanda.'

The young woman looked as if she'd been slapped. 'I don't want to go to no jail, Mr Robinson.'

'I know that, Yolanda. But you got to help me keep you out. You got to tell me what you know.'

'I'm trying. I told you everything.'

'No, Yolanda, I don't think so. And I haven't learned what I need to learn. A name, Yolanda. I want the name.'

'I don't know,' the young woman pleaded. Her voice rose into a whine. 'I don't know. Reggie, he never told me no names.'

'Smart girl like you? Yolanda, I just don't believe you.'

The young woman dropped her head into her hands, shaking back and forth. Her shoulders heaved. Robinson let a momentary silence slide around her, deepening Yolanda's fear, then she said:

'I didn't know about no murder, Detective. Please, you got to believe me. I didn't know there was no harm involved. Where's Sergeant Lion-man? He'll tell you. Please.'

'Sergeant Lion-man can't help you, Yolanda. This woman can. You think about that. We'll be back.'

He led Espy Martinez back into the corridor, slamming the door hard on Yolanda's helpless sniffling.

'This is the part I like,' Robinson said, although Martinez had the impression that he actually liked all the parts of the job.

'What is it that you found—' she started to ask, but Robinson anticipated her question and produced a small plastic bag containing a gold necklace. He handed it to Espy Martinez, who saw the name Sophie and the pair of small diamonds that adorned the *S*.

'That's what Yolanda was wearing.'

'You sure . . .'

'You think it belonged to some other Sophie?'

'No. But . . .'

'Well, we'll get a positive from forensics later. Maybe the son or the neighbors can ID it. But it was hers. Trust me.'

'Okay, Walter. What's the procedure?'

Walter Robinson smiled. 'Well, you've already met Little

Miss Tears and Contrition. The problem is, she's telling the truth. She really doesn't know all that much, although she might know the name. I'm not sure yet. Yolanda's smarter than you might think. Some of those tears might have come from the proverbial crocodile. But, hey, when she got a long look at that briefcase . . . well, we'll see. Cops are one thing. A real live prosecutor, well, that's bound to be a novel experience for her, and I'd bet she's thinking hard right now. On the other hand, over there, behind door number two . . .' Robinson was grinning as he spoke, and Espy Martinez was forced to smile at the game-show host persona the detective mocked, '. . . is Mr Hardcase I Want My Lawyer. Now, I know he's got the information we want. The procedure is simple. Play one against the other.'

'If he's asked for his lawyer, then we're required—'

Robinson made a face. 'Espy, come on. Sure he's asked for his lawyer. He was shouting about his lawyer as soon as I walked into his pawnshop. I just need to make sure he understands the, uh, ramifications of his reluctance. Give him a chance to see the light. The opportunity to do the right thing. He ain't even been asked any real tough questions yet.'

'Well . . .'

'Espy, this is the way it all works. You watch.'

'Walter, I'm not sure I get it.'

'It'll be pretty clear pretty quick. And I'll bet you're a real fast study.'

'We'll see about that. What is it you want me to do?'

Walter Robinson grinned. 'I want you to scare the hell out of him.'

Before Espy Martinez had a chance to reply that she wasn't sure she could scare anyone, Robinson tapped on the glass window to the interrogation room. The two police officers inside immediately rose, and the pawnshop owner called out, 'Hey, where you going?' as they exited, slamming the door shut behind them. Robinson made quick introductions in the hallway.

'Espy Martinez, this is Juan Rodriguez and Lionel Anderson.'

'Sergeant Lion-man?'

'In the flesh.' The sergeant's huge paw enveloped her own hand, pumping it up and down. 'Aren't you the one who put those kids away? The home invasions?'

'My claim to fame,' Martinez replied.

'That was a nice piece of work,' Juan Rodriguez interjected. 'Those kids, they were gonna kill somebody for sure.'

'Not now,' she said.

Both sergeants grinned. 'For sure,' Rodriguez said. 'At least not until they get out.'

Lionel Anderson turned to Walter Robinson. 'Next step?'

'Look, guys,' Robinson whispered swiftly. 'You go in and make Yolanda feel a whole lot better about her chances as long as she cooperates with us. Make her think that just everything's gonna be okay, as long as she keeps her mouth moving. No lies. Got it?'

'Gonna be a pleasure, Walt, old buddy.'

'If there's one thing Lionel here knows,' Juan Rodriguez said to Espy Martinez, 'it's how to make young women feel better about their delicate situations. . . .' He punched his partner on the arm as he spoke, and he drew out the word *feel*, adding a profusion of *e*'s to its center.

'I do have some expertise, ma'am,' Sergeant Anderson said, putting finger to forehead in mock salute.

Then the two uniformed sergeants headed into the first interrogation room. Robinson smiled at Martinez. 'That wasn't a rough assignment,' he said. 'Okay, ready to put the fear of God and the criminal justice system into Mr Reginald I'm A Tough Guy Johnson? Let's go.'

Robinson didn't wait for an answer, but pushed into the room. Martinez jumped to stay close.

Reginald Johnson looked up and scowled. 'You call my lawyer?'

'What's that number again, Reggie?' Walter Robinson asked.

The pawnshop owner merely grunted a response. 'Who she?' he asked.

'Why, Reggie, I'm surprised. You don't recognize her?'

'Never seen her before.'

'You certain?'

'Sure, I'm certain. Who she?'

Robinson smiled once, then he leaned forward, pushing his face close to the pawnshop owner's, hovering over him like a parent about to strike a child. 'Why, Reggie,' Robinson hissed, 'I'm sure you've seen her in your nightmares, 'cause she's the biggest trouble your sorry ass has ever seen. She's the person who's gonna see you do hard time, Reggie. Right up in Raiford Prison. Twenty-four-hour lockup, and I'm just sure there ain't gonna be nobody up there as sweet as your Yolanda. In fact, you'll be lucky if somebody doesn't turn you into *their* Yolanda. You catch my drift, Reggie?'

The words seemed to force the stocky man back hard in his chair. He stole a quick glance at Espy Martinez.

'Your worst dream, Reggie,' Walter Robinson said.

'I ain't done nothing. Don't know about no murder.'

'Is that right?'

'You think I ask all the folks who come through my doors where they got their shit? No way. All I do is figure out the price and write the ticket. Don't need to go about asking no questions.'

'Maybe not, but you know who brought that necklace in. The one Yolanda thought was so fine that she just had to put it around her neck.'

Johnson didn't reply for a moment. 'I can't be telling no police about my business. Wouldn't have no business,' he finally answered, rocking back in his chair, crossing his arms over his chest as if this statement were his final say on the entire matter.

'Oh yes, you can,' Robinson argued. ''Cause your business is now my business, and that's a problem.'

Johnson scowled and grew silent. Espy Martinez sat in a chair at the end of the table, watching the detective as he moved about, walking behind the suspect, leaning over him wordlessly, then stepping back, and finally pulling a chair up close to him. She watched Robinson like she would an accomplished actor on a stage. Every movement he made, every motion, every tone assigned to every word, was calculated to achieve an effect. She watched as he unsettled the pawnshop owner, skillfully undressing him of every arrogance and obstinance. She took a deep breath, fascinated, wondering when she was supposed to interject herself into the performance and doubting whether she would have any of the same skills.

Walter Robinson continued to stare at Reginald Johnson, narrowing his eyes, not wavering, until the pawnshop owner turned abruptly away, snarling an obscenity.

'Sheeeit. Don't know 'bout no murder,' he added. But there was a slight waver in his voice.

The detective let the room fill again with silence. He did not move his eyes away from the suspect. After a moment he slowly exhaled, his breath hissing into the stale room air.

'Maybe I was wrong . . .' Robinson said quietly. 'Maybe I was wrong about you, Reggie.'

Johnson turned back, a look of surprise hitting his face at the sudden change in the detective's attitude.

'Maybe I was wrong. What do you think, Reggie? Was I wrong?'

'Yeah,' he replied eagerly. 'You was wrong.'

Without taking his eyes off the pawnshop owner, Walter Robinson asked: 'What do you think, Miss Martinez? You think I was wrong about Reggie here?'

Espy Martinez was uncertain for an instant as to how to reply, but finally, in as flat and cold a voice as she could manage, she said: 'You're never wrong, Detective.'

'No, maybe this time I was wrong about old Reggie here.'

'I don't think so, Detective,' Martinez said.

'Am I wrong, Reggie?' he asked again.

'Yeah. Shit, yeah. You're wrong.'

Robinson continued to let his gaze bore in hard at the pawnshop owner. He let false hope gather momentum in the little room.

'All this time, I was thinking Reggie here, all he did was take a little bit of stolen goods from the wrong man. And you know, Miss Martinez . . .' He frowned at Reginald Johnson. 'You know, maybe I'm wrong about that. Maybe there weren't no other person, showing up at the Helping Hand late Tuesday last, all eager and anxious and breathing hard and sweating a bit too much and ready to make a deal, any deal, right Reg? No, maybe there weren't no other man at all. Maybe I was all wrong about that Reggie . . .'

He hesitated one instant, just letting the words burrow into the pawnshop owner's confusion, before continuing.

'. . . No, Reggie. Maybe there weren't no other man at

all. Maybe keeping that Yolanda in those fine clothes and driving that fine car and buying all that fine furniture for that fine new house, well, maybe you figured you better work a little bit harder. Maybe you figured you had to put a little bit more cash in the old register. So maybe, Reggie, you didn't need no other man at all. No sir. No, you just took that old G-75 bus right on out to Miami Beach, and you just started doing all those break-ins. Did pretty good at it, right Reggie? Until that old woman Tuesday last, she wakes up and then you got a problem, huh, Reg? A real problem. So you killed her, right, Reggie? That how it happened?'

Robinson suddenly jabbed a finger into the pawnshop owner's face. 'You killed her, you sonofabitch!'

Reginald Johnson looked wildly at the detective, recoiling in fear. 'I didn't kill nobody! I told you! Don't know nothing about no murder!'

Robinson suddenly reached across the table and grabbed Johnson's hands. He forced them onto the table surface with a resounding slap, turning the palms up.

'You're strong, Reg. Got nice big hands. Didn't have no problem at all choking that little old lady, did you? Did you!'

'Don't know nothing about no murder, no old lady!'

He tried to pull his hands back, but the detective held them on the table, pulling Johnson forward, off balance, staring again, harsher.

In the silence that grew in that instant, Espy Martinez felt a heat pour through her body. The words seemed to come from someone else, not her, but she heard them reverberate in the small room.

'Receiving stolen goods, two to five. That's gonna be easy time, medium security. Then comes burglary, five to ten. That's getting a bit more serious, but, time off for good behavior, maybe only do three years. But then you jump up to assault. Now you're in real trouble, Reggie. Jesus, the state attorney, she just *hates* it when old folks get assaulted. So that'll bring you ten to fifteen. And maybe the judge's gonna think hard about retaining jurisdiction on the case, cut that parole board right out of the situation. So no good behavior on that one . . .'

Espy Martinez paused, gathering her breath. She saw the pawnshop owner struggling at the far end of the table. It was as if all the words and numbers added up to so many knots around his chest. She continued, lower, harsher, oddly aware that in some clear, unfamiliar spot within her, she was distinctly enjoying herself.

'. . . But then you really hit the big time, Reggie. Accessory to first-degree murder, fifteen to life. But nobody gets the fifteen, Reggie. Especially when the victim is a little old lady. Everybody gets life, up in Raiford. Not a nice place. Not a nice place at all . . .'

She looked coldly at him.

'And then we're right to the end of the line: first-degree murder. Well, you know what that buys in this state, Reggie. Two thousand two hundred volts of electricity.'

She made a gun shape with her hand and added: 'Zap. You're history.'

Johnson, hands still held on the tabletop by the detective, tried to swivel in his chair toward Martinez.

'What you talking about! Death penalty! I told you I ain't done no murder!'

Espy Martinez leaned forward. 'I got enough to make a case, Reggie. More than enough. Doesn't make any difference, though, how much evidence I have . . .'

'What you mean?' the pawnshop owner asked desperately.

'Little old lady. Never hurt no one. What do you think,

Reggie? What do you think a bunch of nice white middle-class Miamians are gonna say when they see you come walking into that courtroom? All black and angry and tough. You think they're gonna care whether we got *any* evidence at all? No way. Not after I get up and tell all those white folks that it was you strangled the life out of her. That it was your fingers wrapped around her throat, choking her until she was dead! All they're gonna think about is that it could have been their mother, or their aunt Mabel. You think after they hear that, they're gonna give a damn if we have *any* evidence? They're just gonna want to see your sorry ass disappear. So, what do you think that nice white jury's gonna say?'

'I didn't!'

'Guilty. Guilty as charged.'

She hesitated, watching the words slap the pawnshop owner like punches.

'And the judge? Reggie, what do you think that white middle-class judge's gonna do? Somebody who needs all those people to vote for him come next election day?'

'I'm telling you, I didn't do nothing!'

'All those white folks, Reggie. What do you think?'

Again silence gripped the room.

Espy Martinez took a deep breath and pointed at Reginald Johnson. 'Zap,' she said again. 'Goodbye, Reggie.'

Walter Robinson finally let go of the pawnshop owner's arms.

Martinez rose. She looked down at Reginald Johnson with as haughty a glance as she could manage.

'Detective, you keep this piece of shit company. I think I'll go talk some more to Yolanda. She and I, well, we get along a whole lot better, and if I'm gonna make somebody a nice deal, the kind of deal where they get to go on home at night and pick up their life again, well, I'm thinking maybe I'd rather it be that pretty young woman. And I just know that Sergeant Lion-man'd rather have me cut her some slack, rather than this piece of shit . . .'

'You can't give Yolanda no deal! She don't know nothing!'

'You'd be surprised what that gal has picked up, Reggie. Why, she's just filled with all sorts of information.'

'She don't know . . .'

'But she'll be the one to walk.' She said this flatly, nastily.

Walter Robinson smiled and nodded. He was having trouble keeping himself from bursting into applause. Reginald Johnson seemed to calculate quickly in a panic, then he blurted:

'I didn't know where the shit came from! Man calls me up, middle of the night, wants me to meet him at the store make a deal, well, I didn't know! Didn't ask no questions! Just went on down, met him outside, he was waiting, like. That's the truth! Didn't know about no murder.'

'Who, Reggie?' Walter Robinson asked.

'I tell you who, you got to promise—'

'Who! Goddamn it! I'm not promising you anything, you sack of shit! Who?' Robinson screamed into the pawn broker's face.

Reginald Johnson twisted in the seat a final time, like a man trapped beneath a wave, trying to find the surface. Then he slumped forward and said:

'Man's name is Leroy Jefferson.'

'He a junkie?'

'Man likes a pipe, I'm told.'

'He a regular customer of yours?'

'He been in pretty regular last month or so.'

'He got a street name?'

'Yeah. They calls him Hightops because he always wearing those fancy basketball shoes.'

'Where's Hightops live?'

'King Apartments. Number thirteen, I think.'

'Unlucky number,' Walter Robinson said, rising from the table, leaving the pawnshop owner with his head in his hands.

CHAPTER ELEVEN
A Man of Precision

At very nearly the same moment that Walter Robinson and Espy Martinez emerged from the interrogation room with the name of the man they believed had killed Sophie Millstein, Simon Winter was sitting down in a stiff-backed chair across the desk from a young homicide detective named Richards, who seemed unable to decide between acting politely toward the older man or impatient with his questions.

'Thank you for seeing me on such short notice, Detective,' Winter began.

'It's a closed case, Mr Winter. I had to get the file back from records.'

'I appreciate your taking the time.'

'Yeah, well, no big deal, but I don't exactly get your interest in this guy's death.'

Winter decided to lie. 'Well, Stein was related to me – a distant relative – through marriage. And you know how hard it is for people who haven't seen someone in years to accept the fact of his death, much less a suicide. So because I was down here, I got assigned the task of checking it out – even though it's been months. You know how some people are. Kvetching, disbelieving. Never letting things just go, and finally getting around to asking someone to go ask some questions . . .'

'Uh-huh.'

'Families. Sometimes they can be—'

'A major pain. Sure. I got you.'

'There you go,' Winter said with a flagrant shrug.

This falsehood seemed to placate any of Richards's inconvenient anger at having his day interrupted by a curious old man.

'Yeah. I guess. Well, anyway, closed case, Mr Winter. Pretty much cut and dried. One shot. Left a note. Not much for us to do, except tidy up and cart out the body. No big mystery.'

'You were there at the scene?'

'Yeah. My case. Just a matter of collecting the documents and filing a report. I don't really remember it all too much.'

'Who found the body?'

'Cleaning lady, I think I remember. Maybe twenty-four hours postmortem. It's in my summary.'

The young man shoved a brown accordion file across the desk toward Simon Winter. 'Have a look at it. It wasn't anything special or out of the ordinary. You gonna be able to handle the photographs, Mr Winter? They aren't too pleasant.'

'Ahh, I believe so. Thank you, Detective.'

'Well, you take a look. Then I'll answer any questions, if I can. Deaths like these, they all seem to pretty much get lumped together, understand? It's hard to remember specifics. You want coffee?'

'No thanks.'

'Well, I'll be back in a bit.'

He stood up and left Winter holding the file. For a moment the older man hesitated, just letting his fingers creep across the rough brown paper, like a blind man reading braille. He thought of all the case files he'd stuffed with photographs, reports, summaries, and evidence in all his years, and he smiled, delighted to have one in his hands again. He lifted it, measuring its weight. Not much, he thought. Then, with an eagerness that he knew was completely inappropriate, but which he was incapable of denying, he unsnapped the rubberized cord holding it together and looked inside.

He went to the crime scene photos first. There were only a half-dozen eight-by-ten glossy color pictures, perhaps a tenth of what there would have been in a homicide scene. The two most prominent pictures showed an elderly man slumped backward in a brown leather desk chair, his arms thrown out to the sides, almost as if in astonishment. Blood had dripped down between his eyes, from a gunshot wound in his forehead, staining the collar of his sport shirt. There was a clear splatter pattern on the wall behind Herman Stein, marred by flecks of brain and bone. Stein's eyes were open in death, beneath a scarlet and gunpowder-blackened entry wound. His mouth was slightly open, as if in wonderment. He had been nearly bald, with just a few tufts of white hair around his ears. The blood streaking his face made him seem like a gargoyle. Simon Winter studied the pictures carefully.

Tell me something, he said inwardly.

He flipped to another picture. This showed a large .38 caliber pistol dropped to the floor beneath Stein's outflung hand. This was followed by a close-up of Stein's face. Then there was a photograph of an electric typewriter next to the desk. In the platen of the machine was the suicide note. Another close-up picture showed that Rabbi Rubinstein's memory was accurate.

Simon Winter read: 'I am tired of life and miss my beloved Hanna and am going to join her now.'

He put the photographs aside and turned to the detective's summaries. There was a brief description of the scene, and a list of neighbors who had related the facts of Mr Stein's most recent depression. There was a telephone number for Stein's next of kin, a son with the unusual name of G. Washington Stein, and an address at a large New England university. He flipped through the autopsy protocol, which described a most obvious death. There is little medical surprise in what happens when a .38 caliber soft-nosed bullet is fired from a point-blank range into a person's forehead. Blood toxicology was negative, save for traces of ibuprofen – arthritis, Simon Winter thought immediately. Winter saw a short notation on an additional form, mentioning the rabbi's visit to Detective Richards, and he saw a copy of Stein's letter. There was no mention of its contents in any of the detective's conclusions, which were simple: suicide due to mental depression and age.

They would have written the same about me, he thought.

Then he flipped through the file another time, trying to find something. Other than the mention in his own letter, there was nothing linking Herman Stein to Der Schatten-mann.

Simon Winter frowned, just as Detective Richards returned holding a cup of coffee.

'Not much, huh?' said the younger man.

'No, not much.'

'Case like this,' Richards continued, 'we don't really go hunting about for a whole lot. This was pretty much a textbook suicide. A man with no known enemies – even his neighbors said that he was always friendly and polite. History of depression since his wife died a half-dozen years ago. I found some mood-elevating drugs in the bathroom cabinet. That's in the report. . . .'

The detective sighed, then continued.

'And he left a note. A note and a single gunshot wound to the head. Doesn't take a rocket scientist—'

'The gun, did it belong to Stein?'

'Uh, no. Or, at least, no record. No registration. Just another illegal weapon. Must be millions of them in Dade County. I wrote down the serial number. . . .'

Simon Winter copied that figure. 'Any ballistics reports? Fingerprints?'

'What for?'

'Did the cleaning woman ever say she'd seen the weapon before. Or somebody else, you know, to put it in his possession?'

The young detective flipped quickly through the reports.

'Nothing here. But that wouldn't be so unusual. Most folks don't want the cleaning woman to know where they keep their gun. It'll get stolen.'

'True enough,' Simon Winter said. Then he asked: 'The position of the deceased, it didn't bother you some?'

'How so?'

'Well, you're gonna shoot yourself, I guess usually you'd put the gun up like this . . .'

He made his hand into a pistol and held it to the side of his head.

'Or like this . . .'

Again he demonstrated by putting his index finger into his mouth.

'Sure,' Richards replied. 'That's what I'd expect. Never wanted to kill myself, so I never gave it much thought.'

'But holding a large handgun up against your own forehead, like Stein did, that's sort of unusual. I mean, you've got to hold it out there, and then pull the trigger, what, with your thumb maybe, to get enough strength.'

'Yeah. I can see that. What's your point?'

'It's just unusual.'

'Well, suicide is suicide. I mean, he coulda jumped. Lived way up on the tenth floor of that condo. Or swum out into the ocean. It's only a block away. Or walked in front of a bus. We've had all of those. So, yeah, maybe holding that big old thirty-eight like that wasn't how you or I might have done it, but hey, different strokes.'

Richards looked over at Simon Winter closely. 'You got some expertise in this sort of thing, Mr Winter?'

'Used to be a cop. City of Miami. Retired years ago.'

'Hey, my old man was a city cop. Took one in the leg, though, back in the late Sixties. Had to retire too.'

Winter thought for an instant, and then recalled a heavyset man with a florid face.

'I remember. Bank robbery, right? He chased the guy for six blocks, bleeding all the way. Finally got him.'

'Hey, that's right.' The young detective brightened. 'Damn. You got some memory.'

'How's your dad now?'

'Still runs a fishing boat down in Islamorada. Lotsa cold beer and gals who like to get an altogether tan. Has it pretty good.'

'I'm glad to hear that.'

'Hey. Mr Winter, you want me to copy all this stuff for you? Maybe then you'll think of something else.'

'That would be great. But one other quick question . . .'

'Sure. Fire away.'

'The gun. You found it right beneath his hand, right?'

'Yeah. Right there. One bullet gone. Five more in the cylinder.'

'But wouldn't the force of the shot, and his hands flinging backwards . . .'

Simon Winter demonstrated slowly, throwing his hands

out wide and leaning back in his seat.

'. . . Well, wouldn't you expect the gun to be a bit farther away?'

The young detective smiled. 'You're still pretty sharp, Mr Winter. Yeah, I might . . . if it were some little twenty-two or twenty-five. But that old thirty-eight musta weighed a ton. Big as a brick. It wasn't gonna travel far.'

Simon Winter nodded. 'Place was all locked up when the cleaning woman came?'

'Yup. Like I said. She let herself in with a passkey. No mystery there.'

Simon Winter nodded. 'I'd still like those copies.'

'No problem. You just keep them to yourself. They're official police documents. Understand?'

'Hey, the rules haven't changed that much since I sat behind a desk like yours.'

Detective Richards laughed and walked off to a copying machine while Winter sat waiting, thinking of the last moments of Herman Stein. It's all absolutely clear cut and correct, he concluded – and all totally screwed up and impossible. Both at the same time.

It took him several efforts to penetrate the telephone switching system at the University of Massachusetts; each time he'd dialed Professor G. Washington Stein's direct extension, he slid inexorably into telephone limbo. It was not until he managed to get the secretary in the English Literature Department that he was able to get connected. He hated making this sort of phone call; had hated making them when he'd been a detective. But he took some relief from the thought that months had passed since Herman Stein's death, and perhaps some of the rawness of that single gunshot wound had scabbed over.

'Professor Stein?'

'Yes. No extensions. Final papers are due Wednesday. Who is this, please?'

'Professor, my name is Simon Winter. . . .'

'You're not a student?'

'No. I'm an investigator. I'm calling from Miami.'

'An investigator? And what are you investigating?'

Winter paused, trying to think of a concise answer to that question. He couldn't think of one.

'Professor, I apologize for coming to you on a difficult subject, but just prior to his death, your father wrote a letter to my' – he hesitated, trying to think of a word to describe the three old and frightened people in the rabbi's apartment – 'my clients. . . .'

'My father wrote a letter? To whom?'

'A rabbi he didn't know. Another man who'd lived in Berlin during the war until being caught up and shipped to a concentration camp.'

'I see. A letter to a man he didn't know? What was in it?'

'He said he'd recognized a man he had not seen since—'

'The war.'

'That's right. This man—'

'The Shadow Man,' the professor interrupted coldly.

Winter's heart jumped. 'That is correct.'

Professor Stein seemed to be gathering his breath, and for an instant the telephone line was silent. Then he continued, dryly:

'My father often saw Der Schattenmann, Mr Winter. He saw him in his dreams, and then they turned to nightmares and he would awaken shouting, yelling, sweating, and it would take my mother hours to calm him. He saw him in lines at the bank and movie theater crowds and rolling a grocery cart down the aisles of the supermarket. He saw Der Schattenmann in the cars that pulled past us on the freeway and waiting at the local bus stop. Once I took him to a baseball game at Fenway Park, and he saw Der Schattenmann in the rest room. Another time he spotted him in the crowd at a New York Knicks game we were watching on television. The Shadow Man was everywhere, Mr Winter. Everywhere in my father's imagination.'

Simon Winter slumped down in his chair. He was sitting in his own living room, centered on his worn sofa, a pad of paper and several sharpened pencils in front of him on the table, and he suddenly felt as if he was ridiculous.

'So,' Winter started hesitantly, 'if just prior to his death—'

'He told someone he'd seen Der Schattenmann? This would be only slightly unusual, Mr Winter.'

'Slightly?'

'Yes. The only thing out of the ordinary, is that almost always – I can't think of a different occasion that I know of – he would call me, or my brother or sister, with the news of the sighting. And it would be one of us who would go over the circumstances and the memories and slowly, but certainly, talk him out of what he thought he saw. I cannot recall him ever contacting a stranger.'

'You don't think he ever truly saw—'

Again the professor interrupted. 'No. But I spoke with him a day before his death, and he didn't mention anything to me. He was upset. More nervous, more anxious, more depressed than I'd ever heard him before. But he kept speaking about our mother, not Der Schattenmann. I think he might have mentioned him, if he'd seen him.'

'So you could calm him and talk him out of what he thought he saw?'

'Correct.'

'Did he seem scared?'

The professor paused, then replied: 'Perhaps. Perhaps you could add fear into the mix of all the things he was feeling. I remember I was worried, and I called my siblings, and we decided one of us should go down to Miami and visit him, but, of course, by the time we got it all worked out, it was too late.'

Again the professor hesitated, before adding: 'Do I sound cold, Mr Winter? Unfeeling?'

'No,' Winter lied.

'It's an odd thing, Mr Winter. To hate someone you love for doing something to themselves. You feel so many things.'

'I'm sorry to bring it up like this.'

'No, it's all right. In a funny way, it is easier to talk with a stranger than someone you know. Did you ever meet my father, Mr Winter?'

'No.'

'He was an unusual man.'

'How so?'

'He felt debts. He was constantly trying to repay debts.'

'Money?'

'No. Debts of the soul, Mr Winter.' The professor laughed, as if recalling something amusing. 'I'll give you an example, Mr Winter. My full name is George Washington Woodburn Stein. Not your run of the mill, ordinary name, huh?'

'No.'

'I shall tell you the story of how I got my name, and that will help you understand my father a little bit. He was caught, along with my aunt, uncle, and grandparents, in 1942. They were underground in Berlin. . . .'

'Der Schattenmann?'

'Yes. He recognized my uncle, or so my father said. Spotted him in a bunker during an air raid.'

'And?'

'What do you think, Mr Winter? The Gestapo came. Took them away. They all died in the camps.'

'I'm sorry.'

'My father, however, he managed to survive. He was seventeen by the time the war was closing down. Of course, all hell was breaking loose near the end. The S.S. guards marched them all from camp to camp as the front kept changing. I suppose, in their own way, these were as terrible as anything else that had taken place. To have survived so far, through so much, only to be driven into exhaustion with Allied troops only miles away. My father said so many were dying then, just dropping by the side of the road, almost as if the mere hope of survival could kill you.'

'He lived.'

'Yes. But only barely. He said he collapsed in a barracks. It was night and they had marched dozens of useless, absurd miles. Marching to die. They hadn't eaten in days. Typhus, the flu, pneumonia – you name it – was killing them, one right after the other. They could hear artillery in the distance, and he once told me that the sound was like hundreds of people knocking on the great doors of Heaven. He expected to die. When he awoke in the morning, he said he was surprised to see sunlight, and he knew it would be the last time he would see the day, so he crawled from his bed – not a bed, really, a slab of wood in one of the barracks – out the door, knowing that an S.S. guard would shoot him before he got too far, but that it would be worth it, just to feel the sunlight on his face one last time. But the guards had fled during the night. The camp was quiet, save for the sounds of astonishment and death. My father crawled out into the assembly yard. *Arbeit Macht Frei*. That was the slogan. He said he decided he would wait there for his own death. Seventeen, Mr Winter. Seventeen, and waiting in the sunlight to die.'

The professor took a deep breath over the phone.

'I loved my father,' he said. 'But you know, sometimes it seemed as if from the age of seventeen on, he was always waiting to die.'

The professor hesitated, recalling another memory, then added: 'When he moved to Miami Beach, that's what he said. He still wanted to die in the sun. It seemed the right place for him.'

'But your name?' Simon Winter asked.

'He said he fell asleep as the sun rose over him. And after a while he heard an angel speaking above his head. He always said he was so surprised, because the angel spoke in English. My father knew English, because he had grown up in ... well, that's another story. But he knew the language, and he said he heard the angel say: "But here's one that's alive ..." and he opened his eyes expecting to see Heaven, but instead he looked up into the face of Sergeant George Washington Woodburn. A very black face, Mr Winter. A black angel. Sergeant Woodburn was with the Eighty-eighth Tank Battalion. You know what they nicknamed themselves? "Eleanor Roosevelt's niggers," but that's another story too. And so, Herman Stein, my father, he reaches up and touches this Sergeant Woodburn on the cheek and asks, "Have I died?" and Sergeant Woodburn, he says, "No, son, and you ain't." My father always thought this was so funny, later. The sergeant spoke with as thick an Alabama accent as you can imagine, and it had been probably five or six years since my father had heard a word of English, and that was always refined, British, you know very, very upper crusty sort, but he said he could recall every word that sergeant said. So Sergeant Woodburn, he reaches down and picks up my father and carries him right through the camp, shouting "Medic! Medic!" and my father always said all he could remember was these strong arms holding him – he only weighed sixty pounds – and this great black man crying for a doctor and saying, "You ain't dyin' boy. No sir. You ain't gonna die . . ."'

The professor's voice seemed thick with emotion.

'So Sergeant Woodburn carries my father to an aid center and a doctor, all the time saying over and over: "You ain't dying, no sir." And when he awakens again, he's in a hospital, and that is how he lives. And that is how I came to be named for Sergeant George Washington Woodburn. When I was growing up, every couple of years my father and mother would pack us all in the family car and we would drive down to Jefferson City, Alabama, to visit the Woodburns. He became fire chief. Raised six sons, the youngest is a graduate student right here at the university. We'd have these reunions and my father and Chief Woodburn would always tell the same story. And they'd joke, and laugh, and the Chief would try to pick my father up in his arms like he did that day, but he couldn't anymore, and everyone would laugh. He passed away himself just a little over a year ago. We all went to his funeral. Jefferson City, Alabama. It was very hot and my father cried for hours. We all did.'

The professor took another deep breath. Simon Winter could hear tears gathering in his voice.

'My father, you see, Mr Winter, he understood debts.'

Winter did not know exactly what to say. He was fortunate, however, because the professor did not seem to be finished.

'I'm rambling,' he said. 'I apologize.'

'No, not at all. Was your father in academics, like you?'

George Washington Woodburn Stein laughed quickly,

as if relieved to be heading in a different direction. 'Oh, no, not at all! He was a jeweler. The family, in Berlin, had been antique jewel merchants. That was why he'd learned English as a young child. And French as well. They traveled extensively. Very cosmopolitan. They were amongst those Jews in Germany that simply couldn't perceive the extent of the evil about to be delivered to them. The family tree went back centuries. My grand-father must have thought he was more German than the people who finally shipped him to his death.'

'A jeweler?'

'Correct. A man of incredible precision, when he was working on stones. My father had a delicacy, a gift. He was an artist of the exact, Mr Winter. He loved jewels, because they lasted forever, he said. Like a play by Shakespeare – that's my field – or a painting by Rembrandt, or a Mozart piano concerto. Immortal, he would say. The stones are of the earth, and they can live an eternity. Stones were alive, to him. They had personalities and character. He would speak to the settings, as he crafted them. He had hands like a surgeon's – that's what my sister became. Eyes like a sharpshooter. Even at the end of his life, his vision was extraordinary—'

The professor hesitated, a catch in his voice tripping his last words.

'Something is wrong?' Simon Winter asked.

'Well, yes and no.'

'Something is bothering you?'

'Yes. Mr Winter, I don't know if—'

He stopped.

Winter probed gently: 'What is it, Professor Stein?'

The voice on the other end of the telephone was hesitant. 'I don't know you, Mr Winter. I cannot see your face. I am reluctant to speak of doubts with a stranger.'

The professor's language was oddly stilted, increasingly formal.

'I am an old man too,' Winter said abruptly. 'Like your father. I am an old man who was once a detective, and I have been asked by some other old people to find out if this man, this Shadow Man, is actually here on Miami Beach. They are frightened and don't yet have an answer to their fear, professor. They don't know whether to believe your father when he told them he'd seen Der Schattenmann. They do not want to believe he is here. But then, there was another sighting. And another death. And that is why I called you.'

'Another?'

'Yes. Only this was a murder.'

'Someone was killed? But how?'

'A break-in. Apparently a narcotics addict.'

'So, not anyone like the Shadow Man?'

'That's the belief.'

'And the connection to my father's death?'

'Only this: Both your father and this other person believed they spotted the Shadow Man shortly before their deaths.'

The professor hesitated. Surprise lingered in his voice. 'That is remarkable.' He paused again, then added: 'You know, that's the sort of thing my father would have enjoyed, Mr Winter.'

'Enjoyed?'

'Yes. He was a tremendous fan of mystery writers. I don't know exactly how he acquired this taste, but he did. Sir Arthur Conan Doyle and Agatha Christie and P. D. James. He was particularly fond of Harry Kemelman's series about the rabbi who investigated crimes. Do you know those?'

'No, I'm afraid not.'

'They're actually quite intriguing. He forced me to read some once, right about the time I received my doctorate. Said I was in imminent danger of becoming dull. Too many learned, academic texts. Too much studying. I remember him shoving an armful of paperback novels at me and telling me that they were filled with quandaries and MacGuffins and red herrings. I have to admit they are very clever.'

The professor returned to silence. Finally, he said: 'Ask your questions, Mr Winter. Then I will explain what is bothering me.'

Simon Winter took a deep breath. 'The gun. He committed suicide with a thirty-eight. . . .'

'My father abhorred weapons, Mr Winter. I was surprised to learn he had one. He was a gentle man. But it was Miami, and it is a violent place, so I suspected he simply hadn't told anyone.'

'The position he killed himself . . .'

'Yes. A gunshot right above the eyes. That upset me, Mr Winter. My father loved his eyes. They were the avenue to his art. I never thought he would do anything to damage them.'

'I see . . .'

'And another thing. The way the Miami Beach police described how he held the pistol . . .'

'Yes?'

'Well, it would have been hard for him. His hands, you see. All those years working with fine jewelry. All those precise carvings. All those delicate touches. His hands had grown arthritic. Pulling a trigger, especially with his thumb, would have been extremely painful.'

'You said this to the police?'

'Of course. But they pointed out that he'd been depressed and lonely and people in a suicidal frame of mind overcome physical limitations. That, I imagine, is true.'

The two men waited, as if expecting the other to fill in the silence on the phone line.

'What else?' Winter finally asked.

'It was probably nothing, but it truly disturbed me.'

'What?'

'The police didn't attach any importance to it, but you know, families look at these things differently. . . .'

'What is it, Professor?'

'The suicide note.'

'What about it?'

'Well, it was written in my father's style. Direct. To the point. I told you, precise. It was exactly what he would have written if he were about to kill himself. He had long ago made his peace with his children. We knew he loved us. He knew we loved him. There wasn't anything to add to that, unless he was going to go on and on, and that wasn't his style, Mr Winter. No, he was direct. Direct and concise.'

'I see.'

'No,' the professor said abruptly, 'you don't see. The note. The goddamn note . . .' Bitterness scored the professor's voice. Still, he maintained a certain pedantic approach. 'What is a suicide note, Mr Winter? A message. A final statement. Last words. There may only be a few words involved, but they are crucial, are they not?'

'Of course.'

'So, you accept the postulate that he was trying to say something. That this was his last message to me, and my brother and sister and his grandchildren, whom he loved. And through all his sadness and loneliness, despite all our efforts to include him, still this was his final statement on this earth.'

'Yes.'

'Then tell me why,' the professor asked slowly, his own voice deep with renewed despair and confusion, 'tell me why after all those years of marriage, he would not place the final *h* on my mother's name?'

'I'm sorry?'

'Hannah, with an *h*, Mr Winter. Not Hanna. My beloved Hannah ... but misspelled. Misspelled by a man of exactness and precision. So, you tell me, Mr Winter. What message is in that omission? Does it say something to you?'

It did. But Simon Winter did not reply to the professor's anguished questions.

CHAPTER TWELVE

In a Perfect World

The plan was simple: Sergeant Lion-man was to be the uniform. He would knock once, announce, then step aside while a detective borrowed from the Beach robbery division took out the dead bolts with a swing or two of a sledgehammer. The detective was a part-time bodybuilder nicknamed the Lumberjack and accustomed to being called in on arrests that needed the quick destruction of a locked door. Then, when the door was open, Walter Robinson would lead the arrest team into number 13.

In a perfect world, Espy Martinez thought, the suspect will be groggy with drugs or sleep, then disorientated by noise and fear. He should be meek, passive, and willing to surrender without a struggle.

She sat in the dim rear seat of an unmarked police car, staring out across the nighttime black-and-gray-tinted universe of the decrepit housing project. She had never been to anyplace like the King Apartments, especially not in the hours after midnight. Streetlights carved pathetic slices of the night away, as if by holding out a tiny portion of the darkness, they could delay the decay that constantly chewed at the edges of the low-slung, three-story buildings. Despite the hour, she could still hear an occasional shouted obscenity and a child's haphazard cries. A moment after they had arrived, she thought she'd heard a stray gunshot coming from someplace beyond the fringe of the streetlights, whining past, like a lost evil thought. She could just barely make out a graffiti message spray-painted on one tan wall of the apartments: 22 SHARKS RULES. She assumed this was the street gang that extorted money from businesses and controlled the drug trade on Twenty-second Avenue.

In a perfect world, she thought again.

Then she shivered, despite the festering heat.

Walter Robinson turned, right at that moment, and saw her look up at him expectantly. 'You sure you want to be here?' he asked.

She nodded. 'It's my job.'

'Your job is to put this Leroy Jefferson away. Your job is in a courtroom, starting tomorrow morning when we arraign the bastard for Sophie's murder, wearing a sharp blue pin-striped suit and carrying that big old leather briefcase and saying "Your Honor this and Your Honor that and the State requests no bail be set . . ." You don't have to be here,' he said.

She shook her head. 'No. I do. I want to be here.'

Robinson smiled gently and waved his hand in the direction of the King Apartments. 'Espy, why in this entire godforsaken world would anyone want to be here, if they didn't have to?'

He grinned at her and she smiled back.

'Ahh,' she said, 'your point is well taken.' Then she thrust the smile aside and added quietly, 'I just need to see things through. All the way through. From start to finish. Beginning to end. It's my nature.'

'Well, if you insist . . .'

'I insist.'

'. . . Then you wait here until we have the cuffs around

him. You come up and watch me giving him his rights. Maybe we can avoid the usual police brutality charges from the public defender's office if you witness the arrest.'

Again she nodded. Walter Robinson looked at her closely and wondered what it was that she was trying to prove. It was certainly not to impress him, he thought. She had already managed that. But he realized there was some other agenda working within Espy Martinez, and he suspected it would not be too long before he discovered what it was. He continued to watch as she turned her head just slightly, her eyes sweeping across the open courtyard of the King Apartments. For an instant he allowed himself to fix on her profile, the curve of her hair as it swept down next to her cheek, and the girlish way she pushed it back. Then he turned in his own seat and removed his pistol. He checked the clip on the nine-millimeter, then double-checked to see if he had his spare.

'All right,' he said.

'Which one is it?' she asked.

He glanced up at the King Apartments. 'Last one on the left, near the stairwell. Second floor.'

She followed his eyes. There was an exterior set of stairs at either end of the flat, rectangular building. An open-air corridor ran the length of each of the three stories. She thought it was a singularly ugly set of buildings, and wondered how it had ever acquired its distinguished name. The politics of neglect, she thought. Martinez turned away just as Robinson returned his pistol to his shoulder harness. For an instant she tried to imagine what it was like for him or for Sergeant Lion-man or for any other black officer to come in the middle of the night to the King Apartments searching for another black man with a warrant for the first-degree murder of a white person. She wanted to ask Walter Robinson about this, but could not.

Not at that moment. So instead, she spoke words that seemed to jump out of some forgotten part within her:

'Hey, Walter,' she whispered as he was getting out of the cruiser, 'you be careful.'

He laughed his response. 'Careful is my natural state of being.'

The Lumberjack and another detective stepped out of another unmarked car and approached Robinson. Across the street, he saw the two City of Miami sergeants giving instructions to several uniformed officers. They were the backup. After a moment, the two sergeants hurried across the street.

Juan Rodriguez spoke first. 'Lion-man's all set, Walter. A couple of guys around back. The rest, right behind you. Let's do this real quick. In and out. Grab the slime-bucket before his neighbors raise hell. Then we can take our time with the search of his place. *Comprendo*?'

'Sounds good. Who's going around the back?'

'I think the young guys.'

'Come on, Juan, rookies?'

'Hey, they gotta learn. They're okay. Real fire-eaters. Been on the street almost a year. Both of them. And anyway, there's only one little bathroom window on the back end. The perp's gonna have to have wings to get out that way. Walter, buddy, the King Apartments are just like some jail. Hell, most of the places even got bars on the windows. Only difference is, they're trying to keep folks out instead of locking them in. But the effect is pretty much the same. All we got to do is take out the cell door on number thirteen and sweep up what's inside. Like the song says: no place to run, no place to hide.'

'You're making it sound real simple. I like that,' Robinson said. 'All right. Everybody ready? Lion-man, you wearing your vest?'

'Yeah. I put the damn thing on. It's goddamn hot and uncomfortable and it makes me look fat, and I don't like that.'

'Rather have your vanity or a sucking chest wound, Lion-man?' Rodriguez asked sarcastically.

Espy Martinez cut in quickly. 'Ahh, but Sergeant, many women like a big man. If you know what I mean . . .'

The other policemen all grinned as Lionel Anderson tipped his hat toward Martinez, trying to conceal a slight embarrassment at the double entendre.

'Yes ma'am, of course they do. But size where it counts.'

Espy Martinez leaned over and punched the sergeant in the chest. 'Just wear the vest,' she said.

'For you, of course.'

'Maybe for that Miss Yolanda too.'

'Ahh, I had not considered that issue, Miss Martinez.'

'Everybody wear their vest,' Martinez said to the assembled men. Heads nodded. 'Except me,' she continued, 'because I'm staying here where it's safe.'

The men laughed, as if thankful to have whatever tension that had gathered eviscerated by Martinez's lightheartedness. She wished she could tell them all that the joke and the grin and everything else in the nonchalant way she stood in the center of the group was a lie, but she did not. Instead she turned to Walter Robinson. He nodded at her. He knows, she thought.

Robinson held up his hand to get everyone's attention. 'No screw-ups,' he said. 'Everybody take another look at this guy Jefferson's mug shot.'

He passed these around.

Lionel Anderson looked at the picture hard. 'You know, I think I remember this guy. What's his street name?'

'Hightops.'

'Gotta be the same guy. Played a little ball for Carol City

High maybe ten years ago. Strong to the hoop, but no outside touch.'

'He's got a different kinda outside touch now,' Robinson said. 'Assault, burglary, burglary, weapons violations, misdemeanor possession, felony possession reduced. I mean, we're talking a book-length sheet. The all-American bad guy. Probably armed. I mean, definitely armed. Let's just snatch him quick. Any questions?'

There were none. He hadn't expected any. This was well within the policeman's routine: a person who had been wrong for years had finally stepped up and killed someone. The only thing surprising about the arrest was that the suspect hadn't murdered beforehand. Of course, Robinson thought sardonically, I haven't seen his juvenile record. He shrugged inwardly.

'Everybody set? Let's do it.'

He handed the arrest warrant to Lionel Anderson, and the policemen headed off into the King Apartments. Espy Martinez felt a sudden unsettled feeling. She reached down into her pocketbook and took hold of her small semiautomatic pistol. She chambered a round, then exhaled slowly, holding the weapon tightly, bracing it up against her side, waiting for something to happen so that she would not have to stand for long in the encapsulating night that she hated so intensely.

Leroy Jefferson, a young man who did not expect to ever grow old, sat quietly in his underwear at a scarred and stained, shaky wooden kitchen table inside number 13, imagining how his life would improve if he could ever get enough of a stake together to start dealing drugs, rather than simply consuming them. It was a fantasy of the mundane; he pictured himself in newer clothes, driving a large car. He was partial to the color red, and he wondered idly whether his suit or his vehicle should be that shade, only, upon reflection, to decide that perhaps both would not be excessive.

He reached out and toyed with the glass pipe on the table. Leroy Jefferson had long, bony hands. Athlete's hands: the fingers were curved in a predatory fashion, like talons, the veins stood out on the backs, as if pushed up by sinew, muscle, and strength. An artist would probably have thought them beautiful, in a rough-hewn, violent sort of way.

He ran one cracked fingernail down the edge of the pipe.

His girlfriend slept in an adjacent room; he could hear a light snore, almost a wheeze, as she turned over, tangled up naked in a single sweat-damp sheet. They had not been together long, and he did not expect that they would stay together much longer. They had fallen together more out of affection for the drug than for each other. Their coupling was an occasional act of mutual convenience.

Beneath his finger, friction made the glass pipe feel hot, but then, he realized, the whole world was hot. His girlfriend shifted position again noisily, and he wondered how anyone could sleep with the temperature in the small apartment creeping steadily up through the thickest part of the night.

What was it? he asked himself. Seventy-five? Eighty? Ninety fucking degrees? You can't even breathe the air; it was almost like it tasted of bitter wet heat. He wanted a beer from the small refrigerator, but knew there was none. There wasn't even a soda, or a tray of ice. The tap water was brackish and lukewarm. He thought of standing under the shower but had trouble unfolding his long legs from beneath the table and taking a step in that direction. He blamed his lethargy on the heat as well. He stared angrily across at the living room jalousie window, cranked open to let what little breeze there was meandering about Liberty City enter the apartment.

Cold air, he thought to himself. That's what he wanted more than anything. Just nice cold air that would slip over his body like a light shirt. He lifted one of his hands to the back of his neck and swept away some of the sweat that had gathered there. It glistened in his palm. In Miami, he thought, rich people never sweat – unless they want to.

This thought infuriated him, because he knew it was true.

He continued to eye the open window, as if he could force it to provide some relief, almost as if he expected to see the wind as it slid between the glass plates. His frustration made him alert, so that when it was sound that penetrated the window rather than cool air, it only took him a second to realize what was happening.

One set of footsteps, moving unsteadily and haphazardly on the stairwell, that would be a neighbor, stumbling home drunk.

Two sets of footsteps, moving slowly, deliberately, that would be a drug dealer and his muscle, looking to collect on an overdue debt.

But the rat-a-tat-tat of several pairs of heavy shoes moving fast on the stairs could only be one thing; Leroy Jefferson rose sharply, dashing the pipe onto the floor, knocking over his chair and crossing the room in one large stride. His girlfriend snorted once and opened her eyes in surprise as he pushed her aside, reaching for the pistol he kept beneath the mattress. He half whispered, half shouted the word 'Police' just as a fist thundered against the door to apartment number 13, and the same word was shouted out by Sergeant Lion-man. The policeman and the murder suspect had almost spoken in unison.

The girlfriend grabbed the sheet, pulling it toward her breasts and screamed: 'Leroy, no!'

But Leroy Jefferson ignored her. Spinning in a half crouch by the mattress and raising his pistol, he fired two shots from the bedroom, across the living room and into the front door just as it buckled sharply from a sledge-hammer blow, the two pistol reports bracketing the crash of iron against the wooden door frame.

As soon as he had knocked and announced, Sergeant Lion-man had sprung aside, giving the Lumberjack room to swing the sledgehammer. The burly detective howled like an injured animal when, just as he delivered his first blow to the door frame, the second of Leroy Jefferson's shots deflected off the metal plate of the dead-bolt lock and slashed into the bulging bicep of his left arm. Skin, blood, and sinew exploded in a vibrant scarlet mass. He twisted around, the hammer falling with a thud to the corridor floor, slamming backward into a metal grate railing. The Lumberjack continued to wail, his head back, his legs jerking spasmodically, like a runner helplessly trying to accelerate in deep sand. His screams were bursts of unworldly noise that rose through the sudden cacophony of shouts from the other policemen as they dove for cover or threw themselves against the apartment complex cinder-block walls.

The two rookies sent to the rear of the apartment heard the shots, heard the Lumberjack's tortured screams, and sprinted, guns drawn, for the front of the building, where they were immediately sure they were needed.

Sergeant Lion-man, cursing as he saw the detective squirming and quivering with pain, reached down and seized the sledgehammer. He swung back, like a dead pull hitter centering on a lazy fastball, and crashed the hammer into the door frame. The sound of wood splintering, giving way, mingled with another shot from within the apartment. This shot also penetrated the wooden door and creased the air above Sergeant Lion-man's head, and he roared a second vibrant flood of expletives as he smashed the sledgehammer into the frame again.

Walter Robinson grabbed the Lumberjack and pulled him away from the potential line of fire. Behind him, he could hear Juan Rodriguez swearing in Spanish, a torrent of *mierdas* mixed liberally with a Hail Mary and then shouting for Lion-man to keep back. He could hear another member of the arrest team calling in a 10–45, officer down, on his portable radio. Lion-man bellowed again, furious, possessed, and lifted the hammer for a final blow that would separate the door from the frame. Robinson heard, amidst all the jumbled clatter of screams, footsteps, curses, and the sound of glass breaking, a tone that he could not quite decipher in the split second that it took for Sergeant Lion-man to deliver his last assault on the door.

As the door frame cracked and splintered and then suddenly gaped wide, thanks to a resounding kick by Sergeant Lion-man, Robinson rose and burst forward.

He tumbled through the opening, followed immediately by Rodriguez and two other policemen. They were all shouting 'Police! Freeze!' and swinging their weapons right and left, two hands on the grips, as they had all been taught. The first thing they saw was Leroy Jefferson's girlfriend, standing naked in the center of the room, shrieking. She threw a kitchen water tumbler in their direction; it exploded in shards on the wall behind them, and one of the City of Miami officers ducked and fired his weapon at her. He missed. The bullet smashed into the drywall behind her, no more than six inches from her ear, sending a plume of white dust into the air. Juan Rodriguez had the presence of mind to reach out and seize the officer's hand, pushing it down so that he would not fire again, screaming incoherent anger in two different languages as he did so.

Walter Robinson peered about. There was so much confused noise that it obscured his vision. It was almost, he thought, as if he could feel the abrupt absence of his suspect. He turned toward the naked girlfriend, who was standing rigidly, eyes open, making no effort to cover herself, as if astonished to be shot at and still be alive.

'Where is he?' Robinson screamed.

She stared blankly at him.

'Where is he?' Robinson shouted again. This time the girlfriend's head jerked to the side, and he followed the brief look she tossed toward the bathroom.

'Damn,' he said beneath his breath. He vaulted across the room, like a high jumper approaching the bar, and pushed himself against the wall next to the closed bathroom door. He gingerly reached out and tried the knob. Locked. He took a single deep breath, and stepped back, before delivering a massive kick at the flimsy door.

It buckled and sprung open.

He leapt into the tiny bathroom, instantly spotting the broken-out window. He threw aside a chair that had been used to smash the glass. He jumped into the tub, almost slipping on the smooth surface, and reached for the windowsill. He steadied himself and looked out into the night precisely at the spot where the two rookie officers were supposed to be. But he saw only the vague, ghostly shape of Leroy Jefferson, two stories down, rising unsteadily from the backyard dust, illuminated by weak gray light, gun in hand.

He yelled: 'Freeze!'

Jefferson turned, looked up at the window, and then wheeled and ran.

'Goddamn it!' Robinson shouted. 'The bastard jumped.'

And in that moment he realized there was no one outside the apartment, except Espy Martinez.

'Jesus!' he said. 'Espy! Watch out!' he screamed helplessly through the shattered window. Then he pivoted and ran desperately for the front door.

Alone at the edge of the darkness, Espy Martinez started forward, then stopped. She just barely made out Walter Robinson's shouted warning, coming, as it did, out of the night and the noise, but it merely underscored the confusion that she already felt.

Watch out for what?

She had seen the assault on the apartment from her vantage point at the assembled police vehicles; it had played out like some distant theater performed in a strange language, elusive in its meaning. The gunshots, the shouts and yells, the deep booming sound of the sledgehammer against the door – she knew that something had gone wrong, but was incapable in her position of deciphering precisely what that was.

Again she started forward. She thought it important to do something – to move, to act. She could feel insistence racing through her body, making a din within her, smashing up against all the abrupt sensations of doubt and fear that wanted to throw chains around her limbs. As these warring emotions struggled for control, she saw a shadowy figure bounding fast toward her.

Leroy Jefferson sprinted barefoot across the rough dirt and patches of cement that formed the entranceway to the

King Apartments. He had no real idea where he was heading, possessed solely by the idea of escape. Slices of broken glass tore at the soles of his feet, but he ignored them.

He had a sudden flashing memory of being on the court, ahead of everyone, the ball in his hands, rising alone toward the basket. The shouts from the policemen behind him faded away, mingling with distant remembered cheers from a jam-packed gymnasium. The air around him seemed to rush past his ears, like a tropical storm flexing its muscles; he was surprised to realize that for the first time in what seemed like months, he felt cool.

The figure that loomed up in front of him seemed an apparition.

He could see it was a woman; see she was crouched over and that she held something in her hands; see that the something was a weapon. He saw, too, that the woman's mouth was open, and he understood she was screaming something at him, but all these somethings only forced him to move faster. He swerved, but saw her weapon track him. He tried to dodge, to switch direction, but his momentum carried him headlong forward, and he realized, in the same moment, that he had lifted his own pistol and was tugging at the trigger. There were three shots left in the cylinder, and he fired them all. The booming sound of the pistol crashed through the heat.

Espy Martinez saw Jefferson's gun, saw too that it seemed aimed directly at her, and yelled 'Freeze!' for what she thought was the millionth time, and had the sudden idea that the word was completely ridiculous, because it had no effect on the tall, wiry figure that was descending upon her.

She hesitated, and in that moment he fired.

She thought instantly: I'm dead.

And without really recognizing what she was doing, she started pulling hard at the trigger of her own weapon. She did not know if she closed her eyes or not, or if she lifted her hand to shield herself or not, or if she ducked or sidestepped, or whether, in truth, she remained rigid, locked into her crouch, fully expecting a small projectile to pick her up and toss her abruptly into death's eager embrace.

The three bullets from Jefferson's gun buzzed about her. One grabbed at her purse, severing the leather strap, ripping it from her arm. The second tugged like a bored child at the sleeve of her light jacket and passed by harmlessly. The third, howling in what she later supposed was frustration, smashed into the window of the police cruiser behind her, exploding the glass.

Sweat dripped down her face, stinging her eyes, and she was filled with astonishment: no – I'm alive.

She realized that she was still pulling the trigger of her weapon, only the clip had long been emptied. She was unaware that she had fired. There should have been noise. She should have felt the gun bucking in her hand. A faint smell of cordite rose about her, like an unwanted perfume. She had to force herself to stop her finger twitching against the trigger. She looked down at her body, as if taking a quick inventory, astounded that she wasn't bleeding somewhere. In that instant, she abruptly wanted to laugh, and she lifted her eyes. Only then was she able to focus on Leroy Jefferson.

He writhed on the ground, perhaps twenty feet in front of where she stood, kicking up spurts of dirt as he twisted in pain. He clutched at his leg, and she could see blood welling between his fingers. He tried to rise once, bent over, still grasping his smashed kneecap, and he stumbled forward a few feet before falling back, like a thoroughbred with a broken foreleg, trained by instinct to finish a stakes race but unable to comprehend why it cannot run.

She stood, watching him, also unable to move, in that moment equally crippled. She listened to his screams of pain, blood streaking the dusty sidewalk, empty as the clip in her pistol.

Time has a curious elasticity; she was unsure whether she stood looking at the wounded suspect for minutes or seconds before Walter Robinson streaked across the open courtyard and threw himself onto the thrashing man. Sergeant Lion-man was only a few steps behind him, as were the other officers. The gunshots – those fired at her and those she had fired – still rung in her ears, deafening her. She only slowly became aware of the crescendo of sirens that were scoring the night; the bursts of red and blue strobe lights from other police vehicles and ambulances; the squealing of tires.

She watched as Walter Robinson pummeled Leroy Jefferson, finally twisting the suspect's arms back and tightening handcuffs around his wrists savagely. She looked away as Robinson rose and aimed a kick at the shackled man. Her eyes met Sergeant Lion-man's. He was standing in front of her, and it took her an extra moment to realize that he was shouting at her.

'Are you all right? Are you hit? Are you okay?'

She shook her head. 'No, I'm fine,' she replied matter-of-factly.

Anderson threw a huge arm around her shoulders and gently pushed her back a half-dozen feet. He steered her onto the seat of the police cruiser with the shot-out window, sweeping shattered glass away with one hand as he pushed her down.

'Sit here,' he said. 'I'm gonna get the paramedic.'

'No,' she repeated. 'I'm fine.'

She watched as Leroy Jefferson was flipped over onto his back like a beast about to be branded. Two emergency medical technicians wearing blue jumpsuits were tending to his leg. Another, a young blond-haired man, hovered in front of her.

'I'm fine,' she said a third time, before he had a chance to ask the obvious question. She looked up and saw Walter Robinson behind the man. His face was rigid with a succession of pale angers and fears. She smiled at him.

'He missed,' she said.

'Jesus, Espy, I—'

'I got him, though. Is he going to die?'

'Not unless they leave me alone with him. The bastard . . .'

'He was running and he missed. I wonder—'

'Don't think about it. You're okay.' He bent down beside her. 'Jesus,' he said. He wanted very much to put his arm around her, the way the big sergeant had, but he held back. She seemed very small, sitting half in, half out of the patrol car.

And then, to his surprise, she looked at him and laughed out loud. After a second he joined her, hesitant at first, but then giving way. Sergeant Lion-man and Sergeant Rodriguez came up. They started laughing as well, as tension fled from within all of them. It was like the greatest practical joke in the world: to be alive when you should be dead.

After a moment their laughter tapered off, and Espy Martinez let out a deep sigh.

'I'm gonna drive you home,' Walter Robinson said.

'Yes,' she replied. She could feel adrenaline fading from her and a massive exhaustion setting in. She saw the paramedics lifting Leroy Jefferson onto a stretcher, moving him to the open door of an ambulance. She saw another ambulance moving off, its siren cutting through the lights.

'There goes the Lumberjack. Poor bastard ain't gonna be lifting weights no more,' Anderson said. Sergeant Lionman glanced over at the stretcher crew. 'Hey, hold it!' he called out. 'Walter, buddy, you do the honors, huh. Right here. And Miss Martinez, you come witness him getting his rights right now, please. Then maybe we can all get the hell out of here before we have a riot.'

Espy Martinez looked up and saw that a crowd had started to gather on the edge of the lights, milling about.

Walter Robinson nodded, and stepped to the side of the stretcher. 'Leroy Jefferson,' he said, in an even, angry tone of restrained fury, 'you're under arrest. You have the right to remain silent. You have the right to an attorney—'

'I know all the shit,' Jefferson interrupted between pain-clenched teeth. 'What you think I did?'

Robinson stared down with fury that was restrained by only the barest strands of self-control.

'You had to kill her, huh, Leroy? Couldn't just take her stuff. Maybe even knock her out. You could have managed that no problem, right? Big guy like you. She was just a little old lady and you had to go kill her . . .'

'What you talking about?'

'You didn't even know her name, did you, Leroy?'

'Who you talking about? What little old lady?'

'Her name was Sophie Millstein, Leroy. Just a little old lady, living alone on Miami Beach. Trying to live out her years nice and quiet and peaceful. No harm to nobody. And you had to kill her, you sonofabitch. And now you're going away, you motherfucker.'

Leroy Jefferson looked both confused and pained.

Then, abruptly, his lips curled back, half snarl, half

laugh, and he said: 'You more of a fool than I thought. I didn't kill any old lady.'

'Sure you didn't,' Robinson said, icy sarcasm in his voice.

But Leroy Jefferson shook his head. 'All this,' he said. 'All this and it ain't me done it. Damn.' He appeared genuinely confused and saddened. 'All this for the wrong me,' he added.

He dropped his head back onto the stretcher as the paramedics thrust it up into the back of the ambulance none too gently, leaving Walter Robinson standing outside as the doors were slammed closed.

'No, nobody ever does anything,' he said quietly, almost to himself, but Espy Martinez overheard him. He turned toward her. 'Sure he didn't do it,' he said. 'We're going. Now.'

Martinez nodded. She felt completely exhausted. She thought that if it were not for an odd sensation of something not unlike fear, but not precisely fear, that remained echoing within her alongside the suspect's words of denial, she could fall asleep right there.

CHAPTER THIRTEEN

Soddit

He watched the shadows on the whitewashed wall of the hospital corridor; the glow from the fluorescent lights at the nurse's station caught the profile of anyone who walked past, sending a sudden, dark, vaguely human shape skittering across the flat in front of him. At one point he lifted his own hand, to see if he could add to the gray ghostlike forms, but the light angle was wrong.

Walter Robinson shifted in his seat, trying to find a comfortable position, knowing that none were available. He glanced at a clock and saw that the night had almost fled, and he supposed it wouldn't be long before the shadows skulked away, as the day's light penetrated the hospital hallways.

He was exhausted, but anger like adrenaline kept him alert.

He tried to remain fixated on the man occupying the recovery room, thinking it would be simplest to blame Leroy Jefferson for everything that had gone wrong that night. But inwardly Jefferson shared space in his rage with himself. Walter Robinson played over the sequence of events, trying to discern precisely where it had all gone sour, where he had made the mistake that resulted in the shooting. The procedure had been textbook. The setup had been perfect. But getting a cop shot and wounded on what should have been a routine, if tricky, arrest stoked his frustration. The preliminary word on the Lumberjack was not good; extensive muscle and bone tissue damage. A career that had evaporated in a single moment. He had spent a few minutes with the policeman's wife, but his hackneyed words of apology had been ignored. He'd briefed the Beach police brass, and they had made a statement to the press. He had wasted time hanging at the back of the room as two dozen reporters and camera men asked questions, then he crept away to the hallway where he currently sat. He did not know what awaited Leroy Jefferson; in that moment, he wished Espy Martinez had blown the suspect's head off. It would have made for some troublesome paperwork, but probably would have been considerably more satisfying for all involved.

He let this bloodthirsty thought linger within him. Even with everything that had gone wrong, he recognized he should have felt some satisfaction. After all, he'd cleared the case: Jefferson was charged with the first-degree murder of Sophie Millstein. In the Beach homicide offices there was a large chalkboard with active cases listed on it. Sophie Millstein's murder would come off the board. He'd done his job.

Robinson let a whispered expletive slide through his lips.

He leaned his head back against the wall, closing his eyes for a moment, expecting to see the bedlam at the King Apartments played out again, like on a screen behind his eyes, but saw instead himself, holding Espy Martinez by the elbow, walking her slowly up the sidewalk to her duplex with all the stiff-edged formality of some eighteenth century courtier. On the long drive across town, she had fluctuated between a babbling, nonstop excitement, words coupled with obscenities tumbling from her mouth, and moments of dark-ridged silence. One second she had blurted: 'Jesus fucking Christ, I can't believe it, I shot the fucking bastard, didn't I? Right in the fucking leg, Jesus. I mean, it's all so fucking unreal. The motherfucker fired and I fired and I got him. Just fucking well got him, didn't I?'

And when he'd replied, 'That's right. You did,' she lapsed into an electric quiet, as if the interior of the car was vibrating, but there was no sound. He tried to search within himself for some other words to say to her, but was unable to find any, so remained silent. Once, she gasped, and he'd turned to make sure she was all right, only to see her shake her head and stare out at the glow of the city lights as they swept past.

At her house he'd stood on the doorstep, asking her, 'Are you all right? Are you sure you're all right? Should I call someone? You gonna be okay alone?' listening to her reply that she was fine, and all the time wanting to step inside the apartment with her, and being unable to. Like a goddamn teenager on a first date, he berated himself. Maybe the worst first date in the history of the world.

Again he muttered an expletive and opened his eyes. He clenched a fist and raised it in front of his face.

'You going to hit me, or are you saving that for my client?'

Walter Robinson followed the sound of the voice and looked up at the man speaking. He was a lanky, curly-headed man with a ready grin at the corners of his mouth that contradicted an intensity in his eyes. He wore jeans and running shoes without socks and a white knit sport shirt that had a stain on it, and Robinson knew he'd hurried from his bed to get to the hospital. But the attorney also had a loose-limbed insouciance in the way he leaned up against the hallway wall across from the detective,

placing himself where there had only been shadows a few
moments beforehand.

'Hello, Tommy,' Robinson said slowly. 'What are you
doing here?' He knew the answer to this question, but
asked it anyway.

Thomas Alter was about the same age as Walter
Robinson. The detective figured they probably would have
been friends if he were not a senior assistant in the County
Public Defender's Office, which made him and all the local
homicide detectives natural adversaries. One rarely
becomes overly fond of people whose job it is to rip and
rend one's work in the protected cloister of the criminal
courtroom. Respect, certainly. Often a sort of grudging
acknowledgment that they were all part of the same
machinelike process. But a genuine affection was impossible.

'I'm here to make certain that our Mr Jefferson receives
proper medical treatment, which doesn't include giving
you a statement until he's had time to speak with his
attorney, which, for better or for worse, happens to be
yours truly.'

'He's not *our* Mr Jefferson....'

'All right. *My* Mr Jefferson ...'

'Come on, Tommy. He needs to be arraigned, make a
statement of indigency before you get him. In the meantime, if he wants to talk to me ...'

'Yes, ordinarily, yes, Walt. Correct. But not this time.
Jefferson was in court just under a week ago on a lousy
possession charge, which the state intends to drop because
I eviscerated the search warrant. But they haven't got
around to doing it officially, so, Walt, old buddy, I am still
attorney of record. There you have it. You cannot speak to
him without me or someone from my office present at all
times. Got it?'

'If he wants to—'

'At all times. You read him his rights, and I'm telling you he isn't waiving any of them.'

Thomas Alter continued to smile, but his voice had lost any lightness.

Robinson shrugged, trying to hide the irritation that ricocheted about within him.

'At all times,' Alter repeated. 'Got that, Walt?'

'Yes.'

'That means around the clock. Twenty-four hours. Seven days a week.'

'Don't you trust me, Tommy?'

'No.'

'Good. Because I don't trust you either.'

Alter smiled wanly. 'Well, then I suppose we're even.'

'Nope. The one thing we'll never be is even, because I wouldn't be here trying to protect a scumbag like Jefferson.'

'Right. I guess not. Too moral for that, huh?' Alter's voice had a mocking sarcasm attached to it. 'So how you doing, otherwise? Rough night, I hear . . .'

'I would say so.'

'Too bad about the guy who got shot. Friend of yours?'

'No. Not really.'

Alter nodded. 'Is Espy okay?'

Robinson hesitated, then replied, 'Sure. Maybe a little shaky, but she's fine.'

'Good. She's not like some of the sonsofbitches in that office. She's reasonable. Tough but reasonable. And pretty too. Glad she didn't buy it out there in the jungle. Sounds like a close call. Wouldn't go near the King Apartments, personally. Especially after dark. What was she doing out there anyway?'

Robinson didn't reply.

The young public defender looked over at the detective. He smiled. 'Go to bed, Walter. You look tired. This mess will still be waiting for you later. In fact, it's gonna be around for a while.'

Robinson rose. He looked across at Alter, who continued to lean back against the wall. The lawyer glanced down the hallway toward a pair of uniformed officers who sat outside the recovery room. The two cops were watching the detective.

'Tell 'em, Walt.'

'Fuck you, Tommy.'

Alter grinned again, but his eyes were hard. 'No,' he said quietly, 'fuck you, Walter.'

He raised his voice and called out loudly: 'Get this. No one talks to Jefferson except authorized medical personnel and representatives from the Dade County Public Defender's Office! And when you finish your shift, you make sure your replacements know. You got that?'

The words echoed in the corridor, and the two cops stared blankly toward Walter Robinson, who reluctantly nodded.

'Well, thanks, Walt,' Alter said briskly. 'But I think I'll still tape an order to his door.' The lawyer removed a letter with the seal of the P.D.'s office on it. 'Same letter being delivered to the arraignment judge and to Espy Martinez and her fucking boss Lasser, this A.M.,' he added.

'You covering all the bases, Tommy?'

Alter glared at Robinson. 'You think it would be the first time we represented some poor fuck who got the mistaken impression that a homicide detective was his last, greatest, and only true friend in the entire fucking world, and promptly ran his mouth and his ass right onto Death Row? You think it would be the first time some homicide detective that maybe didn't have the strongest case in the world walked into court and got up on the stand and swore to tell the whole fucking truth and said, "Yes sir, Your Honor, the defendant orally waived every fucking constitutional right and then confessed to that murder to me. Privately, yes sir, no problem . . ."? Well, you know what, Walter?'

'What's that, Tommy?'

'It ain't happening this time.'

Robinson felt drained. He wanted fresh air, hoping for a steady breeze that perhaps might carry him like a sailor adrift, home, to his own bed. He abruptly felt like a man at the end of an all-night poker game, who looks down and sees his stake has dwindled and the cards in front of him are nothing but a useless bluff.

Still, he couldn't resist adding an angry statement: 'You know, Tommy, this is a bad dude. He's a junkie and a psychopath and a bad-ass. He's gonna go down. Don't you already have a couple of clients on the Row? How many, Tommy? Two? Three?'

'Just one,' Alter whispered bitterly.

'Really, Tommy? I could have sworn you used to have more. . . .'

'Yeah. I did.'

'Oh, right. I remember. I guess we'd just have to say that one of those clients just fell prey to natural attrition, huh, Tommy? Doesn't that sound like a nice and safe and reasonable way to describe someone being strapped into an electric chair?'

'Fuck you, Walter.'

'He was a cop-killer, right, Tommy?'

'That's right.'

'Not much sympathy in the legal system for cop-killers, huh? That was a tough closing for that jury, wasn't it? Trying to make twelve people feel downright nice and cozy with some bastard that stuck a gun in an undercover cop's mouth after making him strip naked and told him he had enough time for one prayer, right? One prayer before dying, wasn't that what the bastard said? But then he pulled the trigger before the cop even got half the Our Father out . . . Wasn't that the case, Tommy?'

'You know it.'

'Well, my guess is you've already started working on your closing for Jefferson's jury, huh, Tommy? You got something special in mind that maybe explains the really good reason why that rat bastard had to strangle a little old lady? And I'd say our Mr Jefferson is right lucky that all he did tonight was ruin a cop's arm and his career. But it doesn't make a difference, does it?'

'What do you mean?'

'Because he's going to the same place.'

'Death Row? Don't count on it, Detective.'

'No. I meant Hell.'

'Don't count on it,' Thomas Alter repeated coldly. Now even the corners of his mouth had lost the crinkle of familiarity, replaced with a hard-edged coolness that Walter Robinson recognized from a dozen cross-examinations. He felt out of control, like a car skidding on a rain-slick highway. He knew Alter was a formidable opponent and angering him was a mistake. But he continued, letting all the night's exhaustions and frustrations guide his responses.

'No, Tommy. Bet the house. That's where he's headed.'

'Maybe so. But not on this piece of shit case.'

'Really? I got motive, I got opportunity, I got an after-the-fact accomplice and I got an eyewitness at the scene, and I got fifty says you are just totally fucking wrong, counselor.'

Robinson tried to hold his tongue, but could not.

Exhaustion and frustration pummeled him, forcing him to blurt out information that he knew he should have kept to himself.

'Really?' The attorney imitated Robinson's voice. 'And you're covered, Detective.'

'Well, we'll see, won't we.'

'That's right, Walter. We'll see.'

The two men glared at each other. Alter spoke first.

'You know they saved his leg. But that's it. Just saved it. He'll maybe walk about a bit, but that leg ain't never gonna work no more like it used to. . . .' The lawyer slipped into a familiar street talk, as if to diminish the seriousness of what he was saying.

'Breaks my fucking heart,' Robinson replied.

'Yes. Well, I wouldn't expect a man who's going to spend the rest of his life in pain and limping about to cooperate a whole helluva lot with the folks that did that to him.'

'We don't need his cooperation. All we need is for him to take his rightful spot on Death Row.'

Alter smiled again. 'You couldn't be more mistaken, Walter.' He spoke with the overblown confidence of a snake-oil salesman.

Robinson shook his head and turned his back, thought it was almost morning, and if he were fortunate, the sun would just be rising over the edge of the Beach as he drove over the causeway to his apartment, filling the air around him with blades of clear light, slicing away all the stale anger of the night passed, allowing him to think freely about Espy Martinez.

For two days she had been the toast of the State Attorney's Office. Toughness in a courtroom was one thing; toughness in the real world gained a completely different level of respect. The other assistants had busied themselves with a search through a variety of nicknames – Deadeye, Quick-draw, Make My Day Martinez – trying to find one that might stick.

Even Abraham Lasser had made one of his rare pilgrimages from his own office through the warren of desks and cubicles to applaud Espy Martinez on her success, which was an odd thing, when she thought about it; her boss, her coworkers, all congratulating her for not being shot and killed. Lasser had stuck his wiry-haired head around the corner of her door and sang out in a creaky voice: 'Ahh, the young Annie Oakley, I presume?' And then, after shaking her hand and clapping her on the back, lifting her arm up like some fighter in a championship ring, he whispered to her that she should make certain that she nailed Leroy Jefferson to the maximum, a penalty he did not have to spell out for all listening. Then, later that day, he had circulated a memo throughout the office, praising Espy Martinez for her quick-thinking – though she did wonder idly what she had managed to think quickly about – and reminding all the other assistants that they too were sworn law enforcement officers and should arm themselves appropriately, at appropriate moments, so they could take appropriate action, under appropriate circumstances, after using appropriate judgment, as she had. He did not define what he meant by *appropriate*.

Espy Martinez enjoyed the attention, let it distract her from what she was doing. When Walter Robinson called her, she felt a rush of excitement, as if he was the key part of what had taken place.

'So, Espy, how're things?'

'Well, the guys in the office next to me persist in whistling the tune to *High Noon* every time I walk past. Other than that, things are okay.'

He laughed. He could hear a vibrancy in her voice.

'We need to get together, start wrapping the case tight.'

'I know,' she said. 'I haven't been concentrating.'

'Have you spoken with Tommy Alter?'

'Not yet. Well, actually, just once. Jefferson was arraigned in absentia. The hospital won't release him to the jail for another week or so.'

'I took his fingerprints this morning. Alter was there, but wouldn't say anything. He just watched. Jefferson looked like he was in pain, which isn't so bad. Leg's still in traction, but it goes into a cast tomorrow. The doctor said he's looking at maybe two, three more operations down the line. I told the doctor it would be a waste of time. Real loud voice, so that Jefferson and Alter could hear me.'

'That's cold,' she said, laughing.

'Hey, what do they say? All's fair in love and war, and this sure ain't one of those things. . . .'

'What's next?'

'Well, I'm taking the prints to be checked. We should be able to put him right in the apartment. I took his mug shot and made a photo lineup and showed it to my bus drivers and they put Jefferson on the right bus at the right time. I'm gonna take the same photo lineup over to Mr Kadosh tomorrow morning. Because the bastard's in the hospital, a real lineup's out. Then we have the pawnshop owner to testify to the stolen goods. I filed a truckload of charges on poor old Reginald and young Yolanda too. Most of them were bullshit, but enough to keep the two of them toeing the line. Lion-man will be all over their action anyway, to make sure. The search of the King Apartments didn't turn up anything from Sophie's place. He must have dumped it all at the Helping Hand. But still, all in all, it seems pretty tight to me.'

Espy Martinez nodded, but changed her tone: 'Alter

seemed confident. I noticed that.'

'Same to me.'

'Why?'

'I don't know. I can't see a reason, except that he's an arrogant sonofabitch who always acts confident as hell right up to the moment he realizes he's got no defense. Then he'll come whining and begging for a plea bargain. Should be in a couple of weeks. Give him his moment or two.'

'No plea. That came down from the boss.'

'Good. He'll want it, you know. That's what the defense strategy will be: find some little weakness that he can exploit into some worry, so that instead of taking a risk with a jury, we'll settle for the mandatory twenty-five.'

'I don't think the State will agree to that.'

'That's what he'll be shooting for. Anything that keeps Jefferson off Death Row will be a victory for him.'

'I wish we had a confession.'

'Yeah. Make things perfect, wouldn't it? And I would have got one out of the bastard if Alter hadn't shown up.'

'Juries like a confession in a murder case. Makes them feel certain they're doing the right thing. Especially when they have to vote on the death penalty.'

'I know that. But we've got just about everything else.'

'Can we go over it all one more time? Maybe we can see a problem ahead of time if we talk it out? I'd rather be laying in wait for Alter when he comes walking through the door, hat in hand. Makes it easier to say no.'

Robinson grabbed at this opportunity. 'Why don't we make it dinner, or something? I'll bring the case file, we can eat something, go over it slowly . . .'

Espy Martinez hesitated. Her skin flushed red and she felt hot. 'Walter, I don't know about mixing work and . . .'

She didn't finish, but he jumped into the silence.

'Hey. Don't worry about it. A real date would be going to a movie or a play or a concert or a game or something. You know, where I show up at your place wearing a tie and carrying flowers and a box of candy and I open the car door for you. A real date requires nervousness and polite small talk and manners. This is something different. I kinda feel I owe you something for the other night. I mean, you weren't supposed to end up shooting someone. I feel downright guilty about that.'

Martinez smiled, then replied: 'It wasn't your fault.'

'Well, it sure didn't happen the way I had it all worked out in my head.'

'Hey,' she joked, 'do you think I mind if all of a sudden everyone around here thinks I'm dangerous?'

'Dangerous and notorious?'

'That's right. Two-fisted and pistol-packing. A woman to be reckoned with.'

The two of them laughed.

'All right,' she said. 'Tomorrow night.'

'I'll pick you up at your office?'

'No, at my house. You remember how to get there?'

He did.

They did not, of course, end up talking about the case, except in a perfunctory fashion at the start of the evening, almost as if it was something necessary that they had to get out of the way. He took her to an open-air restaurant that overlooked Biscayne Bay, the sort of place where the waiter behaves pretentiously and then serves mediocre food that is obscured by heavy sauces and a spectacular view. As they sat, he could see the blues of the water deepen, traveling from far out in the ocean toward the shore, first a pale, sky color, to a more solid azure, and then finally into the deep navy, almost indistinguishable from black, that heralded the summertime night. City lights blinked on and seemed to score the water surface, as if painted on the rippling waves by an impressionist.

She sat across from him and knew it had all the easy romance of the tropics. She could feel a light breeze blowing through the folds of the loose-fitting dress she wore, touching her skin in hidden places with the familiarity of an old lover. She leaned her head back, then ran a hand through the sweep of her hair. She looked over at Walter Robinson, thought him terrifically handsome, and thought too that were her parents to see her sitting across from him, they would not speak to her for days, unless they were persuaded this meeting was all business. So, in deference to this image and to at least create the illusion of work, she asked:

'Jefferson?'

Robinson smiled. 'Right. A working dinner. I would say things are looking dark for Leroy Jefferson, which might be a pun, but we'll leave race out of this.'

She nodded. 'How so?'

'Well, just before I left the office tonight, I got a call from Harry Harrison – I mean, how does someone get a name like that, anyway? – over in the fingerprints section. Guess whose prints showed up on Sophie Millstein's bureau drawer?'

'Our man Jefferson?'

'None other.'

'Well, that's that, isn't it?'

'Yes. Pretty much so. Harry said he still has to check the prints on the jewelry box, the sliding glass door, and the body print they took from Sophie's throat, but thought we'd like to know what he'd come up with so far.'

'Good-bye, Mr Jefferson.'

'And Kadosh gave us a pretty good identification from the photo lineup.'

'What's pretty good?'

'He picked out Jefferson's mug shot and said he couldn't be certain unless he saw the man in person, but he was pretty sure he was the man. The key thing with the old guy is keeping him away from his wife. He's sort of used to having her tell him everything he thinks, and she has an opinion on everything.'

'Everything?'

'Trust me. Everything.'

'So?'

'So, I can't see the problem. If there is one.'

'Where does that leave us?'

Walter Robinson grinned. 'Actually, right here. Glass of wine?'

Espy Martinez nodded. She watched him pour her glass, then she slowly drank some, letting the cool, fruity taste descend through her. She looked out over the bay and thought for an instant that what she was thinking was like plunging into the waves after sunset.

'Tell me, Walter. Who are you?'

He smiled. 'Who am I? I'm a police detective that's almost got his law degree and—'

She held up her hand. 'No. Not what are you. Who are you?'

Robinson thought he heard an earnestness in her voice, and abruptly realized that she was asking more of him than he'd expected. He felt a momentary reluctance, but then, before he had a chance to check himself, started to speak slowly, quietly, almost as if part of a conspiracy.

'I swim,' he said, lifting a hand toward the bay. 'I swim alone, when no one is watching, far from shore. In deep water. One mile, at least. Two, sometimes.'

He stopped there. He did not describe what he liked to do, which was to drive out to the tip of Key Biscayne to the state park at Cape Florida late in the afternoon, when all the beet-red tourists and the beered-up teenagers had already packed their picnic lunches and were trying to beat the shadows home. He would slide into the water and, taking powerful overhand strokes, push himself against the waves out past the red and white marker buoys, past any boundaries, to where he could feel the conflicting tug of tidal currents pulling at his arms and legs. There he would turn, treading water, and stare back at the key, down toward the rows of condos, or off past the ancient abandoned brick lighthouse, where the ocean joins the bay. He would let the waters rock him, as if they were trying to insist they were safe, when he knew they were not. After a few moments he would take a deep breath and once again battle the rips and flows, dodging the occasional man-o'-war with its lethal sting, ignoring all thoughts of sharks, teasing exhaustion and the inevitable death it would bring, until he was able to touch sand beneath his toes, and he would drag himself back onto the beach, safe again, breathing harshly.

'Why do you swim?' she asked quietly.

'Because when I was growing up in the Grove, none of the black kids ever learned how to swim. There were no pools and the beach was three bus transfers away. We lived in the most watery county in the entire nation – did you know that? – but we never learned how to swim. I remember, every year or so, there was always a story in the paper about some black kid drowning in a canal, where he was fishing or gigging frogs or just playing around. Slipped and fell into four feet of water and panicked and struggled and cried out, but no one was ever there and so they drowned. The white kids never drowned. You see, they had pools behind their homes and were taught. Breast-stroke. Australian crawl. Sidestroke and butterfly. All that happened to them was they got wet and maybe they got yelled at when they got home and tracked water into the house.'

He put his glass of wine down.

'I sound angry. I don't want to sound angry.'

She shook her head. She realized she had been told something important, almost like a clue hidden on a page of a mystery novel and that later she would see why it was important.

'No,' she said. 'It makes it easier for me.'

'Easier for what?'

She didn't reply. What she thought was: understanding what's going to happen.

'So, Espy, now I have a question for you,' Robinson said after a moment's quiet.

'Go ahead. Shoot.' She laughed slightly. 'Maybe that's a bad choice of words for me.'

'Tell me why you're alone.'

'What do you mean?'

He made a small gesture with his hand, as if to say: you're young, you're beautiful, educated, and intelligent – and should be surrounded with suitors. Which she took as a compliment of sorts.

'Because I've never found anyone who—'

She stopped, uncertain how to proceed. For a second she hoped Walter Robinson would step into the silence with some other question, then realized he wouldn't, and so she continued, a small hesitation in her voice. 'I suppose because of my brother.' She took a deep breath. 'My poor dead brother. My poor dead dumb brother.'

'I didn't know, I'm sorry,' he started.

'No. It's okay. It's been almost twelve years. Labor Day

weekend. He was to start law school the next week . . .'

'Car accident?'

'No. Nothing that innocent. He was coming back from a snorkeling trip in the Keys with a couple of college friends. It was getting late, and they stopped at a convenience store to get something to eat. You know, stupid stuff: chips and beers and Ring-Dings and Slim Jims and all that crap that twenty-two-year-old males consume with such passion. Anyway, there they are, it's a little half bodega, half 7-Eleven, just off South Dixie Highway, way down below Kendall, and they've got all this junk and my brother is teasing the little old Cuban lady who's running the store. You know, asking her if she's got a daughter, and if not, is she single, good-natured stuff, and they're both laughing and speaking in Spanish, and he's kidding his friends, because they're Anglos and can't understand what he and the little old lady are talking about, when a guy comes in through the front door wearing a stocking mask and waving a forty-four-caliber Magnum. He screams at everyone to grab the floor and somebody open the register. And everybody just freezes, then they do what he says, but he's impatient, you know, because he's wired on PCP, I guess, or maybe he's just mean, or maybe he doesn't like Latinos, I don't know, but when the old woman hesitates, he just reaches out and pistol-whips her, right across the face. One minute she is joking and flirting with my brother, my poor dumb brother, and the next she is bleeding, her nose busted, her jaw broken. And my brother gets up, just to his knees, and shouts at the guy to stop it, leave her alone, and the guy takes one little look at my brother and laughs just once like he's not sure who's crazier, my brother or himself, and then shoots him, right in the chest. One shot. Boom! The old woman screams and starts praying, and my brother's friends are hugging the floor, figuring they're next. And they would have been, because the bad guy turns to them and points the Magnum and pulls the trigger. Once. Twice. Then he spins and points it at the old woman, and pulls the trigger a third time. Nothing. Click. Click. Click. They're too shocked and scared to realize the bastard only had one bullet in the gun. The bad guy laughs and then he heads out the door with the cash from the register and a bag of Doritos. . . .'

She took another deep breath. 'One bullet and a bag of Doritos.'

'I'm sorry—' Robinson started, but she held up her hand.

'My poor dumb brother who should have kept his mouth shut but that wasn't the kind of guy he was, doesn't even make it to South Miami Hospital.'

'It's okay,' Robinson started, unsure whether he wanted her to continue.

'No,' Martinez said quietly. 'I should get all this out. I was fifteen, home in bed, asleep. I heard my parents crying, and then they went to the hospital. They left me behind. Alone. I sat up all night in the dark waiting for them to come back. I never did see my brother again, except at the funeral, and then he didn't really look like himself, you know. I mean, he wasn't grinning and teasing me like he always did. It was three days before I was to celebrate my *quince*. Do you know what that is?'

'Well, sort of. It's a party Latin girls get when they turn fifteen.'

'Well, yeah, it's a party. But it's more than that. I don't suppose it's quite as big a deal as a bar mitzvah for a Jewish kid, because that's all religion, but it comes close. It's this celebration that announces that now you are a woman. There's tradition and the sense that now you belong to something. It's filled with fancy, frilly dresses and giggling and slow music and chaperones, you know, parents watching all these children behaving like adults. In the Cuban community, it is an important event. You plan it for months. At fifteen, it's the only thing you think about for days and days. But mine turned into my brother's funeral.'

'It must have been difficult,' Robinson said, then thought that sounded stupid because it was so obvious. So instead, he reached across the table and touched Espy Martinez's hand. She immediately grabbed his and held it tightly.

'In my house, you see, my dead brother dominated everything. He was supposed to become a lawyer. Take over my father's business. Become important. Influential. Raise a family and become something. And they never said it, but when he died, that all fell to me. But something else did too.'

'What's that?'

'Revenge.'

'How do you mean?'

'In Cuban society, hell, for almost all Latins, a death like that is a debt. My father and mother, they were made old by his murder. It fell to me.'

'But what could you do?'

'Well, I couldn't just take a gun and shoot someone. I had to find some other way to pay.'

'The killer?'

'Never caught. At least, not officially. A guy fitting his description got busted coming out of a Dairy Mart with the register contents up in Palm Beach County two weeks later, but my brother's friends and the old woman couldn't pick him out of a lineup. The M.O. was the same. Wore the same mask, shouted the same words. Laughed the same way. Fit the pattern. But they couldn't prosecute him for my brother's murder.'

'What happened?'

'He got fifteen then, but did five. He's back in again. I keep tabs on him. I get the prison people to keep running informants through his cell, see if he'll talk, maybe accidentally. Just maybe say what happened to that forty-four Magnum that disappeared. Maybe shoot his mouth off about getting away with murder. I keep my brother's case file in a drawer in my desk. Keep it updated, you know. Addresses. Statements. Whatever it will take, so that if I can ever link him concretely, the case is ready to go.'

She took a deep breath.

'No statute of limitations on first-degree murder. No statute of limitations on revenge.'

She looked at him.

'Obsessive, I suppose. But it's in the blood.'

Again she paused, and he tried to think of something to say. But as he stumbled over his own words, she continued:

'So, I guess, he's why I went to law school. Instead of my poor brother. And he's why I became a prosecutor, so that one day I could get up in front of a jury and point at the bastard and say he's the one that killed him. Killed the little old lady who owned the place too, in reality. She had a weak heart and six months later passed away.'

'I'm sorry,' Robinson said. 'I didn't know.' He realized this was about the stupidest, most trite thing he could say, but couldn't stop himself.

Espy Martinez touched her free hand to her forehead. 'No,' she said, 'it's all right. So there you have it. I'm sorry. We were having fun and then I launched into all this and now you look like someone caught swearing in church.'

She reached out and took a long drink from her wineglass.

'I'd like to make a joke and get us laughing again,' she said.

Walter Robinson thought for a moment, wondered why he felt something was missing, and then realized what it was. Before he could stop himself, he asked the question. 'The suspect in your brother's shooting ... he was black, right?'

Martinez didn't answer right away. Then she nodded. Robinson sighed and started to lean back, thinking to himself: there it is; there it ends. He began to get angry, not with Espy Martinez, or with himself or with anything other than the entire world, when she shot her hand out and grabbed his again, holding him fiercely, like she would if she were dangling on some precipice.

'No,' she said slowly. 'He was him and you are you.'

He leaned back toward her, feeling a rush of excitement.

She smiled. 'My name,' she said. 'Do you know what it means?'

'Espy?'

'No, silly. Esperanza.'

He grinned. 'It's not like I don't know any Spanish at all. It means *hope*.'

She was about to reply, when the waiter arrived with their dinners. He hovered by the table, balancing the plates of food, unable to set them down over their arms, stretched across the table. He coughed and said, 'Excuse me,' and both Espy Martinez and Walter Robinson looked up at him and then laughed.

They ate in a rush, skipped dessert, ignored the offer of coffee. It was as if the simple confessions that they had made to each other had released them from the usual posturing, circling, feints and fakes of connection. She was quiet as he drove her across the city, to her front door.

There, he stopped the car and turned off the engine. She remained in her seat, looking toward the side of the duplex occupied by her parents. She assumed they were watching.

Robinson started to say something, but she wasn't listening.

Instead, she turned to him and whispered with an intensity that surprised herself: 'Take me someplace else, Walter. Anyplace. Anyplace at all. Your place. A hotel. A park. The beach, I don't care. Just someplace different.'

He paused, looking at her. And in that moment they thrust themselves together, embracing, lips meeting electrically, and she pulled him to her, thinking that she was yanking all the loneliness and troubles in her entire life off balance and askew, and hoping that somehow the weight of him pressed against her would stabilize the windstorm of emotions soaring within her.

He took her back to his own apartment. He closed the door behind them, and they grasped at each other on the floor of his living room with the slippery urgency of a pair of lawbreakers worried about discovery. They tugged at each other's clothing with a frantic need that transformed itself into a quick coupling, almost as if they had no time to get to know each other's body. Espy Martinez simply pulled Walter Robinson down on top of her, trying to envelop him; for his part, he felt like a balloon blown to within a micrometer of explosion. That her skin had a particular softness, the curve of her small breasts, the shape of her sex, the taste of the sweat that gathered on her neck – all this was information and knowledge that he was only obliquely aware of as he pushed down toward her with demands that seemed ancient and impossible and were welcomed by her with thrusts of her own.

When he finished, he rolled to the side, breathing hard. He lay back with his forearm across his eyes. After a second he heard her say: 'So, Walter, do you have, like, a bedroom? A bathroom? Kitchen?'

He opened his eyes to see her beside him, lifted up on one elbow, leaning over him, grinning.

'Well, actually, yes, Espy, I do. All the usual and expected conveniences of modern life. A refrigerator. Cable television. Air-conditioning. Wall-to-wall carpeting . . .'

'Yes,' she said, laughing, and letting her hair brush over his chest. 'I found the wall-to-wall carpet. It was right beneath me.'

As she spoke, she lowered her lips to his chest, then lay her cheek on his breast, listening to the rapid-fire beats of his heart.

'Enthusiasm,' he said.

'So, Walter,' she said quietly. 'Who are you?'

He did not answer this time. Instead, he gathered her face in his hands and kissed her slowly. Then he gently pulled her to her feet and then reached down and lifted her up in his arms.

'Bedroom,' he said.

'Romantic,' she replied, still laughing. 'Just don't bump my head.'

This second time, they paced themselves, letting fingers, lips explore each other. 'There's time,' Walter Robinson said. 'There's all the time in the world.'

Afterward he slept. But Espy Martinez felt an odd restlessness. She was both exhausted and depleted, but at the same moment filled with the satisfaction of the smitten. For a short time she watched the detective sleep, studying the relaxed angles of his face, caught by a shaft of moonlight that slid through the window. She held her hand up against his cheek, to see the way the wan light illuminated her pale skin and made his dark flesh glisten. She had the thought that she'd stepped past some sort of fence, then berated herself, thinking that she was allowing herself to muse in racial clichés, and that if she expected to have another night beside Walter Robinson, she should try to shed these thoughts as she had pulled off her clothing; rapidly.

She slid from the bed and quietly maneuvered into the living room. It was a small apartment, in an undistinguished condominium. There was a nice view, looking back toward the bay and the city. She found his desk in one corner, placed so that he could see through the windows toward Miami. There was a picture of an elderly black woman framed in one corner. On the wall were diplomas from the police academy and from Florida International University. There was another picture of a much younger Walter Robinson, dusty, a streak of blood on one cheek, dressed in a football uniform holding a ball aloft. She recognized the colors of Miami High. She turned and saw on his desk a casual mingling of law texts, research and police department reports. She saw his notes on Sophie Millstein's killing.

She continued to move stealthily, naked, through the moonlight.

She whispered again: 'Who are you, Walter Robinson?' As if she could find some paper, some document, that might explain him to her. She went to the kitchen and smiled when she inspected the bachelor's array of cold beers and cold cuts that occupied the shelves. She went back into the living room and noticed for the first time a watercolor on one wall. She approached it and saw that the artist had drawn an expanse of ocean, lit by shafts of sunlight, but that in the distance dark thunderheads had formed, giving the entire painting a sensation of threat. It was difficult in the semidarkness to make out the artist's signature, and she leaned toward it, peering closely, until she saw that it was only two initials: W.R. They were stuck deep in a corner, hidden right at the point where the colors changed from light to dark.

She smiled and wondered where he kept his easel and paints.

Then she returned to the bedroom and slid beneath a sheet next to him. She breathed in deeply, inhaling all the smells of their lovemaking, and closed her eyes, hoping but not really believing that there would be other nights like the one dwindling into morning around her.

He hesitated before touching her, then took a single finger and brushed back the sweep of hair from her forehead. He gently pushed at her shoulder and said, 'Espy, we're gonna be late. It's morning.'

She did not open her eyes, but replied: 'How late?'

'It's eight-thirty already. Late.'

She kept her eyes closed. 'Are you in a hurry, Walter?'

'No,' he said. He smiled. 'Some mornings, you just got to take your time about things.'

She reached out with both arms, like a poor actress mimicking a blind person, feeling the air, until she found his arms and shoulders and she drew him down toward her.

'Do we have time?'

'Probably not,' he said, tugging the sheet away from her, pushing himself toward her.

Afterward they showered and dressed rapidly. He made some coffee, which he handed to her. She took a single swallow and grimaced.

'Jesus, Walter. That's terrible! Is it instant?'

'Uh, yeah. I'm not much of a cook.'

'Well, we'll have to stop and get some real café Cubano on the way to the Justice Building.'

'Do you want me to take you home, get your car?'

'Nope,' she replied. 'Just take me to the office.'

He hesitated, then gestured with his arm, sweeping it about the apartment. It was a lost motion, speaking more of words that were difficult to speak than of anything else. 'Okay,' he said. 'But when can we, I mean, I want to . . .' and then he stopped.

She laughed. 'Get together again?'

'Correct.'

'I don't know, Walter. Where are we going to go with this?'

'I'd like to go further,' he answered.

'So would I.'

They smiled at each other, as if some sort of agreement had been struck.

'Tomorrow, then,' he said. 'I have to work a late shift tonight.'

'Okay,' she replied.

They joked and laughed most of the way to her office. They stopped for coffee and a sweet roll, which seemed hilarious. A cormorant flew low across the bow of his car as they crossed the causeway, which seemed comical. The mid-morning traffic had a rollicking, amusing quality to it. When they pulled to the front of the Justice Building, they were both close to giggling.

She stepped from the car and leaned back. 'Will you call?' she asked.

'Of course. This afternoon. Don't want to forget about Mr Jefferson. Those other fingerprint examinations should be finished by now. I'll call you with Harry Harrison's report.'

'Brought together by Leroy Jefferson. If he only knew.'

Walter Robinson laughed loudly. 'I wonder what he'd say.'

For a moment they looked at each other, each feeling the same, that they were standing at the starting line to something. And it was into that silence that they heard her name being called.

'Espy!'

She turned and Robinson craned across the seat to see who was shouting. High on the steps to the massive courthouse building they could both see the lanky form of Thomas Alter. He waved, and then bounded down the steps toward them.

'Hey, Walt, lucky to catch you here too.'

'Hello, Tommy. Get any killers off today?'

'Glad to see you too. Not yet. But you never know. It's still early.'

He smiled, with just a touch of Cheshire cat grin.

'So, Espy? You guys got your case together? You gonna put the screws to Leroy Jefferson?'

'Tommy, you know the office's policy on discussions. They have to be formal, with a stenographer. But I can tell you off the record that selling any plea is going to be tough, especially to Lasser. He doesn't like it when little old ladies get strangled. Ruins his whole day. So, I'd say no chance. No chance at all.'

'Really? No chance?'

'You heard me.'

He didn't seem fazed by this news. 'Well, I don't suppose, then, you'd like to see this . . .' Alter reached into a briefcase and pulled out a sheaf of papers.

'What's that?' Robinson asked. He had stepped from the car and walked around to the sidewalk, standing next to Martinez.

'Lie detector test,' Alter said abruptly.

'And?'

'Well, guess what?'

'Don't give us that coy crap, Tommy. What are you saying?'

'I'm saying that on this particular test my client demonstrated no signs of deception. None whatsoever. And you know what question we asked him?'

'What?'

'The question was nice and simple: "Did you kill Sophie Millstein in her apartment?" And guess what? He said no, and the machine says he's telling the truth.'

'Bullshit!' Robinson exploded. 'People can con those . . .'

'Well,' Alter replied slowly, 'that's what I thought you'd say. So I used the same guy that her office and your office uses. Vogt Investigations. How long have you guys kept old Bruce and his magical machine on a retainer?'

'Bullshit! I don't care what he passed, he still—'

'You haven't been to your office yet, have you, old buddy?'

'No.'

'Been busy, huh?' Alter grinned at Espy Martinez.

She burst out, furious. 'This is all crap, Tommy, and you know it. A lie detector test doesn't mean a thing! It's not evidence. It's not anything. So cut the crap . . .'

'Interesting report came into the Beach homicide office this morning,' Alter continued, ignoring the anger flushing the faces of the prosecutor and the detective. 'I mean, the sort of thing that just makes you wonder if there could be anything stranger in this odd world. . . .'

'Tommy, cut this shit, before I punch you out.'

'What are you saying, Tommy. What report?'

The defense attorney grinned again. 'It is fun to see you

two self-righteous avengers of society looking so dis-comfited. Perhaps you'll indulge me for a moment while I appreciate this little show.'

'What report?'

'Fingerfuckingprint report, you conceited bastard.'

'How do you—'

'We've got some friends in your office.'

'What are you saying, Tommy?' Martinez demanded, her voice shrill.

'What I'm saying, Espy, is that somebody else killed Sophie. That's what I'm saying.'

'Bullshit!' Robinson interjected. He reached toward the defense attorney, then managed to pull his hands back at the last second.

'Soddit,' Martinez spat out. 'Soddit. C'mon, Tommy, you can do better. The old "some other dude did it" defense. You think I'm so young I've never seen that bullshit before? How about something more original. Something more creative. Not the old Soddit defense . . .'

Alter wheeled toward her, pushing his face down angrily, abruptly shedding all the teasing jocularity he'd employed. 'Oh, you think it's boring? You think it's unoriginal?'

'That's right!'

'Well, guess what, boys and girls,' he said, his voice low, conspiratorial and filled with sarcasm. 'It also happens to be true.'

Alter turned to Walter Robinson.

'The fucking body print. Right from her neck. Right from the fingers that went around old Sophie's throat. That nice little partial thumbprint that your guys lifted from her skin. Guess what? It belongs to somebody. But not to Leroy Jefferson.'

He stepped back.

'So, chew on that, kids. And take a nice look at this lie detector report. And when you're ready to ask real nice and politely for our help in finding Sophie's real killer, well, you just know where I'll be waiting.'

He paused, then added: 'And Walter, old buddy, you bring the fifty you owe me, huh?'

Thomas Alter dropped the lie detector report to the cement sidewalk, where a light breeze riffled the pages as he turned and strode purposefully away.

CHAPTER FOURTEEN
The Missing H

Simon Winter thought: *he*'s here. Somewhere right in front of me. Maybe he's strolling down the wooden boardwalk, or eating an ice cream cone purchased from the vendor on the corner. Perhaps he's in that group waiting in line for a table at the News Café. He could be that man reading the *Herald* on that bench near the bus stop. He could be anyone. But he's here and he's killed at least once, and maybe twice. I don't know how yet. But he has. And he managed to make one killing look like an old man's suicide, and I think he made another killing look like a junkie's frantic handiwork, and I think if he needs to, he will kill again, because he's not having any trouble with murder.

None at all.

Winter took a deep breath and spoke out loud, muttering: 'How do I find you, Shadow Man?'

A teenage couple was walking past, a few feet away. They each wore mirrored sunglasses that glinted in the sun, and they turned when they heard his voice. Then they spoke to each other in Spanish, laughed and wandered off.

They made him angry. Just another old person talking to himself. That's what they think. He started to watch two young women on roller skates dip and swerve amidst the late afternoon crowds on Ocean Drive. The sidewalks were filled with the curious and the trendy, moving between the restaurants and outdoor café that dominate the Art Deco section of South Beach. It is a place of fast cars and neon signs; loud music, bass-heavy salsa or screeching guitar-driven metal, competing against the occasional squeal of tires and blaring horns. No one talks, everyone shouts. Miami, and by extension Miami Beach, honors the immediate, Simon Winter thought. If it's new and noisy and colorful, it's instantly accepted as part of the city's preferred image.

The women on roller skates wore identical tight black lycra shorts and fluorescent pink halter tops. One had dark hair, the other blonde. They moved with a sinuous grace, legs pumping to pick up speed, then relaxing, gliding ahead effortlessly. The crowds parted to let them pass, then closed ranks like some educated but disorganized army.

He sat on a bench across the street, his back to the pallid blue waters that curled effortlessly against a wide expanse of chalky sand. He realized that the street clamor that filled the air obscured the rhythmic music of the ocean surf rolling in against the shore. He could smell the salt air mingling freely with the aromas from a dozen different menus being prepared in as many kitchens. He wondered for a moment why anyone would think that man's sounds or smells were preferable to nature's. He looked down the beach.

How do I find him? he demanded of himself.

From where he waited, he could see the small bandstand at Lummus Park, and as he watched, he saw a half-dozen elderly men and women moving slowly away from the beach; the end-of-the-day retreat. They carried aluminum lawn chairs and folded parasols. The bandstand is a popular place, often crowded, although the gatherings there seemed to grow slightly smaller with each passing month. It is an odd place, a cement slab that radiates blistering summer heat, next to an old, low-slung and faded, institutional green-painted storage building. A microphone and small amplifier are placed outside every day by city workers. Then, one after the other, the old retirees still living on the Beach rise to entertain each other with songs. A sign on the wall limits each singer to three efforts. The songs flow forth nonstop through the wavy hot air, a variety of Eastern European languages coupling with an occasional effort in English and a frequent reliance on Yiddish. It has a touch of the absurd about it, more often than not the old people seem mildly ridiculous, crooning away, mixing verses, dropping phrases, humming the forgotten parts. The singers gesture and pose, arms wide, in imitation of lounge acts everywhere. Only rarely do notes fit music, do tunes correspond with words. The old voices have a raspiness or a tremulousness that crack and fray the songs. Some chant, some keen, others ooze lugubriously. But the singers continue, regardless of the flatness of the voices, because it is memories that they are evoking. Often the singers are overwhelmed by the noise and raucous sounds that emerge from pumped-up jukeboxes and muscular stereo systems across Ocean Drive. But the old people sing on, oblivious to the competition. And when finished, receive the same enthusiastic applause and generous praise from their fellow singers, regardless of whether a word could be heard or not.

Simon Winter shook his head and stood up. He walked slowly down the street, passing the elderly people with their lawn chairs as they headed in one direction, following the two young women on roller skates, who briefly flashed between a pair of shiny red sports cars and then disappeared ahead of him into the dusky remains of the day's light.

His eyes tracked a Miami Beach patrol car that maneuvered slowly through the throng of traffic. He was abruptly reminded of a time he'd been fishing in shallow waters in the upper Keys, flycasting for bonefish, and had spotted the solitary profile of an osprey circling lazily in the air, riding the currents of wind and thermal blasts of heat. He had quickly recognized that the bird was not really hunting. There was no energy in its search. But it was opportunistic; when it spotted a bar jack cruising too close to the surface, it lifted its wings and plummeted, talons outstretched, splashing into the light chop with a resounding explosion, then instantly rising back into the hot air, a rivulet of silvery water streaming from its white wings. It had as little luck fishing that day as he had. Still, as the hours passed and no fish showed, it seemed happy just to curl in great graceful circles in the air, like a part of the sky itself.

It's been a long time since I've been on the water with a fishing rod in hand, hunting, he reminded himself. Ten years perhaps. He tried to remember why it was that he'd quit, but could not recall a reason. It seemed to him that somehow he'd stopped doing all the things that used to make him who he was, and that maybe if he started doing them once again, he wouldn't be so eager to blow his own brains out.

His feet slapped against the dusty sidewalk. He let the osprey fade back into his memory, and turned his thoughts to the man who left the final letter off his wife's name.

I know who killed you, Herman Stein.

You were smarter than he thought, weren't you? Even though you were terrified, and you knew you were going to die, you were still clever enough to leave a message behind. The missing H. It took a long time for someone to figure out what you were trying to say, but I know now.

Simon Winter concentrated on Herman Stein's death, trying to form a portrait of the events in his mind. It was a simple, effective technique, one refined over years of standing above dead bodies. Create a mental moving picture of what happened and then you'll see a way to find the man who did it.

All right, first question: access – how did he get into the apartment?

Front door. Did you open it for him? No, you wouldn't do that. You were elderly and upset and frightened. You wouldn't open the door without checking the peephole first. So how? The hallway. Were you regular and routine, like so many old people? You were a man of precision, Herman Stein, did you go out to the deli on the corner every morning for breakfast and return at the same time after eating the same bagel with cream cheese, cereal and coffee, just like a clock chiming the time? Yes, that would be you. And stalking you would have been easy, even knowing that you were scared and perhaps thinking of taking precautions. And so, all he would have to do is to wait for you to go out, and then take up a position in that hallway, trap you on your return. Is there a stairwell? A fire escape? A closet. Winter knew without going to the dead man's apartment that there was some space that a person could wait in without being seen.

He breathed out slowly. Some of the terror that Herman Stein had felt slid into his own veins.

You knew he was out there, and you knew it wouldn't do any good this time to call your sons or daughter, would it? It was always the same. When you spoke of Der Schattenmann, they persuaded you otherwise. Like the little boy who cried wolf, you knew they would not believe you, even though this time was somehow different, and you were scared right to your core, weren't you? So you wrote the rabbi a letter and put it in the mail.

Because you were all alone and facing death.

So how did you know about the rabbi?

Winter made a mental note of this question. Find an answer, he thought, because if Herman Stein can find out about the rabbi, so can he.

So there you were. He trapped you in the hallway and forced you into the apartment. Then he sat you down in the desk chair. Did he make you type your own death letter? I think so, because that was where you had the idea to leave off the H. Did it give you a moment's satisfaction? Did it strengthen you just a tiny bit, help you to turn toward the gun as he pushed it at your forehead?

Simon Winter thought: Herman Stein, I take my hat off to you. You were a brave man, and no one knows it except me.

The old detective paused. He had reached the entrance to the Sunshine Arms.

Did he talk to you, Herman Stein?

What did he say?

Winter could see the old man sitting stiffly in his desk chair, eyes open wide, seconds before dying. He could see the fear, he could feel the same rush of dizzying anguish that Herman Stein must have felt. To have come so far, only to finally arrive face-to-face with a nightmare.

He stood on the sidewalk. The day's heat still radiated up through the wavy air, but he remained oblivious to the sensation. Instead, in his mind's eye, he started to place the faces of killers he had known onto the vaporous shape across from Herman Stein. He ransacked his memory, right through the long catalogue of crimes. A psychotic who'd used a butcher knife on his wife and children; a contract killer who'd preferred a small caliber pistol shoved up against the base of the skull; a gang enforcer who liked to use a baseball bat, starting with the legs, then moving methodically upward, allowing his frenzy to grow. He mixed into this gallery a few serial killers, a pair of punk teenagers who'd killed for thrills, several rapists who'd discovered a greater, more noxious excitement. One after the other he fit these characters onto the form, only to discard them into the dust heap of his memory.

He lifted his hand to his forehead and wiped away the thin line of sweat that had gathered just below the rim of his old baseball cap.

You're not there, are you, Shadow Man? You're not going to fit into any cop's memory, are you?

Simon Winter glanced over toward Sophie Millstein's empty apartment as he trudged toward his own. Tell me something. Anything, he demanded silently. But the apartment stood blankly, a shaft of final daylight illuminating one wall. He opened his door and stepped inside, letting the cool air flow over him like a clear thought. He congratulated himself for leaving the air conditioner running, worrying only momentarily about the bill from the electric company that would inevitably reflect his wastrel ways. As he stepped into the living room, he saw that there was a message on the telephone answering machine. He wanted something to drink, suddenly parched. He thought he remembered some canned lemonade in the refrigerator, and he took a step in that direction, then stopped, turning toward the machine.

He punched the playback button and after a moment of hissing, electronic noises, heard the rabbi's voice. It sounded distant, tinny. But the anxiety contained in each word was still crystal: 'Mr Winter? Please call me as soon as you can . . .'

There was a momentary hesitation, before the rabbi added:

'It's Irving Silver. He's disappeared.'

There was another pause, and then:

'I was wrong. Oh, my God. We should have let him get a gun. . . .'

And with that the machine clicked off.

CHAPTER FIFTEEN

The Lost Man

In their faces he could see anger and fear vying for control.

Simon Winter gave a small wave and hurried toward Frieda Kroner and Rabbi Rubinstein. They were standing outside the long porch of the Columbus, an old residential hotel a block from the ocean. The flat white walls of the building seemed to glow against the lustrous night black, like the graying embers of a near-dead fire. In the midday, he knew, the porch would have been crowded with the elderly residents of the hotel, patiently taking the sun, but now it was empty, save for two dozen scattered lawn chairs and the two people anxiously waiting for him.

The rabbi was nervously rubbing his free hand across his forehead, as if trying to scratch out a thought. The other hand was clutching a black-bound copy of the Old Testament close to his chest. He saw that Winter had spotted this, and so he said, instead of an introduction: 'In times like these, Detective, the Word of God brings comfort.'

Winter nodded. 'And what does He say?'

'He says to trust in His wisdom.'

That's what He always says, Simon Winter thought.

Frieda Kroner pointed toward the front entrance to the

hotel. 'There is where Irving isn't,' she said. 'He is gone.' She hesitated, then added: 'The Shadow Man got him.'

'How can you be certain?' Winter asked. She did not reply, nor did the rabbi. Instead, she turned and charged up the stairs, her momentum seeming to sweep the others along in her wake. Winter paused as the three of them entered the lobby. On one wall was a fading mural depicting the hotel's namesake arriving at the New World. It had that 1930s stylized feel to it, an immense fiction; all the gestures were heroic, all the figures, natives and Spaniards alike, had a calm and reverential air to them, as if they innately understood the moment in history that they were depicting. There was no hint of strife or blood or terror or any of the things that were to soon follow. In front of the mural there was an old black leather sofa. In the center of it a thin, gray-haired man sat, reading a newspaper in Yiddish. He looked up at them as they entered, then turned back to the paper studiously. But Simon Winter noticed he had placed his eyeglasses on the seat beside him, so that in truth he was listening and watching them. Curiosity, the detective thought, occasionally seems to be the province of either very young or very old age.

'This way,' Frieda Kroner said. She grasped his elbow and steered him toward the corner of the lobby, where a man sat at a small desk adorned with an antiquated plug-in-style telephone switchboard. He was younger than they were, and Hispanic. He shrugged as they approached.

'Mrs Kroner,' he said in heavily accented English. 'What can I say? I have no word from Mr Silver. Not in the slightest.'

'Did the police speak with you?'

'Yes. *Si*, of course. Right after you called them. They ask me if Mr Silver is unusual to not be here, and I say yes, and they ask if I notice anything unusual or funny, but this I do not notice, and so they give me a number and I am supposed to call them if I should know anything, but that is it.'

'Stupid,' she muttered. 'Der Schattenmann is killing us and the police are wondering if there is something unusual. Damn!' She shook her head vigorously. 'I want you to let my friends and I into Mr Silver's apartment.'

'Mrs Kroner, I—'

'Immediately.'

'But this is—'

'José,' she said, drawing herself upright, her face riven with demand, 'right now.' She swung her hand toward the Rabbi. 'This man is a rabbi. You cannot keep him waiting.'

She said this with such authority that the clerk immediately rose, nodding his head toward Rabbi Rubinstein. 'But only for a minute, Mrs Kroner, please.'

The inside of Irving Silver's tiny apartment was immaculate. A few books arranged by height on a shelf, magazines on a coffee table placed carefully, like a display, so that their titles could be easily read. On a bureau top were the expected photographs of distant relatives. Simon Winter slid a hand across the surface. Behind him the rabbi and Mrs Kroner waited expectantly, as if they were anticipating some pronouncement. He moved quickly through the small space; it was only a single bedroom apartment, less even than Sophie Millstein's or his own. The bed was made with hospital corners. He stopped by a cheap linoleum kitchen table and saw that there were two place settings arranged on top. Irving Silver had been expecting company. There was no indication of a struggle, no signs of a break-in. No evidence that Irving Silver had been taken someplace against his will. In short, what

Simon Winter saw was the apartment of a man who might have stepped out to purchase some missing item at the corner store, and who could come walking back through the door at any second.

He turned toward the others.

'You see,' Frieda Kroner said, pointing at the place settings. Then her finger started to waver in the air and he saw her jaw start to quiver around the next words that cracked from between her lips: 'Irving is dead.'

The rabbi turned and threw an arm around Frieda Kroner as her shoulders heaved with yet another sob. But he turned his eyes toward Winter and he nodded.

Behind them, in the hallway, José the desk clerk, shuffled about impatiently. 'Please, Mrs Kroner, is not necessarily possible true,' he said. 'I must lock up, please.'

Back in the lobby, Winter saw that the man reading in front of the mural had disappeared. Frieda Kroner continued to cry as the rabbi steered her toward the exit. But when they reached the sidewalk, she abruptly straightened up, shaking loose from Rabbi Rubinstein's arm. She looked wildly toward the two men, then stepped aside, turned to the empty street and in a loud, furious voice, shouted in her native German: 'You will not win this time!'

The words echoed emptily down the street.

Simon Winter tried to comfort her. 'Mrs Kroner, I don't see anything to suggest——'

She spun about angrily. 'You are a detective and you cannot see?'

The rabbi clapped his hands together in frustration. 'This is how it was. This is how it is!'

'We should have known better,' Frieda Kroner said bitterly. 'Us of all people. If you wait. If you do nothing. If you sit around. Then they will come for you . . .' She hesitated, then shook her head. 'No. Not *they*. *He* will come for you. This time, it is only a he. But it is the same, Detective. If you do nothing . . .'

'Then you will die,' Rabbi Rubinstein said coldly. 'Nothing has changed. He will find us and we will die.'

'Like he found poor Sophie and Mr Stein and now Irving.'

The man's name seemed to snag on her lips.

She stood in the wan light from the entrance to the residential hotel staring intently at the streams of darkness that melded onto the cityscape.

'Irving is gone,' she said. 'The Shadow Man got him.'

'I told you,' Rabbi Rubinstein said quietly. 'I told you. He means to kill us all.'

Frieda Kroner sighed deeply, nodding her head. She trapped a half gasp, half-sob near the back of her throat, and Simon Winter saw her eyes were tinged with red. 'Irving, you must be thinking Mr Winter, is not such a pleasant man, but you are mistaken. There is much kindness within him and good company, especially for an old lonely widow like myself. And now he is gone. I did not think it would happen like this.'

For a moment she seemed to totter on the edge of grief. Then she growled a guttural, angry sound, like some sort of wounded, dangerous beast.

'This is the way it always was,' she added harshly. 'One moment they were right there, at your side, and then, the next, they were gone. Disappeared. Vanished as if a hole had opened up in the bottom of the world and swallowed them up.'

'This is true, Detective,' the rabbi added. 'Soon there will be none of us left and no one will remember the Shadow Man.'

'Back up,' he said. 'Let's start at the beginning. What

makes you so sure Mr Silver has disappeared. What do you mean, gone?'

Frieda Kroner answered sharply. 'Gone means dead. That was how it always was.'

'How?'

Rabbi Rubinstein held up his hand, a small conciliatory motion. 'Frieda, tell Mr Winter. Then he will understand.'

She glared for a moment at the rabbi, then replied:

'Irving is a man of habits. If it is Monday, then he goes to the fish store, the fruit stand, and finally the supermarket. Then he takes his purchases home and he puts them away. Then he goes to the library to read the out-of-town papers, and then he takes a short walk on the boardwalk, and finally he comes home and telephones me and perhaps we go to see a movie because on Monday it is not so crowded as the weekend. If this is Wednesday, then Irving attends the bridge club in the afternoon, after stopping by my place to pick me up, and sometimes staying late. On Thursday, he has a discussion group at the library. On Friday there are services in the evening. These are the things that make up Irving's life now, just as they do mine, and the rabbi's as well. It is not so different for many of the survivors, Mr Winter. We practice order and regimen. It is as if the Nazis somehow installed a clock in each of us, and we must fill it with precision. So, when I arrive at Irving's home and he is not there to attend the bingo at the civic center, as we do on every Tuesday, then I know that Irving is in trouble. And there are only three sorts of trouble out there for people like us, Mr Winter.'

'What are those, Mrs Kroner?'

'There is disease. Disease and age, Mr Winter. Sometimes they seem like the same thing. Perhaps Irving has had a stroke or an accident . . .'

'But we called the hospitals, and they have no record of him,' Rabbi Rubinstein interjected.

'And there is violence. Perhaps some one of these young people who are taking over the Beach with all their noise and fast cars has mugged him in some alleyway...'

'But this the police do not report.' Again the rabbi stepped in.

'And then, of course, there is Der Schattenmann.'

'You spoke with the police?'

'Yes. Of course. Right away,' the rabbi said. 'They told us that they cannot file a missing persons report for twenty-four hours, but they were kind enough to check the accidents and crimes for us. And even then, they said there was nothing much they could do.'

'Not until they find a body. Or some evidence of a crime having been committed,' Frieda Kroner added bitterly. 'An old person on Miami Beach who is not home when he should be is not maybe the crime of the century, Detective. They do not treat this like the Lindbergh kidnapping. They are polite. But that is all. Just polite.'

She hissed, to herself: 'The Shadow Man lives amongst us, and they are polite!'

Simon Winter nodded. He knew this. Absent a kidnapping note, a bloodstained crime scene, or some other overt and unmistakable sign, the police would limit their inquiry to a teletype message to the other local forces and a be-on-the-lookout-for, with perhaps a distribution of a picture at the daily roll calls.

'Tell me, could there be some other explanation for his disappearance?'

'Like what?'

'Fear. Perhaps he went to visit relatives ...'

'Without telling us?'

This didn't seem likely.

'Has he ever experienced forgetfulness? An episode of blackouts?'

The rabbi shook his head angrily. 'We are not senile! None of us, thank God, suffer from dementia! If Irving has disappeared, there can be but one explanation!'

Simon Winter thought hard. All the old people on the Beach were creatures of habit, some in the extreme, like Irving Silver. Like Sophie Millstein. Like Herman Stein. They had all built lives around moments of certainty, as if the inflexible demands of this appointment, this schedule, this meeting, this meal, this medication, all precluded the spontaneity of death from entering their lives.

And, he thought, who is more vulnerable than someone of rigid habit?

Winter shook his head. 'But even if this were the Shadow Man, well, Sophie was attacked in her apartment. Herman Stein died in his apartment. His pattern seems clear—'

Now it was the rabbi's turn to interrupt with an exasperated shake of the head. 'You still do not understand, Mr Winter! Does a shadow have form? Does a shadow have substance? Is it not something that shifts and changes with every motion of the sun or the moon or the earth? That was why he was so frightening, Mr Winter. Back then, back in Berlin . . . If we'd known he liked to ride the trams, well, then we would have avoided the trams. If we knew which streets he walked, or which subway he frequented . . . If we knew which park he took the air in . . . But none of these things were known. Every moment was different. And why would he be different today? If he kills Sophie and poor Mr Stein in their apartments, then the Shadow Man will shift form and find some other location, and that is where Irving lies now. I know it!'

These final words cracked and splintered in the stale

humid air on the street. For a moment the old rabbi was quiet, then he added fiercely: 'He would have fought. Fought hard and long. He would have bit and scratched and used everything he had. Irving was tough. He was a hard man. He took his daily walks. He lifted things and swam in the ocean on warm days. There was still muscle there, and he would have fought hard, like a tiger, because Irving loved life.'

'There were no signs of a fight.'

'I could see that. It means the Shadow Man stole him from the street.'

'That would be difficult. Most of the time this place is crowded. Look at the porch. Ordinarily there would be dozens of people watching the street. . . .'

'This would be difficult for most criminals, yes, Detective, you are correct,' the rabbi said patiently. 'But you must remember: this is what he did, over and over, for all those war years. Quietly and unobtrusively he ended your life. Tell me, Mr Winter, have you not felt your hand slip while it holds a razor, and when you look up into the mirror, see that you have sliced yourself? That there is blood running down your chin? But did you feel the pain of the cut? No, I think not. And that is the sort of man he is.'

Frieda Kroner nodded her head in agreement, then snarled and whispered in a low, angry grunt: 'We must find him. We must find him today or tomorrow or this week or next, but we must find him. Otherwise, he will find us. We must fight back.'

'Even against a shadow,' the rabbi added.

Simon Winter nodded. He thought to himself: *This man is something different*. He felt his imagination start to grind away, mechanical, factoring.

'What was it you said, Mrs Kroner? Last time? He is one of you?'

'That is correct. He must be a survivor as well.'

'Then that is where I will start. And you two also. He will be out there, in a synagogue, at the Holocaust Memorial, at a condo association meeting, as he was with Mr Stein. There must be names, lists of names. Of organizations and congregations. That is where we will start.'

'Yes, yés, I see,' the rabbi said. 'I can contact other rabbis.'

'Good. Eliminate anyone under the age of sixty. . . .'

'He will be older than that. Why not make it sixty-five? Or sixty-eight?'

'Yes. But we are all old, and we all know some people wear their years differently. Some look younger, some older. I think to perform two – maybe three – killings, the Shadow Man will have the strength and appearance of a younger man. Let's keep that in mind.'

The rabbi nodded. 'Like the man on trial in Israel. He was in the papers again today.' Simon Winter's mind's eye quickly formed a picture of a man accused of being a former death camp guard. He had been on the television nightly and in the daily papers. He was a hulking man, thick through the middle, with wide shoulders and arms like wooden pilings. He was balding, and had a roughness about him that was unsettling. Flanked by a pair of armed policemen, the man always wore a prisoner's jumpsuit, but not the attitude or appearance of a prisoner.

'You have seen this man, this Ivan the Terrible?' Rabbi Rubinstein asked, and Winter nodded in reply. 'You can see, can you not, Detective, that this is a man who was never broken? Never crushed? Never beaten down and starved? With us, it is not exactly the same, is it?'

'I don't follow.'

'It is not that we survivors are less . . . I am not sure how to put it, but let me suggest this, Detective: a true survivor wears a mark just as surely as I wear this tattoo.'

He held up his forearm and pulled back the dark shirtsleeve he was wearing.

'See how it has faded with time? But it is still there, is it not? And we are no different inside. There is a mark there. As the years pass, it becomes less. But it is still there and will never totally disappear. You can see it in the slope of the shoulders, or maybe behind the eyes. This I believe is true for all of us.'

'What are you saying?'

'This man, Der Schattenmann, he will say one thing. But he will not have the truth within him. And, if we look hard enough, we will be able to see that.'

'This is correct,' Frieda Kroner added decisively. There was a momentary pause, and then she continued, with a secretary's efficiency. 'I know all of Irving's memberships. The bridge club and the discussion groups ... I can get those lists.'

'Excellent. And addresses. And descriptions, if you can get them. Remember detail. Any little thing could tell us what we need to know.'

'What do you mean, *detail*?' she asked.

'He was a Berliner once. Would he speak with an accent, like you do, Mrs Kroner? That is just a possibility. He may not.'

'Yes. Yes. This makes sense. I can see that, but in the meantime, how do we protect ourselves?'

'Change your routine. If you have been going to the supermarket at three P.M. every Wednesday afternoon for the past ten years, then change. Go at eight A.M. Start taking different routes. If you want to go to the boardwalk for a stroll, fine, just turn and head two blocks in the wrong direction before doubling back. If you are going out, call your destination first. Let them know you are traveling. If you always ride the bus, take a cab. Find someone to accompany you. Move in groups. Travel erratically. Zig-zag. Stop in front of plate-glass windows and spend a few seconds watching the people behind you. Turn suddenly and examine the street you've just walked down. Be alert.'

'This is wise,' said the rabbi.

'He may try to come at you as something familiar, a delivery-man or a postman. Trust no one. Even if you have been going to the same deli and eating the same corned beef at lunch for the last ten years, now you must change. And no longer trust the counterman, even if he's the same face you've seen every day since you moved to the Beach. Think: nothing is safe. Everything could hide a shadow.'

Frieda Kroner narrowed her eyes in appreciation.

'This will keep us alive?' she asked.

'It might. There are no guarantees. A gun is no guarantee. Or a pit bull.'

'Or the police,' she said bitterly.

'That is correct. The police solve crimes that have happened. Rarely do they manage to prevent something from taking place.'

The rabbi interrupted suddenly. 'We could go away. Just leave town perhaps?'

'Forever?'

'No. This is my home now.'

'Then I think it wiser to defend it.'

'Yes. If we had thought that way fifty years ago, sixty years ago perhaps ... No, let us not think of those things. Let us think about staying alive now. Today. Tonight. Tomorrow.'

Winter hesitated before continuing, watching the rabbi's face as it drifted momentarily back in time, seeing the remembrance of evil mark each line and furrow around his eyes, across his forehead, at the corners of his mouth.

'There is one other thing,' Winter added slowly. He saw the rabbi's eyes swing slowly back across the landscape of decades and arrive at the present, recovering an unsettled nervousness.

'What is this one other thing, Mr Winter?'

Winter replied quietly. 'Let's all assume that he knows who you are. And where you live. Let's assume right now that he is confident because he doesn't believe anyone is searching for him. Let's assume he could be planning his next attack right now.'

Frieda Kroner gasped. The rabbi stepped back abruptly. 'Do you think it so, Mr Winter?' he asked with a stroke of panic painted on his words.

'I do not know, but I believe you must consider the worst.'

'But how?' Frieda Kroner demanded.

'Perhaps Mr Silver told him.'

'No. This I do not believe. No matter what the pain. No.'

Winter nodded. 'Perhaps you're right. But there is one other thing that I just remembered.'

'What is that?'

The memory made him feel helpless, impotent and stupid. He wondered for an instant whether Irving Silver might be standing in front of him had he recalled this simple fact a few days earlier. He abruptly pictured himself, standing next to the young black detective amidst the heat and raised voices of the crime scene technicians as they processed Sophie Millstein's apartment. He saw in his mind's eye his own finger pointing toward the telephone stand, and he recalled his words to the young detective.

'Sophie's address book was missing the night of her murder.'

'What?'

'Her telephone address book. It wasn't in its customary location. It was gone.'

'You think Der Schattenmann . . .'

'If he saw it, he might have grabbed it. And you both were in it, because I saw her open it to get your telephone numbers.'

'But we do not know—' the rabbi began, then stopped abruptly. He rocked back and forth on his heels, a faint grin just starting in the corners of his lips. 'This is like a chess game, is it not, Detective?'

'In a way, yes.'

'He has made moves. He has controlled the board. It is as if we have been unable to see his pieces go from square to square. But now, perhaps, it is our turn. There are three of us and we have some tricks left, do we not?'

'I think we do,' Winter said.

'I am not scared,' the rabbi said suddenly to Frieda Kroner. 'No matter what happens, I cannot be scared. I do not think that Irving was either, when he came for him. And I do not think you will be anymore. Have we not seen the worst that this earth can manufacture? Is there some greater terror than Auschwitz?'

Oddly, then, Frieda Kroner smiled as well. 'We lived through that. . . .'

'We can face up to this.'

Simon Winter saw the old man reach out, seize the old woman's hand and give it a small, reassuring shake. He thought he should say something, but could not think of words. After a moment Frieda Kroner turned to him. She did not speak, but he knew that they were all beginning to get ready for whatever the next move was.

Esther Weiss leaned back in her desk chair inside her small

office at the Holocaust Center. She did not seem surprised to see him.

'You have more questions, Mr Winter?'

'Yes,' he replied.

'This is to be expected. When one cracks the lid on Pandora's box, many questions slide out. What is it you need to know?'

'Is there a registry or a list of Holocaust survivors, you know, a directory of sorts, that you have here?'

The young woman raised her eyebrows momentarily, then shook her head. 'A list of survivors?'

'Correct.'

'Like the membership of a club or a social group?'

He paused, but then said, 'Yes, though I realize that sounds odd.'

'That would be anathema, Mr Winter.'

'I'm sorry . . . I don't see—'

She interrupted him swiftly. 'Mr Winter, these people became Holocaust victims *because* they were put on lists. Registers. Directories. Allotments. There are all sorts of innocent words that take on horrific meanings when you connect them to the roundups and transports. No, Mr Winter. There are no more lists, thank God.'

'But here, at the Holocaust Center, and the other memorials . . .'

'We guard the names of the people who have spoken with us, who continue to speak with us, very carefully. Privacy is an important issue for these people, Mr Winter. It is hard to understand how these people can be both unique and special and terribly ordinary, all at the same time. Many have lived simple, unexceptional lives, save for those years swept up in the camps. Consequently, these memories – even though they share them – have a privacy to them that we protect. They do the same at the center in

Washington, and the one in Los Angeles. Yale University keeps their collection of videotaped recollections under lock and key. They have more than two thousand.'

'How many Holocaust survivors are there here on the Beach?'

'On the Beach? This is hard to say. A few years back it was estimated that there were fifteen thousand survivors living in South Florida. From Boca Raton and Fort Lauderdale all the way down to South Beach. But they are growing old. The number dwindles monthly. That is why their recollections are so crucial.'

She eyed him with some apprehension.

'We have no list, Mr Winter. These people come to us.'

He thought hard for a moment, then tried a different tack. 'Suppose I were to backtrack. Try Immigration and Naturalization. Would they have records, you know, from the Forties or early Fifties . . .' His query dwindled as Esther Weiss shook her head.

'I doubt it. Certainly they have records of people entering the U.S. and how it was managed. But an overall compilation? For Holocaust survivors? No. And there were so many different routes here, not just to the U.S., but within the nation after they arrived. From the Lower East Side to Skokie, Illinois, or Detroit or Los Angeles and finally to Miami Beach. These are not official travels, Mr Winter. They are recorded only in the memories of the people who made the trek.'

'But surely there must—'

'Surely what? In Israel they have been attempting to simply document the names of the people killed in the Holocaust. The number is at three million, slightly less than half. No, Mr Winter, lists don't exist. Only disarray and memories of nightmare.'

She paused, examining the consternation in his face.

'There is a question, but you won't ask it. You know something, but you won't say it. You want me to help you, but you won't say why.'

Simon Winter shifted about in his seat. He was dismayed. He berated himself inwardly for thinking the Holocaust would be like some great Department of Motor Vehicles, with names, addresses, telephone numbers, and current photographs. He looked over at Esther Weiss, who was staring at him with anticipation. It was not within his ordinary approach to matters to relinquish information. He stayed quiet for an instant, until the young woman shuffled some papers on the desk in front of her.

'When I came in before . . .' he started slowly.

'After Sophie Millstein's death,' she continued for him. He nodded.

'. . . You recall I was interested in a man Sophie knew only as Der Schattenmann.'

'Of course. The catcher. You were speaking with the other Berliners. I remember.'

'I am afraid that this man, the Shadow Man, is living here on Miami Beach.'

Esther Weiss opened her mouth as if to say something, then stopped. She seemed to take a deep breath before continuing. 'Here?'

The question seemed as suddenly pale as her skin.

'I believe so.'

Hesitancy slipped into the young woman's words. 'But that would be . . .' She shook her head. '. . . incredible. Horrible. I can't believe . . .'

'I think he has killed, Miss Weiss. I think he is stalking survivors. I think he stalked Sophie. And another man, a Herman Stein . . .'

'I knew Mr Stein.'

'And possibly another. Irving Silver.'

She shook her head.

'No. Irving Silver was in here. Two weeks ago. Talking to the camera, recording his memories.'

She reached toward the phone, as if to put something in her hands.

'He is missing.'

'Have you spoken with the police?'

'I haven't. Others have.'

'What do they say?'

He shrugged. 'Unless there is evidence of a crime . . .'

'But the Shadow Man? Here? Someone should . . .'

'What, Miss Weiss? Someone should investigate? Certainly. The police? The Justice Department? The damn Supreme Court?'

'Yes, yes. They have special investigations at the Justice Department. They have found Nazis . . .'

'Is this man a war criminal, Miss Weiss? It would be easier if he was.'

She stopped. 'Of course he is,' she said briskly.

'Are you certain?'

'He collaborated. He helped. Without him . . .' She looked at Simon Winter sharply. 'Surely that must constitute a war crime.'

'I wonder.'

Esther Weiss exhaled slowly. 'I think I see your point. And where would the evidence be? The proof?'

'I suspect the proof is mostly dead.'

She nodded. 'I see,' she said. She leaned back, rubbing her hand across her forehead. For a moment she turned toward the window, then she swiveled back around, facing him.

'What is going on here, Mr Winter? Please tell me what is going on?'

But that was a question he wasn't yet prepared to answer.

Simon Winter left the Holocaust Center with the promise of assistance and the names of some two dozen scholars who had specialized in studying the survivors. Mostly they were academicians and sociologists, with university listings. Some were associated with legitimate and well-known Jewish organizations. A few were independent, authors working on various accounts of the Holocaust. The problem was, as Simon Winter looked at the list, his hand by the telephone in his apartment, they could tell him much about the past, while he was trying to probe the present and divine the future. He stared at his list and checked off the three that lived in South Florida.

A secretary at the European Studies Department at the University of Miami took his name and number, but sounded extremely skeptical that any professor would return the call of a retired detective purposely vague about the nature of his inquiry. The second man was a writer, living in Plantation, working on a book about the collaboration of the Vichy government in shipping out thousands of French Jews to die in Germany.

'I can tell you about the south of France,' the man told Winter regretfully, 'but Berlin, no.'

The man hesitated, then added, 'Of course, like everyone who studies the Holocaust, I can tell you about death. Deaths by the hundreds, thousands, murder as commonplace as the sun rising in the morning or setting at night. Murder as a train schedule, regular and routine. Is that what you're interested in, Mr Winter?'

Simon Winter hung up, understanding that he needed something different, something unique, some observation or some connection, something that would pitch him out of the darkness of all the memories into the specifics of finding the Shadow Man. He thought: There must be some conjunction between the past and present that I can grasp. Something physical. Something palpable.

He could see none. He slammed a fist against the table. Impatience filled him.

Taking a deep breath, he dialed the third number. He almost slammed the receiver down when the mechanical sound of an operator informed him that the number had been changed. He noted the new listing, and then called that. He almost hung up on the fifth unanswered ring, only to hear a gruff 'Hello?' on the seventh.

'Is this Mr Rosen? L. Rosen?'

There was a hesitation, then a reply. 'Louis Rosen. Who is this? If you're selling subscriptions or insurance and seeking a donation, forget it.' The man spoke sharply.

'No,' Winter said. He quickly introduced himself and explained, 'I got your number from the Holocaust Center.'

Again the speaker paused. 'Those numbers are supposed to be confidential.'

'I believe they are, but these are unusual circumstances.'

'Unusual? What could be so unusual that they would break a promise of confidentiality?' The man's voice didn't soften, but gathered an edge of curiosity.

'I have reason to believe that a man who operated in Berlin as a catcher is living in South Florida.'

Rosen hesitated. A silence clung to the line before he answered in a steady, cold, but compelling tone.

'That is intriguing. A catcher? Only a few survived. Same as the Kapos in the camps. If you could find this man, it would be truly interesting. There are so many questions.'

'What sort of questions?'

'All questions that begin with the great Why, Mr Winter.'

'What do you suppose the answer to that might be, Mr Rosen?'

'I would be speculating. My area of study is Poland. The Warsaw Ghetto.'

'You had family?'

'Of course. And I too.'

'I see.'

'But that is a different story, is it not, Mr Winter?'

'Yes. But could you speculate what sort of personality I am looking for?'

Rosen seemed to be gathering his thoughts before he replied. 'That is a fascinating question, Mr Winter. What sort of personality? Do you truly think you want to open that particular door, Mr Winter?'

'I need to know. I need something to grasp hold of.'

'This, of course, is the great How at the bottom of all questions about the Holocaust,' Rosen continued, his voice sinking a bit deeper. 'It stands only a step closer to the surface than the great Why.'

'I'm only beginning to understand,' Winter said.

'No one ever really understands,' Rosen said coldly. 'No one who was not there. The numbers were so immense. The cruelty so common. The evil so complete.'

Simon Winter was silent. He could sense the man on the other end thinking.

'And so you want to know about a catcher? Not a fanatic. Not a Nazi. Closer to what the papers like to think of as a criminal psychopath. Remorseless. Relentless. Do you not think they would first excuse themselves by arguing they did what they did in order to save themselves and their own families?'

'That would be reasonable.'

'But it is of course untrue. Most didn't save anyone, including themselves. Only the truly clever ones, I suppose. And they would be a special breed, would they not? To survive? High odds.'

'Yes.'

'So, right away, you know you are dealing with a systemology of lies, are you not, Mr Winter? A person who cannot be self-delusional, because only someone who saw clearly what was happening could take the necessary steps to remain alive. But someone comfortable with distortions. Someone who embraces deception. But that would not be all, would it?'

'I'm listening.'

'There would have to be something beyond simple expediency, would there not? A ferocity. A steel will to live. The catcher would be someone who would never find anyone's life to be even remotely as important as their own. So, perhaps, you will be looking also for a man of some ego. A man who thinks he has done great things. This will not be a stupid man. Not like some dull-witted, hulking camp guard. Not even the accountant's mentality of some S.S. bureaucrat that made certain the transport trains ran on schedule. For a catcher to survive required true genius. Creativity. Do you not see that?'

'Yes. But how would I find this person? Here, among all the survivors?'

Rosen paused again, then laughed briefly.

'Oh, this would be impossible, Mr Winter. Like a needle in the proverbial haystack. Among thousands, one is not precisely who he says he is. But still, he would be expert. He would know everything that all the survivors know. He would have all their own terrors memorized, because he participated in them. He would have access to all the same nightmares, but not wake up in the middle of the night shouting the name of some long-lost relative who went to the gas. You see, Mr Winter, he would be completely intact, completely authentic. Yet intrinsically wrong. And somewhere within him a hatred so virulent ... It would be fascinating. Fascinating.'

'I must find him.'

'It is a him? Some of the catchers were women. You have a name?'

'Only a nom de guerre. Der Schattenmann.'

The name didn't seem to register.

'And you believe he is here?'

'Yes.'

Rosen's voice maintained an evenness as he spoke. 'And you want desperately to find him? Why would that be?'

'I believe he has killed.'

'Ah, now that is interesting. Killed whom?'

'Someone who might have recognized him.'

'This makes perfectly reasonable sense. And your involvement?'

'The victim was my neighbor.'

'Ahh, this too makes sense. Revenge?'

'I want to stop him.'

Rosen again grew silent on the other end of the line, and Winter thought for a second or two that he should say something, but did not, and into that space the man finally spoke quietly, deliberately, saying: 'I do not think you will be able to.'

'Why is that?' Winter asked.

'Because he must be an expert in death. All kinds of death.'

'So am I.'

'So is Time, Mr Winter. And Time has a better chance than you.'

*

Simon Winter rose from his table and walked to the window. Late afternoon sunlight filled the courtyard of the Sunshine Arms. The trumpeting cherub seemed inanely pleased, basking in the end-of-day heat, before the oppressive night humidity settled on the city. For the first time since Sophie Millstein had knocked at his door, Simon Winter felt a sense of defeat. All he'd heard, from every voice, was the same thing: death and impossibility. He lifted a hand to his forehead and rubbed hard, turning the skin red with frustration. This will kill me, he thought. I will die from impotent futility. This thought made him smile ruefully to himself when he recognized that that was precisely what he had been preparing to do when Sophie Millstein knocked on his door.

He decided that he would take a walk to see if movement could spur loose some idea for a productive avenue of inquiry, and so he turned and grabbed his battered Dolphins baseball hat and had his hand on the doorknob when behind him the telephone rang. He paused, wondering whether he should let the machine take it, then decided this was wrong, and bounded across the room, sweeping the receiver off the hook just as the machine went into its recorded message.

'No, I'm here, hang on,' he said over his own metallic taped voice.

'Mr Winter?' It was Frieda Kroner.

'Yes, Mrs Kroner, what is it?'

'Irving,' she said. Her words were iron-hard. 'The lifeguard station at South Point. The very last one before the jetty. We will meet you there.'

He saw a trio of police cars parked on a sandy strip next to the entrance to the beach. Off to the side was a small park, with a meandering exercise course wandering through it. The park had a half-dozen picnic areas and a set of swings and seesaws; it was a popular place on weekends; many of the immigrant families that clung to the tip of South Beach in narrow, low-slung apartments, used the spot for parties. It was a favorite park for the homeless as well, because it wasn't well-patroled at night, and a favorite too for fashion photographers shooting magazine layouts, because the park abutted Government Cut, the wide channel used by the cruise ships to head out into the open ocean. It sometimes had little moments of theater, where some man whose hopes and clothes were in tatters watched hungrily as chicken and plaintains were grilled and children played, a few feet away from where a model wearing thousands of dollars worth of evening wear and jewels pranced and preened for a cameraman.

From the long jetty one could see for miles out to sea, or look back toward the clear skyline of the city. Across the Cut was Fisher Island, a condominium complex serviced by its own ferry, populated by the wealthy, the very wealthy, and the obscenely rich. The jetty was also popular with fishermen, although the beach itself received less attention than the other spots at South Point. By virtue of being at the tip of Miami Beach, it gathered the roughest water and the most dangerous riptides. Some surfers liked it. The tourists were usually warned to move a mile or so up the expanse of sand. There was a boardwalk that led out to the jetty. Once he was on that, he quickly spotted the solitary lifeguard station at the end of the beach.

He saw a half-dozen blue-uniformed police officers milling about the faded green wood of the lifeguard stand. At the same time, he spotted Frieda Kroner and Rabbi Rubinstein standing apart, perhaps twenty feet away, watching the policemen, who seemed unsure what to do. A single crime scene technician, in a jacket and tie despite the heat, was bent over the sand, but he could not see what the man was examining. There was another man in a suit, leaning over, but his back was to Winter, who couldn't make out what the man was searching for.

He hurried forward, his basketball shoes making a clopping sound on the wooden boardwalk, like a horse trotting on pavement.

The rabbi turned as he approached, but Frieda Kroner kept watching the policemen.

'Mr Winter,' he said slowly, 'thank you for coming.'

'What is it?'

'They called us. Frieda, actually.'

'Did they find Mr Silver?'

'No,' Frieda Kroner said, not taking her eyes off the policemen. 'They found his clothes.'

'What?'

The rabbi shook his head. 'The policeman called her. Apparently some kid, a teenager, tried to use a credit card at a shopping center, and the clerk selling the video games didn't think this child, whose name turned out to be Ramón or José or Eduardo, looked much like an Irving, and so she summoned a policeman. And the teenager says this, and then says that, and lies this way and that, but soon enough gets around to telling the truth when someone gets a bit tough with him, and he says he finds this wallet with the credit card. They do not believe him, but he insists, and so the police bring him down here and he shows them.'

'What?'

'Irving's clothes. Right on the beach, as if he left them there.'

'And the wallet?'

'It was on top.'

Simon Winter nodded.

'This is where he killed him,' Frieda Kroner said quietly.

The old detective took a deep breath, thinking, *I don't think so*, and stepped away from the rabbi and Mrs Kroner and started to pace across the sand. With each step he grew increasingly angry, raging away within himself, once again feeling the same incompetence and stupidity. And within each step of anger, another voice within him tried to calm him, tried to force himself to stay alert, because, he thought, perhaps there is something here to learn, and he knew that frustration, perhaps better than anything else, could serve to blind him to knowledge.

Two of the uniformed officers peeled away from the group and stepped in front of him.

'This area is closed, Old-Timer,' one of them said with the arrogance of youth.

'Who's in charge?' Winter demanded sharply.

'Detective's in charge. Who wants to know?' the patrolman replied with an edge.

Winter wanted to reach out and shove the younger man aside, but hesitated, and in that second heard a voice that seemed to be familiar:

'I am, Mr Winter.'

He looked past the young patrolman's shoulder and saw Walter Robinson slowly rising from the blond sand beach. Robinson gestured at the patrolman. 'Let him come over.'

Simon Winter stepped across the sand. Walter Robinson did not offer his hand, but said instead: 'I thought you would be here. If not, I would have found you.'

'Why is that?' Winter asked.

The young detective didn't reply, except to ask a question. 'You knew Mr Silver?'

'Yes.'

'And Sophie Millstein as well.'

'That is obvious, Detective.'

Robinson grasped Winter by the elbow and led him to where a crime scene technician was taking a few pictures.

The technician looked up at Robinson. 'Come on, Walt. Let me bag this shit and let's get back to real work.'

Walter Robinson shook his head.

'All right, Mr Winter,' he said quietly. 'You were a detective once. What do you see?'

The technician overheard this question and interrupted with his own answer: 'Walter, come on. How obvious can things be? Old man wants to end it all, comes on down here at night, no one around, folds up his clothing nice and neat and heads into the surf. Body will turn up in a couple of days up the beach a few miles or wherever the currents wanna dump it. Should be calling the Coast Guard to keep an eye out.'

Robinson glared at the technician. 'That's what you see,' he said coldly. 'I'm interested in what this gentleman sees.'

Winter was studying the beach carefully. He saw Irving Silver's clothes, folded just as the technician said, prepared like a man afraid of making a mess in death.

'The wallet was right on top?'

'Yes,' Robinson said.

'Anything on the beach?'

'Not that we can find.'

'No note?'

'No.'

'Have you examined the clothing?'

'Just in its current position.'

Winter knelt down beside the clothes. 'May I?' he asked.

Robinson squatted beside him. He held up a plastic evidence bag. 'Go ahead,' he said.

There was a straw porkpie hat. Simon Winter picked it up and turned it over. He saw the initials I.S. scratched into the dark-stained sweatband. He pointed at these to Robinson, then dropped the hat into an evidence bag. Then he picked up a floral-print polyester shirt. The flowers were greens and blues and vinelike, entwined in design, making the pattern a maze of variegated shapes and colors. He started to pass the fabric beneath his eyes slowly, feeling it between two fingers, until he reached the collar, and there he stopped. He could feel his heart suddenly accelerate, and for a moment he felt dizzy.

'There,' he said quietly, almost a whisper.

Robinson leaned over and touched the fabric where Winter was pointing. He picked up the shirt and held it up into the fading light, squinting as he examined the texture.

The young detective nodded, letting out a long hiss of breath. 'Perhaps,' he said. 'I think you're maybe right.'

Winter stood up and looked out to sea. Each wave seemed to reach up and catch a piece of the fast-dropping night, then thrust the darkness up onto the shoreline.

'It's blood,' Winter said. 'Irving Silver's blood.'

'There's not much,' Robinson acknowledged slowly. 'It could be nothing more than a shaving cut.' Then he turned to the technician. 'Collect all this stuff carefully.' He waved at the uniformed officers. 'I want this whole area taped off. It might be a homicide scene.'

Simon Winter remained silent for a moment, watching the ocean, feeling the onshore breeze start to dwindle, making space for the oppressive summer night.

'He's not there,' he said softly.

'Who isn't there?' Walter Robinson asked.

'Irving Silver.' Winter raised a hand and stretched it toward the ocean. 'That is what it is supposed to seem like.

That he's out there drowned and disappeared. Swallowed up. But he isn't.'

'Where is he, then?' the young detective asked.

'Somewhere else. Somewhere distant and lost. Out in the Everglades maybe.'

'A body one place. Clothing here?'

'Correct.'

Walter Robinson whistled softly and stared out at the ocean as well. 'That would be clever. It would really screw us up.' He hesitated, then added: 'I think you may be right.'

Winter turned then, and looked at the young detective. 'You said you were going to find me. Why?'

'Because,' Walter Robinson replied slowly, 'I have lately become interested in history.'

CHAPTER SIXTEEN

A Legal Game of Chicken

There was a pay telephone across from the nurse's station inside the locked ward at Jackson Memorial Hospital, and Espy Martinez paused there. She quickly dialed the number of the Miami Beach Homicide Unit. For the third time that afternoon she was forced to leave a message for Walter Robinson. She hung up the receiver with an irritated snap to her wrist, banging it down. Then she took a deep breath and eyed the corridor that led to Leroy Jefferson's room.

She wondered for an instant whether she was closer to the truth or about to lose sight of it completely. Then she paced down the hallway, listening to the smacking sound her heels made against the polished linoleum floor. Someone was crying in one of the rooms she passed, but she could not see who it was. The sound of sobbing, however, seemed to keep cadence with her quick-march down the corridor.

The prison guard on duty at the wire-mesh gate was an older man. She recognized him from a half-dozen courtrooms. He had a brushy crew-cut gray shock of hair and thick forearms adorned with intricate tattoos. He gave her a little wave and a crooked smile as she approached.

'Hi, Mike,' she said. 'This must be easier than hauling

guys back and forth between the jail and the Justice Building.'

'Well,' he said, 'all I got to do here is make sure I don't catch something, and sit around reading the paper.'

'Any good news?'

'Never is.'

'Feeling okay?'

'Sure am.'

'Then sounds to me like you've got easy duty.'

'You got that right, Miss Martinez.'

'Is Alter here?'

'Just a couple of minutes ago. Went in with the doctor.'

She started to sign in on a log sheet attached to a clipboard when the guard whispered, 'I think poor Leroy's having a bit of trouble with the pain today, you know, counselor? He's been on that buzzer to the nurse's station all morning. I think maybe you shooting up his leg and him not being allowed no crack pipe, well, maybe it's made him a tad *tense*, if you catch my drift, Miss Martinez.'

'Uh-huh,' she said, nodding.

The guard grinned. 'I mean, he might be just a little bit rocky today. You might squeeze him a little bit, if you get the chance, know what I mean?'

Espy Martinez managed to smile, despite the feeling that it was going to be herself that was squeezed, not Leroy Jefferson. She put her index finger to her temple, making a small salute. Prison guards, she thought, know everything and have a remarkable ability to sense the direction of any wind that blows through the justice system.

As she pushed her way into the hospital room, she heard the sound of retching, and then a long, complaining, 'Sheeit.' She summoned a wry, mocking, inquisitive look and stepped into the room. She immediately looked at Leroy Jefferson, his leg still immobilized in traction, struggling to sit up in bed. As he turned to face her, she saw a thin line of perspiration gathered at his forehead. He wiped the back of his hand across his lips.

'Not feeling too good, huh, Mr Jefferson?'

The accused man scowled, then he bent over and spat into a bedside wastebasket.

'Bitch that shot me,' he said beneath his breath.

'He's okay,' Thomas Alter said quickly, rising from a steel folding chair. 'Isn't that right, Doctor?'

A young white-jacketed physician was standing beside Jefferson. He nodded. 'The discomfort is normal.'

'Normal, shit,' Jefferson said. 'I wanna another shot.'

The doctor glanced at his watch, then down at his chart, and shook his head. 'Nope. Not for at least ninety minutes. Maybe two hours.' He said this coldly, without feeling. As he spoke, Martinez saw a wave of hurt and nausea wash over Jefferson's face. He started to bend toward the side of the bed and the wastebasket, then managed to stop, pushing himself back hard, as if tired. 'Ain't got nothin' left in me,' he whispered. An intravenous tube running from a stanchion down into his arm rattled. Martinez looked away for a moment, absorbing the stark surroundings in the small room. White walls. A gray steel grate over a dirt-streaked window, so that even the day's sunshine seemed smudged as it crept into the room. A single, utilitarian bed, and bedside table. A paper cup and a cheap plastic jug for water. As bleak as the jail cell that awaited him barely a block away.

Alter looked irritatedly at the young physician, who replaced the chart at the bottom of the bed. 'I think he could use something,' the attorney said.

The doctor looked up. 'You're the lawyer, right?'

'Correct.'

'Well, stick to the fucking law, then,' he said quietly. The doctor looked over at Espy Martinez. 'My brother-in-law's a cop,' he said. He jerked a thumb toward Leroy Jefferson. 'He's okay. His leg hurts like hell, and he's in withdrawal. So he's feeling mighty sick, and every time he makes a move for that wastebasket, it must feel like someone's sticking a knife in that knee and twisting it around. But it isn't anything that will kill him. It just isn't making him happy. Making him happy isn't exactly my job. Keeping him alive was.' The doctor slid past her and out the door.

Leroy Jefferson's hands were clenched tight, into balls. 'I ain't never gonna walk right again 'cause of you,' he said.

She shook her head. 'Breaks my heart,' she replied. 'I told you to freeze. And instead you tried to shoot me. Screw you.'

Leroy Jefferson scowled again, and started to speak, but was cut off by Thomas Alter.

'That's not the purpose of this meeting,' the public defender said.

'That's right,' Martinez said. 'The purpose of this meeting is to determine whether or not I think this defendant has the capacity somewhere within him to tell the truth, which, right now, I seriously doubt.'

Alter waved his arm dramatically, like some overwrought actor on a dinner theater stage. 'Then get out. Take him to trial. Do what you want, but you won't get his help, and it sure looks to me like you're going to need it.'

Espy Martinez managed to grip hold of herself, and spoke quietly. 'Look, the lie detector test is persuasive, but not conclusive.'

'You gonna put an innocent man in jail?' Leroy Jefferson demanded. She ignored him.

'What about the fingerprint?' Alter asked. 'How're you going to get around that?'

She didn't answer this, but instead said, 'So maybe it wasn't his hands around Sophie's throat. But there's clear-cut evidence he was in Sophie's room, and that he stole items. So, perhaps he had an accomplice. Perhaps there were two of them there that night. That still makes him guilty of felony murder.' She looked over at Jefferson. 'Penalty for felony murder in this state, in case you weren't aware, is the chair.'

'Shit,' Jefferson said. 'Didn't kill nobody and didn't have nobody with me.'

Alter glared at his client and said, 'Just shut up and let me and the prosecutor talk. What are you saying?'

'I'm saying that before I go any further, I want to know what you mean by help. Give me some proffer of your client's evidence.'

'Not without a guarantee.'

'What sort of guarantee?'

'That he gets a deal. No prison time.'

'Forget it.'

'Then go screw yourself. Find that old woman's killer without him.'

'That's what we'll do.'

'Sure you will. Good luck. You got any idea who left that partial on her throat?'

'I'm not answering that sort of question.'

'I didn't think you did,' Alter said, smiling, relaxing. He turned to Leroy Jefferson. 'You just keep your mouth shut, Leroy. Dealing with the state is just the same as waiting for that shot of painkiller. It hurts. You feel sick. But eventually they come to you. And then everything is all right.'

Jefferson seemed gray and pale. He nodded. 'I saw him,' he said.

'Saw who?' Martinez asked quickly.

'I said keep your mouth shut!' Alter shouted.

Leroy Jefferson leaned back on a pillow. A single rivulet of perspiration ran down his cheek, but he grinned at Espy Martinez.

'Gonna need me,' he said. 'Ain't gonna find no killer, 'less I show you who. I saw him good. I saw him kill that old lady.'

Martinez clenched her own teeth together. 'You know I've filed enough charges against you to keep you up in Raiford Prison for a thousand years. Ten thousand years. Forever. Until you shrivel up and rot away. And that's where you're gonna be.'

Jefferson just shook his head and repeated: 'Gonna need old Leroy. You go ask that detective, he tell you.'

Martinez looked over at Alter.

The public defender shrugged. 'What can I say, Espy? He's telling you the way it is.'

'Really? Why is it that I don't find it easy to believe Mr Jefferson? Maybe because he's a strung-out, lying—'

'You're going to have to believe him, Espy, because he was the one that was there.'

'Yeah, him and one of his junkie buddies. The only deal I'll cut will be to life in prison. He gets to save his sorry ass by testifying against whatever low-life friend of his killed Sophie Millstein.'

'Weren't no friend, I tol' you,' Jefferson said, smugness penetrating through the pain. 'Were a white guy. An old white guy.'

Thomas Alter smiled again. 'I think we've helped Miss Martinez out quite enough already.'

'You're saying that . . .'

'He was there. He saw the killing. He ran away. What more do you need to know, Espy? There's your precious proffer.'

'You mean this low-life witnessed a murder then robbed

the victim before the neighbors got there? Is that what you're saying?'

She was unable to conceal the astonishment in her voice.

'You figure it out,' Alter replied with a shrug. 'Life sure is strange.'

They were all silent for a moment.

'Nice seeing you, prosecutor,' Thomas Alter said. 'You get back to me, okay? We're not going anywhere. And now you know the score.'

Espy Martinez stared hard at Thomas Alter, letting her eyes burrow into his, until he finally let his self-satisfied grin slide from his lips.

'You think I'd cut this piece of garbage a deal after he almost killed a cop and almost killed me? You think he's gonna walk on those charges?'

Alter sat quietly, infuriatingly, in his chair, as if assessing both what she'd said and how angry she was.

'I don't think anything, Espy. All I think is that Mr Jefferson knows something that you're gonna want to know, and the price of that knowledge is steep. But then again, the cost of enlightenment is always high. See? I can be a philosopher.'

'That's right. The price is right up there. You see? I'm a fucking philosopher too,' Leroy Jefferson cackled, although the last words were twisted with a sudden twinge of pain that made the corner of his lip twitch.

'Better not price yourself right out of the market, Tommy,' Martinez said briskly.

'Please shut the door on your way out,' the public defender replied.

As usual, the summons to Abe Lasser's office was written in red ink to underscore the urgency of the request. All of

Lasser's summonses were urgent, she thought, whether they really were or not. She quickly flipped through her other messages, looking for one from Walter Robinson, but there were none. For a second she managed enough distance to wonder whether she was anxious to hear from her lover or from the detective working the case. She didn't know the answer to this question but suspected that each desire hummed like a tuning fork within her, each a different tone, but equally insistent.

Lasser was standing by his window when she entered his office, staring out over the city.

'You know, during the riots, I was standing right up here, right at this window, and I could see all the way to the tire store, the big discount one on Twenty-first Avenue. I had some binoculars and I even saw the guys set the place on fire. They were running right around the side and then they stopped and they piled up some debris and I saw them toss some gasoline on it. Like some sort of demented troop of evil urban Boy Scouts.' He pointed and laughed, although not at anything particularly funny. 'It was four blocks away, and it seemed like something I was watching on television.'

He turned from the window.

'Damndest thing,' he continued. 'These little antlike figures way down there, scurrying about, torching that big old warehouse. Thing burned for almost two days. And here I was, chief felony prosecutor for the county, witnessing the whole rotten thing from my window and not able to do a damn thing about it.'

She nodded, thinking: There's going to be a point somewhere.

'Like watching an accident happen, but worse, because this wasn't an accident, it was a crime. Much worse. Deliberate, destructive. No act of God. An act of man.'

He stepped away from the window.

'Acts of God, we leave to higher authorities, Espy. But acts of man, those are precisely why we're here. They're our job.' He smiled. 'I sound like a philosopher,' he said.

'Tommy Alter said the same thing to me, barely an hour ago.'

Lasser grinned. 'Really? Stands to reason, I guess.'

He moved behind his desk. He had removed his suit coat, and she saw that his white dress shirt was tapered to his waist, obviously tailored. She kept quiet while Lasser picked up the copy of the lie detector report.

'I hate these fucking things,' he said. He dropped it to the desktop as if it were infectious. The pages flapped momentarily. 'So, Espy, do you feel like you're standing at a window about to watch a crime take place and unable to do anything about it? If this scumbag Leroy Jefferson walks, it will be a crime. As sure as I'm standing here now, it will be just like an arson. It will be like putting a match to some flammable bit of material. Sure, he may smolder and smoke for some time. A week. A month. Maybe six months. But then he will go and do precisely what this damn report says he didn't do: kill some harmless little old lady. You understand that, Espy?'

'Yes sir.'

'You've met Mr Jefferson. What is the prognosis for him becoming a contributing member of society?'

These last words were spoken with unbridled sarcasm.

'The prognosis is dim, sir.'

Abe Lasser burst out laughing. 'Dim. Yes, I'd say. More like nonexistent.'

He sat down suddenly and immediately rocked back in his chair. 'Maybe, Espy, we'll get lucky. Perhaps fucking Leroy Jefferson will kill some other scumbag instead of some tax-paying, God-fearing, innocent member of our community, though I doubt it, because the slimeball seems to like robbing little old ladies, and I would suspect that he will return to that profession just as quickly as he can.'

He hesitated, then added, 'Even if he is limping along thanks to your twenty-five caliber arrest. So, tell me, Espy, do you feel lucky? Is there some little Hispanic leprechaun guiding the Martinez family fortunes, set to deliver some good luck in your direction? Or perhaps a fairy godmother that will sing bibbidy-bobbity-boo, wave her magic wand, and send Leroy Jefferson off to kill one of his own ilk, instead of someone's beloved grandmother?'

'I don't think so, sir.'

Lasser spun about in his chair. 'Ahh, such a pity.'

He stopped and bent toward the desk, poking at the lie detector test. 'Got to admit, fucking Tommy Alter knows what he's doing. Gets our own man to run the fucking test. A nice touch, that. I've got to remember that, you know, so that the day that Tommy comes in here, hat in hand, we get a little payback. Just between us philosophers.' He swiveled about, leaning back, placing his hands behind his head.

'So what're you going to do, Espy?' Lasser asked abruptly.

'I'm sorry, what am I—'

'Right. What are you going to do? Your case. Your decision. I'm merely here to, uh, assist you.'

Espy Martinez felt her skin flush. 'I thought. . .'

'You thought I'd make the call?'

'Yes.'

He shook his head. 'No. Your case. Your call. I only present certain guidelines. Like this: Jefferson is charged with two counts of attempted murder for shooting at you and at that detective. Seems to me that those transactions have nothing to do with Sophie Millstein's murder.'

'Yes.'

'But on the other hand, an actual murder, especially a heinous one, such as Sophie Millstein's, well, that case takes significant precedence over a shootout, even one as dramatic as Mr Jefferson's.'

'I see.'

'Do you, Espy?'

She could feel a solitary anger winding up within her, and she did not think she could control it from spilling forth. 'I see that it is my butt on the line.'

Lasser nodded. 'Inelegantly put, but accurate.'

She breathed in harshly. It seemed as if the office was suddenly hot. 'If Jefferson provides us with Sophie's killer . . .'

'Then you're a hero, with the headlines to prove it.'

'But if it is all bullshit and I cut him a deal and then he goes out and kills someone . . .'

'Then the news stories won't be quite so laudatory, will they?'

'No. They won't.'

Lasser continued to rock in the chair. 'It would be better if Walter Robinson could make a case without Jefferson. Any chance of that?'

'I don't know. It's like starting from scratch. I don't even think he's got a lead. We were all set to start putting Jefferson in the electric chair, when it all went to hell with that report.'

'Nasty little device, the polygraph machine. Makes everything gray and fuzzy. Not clear-cut and pristine.'

'So, I'm not sure what Walter can come up with.'

'Trail is cold already. Have you ever seen the statistics on solving homicides? Every day that passes without an arrest . . .'

The chief prosecutor held up his hand, then, as he spoke, he started to curve it downward, like measuring the fall off a cliff. 'Maybe that partial thumbprint the killer left behind?'

'I believe he's already run it through the computer with negative results. I think he did that first.'

'So Sophie's killer isn't a criminal who's been finger-printed recently. That's a bad sign.'

'Apparently not.'

Lasser continued, 'Tough sledding, then. Of course, the converse is true for Tommy Alter and Leroy Jefferson. If Robinson can somehow, magically, get headed in the right direction, well, then the value of some murderous junkie's testimony diminishes rapidly, doesn't it?'

'Yes.'

'I'd like to see that,' Lasser said, tilting backward, as if daydreaming, his eyes for a moment sweeping the ceiling. 'Like to see old complacent Tommy Alter's face when we tell him we don't need Mr Leroy Jefferson. That would give me pleasure.'

'Jefferson claims to be an eyewitness to the killing.'

'He does? Ah well, would that all the witnesses in the world were saints, virgins, or Boy Scouts. That makes it sticky, doesn't it?'

'How so?'

'Well, that would be a difficult explanation to make to the Millstein family and to some whore scribbler over at the *Miami Herald* who finds out about all this and who calls us up on the phone one day with a uniquely nasty set of questions – you know, having to admit that the state rejected an *eyewitness's* testimony because he was, shall we say, unsavory? I don't think that particular explanation would look good in print.'

'No sir. Me neither.'

'They will find out, Espy. You know that, don't you? The *Herald* will find out. The bastards always do.' He cleared his throat. 'A tricky situation, Espy. Tricky.' Lasser glanced down at a file on his desk. He picked it up and thumbed through it almost haphazardly, as if distracted. 'You'll let me know what you decide to do, won't you?'

She kept her anger under check. 'Yes sir. As soon as I make a decision.'

'Don't hesitate.'

'No sir.'

'And, Espy, keep one thing in mind as you work your way through the minefield. One priority. . . .'

'What is that, sir?'

'We find, we prosecute, we convict, Sophie Millstein's killer. I made that promise. To a fucking rabbi, of all people. What could I have been thinking? Bad lesson there, Espy. If you're going to promise something that may be well-nigh impossible, better make that promise to someone who doesn't count for much either in this life and especially not in the next. So, unfortunate as it seems, I mean to keep that promise.' He looked up from the papers on his desk quickly and jabbed a finger at her. 'You're going to keep it for me.'

Espy Martinez nodded, but felt only slippery black ice within.

Lasser laughed, but the sound only slightly diminished the tension in the room.

'Lighten up, Espy,' he said, although she realized there was nothing to lighten up about. 'This is what makes criminal law so intriguing.' He smiled. 'It has a certain existential quality to it. Life gambles, I like to call them. It is sometimes like we're caught up in a game of high-speed chicken, souped-up situations racing headlong right at each other, wondering who's going to flinch first, played out in suits and ties, in wood-trimmed courtrooms, with rules and judges and all the trappings of civilization, but where we're really talking about something almost primitive, something ancient, aren't we?'

'What would that be?' she asked bitterly. She felt utterly alone.

'That would be justice,' Lasser replied offhandedly.

CHAPTER SEVENTEEN

Not Something from the World He Knew

About an hour after beginning to listen to the two old people tell him a story so hard to imagine that even the jaded homicide detective within him rebelled, Walter Robinson held up his hand, bringing a halt to their conversation. He realized he needed a moment to think, a moment to absorb what he'd heard, and so he suggested that he bring them all coffee, or a soft drink.

Frieda Kroner scowled. 'We drink coffee while *he* plans!' she said angrily. Rabbi Rubinstein added quickly, 'I think we should continue.'

Robinson glanced over at Simon Winter, who had said little since they'd all returned to the Beach Homicide offices. But the old detective shook his head. Robinson stared hard at the older man, who realized in that second that he was being asked for help, and so, quickly, changed his mind. 'Maybe a soda,' Winter said.

The rabbi and Frieda Kroner swiveled in their seats at the sound of his voice. Frieda Kroner frowned and started to say something, but the rabbi diplomatically shushed her before the words tumbled out. 'Perhaps coffee. With sugar and milk,' he said, and the old woman at his side reluctantly nodded. 'Two sugars,' she muttered. 'To put sweetness back in my life.'

'All right,' Walter Robinson nodded. 'Just take five. I'll be right back.'

He left them all sitting in one of the interview rooms, walking swiftly out into the corridor. For a moment he felt an immense exhaustion sweep over him, and he leaned back against a wall, closing his eyes. He wanted to blank his imagination, but could not. For a long, spinning second, he found himself wondering what it must have been like, packed tightly into a cattle car, the press of people choking away his breath. Work Makes Free, he thought suddenly. He opened his eyes and wheezed like a man at the end of a long run.

From down the corridor he heard the sound of a young woman crying. He welcomed the distraction. It was a long, steady sound of someone slowly sliding down grief's slope, not urgent, but desperate. He knew the case; a twenty-one-year-old mother of three small children, the oldest being five, had left them unattended in her small apartment while she went to the corner store for diapers and groceries. She was Nicaraguan, and had only been in the country for a few months – which is to say, just long enough for her husband to disappear, and not long enough to find any friends who might help her out with babysitting – and the rattrap that she lived in was a place that would never show up on any of the Chamber of Commerce's idyllic photographs of bikinied, suntanned, happy-go-lucky Miami Beach. At the young woman's apartment, there were no screens on the windows and the air-conditioning was out, so they were left wide open to the day's heat. While she was gone, the three-year-old had climbed out of the crib she'd placed him in, and managed to get up to the windowsill, trying to catch some stray breath of fresh air, or maybe just interested and curious in the street noises because that is the way children are. Perched high, he had lost his balance and tumbled out, head first from the third story of the apartment building, landing on the cement of the sidewalk just as his mother approached the building, so that she had had one horrible vision of her child whirling through the air, before landing with an unholy crunch almost at her feet.

She had screamed then, but since arriving at the homicide offices, had retreated into a wordlessness interrupted only by an occasional cry for Santa María, Madre del Dios, and tightly clutching her rosary beads.

Walter Robinson let out a long, slow sigh. The young woman doesn't understand, he thought. She barely understands this death, and she doesn't understand this country, and she probably wouldn't understand much anyway because she is poor and uneducated and alone, and surely she doesn't understand why the *policia* have taken her two other children away and are getting ready to charge her with criminal negligence. After all, she was going to the store to buy them milk with the few remaining dollars she had because she loves them.

He shook himself off the wall and let the young immigrant woman's cries drift into the background realm of noise that is more or less commonplace in police stations, even modern ones with recessed lighting and industrial carpeting on the floors. It was sad, but sadness was the norm, and he knew that no one in uniform or carrying a badge ever allowed these sadnesses to accumulate within them, although he recognized that each one probably made some little scratch somewhere on the psyche. He started to walk down the corridor briskly, standing aside when another interview room door opened and two detectives emerged, struggling with a handcuffed teenager.

'Come on, tough guy,' one detective said, but the teenager, his face pockmarked with acne, framed by ringlets of long stringy hair, sporting a tattoo extolling the virtues of a heavy-metal rock band high on the considerable muscle of his arm, instead of following orders, slammed back into the detective. The three of them abruptly tangled up, teetered for a moment as they all lost balance and then fell to the floor.

As Robinson stepped quickly toward them, the three men struggled briefly. The teenager's legs flailed out as he tried to kick at the detectives. They, in turn, rolled over on top of the suspect in a practiced fashion, immediately gaining the advantage. He stopped a few feet back from the fighting men. It reminded him, in an odd way, of contentious brothers, where the older ones sit on the youngest until he stops fighting back.

'Need help?' Robinson asked, almost offhandedly.

'Ahh, no thanks, Walt, buddy,' one of the detectives replied as he calmly reached down and grabbed a handful of long, stringy black hair, then slammed the teenager's face hard against the floor.

'Fucking asshole cop!' the kid yelled.

The policeman slammed him again.

'Motherfucker!'

The second detective maneuvered around, placed one knee square in the teenager's back and twisted his arms savagely.

'Got that right, at least,' he said between clenched teeth, irritated more than angry.

'You sure you don't need a hand?' Robinson asked again.

'Not for this punk cocksucker,' the detective replied.

'Fuck you!' the kid yelled. But his desire to continue struggling was fast diminishing, as his face was bashed into the floor. 'Fuck you both!' the kid managed between slams.

'What's the deal?' Robinson asked.

'Fucking punk kid got burned in a drug deal. Fuck, some drug deal. Fifty bucks worth of rock. Goes home, gets a nine-millimeter out of his daddy's bedside table, and goes and finds the kid who burned him. Shoots him right on the street, right in the head, right in front of Miami Beach High, just as school's getting out. Sort of an unusual extracurricular activity, huh? Made a real pretty show. I mean, kinda like *Miami Vice* usta be, except no flashy clothes and trendy haircuts and no fast cars and no speedboats. But real live blood all over the fucking place. Over fifty fucking bucks, you dumb punk.' The detective had slammed the kid's head down with each word of the final sentence, keeping time with the sentiment.

'And you don't look like Don Johnson,' Walter Robinson said.

The detective, a young man, smiled and shrugged. 'But hey, I'm trying.'

The teenager went limp. The two detectives pulled him to his feet, and the kid snarled. 'Fuck you, cop,' he said again. He leaned his head back as a bright stream of blood ran down over his lips and chin. 'You broke my fucking nose!' he whined. 'Motherfuckers!'

'No, we didn't,' the younger detective answered calmly. 'The floor did.'

'Fuck you,' the kid repeated as the older detective laughed at the younger's disingenuous statement.

'Can't you come up with something original, asshole?' the older of the detectives complained sarcastically. 'I mean, punk, don't you figure we've had enough people telling us to go fuck ourselves like almost every minute or at the very least every hour, on the hour, every fucking day, like so much that it don't mean a helluva lot to us anymore? I mean, it just doesn't cut it, insultwise. Like sticks and stones can break my bones, you know, that sort of thing. So, how about something clever. Show off that intelligence of yours. Be original, punk. Say something that will really piss us off. Give us that satisfaction, at least.'

'Fuck you,' the surprised teenager replied.

The older detective turned to Walter Robinson. 'Makes you wonder about the younger generation, doesn't it, Walt?' He grinned. 'Too much television. Kills the mind. Too much loud music. Dulls the senses. Right, punk?'

'Fuck you,' the kid repeated sluggishly.

'See what I mean?' the detective said. He gave the teenager's arms another jerk and twist.

'Owww!' the kid yelled. 'Fuck you. I'm gonna do juvie time anyway, asshole.'

'For first fucking degree murder? No way, punk,' the detective said. He started to half shove, half pull the suspect down the corridor, toward the elevator that would transport them to the lockup, where the teenager would stew for a few hours, while the inevitable stack of paperwork was completed.

The second detective paused next to Robinson and dusted the residue from the small struggle off his suit. As he swept his hands across the fabric, he whispered, 'Fucking kid is probably right. The kid he shot is in a coma but probably will pull through, although he ain't gonna have a real excellent life from now on, and we'll have to lower the charges to attempted homicide and assault with a deadly. What a world, huh, Walt? Shoot somebody over a measly fifty bucks worth of rock and end up with some judge saying "Naughty, naughty, please don't do it again . . ." Ah, well, we'll give it a shot. Try to persuade them to treat him like an adult. Except he's just barely sixteen. Shit.

Sixteen going on twenty-six.' Then, without waiting for a response, hurried after his partner and the suspect.

Walter Robinson watched the trio move out of his sight, and thought: *This I understand.* In his world, a baby left alone and falling from a windowsill, a teenager who attempts murder and expects to get away with it – these were the events of every day. There was nothing shocking, nothing unique, nothing even remotely exceptional about these crimes. They just happened. Tomorrow there would be other crimes, just like them. The detective's eyes fastened on the door to the interview room, where the two old survivors and an ancient policeman waited for him to return with coffee so they could continue telling a tale of a hatred and evil so virulent that he was having trouble imagining it. He realized that there was not one word of what they had told him that he could grasp hold of with any familiarity. All he knew was that he'd been plunged into a system of murder that even unsettled him, and he wondered for a moment whether or not there wasn't a Shadow Man that lurked on the edges of everyone's history, somewhere.

He asked himself suddenly: How do you find a criminal who is not a criminal like any other?

Good question, he thought. He did not know that Simon Winter had posed the identical question of himself days earlier.

How do you find this man?

Find his mistake. He's made one somewhere.

How do you find his mistake?

Figure him out. Understand the Shadow Man, and you'll see where he made an error.

Understand? What sort of man hates the way he does?

This question made Walter Robinson breathe out sharply. He did not know the answer, but suspected the old people waiting in the room could show him.

He shook his head. You're thinking too much, he told himself. He tried to shrug it all off. He hurried toward his own desk. He knew there was a telephone call he very much wanted to make.

Espy Martinez grabbed the telephone receiver before the first ring had been completed. 'Yes?'

'Espy . . .'

'Walter, Jesus, I've been trying to reach you.'

'I know. I'm sorry. I was at a crime scene, and now I've got these people in an interview room.'

He stopped there, and both of them were silent for a moment.

'I wanted to talk to you,' he said. 'I just wanted to talk.'

She laughed, relief in her voice. 'That would be nice, you know. Just to talk about you and me. Us. Or maybe the weather . . .'

'It's goddamn hot . . .'

'Or how about sports? Are the Dolphins going to win the pennant?'

He grinned. 'Good idea, but wrong sport.'

'Okay, how about the future?'

'Our future? Or Leroy Jefferson's?'

'Good question. Leroy fucking Jefferson.'

Walter Robinson smiled. 'You're beginning to sound like a cop. Maybe we should just call him Leroy F. Jefferson. Or F. Leroy Jefferson, if you want to make it sound classier.'

She shook her head. 'It's inevitable, I guess. Business first. I went to see Alter and his delightful client. What a sweet guy, Mr Jefferson. Outgoing. Pleasant. Gives one a real sense of optimism about the world we live in.'

'That bad, huh?'

'Well guess what? You know what he is? Leroy fucking Jefferson, the *eyewitness*.'

'He saw the murder? He was there?'

'Yeah. And then like the good citizen he aspires to be, he immediately robbed poor Sophie Millstein. Her body wasn't even cold.'

'Jesus Christ what a—'

'No kidding. The problem is, the killer was—'

'An old white guy,' Robinson blurted.

'How did you—'

'I think,' Robinson said slowly, 'that you better come over here and listen to the people I've got in the interview room.'

'How did— I'm not sure I get it. But I'll be right over.'

'There was an old-timer at the scene that night. Sophie's neighbor. He told me that she was scared. Scared of someone she knew fifty years ago. Fifty years and in another world. And I just goddamn ignored him then, instead of paying attention. So, after we got the lie detector report, I came back here and went over my notes and saw his name and, well, it's pretty far out, but maybe, just maybe, she had reason to be scared. Damn it!'

'What?'

'It's not the first damn rule of being a homicide detective, but it damn well ought to be.'

'What's that?'

'Listen to everyone, and don't discard anything, just because it doesn't seem to fit right away, because maybe it will before everything is over.'

Martinez felt a surge of excitement. 'Do you think maybe you have a lead. Something good? I'd love to tell Alter and Jefferson to get lost.'

'Don't get your hopes up, Espy. What we've got are some scared old people and maybe a killer like none I've ever heard of. Like nobody's ever heard of.'

He stopped there, hesitating, his mind churning. Then he added, 'But if Leroy fucking Jefferson saw him, damn, that's something. That's something we can use.'

Espy Martinez rose at her desk. 'All right, I'm on my way.'

'Great. Hurry. These old folks might start getting worn-out.'

'And afterward . . .'

Walter Robinson smiled, and the tone of his voice lifted slightly. 'Well, afterward, we can go discuss the case, or whatever you want. Although, I seem to recall that the last time we discussed the case, things were, well, pretty damn convivial. But if you want to talk about the weather, well, hell, let's see where that leads us.'

Martinez flushed and grinned. She hung up the telephone, stuffed some papers in her briefcase, and hurried from her office. It was late, and there were only a few prosecutors and secretaries left about. She bounded down the stalled escalators in the Justice Building, passing empty, darkened courtrooms, waving at the guard by the front doors, who hardly looked up from his copy of *Penthouse*, so intent was he on the breasts and genitals exposed on the glossy pages that he looked for all the world like a student cramming for an exam. Outside, the night air was thick with heat, lustrous with city lights that delivered glowing illumination. Her eagerness overcame her usual unsettled fear; she rushed for her car with a determination and desire, feeling as if she was heading toward, if not solutions, at least the beginnings of some answers to a wide variety of questions.

Simon Winter kept his mouth shut and watched as the rabbi and Frieda Kroner patiently repeated their story for the young woman from the prosecutor's office. He noticed a glance or two, shared between Espy Martinez and Walter Robinson, and suspected there was more there than professional friendship, but he did not really concern himself with this, other than to note inwardly that Espy Martinez seemed every bit as beautiful as his landlord's daughter, and this made him slightly envious. As for himself, he contributed as little as possible.

When Herman Stein's death came up, both the old survivors turned to him, and he realized he was supposed to say something, so he did: 'Stein was murdered.'

Walter Robinson shook his head just slightly. 'A closed-door suicide?'

'He misspelled his wife's name.'

'But surely he was tense, depressed, anxious. . . .' Espy Martinez interrupted.

Winter looked at her, searching her face with his eyes, examining the curve in her brows, the shape of her eyes, looking for signs of something other than youth and inexperience. 'Yes, he was those things.'

'And you don't think that could have caused him to make a mistake?'

'Not in a million years. Not that mistake.'

Martinez shot a quick glance over at Robinson. But he had leaned back in his chair, lowering his chin to his chest in thought, but still staring right at Simon Winter.

'Walter?' she asked. 'What do you think?'

'I think people make mistakes all the time,' he said slowly. 'But I don't think the mistake on that note was made by Herman Stein, unless he meant to.'

Frieda Kroner immediately slapped her hand hard on the wooden surface of the table in the interview room. It made a sound like a pistol shot. 'Ach! I told you so! So, you believe, do you Mr Young Detective?

So now you are beginning to see?'

'I'm still here,' Robinson replied quietly. 'I'm still listening.' But inwardly, Walter Robinson was churning, filled with an abrupt, torrential surge of anxiety. For a moment he tried to concentrate on the two old people, masking the surge of suspicion within him, but this was difficult as his imagination began to fill with an unsettling, eerie dread. He worked hard to stifle this concern, thrusting it aside for the moment, knowing that he would revisit it before long.

'I know what you're thinking,' Winter said quietly. 'It has just occurred to me as well.'

Robinson turned to the ancient detective and measured the look on his face. There was no doubt in his mind that Winter was correct. He had been struck by the same horrific thought at the same moment. Robinson nodded to the elder man, like forging a link or grasping each other's hand and shaking, as if an agreement had just been struck between the two of them.

'What are you saying?' Espy Martinez asked.

'I'll explain later,' Robinson replied. 'Please,' he gestured toward the rabbi and Frieda Kroner. 'Please continue.'

But the rabbi held up his hand. 'There is something? Something different?' He quickly looked over at Winter. 'Something has just taken place, and I want to know what it is.'

For a moment everyone in the room was silent.

From somewhere else in the police headquarters came the noise of shouting, momentarily overcoming the soundproofing, but it receded quickly. The rabbi folded his arms across his chest, awaiting an answer to his question. Frieda Kroner saw him do this and once again she slapped the wooden tabletop.

'Mr Winter, Detective Robinson, what is it?' she demanded. 'I may be old, but I am not like a child to be told little lies and have things hidden from me because of who I am. So please, if this is something to do with poor Sophie or Mr Stein and now my dear Irving, please, you are to tell me now!'

'Frieda is absolutely right,' Rabbi Rubinstein said sharply. 'You have seen something. Perhaps a little light on the Shadow? I hope . . . .'

Simon Winter shook his head. 'No. Nothing this fortunate.' He looked over at Walter Robinson and then at Espy Martinez, who had a look of confusion on her face.

'Walter, what the hell's going on?' she asked. 'Did I miss something?'

Robinson shrugged and smiled, but not at anything even the slightest bit amusing. 'It was simply a detective's thing. A click, you know. An observation. A worry. Mr Winter and I . . .'

'. . . saw the same thing at the same time,' Winter said, completing his sentence.

'And what was it that you saw?' Rabbi Rubinstein questioned.

The old detective and the young detective shared a quick glance. Then Winter turned to the rabbi and Mrs Kroner. 'I apologize. I should have seen this from the start. I am not as sharp as I once was. I'm sorry.'

The rabbi made a quick, impatient gesture. 'Mr Winter, what is it?'

'Herman Stein dies in a locked room. Sophie dies, and the police immediately go searching for the junkie that killed her. Irving Silver disappears into the ocean, or so it appears. And we think you two will be next. But it occurs to Detective Robinson all of a sudden – and this, Mrs Kroner, is what makes him shift about in his seat and maybe feel a little sweat on the back of his neck and a little twinge in the bottom of his stomach – it occurs to him that maybe, just maybe, Herman Stein wasn't the first. Am I right, Detective?'

Walter Robinson slowly nodded in agreement. 'You're doing fine,' he said softly.

Espy Martinez inadvertently lifted her hand to her mouth, covering it in surprise, unaware that she had made this motion like a hundred Hollywood actresses.

Frieda Kroner's face seemed to collapse.

Rabbi Rubinstein slid back in his chair, as if pushing himself back from the table, away from what Simon Winter was saying.

'You see,' Winter continued, 'what the detective thought was this: *Why is this man starting to murder now?* And the obvious answer is: *He isn't.*'

Winter looked around at the others, finally resting on the two other old people. 'Do you think perhaps that you are the last remaining Berliners that know of the Shadow Man? Or could there be others, that you do not know about? Do you think maybe there were once twenty? A hundred and twenty? A thousand and twenty? How many survived the basement? The train transport? Then survived the camps? Then found their way through the maze to the world here? How many people may have caught a glimpse of him, in an alley, at Gestapo headquarters, on a tram or in a shelter when the bombs were falling? Do you not think that he has spent every waking moment since the last bullet was shot and the last fire of the war doused, thinking of all those faces, frightened that this one or that one will be the person who rises up and exposes him? And what would that make him do?'

The others remained quiet, unwilling to put words to this question.

Simon Winter turned to Walter Robinson. 'Does that pretty much sum up what you thought?'

He nodded. 'Pretty much. Except it could be worse.'

'Worse?' Espy Martinez asked. 'How?'

'Accept for a moment that this Shadow Man exists and that he's killed maybe three times successfully. How many others? Over how many years? In how many places? Did he retire to Miami Beach last year? Or twenty-five years ago? Where has he been and how many people have lost their lives? We know nothing, except who he was once, fifty years ago, in Berlin, in the middle of a war, and even then, we have no name, no identification, no fingerprints or identifying marks. We have only these people's recollections. Recollections based on terror and a momentary glimpse of someone when they were little more than children themselves. How do you connect the present to the past?'

Espy Martinez took a deep breath. 'I know how,' she said quietly.

The others all swiveled and looked at her.

'Mr Leroy fucking Jefferson,' she said.

It took several moments for Frieda Kroner to respond: 'This is an unusual name for a person to have. . . .' And Espy Martinez realized that she had automatically attached the obscenity to the suspect's name without considering the more delicate ears of the older people, who did not use the word *fuck* with the same constancy as virtually everyone connected to the criminal justice system. She immediately apologized.

'I'm sorry, Mrs Kroner. Leroy Jefferson is the man Detective Robinson originally charged with Sophie Millstein's murder. Apparently he was at her apartment – or just outside it – and witnessed this Shadow Man enter and commit the crime.'

'So,' the rabbi said slowly, 'this man can tell us what the Shadow Man looks like today. He can describe him?'

'Yes. I believe so.'

'Identikit,' Winter said. 'A police artist could work with him and come up with something current. That would be a start. Can he provide other information? A license plate maybe?'

'I don't know,' Martinez replied. 'Not yet. The price of Mr Jefferson's cooperation is high.'

'How high?' Robinson interrupted.

'He wants to walk.'

'Shit!' the detective muttered.

'Walk?' Frieda Kroner asked. 'He is crippled?'

'What he wants is to be released from pending charges. Freed.'

'Ahh, I see. And this is a problem?'

Espy Martinez nodded. 'He shot and wounded a policeman.'

'He must be an awful man to do such a thing,' she said.

'Indeed,' Martinez replied.

Simon Winter was thinking quickly. 'If we had a good picture, you know, something reasonably close . . .'

Martinez turned to him. 'Yes? With that picture what?'

'Well, first off, it would go a long ways toward helping the rabbi and Mrs Kroner. It would help them to be prepared. They wouldn't be sitting around waiting to recognize some man they only saw for seconds fifty years ago. They would know what the man stalking them looks like. That would be an immense advantage. Help level the playing field.'

'This is true,' Mrs Kroner said. 'We would not be so vulnerable.'

'But more, it gives me an idea or two.'

'I think I know what you're thinking,' Walter Robinson said slowly. 'You're thinking that there is one thing in the entire world that this man is frightened of, and makes him act quickly, and one thing only: losing his anonymity. Correct?'

Simon Winter nodded and smiled. 'We seem to think alike.'

'And,' Robinson continued, 'if we can threaten that anonymity, then perhaps we can do something else.'

'What would that be?' Rabbi Rubinstein asked quickly.

Simon Winter answered coldly for the both of them. 'Set a trap.'

CHAPTER EIGHTEEN

Playing the Hand That's Dealt

The Lumberjack lived in a modest three-bed, two-bath house on a quiet cul-de-sac in North Miami, a suburban neighborhood where every other house had a powerboat on a trailer parked by the side, and where the residents lived from barbecue to barbecue, weekend to weekend. It was clean, kept up, a place where policemen and firemen and city workers spent their money in sturdy, stolid pursuit of upward mobility in single-story, cinder-block homes with small, in-ground pools in the rear. The rooftops were flat white or red tile. Lawns were mowed, hedges trimmed. The late-model four-wheel-drive trucks that towed all the powerboats to the water some three or four miles away were all polished brightly, glistening in the midday sun.

An occasional dog barked, as Walter Robinson rolled slowly down the street, looking for the Lumberjack's address. He assumed that the dogs were barking at his skin; no blacks in this neighborhood, he thought. Just the mixing of white and Hispanic that has a certain inevitability in Dade County. The middle-class blacks in the same economic sphere as the Lumberjack tended to bunch together in their own neighborhoods, where there weren't quite as many shade trees, or books for the elementary school library, where there were a few more brown spots on the lawns, and bank loans were a little harder to come by. These neighborhoods were always a little closer to Liberty City or Overtown, a little closer to the edges of poverty. He had an odd thought as he pulled in front of the Lumberjack's house. He remembered all the early explorers who set out for the New World overcoming their fear that the world was flat and that they would sail off the rim into oblivion. This was the sort of historical information that his mother, the dutiful teacher, would speak of over dinner, when she wasn't patiently but insistently correcting his table manners. They were wrong, he thought. The world is round. But it is the people in it who manufacture the edges, making it frighteningly easy to sail off the brink, where there are still monsters waiting eagerly to swallow you up.

Heat like an angry complaint greeted him as he stepped from his car. The walkway to the Lumberjack's house glowed, filmy air hovering just above the cement. He saw a wooden swing set around one side of the house, and in front there was a small collection of bicycles and tricycles abandoned by the garage door. Across the street a middle-aged woman, wearing cut-off Mickey Mouse jeans and a T-shirt was cutting the lawn. She stopped, shutting off the mower, as he stepped from the car. He could feel her eyes tracking him as he approached the house.

He rang the bell and waited, hearing a set of harried footsteps after a moment or two. The door swung open and a young woman stared out. She wore baggy long shorts and a bathing suit top and had her dark hair pinned back sharply. A baby clutching a bottle was draped on her hip.

'Yes?'

'I'm Detective Robinson. Can I see your husband?'

She hesitated, without smiling. 'He's still in some pain,' she said.

'I need to see him,' Robinson repeated.

'He needs to rest,' she whispered.

Before he could reply, a voice bellowed from within the house: 'Honey, who is it?'

The Lumberjack's wife seemed to want to close the door, but instead, she swung it open, calling out at the same time, 'It's Detective Robinson, here to see you.' She jerked her head toward the rear of the house, and Robinson stepped in. He saw immediately that, for a house with small children, it was extremely neat. There were trimmed plants in an étagère, no toys underfoot. In the entranceway there was a large crucifix hanging over a blessing. He passed the expected wall decorations: framed photographs of babies and parents, a selection of posters advertising forgettable art shows.

One thing surprised him as he entered the living room. On the wall above the matching sofa and love-seat set was a large, brightly colored painting, realism in the primitive Haitian school, obviously painted by someone with little education and great talent. It was a marketplace scene, great splashes of vibrant color interrupted by the resonant blacks of the faces of the country people populating the market. It was striking, fascinating in a way, because it pulled him momentarily into that small world, as if allowing him to sense a little bit of the story of each character on the canvas. He stared at it, astonished to see it in the Lumberjack's home. He had seen many of these paintings, usually hanging in the trendier art galleries in the rich sections of South Miami and Coral Gables. They had an odd attraction for the wealthy; a combination of something native and something articulate; the better examples of art from the impoverished Caribbean country were destined for the walls of the million-dollar homes overlooking Biscayne Bay.

'Kinda different, huh?' the Lumberjack said quietly. He had entered the room from a side door.

Walter Robinson turned away. 'It's a nice piece,' he said.

'Wouldn't have expected it here, huh?'

'No,' Robinson said slowly.

'My wife was an art student a couple of centuries ago, like before kids and mortgages and all that, and she picked it up on a trip down there. Never could understand why anyone would want to go to Haiti on vacation, you know? Just a lot of people getting poorer every second of the day. That's why they're forever trying to come over here.'

'Coast Guard cutter stopped another boatload just off Key Biscayne the other day,' Robinson said.

'Well, there you have it,' the Lumberjack replied. 'Anyway, the wife hauls that sucker around, everywhere she went, always saying someday it'd be worth something. You know what? Sucker would go for ten, maybe fifteen grand now. Best investment we ever made, even if it is kinda strange hanging there. I got to insure it. Hell, I'd rather have a new Aquasport twenty-footer. But, hey, you get used to everything after a while.'

'I suppose so.'

'Well, what do I know? Kinda ironic, though, isn't it?'

'Why's that?'

'Well, hell, some poor sucker painted that thing and maybe got a few bucks for it, maybe enough for a meal or a new chicken or a tank of gas or something. But that's it. And his painting, well, it makes it all the way here to the States, nice and easy. He'd probably be willing to die to get here, just like so many of those poor suckers. And you know the damn painting's worth more than he ever will be. Now, that's irony, huh?'

'Yes. It is.'

'Hell, you can bet those paintings don't got to come across the ocean in some handmade, falling-apart boat that's more likely to sink fifty miles from shore than it is to land on Miami Beach, huh?'

The Lumberjack turned and settled gingerly into an easy chair.

'You an art lover, Walter?'

'It's an interest of mine.'

'Never did much for me. But hey, what do I know? The wife usta take me to shows and such. I learned to keep my mouth shut. Just stand around, nod, drink the imported fizzy water, and eat the hors d'oeuvres. Agree with everybody. Easier that way, especially when you don't know shit.'

His arm was still encased in a case that rose up to his neck. The cast forced the arm out ninety degrees from his body, so that the Lumberjack looked like a particularly gangly bird, hopping about with a broken wing.

He grimaced as he shifted position.

'Sucker still hurts,' he said.

'What's the word?'

'No more fucking surgery, thank goodness. Four months trussed up like a fucking puppet, then maybe six, eight months rehab. Then, maybe, just maybe, back on the job. But it's dicey, you know? No one really knows what the fucking arm will do until we try to do it.'

'How're you doing?'

'Wife going crazy with me around. Kids getting a bit tired of it too. I mean, I'm like a fucking kid myself. Can't drive anywheres. Can't do much of anything. Watching a lot of television. What the hell do people see in those soaps anyway?'

Walter Robinson didn't answer, and the Lumberjack smiled. 'Going a little crazy myself,' he added.

The Lumberjack leaned back, then squirmed around.

'Can't fucking get comfortable,' he said. After a few seconds spent shifting position, he looked across the room and one eyebrow arched up. 'So, Walter, you didn't drive all the way out here just to see how I was doing, did you? I mean, that would have been okay, if you did, but hey, we weren't big buddies or anything, so I'm thinking there has to be some other reason, right?'

Robinson nodded his head, just as the Lumberjack's wife came into the room. 'Baby's napping,' she said. 'Thank the Lord. Don't make a sound for an hour or so.' She looked over at Robinson, as if she were expecting him to start singing or dancing.

'There's a problem with the case against Leroy Jefferson. I just wanted you to hear it from me instead of someone else.'

'Problem?' asked the wife.

'What sort of fucking problem?' the Lumberjack asked, his voice cramping into a demanding guttural sound.

'Jefferson has been cleared as a suspect in that old woman's murder. But he can provide substantial information in that case, and in perhaps two other homicides. Very substantial information.'

'What are you saying?'

'I'm saying he's about to get a deal.'

'Fuck! What sort of deal? I'll tell you the deal that motherfucker ought to get! I'd like to take my revolver and shove it right up his ass and pull the trigger. That's the deal I'd give the bastard.'

'You're going to wake up the baby,' the wife said softly. The Lumberjack stared over at her. He opened his mouth, but stopped before words came out. He turned back to Walter Robinson. His eyes had narrowed.

'Tell me what you're saying?' he demanded again.

'I'm saying he may walk in return for cooperation.'

The Lumberjack slammed back in the seat, and Robinson knew the motion must have sent rivets of pain through his arm. The policeman snarled, and a sound like a mean dog slowly slid between his teeth.

'He's going to shoot me and get away with it?'

'We're trying to squeeze him. Going to dangle lessers in front of him, see if he'll do some time—' Robinson stopped abruptly as he saw a dark glare form on the Lumberjack's face. 'But you know the deal. You know the priorities. You know the way this works.'

'Yes. Fuck, though, I never thought it'd be me getting screwed.'

The Lumberjack hissed breath out slowly.

'I don't think I like it. Not one little fucking bit. And I don't think it'd go down real sweet with the rest of the fucking department. I mean, cops are generally unhappy when other cops get shot, right, Walter? I don't think the rest of the department's gonna be too pleased when the shooter takes a hike, courtesy of the fucking state attorney.'

'He's gonna clear a homicide. He's gonna help us take a real bad guy off the street.'

'Yeah, and put another one out there,' the Lumberjack replied.

Walter Robinson was uncomfortable answering this. It was fundamentally true.

'I'm sorry,' he said. 'I just thought you'd want to hear it from me.'

'Yeah, well, thanks a whole fucking lot.' The Lumberjack turned away momentarily, then swiveled his head quickly, staring hard at Robinson. 'This your deal, Walter? This your idea?'

Robinson paused before replying. He thought abruptly of the rabbi and Frieda Kroner, and then had a sudden, chilling vision of the Shadow Man himself, stalking them. Then, just as swiftly, he thought of Espy Martinez, and he knew he didn't want the Lumberjack's anger and resentment poured out all over her, so he gritted his teeth and answered: 'Yeah. Sure. It's my deal.'

'Gonna clear some cases, huh? Maybe make your fucking star rise a bit, right? Gonna get one of those department commendations, maybe a promotion, huh? Lead the pack in homicide with cleared cases. Maybe get the fucking newspapers to write you up. The new, black star on the Beach, right?'

Robinson tried to ignore the racial comment. 'No. Maybe going to keep someone from killing again. That's the deal.'

'Sure,' the Lumberjack said sarcastically. 'Sure. And you don't give a damn that it gets you ahead.'

'You're wrong.'

'Sure I am,' the policeman said. 'Took me nine years in uniform to get my gold shield, then I get stuck in robbery and car theft for another three years. How's that for affirmative action? How long did it take you, Walter? And you went straight to fucking homicide. Big-time move, Walter. No time in the trenches for you, huh? And now I may never work again, thanks a lot.'

Both men were silent. The Lumberjack seemed to be chewing something. 'You do what you've got to do,' he said. 'That's the territory. I understand. Do what you have to.'

Walter Robinson rose. 'Okay,' he said. 'Thanks.'

'And I'll do what I have to do,' the Lumberjack replied.

Robinson stopped. 'What do you mean by that?'

'Nothing. Not a single fucking thing. Now get out.'

'What did you mean?'

'I told you. Not a fucking thing. Door's that way.'

He wanted to say something else, but couldn't. He stepped out of the living room and reached the front door. As he swung it open, the Lumberjack's wife came up behind him.

'Detective?' she said quietly.

He turned. 'Yes.'

'It was your arrest he agreed to help out on. Your plan. And you almost got him killed. He may be disabled forever thanks to you. And now you're going to let the slimeball who did it go free? I hope you rot in Hell, Detective.' She said the word *Detective*, but he suspected within the anger that flared in her eyes, the Lumberjack's wife had an altogether different word in mind. He wondered why she didn't use it.

'Get out of my house,' she said. He thought he heard a rolling *n* sound stopped at the end of her sentence, as if she were battling to avoid the racial epithet. But then, he thought abruptly, maybe he was wrong. Maybe she was only furious and she didn't have the slightest intention of calling him a name. Maybe she never noticed that she lived in a world that was both as segregated and frightened of blacks as any pre-Civil War plantation. Maybe, but he doubted it. He thought that this was the nature of Miami; it is a place where people think *nigger* but won't say it out loud. He was instantly overcome by the need to get out, get away, get back to his job. He simply nodded, stepping out of the cool central air-conditioning, into the unrelenting midday, summer heat, feeling as if he'd somehow tracked dirt into the spotless home. As she slammed the door behind him, he heard the clamor of the baby awakening with tears.

Espy Martinez hated the sound of glee that Tommy Alter was unable to conceal in his voice.

'Knew you'd come to reason, Espy,' he said.

'No, Tommy, that's incorrect. It's expediency. Not reason.'

The two of them were sitting in a corner of the cafeteria at the Justice Building. Untouched coffee steamed from cups in front of them. A few other prosecutors and public defenders occupied other tables, rarely mingling, and when they did come together, generally it was either to trade insults, challenges, or rivet together an arrangement, just as Martinez and Alter were doing. These other attorneys would glance over at the two of them occasionally, but through tacit understanding of the process, no one sat at the closest tables, creating a buffer zone about them.

'Well, whatever you want to call it. What's the offer?'

'He's got to do some time, Tommy. He can't shoot a police officer and walk away from it.'

'Why not? Police arrive to arrest him for something he didn't do. They're the ones smashing down his door, waving their weapons. He's lucky he didn't get shot then. He's lucky *you* didn't kill him for something he didn't do. Seems to me you guys ought to be apologizing to him.'

'He witnessed a murder and then robbed the victim. Somehow, I don't think apologies would be completely appropriate.'

'Well, no time, that's our position. He'll take probationary time, if you want. Plead to some lessers. Burglary. Assault. But he isn't going upstate. Not after helping you folks find a killer. Maybe even stopping someone before they kill again.'

Espy Martinez inhaled sharply. 'What are you saying, Tommy? Kill again? What has he said to you? Do you know something?'

'Did I touch a nerve there, Espy? No, I can't say I know anything for certain. Just speculating, you know. Figure that there had to be a reason that old woman got killed, and maybe that same reason will apply to someone else. Just a guess.'

Martinez hesitated and Alter smiled.

'You're going to get what you want, Espy. A real, live witness. It may not be the best deal in the world, but it isn't the worst deal that's ever been made in this building.'

'He assists completely. Full statement. Description. Works with the artist. Does just anything that Walter Robinson asks him to do, and then he's available for a trial and he testifies truthfully when called. Got that? Any failure to appear, any reluctance, any false or misleading statement, any unexplained absence, any goddamn slip of the tongue, and he goes away. A long trip for a long time, got it, Tommy?'

'That's acceptable. Shall we shake on it?'

'I don't want to shake your hand, Tommy.'

He laughed. 'Somehow, I didn't think so. Relax, Espy. He'll help you bring your man in, and then think what a fucking hero you're gonna be. Just keep that in mind when we go to the judge. I'll make sure it's on his docket for the morning. They can bring Jefferson over early. He's just graduated to a wheelchair.'

Espy Martinez nodded. 'I want to do this during his regular calendar call – as quietly as possible. Just a quick plea colloquy and then out he goes with the detective.'

Alter smiled and rose. 'Sure. Makes sense to me.'

'We have to maintain the integrity of the investigation.'

'What a nice, important-sounding phrase that is. Sure you do.'

'Tommy, don't get me angrier than I already am.'

'Now, why would I want to do that?' he asked. He didn't wait for an answer. Instead he turned away and started across the cafeteria. Martinez saw him make a fist and punch the air in satisfaction. She tried to keep in mind the two old people on the Beach, trying to persuade herself that what she was doing verged on the medicinal; it would keep them alive.

There was one lanky teenager who appeared to have a little more quickness and a little more lift, and when the ball was in his hands, he seemed to move effortlessly toward the basket. From his seat on a bench, just inside the chain-link fence, Simon Winter watched as the teenager dominated the game, sliding remorselessly past bigger players.

He thought: I was like that once.

And then, smiling, he tried to envision what he would have done to stop the teenager. This was technical thinking, the language of precision placed within the fluid context of the basketball court, and he realized that indulging in these fantasies was like fulfilling a child's need for candy; not altogether necessary for life, but something that delivers a momentary pleasure. He studied the teenager carefully. The young man was tall, nearly six-four, but that would still have given Simon Winter a slight height advantage. First rule, he told himself, deny him the ball. Beat him to that spot at the top of the key where he likes to receive the pass, then don't let him turn and square up to the basket. Make him get the ball on the wing, where he has a little less room to maneuver. Force him onto his left hand – he seems to be less confident in that direction – and when he pulls up for the jump shot, he doesn't seem to rise as swiftly. Take away the baseline, so he can't bring it around to his right. Insist he settle for that drop-step, fadeaway jumper, Winter concluded. He will make some, but most will rim out. Keep your feet moving and make him work hard for everything he gets and eventually he will slow down and start searching for a pass, and when that happens, you know you will have done your job.

Winter nodded and smiled. Playing the game in his head always resulted in the same thing: victory.

On the court before him, Winter saw the teenager knife between two defenders and deposit the ball with a gentle, soft touch. He thought to himself: the young man knows how to play. A smashing, backboard-rattling dunk may be impressive, but the real players recognize and admire the move that gets one there, not the result.

'Is this your game, Mr Winter?'

Simon Winter pivoted in his seat at the sound of the voice. 'It was once, Detective.'

Walter Robinson slid onto the bench next to him. 'Not me,' he said. 'I wouldn't play the game. It was always what everyone expected: you're black, athletic – surely you must play basketball. Instead, I played a little high school football. I was a tight end on a real good team. Won the city championship.'

'That must have been nice.'

'Probably the best day you could ever have. Seventeen, going on eighteen, walking off the field bloody, dazed, and exhausted, but the winners. Nothing like it, ever again. Has a sort of purity to it.'

'Were you good, Detective?'

'Not bad. Not bad at all. But not nearly big enough to play the position in college. Tight end is an odd job, Mr Winter. Most of the time you're fighting it out on the line, smashing linebackers, defensive ends, another drone defending the glory boys at running back and quarterback. But every so often, kinda like a reward for all that hard work, you're cut loose downfield, and you explode out into the secondary, finally on your own, and the ball is zipping your way. There's always this great moment, defenders surrounding you, ball heading toward your hands, that you realize it's up to you. If you drop it, it's back to the salt mines. Back to being the worker bee. But catch that ball and you're free to do what you want, make of it what you can. Those were the moments I liked.'

'There is poetry in sport,' Winter said, smiling.

'And metaphor as well,' Robinson added.

'How did you find me here?'

'The Kadoshes. They told me you liked to come down here to the park after dark and watch the basketball games.'

'I didn't think they were that observant.'

Robinson grinned and Winter shrugged, adding, 'Of course. You're right. Lesson one: The neighbors always know more than they let on. There you have it. So, that explains how you found me. Now the question is why?'

'Because Leroy Jefferson goes to court tomorrow morning and by noon will be sitting next to a police artist, giving us a description and a statement, and once we have that, then we must take the next step.'

'Baiting the trap.'

'Exactly.'

'I think we must be very cautious,' Simon Winter said.

'Yes. Why?'

'Because, Detective, we are in an extremely vulnerable position.'

Walter Robinson nodded. 'Go on,' he said.

'We must find this man. We must find him this time. We have this one chance and we can't screw it up.'

'Keep going,' the detective said.

Simon Winter paused, watching the players pivot and weave on the court in front of him. The sodium vapor lights gave their skin a yellowish tone, almost as if the sweat and muscles were sickly and the struggle they made over the ball was against some odd disease.

'If we do not identify and stop the Shadow Man, if we merely spook him, he'll disappear. He can go anywhere. Be anything. If he slips past us, there is no telling where he will go. You see, we know nothing of his roots, of his history, not since the end of the war. So we know nothing of his resources. How do you pursue someone without substance? Do you think he'll leave behind a trail that we could follow? I doubt it. Not if he's reached this point after so many years. So I think we should assume that this man Leroy Jefferson is going to provide us with our one and best hope. We must get him this time.'

'You've been thinking about this?'

Winter nodded, then looked over at Robinson.

'As have you. In fact, I bet that's why you came tonight to see me.'

Robinson extended his feet and stretched backward, relaxing. 'You had quite a reputation in the City of Miami department.'

'You pulled my service record?'

'Of course. Wanted to know who I was dealing with.'

'That's all crap, you know. Solved this case. Made this arrest. Received this commendation. Doesn't tell you about who I am.'

'No, that's true. So, who are you, Mr Winter?'

Simon Winter paused. Then he pointed out at the game. 'See the kid with the ball?'

Walter Robinson nodded. 'The kid draining the twenty-footers?'

'Yes. That one.'

'Uh-huh. What about him?'

'He wouldn't score like that on me.'

Robinson started to laugh, then stopped, and instead he watched the teenager play, saw the quickness in his first step, saw the burst of speed as he made a crossover dribble.

'Out muscle him?' he asked after a moment.

'No. Just start taking things away, one by one. And then, when he doesn't expect it, force him into the double-team. Catch him unawares. He'll turn the ball over.'

Robinson breathed out slowly. 'Difficult.'

'But the only way.'

'You're right.'

'That's how you think we should do it?'

'Yes. The trap must have a fine line. Invisible defense. The Shadow Man must think something is available to him. Success. But really he is doing what we want. Where we are waiting. That's how it must work.'

The two men were silent.

'The two old people, Rabbi Rubinstein and Frieda Kroner . . .'

'Don't worry about them. When the time comes, they will do what they have to.'

'I've put a squad car in front of each of their apartments twenty-four hours.'

'No. You have to take those away. We can't make him warier than he already is.'

'But what if—'

'They understand the risk. They're the bait, and they understand.'

'I don't like that.'

'How else would you do it?'

Walter Robinson paused. 'I still don't like it, much,' he said finally.

Winter smiled. 'You see, that's the advantage I have over you, Detective. I don't work for anyone. No City of Miami Beach paycheck for me. I don't have to worry about anything except succeeding. I don't have to worry about what it will look like in the papers or to my superiors or anything. When I said we could set a trap, that's what I meant. And a trap requires bait. It has to be fresh and attractive and it always runs the risk of being eaten, doesn't it? That maybe the springs on the trap won't slam shut at precisely the correct moment, and maybe the quarry will race away after robbing the trap of bait. So, my recommendation to you, Detective, is that you play this very close to the vest. That your friend, Miss Martinez, and you keep this to yourselves. Then if it all goes wrong, you can blame it on me.'

'I wouldn't do that.'

'Sure you would. And it would be okay. I'm just a crazy old ex-cop, and it wouldn't bother me in the slightest. Hell, probably make my life more exciting.'

'I still wouldn't do it.'

'Why not? I'm old, Detective Robinson. And you know what? Nothing frightens me anymore. Got that? Nothing. Except maybe not catching this son of a bitch.'

Simon Winter smiled and applauded a nice shot on the court in front of them. 'I don't think I want this guy to outlive me.'

'I think you've got some good years left.'

The old man laughed out loud. 'Well, at least they are years, even if I wouldn't leap to characterize them as *good*.'

'All right. I'll pull the squad cars. What then?'

Winter's voice gained a certain coldness with his

response: 'Then we force him to make a move.'

'How did you imagine that going down?'

'Well, ordinarily, with a picture of a suspect, you'd be likely to flood the place with it. Get it on the television news and make the *Herald* run it on their front page. Post that picture everywhere, right? Hope maybe someone will make a call.'

'That's the standard drill.'

'Won't work with this guy, will it?'

'No,' Robinson said. 'Not from what I'm beginning to see. All that would do is make him take off.'

'Of course, if we scared him off, that might save Frieda Kroner and Rabbi Rubinstein. Scare him off and they might live out their lives in peace.'

'Always looking over their shoulder, expecting him back.'

'But alive.'

'True enough. But alive.'

Both men were quiet for a moment. The air around them was filled with the sounds of the game, voices raised, the slap of bodies coming together, the chain of the net rattling as the ball slipped through.

'So, we don't do what is standard,' Robinson said. 'What do we do?'

Winter smiled. 'I had an idea,' he said carefully. 'You see, *he* won't know that we have his picture, and he won't know that we're waiting for him. So what we do is very subtle. We *suggest* something. We do just enough to make him move rapidly, maybe before he is quite ready.'

'I follow. What sort of suggestion?'

'At services one evening, perhaps the local rabbis make references to, oh, say, the shadow that has fallen over the community. At the Holocaust Center, we post a sign requesting anyone with any knowledge of wartime Berlin to contact Rabbi Rubinstein. Maybe have that same announcement made at a few of the condo association meetings. Just enough so that the right words and sensations creep back to him and he thinks he must make a move. But not so much that he decides to flee.'

Walter Robinson nodded his head. 'This seems tricky,' he said quietly.

'Have you ever been on the flats off Key Biscayne, fishing for bonefish, Detective? It's a great sport. The fish are very skittish in shallow water, attuned to every sound and motion, anticipating threats. But they are hungry, and the flats are where they find the shrimp and small crabs they consider delicacies, so that is why they are there. The water is gray-blue, a hundred colors, changing with every breath of air, and the fish appear like the slightest small alteration in the color scheme. One writer once called them ghosts. You stare at the water for hours, and then, suddenly, you'll see that little motion, that minuscule departure in tone, that indicates a fish. Then you cast, and if you lay the fly just gently, a foot or so in front of that indistinct shape, you will hook a bonefish, which is something sportsmen all over the world look forward to.'

'I've heard that,' Walter Robinson replied.

'You should learn to fish, Detective,' Simon Winter said. 'It will help you understand, as it did for me.'

Robinson grinned in spite of an unsettled nervousness inside. 'When this is over, will you teach me?'

'It would be my pleasure.'

Robinson hesitated, before asking: 'This is like fishing?'

The older man smiled. 'Precisely.'

CHAPTER NINETEEN
The Cherub's Warning

The game had ended and Walter Robinson insisted that Simon Winter accompany him back to the Sunshine Arms. They rode through the nighttime world of downtown Miami Beach in the detective's unmarked cruiser. Winter kept glancing at the small computer unit attached to the center of the dashboard and finally said, with a small, wry grin:

'That damn thing really makes me feel old.'

He looked up, his eyes gathering in the street life they rolled past. The older detective sighed slowly.

'What?'

'You know, look at this. See what's happening?'

Robinson let his eyes rest on a tangle of white limousines and gleaming, dark luxury cars double-parked midway down the block outside a nightclub. The club had a large, two-story purple and red neon palm tree flashing above its front door. There was a crowd of people on the sidewalk, mostly young, white or Hispanic, upwardly mobile, early twenties. They were just out of college, newly minted with an MBA or a law degree, and searching for a little diversion on their way to their first big score. They mingled with the older but trying to appear young types. There was a smattering of a category that seemed unique to Miami, the drug-culture hangers on; young men in particular, who affected the airs of a *narcotrafficista*: gaudy shirt open to the waist, gold chain around the neck, fine linen suit, as if this successfully concealed the realities of their lives as clerks and accountants. It was like a masquerade, where everyone portrayed some exotic, wealthy, heartless Colombian hit man, which, of course, helped to hide the few but legitimate killers that were mixed amidst the crowd, in the same outfits. The women, for the most part, seemed to favor high, spiked heels and hair flounced into manes. They dressed in spangles and silks, peacocks as colorful as the sign that blinked above them. As Simon Winter and Walter Robinson slid past, the bass-heavy sound of rock and roll with a Latin accent shook the car.

'What do you see, old-timer?' Robinson used the word to poke fun at Winter, who recognized this immediately, and so replied in a fake-crotchety-old voice filled with wheezing and accented with pseudo-irritation.

'What I see is change, young fella. On one side of the street, the Broadway Delicatessen. Used to serve the best chicken soup on the Beach. Probably still does. Next to it, there's a grocery, where the old folks like me get fresh fruits and meats that haven't been collecting frostburn for a month. The sort of place where they know your name and if you're perhaps a little short of cash one week, will wait until the Social Security checks come in for you to pay.'

Simon Winter paused, then resumed, in his normal tone of voice: 'A year from now, maybe two, they won't be there, will they? You see, that nightclub is hot, and that means competition, and the space across the street suddenly has value, because – and you know this, Detective – a new dollar always seems to be worth more in our society than an old one.'

Robinson nodded. He let his eyes trail into the crowd outside the nightclub. He saw a bouncer muscling a rowdy client, a man dressed in a white suit that cost considerably more than a detective's weekly paycheck. He saw that Winter had seen the same scuffle.

'Too much cocaine. The problem with cocaine is it makes you do incredibly stupid things and makes you think you're incredibly smart to do them.'

Winter laughed. They continued driving, leaving the crowded sidewalk in the rearview mirror. Simon Winter gestured for Robinson to turn.

'Wrong direction,' the younger man said as he turned the wheel, obligingly.

'I just wanted to see something,' Winter said. In a moment they turned again, so that they were traveling adjacent to the beach, and beyond, to the ocean. 'Always liked this,' Winter said slowly. 'Older I get, the more I like it.'

'What's that?' Robinson was trying to drive and to stare past the older man, out at the great expanse of black sea.

'No matter how many hotels and nightclubs and condos we put up, the sea is always there. Can't do anything about it. Can't fill it in. Can't pave it over. That's what I like. Do you like the ocean, Detective?'

'When I was young, growing up, no, I hated it. But now I've changed.'

'Good.'

Robinson nodded, and turned the car again. Within a few minutes he had located the Sunshine Arms and pulled to a stop by the entranceway. Winter put his hand on the door handle, then hesitated.

'Do you think about the men you pursue, Detective?'

'Sometimes. But more often, they're an object rather than a personality. They're the culmination of a set of facts, or a series of observations. They're more like conclusions than people.'

'For me, the bad guys would get under the skin, you know? They would stop being a case file number, and become something very different. And then, there were always a couple that became special.'

'They stay with you?'

'Forever.'

'I don't know if I've ever had one like that.'

'How many open cases do you have?'

'Lost count, Mr Winter. They seem to pile up rapidly. And my clearance rate is ahead of all the other detectives in the bureau.'

Simon Winter shook his head. 'In my time, every homicide was something at least a little special.'

'Not anymore.'

'What do you think of the Shadow Man?'

'I don't know yet. It's hard to get a feel for him. I'll say this, though. He's got me a bit more antsy than any other case I've ever worked. You know how it is: usually you have a pretty damn good idea precisely what you're looking for, even if you don't have a name and a face to find. You know what sort of person it is. Character traits, psychology – whatever – it fits into the normal scheme of things. No surprises. This guy seems a little different.'

He paused, then corrected himself. 'No, a lot different.'

'Why are we hunting him, Walter?'

This was the first time Simon Winter used Robinson's first name, which the younger detective noted.

'Because we think he's killed one, two, maybe three or more times.'

'Serial killer?'

'Well, not exactly. He sure as hell doesn't fit any FBI profile I've ever seen. But multiple homicides. Isn't that a good enough reason?'

'It's a good reason, but the wrong one.'

'Want to run that by me again?'

'It's the wrong reason. You're here because this is your job. To serve and protect. I'm here because he's killed my neighbor, and that makes me feel a debt, and because he may kill these other people, whom I cannot even consider friends, but whom I've made some promises to. But those aren't really good reasons, any more than yours are. I don't think you or I, or your pretty friend in the State Attorney's Office, will ever grasp the best reason. The rabbi, he knows, and so does Frieda Kroner. You see, we can comprehend one dead body, or two or even twenty and say: there's a criminal that needs to be stopped. But they see the Shadow Man and they see hundreds, thousands, millions all going to their death. They see their brothers and mothers and fathers and uncles, aunts, nieces, nephews, neighbors, friends, acquaintances, and everyone else. You think those deaths will even be anything but numbers to us? But they're not numbers to those people, are they?'

Simon Winter opened the door and stepped to the sidewalk. He leaned back toward Walter Robinson.

'Shouldn't let old men muse on these things. Just muddies the waters, huh?'

Robinson nodded slowly. 'I think,' he said carefully, 'that you and I should catch this man, and then consider what he's done.' Again he paused, then added: 'Everything he's done.'

'Yes,' Simon Winter said. 'We should catch him.'

He straightened up and closed the door. He gave the detective a small wave as the cruiser pulled away. He watched the taillights disappear into the darkness down the street, blinking once and then turning aside, leaving him alone on the sidewalk. There was a richness to the air, as if the tropical night somehow was concocted with a small portion of molasses or maple syrup. He thought this a deceptive thing; the warmth made one ignore the dangers after the sun had set. He suddenly started talking inwardly with his anonymous quarry: Did you do your best worst work after dark? Is that when you became truly dangerous? People are more vulnerable in the nighttime; is that when you came for them? A night like this one?

He thought to himself: yes.

Simon Winter listened to the distant street noises blending with the inevitable sounds from the apartments on his block, television sets, music, voices raised in an anonymous argument. No children crying, he realized. Not in his part of the city. We are all old here, he said to himself, and the noises we make are old noises.

Winter took a step toward his apartment, then stopped and stared over at the empty fountain and the dancing cherub in the center.

'So,' he said out loud, 'what tune do you have for me this evening? Something lively, I suppose? Something to cheer me up?'

The cherub continued to play soundlessly.

'Well then,' Winter asked abruptly, 'what have you seen tonight? Anything different? Anything unusual?'

He stared at the statue, meeting the cherub's dead eyes, as if waiting for a reply. He stayed like this for a few seconds, then swung about abruptly, surveying the entire courtyard. The murdered Sophie's apartment remained dark, and above her, only the blue-gray glow of the television illuminated the Kadoshes. As he watched, a single light in old Finkel's apartment switched off. He pivoted, fixing on the windows of his own place. The darkness within seemed liquid, shifting like the ocean he'd gone out of his way to see only a few minutes earlier. Slowly, he moved his gaze around the courtyard, turning a full circle as he examined the shadows and shapes, inspecting each corner, probing each angle.

There is nothing here, he told himself.

Have you gone crazy?

You are alone and tired, and you should get to bed.

He took a step forward, then stopped.

A night like this one, he repeated to himself.

For a moment he breathed in hard.

But he doesn't know me, Simon Winter insisted. He doesn't know I'm out here, and he doesn't know I'm looking for him. He thinks his enemies are old, frail survivors, with fragile recollections and shaky memories that may have endured through the decades. Those are his targets. Not you. He doesn't know about you.

Or does he?

He realized, in that moment, that he'd unconsciously raised his right hand to his left breast, as if he was wearing the shoulder holster with his old revolver, as he had for so many years.

There is nothing here, and you are alone, he insisted, and you are being foolish. Then he corrected himself: being cautious is never foolish. You may embarrass yourself by trusting your instincts, but that is all you will do, and the alternative is far worse.

He took several steps forward, hating instantly the sound that his shoes made on the sidewalk. Like a drumroll, he complained. Move quietly. He gingerly stepped onto the grass strip next to the walkway, muffling the sound as he approached the building.

He paused outside the front door, his hand a few inches away from the door handle. Slowly, he pulled his fingers back.

If you open that door, he will hear it, he told himself. He will know the sound, and he will gather himself and be ready.

He will be expecting you to arrive home like any tired old man, hurrying to bed and a few hours of fitful sleep. He will expect you to jerk the front door open, fumble about impatiently in the vestibule until you find the key to your apartment, and then barrel ahead, right in.

Simon Winter retreated from the doorway, sliding into a shadow of his own.

He leaned against the side of the building and listened, but could only hear the normal night sounds that he expected. He searched through these noises, trying to find something out of the ordinary, which would tell him something other than the fear that he felt easing through his body like some infectious disease.

All right, he said. Where would he be?

In the vestibule? No. The light is on and he doesn't know the habits of the other tenants. There's no place to hide there, not like Herman Stein's building.

Then inside?

Yes. Inside.

How?

That's obvious: the patio door. Just like Sophie's. Same shabby lock that will break at the mere insinuation of a screwdriver.

Once inside, where?

Simon Winter searched the memory of his own small apartment like a general poring over a map. Not the kitchen; the streetlight reflects off the white linoleum, making it bright. Not the bathroom either; not enough room to maneuver in that small space. The living room, then, or the bedroom? One or the other. He continued to think hard, then told himself: not the bedroom. He would expect me to flick on the lights as I enter, and other than the narrow, small closet jammed with clothes and boxes and otherwise useless junk, the lights would destroy any hiding place. So it has to be the living room. Maximum surprise.

Winter began snaking his way around the side of the building, heading carefully, noiselessly, to the back. He heard a small dog yapping from another apartment, down the block. As he moved around the corner, he picked up some speed. He can't hear me now, Winter told himself. He slid up against the back fence, dodging the wan light coming from the neighboring apartment complex, homing in on the small tile patio in the rear of his apartment. Something rattled about in a garbage can, near the back alley. A cat, he thought. Or a rat.

As he moved he carried on an imaginary conversation with his quarry: What will you be carrying? A gun? Perhaps. Something small and efficient. Twenty-two or .25 caliber, an assassin's weapon. But you still wouldn't like the noise it would make, would you? Draw attention rapidly, no matter how silent you thought it was. That's always a problem in Miami and on the Beach. People know the sound a gun makes. No one says: 'What was that?' or 'Was that a car backfiring?' Not in South Florida. They know gunshots. So maybe you'd carry the gun just for show. Just for the threat. But you wouldn't want to use it, would you? You'd rather use your hands, like you did with Sophie. That's what you like, isn't it? To be close when they die, isn't that right? You like the sounds of life departing, the smells of death. You like that feeling that comes over you when you steal that final breath, don't you? It wasn't the same thing when you watched them packed shoulder to shoulder, tears to tears in a cattle car, that mustn't have been nearly as satisfying, but you were younger then, and probably only beginning to understand the marriage you'd made with murder. Back then, you were still experimenting with what you liked, weren't you?

He stopped.

But I'm too big, he thought. If you've come hunting for me, then you know that I'm not small, like a child, like Sophie was, or wizened, nervous, and filled with fear, like Herman Stein and Irving Silver. No, I'm not somebody you quite know, am I? And this has made you wary, and so you will move quickly and efficiently when you have the opportunity, won't you? You will want to know why I'm hunting you, you will have a dozen, a hundred questions, but given the choice between information and just removing the threat, you will take the easier course, right?

A knife.

Simon Winter nodded to himself.

He is probably a knife man. That would be quiet enough for him. He would not like the blood, not like the struggle, because he would know that every second we're together and he's searching with that blade for my heart, he could be leaving some bit of incriminating evidence behind. But he would accept this worry, just to remove the threat he feels.

Winter felt his pulse accelerate, then slow, as he grew cold within himself.

So, it will be a knife. Delivered without hesitation.

He continued to move closer to the patio.

But you won't expect this, will you? You won't expect me to come in the same way you did. You'll be waiting in the living room, near the front door. It swings to the right, so there's a large dead spot to the left, which remains dark, blocked off from the vestibule light by the solid wood door as it opens. You will have seen that spot, won't you? You will have seen that right from the first minute you were inside, and that's where you'll be, because you will think that I will step inside, right into your path unawares, not seeing you until I shut the door right on my own death and not seeing the knife until it bites through my solar plexus, thrusting upward just as you were taught once, weren't you? That's what you think will happen, that's what they showed you, didn't they? All those men in black uniforms so many years ago. Make a single thrust and make it work. Draw the victim in on top of you, pulling him off balance, so that his own weight against the blade kills him.

He was only a few feet from the sliding glass door, and he crouched down.

The gun is in the drawer of the bedside table. Did he go in there and search for it? You damn old fool, he berated himself. Leaving the weapon precisely where any two-bit crook or break-in artist would look first. But did he do that? Or is he simply waiting for you now?

Simon Winter realized that was a chance he'd take.

The patio door would crash back, making a racket, but he could cross the kitchen space in a single stride, heading directly for his weapon. At least this small element of surprise would be his, he thought. Then he corrected himself: *unless* he was watching, and he saw your hesitation in the courtyard.

What then?

He didn't want to think of this. He reached out slowly and just touched the sliding door. A residual part of him thought: This is all crazy – you are alone. But the door moved. He pulled on it as quietly as he could, and it slid an inch, just past the lock, which rattled slightly, as the door traveled on its runners. He realized in a second that the lock had been broken, and then he rose and threw the door back, slamming it hard. In the same motion, he vaulted through the kitchen, heading for the bedside table and the gun he hoped was there.

From the living room, a darkness to his left, there was an explosion of sound, a smashing noise of alarm that he ignored as he soared toward his weapon. He reached out through the blackness of the apartment for the bedside table. His hand found the knob and he jerked it open, hearing the gun within the drawer thud against the wooden frame. He thought himself fumbling, hurrying, wrapping his hand around the familiar shape. He slipped as he spun around, facing the nighttime that had chased him into the room, sliding down to a sitting position on the floor. He brought the gun up to his eyes, two hands on the weapon, into a shooting position, his ears listening for the hurried sounds of attack.

There were none.

His breathing filled the room, a cacophony of tension.

In his haste he had knocked the reading lamp to the floor, sending the shade skittering across the room. He found the lamp with his foot, then slowly he reached over and switched it on.

The room flooded with light.

Like a sailor raising a beacon against a storm, he lifted the lamp up as he slowly climbed to his feet. He could see his own shadow streaking away from him, toward the living room. He set the lamp down, and stepped forward gingerly, searching for the wall switches as he moved. He could see a thin shaft of light coming from the living room. He continued forward, keeping the wall at his back, the pistol raised in firing position, hammer cocked. He moved slowly and deliberately around the corner, ready to formulate the command to freeze, halt, whatever, his own training coming back after lying dormant for so long.

But he quickly saw that he wouldn't need the word.

Simon Winter breathed out slowly, staring at the sliver of light from the apartment vestibule. The front door was cracked open about six inches.

He moved forward, ready to pursue the man across the night, then stopped himself, recognizing he would already be gone.

He let air whistle between his teeth.

So, he spoke inwardly, you were waiting right where I thought.

He shook his head. But I didn't think you'd be that smart. Or be able to move that quickly. You heard the noise behind you, and instead of letting it cripple you with surprise, you acted instantly, and you saved yourself.

This impressed the old detective. Not many people can function with an animal's cunning or instinctive sense of preservation, knowing to flee at the first sound that is unexpected. People are generally more clumsy and hesitant.

But not the Shadow Man.

So, he thought, now you are already away, racing ahead. And you are more than a little concerned, aren't you, because now you know I'm not like Sophie or the others. I'm a little closer to you, aren't I? And that probably will keep you awake tonight, but it will also make you more careful the next time. And it will make you decide that maybe the next victim should be someone a little easier, correct? But you will be worried too, perhaps for the first time in how many years? Truly worried, because you will know that I know something about you, and that frightens you more than anything, doesn't it? But you will reassure yourself, because you know that you're still hidden, that I do not know your name or your face. Your anonymity is intact, and that will help you finally fall asleep, feeling your safety is secure. What you don't know is that soon I'm going to take that away from you too.

Simon Winter nodded, almost congratulatory. I'm beginning to know you, he said to himself. But the sensation of satisfaction was short-lived, because he realized now that the Shadow Man knew just as much about him, as well.

There were several messages waiting for Walter Robinson when he returned to his desk in the homicide offices. He flipped through these rapidly. A few had to do with other open cases he had. There was one from a Mark Galin at the *Miami Herald*, but he didn't know the reporter, although he had a vague recollection of reading his byline. It was late, however, and he knew the only message he would return was from Espy Martinez.

She sounded groggy when she picked up the telephone.

'Espy? It's Walter. Were you asleep?'

'No,' she lied. 'Well, maybe a little. Where are you?'

'In my office. I'm sorry. I shouldn't have awakened you.'

'It's okay.' She was stretched out in her bed, like a cat awakening from a perch on a sun-strewn shelf. 'I tried to reach you earlier. Where were you?'

'Out getting to know our Mr Winter. An interesting guy.'

'Sharp?'

'As sharp as they come. You should see his service record. Nothing but commendations and awards. I think we've got something worked out. What about you?'

'Jefferson gets his deal tomorrow morning. As short and sweet as I can make it. Zip, zip, zip, so I don't have to spend too much time watching Tommy Alter pat himself on the back for finally finding someone to represent who's more important alive than wasting away on Death Row. Then, as soon as the plea is finished, you get him. Will you meet me there?'

Robinson hesitated. 'Uh, yes. Sure.'

She sat up in the bed. 'What is it?'

He smiled. 'I guess my adrenaline is pumping away. You know, you get so used to working late at night that you forget other people aren't quite so midnight-orientated. Maybe in my next life I should come back as a vampire. Or a werewolf, howling at the moon. Something who skulks around after dark. So, forget it. I'll meet you there in the morning.'

'Wasn't there a horror movie about—'

'Yeah. It was called *Blacula*. Dracula with an Afro. It set race relations back maybe a hundred years. Not one of Hollywood's finest. I saw it when I was a kid. All the kids in my neighborhood thought it was pretty funny. So, anyway, go to sleep. I'll see you at the hearing.'

'No,' Espy Martinez said softly. 'You were going to say something. What was it?'

Walter Robinson hesitated once more, then shrugged. He told himself that tumbling off a cliff was easier if you just jumped. 'Well,' he said slowly, 'I know it's late, but I was sort of hoping I could drive you. In the morning, that is.'

He stopped, embarrassed. Then he quickly added: 'Oh, look, forget it. We can get together tomorrow. Or this weekend. I can hold my libido in check until then. It's late. Go back to sleep.'

Espy Martinez had sat up in her bed and, holding the telephone in one hand, was searching around the bed for a hairbrush with the other.

'You can't come here,' she said. She pictured her

parents asleep or, more likely, trying to listen through the thin walls that separated the two duplexes. 'Don't ask why, because it's complicated and all wrapped up not in who we are, but who we might seem to be.'

'You lost me,' Robinson replied.

'No,' she continued. 'I'll come to your place.'

He hesitated, caught between practicality and desire. 'Maybe you shouldn't. You'll need to be fresh in the morning. On top of things.'

She laughed. 'There's a good dirty pun in that last statement.'

He grinned. 'You know what I meant. Or at least what I thought I meant.'

'Walter,' she said slowly as she began sliding the brush through her hair, 'I need to say something.'

'Go ahead.'

'We play by so many rules and regulations. That's what our jobs are: enforcing the rules. Policeman and prosecutor. And in my family, there were always expectations, which are precisely the same thing as rules. The dutiful daughter filling in for the murdered son ...' She took a deep breath and continued: 'So, maybe in a little way, you, who you are, and me, being myself, well, we're a little outside all the accepteds and normals. And so, if I want to come over there and be with you, I think that's a good thing, maybe because it's not right and reasonable. What's reasonable is getting a good night's sleep. Well, maybe I don't want what's reasonable. Not all the time. Not tonight. Maybe what I want is something far different.'

She stopped. 'Jesus,' she whistled slowly. 'What a speech. I should save all that for the judge. Did I make any sense at all?'

He wanted to say: *more than I could ever have hoped for.*

But instead he answered: 'I'll be waiting for you. Please hurry.'

And so, she did.

CHAPTER TWENTY
The Freed Man

Espy Martinez left Walter Robinson asleep in his bed. He had tossed and turned throughout the night, once calling out a name that she did not recognize before falling back into a deep, solid sleep. She slid gingerly from his side, dressing quietly in the thin morning light, then carrying her shoes until she reached the hallway outside his apartment. Leaving him like some cat burglar who'd robbed his night of passion, gave her a sense of accomplishment, made her feel unpredictable and perhaps a little mysterious, and she enjoyed this.

But by the time she reached the Justice Building downtown, she'd let these sensations slip away from her, replacing them with the tough edge that she suspected she'd need in that morning's hearing. She parked her car and then paced swiftly through the lot, letting her heels click determinedly against the macadam, her stride purposeful and directed, giving her the appearance of someone who knew not only where she was going, but someone who wouldn't tolerate any departures from her pre-established route. She nodded at other attorneys and court personnel heading into the building, still moving quickly; if not precisely eager to confront the morning's task, at least prepared inwardly to accept it and move on.

The escalator deposited her in the center of the fourth floor, in the midst of a jam of people waiting outside the entranceways to the eight courtrooms located there. Occasionally a bailiff would emerge through one of the sally-port doors and call out a name in an exasperated voice. Clutches of people circled around various lawyers; defendants and their families with eager, worried expressions, cops in uniform, cops in plainclothes biding time, drinking coffee from plastic cups, waiting their turns. The hallway was a sea of people, all gathered for different cases, filled with fear, doubt, disgust, anger, a cacophony of emotions. She could hear laughter and sobs, often coming from competing groups. The lawyers in her office likened calendar calls to cattle roundups, complete with similar deep lowing noises. She could hear at least a half-dozen different languages being spoken loudly; Spanish, Haitian-French, Jamaican patois, tourist German, and many English variations, ranging from the deep-South drawl to New Yorkese. She pushed through the crowd of people until she found the right courtroom, then hesitated briefly before heading inside. As she paused, she heard a voice say:

'There she is, there she is! I told you, I told you, we should go get seats.'

She turned and saw an elderly woman standing between two white-haired men. The men wore the basic Miami retiree outfit: Bermuda shorts, checked shirts, and porkpie hats. The woman had on a flower-print dress and a cardigan sweater with stripes. One of the men brandished a cane.

Buzzards, she thought instantly. She smiled in their direction. All courthouses attract a percentage of older people, who perch inside the courtrooms, following the various cases with the determination of soap-opera addicts. They come to know the jail and court personnel, have opinions on the cases, review the performance of prosecutors and defense attorneys, critique the jurors' decisions, cheer when bad guys are sentenced. Mostly, they were harmless, fixtures with an occasionally astute observation or two. More often than not, they fell asleep during the longer hearings, and sometimes their snoring had to be interrupted by a quick shake on the shoulder by an irate bailiff. Some had been hanging around the courthouse for years, long enough to see some defendants several times. Like their nickname, they arrived early, roosted on the sidelines, then disappeared at night. Espy Martinez had always tried to be friendly to them, call them by their first names when she knew them, which made her popular amidst a group seemingly oblivious to the brutish comments made by most of the younger, less experienced lawyers.

'Hi, Espy,' the woman said. 'All the excitement's for you, dear.'

'What?' she asked stupidly.

'Why, your case was in the paper this morning,' the woman continued. 'Right on page one of the Local section. That's what's brought out the crowd.'

'I've got it here,' said one of the men. He put down his cane and began searching through a tattered newspaper. 'See?'

He thrust the newspaper at her, and her eyes fell on the story, played across the middle of the page: ACCUSED MAN CLEARED IN KILLING; PLEA SEEN IN COP-SHOOTING CASE.

'Shit!' The expletive burst from her lips.

'Is there a problem, dear?' the old woman asked.

She shook her head, but this was a lie. 'Can I keep this?' she asked.

The old man nodded his head, touching his index finger to his cap rim.

'We've got to get in,' the other old man said. 'Otherwise all the good seats will be taken.'

'Is it true, dear?' the old woman asked. 'The story says he's going to help you on another case, that's why he's getting a deal. Is it right? I hate it when these awful men get deals. I wish you'd just put them in jail, Espy dear. Even if he is going to help, I still wish you'd make him go to prison, because I think he's not a very nice man, is he? Not this man, no. A bad man. Are you sure you've got to do this?'

Espy Martinez didn't reply. Instead she scanned the story. There were few details, other than the essential one that Leroy Jefferson was cleared of killing Sophie Millstein and was expected in court that morning. The story didn't directly link his cooperation to the investigation of her death, but that inference was obvious. There was a predictable statement from Abe Lasser about preferring witnesses to be holy men, but sometimes being forced to take what was available. She recognized his comment for what Lasser termed *midnight quotes* – which were color-fully phrased truisms that sated some *Herald* reporter who called late at night, long after office hours.

She grimaced. It wasn't a long story, but it was more than enough to draw attention to something she'd wanted handled quietly.

'Damn,' she said again. 'Damn your eyes, Tommy Alter. Couldn't keep your mouth shut.' She looked at the three old people. 'Have you seen the *Herald* reporter? Or any television crews . . .?'

They all nodded in unison.

'Already inside,' the old woman said.

'Come on.' The old man tugged at her sleeve. 'We won't get seats. It's packed in there and I want to get a seat.'

The trio of buzzards hopped across the corridor, leaving her standing outside, clutching the paper. She squeezed it tightly, hoping to force some of the fury she felt out through her fingers, hoping to maintain her composure. Then she turned abruptly and followed the old people into the courtroom.

A single television camera lurked in one corner. The cameraman spun and tracked her like a determined sniper as she pushed her way down the center aisle. It was a dark place, a sort of hybrid between the old churchlike style of some courtrooms, with wooden pews and deep, brown oaken benches and railings, and the ultramodern, offset lighting, theater style that was becoming increasingly prevalent. The effect was of a high-ceilinged room with a limpid off-white light, that was neither auditorium nor living room. It was as if the courtroom had been designed to make everyone sitting in it uncomfortable, forced to strain to see properly in the dim light and lean forward to catch the words spoken amidst the poor acoustics. In Florida, she understood, it just went to show that on any public construction project, it makes much more sense to hand your inevitable bribe money to actually competent workmen and not waste it paying off the vast number of inept contractors, regardless of how many city councilmen they might happen to be related to.

She saw Tommy Alter sitting behind a defense table with two other public defenders. She stepped up behind him. 'You son of a bitch,' she whispered. 'This wasn't supposed to be a goddamn carnival.'

He spun around to face her. 'Well, good morning to you too, Espy.'

'You promised me,' she said bitterly. 'This was going to stay quiet until we'd finished with Jefferson. I've half a mind to walk on the whole deal. Reinstate the charges, you bastard. Let your precious client spend some more time waiting in jail. How about that? Maybe let him do six months in county lockup while I screw around with the case? Would he like that?'

Alter eyed her narrowly. 'As usual, you leap to a conclusion and it's incorrect.'

'What's incorrect?'

'I didn't call the fucking *Herald*, Espy. And when they called me, I wouldn't talk to them.'

'Then who would? Who knew?'

Tommy Alter smiled slowly. 'Well, I've got one guess. It's your guy, Espy.'

'Walter? Don't be crazy, he wouldn't—'

'No,' Alter interrupted. 'Not Walter Robinson. How about your friend and mine, the Lumberjack? He's the one quoted in the paper saying he's none too happy about all this. Think maybe he made that call? Think maybe he doesn't care what he screws up, as long as he gets his precious opinion heard?'

She stopped, still clutching the newspaper in her hand.

Alter's smile slid into a grin. 'Good guess, huh?'

She straightened up, nodding. 'All right,' she said. 'We'll do it. But no comments to the press afterward. Got that, Tommy? You've been doing such a fine job keeping your tongue from flying about uncontrollably. Let's try to keep it up, okay?'

Alter lost grip of his grin and flushed. He started to reply angrily, but stopped himself. 'Let's just get it on the record,' he said after a moment.

Behind her the bailiff was singing out, 'All rise,' and without replying, she stepped over to the prosecution table. She watched as the judge, a small, wiry man with a bald, monkish pate and an upper lip that seemed surgically fixed into a sarcastic leer, swept into the courtroom like some emperor in a hurry. After seating himself, the judge peered out at the cameraman, one eyebrow shooting up, then took in the filled courtroom. The raised eyebrow degenerated into an irritated scowl. He motioned to his bailiff, whispered something to the man, and then waved at Alter and Martinez to approach, with much the same motion one might use with a poorly trained puppy who'd made a mess on an Oriental carpet.

They dutifully gathered at the front of the bench.

'All right,' the judge said. 'I've got a heavy calendar today and I want to get through it quickly because I'm in trial this afternoon. You two are the main show. Let's do your Mr Jefferson first. This is a plea, I gather?'

Martinez nodded. 'Yes, Your Honor. A plea contingent upon cooperation with investigators. It was supposed to be quiet.'

'I understand, Miss Martinez. You'd prefer not to let slide too many details of your ongoing investigation into the waiting notebooks of our local champions of the First Amendment. Correct?'

'Correct.'

'All right, then, if this is satisfactory with you, Mr Alter, we'll limit the plea colloquy simply to what needs to be on the record. I will give my standard "If you do not cooperate, I will send you to Raiford or Hell" speech, and then I can get on with business and you can take the circus out into the hallway, so that you can successfully lie to, mislead, or deceive the press out of my presence.'

'That's fine, Your Honor,' Alter said.

'I will postpone any sentencing on the plea until I receive memos from the two of you detailing the cooperation Mr Jefferson provides. That's the sword you hold over his neck, Miss Martinez. But likewise, I understand that in return for his cooperation, Mr Jefferson receives a makable cash bond and then one of those lovely get-out-of-jail-free cards, correct, Mr Alter?'

'That's the arrangement.'

The judge expelled a burst of air. 'I hope he's worth it, Miss Martinez.'

The judge rocked back in his high-backed leather chair as the bailiff intoned, 'The State versus Leroy Jefferson.' Espy Martinez turned to take her place at the prosecution's table and saw Jefferson being wheeled into the courtroom through a side door by a corrections officer. Jefferson frowned at her, but greeted Tommy Alter with a soul-shake.

'We're here on a plea?' the judge asked loudly.

'Correct, Your Honor,' she replied. 'Because Mr Jefferson has agreed to provide substantial cooperation on several unrelated cases, and because our office has developed information indicating he was not responsible for the homicide he was initially charged with, a plea agreement has been worked out.'

'Is that your understanding, Mr Alter?'

'Yes, Your Honor.'

'All right, Miss Martinez. Please read the charges.'

She did this swiftly, racing through the assault, robbery, resisting arrest with violence, and a few other, incidental charges designed to pad out the length of the plea, but which would not change the actual nature of the agreement. The idea was to have him say *guilty* enough times that the actual meaning of the arrangement was obscured. She watched as the court stenographer's fingers flew above her recording machine. She finished and the judge gestured at Leroy Jefferson. Alter maneuvered the wheelchair to the center of the courtroom.

'All right, Mr Jefferson. For the record, please state your name and address.'

'Leroy Jefferson. King Apartments. Number thirteen.'

'How long have you lived there?'

'Couple of years.'

'Mr Jefferson, are you currently on any narcotic substance?'

'Just what they give me for the pain in my leg.'

'How much education do you have?'

'I went to high school.'

'How far?'

'I got my diploma.'

'Really? Do you suffer from any mental impairment or illness that would prevent you from comprehending the arrangement your attorney has entered into with the State?'

'What?'

'You sick, Mr Jefferson? Are you crazy? Do you understand the plea?'

'I done pleas before, Your Honor. I know what they are.'

'Good. You understand that by failing to live up to your part of the agreement, that I can rescind the plea and sentence you to over one hundred years in prison? I want you to have no doubt at all, that's what I will do.'

'I'm gonna help them, best I can.'

'Good. But you understand that in order to obtain the benefit of this agreement, you must help them to their satisfaction.'

'They'll be satisfied. I promise that.'

'Good. Now you're pleading guilty, because you are guilty, correct, Mr Jefferson?'

'Yes. 'Cept I didn't do what they said I did when they came for me. Had nothing to do with that killing . . .'

'I understand.'

'I ought to sue them for shooting me.'

'Talk to your lawyer, Mr Jefferson. But personally, I think you're lucky to be standing here today.'

'Ain't standing, Your Honor.'

The judge smiled, caught in a sarcasm he appreciated. 'True enough. All right, Mr Jefferson. As the clerk reads the charges, you say the word *guilty*. Miss Martinez, I assume you have plans for Mr Jefferson?'

'Yes, Your Honor.'

'Well, you can pick him up at your convenience at the jail. Madam clerk, start reading. And you, Mr Jefferson, one thing . . .'

'What's that, Your Honor?'

'Don't let me see you again. Don't screw up. You've got an opportunity here, don't mess it up. Because the alternative is a very long time in a very unpleasant place, and I will send you there just as quickly as you can curse out my name. Do you understand that, Mr Jefferson?'

He nodded.

'Good. Then let's hear some guiltys.'

The clerk began reading and Leroy Jefferson began answering. Espy Martinez took a quick glance back over her shoulder at the packed courtroom. Her eyes fell on the trio of old people, and she saw that they were surrounded by a dozen other retirees, all staring at her or Leroy Jefferson, hanging on every word. She swept her gaze about, lingering on other defendants, witnesses, police-men, and attorneys occupying every seat or leaning against every inch of free wall space, all waiting for her case to finish so they could get on with their own. She thought the justice system was like the sea; her own small wave had curled up and crashed against the sand, and now it was dissolving, racing back toward the ocean, while another wavelet was gathering to make its own assault on the shore. She heard the last guilty, turned back and saw Jefferson being pushed out of the courtroom, and she gathered her papers, stuffing them into a briefcase, aware that the camera was tracking her again, feeling oddly as if it was not the only eyes following her path. She ignored this sensation.

Walter Robinson and Espy Martinez sat in the front seat of his unmarked cruiser, while Leroy Jefferson and Tommy Alter occupied the back. The midday sun filled the interior, glistening off the white hood. The air conditioner labored to overcome the heat. The bay stretched out on either side of them, reflecting shafts of sunlight. Robinson took a quick glance in the rearview mirror and saw that Jefferson was uncomfortably squirming in his seat – there was little room to stretch out his leg, which was still heavily wrapped in bandages. His wheelchair had been jammed into the trunk.

Robinson knew there was a large pothole in the right-hand lane of the Julia Tuttle Causeway, so he steered directly for it. The worn shock absorbers on the car thumped as he dumped the right tire into the pothole. Leroy Jefferson grimaced.

'Hey, Leroy,' Robinson said cheerfully. 'What number bus runs over the causeway to Liberty City?'

'That's the G-75,' Jefferson answered.

'That's right. That's the one you rode that night, right? After you saw Sophie Millstein get waxed, right, Leroy? Rode it right back to Liberty City. All that hot stuff in your hands. What were you thinking, Leroy? What'd you think about what you saw?'

'Don't answer that,' Tommy Alter said quickly.

'He's gonna have to answer. That's the deal.'

Alter hesitated. 'Okay,' he said slowly. 'Go ahead.'

'Didn't think nothing,' Jefferson replied.

'Not good enough, counselor. I think you're going to have to inform your client that he's to be forthcoming.

Expansive. Descriptive. A veritable poet, a wordsmith, when it comes to Sophie Millstein's murder and everything he saw that night. You tell him that, Tommy. Don't want to have to turn right around and head back to the judge's chambers.'

'He'll tell you what you want to know. When we get there.'

Espy Martinez said nothing, but watched Walter Robinson's face. The detective nodded.

'Okay. I can wait a few minutes. So, how's it feel to be free, Leroy? You got some plans for tonight? Little celebration, maybe? Got some friends gonna come over, have a little party?'

'Ain't got no friends. Ain't got no party.'

'Oh come on, Leroy. Not too many folks are slick enough to talk their way out of shooting a policeman. You're gonna be an important man on your block. People likely will look up to you. I'm sure there'll be some sort of celebration.'

Robinson's cynicism filled the car. Jefferson merely shrugged.

'Come on, Leroy. Not even a little one? Maybe invite over your friends from the Helping Hand?'

'I told you, they ain't my friends.'

'Well, then how about an-all-by-yourself party, what do you think?'

'What you mean?'

'I mean, I know you've got some little stash hidden so good we couldn't find it when we tossed your apartment. Under a false board maybe or behind a loose cinder block. It's somewhere in that apartment, ain't it, Leroy? Just waiting for you, right? Nice and patient and ready, just like some really good and faithful friend, right? I mean, who needs other folks when you've got that pipe, right? That's why you were so eager to get out, huh? Gonna fire up that pipe, get yourself high again. That'll get rid of the pain, no shit.'

'You crazy.'

'Maybe. Maybe. You keep that in mind, Leroy. Maybe I'm a little crazy.'

Walter Robinson abruptly slammed the steering wheel to the right, jerking the car onto the rough shoulder next to the highway, sending a rooster tail of dirt and dust up behind them, instantly making all four passengers bounce wildly about, crying out, as the car fishtailed. He accelerated on the gravel and coral shoulder. The stony road made the car sway and heave, kicking up bullets of rock. Martinez clamped her mouth shut and held on as Robinson swerved between two cars, back onto the pavement. Behind them a driver leaned on his horn in frightened irritation.

'Come on, Walter, what are you trying to prove?' Alter demanded. 'Just drive the car.'

Robinson didn't reply. Something about Leroy Jefferson simply angered him; perhaps it was the sensation that the suspect was getting away with something, perhaps it was the self-satisfied, frustrating way Jefferson grinned at him. Robinson had one extreme thought: I know where that smile comes from. It was simple: Jefferson was ready to kill Sophie Millstein. All those break-ins that they knew he did, but couldn't prove. He was ready to start escalating the violence. Making the jump from robbery to armed robbery and then to murder. He would have done her for sure. But he didn't have to, because someone else was there, beating him to it, and he thought this was all some great cosmic joke. Funniest thing he'd ever seen. Walter Robinson breathed out slowly, gritted his teeth and tossed the car around the off-ramp, the engine racing as he headed toward Miami Beach police headquarters.

They sat in one of the ubiquitous interrogation rooms, starting slowly, pausing over details, lingering over each component of the night Sophie Millstein died. Walter Robinson's thinking was simple. He wanted to get Jefferson's memory working hard, and, at the same time, he wanted to both relax and exhaust the man. Even with Tommy Alter's presence loosely guarding the words that his client spoke, Robinson thought he might be able to slide in some question, extract an answer that might inadvertently tie Leroy Jefferson to all the unsolved break-ins that preceded Sophie Millstein's murder. Or at least something that he might be able to develop later into a piece of evidence that would support an indictment. It would be nice, he thought, to arrive at Jefferson's house some fresh morning with a brand new warrant for some crimes that were not part of the arrangement. Consequently, Robinson adopted a tedious, painstaking style, designed to bore everyone in the room. He asked about the weather, he asked about the bus rides. He made Jefferson describe the clothing he was wearing, and made Jefferson recall where he purchased his sneakers and why he bought that brand and how he was nicknamed Hightops and how he first got introduced to crack cocaine, and every other question he could think of that only occasionally bordered on the relevant.

He drew this out for several hours, letting the Identikit technician sit in a corner, waiting for his turn. The technician was a veteran, and well aware of what was going on. He kept his mouth closed. Occasionally Tommy Alter would impatiently interrupt, as the day dwindled around them, marked only by the single wall clock high on the ceiling of the interrogation room. Eventually the public defender rose, said he was going to get a cup of coffee and a newspaper to read, and asked if anyone else needed anything.

'I want something to eat,' Jefferson said.

Walter Robinson pulled out his wallet and said, 'Tommy, why don't you get your client a sandwich and a soda from the deli across the street. Maybe better get everyone a sandwich. Miss Martinez, maybe you can go along and give him a hand.'

Espy Martinez started to object, but then recognized that Robinson probably had a reason for asking her to escort Alter, and the reason probably was to delay his return as much as possible, so she nodded.

'You're going to stick to the same material?' Alter asked.

'Yeah. Just going through it all slowly.'

'Okay. We'll be back in a few minutes. Leroy, don't answer any question you're not comfortable with.'

'No problem.'

Alter exited, trailed by Espy Martinez. After a second or so of quiet, Walter Robinson started asking more cogent questions.

'Tell me, Leroy, did you always ride the bus when you did a break-in?'

Jefferson was slumped back in his seat, slightly distracted, toying with a pack of cigarettes, obviously feeling pretty confident and slightly bored. He shrugged. 'Didn't have no car.'

'Same bus every time?'

'It took me where I wanted to go.'

'Weren't you scared some bus driver might remember you?'

'Nah. They change drivers around so much. And I went on different nights. And I was always careful, you know, to come out when the evening shift was driving and leave when the next shift took over.'

'That was smart.'

'I ain't stupid like some junkies.'

'Why the same neighborhood each time?'

'Old people. Old buildings. Old locks. Weren't nobody gonna have a gun, come surprise me. I never carried my gun myself.'

Walter Robinson nodded. 'Sure. Makes sense. So, tell me how come you picked Sophie's place?'

'Oh, man, it was easy. I'd noticed it on another trip. Got that alley down the back. Not much light. Those patio doors, all you got to do is jam them up and off their runners and makes no difference what sort of lock they got. You're in.'

'So, tell me about that night.'

'It weren't too late, you know. Maybe midnight. I was right in the back, hiding next to the garbage cans. It was nice and quiet. No lights on, except upstairs, and they was watching the television real loud, which was gonna cover up any noise I made.'

'Did you know she was inside?'

Jefferson shook his head. 'Weren't no lights or sounds or nothing. I thought the place was empty for sure.'

Robinson nodded again. Sure, he said to himself. Sure you thought it was empty. Like hell. But he didn't say this out loud. He merely made a mental check note next to the lie and continued.

'So you were out back. How long were you there?'

'Maybe half hour. Maybe a little more. I took my time about these things. Lot of guys, you know, they just smash their way right in. Me, I was more careful. Didn't want to get busted.'

'And what happened?'

'Man, dude scared the shit outta me. I was just starting

to get ready, you know, sneak across, do my thing, when I saw this little movement off to my side. I froze. Didn't make a move. I was already ducked down, you know, being careful. He must have been there watching, maybe ten feet away. I don't know how long he'd been there, man, the dude was so quiet, didn't even hear his breathing. I thought he musta seen me for sure, but I guess not because maybe he was watching that apartment so close and like he didn't expect anyone to be doing the same thing. Where I was, it was like a little black hole, no light in there at all, and I was hidden pretty good.'

'So, you didn't see him arrive?'

'No, man. Man moved like a spook. Maybe like some damn ghost, he be so quiet. I don't know how long he was hanging there. Coulda been a couple of minutes, coulda been an hour. At least as long as me.'

'Tell me what you saw.'

'Dude slides across the patio, right up to the old lady's place. Man was slick, I'll tell you. Didn't make a sound. Not like some old guy bumbling and fumbling, you know. Dude had done this thing before, the way he moved. Damn, he had that sliding door open so quick, just like it wasn't even locked. Made one little noise, when he broke the lock, you know, then he was inside.'

'What did you do?'

'Well, man, first thing I thought was to run, you know? Try someplace else, because I figured this old guy was gonna clean that apartment out. He was a pro, you could tell, and there weren't gonna be nothing left for me. But I was curious too, you know? Sort of wanted to see what was gonna go down.'

'Sure. Makes sense.'

'I mean, like it was almost like I thought I might learn something.' Leroy Jefferson laughed briefly. 'Man, I learned something all right.'

'So, what did you do?'

'Moved right across the yard there, right up to the door. Couldn't see shit, so I stepped inside, real quiet. Into the kitchen there.'

'Because you wanted to learn something?'

'That's right.'

Robinson thought to himself: not because you thought you might be able to pop the old man after he'd done all the work for you. You were gonna take him off, right then. Good thing you didn't try it, because the Shadow Man would have killed you so fast, you wouldn't even have known you were dying. But he said: 'Go ahead. What happened then?'

'I heard them. Sound was coming from the bedroom. Weren't a lot of noise, but man, I knew what was happening. Old dude was killing her. It weren't like no fight, weren't even like much of a struggle. Just real quick, like the dude still knew what he was doing. I heard her make a sound like a little scream maybe, but not real loud and that was it for her. And I heard a cat too, you know that meowing noise they make. I heard that too. I slide down into the corner, trying to stay where it's hidden, you know? I think, shit man, he's killing somebody, let's get the fuck outta here, but before I can run, I see the dude again. Only a couple of feet away, man, he was moving fast, but just as quiet as before and he's out the door and gone.'

'What did you do?'

'Well, I real quick stuck my head in, saw the old lady all tangled up in her sheets. Weren't much light in there, just streetlights, you know, coming through the window, but enough to see that jewelry box, so I grabbed a few things.'

'You were in a hurry?'

'Sure. Jesus, man, just wanted to get outta there. But,

like, this old dude had given me an easy score, and after all, that was why I was there in the first place, so shit, I wanted to, what you say, take advantage of the opportunity. But I musta made too much noise with the drawers and things, because I heard a door open upstairs, and then footsteps, and knocking on the front door. Figured I better get moving then, grabbed a few more things, anything, you know, anything that would fit in the pillowcase and might be worth something, and got outta there. Shouldn't have been so damn greedy, you know? If I'da left right then, when I heard the knocking, nobody'd have seen me. But man, when you're looking to make some money, sometimes you don't think right.'

'The necklace?'

'Yeah. I saw it as I was leaving. Saw those diamonds. Man, even in the dark they were glowing. Figured I could get something for them, so I grabbed it quick from her neck.'

Walter Robinson thought: postmortem scratch explained. 'And what happened next.'

'Fucking old-timer sees me running. Gets a good look too. Starts shouting for the cops. That's it, you know the rest.'

'Let's go back to the man you saw commit the crime . . .'

'Man was cold. Gave me the shakes. Don't want to see him again. Goes in, strangles an old lady, no reason I could see. Don't even steal nothing. Man was cold.'

Walter Robinson paused. Jefferson had shifted about in his seat, sitting up, arms on the table in front of him, a nervous electric tension in his voice as he described the killing. Jefferson's easygoing confident manner had changed, and he sensed some frightened urgency on the man's face.

'When I thought about it, later, you know, after I got my

money from Reggie and was getting some smoke down, it kinda freaked me, you know. I mean, dude was just a killer, that's all.'

Walter Robinson realized that in the generously psychopathic world that Leroy Jefferson occupied, a murder without some obvious profit connected to it was unsettling. There were probably dozens of killings that Leroy Jefferson wouldn't have thought twice about. But this one made him anxious.

'Don't want to run into that dude on a dark night,' Jefferson joked, leaning back in his seat. 'You better be thinking the same, Detective. Man was a stone-cold killer.'

'Did you ever hear him say anything?'

'No. Just quiet. Cool. Moved so easy.'

'Okay, but you'd know him if you saw him again?'

'Sure. I got a real good look at him. Hell, better than the old-timer got looking at me, when I was running. This dude didn't move real fast, you see? Deliberate-like. Took his time to do things right. So I got a real good look at him. Both outside, and when he went right by me in the apartment. Good thing he didn't see me. Guess he weren't expecting no black man on his tail.'

Walter Robinson nodded again. He still has a black man on his tail, and he doesn't know it. The detective gestured over at the Identikit technician, who stretched like a dog awakened from a place next to a fire, and then approached with his valise.

'All yours, now,' Robinson said.

'Okay, Mr Jefferson,' the technician said. 'We're going to go real slow. You just form a mental picture of the man you saw. And I'm gonna show you a bunch of different facial shapes. And pretty soon, we're gonna have a picture of this guy.'

Jefferson made a small gesture with his hand. 'Sounds fine to me.'

The technician produced a series of overlays on clear plastic sheets of paper. 'Let's start with the chin,' he said. 'I'll show you these forms, and you concentrate on what you remember, and stop me when I get the right one.'

'Hey, Detective,' Jefferson said. 'You bust this guy, you gonna be looking for the death penalty, same as you were with me?'

'Absolutely.'

Leroy Jefferson nodded his head, wrinkling his chin as he thought hard. He turned his eyes to the plastic overlays.

'Didn't ever think I'd be helping the cops put the juice to no one,' he said. 'But the dude was a killer. No doubt about it.' He pointed at one of the shapes displayed on the table in front of him. 'Let's start with that one,' he said.

Walter Robinson shifted in his seat and watched as the painstaking process of giving a face to the Shadow Man began.

Tommy Alter gave up after a few more hours, leaving after extracting a promise from Walter Robinson that Jefferson would be given a ride back to his home and that the ride would be direct and smooth. The Identikit technician was thorough and refused to be hurried, a man who enjoyed his work in the same way that an artist does as shapes take form on the canvas.

It was late when Espy Martinez and Walter Robinson stole a moment alone in the corridor outside the inter-rogation room.

'I'm exhausted,' she said.

'Why don't you go home?'

She smiled. 'Home for me is two things: boring or frustrating. Boring because I live alone and there's nothing there that makes me feel like who I really want to be; frustrating because no sooner will I close the door before the phone will ring and it will be my parents calling from their half of the duplex. My mother will want to know what I'm doing and who I'm doing it with and a dozen other questions I don't want to answer.'

She shook her head. 'Too tired to really sort these things out, Walter. But being with you is, I don't know, an adventure. Something way outside all the things I've ever done. I always did what was expected of me. And this isn't and I like that. I like it a lot.' She reached out and just touched her fingers against his hand. 'Is that wrong?'

'I don't know,' he replied. 'I'm not sure what I think, if I think anything at all.'

'It did come out wrong,' she said. 'I'm sorry. Can't we talk at some other time, when we're not so tired?'

'Yes,' he said. 'That would be wise.'

'I want to make this work,' she said.

'Me too.'

She paused. 'I don't want to go home tonight.'

He nodded. He was troubled, but desire overcame whatever doubts he had. He recognized this, thought himself slightly weak, and then thought that was stupid because thinking too much about any relationship was likely to doom it, and there was a great deal that remained to happen with Espy Martinez that he wanted to happen. So, instead, he reached into his pocket and pulled out his key chain. He worked the apartment key off the ring and handed it to her.

'I have the chauffeur duty with our man Leroy. You go back to my place and wait up for me, okay?'

'Would you like me to go with you?'

'No.' He smiled. 'It will give me the opportunity to needle the creep without feeling guilty that I might be violating the spirit of his agreement with the State of Florida.'

'Okay,' she said. 'Just don't make him so pissed that he decides to run away.'

'Isn't running anywheres, thanks to that little twenty-five caliber you tote around in your handbag.'

'It's still there,' she said. She hesitated. 'And tomorrow?'

'Tomorrow we start on Simon Winter's plan. We'll go see him and the other old folks with our picture.'

As he said this, the door to the interrogation room opened and the technician emerged. He was holding a white sheet of paper in his hand, staring down at it with an appraiser's eye. He saw the two of them look up at him and he said: 'Jefferson wasn't too good with the eyes. I think that's because he never got a full face look at this man. According to his story, mostly it was profiles, maybe three quarters front. Never did look the man in the eyes, which is probably a good thing for him. Other than that, I think this came out okay. What do you think?'

Walter Robinson took the drawing and held it in front of him so that they both could look at it. What they saw was a picture of a tall, big-chested elderly man who wore his years with the firmness of a person considerably younger. His chin was sturdy, like a boxer's, with skin that remained tight. He had high-set cheekbones and a wide brow, giving the portrait the appearance of a man looking far into the distance. His hair was white, closely cropped like a soldier's, but thick.

'This is good,' he said quietly.

'Hell, Walter, you could do the same.' The technician was aware of Robinson's hobby.

'So, that's the Shadow Man,' Espy Martinez said.

'I don't think the eyes are right,' the technician repeated.

'I just couldn't get them.'

The eyes in the drawing were dull, vacant.

'No,' the detective said. 'These could be anyone's eyes. Not a killer's.'

Eyes like razors, he thought. Walter Robinson held the picture in his hands and wondered what the rabbi and Frieda Kroner would say when they saw it.

The King Apartments looked very much the same as they did the night Walter Robinson arrived there to arrest Leroy Jefferson. He pulled his vehicle to the curb, crunching over some broken glass. There were midnight noises throughout the distance, all accompanied by the faraway sound of a fire engine with its deep-throated horn sounding urgently as it pushed through the inner city night.

'Home sweet home,' Robinson said.

Jefferson nodded. 'Ain't much, is it?'

'Can't say it is.'

'Maybe I'll get someplace new now. This place got a lot of bad luck connected to it.'

'What sort of bad luck, Leroy?'

'It's bad luck to get busted,' he replied, grinning. 'Even if you do find a way out.'

Robinson exited the car, retrieved the wheelchair from the trunk, and opened the rear door so that Jefferson could swing himself out, into the seat. This the man did, with an agility that made Robinson believe the pain in his leg had diminished some. Either that or he was eager to find what he knew was waiting for him.

'You want me to help you upstairs?' he asked.

Jefferson shook his head, still grinning. 'Ain't too interested in having my neighbors know I been helping the police. They don't consider this a necessarily good thing, you know.'

'Not part of the local idea of civic duty, huh?'

'You got that right.'

'How're you going to get up the stairs?'

'Maybe somebody's fixed the elevator. If not, I'll figure it out. Ain't your business anyways.'

Jefferson gave the wheels a push and rolled a few feet away, up onto the walkway. Then he spun the chair about and looked back at the detective.

'I did what you asked, right?'

'Yes. So far, so good.'

'I told you I'd keep my part of the bargain.'

'Just keep keeping it.'

'You ain't got enough trust in human nature, detective.' Jefferson laughed. 'Can't even tell when somebody's helping you out. Wouldn't have no case against that old dude, 'cept for me.'

'You just keep cooperating, Leroy. Don't move. Don't go anywhere. And don't get into any trouble. Got that?'

'Sure.'

Jefferson laughed. The sound echoed down the street. He rolled the wheelchair back a foot or two, then added: 'You know, you ain't so far from all this, Detective. Put on that suit, act like the man, but truth is, could be you right here and me right there.'

Walter Robinson shook his head. 'Nope. You're wrong.'

But he didn't know whether this was true or not. He did know, however, that Espy Martinez was waiting for him, and he thought that more than anything else, at that moment right then, he wanted to get out of Liberty City, wanted to leave the King Apartments and return to the other world he lived in.

Leroy Jefferson laughed again, mocking the detective. He could feel a surge of exhilaration within him, and for the first time, as he measured the distance between himself and the detective, truly thought that he'd managed to beat the system.

'It feels real good to be free,' he said. 'Be seeing you.' He spun the chair again and eagerly started rolling toward the apartment building. He did not look back as Robinson scowled, irritated but accepting, and climbed into the cruiser, quickly slamming the car into gear and accelerating through the coffee-black night.

To his surprise, the elevator was operating.

Leroy Jefferson thought this was a good sign, as the dull steel doors jerked to a close. There was a momentary pause, then a grinding sound before the elevator rose. The interior light dimmed once as it reached the second floor, and the doors seemed oddly reluctant to open, but eventually they did, and he pushed himself out onto the landing, thinking that everything around him was working quite as well as it ever had.

He maneuvered down the landing toward his apartment, breathing raspily with the exertion required to push the wheelchair. He could feel sticky sweat beneath his arms, dripping down his forehead across his cheeks and finally dropping from his chin to his chest. It was an irritating sweat, caused by hard work and humid, still summer air, not the genuine sweat of athletic motion. He gritted his teeth and thought: ain't never gonna be running up no court on a fast break again, and he inwardly cursed Espy Martinez and her unlucky shot, which had left him in such awkward pain. He slapped at the wheelchair and reminded himself that the doctors had estimated he'd be out of it within a month or so, which he wanted, because until he had his motion back, he didn't see much of an opportunity to create any income.

He knew he'd be all right for a while. He smiled to

himself. Fucking detective was right. He kept a private stash behind a loose tile in the bathroom, two hundred dollars and a similar amount of rock cocaine in a plastic bag, thrust down between the plumbing pipes where it couldn't be seen even if you found the right tile. You had to snake your arm way down and know what you were looking for. He thought: maybe take a little taste, sell the rest. Gonna be okay just as soon as I get back on my feet, even with a limp. Things gonna work out. They always do.

He lifted a hand and wiped the sweat from his forehead, concentrating on the stash.

Just a little taste, he repeated to himself.

He paused outside the door to his apartment. The tattered remains of yellow police tape hung limply from the cracked and splintered door frame. The door itself had been replaced, but ineffectively. He reached out and pushed at it, and it swung open. Unlocked.

'Goddamn junkies, probably stole everything,' he said out loud.

He shifted about in the seat of the wheelchair and bellowed back over his shoulder: 'You fucking people. Got no respect for other folks' shit!'

There was no one outside to hear his complaint, but from a distant room he heard one voice yell, 'Fuck you!' and from the opposite end of the corridor another shouted, 'Shut the fuck up!'

He waited for a moment, to see if there were any other responses, but silence gripped the neighborhood. He couldn't see anyone on the street, or on any of the landings. He felt alone, which did not bother him, because he was not eager to share what he had waiting for him inside behind that false tile.

He remembered what Walter Robinson had said: home sweet home.

He pushed the door wide and rolled himself inside.

The apartment was hot, still, as if a month's oppressive days were collected within the walls. He slammed the door back shut behind him and reached out for the wall light switch.

His hand did not reach the wall. It was interrupted by an iron grip clamping down on his forearm.

In the same instant he heard an ice voice: 'No, I don't think we need any light quite yet, Mr Jefferson.'

Fear like a runaway engine accelerated through him. 'Who are you?' he choked.

The voice had moved around behind him and made a small laugh before answering. 'But you know, don't you, Mr Jefferson?'

The man seemed to pause, then he asked:

'You tell me: Who am I?'

At the same time as these words slid about in the darkness of the apartment, Jefferson was suddenly jerked backward, as the man released his arm and shifted his grip, throwing a muscled forearm across Jefferson's forehead, tugging his head back, exposing his neck. He gasped, reaching up involuntarily as he felt a knife-icicle at his exposed throat.

'No, Mr Jefferson, put your hands down. Don't make me kill you before we've had a chance to talk.'

His own hands, fingers straining toward the blade, stopped in midair. Slowly he dropped them to the wheels at his side. His mind was moving quickly now, roaring past all the fear, trying to think of something to do. He opened his mouth to call for help, but then stopped, shutting it with a snap. Ain't no one gonna come, no matter what you say, he reminded himself. And maybe the dude'll cut your throat before you get the second word out. He remembered the choking cry that was all that Sophie Millstein managed before death. It made him shudder; he could sense fear loosening his control over his bowels, but he fought this, breathing hard and fast, controlling the quiver that found his hands, the twitch that discovered his eyelids. Talk your way out, he told himself. Keep talking. Make a deal.

'That's better,' the voice said. 'Now slowly bring your hands behind the chair, wrists together.'

'You don't gotta do that, man. I'm gonna tell you whatever you need to know.'

'Excellent, Mr Jefferson. That is very reassuring. Now move your hands back slowly. Think of it this way: Any knot I tie, I can always untie. Alexander the Great proved that. Do you know who Alexander is, Mr Jefferson? No? I didn't think so. But you do know this, don't you: It's always wiser to indulge a man who holds a knife at your throat.'

The flat voice seemed patient, cold, with only a slight urgency at its fringe. But the knife blade bit against his skin, its demands obvious. The pressure increased just slightly, enough to draw a small line of blood. Jefferson pushed his hands behind him, as asked. He felt the knife slide around his throat, to his ear, to the nape of his neck, before easing away. He had a momentary urge to jump right then, to fight back, but just as swiftly the urge departed. He told himself: stay cool. You can't run and you can't fight. There was a ripping sound and he felt his hands being bound with duct tape.

When his arms were immobilized, Jefferson felt the chair being wheeled into the center of the room. He waited, breathing like a runner trying to catch the leaders in a race.

'Who are you, man? What you want? What you got to tie me up for? I ain't going nowheres.'

'That's correct, Mr Jefferson.'

'Who are you, man? What's the deal?'

'No, Mr Jefferson. That's my question for you: *Who am I?*'

'Man, I got no idea. Some crazy white dude, that's who you are.'

The voice laughed again. 'Not a good start, Mr Jefferson. Why would you lie to me?'

The man leaned down and poked with the knife blade at the bandages on Jefferson's ruined knee, sending a rainbow of hurt through his body.

'Jesus, man! What you doing? I don't know shit!'

'Who am I, Mr Jefferson?'

He poked again at the leg, and Leroy Jefferson gritted his teeth.

'Who am I, Mr Jefferson?'

'I don't know. I ain't never seen you before.'

'I hate lies. Once again, who am I, Mr Jefferson?'

'I don't know, I don't know, Jesus, why you doing this?' Leroy Jefferson's reply was high-pitched with anxiety.

The visitor sighed. Jefferson felt the knife on his leg, tightened his stomach muscles against the expected pain, but instead the voice simply continued.

'I saw you today, Mr Jefferson. In the courtroom, pleading guilty to all those phony charges. I had had such high hopes for you, Mr Jefferson, when I read of your arrest. Imagine my surprise this morning when I saw in the paper that you'd been cleared of Mrs Millstein's murder – and that you were going to help the police in their inquiries. Of course, the story didn't say what inquiries those might be, but I thought it better to err on the side of safety. So I hurried right over to the courtroom and took my seat right with the rest of the curious and the concerned in the back, and waited for you to come out.

You appeared preoccupied, Mr Jefferson. All eager to get on with your business and not attentive to your surroundings. That's a bad habit for anyone of a criminal persuasion, don't you think? Always smarter to take stock of who's who and what's what, even in a crowded courtroom. Should have taken the time to go over each and every one of the faces that were packed inside. But you didn't do that, did you, Mr Jefferson? Instead you conveniently provided me with your address. So, I came on over and decided to wait for you here, Mr Jefferson. Because I had some questions and I have some doubts and I hate uncertainty. You're a professional criminal, Mr Jefferson. Don't you think that is always the smartest approach: assume the worst. Assume there's a problem. And if there isn't, well, then you're pleasantly surprised. Isn't that right, Mr Jefferson?'

'Man, I don't know what the hell you're talking about—'

The last words he spoke were swallowed by a sharp pain as the knife blade probed the bandages again, searching for skin and muscle. He breathed out harshly:

'Goddamn it, that hurts, man, I don't know what, you're crazy, just leave me alone . . .'

'Who am I, Mr Jefferson?'

Leroy Jefferson didn't answer. Tears of pain cluttered his face, running down his cheeks. Very little that the man said to him was clear. All he could taste was an acid dryness in his mouth.

'You a killer,' Leroy Jefferson said.

The man hesitated, and Jefferson heard him inhale deeply.

'That's a start,' said the man. 'Here is a simple question: who is Simon Winter?'

Leroy Jefferson was confused. He licked the sweat from

his lips. 'I don't know that name.'

Pain like a rocket soared through him and he gasped out in the darkness, a scream rising within him, racing toward his lips, only to stop, gurgling in his throat when he heard the man say: 'Stay quiet!'

His leg was aflame. The knife had scraped through the wrappings, twisting at flesh. Leroy Jefferson tried to bend forward, twisting against the confinements of the duct tape and the wheelchair. 'Jesus,' he said. 'Don't do that, man. Please don't do that.'

'Who am I, Mr Jefferson?'

'Please, please, whatever, just don't do that again . . .'

'That was only a start, Mr Jefferson. I'll try again. Who is Simon Winter and what does he know about me?'

Leroy Jefferson let words burst through his lips, a torrent of fear, almost as if he could already sense the burning in his leg as the knife ripped at tendons and nerves.

'Man, I don't know! I never heard that name before!'

For a moment the man was silent and Leroy Jefferson searched through the darkness for the knife. He felt the man shifting next to him, reaching at the damaged leg, and he quickly added: 'That's the truth, man. I got no idea, don't hurt me again!'

'All right,' the voice said after a pause. 'I did not think you necessarily knew the answer to that question.' There was another silence before the voice continued, 'Mr Jefferson, you must have the patience of a spider. Spin your web and wait for your prey to deliver itself to you.'

The voice hesitated, then continued: 'Isn't that right, Mr Jefferson?'

He answered quickly. 'Sure. Yes. What you say.'

A small, bitter laugh creased the darkness. 'Who am I, Mr Jefferson?'

'Please, I don't know. I don't wanta know, and even if I did know, I wouldn't tell nobody.'

'Do you think I'm a criminal, like you, Mr Jefferson?'

'No, yes, man, I don't know . . .'

'You think I'm some parasite that kills and robs to support a disgusting drug habit? You think I'm like you?'

'No, no, that's not what I meant.'

'Then, who am I, Mr Jefferson?'

Leroy Jefferson sobbed his response, a plaintive plea mingled with the aching pain that came in waves from his ravaged leg. 'I don't know, I don't know . . .'

He heard the man start to move about the apartment, circling him, and he swiveled his head, trying to follow the shape as it traveled through the shadows in the living room. After a moment the voice asked, in a steady, mildly curious voice:

'Tell me, if you were to die tonight, right here, right in the next two seconds, Mr Jefferson, would the world even hesitate for a second to note your passing?'

'Man, please, I'll tell you what you want, but I don't know what you're saying. You talking crazy talk. I don't understand. I just don't understand.'

'I have been a part of great things, Mr Jefferson. Some of the greatest moments this world has ever seen. Unforgettable events. Incredible times.'

The voice emptied the room of everything except fear. Leroy Jefferson could see the man's outline as he moved past the diffuse, weak light tossed haphazardly into the room through the living room window by a streetlight lurking somewhere distant.

'Who am I, Mr Jefferson?'

He shook his head in the darkness. 'Oh, please don't ask me that! Man, I don't know who you are!'

The voice again slid a small, coarse laugh into the still air around him. It seemed to come from several spots at once, and Leroy Jefferson pivoted his head about, trying to find where the man stood in the ink-dark spots of the room. Again he wanted to cry out, but he knew it would be useless. He shivered deeply, and waited for the voice to ask another question. He felt confused, afraid. He barely understood what the man was asking. The language was beyond his experience. But then, so was the pain in his leg, which throbbed and gnawed at him, keeping pace with his heartbeats and the fear that ricocheted about within him.

'All right,' the man said. He continued moving from side to side, sometimes pausing behind the wheelchair. Leroy Jefferson pivoted nervously. 'Let's talk about your deal with the State of Florida. What sort of deal is it, Mr Jefferson?'

'I got to tell them what I know about some crimes.'

'Good. That's helpful. What crimes, Mr Jefferson?'

'Break-ins. Robberies. Bunch of them on Miami Beach.'

'Good. Keep going.'

'Man, that's it! Whole pile of little shit crimes, some robberies, like I said. Maybe rat on some coke dealers too, that's what they want from me.'

The voice moved around behind him. 'No, that doesn't make much sense, Mr Jefferson.'

'I'm telling you the truth ...'

The man laughed. 'You insult me, Mr Jefferson. You insult the truth.'

He suddenly felt the pressure of the knife against his cheek and he wanted to scream. The man must have anticipated this, because he whispered into Jefferson's ear: 'Don't shout. Don't yell. Don't do something that might make me want to end this.'

He bit back terror and nodded.

There was a second's delay before the man spoke. 'How strong are you, Mr Jefferson? Remember, don't shout out. You remember that, don't you?'

Jefferson nodded.

'Good,' the man said. Then he slowly drew the tip of the knife across Leroy Jefferson's cheek, cutting a deep furrow in the skin.

Jefferson clenched down on his lip to avoid screaming. Salty blood ran into the corner of his mouth.

'Don't lie to me, Mr Jefferson. I truly despise being lied to.'

The voice was never raised. It stayed a low, cold tone.

Jefferson thought he should say something, but he was preoccupied with the knife blade, which tickled at his other cheek.

'One should always use their anger constructively, Mr Jefferson.'

The knife tip dug into his skin again, and was drawn slowly across the cheek, parting the flesh. Pain redoubled, and for an instant he thought he might pass out.

The man sighed, and moved to the side of the wheel-chair. For just an instant his profile was caught in a wayward shaft of weak light. His white hair glistened, almost as if it were electric.

'There is a great difference between being old and being experienced, Mr Jefferson.' The man bent down over him. 'Now consider what has happened. I've been quite patient with you. I'm not asking for something you cannot provide. All I demand is a little bit of honest inform-ation.'

'I'm trying, please, I'm trying . . .'

'I don't think you're trying quite hard enough, Mr Jefferson.'

'I will. I promise.'

'Who knows about Der Schattenmann, Mr Jefferson?'

'Man, please, I don't know that name.'

'Who is searching for him? Is it the police, Mr Jefferson? Or that attractive young prosecutor? The old people, I know about. But who else? How is it that you are involved in all this? Did you see me that night, Mr Jefferson? I want to know and I want to know now. These are not unreasonable questions, Mr Jefferson, but still, you persist in evasion. Because of that, you've forced me to deliver to you a pair of scars, one in either cheek. The wounds will heal, Mr Jefferson, but the scars will remain to remind you of the evils of obstinacy. And you've forced me to probe about in your damaged knee. Do you not think I could ruin it completely, Mr Jefferson? Perhaps I could just start to work the knife blade into all those healing sutures. What do you suppose that might feel like?'

'Please don't, man, I'm trying to help . . .'

'Are you, Mr Jefferson? I'm not impressed. Mr Silver didn't lie, when I spoke with him under similar circumstances, although I would not characterize his behavior as completely forthcoming. But he had friends he wanted to protect, and so his reluctance was understandable. As was his death. And Mr Stein, well, that was a meeting doomed from the start, right from the second he saw me, same as Mrs Millstein. These were people that I knew, Mr Jefferson. People I have known for decades. Since I was even younger than you. And they died, Mr Jefferson, just as they always died. Quietly and obediently.'

'I don't know what you're saying, man. Please leave me alone.'

'I asked them the same question, Mr Jefferson. They knew the answer.'

'I'm sorry, please. I'm sorry . . .'

'Who am I, Mr Jefferson?'

Again he sobbed, his voice shut down from pain and fear. He did not reply.

After a moment he heard from behind him:

'I have more questions. You see, Mr Jefferson, I know that the State of Florida wouldn't cut you a deal after you shot a policeman unless there was someone really special that they were hunting for. Someone who really mattered, mattered enough for them to do something I'm sure they found extremely unpleasant and distasteful. And that was letting you go. Nasty bit of work, that. Letting a junkie who almost murdered a policeman walk free. Must stick in the throat of every policeman and prosecutor in town. So, somehow I just don't think that you're helping them out on a bunch of insignificant crimes. No, there's someone out there much more important, isn't there?'

'Please, man.'

'Much more important, correct?'

'Yes, man, whatever you say!'

'That someone, of course, is me. It has always been me, but they never knew it.'

The man in the darkness seemed to take a deep breath.

'So, now, Mr Jefferson, I want the truth. Do you know no one has ever managed to refuse me, in all these years of asking questions. No one asked – no one! – has ever not answered. A remarkable record, that, don't you think? It was always so easy. People are so vulnerable. They want to 'live, and when you can take that away from them, it gives you all the power you need. You know something, Mr Jefferson? They always told me. Back then, late at night. There were sirens in the distance from the air raids, and the streets were bombed out. A city of death. It wasn't all that different from your own neighborhood, Mr Jefferson, which is a curious and interesting thing, don't you think? We've come so far, and yet, not really, have we? Anyway,

Mr Jefferson, they always told me what I wanted to know. *Where was the money? The jewelry? And where were their relatives? Their neighbors? Their friends? Where were the others hiding?* They always told me something that I needed to know, and they were smart people, Mr Jefferson. Smarter than you. Educated. Resourceful. But I caught them, just as I've caught you. And then they told me what I wanted, and so will you.'

Leroy Jefferson heard his own raspy breathing fill the room.

'Consider your situation for a second . . .' the voice continued. It seemed to come from everywhere at once, and he felt wildly disorientated, adrift, as if he were not in his own apartment, in the part of the city he claimed as his own, where he'd grown up and spent almost all his waking hours, but was someplace else, drowning someplace far from shore. 'You're already crippled, and now I've disfigured you with scars. What remains?' He pressed the blade up against Leroy Jefferson's lips. '. . Or maybe you'd prefer to be blind, Mr Jefferson? I could take your eyes. I've done that before. Are you willing to go through the rest of your life as a blind, dumb cripple? What sort of life would that be, Mr Jefferson? Especially for someone of, shall we say, your economic and social background? I can deliver that, you know . . .'

Leroy Jefferson saw the knife blade hovering in front of his face, reflecting the small light in the room.

'. . . Or maybe something else, something important . . .'

The man abruptly dropped the knife down, pressing the flat of the blade hard against Leroy Jefferson's crotch.

'Isn't it remarkable how many different ways there are to hurt a man? Physically. Mentally. Emotionally . . .' The knife pressed down sickeningly, and Leroy Jefferson thought he might vomit.

'. . . And some injuries accomplish all three. Right, Mr Jefferson?'

Leroy Jefferson wouldn't allow himself to answer this question. Fear like a mist obscured his thoughts. He felt himself ensnared in some net that threatened to choke him no matter how he twisted or squirmed. He tried to force himself to think clearly, but it was difficult, with the man's even, cold voice echoing in his ears and the knife blade dancing around his body. Leroy Jefferson felt trapped within a whirlpool of pain and terror; he knew little, except that if he told this man the truth, if he told him that he had seen him before and seen him kill Sophie Millstein and that he had told these things to Walter Robinson and Espy Martinez and had provided them with his picture and had agreed to testify against him at a trial, then the man would surely kill him. And then he would probably kill the detective and the prosecutor and anyone else that threatened him. He knew this with a clarity that defied all the hurt that surged throughout his body, knew it because he recognized if it were he standing over some similar witness with a blade of his own, anger and fear and the threat of arrest might force him to do much the same, and this gave him a certainty that was as unwelcome in the small, hot room, as was the visitor himself.

He felt tears welling up in his eyes, dripping down, mingling with the blood on his cheeks.

'So, Mr Jefferson, who am I?'

The question rang in his ear, urgent, terrifying. He took a sharp, deep breath, trying to contain himself. He knew, in that second, that nothing he said was going to make any difference whatsoever. The visitor was going to kill him. There was nothing he could say or do, that might save his life. All he could do, by telling the man what he wanted, was prolong it perhaps a few minutes. Maybe only a few seconds.

The thought pushed panic through him. He pulled at the duct tape that seized his hands, but could not break it. In the silence in the room, he felt the man maneuver around him, like a wayward breath of cold wind on a hot day. He swallowed hard, the dryness in his throat as parched as if he'd held a red-hot coal on his tongue. And in that second, abruptly, surprisingly, an entirely different sensation settled over his heart.

Leroy Jefferson felt a sudden, complete calm settle within him.

There was, he realized, no way out.

He could not fight. He knew no one would answer his call for help. And he knew no lie, nor no truth, could save him.

He thought he should be scared, but instead felt filled with an acceptance that bordered on defiance. He understood, in that second, that he had done precious little in his life that amounted to anything good or anything that anyone would have considered brave or even honest, and that now, facing his death, it saddened him to realize that no one would see him become these things. He would have liked it if someone like Walter Robinson or maybe Espy Martinez could have seen him change, in that moment, and that they realized that he had fought to protect them and maybe even had saved their lives. In that moment he hoped that when he was found, that they understood that he had died being something that he had never been before.

'*Who am I*, Mr Jefferson?'

He finally knew the answer to this question: death.

But he decided he was not going to give the man and his knife the satisfaction of a reply. Instead Leroy Jefferson spoke out in a determined voice that pushed past the parched thickness of fear. 'Old man, I don't know about all those other people. Maybe they told you what you wanted to know. Maybe they didn't. That be their business. But I know this: I ain't gonna tell you shit.'

And then he quietly surrendered to the relentless agony that awaited him.

CHAPTER TWENTY-ONE

Hatred

Simon Winter thought: I could have had him.

But then, in the next second, he realized: He could have had me.

'Stalemate,' he whispered out loud.

The old detective sat deep in an armchair, heavy in thought, amidst the rows of books and periodicals of the Miami Beach Library. Fluorescent lights and steadily droning air-conditioning gave the room an independence from the blistering day outside. For a library, there was significantly less devotion to utter silence than one might have expected. Sturdy shoes clicked against the linoleum floor; an old man snored, a newspaper fluttered open on his lap; occasionally raised voices ruptured the still air as one elderly woman sought to explain something to another, defying the hearing loss that afflicted both. The room had a busyness to it that would have irked any true scholar; but it served a slightly different purpose, existing both as a place where information was gathered, and as a cool, well-lit world where some of the older people living on the Beach could meet and spend a few unconcerned hours surrounded by safety.

This, he recognized, was more or less the same reason he was there. In the twenty-four hours since the Shadow

Man had fled from his apartment, Winter had decided several things. First, for the time being he was going to keep quiet about this new threat to himself. Secondly, he knew he was going to have to work harder and faster.

He had encircled himself with texts on the Holocaust, of which, understandably, there were many collected at the Miami Beach Library. He was riven with frustration. He was unable to shake the belief that somewhere in the past there was some bit of information that would open the door to the present. He was simply at a loss as to how to find that piece of history. All the books piled beside him, spread about on a small table and gathered at his feet, told him immense amounts about Nazis. They told him about what the Nazis did, and how they did it and where they did it and to whom they did it. He thought it an odd thing, to create, as they had, a world dedicated so completely to terror that it became commonplace and routine, and wondered if this were not amongst their greatest evils. But this observation did nothing to assist him in his pursuit of the Shadow Man; it told him nothing about what he felt he needed: some light that might penetrate the man's psyche. None of the books helped him in this pursuit. Some, admittedly, sought to examine the personalities behind the acts of men in black uniforms. There were political explanations describing how men came to join the Nazi Party, how they decided to participate in S.S. actions, how they came to justify murder and genocide. These political explanations dovetailed with psychological profiles, but none of these even came close to touching the soul of the Shadow Man, because, as Frieda Kroner and Rabbi Rubinstein had pointed out, he was never a Nazi, he was supposed to be one of their prey. Yet he managed to reverse that equation somehow, and emerge from events that had left their marks on everyone connected to them.

He was something entirely different, a unique player at the game of evil.

Simon Winter closed another thick history book with a snap that echoed in the large room.

If I do not understand this man, even if only a little bit, then he will slip past me again, Winter thought. He is not a man that has ever made the same mistake twice.

He slid deeper into his chair, dropping his head into his hands. He abruptly pictured himself standing outside his apartment, next to the trumpeting cherub, the night before, and he wondered what was it that had told him something was wrong.

Luck? Instinct? The old detective's sixth sense?

Winter exhaled slowly.

There had been no sound. No footstep. No tortured breathing.

There was not a light on that should have been off. No window open that should have been closed. He'd discovered the door ajar in the rear only after persuading himself that the Shadow Man was inside.

The night had been like every other. The darkness held the heat. The city pulsed on as it did every evening.

The only thing that was out of place was that a man with a knife had been waiting for him, and that if he'd not been overcome suddenly by some ancient sensation of dread and danger, he would no longer be hunting for the Shadow Man. He wondered where that sensation had come from, and did not know, but knew that he would be foolish to think that he would ever be fortunate enough again to have it come to his rescue as it had the previous night.

You should be dead, Simon Winter, he told himself.

He looked up suddenly, his eyes sweeping the room filled with old folks, reading books, magazines, newspapers. Some simply sat, lost in dreams of faraway times.

His eyes widened and he felt a sudden surge of fear tumble through his body.

Are you here?

Am I hunting you, or are you hunting me?

He fought off the urge to rise and run, steeling himself inwardly, forcing himself to examine all the people within the range of his eyes. The man in the hat poring over the *Herald*. The wizened man who seemed to be studying the ceiling. Another man, wearing white socks and black oxfords beneath madras shorts, who walked slowly past, carrying a pair of detective novels, one in either hand.

Winter half rose and stared behind him, at the people gathered in other chairs, at other desks, partially hidden by the stacks of books and reading cubicles. Then he settled back into his chair. He took a moment to compose himself.

He smiled.

How did you know about me?

He knew the answer to that: Irving Silver.

But what did he tell you?

Just enough to make you decide to kill me.

But what do you really know about me? You weren't inside the apartment long enough, were you? There were no signs that you took the time to discover who I really am. Drawers weren't ransacked. Clothing untouched. You didn't find the gun, and you still don't know that I have it, and that I will use it, and that once, a long time ago, I was an expert with it, and that I doubt it will fail me should I call upon our old camaraderie. No, you were merely going to kill me because you thought I was a threat, and it was easier for you to do that than anything else.

Simon Winter nodded. You arrogant bastard.

But it wasn't as easy as you thought it would be, and now you're probably a little bit worried, and that's something I can use. And you probably want to learn more about me, don't you? Well, that might prove harder than you think. So, for now at least, you are in the dark. Perhaps not as much as I am, but still, you are groping about, and that may make you take a chance you wouldn't ordinarily consider.

Winter felt himself fill with harshness.

They were always easy, weren't they? Once they were young and scared or old and scared, but always they were lost and desperate, and you were never that way, were you? No, you were always in control. But you made a mistake when you killed Sophie Millstein because you never imagined her neighbor would rise up against you. You never thought that there might be someone out there in this great wide world who would consider finding you as immense a challenge as you consider staying hidden. And it never occurred to you that this man who decides to hunt you would come from a world you do not know. And I too know a great deal about the ways of death, and maybe just as much as you, and I too am old, and have not so much time left that I care about, so that makes me unpredictable and that also makes me a dangerous man, and you've never been faced by a dangerous man, have you?

Winter reached out and seized a ballpoint pen and a pad of yellow legal-sized paper and started to scratch some notes to himself.

What do I know? he asked himself. Then he answered the question: more than I think.

I know you are old, but appear perhaps younger. I know you are strong, because the years have been good to you.

Why do you kill?

To stay hidden.

Winter paused. That's not enough, is it? There's much more to it than simply staying safe, isn't there?

He smiled. You like it, don't you? You like the idea that someone might recognize you? When Sophie Millstein spotted you outside the ice cream store in the middle of the Lincoln Road Mall, it didn't send a shiver of fear through your body, did it? No, the shiver you felt was pleasure, because you were once again in the hunt and that is what you like, isn't it?

An awful thought occurred to Simon Winter at that moment, and for a second his pen quivered above the yellow legal pad. Maybe Sophie Millstein didn't spot you by accident. Maybe you'd been hunting her for some time. And the others too. How many?

He gritted his teeth. Everything seems to be one thing, then it turns into other possibilities. He admonished himself: stick close to what you can grasp.

All right. He kept talking to himself, maneuvering through the maze of contradictions that might be the Shadow Man. All right, what else do you know? I know he doesn't fear the police, because he came after me without much preparation. He was simply going to cut the life out of me, and then leave my remains for Detective Robinson to clean up. So, he does not think he can be arrested. Why?

The answer to that question was immediately clear.

Because he is not a criminal.

If I were to discover your name today, what would it tell me? That you've never been arrested. Never finger-printed. Never typed into any criminal data bank for suspicion of any crime. Never cheated on your taxes. Never made a late payment or defaulted on a loan or returned a rental car late. Never pulled over for driving under the influence. Never even received a speeding ticket. You've lead a quiet, unnoticed existence; an exemplary life with one small exception: you kill people.

Simon Winter breathed out slowly. He nodded to himself. That's what makes you feel safe. You know that the police operate in a world circumscribed by routine. He was reminded of Claude Rains's famous line in *Casablanca*: 'Round up the usual suspects.' But you'd never get caught in that corral, would you? Because you don't fit into what we were taught to look for. Leroy Jefferson did, and that was why Detective Robinson was so expert at finding him. But you're not some low-life, crack-addled junkie, are you?

He put the writing pad down on the arm of the chair. He wondered whether Walter Robinson had managed to get his composite drawing prepared. He was suddenly overcome with the desire to see the man he'd been so close to for those few seconds in the darkness of his apartment. I am beginning to understand you, Shadow Man, he whispered to himself. And the more I understand, the more light falls across your shadow.

He looked at the books gathered about him, and abruptly was struck with an idea. I'm looking in the wrong place, he thought. I'm asking the wrong people. The rabbi, Frieda Kroner, Esther at the Holocaust Center, all the historians – they're all the wrong people. They know only of the fear and the threat the Shadow Man created. I must find one of the men who helped create the Shadow Man.

Simon Winter picked up a book from the stack beside him titled: *The Encyclopedia of the Third Reich*. He flipped through it swiftly, until he found an organizational chart. He wrote down some numbers and designations on his sheet of notes, and then took a deep breath.

A long shot, he thought. But I've seen longer. And it's something you wouldn't expect, would you?

He collected his things and rose. There was a bank of telephones just outside the library, and he repeated the numbers for Esther Weiss at the Holocaust Center and for the historians he'd spoken with as well. For a moment he saw his reflection in the plate-glass window of the library front door and noticed his lips had been moving as he'd kept up his one-sided conversation. This amused him. Old people are forever talking to themselves, because no one else will listen. It is a part of the harmless madness that age brings. Sometimes they talk to absent children, or long-lost friends, or missing brothers and sisters. On occasion they converse with God. Often they speak animatedly to ghosts. Me, he thought, smiling to himself, I talk to a hidden killer.

Walter Robinson, too, was frustrated.

The composite drawing of the Shadow Man stared back at him from his desktop. The Identikit technician had drawn the face with a small, almost mocking grin, which irked the detective immeasurably. Not the drawing per se, but the smile, because it spoke of elusiveness and ano-nymity.

He had begun to perform several routine chores of detection, the sorts of tasks that detectives everywhere do, and which they are accustomed to meeting some successes with. But so far his own efforts had been fruitless. He had faxed the partial thumbprint taken from Sophie Millstein's throat to the FBI labs in Maryland, to see if their computer could come up with a match. The marriage of fingerprint technology and computers has been slow in developing. For years matches were performed by human eyes. This, of course, required the detective seeking a match to know who his suspect was, so that a technician could then compare the crime scene print with a properly taken exemplar. Only in the last few years has computer technol-ogy been created allowing an unknown print to be fed into a machine and an identity plucked from the millions of prints taken from the fringe population. Dade County's computer, a smaller version of one operated by the FBI, had already failed. Robinson did not hold out much hope that the agency would be any different. And, owing to the immensity of the FBI sample, the examination would take upward of a week, and he did not know if he had a week to spare.

He'd spent several irritating hours at a computer screen, searching through records for some sign of the Shadow Man. There had been two entries with the word *shadow* under known aliases, but one of these was a Hispanic hit man in his late twenties, presumed dead himself, a victim of the usual narcotics dispute, and the other was a rapist working in the Pensacola area, who had been given the sobriquet by the local newspaper. He'd tried some variations on the phrase, but without success. He'd even been clever enough to tie into the Miami Beach tax rolls, using the German *Schattenmann*, but this had been a dead end.

He had tried entering the national criminal computer data base, with key words such as *Holocaust* and *Jewish*, but the one had been negative and the other had produced a lengthy list of various synagogue and cemetery desecrations, also listed under *Hate Crimes*.

He had tried the word *Berlin* with an equal lack of success. Efforts with *Auschwitz* and *Gestapo* and other links were hopeless.

He had not actually expected any success, but every time his computer blinked the reply NO ENTRY FOUND, it renewed his frustration.

He had also gone back into the Miami Beach department's cold case file, wondering whether there might be other signs of the Shadow Man's work in ancient cases, but so far he'd been unable to find anything. Certainly there

were unsolved homicides with Jewish victims, and probably some of these were Holocaust survivors, but whether
they'd once come from Berlin, and how and where they'd
survived the Holocaust, were not the sort of details
contained in the files. Backtracking through cases five, ten,
perhaps twenty years old, would take days. He had held the
files in his hands and thought to himself that surely one,
two, maybe more, could be the Shadow Man's handiwork.
For an instant he thought of the men and women the
Shadow Man had trapped in wartime Germany, and he
realized the cases he held were as lost to him as those
murders were.

The thought made him swear loudly, a torrent of
obscenities, heard by no one.

Walter Robinson rose from his seat and started to stalk
around the desks in the homicide office with all the
intensity of a newly captured wildcat, hoping that motion
might dislodge some thought that would lead him into a
profitable electronic avenue. Every detective keeps in
mind such salient memories, such as the Son of Sam case
in New York, solved when someone finally checked on
every parking ticket issued near one of the crime scenes.
He moved from one side of the room to the other, stopping
once to spend a minute or two staring out the window
across the city, which baked beneath the midday sun.
Then he hiked back to his desk, picked up the composite
drawing, and holding it in front of him, continued pacing
around the room.

He looked up only when he heard the voice ask him: 'Is
that our man?'

Simon Winter was standing across from him. Robinson
nodded, covered the space between them in a quick step
and handed the old detective the picture. Winter held it in
his hands for a moment, staring hard at the lines of the

drawing. His eyes seemed to absorb every detail, imprint-
ing them on his own memory. Then he smiled cheerlessly:

'Pleased to meet you, you sonofabitch.'

What he did not say was: So, you're the man who tried
to kill me.

'Now,' Robinson said, almost offhandedly, 'all we have
to do is put a name to that face.'

'A name . . .'

'Then I'll nail the bastard. You can take that to the bank.
That's all I need. A name. Then his next stop will be the
Dade County Jail. A brief stopover on the bumpy ride to
Death Row.'

Winter nodded. 'Tell me, Walter, have you ever hunted
a man involved in multiple homicides?'

'Yes and no,' the detective replied. 'That is, I busted a
drug dealer once who'd killed four or five rivals. And I was
part of the team that nailed that serial rapist who was
working up in Surfside. We always thought there were
probably some homicides that we could have made him
on, especially up in Broward County, but nothing came of
it, and he went away with a zillion-year sentence. But I
know what you're really asking. You want to know about
Ted Bundy and Charlie Manson and John Gacy and the
Boston Strangler and all the others, and you're wondering
whether I've ever participated in one of those investigations, and the answer to that is no, I haven't. Did you?'

The older man smiled. 'I took a confession once, a guy
sat across from me, smoking cigarettes, drinking Coca-
Colas. That was back when they came in those six-and-
a-half-ounce bottles, and you could polish off one of those
suckers in a gulp or two. It was hot, and there was only this
little fan running in a corner of the room, and it was late
at night, and it seemed like every time I got that guy
another Coke, he'd confess to another killing. Little boys,

mostly. He liked little boys. This was down in the southern part of the county, not too far from where the Everglades reach down and touch the bay. Redneck country. He was a transplanted good old boy. Should have been humming "Dixie". Couple of scraggly tattoos, three-day-old beard, beat-up baseball hat. Could hardly read and write. He got up to maybe seventeen, eighteen confessed killings by the time the sun came up, and so we took him out. He was going to give us the tour, you know? I felt like a bus driver at a goddamn tourist trap, like some sort of nightmare sightseer, thinking about what sort of final hours those kids had had with this bastard. We used a Jeep at first, then that got stuck, so we had to switch to one of those swamp buggies, the ones they use for crossing the hammocks, with a big old airplane engine in the back roaring away. He was trying to show us where he'd left the bodies, but hell, there'd been so much rain and sun, and that place, well, everything looks pretty much alike, and he wasn't the brightest light ever either, so we didn't come up with much. Ended up just charging him with the one case that we'd made him on. He went to the chair, always claiming there were others out there. Lots of others. And, you know, every so often some hunter or fisherman came across some bones out in the woods and muck, and I used to think maybe it was that guy's handiwork, but there was no way of telling.'

Simon Winter shook his head as he ransacked the memory.

'It bothered me for years. It still bothers me. All I could think about was all the people out there, mothers, fathers, brothers, sisters, hell I don't know, who didn't get an answer from me. You know, that's one of the most important jobs a policeman can provide: certainty. When you can give it out, no matter how terrible it is, then you must do it, because it is a helluva lot easier for people to live with even if it's the worst certainty in the world, than to be left not knowing. Damn that swamp. It can cover up anything.'

Walter Robinson nodded. 'Now we could fly over those spots in a helicopter, shooting the terrain with an infrared camera, and pick up the heat from a decomposing body.'

Winter sighed. 'Science is wonderful.'

'So . . .'

'Well, I remember thinking, listening to this guy, wondering when he was gonna quit, and he never quite did. You get this sensation that you've been dropped down a well. It's dark and dank and you might never get out, and even if you do, all you'll remember is the nightmare. I think our guy is a little like that.'

Robinson took a deep breath. 'I'm having some trouble sleeping. Even with . . .' He paused and Simon Winter filled in for him:

'. . . pleasant company?'

'That's right. Even with company. That obvious, is it?'

Winter grinned. 'I was a detective once.'

Robinson gave a small shrug. 'I had nightmares the other night.'

'What sort of nightmares?'

'Pretty much what you'd expect. Where you're watching someone drown and you can't do anything about it. That sort of thing.'

'You know what used to frighten me the most?'

'What?'

'That there were other guys, like this good old boy that killed seventeen, eighteen, or maybe more kids, and that they were out there and not only could I never get them, but that they'd live and do these terrible things to poor children who never had a chance, and then they'd grow progressively more awful and get old and finally die peacefully in their sleep, never touched, never threatened, never anything other than one hundred percent evil. And now, I'm old too, and I worry that maybe there isn't a Heaven and there isn't a Hell. Because, goddamn it, it truly bothers me to think that if we can't catch these guys on this earth, they can just disappear into the great oblivion without being held in the slightest way accountable. That's what gives me nightmares.'

Walter Robinson rubbed a finger across his forehead. 'I hadn't thought of it that way.'

'That's what makes this job so important, Walter. We like to think that there's a higher court. We hope there is, but there just might not be, and if there isn't, then it's completely up to us. Just us. Nobody else.'

'You're a philosopher, Simon.'

'Of course. All old men are.'

'They *are* out there, you know. That's what we've learned, since you retired. Not just one or two, but more than we can count. Perverts of every stripe and color. Killers of unique styles and approaches.'

'But this guy,' Winter glanced down at the composite drawing, 'this guy isn't a sex fiend or a pervert or some star-crossed megalomaniac. He's not Bundy and he's not Gacy and he's not Charlie Manson. Something else motivates him.'

'What do you think that is?'

'Hate.'

'He hates his victims? But he barely knows them.'

'No, he knows them well. Not them exactly, but who they are. But more importantly, he hates what they mean to him. They share a past. But I'll wager his hate goes back further. And what he wants to kill is history.'

'What do you mean?'

'I mean, he has never known anything other than anger.'

The younger man slowly bent his head to the picture. 'That makes sense,' he said after a moment. 'Maybe that's what has me screwed up.'

'How so?'

'I can understand perversion. I can understand blowing away the competition. I can understand shooting your husband for cheating on you. I've always been able to understand just about every reason for murder there is. But not this guy. Not yet. And that has me worried, Simon.'

The old detective smiled. 'I think,' he said, 'that perhaps I have not given you enough credit.' Then he scratched at his head in a mock curious motion. 'So, maybe if that is what moves this guy, don't you think we might try to find the source?'

'The source of his hatred?'

'Precisely.'

Winter reached into a small backpack that he carried, which contained some books and his notepad, and which made him think of himself as the oddest student walking the earth. He handed a piece of paper to Walter Robinson, who glanced at it quickly, then looked up with some confusion.

'What's this mean?' the detective asked. Then he read in a halting tone:

'Geheime Staatspolizei Gbh. thirteen; Sec. 101.'

He looked up. 'That's German, right?'

'Correct,' Winter said. 'That's my best guess as the military designation for the Jewish Bureau of Investigation. That's where the catchers worked. That was where our man got his training and discovered his vocation. I made a couple of calls too, over to the Holocaust Center and to a historian or two. They helped out. Now, what we need to do is find someone in Germany who has a list of the men who operated that section. Because someone else still alive will remember the Shadow Man, and maybe they'll know his name. The name may be changed, but it will be a start.'

Robinson shook his head. 'Do you think they kept a list of the killers they had working for them?'

'Yes. No. Maybe. I'll tell you what I've learned. I've learned that during the war the Germans kept lists and records of just about every damn crazy thing. They created this world that was completely upside down, where the laws protected the guilty and the criminals ran the courts. And because it was so bizarre, they became devoted to organization. Organization means paperwork. Sophie told me, right before she was killed, and I didn't hear her: *Even when they were going to kill you, the Nazis had paperwork.'* So, I'd guess somewhere there is a list of the men who were in charge of the catchers. All the captains, lieutenants, and sergeants that handled all that paperwork. And now that there's no more East Germany, there are a lot of documents floating around over there. It's worth a try.'

'But how . . .'

'Haven't you ever made an international inquiry before?'

'Well, sure. On that Colombian drug dealer I told you about. Contacted their police liaison . . .'

'So, let's do the same. In Germany. Same time, let's get in touch with the office of Special Prosecutions in the Justice Department. You know, it seems like every so often an old Nazi turns up, and there's someone who deals with it. They would likely have a contact with the Germans.'

'I don't know, Simon. Seems to me we should be concentrating here . . .'

'Here, we're searching for a shadow. Over there, there's someone who knows this man as flesh and blood.'

'Fifty years ago.'

'But knows him, and that is something we will find valuable when we spring the trap.'

'You're sure? They could all be dead. And they might not be willing to talk.'

'Always possible, but if we don't try . . .'

'Then we won't know. Okay, I'm with you on that.'

'Think of it this way. If you were a reporter at the *Herald* and you got a tip the Shadow Man was here, wouldn't you make those calls?'

'Probably.'

'Well, we're not doing anything different. And we've got more resources. Why not get Miss Martinez to use her weight. State Attorney's Office will carry some impact with the German police. And remember, they're always sending those damn German tourists over here to Miami Beach. They might be eager to help.'

Simon Winter smiled.

'The way I figure it,' he continued. 'When the Shadow Man walks into our trap, the spotlight we shine on him should be bright enough so that there is no way out.'

Walter Robinson shrugged, and considered this to be an impossible idea. And then, just as swiftly, thought: Why not?

CHAPTER TWENTY-TWO

The Expected Call

Espy Martinez worked the telephones steadily, doggedly, not altogether certain that she would find what they needed, but also not certain that they wouldn't.

As Walter Robinson and Simon Winter suggested, she had started with Special Prosecutions at the Justice Department in Washington, only to discover that this was a misnomer at best; she'd learned that Special Prosecutions was the smallest of offices, no longer manned on a full-time basis. It was more a designation assigned to whatever career attorney happened to be given a case file about a suspected Nazi. It had once been an actual office, but now had an accidental quality to it; as the years passed, it slipped out of the mainstream, dying out with the same ceaseless erosion that time had brought to the people it was supposed to hunt. There were only two active cases being handled: an allegation that a butcher in Milwaukee had once been a guard at the Treblinka concentration camp, and another, that a priest in a monastery in Minnesota had fifty years ago been a member of an S.S. Einsatzgruppen extermination squad in Poland. Both cases had been referred to the Immigration and Naturalization Service, where, as best as Espy Martinez could determine, they were shelved, awaiting the bureaucratic convenience that old age brings with death.

The State Department had been slightly more helpful; after a half-dozen calls, shuttling from office to office, a secretary had provided her with the police liaison number at the U.S. Embassy in Bonn.

She had persisted, working through the late afternoon and into the night, and finally was connected to a pseudomilitary type with an outgoing, friendly voice, who by happenstance was a native of Tallahassee, and therefore delighted to speak with someone from his home state. The liaison confirmed for her that German authorities would probably be willing, but hardly enthusiastic, to help her in her search – but only after she provided them with a name.

'These are Nazis I'm looking for,' she said.

'Yes, ma'am, I understand that,' the police liaison replied. 'The police over here are cracking down on all sorts of neo-Nazi operations.'

'I'm not interested in neo-Nazis,' she said, thinking that somehow the long distance and the lateness of the hour were obscuring her words. 'These would be real Nazis. Original Nazis, World War Two Nazis.'

'Oh,' the liaison answered. 'Well, that might be a problem.'

'How so?'

'Well, after the war the Allies, and then subsequently the West German authorities, designated a number of war criminals. But these were the upper echelon types. The guys that had stuff to do with theory and planning. The people who carried out the orders, well, they were reassimilated mostly.'

'You mean they just went back to doing whatever they were doing before the war?'

'Yes, ma'am. That was pretty much it. You see, if they'd tried to prosecute everybody who'd been a Nazi or worked for them, or helped in some way or another, hell, I guess they'd still be holding trials today. Now, of course, you got your exceptions to this. The concentration camp officials. People who participated in mass executions. That sort of thing. But I haven't heard of any of those cases being brought to trial, not for some time. You go through the Bundestag votes on this stuff, and you'll find a tangle of amnesties and pardons and redefinitions of what crimes were what. Then you'll find all sorts of statutes of limitations. Hell, they've even voted a couple of times on different laws trying to define what a murder was, during wartime.'

The police liaison, paused, then added:

'Memory's a funny thing, ma'am. Seems like the further we get from the war, the less people want to remember. Then you got all these new fascists demonstrating in the streets about foreigners, and committing assaults and even murders and waving swastikas and reading *Mein Kampf*. Authorities are pretty nervous about them.'

'But lists . . . memberships, all the documentation . . .'

'Oh, you're right about that, ma'am. There's a list, somewhere. Probably one with all the names on it that you're interested in. But finding it, well, that's the problem. They have a huge documents center here, but they're still sorting and cataloguing. Big job too, now that there are millions of other papers being sent over by the Russians and what used to be the East Germans. If you came over here, and if you were real persistent, I suspect you'd find someone over in that document center who could find what you needed. You get the names, then my police contacts would find them, if they're still alive. But that's a big job. You got some time on this, ma'am?'

'Not much.'

The liaison seemed pessimistic. 'You see, ma'am, the problem is, what you're looking for isn't considered a police matter. Not anymore. Now, it's a matter for historians. The world pretty much wants to get along and get ahead. Hell, you know over here it's a big damn issue what they say about that era in the classrooms. There's a significant percentage of people who either don't want it talked about at all or don't think it was all that damn bad. Except for the losing part, that is.'

Espy Martinez sighed, wondering at what point murder slipped from the province of the police and prosecutors and became something for doctoral candidates.

The police liaison, with his slow North Florida drawl, seemed to hesitate, as if thinking.

'Well, miss, I'm not supposed to suggest this . . .'

Martinez sat up abruptly. 'What is it?'

'Well, it seems to me you ought to try your questions on the only folks that are still real active in hunting Nazis. The kinda people who ain't all that interested in what the Bundestag says is a crime or not. I mean, there are a few people who think some crimes committed back then still deserve the world's attention.'

'Who might that be?'

'I'm not giving you this number,' the police liaison said. 'I don't know you, and I will deny it should it ever come up. Politics, you know. We cooperate with the Germans. Best of friends about just about everything. But they get very touchy when it comes to former Nazis. Not what you'd call naturally forthcoming. Especially when the request comes from outside the borders. Don't like to be reminded of all those things much. And they aren't real fond of this old guy. He and his people have a way of reminding them about their, how shall we put it, uh, darker side.'

'The number?'

'In fact, that's all they do. Remind people. Seems like an honorable thing to me, but then, anybody who's ever been a victim of any crime, much less the greatest crime ever committed, has a long memory.'

'Who is it?'

'In Vienna. There is a place called the Simon Wiesenthal Center. Really just the old guy, who thank the Lord has a memory that will go on forever, and a few dedicated folks that work for him. But if anyone knows who operated that section in Berlin in 1943, well, they might. And they're gonna be a whole helluva lot more likely to help you when they learn what it is you're looking for. Then, maybe you get lucky, get a name or two, get back to me, and I'll get my police friends to provide us with an address before they get too suspicious.'

The police liaison gave her a number and then disconnected the line. Espy Martinez thought, We all have memories of nightmare, and wondered why it was that the world was so eager to forget them. For an instant she was reminded of her murdered brother, and told herself that she would never forget what happened to him, no matter what arrived in her life. Then, just as swiftly, she wondered whether that was a wise thing. Then, because she did not like to examine herself as much as all that, she stared down at the number and picked up the receiver.

As with most international calls, it took her some time to get through, and then she was forced to leave a message, so that it was nearly an hour before someone returned the call. The someone was a young woman, who sounded to be the same age as her, although the woman spoke in English tinged with education and a distinctive accent that Espy Martinez could not categorize. It was not German. She identified herself as Edie Wasserman, and said she was a worker at the center. The center's namesake, she said quickly, was receiving an award in Israel, and unavailable.

'But what is it that you are interested in, Miss Martinez?'

'I am trying to find someone who worked in a particular section in Berlin, during the war.'

'Do you have the section number?'

'Yes, as best as we can figure it out. Section 101, Geheime Staatspolizei . . .'

'The Gestapo. They were better at destroying records than many other groups. The S.S. for example. Their cruelty sometimes seemed matched only by their arrogance. Yes. So, you are interested in the Gestapo in Berlin in 1943. This is curious. A prosecutor in Miami today wonders about the Gestapo in Berlin long before she was born. Most unusual. What is this particular section?'

'The Jewish Bureau of Investigation,' Espy Martinez answered.

There was a pause from the young woman on the end of the line so distant. When she replied, it was slowly.

'Yes, we know of this section,' she said. 'The catchers?'

'Yes.'

'A prosecutor in Miami, Florida, in the United States of America calls us one day, how do you say? Out of the blue? Interested in the catchers? This is most intriguing, Miss Martinez. What is it that you wish to know?'

'I am seeking information about an individual who was called the Shadow Man . . .'

'Der Schattenmann is dead, Miss Martinez.'

Again silence slipped into the air in front of her.

'Why do you say that?'

'Because when a woman named Kubler who had been known as the Blonde Ghost, who did much the same as Der Schattenmann, was arrested and tried, she was asked what became of some of the other catchers, and she said they were shipped east on the last few transports. You know what that meant, do you not, Miss Martinez? It meant you were dead.'

'But you know of that section?'

'Yes. Much information came out of the records of Kubler's trial, which were only recently available, because she was tried and imprisoned in East Germany. Many names that we did not know. Some other documents are given to us privately. But Gestapo records are quite precious, Miss Martinez. And therefore, alas, not complete. But why is it that you are interested in this man who is by all accounts dead today? You are not a historian or a journalist?'

'Because I don't think he is dead.'

'Der Schattenmann alive? You have proof?'

'I have deaths, Miss Wasserman. People who believe they saw this man here, and then were killed.'

'People? Who could recognize Der Schattenmann?'

'A handful of survivors.'

Espy Martinez could hear the young woman's sharp intake of breath, followed by a long silence, before she said: 'I must know more. I will help you however I can, but we must know more. If this man is alive, then he must be found and punished. This is important, Miss Martinez. Critical.'

'Names. I need names. If we can find out who he once was, then perhaps we can find out who he is now.'

'Yes, yes,' Wasserman answered. 'I will do this now. I will call you back when I get some information. Names.'

She hung up, leaving Espy Martinez to think that she was making some progress. She thought of calling Walter Robinson to update him, but decided to hold off until she actually knew something. So, instead, she paced about her

small office impatiently, fiddling with other cases that she
had pending that had been neglected and forgotten. This
simply enervated her more, and before too long she thrust
these files aside and simply sat at her desk, staring at the
telephone. Time seemed to fray the edges of Espy Martinez's patience as she waited for the woman in Austria to
call back.

It was past one when the phone finally rang.

'Miss Martinez?'

'Miss Wasserman?'

'I have some names for you, but I must extract a promise
first.'

'What is that?'

'That if this is true, if you succeed in finding the Shadow
Man alive, that you will share what you learn with us. Not
merely who he is, but how he escaped death in 1944 and
how he arrived in the United States. All the details of his
past, Miss Martinez. There is nothing that would not
interest us.' She paused, then added: 'He sent many to
their deaths, Miss Martinez. And there are some we
believe he may have killed himself. This is a man who
many will want to see brought to justice.'

'That is what I'm trying to do, Miss Wasserman,' Espy
Martinez said.

'I think we may not be speaking of the same justices.'

'I will provide you with all the information I can, as long
as I don't jeopardize my case here. You are interested in
deaths that took place fifty years ago. But I want to
prosecute him for killings that are here and now.'

'I understand.'

Again the woman hesitated. 'There is a sensation, Miss
Martinez, when you finally get close to one of these men.
S.S. men, usually. Camp personnel. There is a special
coldness about them. Perhaps it comes from living with

such immense lies for so long that they come to not believe
they did anything wrong . . .'

There was another silence, before the woman concluded:

'Here are five names from our files, which is the best I
can do on such short notice. I will keep working, though.
Two men held the equivalent rank of major, which would
have meant they were in their thirties or forties back in
1943, so I would not expect much from them, if they are
still alive. The other three were a captain and two
sergeants. They, perhaps, would have been younger, but of
less importance. Good luck. I doubt they will cooperate,
even if they do know something. But one never knows.'

Espy Martinez wrote down the names. She stared at
them, slowly drinking coffee, as she waited for morning in
Berlin. At eight A.M. overseas, she dialed the number for
the police liaison in Bonn. To her surprise, he was at his
desk.

'Any success, Miss Martinez?'

'Perhaps. You were right. They were eager to help . . .'

'Good. I thought they might.'

'I have some names. Could you get them run through
some sort of data bank? Tax rolls? Driver's licenses? All
would be elderly . . .'

'Let me see what I can do. Stick by your phone. I'll
simply tell the police these names have come up in a
Stateside murder investigation. I'll tell them we're looking
for some next of kin, or something. The police will be
wary, but we'll see.'

She rocked back in her seat and watched the second
hand of her wall clock sweep about. Exhaustion began to
cling to her thoughts, and she rubbed a hand across her
face. She put her head down on her desk.

The ringing of the telephone awakened her. Startled,

she almost lost her balance on her seat as she reached out for the receiver. She glanced at the clock and saw that it was nearly five A.M., and she felt a momentary dizziness as she answered the phone. It was the police liaison in Bonn.

'Miss Martinez?'

'Yes.'

'Well, burning the midnight oil, I see. You must really want this guy something fierce. What's the weather like home in Florida?'

She shook the sleep from her eyes as quickly as possible. 'Well, as best as I can tell, the weather is a constant sixty-eight degrees here in the Justice Building. I haven't been out for hours.'

'I miss it, you know. No palm trees over here. None of that good old Florida sticky goddamn hot either. Don't know how nice it is until you land someplace cold, like Germany.'

'I guess not.'

'Well, here's what I have for you. Of those five names, only two seemed to produce any possibilities, when I factored in age and location. Those were the men you thought held the sergeant's ranks. One of the guys, Friedman, well, that's like Smith in New York. List ran into the hundreds. The other, well, Wilmschmidt, is a little less common. Still, got a couple of dozen names across the country. I can fax you the entire list for both.'

'Okay,' she said wearily. 'That would be fine. I can start . . .'

'Well, I'll send you those, but there was one name that kinda jumped out at me that I figure you might want to start with.'

Espy Martinez straightened up. 'How so?'

'Well, age would be right and he's still living in a Berlin suburb, but more importantly, the records check showed he's a retired policeman. On the force dating back to the 1940s. Remember what I said about assimilation during the Occupation?'

'Of course.'

'Well, Miss Martinez, you got to understand what this country looked like in 1945. Just death and rubble. That was pretty much it. You remember your history? The Berlin airlift? Anyway, someone had to keep order, and so the Allies generally picked the people with experience. So, even if you were Gestapo once, it wasn't hard to make the leap to the postwar police. I'm just guessing now, but that would be my first choice for your mystery man. You've been pretty damn lucky so far, why not try him?'

She took the number down and gave the police liaison the fax number for the Dade State Attorney's Office. She looked at the number for a moment, trying to collect her wits, shaking the residual exhaustion from her consciousness.

Why not? she asked herself. Worth a try.

She dialed the number, not at all certain what she would say.

It rang a half dozen times before being answered.

'*Hallo?*'

'Hello. I'm trying to reach a gentleman named Klaus Wilmschmidt. Is this he?'

'*Was ist das? Ich spreche kein Englisch. Eine Minute . . .*'

The phone was silent, then a hesitant, younger voice came on.

'Hello? What is this, please?'

'Do you speak English?'

'Yes. Who is this, please?'

'My name is Martinez. I am a prosecutor with the Dade State Attorney's Office in Miami, Florida. I am in the midst of a murder investigation and I believe that a Mr

Klaus Wilmschmidt can provide us with some relevant information. I'm trying to reach him.'

'Yes, this is his home. I am his daughter. But murder? What is this? He has never been to the United States.'

Espy Martinez heard someone in the background asking a question in German, and the daughter hushed the man as she continued.

'The information we are searching for dates back fifty years ago. To Gestapo Section 101 in Berlin, during the war. Is that where your father worked?'

There was no reply.

'Miss Wilmschmidt?'

Again the line was silent.

'Miss Wilmschmidt?'

She heard a burst of German being spoken on the other end, a quick, snapping exchange before the daughter replied: 'Those times are past. He cannot help you. I will not allow it.' The woman's voice quavered.

Espy Martinez spoke swiftly. 'I'm trying to find out about a man who worked in that section. A man who may have committed murders today. It's important. Your father may simply have some information—'

'He will not speak of those times. They are gone, Miss . . . I did not get your name . . .'

'Martinez.'

'. . . Miss Martinez. He is old and those times are long ago in our history and he has lived a good life, Miss Martinez. He was a policeman and a fine man. I will not bring those times up to him. Now he is old and he is not well, Miss Martinez. He is not well, and deserves to live out his time on this earth in peace. So I will not help you, no.'

'Miss Wilmschmidt, please, just one question. Just ask him if he knew of a man called Der Schattenmann? If the answer is no, then—'

'I will not. He is not well. He deserves peace.'

'Miss Wilmschmidt . . .'

Before she could complete her plea, she again heard the gruff voice in the background demanding something in German, followed by a racking series of coughs. She heard the young woman angrily reply, and there was a sharp exchange of heated words before the daughter's voice once again came over the line.

'What was the name you spoke, Miss Martinez?'

'Der Schattenmann.'

Martinez heard the woman turn away from the phone and utter the name. Then there was silence. After a considerable pause, she heard more German echo over the distance. Then the young woman came back on the line. There was an odd hesitancy in her voice, as if she had seen something she was unsure about, but that might be terrifying.

'Miss Martinez?'

'Yes?' She heard the policeman's daughter battle a sob.

'My father says he will speak with you, if you will come here so that he may see your face.'

'He knows?'

'I am surprised. He has never spoken of those times, not at least with any—' She stopped, gasping a quick breath, before continuing. 'You will come here? He cannot travel. He is far too ill. But he will speak to you.'

Again the woman paused. In the background, once again, Espy Martinez heard German being spoken.

'This is the most unusual thing to say.' The voice on the phone had a tremor within it.

'What is that?' Espy Martinez asked.

'He said he has been waiting every day for fifty years for your phone call.'

CHAPTER TWENTY-THREE

The Man Who Once Taught Death

Walter Robinson was standing a few feet away from the bodies of an elderly man and woman. They were side by side, stretched out on their bed, inside an expensive, well-kept apartment that overlooked the ocean. The man wore a tuxedo, the woman a slightly dated, long, off-white satin evening dress, and they gave the appearance of a couple just returned from a New Year's Eve celebration. The woman's makeup was carefully applied, and diamond earrings glistened every time a police photographer snapped a picture. The man seemed to have trimmed his brushy, white mustache and slicked his hair down. He had taken care to fold a bright red silk breast-pocket handkerchief so that it splashed color across the black jacket, giving him a rakish, devil-may-care look even in death.

An empty vial of sleeping tablets was placed on a bedside table, next to two half-filled champagne flutes. A bottle of Perrier Jouet, with the etched flowers on the green glass, stood at solitary attention in a puddle of water inside a silver ice bucket.

He wished they'd left a suicide note, but couldn't find

one. The couple, however, had taken the time to arrange all their important papers, insurance policies, copies of their wills, their mortgage, their bank statements, in a neat pile on a dining room table. He noticed that on their balcony there was a table with some potted plants, and he stepped outside and touched the dirt in each planter and felt that it was damp. He took a long, deep breath of the humid predawn air. He looked out toward the sea, feeling the darkness around him thin ever so slightly as the minutes crept toward morning.

He stepped back inside. In the bedroom, the lead detective was making notes on the double suicide, and Robinson approached him.

'They watered the plants too,' he said.

'I guess they took care of everything,' said the other detective. 'They even left a stack of envelopes addressed to relatives, and a list of instructions for the funeral home.'

'Any idea why?'

The detective nodded. 'Right on top.'

He handed Walter Robinson a manila envelope and Robinson pulled out the papers contained inside. These were reports and a letter from a medical office clipped to a small booklet entitled *Understanding Alzheimer's Disease*.

'I guess they understood, all right,' the detective said. 'It wasn't too hard to see what was coming down the pike. Easier to go now, than try to fight that disease.'

Robinson shook his head. 'Can't see it,' he said. 'Can't see giving up a minute of life, no matter how lousy.'

'Hell, Walt, what's so special about life anyway?'

Robinson was about to answer this question when the pager on his belt went off. He went into the kitchen to answer his call.

The Beach message center operator had a crass, businesslike voice. 'Detective, I have two messages. They came in almost simultaneously.'

'Yes?'

'You're to call A.S.A. Martinez at her office. And I have an urgent request that you meet with a Sergeant Lionel Anderson of the City of Miami police.'

'Lion-man?'

'He gave me this address: King Apartments. Said you'd know which one. Said you have a problem with a witness.'

'A problem?'

'That's what he said. He didn't say what sort of problem.'

Robinson disconnected the operator and called Espy Martinez. When she picked up the telephone, he joked: 'Isn't there some song about working hard just so's you can end up on the late shift?'

She smiled through her exhaustion. 'I don't want to make a practice out of it.'

'Any luck?'

'Yes. I think so.'

His eyebrows shot upward and surprise curled around the edges of his reply. 'Really? What have you got?'

'A man who knew the Shadow Man, way back, during the war.'

'Where is he?'

'Berlin. And he's old and sick and he has a daughter who doesn't want him to talk to anyone about those times. He'll only talk face-to-face.'

'Go,' Robinson said impulsively. 'Go right now.'

Martinez breathed out slowly. 'That's what I thought too.'

'Just go and talk to the man. Whatever we learn—'

'I made a reservation. Could you come?'

'That would be nice. But I don't think so. The brass

would never authorize this sort of potential wild goose chase.'

'Do you think it is?'

'No. Because nothing in this case is as it seems. So, go find this old man and talk to him. Can you fly out today?'

'There's an afternoon flight that connects in London. I can sleep on the plane.'

'Talk to him, then come back. Maybe you'll get a name, and all I'll have to do is look the bastard up in the phone book, get a nice arrest warrant, and everyone can go back to working normal hours.'

'Nothing in the world is ever that easy. What will you do while I go gallivanting about Europe?'

'Well, right now, I'm going over to see our main witness. I got a message that there's some problem with Jefferson.'

'Mr Leroy fucking Jefferson. What sort of problem?'

'Won't know until I get there. He's probably complaining because crack cocaine prices went up while he was in jail and he wants to hold me personally responsible. Going right now. Let me know when your return flight arrives and I'll meet you. And let me know what this guy says. What was he, a Nazi?'

'A Nazi and a cop.'

Walter Robinson smiled. 'Hell. That's what every punk we arrest and every lawyer who represents them accuses us of being. It might be interesting to meet someone who actually was.'

Early dawn light seemed to chase him across the causeway, dogging his steps as he drove from the Beach to Liberty City and the King Apartments. The routine fatigue of a night spent in the presence of unremarkable death made him feel as if his reactions had slowed and his thinking dulled, almost like a man close to the legal point of intoxication, but not quite. He had a certain light-headedness, which made his concentration wander. He wished he were joining Espy Martinez at the airport, but realized this was impossible. And he had a vague, unfocused fear that seemed to halo his thoughts whenever he worried about Frieda Kroner and Rabbi Rubinstein. He had only partially heeded Simon Winter's suggestion that they be left without police protection. He had ordered a pair of unmarked cars manned by officers out of uniform to watch their apartments. He did not know for certain whether the Shadow Man was stalking them, but he suspected he was, in a steady, unimpulsive way. Still, even if so, he had the sense that he was making progress; he had a picture and a description and a witness and the partial thumbprint as evidence. Enough for a conviction. Now, all that remained was a name, and he thought that would arrive soon enough, especially after they set in motion Winter's scheme to flush the Shadow Man from hiding.

So, if not altogether confident, he at least felt things were in hand, and he yawned once or twice and rubbed his forehead as he rolled slowly down Twenty-second Avenue and turned toward Leroy Jefferson's home.

He saw the gathered police cruisers first; this made all the exhaustion flee from his eyes. Then he spotted the crime scene technicians' van, which gave him an electric shock of anxiety. He pulled his car to the curb sharply and pushed his way through a small gathering of the curious, the pale early morning light giving their skin a wan, lukewarm pallor. He waved at the uniformed officers holding the crowd back on the sidewalk and hurried toward the apartment building. He ignored the dilapidated elevator, choosing instead to bound up the exterior stairs.

He saw Juan Rodriguez and Lionel Anderson standing amidst a half-dozen other policemen outside the door to

Jefferson's apartment. There were several plainclothes men working the area, one with a fingerprint kit, going over the door.

Sergeant Lion-man saw him first and directed a small, helpless gesture at the apartment.

'Where's Jefferson?' Walter Robinson demanded.

'Inside,' Anderson replied. 'What's left of him.'

Rodriguez stepped aside, to allow him to enter the room. 'Watch your step, Walt, amigo. There's blood pretty much every fucking place.'

The light pouring through the doorway glinted off the tubular steel frame of the wheelchair. There was a thick, stifling sense of warmth and blood, a mustiness in the air as if the room had been superheated by both the tropical summer and murder. Robinson moved slowly toward the body; he forced himself to compartmentalize, to try and see every single detail inside the room in separate and complete fashion; Jefferson's eyes remained open; he'd watched his own murder. Robinson shuddered and stared hard at the duct tape that encircled Jefferson's wrists, and saw that a second strip had been placed across Jefferson's mouth, to keep him silent. The gray tape was streaked with vibrant red around the edges, caked up at the corners of his mouth. His eyes took in a sea of deep crimson blood that stained the floor beneath the chair. He saw that the bandages on Jefferson's ruined knee were ripped and torn, and he thought it obvious that Jefferson had known real pain in his last moments.

He felt an odd combination of sadness and anger. He wanted to curse at Jefferson, to grab him by the shoulders and shake him back to life. Instead, he swore beneath his breath, a quiet flood of obscenities as he took in the murder scene and felt all the confidence he'd had on the drive across the bay unraveling.

A flashbulb went off, and Robinson saw the medical examiner lean down next to the body and gently lift the dead man's head, examining a long scarlet slice in the skin of the throat.

'Is that what killed him?' the detective asked.

'Maybe. Maybe not. Hard to say,' the medical examiner replied, shaking his head.

'What, then?'

The medical examiner stood up slowly. 'I think he drowned.'

'Drowned? How?'

'Cut someone in the throat just right, tip the head back, and it just pours back down the airways, filling the lungs. Not a nice way to go. Takes a few minutes. Don't lose consciousness. But that's just an educated guess for right now. Look at this guy. He's been sliced up like someone took a Cuisinart to him. A lot of little cuts that won't kill you.'

A detective moving near the side of the room looked up. 'Sort of like one of those late night television commercials, you know? For the Veg-O-Matic. Slices, dices, chops – whatever.'

A couple of cops laughed, and continued inspecting the room.

'Your witness, right?' the medical examiner asked.

'Yes.'

'Not anymore. What was it, a drug case? I haven't seen this sort of thing since the late seventies, when the Colombians and the Cubans were arguing about who owned the cocaine trade. They were partial to knives. Especially those electric ones – you know, the type your mother-in-law gives you for Christmas. They used to like to use those on each other. Slowly. Not exactly what your mother-in-law had in mind.'

'No, not a drug case. A murder investigation.'

'Really? I'd swear it was a drug case. You don't usually see somebody get tortured like this if the general idea is to shut them up. Usually just a nice quick bullet.'

'This isn't the usual sort of case.'

'Well, somebody sure took their sweet time about all this. Somebody who sure enjoys their work.'

Before he could reply, one of the other detectives joined in. 'Hey, Walt, you know we found some crack cocaine spread around. Just a little, you know. And this guy had a long history of burning other dealers. I mean, maybe he was helping you, but he sure had a lot of bad-ass enemies out here in the real world. A lot of guys capable of carving up old Leroy there without too much thought and not a whole lot of concern over the poor slob. The guy he was helping you on, you sure that dude knew enough to come over here and do him like this?'

'I don't know. I didn't think he knew anything about Jefferson.'

'Well, Jefferson made the paper the other day. Maybe that tipped him off.'

'I still don't see how he made the connection. Shit.'

'This guy you're looking for ... he a black guy? On the Beach?'

'No. He's a white guy. An old white guy.'

A couple of the other detectives working the room stopped when they heard this. One shook his head in an exaggerated fashion.

'You think an old white guy came down here to the jungle in the middle of the night and did this? Not fucking likely,' the detective said. 'I mean, don't want to rain on your parade, Walt, but an old white guy? Down here? After dark?'

'No. I think he did.'

'Well, maybe. Maybe once in a zillion years some old-timer could come down here and not get taken off himself. I'm not saying it couldn't happen, but hey, Walt, get real. My money is on the neighborhood crack distributors. This looks like the sort of thing they'd get hot for.'

'Have you got any witnesses?'Robinson asked, 'Anybody in the building see or hear anything?'

The detective smiled. 'In the King Apartments? Somebody see something and then tell us about it? Forget it. And anyway, after what they did to Leroy, here, do you think someone else is going to be real interested in shooting their mouth off, and maybe taking their turn trying to explain why they talked to the cops to someone as handy with a knife as the psycho that did this?'

Robinson shook his head, and thought: It's useless.

He stepped away from the macabre tableau in the center of the room, and leaned up against a wall, thinking that he was completely, totally certain that the Shadow Man had found a way into the apartment, and was waiting for Jefferson, and that each slice in the junkie's body was like some exotic signature that only he could read. He recognized a fundamental truism in the responses of the other policemen: It didn't make sense that an elderly white man from Miami Beach would come to the center of the inner city to kill a low-life junkie and wannabe drug dealer, but he was certain that was what had happened. He also knew that anyone killing Leroy Jefferson was likely to get away with it. No one cared much about Leroy Jefferson either in life or death.

He took a deep breath.

Leroy Jefferson is merely dead, he told himself. The detectives working the case will shake a few informants, try to play one gang against another, see if they can't come up with a name that way. But they aren't really going to care, any more than he would. They'll maybe put in a little extra effort because he was a State's witness, but they understand the drill. You play on the fringe, you got to accept what's coming to you, and there was no one in the world who would say that, in a perverse way, Leroy Jefferson, Leroy fucking Jefferson, hadn't gotten precisely what the heavens were always expected to deliver to him. He'd only received it a little slower and more painfully than was the norm. A bullet in a drive-by shooting would have been statistically more appropriate. He thought there hadn't been much to like about Leroy Jefferson, but more, he hated how close they were, just as the murdered man had said. Could it have been me? Walter Robinson asked himself. If I'd taken a wrong step, made a bad decision, then I might have ended up like this: no suit, no badge, no lover, no future.

He looked over at the body and thought: No matter how far you travel away from this, it will always be there. It was like staring into a nightmare, one that was much closer to him than the vision the old couple laying peacefully on their bed had created earlier in the morning. He tried to imagine himself and Espy Martinez, old, together and drinking champagne as they swallowed handfuls of sleeping tablets.

Walter Robinson let out a long, slow sigh.

He felt an abrupt chill, almost as if some bizarrely lost cold wind had singled him out from all the other policemen processing the room. He looked up toward the open eyes of Leroy Jefferson and thought: Was he waiting here for you when I dropped you off?

He knew the answer to this.

He remembered his offer to accompany Jefferson to the apartment, and in that second he imagined himself reaching for his weapon as the Shadow Man reached for him. He wondered: Would I have made it?

He did not think so.

He asked himself: Would he kill a cop too?

Again the answer was yes. He did not think the Shadow Man cared the slightest for the ordinary conventions of criminality, which held out that killing policemen was a considerably worse crime than eviscerating a drug-dealing State's witness.

He will kill anyone whom he perceives as a threat.

Robinson shuddered involuntarily, then looked around the room to see if any of the other policemen had seen the quiver in his shoulders. His eyes met Sergeant Lion-man's, and for just an instant the two of them locked, and the burly policeman nodded in understanding. Robinson breathed in hard, and saw the medical examiner hover again around the dead man's body.

One of the other detectives saw the same. 'What's so interesting, Doc?' he called out.

The medical examiner was a small, bookish man, with delicate features and a bald spot on his head that glistened with sweat. He sometimes whistled while he worked on a body, a detail that caused no end of amusement amongst homicide detectives.

'I was just looking at this tape around the victim's lips,' he replied. 'Very strange.'

'What's so strange?' the detective asked. The other men stopped working and looked his way.

'Well, for one thing, I don't understand all this blood caked up here and here. See, if the killer put the tape on his mouth to shut him up, then cuts his throat so's he drowns, well, all the blood would be where most of it is. There wouldn't be any on his mouth. Gravity, you know. Liquid flows downhill.'

'So, what are you saying?' Walter Robinson heard someone ask.

'I'm saying, something else caused this blood.'

'Maybe he smashed him in the mouth before slapping on the tape?'

'Maybe. But no other external signs of a beating. Just signs of knife work.'

The medical examiner whistled for a moment, a vaguely recognizable tune from a Broadway show. Then he reached out and put his fingers around the edge of the tape.

'Just can't stand waiting,' he said quietly. 'Never could, even when I was a kid. Birthdays. Christmas. Always wanted to see what was inside those packages.' As he said this, he ripped the tape from the dead man's lips. It made a sucking sound.

The other men turned and looked. For a moment Robinson's vision was obscured by the medical examiner's body.

'I'll be damned.' The medical examiner stepped back. 'Well, I guess it's safe to say that someone was displeased with the victim's conversational style.'

The doctor turned toward Walter Robinson, who saw that he held Leroy Jefferson's tongue in his hand. It had been sliced out at its roots.

By the time she was settled into her connecting flight from London to Berlin, Espy Martinez was snared by the inevitable tug of conflicting sensations: exhausted by erratic sleep and air travel, energized by the thought that she was doing something that might matter. She found her daydreams filled with successes; imagined headlines, envisioned the accolades from her officemates. She pictured herself and Walter Robinson linked by good fortune and public prosperity, and thought that high-profile triumph would allow her to force him upon her reluctant, antique

parents, creating an avenue where even their prejudice
would have to take a backseat to accolades.

She did not really think of the Shadow Man as anything
other than a device for advancement. Ambitions in love
and career were all she could concentrate on, as the jet
engines droned outside and she sliced through the dark
European sky. That she was thousands of miles from her
home, and from the case in hand, was lost on her. She saw
nothing unique in her destination, only that there was a
witness that needed to be interviewed and that he might
provide her with a name, and that might be all that she and
Walter Robinson needed.

As the lateness of the hour settled on her, she worked on
her list of questions for the old man she had traveled to see.
She did not understand that she was somehow stepping
into the history of nightmare. Simon Winter would have,
as would the rabbi and Frieda Kroner. Walter Robinson
might have begun to comprehend this, but as her flight
began its approach into Berlin's airport, he was fighting
nausea in a sterile autopsy chamber at the Dade County
Medical Examiner's Office, watching as the physician
carefully documented each of the dozens of slices in Leroy
Jefferson's body, thinking, as each was noted on a form,
that he could no longer underestimate the man he was
hunting.

She exchanged some money at a kiosk inside the
terminal and took a cab to the Hilton Hotel. She left
instructions with the desk clerk that she should be awakened at eight in the morning, which was an hour before the
police liaison from Bonn was scheduled to meet her.

For a moment, before crawling into bed, she looked out
the window of her hotel room. What she saw was a modern
city spread out under a night sky. She did not feel that far
from home.

*

Timothy Schultz, the police liaison, was waiting for her in the lobby of the hotel. He was a thickset man, in his fifties, with close-cropped, military-style hair and a pleasant southern accent. As she exited the elevator, he rose from an overstuffed chair and advanced on her, hand extended.

'Well, hell, Miss Martinez,' he said, 'it sure is nice to meet someone from the great State of Florida, even if it is the wrong end of it.'

'Glad to meet you, Mr Schultz. Let me thank you again for all your help.'

'No big deal. And anyway, most of the time I spend handling FBI queries about terrorists and international jewel thieves and all sorts of business scams. So, I got to admit, your request sure was a whole helluva lot more interesting than the usual thing come knocking over the telex. Wouldn't have missed this for the world.'

'The daughter said she would translate for me. . . .'

'Well, then I'll just sort of back her up.'

Espy Martinez nodded, her mouth open slightly, as if to ask something, but the police liaison anticipated it.

'I know, I know. I know what y'all are thinking. You're thinking how is it this good old boy from Pensacola lands over here, and he sure doesn't sound like he can talk one word of the lingo, ain't that right, Miss Martinez?'

'Well, the thought crossed my mind.'

'Not too complicated. My grandparents were both German immigrants and I grew up in their house, 'cause my daddy ran out on us when I was still little. The old folks kept up the language, and so I learned it young. There you have it.'

They started to walk across the lobby.

'You want me to give you the scenic tour, Miss Martinez? Or are you in a hurry to talk to this old guy before his daughter gets him to change his mind?'

'Mr Schultz, tourism isn't what I'm here for.'

He nodded and shrugged. 'I'm thinking you're gonna get a different kind of tour,' he said.

They drove through the city, and despite Espy Martinez's quiet attempts to focus on the upcoming interview, the police liaison kept up a steady travelogue, pointing out the sights of the city. Where the wall once stood, parks, buildings, and a river flowed past the windshield. She found herself looking up occasionally when something he said spurred some memory. He drove her past the Iranische Strasse address of the Jewish Bureau of Investigation, but the building had been replaced by a modern office complex. Schultz explained to her that Berlin, like many European cities, had more lives than the proverbial cat; centuries of building had made it old and venerable, only to have the war turn it into a bombed-out world of rubble. The fifty years since the war had been filled with rebuilding, but hampered by the years spent divided between East and West. The result was an odd hodgepodge of architectures and ages. He laughed, and asked her to envision Miami fifty years earlier.

The old Nazi lived in tract housing outside the center of the city. It had a determined suburban feel to it, slightly alien, as if a poor model of an American concept. There was an insistent uniformity to the houses: white stucco, with dark slate roofs, trim gardens and shrubs, uncluttered streets. There was an orderliness to it all that made her feel uncomfortable.

Schultz noticed this, and said, 'You got to remember, Miss Martinez. The Germans like things lined up and at attention. Everything in its place.' He pulled to a stop in front of one of the homes. 'Here we go,' he said. 'Should be interesting.'

They were a few feet from the front door when it cracked open slowly, and she saw a striking woman standing hesitantly in the portal.

'Miss Wilmschmidt?'

The woman nodded. There was an awkward moment when she did not open the door, but then, as if still doubtful about what she was allowing to happen, the woman swung the door wide and gestured for them to enter. She was tall, in her mid-thirties, but thin-waisted, like a fashion model, with a wave of reddish-brown hair gently littered with gray, which only made her seem more elegant. She wore fashionable eyeglasses that hung from a retaining strap down onto an expensive white silk shirt. Her clothes, though, reflected her attitude: a chocolate skirt and dark stockings, a black blazer. Despite her stylishness, she had a spinster librarian's quality to her, a cold, tight, angry attitude. As Espy Martinez and the police liaison stepped into the small house, the woman said: 'I wish you were not here, Miss Martinez. I wish that this was not happening.'

'I'm sorry to intrude,' Martinez answered. 'I appreciate whatever help your father—'

'He is sick. I do not know the word in English. He cannot breathe. Because of the smoking. I do not know what you would call it.'

'Emphysema?'

'Perhaps that is it. He is not supposed to become excited. That you understand.'

'Of course. We'll try to keep this short.'

'That would be good. I am supposed to return to the bank this afternoon. That is where I work.'

'I'll try to be brief.'

The daughter nodded, although clearly she did not believe this. At the same moment, there was a burst in

German, which echoed from the rear of the house: 'Maria! *Bring sie herein!*'

The woman hesitated. 'Already he is too excited,' she said.

'*Bring sie herein!*'

Maria Wilmschmidt swung her hand halfheartedly in the direction of the voice. Espy Martinez heard a series of painful coughs as they maneuvered through the narrow central corridor of the small, two-bedroom house.

The old Nazi lay in pajamas and dark dressing gown on a single, wooden-frame bed inside a still, cramped room. A sole window, framed by thick white curtains, allowed some gray daylight to enter the room. There were no pictures on the walls. The only other furniture was a beaten brown bureau and a bedside table littered with vials of pills and a water jug. A tall oxygen tank with a pale green mask stood next to the bed. In a corner a television set played soundlessly. The old man had been watching reruns of American television shows. In one corner, as if thrown there, was a pile of magazines and paperback books.

'Mr Wilmschmidt, I am Espy Martinez . . .'

She could see the blue tinge to his nose and the red flush of his cheeks caused by blood vessels starved for air. He wheezed harshly as he waved her into the room. She saw that he had large hands, with long, aristocratic fingers, though they were stained yellow at the nails. She realized that he had once been a large, thick man, but no longer; the disease that robbed him of air had gnawed away at his body as well, so that flaps of flaccid skin hung from his bones, giving her the impression that he was someone who was being devoured from within by his own illness.

'*Maria, bring Stühle für die Gäste!*' Bring chairs for the guests! He coughed.

As the daughter responded, Espy Martinez thought him a man who never asked, only ordered. In a moment the daughter returned with three steel folding chairs, which she arranged by the bed.

Martinez sat down, nodded toward the daughter for translation, and said: 'Mr Wilmschmidt, I am investigating several murders that have been committed by a man once known here in Berlin as the Shadow Man. We do not know his current identity, so we are searching for anyone who might have known him and who can tell us about him.'

The daughter dutifully translated.

The old man nodded. 'So, he kills still, even today,' he replied.

'Yes,' Martinez said after listening to the translation.

'I am not surprised. *Er hat sein Handwerk gut gelernt.*' He learned his trade well.

'Who trained him?'

The old man hesitated, then smiled. 'I did.'

There was a momentary pause, and the daughter gasped and spoke rapidly to her father in German: 'You should not speak of this! *Das bringt nichts Gutes!*' No good will come of it! 'You did only what you were told, nothing more! You did what others did, you were no different! Why should you help these people? *Das bringt nichts Gutes!*' she implored.

Espy Martinez glanced at Timothy Schultz, but he was listening intently for the old man's reply.

'Just because I did what I was ordered, do you think it means nothing?'

The daughter shook her head, but didn't answer.

He turned to Espy Martinez: 'My daughter is ashamed of the past and that makes her frightened. She worries what the neighbors will think. She worries what her employers at the bank will think. She worries what the world will think. I do not have so much time that I worry at all. We did what we did! The world trembled and rose up against us! And so, we were defeated, but the ideas, they have never died, have they? Whether they were right or wrong, they still live, do they not? You Americans should understand this better than anyone else. Do you understand Miss Martinez?'

'Of course,' she replied, after hearing the translation.

'*Nichts verstehen Sie!*' You understand nothing!

The old man snorted, and this turned into a protracted cough.

'You cannot understand,' he said, with a small snarl that maneuvered on his face into a twisted grin. 'I was a policeman! I did not make the laws, only enforced them. When the laws changed, I enforced the new laws. If the laws changed tomorrow, then I would change tomorrow.'

Espy Martinez didn't reply, other than to think that he had already contradicted himself.

He coughed again and reached for the oxygen mask. There was a hissing sound as he turned on the bottle and drew in several long draughts.

He peered at Espy Martinez over the edge of the mask.

'*Der Schattenmann lebt also noch und bringt noch immer den Tod.* So, the Shadow Man lives and still brings death. I knew this. Without you telling me this was so, I knew it. I have known this was true for years. I was the last of our group to see him, but I knew then that he would not die. Will it be you that kills him, Miss Martinez?'

'No. I merely want to arrest him and prosecute him in a court of law. . . .'

The old man shook his head violently. 'There are no laws for the Shadow Man, Miss Martinez. For me, yes. For you, yes. But for him, no. Tell me again, Miss Martinez: Will it be you that kills him?'

'No. It will be the State.'

The old man laughed. A brittle sound in the small room. 'And so, it was the same with us.'

'These are not the same things.'

He laughed again, mocking her. 'Of course not.'

She stopped, eyeing the old man. 'You said you would help me,' she said after a momentary silence.

'No. I told you I would tell you of the Shadow Man. I have been waiting all these years for someone to come to me and ask of him. I knew that this would happen before I died. I did not know who it would be. Sometimes I thought it would be some Jews, perhaps the ones that still hunt for the old ones. I thought it might perhaps be a policeman, like I was. Or maybe a journalist, or a student, or a scholar, someone who studies these great and evil things. Someone who wants to know about death. This is what I thought. This I expected, every day. When the telephone rang, I told myself, this will be the one. If there was a knock at the door, I thought, now they have finally found me and come to learn. Even as the years passed, Miss Martinez, I knew someone would come. I knew this.'

'How did you know?'

'Because a man like the Shadow Man cannot exist in silence.'

'You taught him?'

Klaus Wilmschmidt stared hard at her. Then he slowly reached toward a bedside table, opened a drawer, and produced a long, thin, black-handled dagger, with a death's-head skull adorning the tip of the grip. He held the blade gingerly, letting his finger slide down the steel.

'This, this would be used for ceremonial purposes, Miss Martinez. A killer's knife would be thicker, double-bladed, with a wider grip, so that you can turn it more easily.'

He stared at her.

'Do you know how many ways there are to kill a man with a knife, Miss Martinez? Do you know that it is different from behind . . .' He drew the blade slowly from right to left in the air in front of him. '. . . than it is from the front?' He suddenly jabbed the knife upward, twisting as it slashed the space between them.

She said nothing, and he laughed again.

'Will it not make you a better policeman, Miss Martinez?'

'What?'

'The more you know about death, the better you will be at detecting it. Is this not so? It was for me. And for many others, like me. I think you probably know some men like me, Miss Martinez. It is just that it is not always so pleasant to admit it.'

He laughed again.

'*Sie glauben wohl ich bin ein böser alter Mann,*' he said. I must seem to you to be a terrible old man. When his daughter hesitated, in her translation, he grunted at her, gesturing with the knife. 'And perhaps I am so. But I will tell you a story, about the Shadow Man, and then you may do with it what you will.'

'Maybe it would be better if I just asked questions—' Martinez started, but the sick man's glare made her stop. The daughter managed to blurt out a few words in German, and then halted as abruptly.

'*Ich erzähle Ihnen jetzt die Geschichte,*' he said. I will tell the story. He reached to his side and seized the oxygen mask, cupping it across his face, breathing deeply.

'It was 1941 when I was transferred into Section 101, and I had just been promoted to the rank of sergeant. Sergeant! Not bad for the son of a coal hauler whose wife had to take in laundry to help make ends meet. These people, my parents, my daughter never knows of them, because they die in an air raid in 'forty-two.'

The old man stared at his daughter.

'*Du weisst ja was Seide ist,*' he said sharply. You know silk. 'Silk and Mercedes cars, because of your international bank. You know money. We knew none of that! I was raised poor and shall die poor!'

The daughter did not translate this, but Schultz did, quietly, beneath his breath. Espy Martinez saw the daughter's face constrict, and she knew that she was glimpsing some longtime pain between them.

'You do not care,' the old Nazi continued. 'And so, I do not care either.' He turned away from his daughter and back to Espy Martinez.

'The transports were running constantly then. Round-ups daily. Sometimes twice a day.'

'Roundups?'

'Jews. Transports to the East. To the camps.' He smiled. '*Diese Züge waren immer pünktlich.*' Those trains always ran on time.

Espy Martinez tried to keep a poker face. 'The Shadow Man?'

Klaus Wilmschmidt turned away, just for an instant, his eyes searching out the window. He stared at the glass.

'I can see nothing,' he said bitterly. 'I lie here, and all I can see is a corner of the neighbor's house and a little piece of the sky past it. There is no light.' He spoke the last words rapidly, and he reached across for the oxygen mask again, as breath started to wheeze from his chest.

In a moment he turned back to Espy Martinez.

'The Shadow Man was in the major's office. I was called in . . .'

On his bed, the old man lurched into a position approximating a man snapping to attention.

'. . . The major knew something. That he was different.

I only saw the boy sitting there. He was dressed like a workman. Heavy boots. Woolen pants and coat. He had a hat pulled down, so it was hard to see his face. The major says to me: "This Jew will help us. He will catch other Jews for us. . . ." and I salute. This is something I expect. But what comes next is unusual, because the major, he turns to the Jew and he says, "Willem, you are a Jew, are you not?" as if he is joking. And this boy, he is perhaps nineteen, twenty years of age, he makes a face like some beast in the zoo. Filled with anger and capture. And after a moment, he replies, "Yes, Herr Major, I am a Jew!" and the major, he laughs and turns to me and says, "Willem is not much of a Jew, Sergeant. Just the littlest bit. What bit is that, Willem?" and the boy, he answers, "My grandmother, damn her."'

The old man looked at Espy Martinez.

'You are a woman of laws, correct?'

'Yes. I am a lawyer and a prosecutor. . . .'

'*Sie haben keine Gesetze wie wir sie hatten! Die Rassengesetze!*' You have no laws like we had. The race laws. He laughed. 'Poor Shadow Man! A half-Jewish grandmother who renounced her religion when she married before the first war. Who died before he was born. What a great joke that was, was it not, Miss Martinez? This woman whom he never knew put her blood in his veins, and because of that, he was to die. *Ist das nicht ein guter Witz?*' Is that not a great joke? 'Can you not see the devil's own hand making sport of the poor Shadow Man?'

He paused, as if waiting for an answer, but she did not reply, so he continued.

'So, the major, he turns to me again, and he says, "Willem can be a very useful boy. He will find Jews for us. And he will do other things too. For me. Is that not correct, Willem?" and the boy replies, "Yes, Herr Major." I do not know, but I suspect the major knows of this boy, and has experience with him in the past. I do not ask this, because the major gives me my orders: I am to train the boy. Surveillance. Pursuit. Weapons. Techniques of detection. Even some code work. Also forgery, which he has quite a fine hand for. *'Der Junge soll das Geschäft der Gestapo lernen!'* The boy is to learn to be Gestapo! 'A Jew! And so, I teach him, and do you know, Miss Martinez, no teacher ever had a pupil quite like him.'

'Why is that?'

'Because he understands always, he can be on the next transport. And because he hates so fully and completely.'

'The major, why did he . . .'

'Because the major was a smart man. A brilliant man! Still today, I salute when I remember him. He knew that finding Jews was his job. But he knew too that it would be useful to have a man like the Shadow Man always ready, always expert, for whatever task you might have. Did you want a document stolen? A rival murdered? What better man than the Shadow Man to perform any small, deadly task the major might have had. Because, Miss Martinez — *er war bereits tot!'* He was dead already! 'All the Jews were. And he knew he owed his life only to his special capabilities.'

Again the old Nazi smiled.

'We were killers together, Miss Martinez. He and I. Student and teacher. But he was far superior to me. . . .' The man on the bed rubbed a hand across his forehead. 'I felt guilt. He did not.'

Again he paused.

'He was our perfect killer, and you know what else, Miss Martinez?'

'What?'

'The Shadow Man truly enjoyed his job. Behind all his hate, he loved bringing death. Especially to the people he blamed for his own blood.'

'What happened to him?'

Klaus Wilmschmidt nodded his head. 'He was clever. He stole. Diamonds, gold, jewels, whatever. He stole from the people he found. Then he saw to their deaths. He knew, you see, Miss Martinez, he knew his own existence relied on his ability to detect Jews and to perform the major's special tasks. As the number of Jews to catch dwindled, in 'forty-three and 'forty-four, his own existence became more precarious. And so, he took precautions.'

'What do you mean?'

'He took steps to survive, Miss Martinez. We all did. No one believed, anymore. When you can hear Russian artillery, it is hard to believe. But long before that, we knew. When you have helped create the lies, Miss Martinez, you would be quite a fool to believe them yourself.'

'The Shadow Man?'

'He and I had an agreement. A mutual convenience. Of what he'd stolen, I was to receive half. And papers. He was quite the forger, Miss Martinez. And, of course, I was able to help obtain stamps and proper forms. So, when the time was right, we could disappear. Become something new. I was to be Wehrmacht. A soldier wounded on the Western front and disabled. *Ein ehrbarer Mann.*' An honorable man. 'A soldier who merely followed orders and now wanted to go home in peace. Not Gestapo. And this, one day, when all was finished, I became. Handed myself in to the British.'

'But the Shadow Man?'

'His task was more complicated. And, he was more clever than I. He searched for a man. Every day, he hunted. A man to become.'

'I don't understand.'

'A different identity. A Jew, like himself. Of close to the same age, size, education. With the same coloring. And, when he found this man, he did not put him on the transport, although that is what the records said. No, he killed him, himself. And he kept this man's person safe for his own use. He began to starve himself. . . .'

'Starved?'

'Yes. To become, you see! And he had his arm tattooed with a number as they did at the camps. And then, one day, he disappeared. A wise choice, that day.'

Again the old man laughed, which prompted a coughing fit.

'It was wise, because that day the major, his protector, was drunk and asleep when the bombers came over, and did not awaken in time to go to the shelter, and so, when he did awaken – *er war bereits fest auf dem Weg zur Hölle.*' He was already fast on his way to Hell!

Wilmschmidt again choked on his laugh, reached for the oxygen, then smiled toward Espy Martinez.

'A good plan. I suspect he'd sewn his money into his coat. A rich man! He probably headed west, toward the Allies. I did. You did not want to be questioned by the Russians. But the Americans, like you, and the English, they still wanted to be fair. And if you landed with them, complete with a tale of escaping from a camp, starved and tattooed, would you not be embraced? *Zumindest glaubte man Ihnen?*' At least believed?

Espy Martinez didn't answer. Her own throat felt tight and dry, and the small room seemed filled with an illness different from the one that racked the body of the old Nazi. She felt a thickness, a dullness, as if sorting through the story she'd heard would require a razor, and she had none.

'And so, he escaped?' she asked.

'He escaped. I was sure of it. I escaped, doing much the same.'

She stumbled internally, thinking hard.

'So that is how he came to be,' she said. She abruptly reached down into her leather satchel and removed a copy of the composite drawing that Leroy Jefferson had created. She thrust it toward the old man, who held it in front of him. After a second staring at it, he burst into a harsh, raucous laugh. He shook the picture in front of himself and said: '*Es ist so gut, dich zu sehen, mein alter Freund!*' It is so good to see you, my old friend!

Then he turned to Martinez. 'He has changed less than I would have thought.'

Martinez nodded. 'You've told me about the past,' she said. 'How do I find him? Now. Today.'

Klaus Wilmschmidt lay back on his bed, eyeing her. He lifted a hand and gestured toward the vials of pills, the oxygen, and then toward himself.

'I am dying, Miss Martinez. I am in pain, and I can count the breaths I have left.'

Maria Wilmschmidt sobbed slightly as she translated.

'*Gibt es einen Himmel?* Is there a Heaven, Miss Martinez?'

'I do not know.'

'Perhaps. Perhaps not. So, once I was part of terrible things, Miss Martinez. Things you cannot begin to understand. I hear cries at night. I see faces on these walls. Ghosts in this little room, Miss Martinez. They are here with me. More every day. They call to me, and soon enough I will try to take a breath, but I will not be able. I will grab for the oxygen, but it will not work. And I will choke and die. That is what is left for me.'

He paused, gathering himself.

'So, I wonder, can I die with what I know about this man? Tell me, Miss Martinez, will I now know peace? Now that I have spoken of him, and what we did?'

'I don't know,' she answered, but she did.

The old man seemed to grow smaller, darker, as if night and fog had covered him like a coat. His breathing was raspy, erratic.

'Find the Shadow Man? That I cannot do, Miss Martinez.'

'But—'

'But I do know the name of the man who he became.'

'Tell me!' she demanded quickly, as if she needed to know before the man on the bed coughed again.

He grinned, his face not unlike the death's head on the dagger he'd waved about earlier.

'Yes,' he said. 'I can tell you the name. And I can tell you something else.'

'What is that?'

Klaus Wilmschmidt, the dying man, whispered his response: *'Ich weiss was für eine Nummer der Schattenmann auf seinem Arm hat . . .'*

The old man's daughter paused for an instant, breathing once harshly, before she quietly translated: 'I know the number the Shadow Man tattooed on his arm.'

CHAPTER TWENTY-FOUR
The Historian

Simon Winter and Walter Robinson, standing slightly apart, watched as the rabbi and Frieda Kroner examined the composite drawing of the Shadow Man. The old people were quiet, studious, like a pair of scholars poring over some faded ancient hieroglyph, before they each sat back abruptly. Frieda Kroner had a slightly wild, runaway look on her face as she declared:

'That is him. Except for the chin. It should be much stronger. . . .'

'The eyebrows are not quite right. They should be more pinched, as if angry all the time,' Rabbi Rubinstein said stiffly. 'That would make his eyes more, I do not know, what Frieda? Do you remember his eyes?'

'Yes,' she nodded. 'Narrow, like a vicious dog's.'

'But the rest?' Robinson asked.

'The rest is the man we saw fifty years ago.' Frieda Kroner said this in a firm, fierce voice. She turned to the rabbi. 'Older. No longer young. Like us. Is this not so?'

'Yes. That is the Shadow Man,' the rabbi agreed. He reached across and placed his hand on her arm. He turned to the detective. 'I would know him in an instant.'

'I also,' Frieda Kroner added. She took a deep breath. 'And, I am thinking, so would have poor Sophie and

Irving. If our memories told us short or tall, thin or thick, dark or light, this was because so much was in there cluttered about and made it difficult to remember. But now, seeing this, I can say, that is him.'

She shivered, but spoke in a firm, determined voice.

'So, Detective – and you too, Mr Winter – you think he is out there tonight,' she gestured toward the windows and beyond, 'searching for us, as he did the others?'

Simon Winter nodded.

Frieda Kroner laughed slightly, as if this were amusing. 'So, perhaps it will be difficult to sleep. I remember this was the same, once before. A long time ago.'

Walter Robinson had been controlling himself with difficulty, watching the old couple. 'I've changed my mind,' he said. 'I think the risk is simply too great. This man is almost a professional killer. More than that. A homicidal psychopath. I think what would be wisest would be for each of you to visit relatives and let me use what information I already have to find him. That way you'll be safe and I won't have to worry about protecting the two of you. We can slip you out of town, and still trap him when he makes some sort of move toward the apartment here, or yours, Mrs Kroner. But the important thing is, we won't have another death.'

The rabbi curved an eyebrow up in surprise when he heard this. Simon Winter started to speak, but then held back. Frieda Kroner snorted.

'No,' Robinson continued, holding up a hand to cut her off. 'I think the first priority should be maintaining your safety.'

The rabbi eyed the young detective and said: 'Again, Detective Robinson, I do not think you are saying everything you know. Leave? Leave now? Why is it that you are suddenly so insistent.'

'I just want to keep you safe.'

The rabbi shook his head. 'That is not it,' he said briskly.

Frieda Kroner had been watching Robinson carefully as he spoke. She suddenly smiled.

'I know,' she said, like a child who has guessed which hand holds a concealed sweet. 'I know why the detective is saying these things.'

Robinson turned to face her. 'Mrs Kroner, I simply want—'

She shook her head, as if to replace the smile there with some iron-hard attitude.

'You have seen something, have you not? You have seen something about the Shadow Man, and you will not share it with us because you do not want to frighten us. As if there is something more terrible than what we have already seen. I have seen more of death than you, Detective, even if you live to be a hundred years old. You still do not understand us, do you, Detective?'

Walter Robinson was at a loss for an answer.

The rabbi spoke quietly then. 'I think,' he said slowly, 'that sometimes this frightens me more than anything.'

Frieda Kroner nodded. 'You look at us and you see an old lady and an old man because you are young, and that means you are filled with all the prejudices of the young—' She held up her hand as Robinson started to protest. 'Don't interrupt me, Detective.'

He stopped.

'All right,' she said firmly. 'So tell me now. What is it you have seen?'

Robinson shrugged before replying. He thought, in that moment, that just as it was unwise to underestimate the Shadow Man, so might it be unwise to underestimate the old people sitting before him.

'I have no real proof—' he started.

'But, there is a but coming right here, correct?' the rabbi said with a slight sardonic smile. 'There always seems to be a *but*.'

'Yes. You remember the man who saw the Shadow Man in Sophie's apartment?'

'The drug addict? Mr Jefferson?' Frieda Kroner said.

'He was found murdered early this morning in his apartment in Liberty City.'

'Murdered? How?'

'Tied into his wheelchair and tortured with a knife.'

Both the rabbi and Frieda Kroner were silent as they absorbed this news.

'The city police aren't certain that he wasn't the victim of the neighborhood drug dealers. In that part of the city revenge is frequent and it can be vicious, and there are indications that he was on many lists of people easily capable of murder. . . .'

'You do not think this?' the rabbi asked.

'No. I think we all know who is responsible.'

'Mr Jefferson, he was—' Frieda Kroner started, but again she was cut off by the young policeman.

'Jefferson died hard, Mrs Kroner. Died hard and slow and in more pain than even he deserved. He was tortured, because someone wanted to know what he knew. And he was subsequently mutilated. I will not have either you or the rabbi in the same danger. Look at it from my point of view: it would mean my career, if something went wrong and this man reached either of you. And I could never forgive myself. So, no, I want the two of you safe.'

Simon Winter had been startled by the news of Jefferson's death, but had hid his surprise behind a poker face. He watched Robinson carefully and saw that he was genuinely shaken. So, when he did speak, it was softly.

'You say Jefferson was mutilated? How?'

'I'd rather not go into the details, Mr Winter.'

'Well, he was tortured for a reason and then mutilated for a reason, because I think this man does everything for a reason, and so everything he does should tell us something and maybe help us think ahead as to what he will do next. So, I ask again, how was he mutilated?'

Robinson hesitated a moment, listening to the coldness in the older man's voice. 'His tongue was cut out.'

Frieda Kroner gasped and put her hand to her mouth. The rabbi shook his head.

'That is awful,' the rabbi said.

But Simon Winter's eyes had narrowed and he was thinking quickly. He spoke in a low, confident tone.

'Well, I'll be damned,' he said. The others looked at him. 'You wouldn't have expected it of a low-life like Jefferson, would you? Not in a million years.'

'What?'

'That Jefferson didn't tell the Shadow Man what he went there to learn.'

'Which was?'

'What do the authorities know? How hard are you looking for him? How close are you to finding him? What evidence is there that he exists? I can think of a dozen questions that would take the Shadow Man out in the middle of the night.'

Winter hesitated, shaking his head. 'It also says this to me: that Leroy Jefferson didn't tell the Shadow Man about the composite drawing. So we still have that working for us.'

Walter Robinson thought hard for a moment, then nodded. 'I think you're probably right,' he said. 'Poor old Leroy.' He hesitated another second, then added: 'Of course, the mutilation could mean that the Shadow Man was simply angry at Jefferson *for* talking, and this was his way of showing it.'

'Organized crime hit men have certain signatures,' Simon Winter said quietly. 'They do things that are supposed to leave a message. I don't think the Shadow Man does the same. His killings try for the concealment of routine. This time, I think he was frustrated. Frustrated, and perhaps you can see a touch of the racist as well. Leroy Jefferson wasn't anything to him other than an unfortunate obstacle. I think we should try to move quickly now. He is moving fast. So should we.'

Walter Robinson thought hard about what Winter had said, and nodded. 'Simon, I think you're correct. All the more reason to get Mrs Kroner and the rabbi out of Miami Beach today. This minute. Right now.'

When Winter looked blankly at him, Robinson added in an exasperated tone: 'Damn it! The two of them are what holds it all together, right? Without them, what do we have? Herman Stein becomes a suicide again, forever. Sophie Millstein goes into the books as unsolved, assailant unknown. Just another goddamn statistic. And Irving Silver, he remains wherever he is. Missing. Period. Not even classified beyond disappeared, possible drowning. How many others are there out there in the same damn category? The only thing that points at one man and murder are these old folks! Without them, we never get into a court of law.'

Winter took a moment before replying. 'I know that.' He was about to add to that statement, when Frieda Kroner interrupted.

She had paled slightly, and she was shaking her head vigorously back and forth. 'I will not go,' she said.

Robinson turned to her. 'Please, Mrs Kroner. I know your intentions are admirable, but this is not the time. I believe you are in great danger, and I believe you are essential to any ultimate prosecution of this killer. Please let me help you—'

'I can only be helped one way, Detective. Find the Shadow Man.'

'Mrs Kroner—'

'No!' she replied angrily. 'No! No! *No!* We spoke of leaving before and decided against it.' Her words drove her to her feet. 'I will not hide! I will not flee! If he comes for me and I am alone, then I will fight him alone. He may kill me, but I will give him a battle he won't soon forget! I tried to hide from this man once and it cost me my entire family! Not again! Do you understand that, Detective?'

She took a deep breath.

'I am scared. That is true. I am old as well. And perhaps I am not as strong as I once was. But I am not so ancient and weak and feeble that I cannot make my own choices, and my choice is to stay whatever happens!'

She turned toward the rabbi. 'Rabbi, this is simply me, the stubborn old woman speaking. You must make your own decision—'

He interrupted her. 'And my decision is the same.' He reached out and grasped hold of her hand. 'My dear and old friend. Whatever there is that threatens us, we shall face together. You will pack a bag or two and move into the guest room here for a week or so or however long it takes for this to end. Then we can face whatever arrives together.'

He turned to Walter Robinson. 'We have lost much to this man. Families, and now friends and there are but the two of us left. I do not know if together we can be stronger than he, but I am certain that we must try. So thank you, Detective, for your concern for our safety. But here is where we stay.'

Robinson opened his mouth to say something, but Winter cut off his reply. 'Listen to them, Walter,' he whispered.

Robinson turned to the old detective, angry for an instant, but then he let the anger slip away, replaced by the advantage he thought keeping the two old people close would give him. 'All right,' he said. 'But you will be protected. By me. I'm going to have an officer assigned here, around the clock.'

He picked up the composite drawing.

'It's time to let this do us some good.'

The plan was simple. That evening at services in two dozen different temples and synagogues, a brief, potent message was to be read:

A person known only as the Shadow Man, who is alleged to have committed crimes against our people in Berlin during the great darkness, is suspected of coming to live amongst us once again, here on Miami Beach. Anyone with any information about this individual is urged to contact Rabbi Chaim Rubinstein or Detective Walter Robinson of the Miami Beach police.

Nothing was to be mentioned concerning the murders. Simon Winter thought the announcement already too specific, and ran the risk of scaring the Shadow Man out of the territory, but Walter Robinson had insisted the wording be direct, half hoping that precisely that would occur, and then he could take his time to find the man wherever he went, leaving the two old people safe. He also did not think that the Shadow Man was likely to hear the message directly; he did not think the man spent any time observing any religious niceties. So, he thought, the

Shadow Man will learn of the announcement secondhand. A conversation in a lobby, or on an elevator. Perhaps in a restaurant or at a newsstand. And just the reconstruction of the announcement, he hoped, would prompt the man to take steps without caution. That was all he wanted; for the man to act without thinking once, without preparing once. This time, Robinson was certain, he would be there.

More critically, both the old and the young detective agreed, the Shadow Man would still not know his anonymity was compromised. It was merely a question of putting a name to the picture.

Winter had suggested adding a further element to the plan, which Robinson had thought a wise one. The two of them were each to take the composite picture of the Shadow Man to the heads of several condo associations, including the one that Herman Stein belonged to. The idea was that by showing the picture quietly, someone might point them in the right direction.

When Walter Robinson returned to his office, before heading out on this task, he discovered that Espy Martinez had called. She had listed her arriving flight information and the cryptic message: 'Some success.'

He did not allow himself to speculate on what this might be, although he passed this news on to Simon Winter as the two of them drove north, up Miami Beach, into a world of high-rise apartment buildings.

'The name,' he answered for the detective. 'She got the name.'

'He won't still be using it,' Robinson replied.

'Maybe not. Probably not. But look, if he suddenly disappears, at least you'll have something to start with in records. Immigration records. Tax records. Records from relief organizations after the war. It'll turn you into a historian. My guess is, he rode that name into the States before changing it. Maybe there's something in social security. You never know.'

'Sounds like a lot of work.'

'And people think being a homicide detective is all glamour and glory, huh?'

Robinson laughed briefly. He had left the old couple in the rabbi's apartment, preparing tea for the uniformed Miami Beach officer assigned to watching them. What he had told the watchdog was simple: no one allowed inside unless authorized by him, personally, or carrying a recognizable badge. He had taken a copy of the composite drawing and taped it to the front door, next to the peephole. He had thought there are few advantages to high-rise condominiums, but one is that when one shuts the door, the apartments have the same safety characteristics as a cave. Only one way in and out. This allowed him to feel as if things were slightly under control.

'But,' Simon Winter continued, 'I don't think you find this guy through conventional methods. Never have. I think he finds you. What we have to do is beat him to the spot.'

'That's a basketball term, right?'

'Precisely. When you're playing defense against a good player, you try to anticipate where he wants to set up on the court. And then you simply get there first.' Winter paused, then added: 'He's never experienced that sort of unpleasantness before.'

'At least, not that we know of,' Robinson said.

They entered into the concrete canyon sections of Miami Beach, where huge, ungainly high rises seemed to compete with the clouds at blocking out the sun. Like any city, the buildings give one the sensation of uniformity. Stack after stack of similar apartments, people living in vertical hives, their own identity and uniqueness competing against a world of identical shapes, angles, and sizes.

The first place they visited was Herman Stein's condominium, and the association head, a robust, bald-headed man, glanced at the picture they presented him with, but shook his head negatively. He pointed out that the association had over a thousand members, representing hundreds of apartments, and the picture, as best as he could say, didn't resemble any of them. This did not surprise Simon Winter. Nor was he surprised when the next two apartment complex association heads said much the same thing.

'Stein said he spotted the Shadow Man at a meeting,' Robinson said, frustrated after several hours with negative results. 'You know what we could do? Get lists from every building, find all the single residents, then go door to door until we come face-to-face with the bastard. He'll be on some list.'

'Yeah,' Winter said. 'I thought he might be on a list too. But I couldn't find the right one. That might work.'

The tone in his voice indicated that he didn't have any doubt that it wouldn't work.

Robinson glanced at his watch. He didn't want to be late for Espy Martinez's arrival. It was late in the day, and red streaks filled the sky to the west. Tendrils of night were already starting to creep through the shadows thrown by the high rises.

'I'm going to the airport,' he said. 'Want me to drop you someplace?'

Simon Winter was abruptly struck with an idea. He nodded and gave the young detective an address. Then he folded up a copy of the composite drawing and slipped it into his pocket.

Walter Robinson pulled the car to the curb. 'Something

will happen soon,' he said. 'They read that announcement tonight.' He looked down at his watch again. 'Actually, any minute now. Should shake something loose in the next couple of days. And let's see what Espy found out.'

'Call me when you know something. I'm going to be home after I stop in here.'

'What's this?'

'Oh, a long shot,' the old detective said, stepping back from the unmarked car. 'And they've probably all gone home.'

Walter Robinson eyed the older man. Overhead, a jet had turned on its final approach into Miami International Airport, and its route was carrying it over the midsection of the Beach. It was still too high for the engines to be heard, and the plane seemed to be floating across the darkening sky.

'How long a shot?' he asked.

Winter had started to turn away, but when he heard the question, he faced about and made a slightly dismissive gesture with his hand, as if to say not worth the detective's time and effort. Robinson saw this, saw precisely what the motion was supposed to create within him, fought off the urge to pull the car out into traffic and head to the airport, which was where a large part of him eagerly wanted to go. Instead, he slipped the car's gear shift into park and jumped out from behind the wheel. Simon Winter, a few feet away on the sidewalk, paused and grinned.

'What, don't trust me?'

'It's not that,' Robinson said as he caught up with the older man. He didn't add to that statement. Instead, he asked, 'What is this place?'

'This is the Holocaust Center,' Winter answered. 'But more importantly, it's the only place I've been to, since all this started, where the past meets the present. Other than over several dead bodies, that is.'

He pushed his way into the office building, trailed by the younger detective.

The receptionist was collecting her things when they came through the door, frowned impatiently, but was impressed when Robinson flashed his badge. It only took a few seconds for them to be swept into Esther Weiss's office, where the young woman stood beside her small desk. She greeted Simon Winter rapidly, with both familiarity and crispness. She too had been preparing to depart.

'Mr Winter, have you had any success? Are you still persuaded this man is here?'

Winter introduced Walter Robinson and Esther Weiss asked: 'Are the police now believing the Shadow Man is here?'

Robinson answered this swiftly. 'Yes.'

The center director shuddered slightly, placed her small briefcase on her desk and sat down. 'This is a terrible thing. I never thought such a thing possible. He must be found and brought to justice. There are courts in Israel. And Germany . . .'

'I'm more interested in a court across town,' Robinson said.

Esther Weiss nodded. 'Of course. He must be brought to justice.' She seemed about to add to that statement when Simon Winter stopped her.

He had had that conversation with the young woman before, and part of the advantage of old age, he thought, was insisting that roads once traveled did not need to be traversed again. So, following his instincts, he reached inside his jacket pocket and unfolded the composite picture of the Shadow Man. He thrust it across the desk at Esther Weiss without saying anything. She reached out, spreading the picture on the desk in front of her. She stared hard at the drawing, just as everyone else had, but when she looked up, there was a slight twitch at the corner of her right eyelid and a tremor crept into her words:

'But I know this man,' she said slowly, as if confused. She recoiled from the drawing as if it were a current of electricity. 'At least, I have seen him once, twice, a few times before . . .'

Espy Martinez was surprised that Walter Robinson wasn't at the International Arrivals terminal to meet her. She was in that unsettled state caused by traveling across large time zones; she was uncertain whether she was exhausted or energized. She went directly to a telephone and called his office, only to learn that he had not checked in since he was at the rabbi's apartment.

She debated whether to head home, the thought of a shower and a change of clothing, and perhaps a nap as well, being a powerful attraction. But she had the sensation that things were taking place, and she felt slightly on the forgotten side of events, which surprised her; written on a piece of paper inside her briefcase were a name and a number and, she thought, maybe all they needed to find the man they hunted.

She took one last quick glance around the airport terminal, but did not see Walter Robinson. She insisted to herself that she shouldn't feel irritated, that after all there were higher priorities than being met at the airport, and she wondered if perhaps he hadn't received her phone message, or that the arrival time could have been garbled. She filled herself with excuses, which made her forget, momentarily, any fatigue, and headed outside.

She stood, waving for a cab, amidst the noxious combination of exhaust fumes and syrupy evening heat that filled the half-enclosed waiting area. She climbed into the backseat of the taxi, gave her home address and leaned back, letting the tropical air slide around her. But before the cab managed to reach the airport exit, she changed her mind, and pitching forward, speaking in rapid-fire Spanish, told the driver to take her to the rabbi's apartment on Miami Beach.

Simon Winter had grasped Esther Weiss by the arm. With his free hand he thumped hard on the composite drawing.

'Who?' he demanded. 'Who is it!'

Walter Robinson had jumped forward, gesturing, his voice urgent with a cold, harsh hope. 'Where have you seen this man?' he asked, his words trampling the same furious questions by the older detective.

Esther Weiss stared crazily at the two men. 'This is him?' she asked, high-pitched.

'Yes,' Robinson replied. 'Where have you seen this man?' he repeated.

Esther Weiss's mouth opened slightly in astonishment, and Simon Winter could see the formulation of fear behind her eyes. He released his grip on the woman's arm, and she slid into her desk chair, still wide-eyed, staring at the two men.

'But here,' she answered slowly. 'Right here . . .'

Winter was about to speak, but Robinson beat him to the punch. The young man's words were measured, slow, still colored with a cool appreciation of good fortune. 'When, how, tell me what you know, right now,' he said. 'Leave nothing out. Not the smallest detail. Anything could help us.'

'This is the Shadow Man?' the woman asked again.

'Yes,' Simon Winter said.

'But this man is a historian,' she replied. 'With impeccable credentials . . .'

'No, I think not,' Winter said quietly. 'Or perhaps he is both. But this is the man we are searching for.'

'Start at the beginning,' Robinson said. 'A name. An address. How is it you know him?'

'He studies the tapes,' she said. 'We allow scholars to study the tapes privately. Scholars and historians and social scientists . . .'

'I know that,' Simon Winter said impatiently. 'But this man. Who is he?'

'I have his name on file,' Esther Weiss coughed as she spoke. 'I have it written down. And an address. I have these things. A résumé too, I think. We keep all these things in the confidential files. You remember, Mr Winter? I gave you some names once before . . .'

'Yes. I remember. Was he on that list?'

'I can't recall,' the young woman said. 'I gave it to you. I just don't remember.'

Walter Robinson interjected himself smoothly. 'But now you can go to the file, correct? You can go to the list of scholars and pick this man out? Is he on a Rolodex? In an address book? Now, Miss Weiss, if you please.'

'I can't believe—'

'Now, Miss Weiss.'

She hesitated, then acquiesced: 'Yes. Of course. Right away.'

The center director unsteadily moved to a black, lateral file cabinet tucked into a corner of the small office. She rolled the top drawer open and began searching through the collected papers. After a moment she muttered, 'There are more than a hundred people authorized to examine the tapes.'

As she continued to search, Simon Winter asked: 'Is there a procedure for getting this authorization? I mean, does somebody get checked out?'

'Yes and no,' the young woman replied. 'If someone's credentials seem in order, then approval is pretty much routine. The scholar must submit a statement as to why they need access to the tapes, and describe any use they intend for them. They must also sign a waiver and a confidentiality clause. We are strict about prohibiting any commercialization of the memories we have on tape. But what we're mainly interested in avoiding are the revisionists.'

'The what?' Robinson asked.

'The people who deny the Holocaust ever took place.'

'Are they crazy?' Robinson blurted out. 'I mean, how can someone—'

Esther Weiss looked up, a small manila folder in her hand. 'There are many people who want to deny the existence of the greatest crime of history, Detective. People who would explain away gas chambers as delousing units. People who would say that ovens were for baking bread, not people. There are those who think Hitler was a saint and that all the memories of his terror are so many conspiracies.' She took a deep breath. 'Rational people would say these views are madness. But it is not so simple. Surely, Detective, you can understand that?'

He could not, but he did not say so.

Esther Weiss put her hand to her forehead for a moment, as if shielding her eyes from something she did not want to see. Then she handed the manila envelope to Simon Winter.

'This is the man that resembles your drawing,' she said.

The old detective opened the file and drew out several sheets of paper. The first was a form requesting access to the tapes. Attached to that was a letter, a curriculum vitae and waiver forms, signed.

At the top of the résumé was a name: David Isaacson.

Beneath that was a Miami Beach address.

'What do you remember of this man?' Robinson asked.

'He was in, I don't know how many times. He was very quiet and not outgoing in the slightest. I only spoke to him once, the first time. He told me that he too was a survivor, and I asked him to contribute his own memories to the tapes, and he agreed, but said it would have to wait until he finished his memoir. That's what he was working on. His memoir. He said it was to be privately published. After his death. He said it was for his family, so there would always be a record for them to remember.'

She hesitated, then added: 'I thought this was admirable.'

'Is there a log, showing numbers of times visited?'

'If we collect the staff, perhaps we could piece that together. But once someone has access, they are given their privacy with the materials.'

'How did he get approval?'

'See the other letter?'

Winter and Robinson both looked down at the letter clipped to the file. It was from the Holocaust Memorial organization in Los Angeles, and it was signed by an associate director. It asked that all scholarly perquisites be permitted for Mr Isaacson, who had done similar work with materials in Los Angeles.

'You called? Checked this out?'

'No,' Esther Weiss said hesitantly. 'It was signed by the associate director.'

Walter Robinson nodded. 'Don't worry,' he said slowly. 'It makes no difference.'

Simon Winter looked up. 'So, these other things on the résumé. The degrees from New York University and the University of Chicago. The publications, and all that. You didn't check ...'

'Why?' she replied. 'Why? It was clear he wasn't a revisionist! He even showed me the tattoo on his arm!'

Winter held up his hand. He could see the young woman's face was drawn. She had paled and seemed to be teetering on the edge of panic.

'I didn't know,' she said. 'How could I have known?'

Winter didn't answer that question. All he could think about was the Shadow Man. Polite. Quiet. Doing nothing to draw attention to himself, examining tape after tape, looking for anyone who might have known him.

Hunting, the old man thought.

The same thoughts filtered through Walter Robinson. But he took the time to answer Esther Weiss's question. 'You were never meant to know,' he said. He paused, and added firmly: 'But don't worry. This is ending now.'

He looked down at the address. Then he reached across the desk and picked up the telephone. He dialed the Beach police headquarters, identified himself briskly, and demanded to speak directly with the captain in charge of the special weapons and tactics squad.

CHAPTER TWENTY-FIVE
The Tattoo

Both Simon Winter and Walter Robinson underestimated the impact that the announcement would have on the community of survivors. As evening passed into night, telephones throughout Miami Beach were ringing. At the few old Deco-style hotels that had not been taken over by the youth movement and still catered to the elderly, knots of people up past their usual bedtimes stood in the lobbies, or on the wide, outdoor porches, loudly discussing what they had heard. At Wolfie's Restaurant, not far from the Lincoln Road Mall, there was an argument going, which turned abrasive and strident. It caused some of the younger people and several foreign tourists visiting the landmark to turn their heads, wondering why the ordinarily quiet, placid old folks were raising their voices. A stranger overhearing the heated talk would have seen anger in several faces, but had they looked closer, would have seen fear as well. A deep, blackened fear, rising through long-held memory; although there were precious few who had ever heard of the Shadow Man, every man and woman was scarred by a recollection of a similar terror, whether it was Gestapo or S.S. or merely the awful knowledge that they had done what they were ordered to do, and voluntarily delivered themselves to the machine of evil.

And so, the idea that a piston in this machine was living among them created an unsettled sensation, a step or two on the road to panic, that summoned remembered nightmare in all their voices, sounds that went unheard and unrecognized by the young and the trendy occupants of the Miami Beach scene on their way to the dance clubs and night spots, but which fairly shouted to those older people.

Espy Martinez was peripherally aware of the stir that had been created. She sat in the living room of the rabbi's apartment and listened as he and Frieda Kroner handled phone call after phone call. She quickly understood that these were not calls containing information, but pleas for reassurance. This the rabbi handled expertly, speaking in a soothing, practiced voice, listening, letting memories drop around him like so many invisible petals from dying plants.

She listened as she overheard him say:

'No, Sylvia, it is just this one man . . .'

'Yes, the authorities are searching for him. We will find him . . .'

'I agree. This is a terrible thing. Who would have thought it?'

And then he hung up, turned toward her as if to say something, and the telephone rang again. He picked it up, smiled wanly, and said: 'Of course, Mr Fielding. Of course I remember you. Ahh, I see. You heard as well. Is there something you know? No? Oh, I see. Of course. Of course . . .'

The rabbi shrugged, and continued to speak with his caller.

Martinez turned to where the uniformed Beach police officer was busy reading the Sports section of that morning's paper. She opened her mouth to say something, then stopped. Instead, she rose to her feet and walked to the patio doors, staring out for a moment. The horizon seemed to glow with a dull silver intensity created by the city's lights. She wondered where Walter Robinson was, and wished she were with him.

He and Simon Winter were sitting in a briefing room at the Beach police headquarters, discussing arrest procedures with the SWAT captain and his nine-man team.

'In and out. I don't want to give this guy even one second. Full restraints as soon as we have control, I mean hands pinned, and legs too.'

'No problem,' replied the SWAT captain with an offhand wave. He seemed singularly unimpressed with the need for a tactical squad to arrest one elderly man. 'You have a judge sign a warrant?'

'Got it right here.' Robinson paused. 'I had trouble with my last arrest,' he understated.

'Heard that,' the SWAT captain replied. 'But you followed established procedure. These things happen.' He was an experienced policeman, who wore his military training every waking minute and probably snored in his bed at night to a marching cadence. Square-shouldered and close-cropped, he was the type of person who considered discipline a virtue beyond intelligence and who was forced to quit coaching his son's Little League team because of too insistent an approach to victory.

'The man we're arresting should be considered armed and extremely dangerous.'

'Everyone we arrest fits that category,' he replied matter-of-factly. 'Automatic weapons?'

'No. I don't believe so.'

'Well, there you have it. Likely to surrender when confronted?'

'Hard to say.'

'Likely to run?'

'More likely to disappear,' Simon Winter added softly, but with just enough force for the SWAT captain to hear him. The captain turned to him.

'That would be a first for me, old-timer,' he said condescendingly.

'This is a case of firsts,' Winter replied.

The captain unfolded himself from the briefing chair, and as he did, the nine members of his team rose with him.

'Whenever you're ready,' he said confidently.

Walter Robinson nodded. He went to a wall telephone and tried Espy Martinez's home for the tenth time, only to once again get her answering machine. Then he dialed the number for the rabbi's apartment. This was the fourth time he'd tried this number, only to be frustrated by the busy signal. He had the authority to get the phone company to interrupt, but he was reluctant to use that. He merely wanted to inform the rabbi that they'd had a break in the case, thinking that even without a lengthy explanation, this news would reassure the old couple. Simon Winter had concurred in this view.

He was surprised when the phone rang and the rabbi's voice was immediately there.

'Yes, this is Rabbi Rubinstein. Who's calling, please?'

'Rabbi, it's Detective Robinson.'

'Ah, Detective. Your announcement has had some effect. The phone is ringing off the hook.'

'I've been trying to get through. Any information?'

'No. Only people upset, which is understandable. But I am still optimistic someone will know something. It seems as if they will be calling all through the night.'

'Look, Rabbi, Mr Winter and I have found something

out, no, don't interrupt, I don't want to go into detail right now. I will call you later, but we may have made some progress. Just sit tight, you and Mrs Kroner, okay? Is the officer still there.'

'Yes.'

'Make sure he stays alert.'

'Of course. But you say you have discovered something? This is good news. What sort of progress?'

'Really, I'd rather discuss it later, in case it amounts to nothing.'

The rabbi hesitated. 'All right,' he said after a moment. 'Do you wish to speak with Miss Martinez? She is here.'

Walter Robinson smiled and felt his stomach leap. 'Yes,' he said rapidly. There was a momentary pause before he heard her voice.

'Walter?'

'Espy, I've been trying to reach you. I'm sorry I missed the flight, but we've had a break. I've got a name and address—'

'Are you heading there now?'

'Yes. Stay there. I'll call you when we're finished.'

Espy Martinez felt a surge of excitement. She wanted to accompany the arrest team, but she was also aware that Walter Robinson had not asked her to.

'I want to be there,' she said firmly.

'Espy, last time I allowed you to go on an arrest in the middle of the night, I nearly got you shot. Not this time.'

She started to protest, but stopped.

'Your trip—' he started to ask.

'I learned some things,' she said. 'Fascinating things. I mean, I never knew. You study history in high school, college, but you don't really know it until you come face-to-face with it. That's what happened. This guy, Walter, the Shadow Man, he was carefully trained by the Gestapo.

All sorts of techniques. Surveillance. Forgery. Murder.
You name it. A mean customer, Walter, be careful.'

Robinson had a vision of Leroy Jefferson in his wheelchair and thought: *beyond* mean. He realized that Espy
Martinez knew nothing of what had happened to their
witness and was about to tell her, and then decided against
it. He could see the SWAT team strapping body armor
into place, stamping their feet like a collection of quarter-
horses before a roundup, and he realized he had to go.

'They trained him?'

'Made him into an expert. Can you imagine that? And
these guys, Walter, they were the best, if you could call it
that, and the man that told me all this says that he was the
best of the best. So, play it safe, okay.'

'Of course.'

He was about to hang up, but she stopped him, lowering
her voice. 'There's one other thing, Walter. It might be
helpful. . . .'

'What?'

'He had a death camp number tattooed on his arm. That
was one of the ways he disguised himself near the end,
when all hell was breaking loose over there and all the rats
were leaving the sinking ship. I have the number. He may
have changed his identity a million times, but I don't think
he'll change that number. If you get your hands on him—'

'What is it?'

'A26510,' she said.

He wrote this down.

A block from the address of the man who said he was
writing his memoirs, the SWAT team captain transferred
from the van carrying his squad and into the unmarked
patrol car that Walter Robinson drove. The SWAT captain
hurriedly tossed himself into the rear seat, moving as

swiftly as his body armor would allow.

'All right, Walt,' he said. 'Let's drive by.'

Walter Robinson wordlessly put the car in gear and they slowly drove down a dark, small side street in the midst of a modest residential area. The section of Miami Beach around Forty-first Street is an odd collection of houses; some, which abut the waterway that carves through the beach, were million-dollar homes. Others were large, elegant, two-story designs, with deco touches, and red barrel-tiled roofs, eagerly sought after by many of the young professional types moving back to Miami Beach. But interspersed with these, on streets with less imposing palm trees and pockmarked, gravelly roads, were far humbler houses, low-slung, with flat brick tiles, old jalousie windows, and a depressing uniformity. They were often what realtors liked to term 'starter houses,' which meant they could be afforded by couples just starting out and not being bankrolled by a parent, or the old and finishing-up people who still wanted to call the Beach home, and who had not yet been chased by fear of crime into the high-rise condos. Many were in that realtor's euphemistic category of *handyman's specials*, which indicated that years of constant heat and sun pounding away each day had caused the wooden floors to buckle and warp – or the cement foundations to crack and sway. It was not unusual for one of these houses, as old as their occupants and suffering from as many of the ills and pains of age, to lurk in the shadows thrown by some large, landscaped, remodeled home housing a doctor, a lawyer, or a well-heeled businessman and his family, sitting on the backside of progress like a poor reminder of neglect.

The address that Walter Robinson held in his hand was for one of those houses.

He slowly crunched the car to the hard coral-rock curb

across the street. The house in question was set back from
the street about twenty yards, with a desultory pair of
scraggly bushes guarding the front door.

'Window bars,' Simon Winter said.

He'd been silent most of the ride, thinking hard about
the man they were narrowing in upon.

'Probably around back as well,' the SWAT captain said.
'And dead-lock bolts on the doors. There'll be a side door,
or one in the rear, but most likely by the side where those
garbage cans are located. But that's it. Two bedrooms, two
baths, no central air, so those window units are on and
going strong, and making a racket that will cover any noise
we make. See any signs of an animal?'

'No fence. Hold it . . .'

The three men froze in position as they saw a figure
cross in front of a front window. A tall man. Moments later
a shorter shape followed. In a moment the front room of
the house filled with the unmistakable glow from a
television set.

'He's got a wife,' Winter said. 'I'll be damned.'

'You want her taken as well?' asked the SWAT captain.

'Yes,' Robinson said. 'She may have helped him.'

'She may also know nothing,' Winter said.

'Well, we can find that out back at headquarters.'

The SWAT captain took another long look, and then
gestured for Walter Robinson to move the car ahead. He
did this, not flipping on the headlights until they were a
half block away from the target house.

'No sweat,' the captain said, leaning back in his seat.
'Two in back, two at the side, then the rest of the team goes
in through the front door. He won't know what hit him.'

'That's what I thought would happen the last time,'
Walter Robinson said.

'So what happened to that guy, the one that gave you the

trouble before?' the SWAT captain asked.

'He ran into the guy in that house,' Robinson replied.

Simon Winter listened with half an ear to the SWAT captain brief his team one final time about the layout and the approach. He realized that Walter Robinson was allowing him along on the arrest as a courtesy, and realized as well that he had to stay in the rear, away from the actual action. A part of him wished that it were he going through the door first, but he realized this was simply his own ego speaking to him. He felt an odd mix of emotions; an excitement that the man that had dominated his thoughts was so close, but a bittersweet recognition that once handcuffs were slapped around the Shadow Man's wrists, his own participation in the event would fade. He thought that he should be pleased, that it was his work that ultimately provided the connection between composite drawing and name and address, and he understood that in all likelihood he would get the instant attention and notoriety that newspapers and television bring. But this would diminish as the days went past, and he had the unsettling thought that a few weeks after the Shadow Man was arrested, he would inexorably return to precisely the same position he was in when Sophie Millstein had knocked on his door with terror in her eyes.

He remembered that position wryly: sitting on his couch with his revolver barrel in his mouth and finger on the trigger.

Without thinking, he lifted his hand to his left, where the pistol now rode in his old shoulder harness, concealed beneath a light windbreaker that was making him sweat as if nervous, which he hoped had so far gone unnoticed. He did not think that Walter Robinson realized he wore it. He did not care. The weight beneath his armpit was as reassuring as an old friend's handshake.

He turned away from the SWAT team as he heard the clickings and clackings of men checking weapons, and stared up past the dingy pale green streetlight glow toward the wide expanse of night sky, and tried to think what it was that he had learned that would speak to him in the days to come. For an instant he turned toward the young detective and measured him, finding a bit of envy reverberating around within himself. He wanted to have it all to do over again. Every moment. Every frustration. Every pain.

He thought he would not trade any of it, and he bit down on his lip at the thought that in a short amount of time he would once again be finished, useful to no one again, and alone.

'Simon? You all set? Ready to get this guy now?'

He turned toward Robinson's voice. He saw an enthusiasm in the younger man's eyes.

'Absolutely,' he said.

'Good,' Walter Robinson said, putting his hand out and grabbing the older man by the arm, a gesture he recognized sprung in part from excitement, and perhaps affection. 'Tomorrow, maybe we can go fishing. Or the day after. You promised, remember?'

'I'd like that,' Winter said quietly.

They moved to the unmarked car.

'This bring back memories?' Robinson asked.

'You get to be my age,' Winter replied, smiling slowly, 'and everything brings back memories. Spend more time looking backward than forward.'

'Not you,' said the younger man. 'Come on, Simon. Let's finish this guy now. Put the cuffs on him and the fear of God inside him. You and I. Show him he ain't so goddamn smart after all.'

'I'd like that,' the old detective replied, although he did not know whether he was lying or not.

They chose a vantage point around the corner from the small house, shielded from sight by an eight-foot-high stucco wall that enclosed the target's neighbor's small estate. The SWAT captain made one final check, adjusting the earpiece on his intercom set, made the men count off, and then, with a small chopping motion of his hand, sent the team into action.

The squad barreled around the corner and swooped down the street. Their black jumpsuits blended with the inky midnight air. Robinson, poised just behind the SWAT captain, waited like a sprinter at the start of a race, muscles tightening while listening for the starter's gun.

The SWAT captain listened, hunched over, then repeated out loud in a soft voice: 'Back door team in place. No sign of activity. Side door team, ready. Okay, here we go!'

The front door group swung out and down the street on the run, their boots slapping the sidewalk like a drummer beating a reveille.

Walter Robinson held out his hand to restrain Simon Winter for a moment or two, then the two of them lurched forward, just behind the quick-moving dark shapes. The ground beneath their feet seemed to evaporate, and Robinson was hardly aware of the energy he was expending. He had a flash, a momentary memory of his own, cutting down the center of a football field, reaching for the ball suspended in the air, the roar of the spectators dull and distant in his ears. But then this passed and he found his own vision tunneled in on the front door, where a burly SWAT member was readying a door-buster.

'Police! Freeze!' the SWAT captain shouted.

And as Robinson watched, the man swung the thick black steel door-buster and there was a resounding crash and splintering of wood.

A few feet behind Robinson, Simon Winter moved swiftly, his breath coming in jagged pulses.

He immediately heard a high-pitched scream of shock and panic, and glass breaking, and he heard the SWAT captain yelling, above the sudden cacophony, 'Go! Go! Go!' and he saw the team members pouring through the shattered door into the house. Robinson had surged ahead as well, trailing the team by a few feet, gun in his outstretched hand. The air was filled with voices, all shouting commands, and he pushed himself toward the entrance of the house and the light that was pouring out into the night like a dam that had sprung a leak.

Simon Winter heard Robinson screaming: 'Get down! Get down on the floor! Hands behind your head!'

These words mingled with the woman's frightened cries, sounds that resembled nothing human other than the emotion of fear that engendered them.

Winter vaulted through the door and saw the SWAT captain and one of his men bent over a large man on the floor of the modest house. Robinson, gun pushed up against the man's ear, was shouting commands. To the side, two of the SWAT team held a small, thin, elderly woman. Her white hair had been pinned back and had come loose, so that it flew around her face. She was crying piteously, 'What have we done? What have we done?'

The SWAT captain watched as Robinson snapped handcuffs around the supine man's wrists and then half rose.

'We're clear,' the captain said with satisfaction. He turned to Robinson. 'Told you so. Piece of cake. So this is the tough old killer you've been hunting?' In a corner of the room the television set was blaring loudly, a late night talk-show host was making jokes. The SWAT captain gestured for one of his men to shut it off.

Walter Robinson jerked the man to his seat and spoke rapidly. 'David Isaacson, you're under arrest for murder.'

Simon Winter saw the man's face for the first time. Light seemed to slice across the fear in the man's eyes, leaving a scar.

'What have I done?' the man asked.

'Shadow Man!' Robinson fairly spat the words as he jerked him up to his feet. The detective seemed to rattle the man, pushing his face right up to the suspect's. Then he thrust him into a nearby armchair. 'You're going away. I'm going to see you on Death Row.'

Simon Winter stepped forward then and stared hard at the man in the chair.

'Oh, my God,' he said slowly, softly. He reached out and seized Walter Robinson's arm. The young detective turned briskly, irritated at being stopped, and then hesitated when he saw Winter's eyes.

'What is it?' he asked angrily.

Winter felt his mouth grow dry, and the words he spoke seemed to crack and splinter like the door to the house. 'Walter, look at him, goddamn it!'

'What?'

'Look at his face! The damn picture! He doesn't look a thing like the goddamn composite!'

For the first time Walter Robinson turned back to the man he'd arrested and stared hard into his face. 'No,' he said slowly, 'Simon you're wrong. The build is the same, the hair—'

'Look at him! That's not the man Esther Weiss picked out!'

Walter Robinson, a man who sometimes arrogantly

prided himself on remaining calm under the most difficult of situations, felt a touch of panic soar through him, unwanted, unwieldy, and almost out of control. His eyes widened as if trying to take in the contradiction between the picture and the man sitting before him.

'Who are you?' he demanded.

'I am David Isaacson,' the man stammered in reply. 'What have I done?' he asked again.

'Where do you come from?'

The man looked confused, and so Simon Winter stepped forward.

'How long have you been here?'

'On Miami Beach, some twenty years.'

'Before that?'

'In New York City. I was a furrier.'

'And before that?'

'From Poland, once, many years ago when I was young.'

The man's wife finally managed to pull loose from the SWAT team members and threw herself next to her husband. 'David, what is it, what is it?' she cried, clinging hysterically. She turned to the policemen and shouted with bitter anger: 'Gestapo! Nazis!'

The room grew quiet for an instant, save for the woman's sobs.

'Are you a survivor?' Simon Winter asked abruptly.

The man nodded. 'What is this?' he asked, as if sliding into shock.

Robinson stepped over to David Isaacson, grabbed his forearm and pulled it forward, rotating it slightly. He ripped the man's shirt as he pushed it up. In almost the same motion, he reached into his pocket and pulled out the paper on which he'd written the number Espy Martinez gave him. He thrust the paper down next to the purple-blue tattoo on the man's wizened forearm, and saw immediately that the two numbers were different.

'Oh, my God,' he said slowly.

'Gestapo!' the wife cried out again.

Simon Winter saw the same and turned, staring back through the smashed door, out into the night, which seemed to mock them with every shadow.

You're close, he thought. You're close. But where?

CHAPTER TWENTY-SIX

The Teakettle

The Shadow Man stood silently in a darkened space at the edge of an alleyway, just past the lip of light tossed onto the sidewalk by the fluorescent sign of a vacant pharmacy. He looked up at the sixth floor of the rabbi's apartment building.

The side of him that usually spoke of caution argued that he was unwise to stand there, even for a moment, even if unseen and undetected. He sometimes thought listening to this voice within him was like having some overly protective angel perched on his shoulder. This time, the voice was shrill, insistent, and it demanded that he leave, and leave that instant.

Pack a bag. Check into a hotel by the airport. Fly out on the first plane in the morning.

He shook his head.

I have unfinished business, he argued to himself. It awaits me up in that building.

What business? Stay safe. You have used up this life, as you have used up others before. These years on Miami Beach have been pleasant and profitable, but they have finished now. You knew this time might arrive, and now it has. Too many people are circling around, looking under rocks, checking behind doors, searching for you. You have heard people speaking about the Shadow Man as if they knew you. It is time to fade away and become someone new.

He leaned back farther into the darkness of the alleyway, pushing his back against a dingy gray wall.

Los Angeles will be nice, he told himself. There was an apartment, bank accounts, and a different identity awaiting him there. Chicago would be acceptable as well. The groundwork for a similar arrangement was established in that city. In Los Angeles, I will have to get a car. Everyone there drives. But in Chicago, that won't be necessary. In Los Angeles, he was to be a retired businessman; in Chicago, he was already known as a retired investor. He considered the two situations, unable to make up his mind. It made no difference, really, he told himself. As soon as he took up either one identity or the next, he would start in building the framework for a third in some new city, so that there was always more than a single option awaiting him. Perhaps Phoenix or Tucson, he thought. Someplace warm. He did not like the idea of a winter in Chicago. He realized he would have to do some research. He did not know whether either of those cities had the type of elderly Jewish community he could tap into. Were there survivors there? he wondered.

Deep in the distant night, an auto alarm system klaxon horn severed the still heat. He listened for a moment, until it abruptly disappeared.

He spat on the ground, suddenly furious.

I have enjoyed it here, he whispered to himself. All these years, I have been comfortable. He liked the way the tropical nighttime had a richness to its darkness that seemed to cloak all his angers.

He considered the list of enemies arrayed against him. He dismissed the policeman and the prosecutor swiftly, making a small, involuntary motion with his hand, as if carving a piece of the dark air in front of him. He never feared the police. He believed they were too stolid and unimaginative to catch him. They searched for evidence and clues, and never understood that he was more of an idea. Although this was perhaps as close as they had ever been – as close as anyone had been since 1944 – he still considered them too many steps behind him. But his cautious side reminded him: Never before had the police actually known he existed. This made him pause, until his arrogant persona recalled that this was precisely the reason he'd taken so much trouble over the years to always have at least two different identities available. That he'd infrequently needed to hurry was testimony to his careful planning. And, he thought harshly, this is really no different.

But then he pictured the old detective, the neighbor, which made him hesitate. This man worried him more, mostly because he did not completely understand why he was in the picture at all, and because he was neither official nor someone like his usual quarry. The Shadow Man conjured up a vision of Simon Winter and made a quick assessment. He seems dogged and intelligent. He has instincts that are formidable. But he is not here tonight, and will be left clutching at emptiness in the morning. So, the Shadow Man thought, he is perhaps dangerous, but he will remain too slow and out of step. And what really are his resources? A cleverness and some experience. Enough to find me? No.

Still, he shook his head and told himself: You should have killed him that night in his apartment. He was lucky.

He won't be lucky again.

The Shadow Man took a deep breath of air and pictured the old pair up in the apartment.

They are the real danger, he told himself. They always have been. They always will be.

A star shell of fury burst within his chest, stoked by long memory.

They have always been to blame. Since the very beginning.

They are the only ones who remember.

They are the only ones who can pick me out.

For a moment he shifted his feet, then forced himself to remain under control, although he felt withering rage resounding throughout his body. How many were left? he wondered suddenly. These two? Others? How many more can there be, who can recall the Shadow Man?

Perhaps none.

He allowed himself a small smile.

Maybe these are the last two who ever saw the Shadow Man. He had spent much time, in archives and memorials, among documents and videotapes, reading books and studying faces. Years of work. Killing work. It was inevitable, he told himself. Inevitable that someday you would find the end of the line. The last Jews from Berlin. And perhaps they were right there in front of him, waiting in that sixth-floor apartment.

This thought filled him with a familiar and welcome desire.

And so, even if his cautious side told him that escape was wise, and had been insisting this since earlier in the evening, when he'd first overheard someone say 'Shadow Man' as he'd stepped onto the elevator in his own condominium and had patiently listened to the conversation beside him and learned of the announcement made in those places of worship, his sense of fury told him that he could not depart for any of the other lives he'd so carefully established knowing that those two old people were left behind to bedevil him on some future date.

Inwardly, he smiled.

I will enjoy ending them, he thought. Perhaps it will be a beginning for myself.

The Shadow Man collected himself. He compromised with his cautious side: I will leave by midday. I will finish this and then I will not hesitate, I will depart.

He told himself that truly there was not that much to worry about.

I have prepared this well. There has been no hurry to this collection. I have been inside the rabbi's building three separate times, been to the roof and been to the basement. I have examined the electrical system and the circuit breaker box, and I have stood outside the rabbi's apartment. I have even checked the old microfilm of the architect's plans filed with the City of Miami Beach, showing the layout of the rooms inside. I have prepared a plan and it will work.

It has always worked.

He remembered a time, many years earlier. It came back to him slowly, a memory that seemed like a dream that faded in the first moments of awakening. He could picture a family, and he could picture the upstairs, attic flat that he knew they hid in. Two small children, who cried when the bombers came over; a mother and father, grandparents, a cousin; all jammed into two little rooms. He tried to remember their names, but was unable. He remembered they had pleaded hard for their lives, and paid handsomely. And then they had died, like all the others. They were like rats, he thought, holed up in some deep crevasse. But he knew how to bring them out into the open.

He looked up at the apartment building.

I have done this many times before.

He reached down and picked up a small bag at his feet

that held several important items. Hefting this, he once again stared up at the building.

Judenfrei, he thought to himself. That was what the Reichsführer once had promised to the entire world. And that is the same promise I made to myself. Perhaps tonight I will finally be *Judenfrei*.

He visualized the old woman and the old rabbi.

His face seemed to slide then into a cold, frozen visage, one of determination and duty. He stepped slightly forward. From the edge of the alley, he carefully searched the empty street. There was some traffic a few blocks away, but nothing that overly concerned him. And so, moving from darkness to darkness, he eagerly crossed toward his targets.

They do not know it, he reminded himself. None of them ever knew it. But they have already been dead for days.

Simon Winter watched wordlessly as Walter Robinson tried to sort through the confusion caused by the arrest of David Isaacson. The elderly man and his wife sat on a bench in the corner of the homicide offices, alternately scowling, threatening to call their attorney – though clearly they had none, especially one who would arise in the middle of the night to help them – and grudgingly offering up the occasional morsel of information. These came more readily after Walter Robinson assured them that the city would pay for the repair of their front door and any items broken in the mistaken arrest. This back and forth between the angry couple and the detective went on for some time, moments that drove Simon Winter toward frustration.

It was deep into the night and heading toward morning when Robinson finally slipped away from the couple and approached Simon Winter. Behind the detective an overly solicitous, cloyingly polite, uniformed officer was helping the Isaacsons to their feet, ushering them out of the offices and to a squad car and a chauffeured ride home.

'Well?' Winter asked.

'Well, shit,' Robinson replied, sitting down heavily in a seat next to the old man. 'Aren't you tired, Simon? Don't you want to go home and go to bed and wish maybe this mess would just get up and disappear while you slept?'

'That sounds unlikely,' Winter replied, though he smiled through the lateness of the hour.

'No shit,' Robinson said. He laughed, self-mocking. 'Man, have I made a pile of crap here that's gonna take me a month to straighten out. . . .'

'A month in triplicate,' Winter said. The young detective snorted another laugh.

'You're right about that. Man, Simon, you don't have any idea the forms I'm gonna be filling out. And then I'm gonna get my butt hauled in front of every brass-assed superior officer in need of chewing somebody out. And that's a big number. And then there's the department lawyers. Gotta give them their shot . . .'

'He planned it, you know,' Winter said softly. 'He knew somebody might make the connection, and so instead of making up a phony name and address, he used a real person. He had a choice between creating a fiction that maybe we could backtrack from or that might have drawn someone's attention, and a confusion that would create a mess, and he selected wisely, I think. And he picked out someone that resembled him, if only slightly. What do you think? Think he saw Isaacson at some meeting? On a videotape? Strolling on the beach? In a synagogue? Grocery store? Restaurant? Picked him out of some crowd without the guy even having the slightest idea what he was contributing to?'

'Somewhere, you're right about that. Maybe Isaacson will be able to figure it out for us after he's calmed down. But I doubt it. Anyway, it ain't gonna happen tonight.'

Walter Robinson let slide a long, deep breath. 'The Shadow Man seems to have a good idea how bureaucracies like the police department work. Think he was a cop once?'

'Remember who trained him. Where could you find a more devoted bureaucracy than Nazi Germany?'

'Maybe right here on Miami Beach,' Robinson said bitterly, pushing haphazardly at some forms on his desk. 'Ah, hell, that's not true. But I see what you're driving at. The fucker's smart, isn't he?'

'Yes. And you know, all that preparation tells me something else.'

Robinson nodded, not listening for an answer, but providing one himself: 'That the Shadow Man has an exit door all ready and open, and once he walks through it . . .'

'He's gone.'

'That occurred to me as well.' Robinson leaned back. 'I made a call,' he said slowly, 'just wanted to check something out. While the Isaacsons were stewing over there. I called out to Los Angeles and got the director of the Holocaust Center out there on the phone. You know the letter that Esther Weiss had? Signed by an associate director?'

'No such person, right?'

'Right. Letterhead was proper, though.'

'That's easy enough. Just write them a letter, requesting any old thing, get something back on their nice official stationery, head to a copy machine and bingo, there you have it. Hell, you could take it off a fund-raising letter.'

'That's what I thought too.'

'So,' Simon Winter said slowly, 'where does all this leave us?'

Robinson paused. 'Maybe the old folks will turn up something. Or maybe he'll make a move for them. Or something. The phone was ringing off the hook at the rabbi's earlier. Maybe the announcement will do some good, other than scaring the hell out of everybody. Otherwise, well, we're not exactly at square one, but what the hell square we're on, I don't know.'

Winter nodded. He held his hand out and grasped a piece of the air between them. 'He seems close, and then, nothing,' he said. 'We just have to grab faster.'

'We have to find someone to grab at,' Robinson said.

He leaned back, rocking in the swivel chair at his desk.

'All right, Simon. Tomorrow, you and I, we start in again with the composite.' He smiled. 'Instead of going fishing. That still seems our best chance. What do you think?'

'Legwork never hurts a case,' the old detective replied, though he doubted he had the time and energy for it.

'We should head home now,' Robinson said. 'I'll drop you off. And tomorrow, don't wear that gun, okay? I'm trusting you that you've got a proper license somewhere. But I sure as hell know you haven't got a permit to carry a concealed weapon.'

Simon Winter managed a small grin. He rose. The thought of sleep wasn't unattractive, and there, within the brightness of the police headquarters, any sense of urgency dissipated slightly as fatigue nibbled at his imagination.

With an effort not unlike a diver launching himself from a high board, Robinson kicked himself up and out of his seat. 'Let's go before the sun comes up,' he said.

The two men rode the elevator down to the ground floor

in late night silence, each filled with their own thoughts. When they stepped outside the cocoon of the police building, a wet warmth seemed to drape over them, as if there had been a storm nearby that had deluged some close area but just missed them. They walked through the lights to the detective's unmarked car and slid into their seats, staying just the smallest step ahead of exhaustion. Robinson slowly ground the starter on the car and gunned the engine twice, as if that could invigorate him as well. The police dispatcher's voice scratched through the radio speaker, and Robinson leaned forward, reaching for the knob to shut off the irritating, tinny sound, only to have his forearm seized by Winter.

He looked up at the old man, whose eyes had abruptly widened, and in the same moment, Robinson felt a surge of electric energy race through his own body, past all the frustrations and weariness, rendering him abruptly and completely alert.

Winter's voice was hard-edged, but almost breathless. 'That was the rabbi's place, goddamn it! That was the rabbi's address she just gave. I heard it! She just moved a goddamn hook and ladder company to the rabbi's apartment building!'

Robinson thrust the car in gear and smashed down on the gas pedal.

'Who's there? Goddamn it! Who's there?' Winter shouted, as if he couldn't remember.

Walter Robinson didn't reply. He knew. Two old people, one young and probably inexperienced police officer, and Espy Martinez.

And one other.

Espy Martinez had fallen asleep on the living room couch shortly after the two survivors had departed for their respective bedrooms. The police officer detailed to watching over them had repaired to the kitchen area, where he sipped coffee, tried to read a novel that the rabbi had recommended, and half dozed while counting the minutes before his shift changed and someone else would get assigned to a task he considered slightly glorified baby-sitting, and which had bored the interest out of him within five minutes of his arrival.

When the ringing of the condominium's fire alarm system had suddenly creased the air, he'd been on the verge of sleep, and he shot to his feet unsteadily, cursing in surprise.

Espy Martinez also rose up, a fear falling through her stomach, thrashing about in the semidarkness and disorientation of awakening in an unfamiliar room.

In the guest bedroom, Frieda Kroner had been having an unsettling dream, one that touched the shores of nightmare, where she had seen herself in a space she couldn't recognize and that seemed to grow increasingly smaller around her. Every time she tried to find the exit door, it seemed to move, just as she reached for the doorknob. The alarm bell sliced across this sweat-soaked sleep, and she awakened, shouting in German, 'Air raid! Air raid! Get to the shelters!' until a few seconds passed and she remembered where and what year it was.

The rabbi, as well, awakened abruptly, shivering as if cold, the ringing bell beating on him like a fighter's flurry of punches. He reached for his dressing gown and hurried from his bedroom.

The four people came together in near-panic and surprise in the living room.

The young officer spoke first. His voice was slightly on the high edge and rapid, as if the words were trying to keep up with his heartbeat. 'Look, everyone stay calm, just stay calm.' He said this, but of course his tone implied the opposite. 'Okay, stay together, and we'll head out, right now. . . .'

Espy Martinez took a step toward the door, only to be stopped by Frieda Kroner grabbing her arm.

'No!' the old woman shouted. 'No! It is him! He is here!'

The others turned to face her.

'It's the goddamn fire alarm,' the young policeman said. 'Let's stick together and get the hell outside.'

Frieda Kroner stamped her foot. 'It is him! We are being attacked!'

The policeman looked at her like she was crazy. 'It's a fire, damn it! We may not have much time!'

The rabbi spoke then, his voice quavering, but filled with calm. 'Frieda is correct. It is him. He is here.' He turned toward Espy Martinez. 'Do not move, Miss Martinez.'

The young policeman stared at the old people. He tried to force reason and calm into his voice, but these emotions were frayed. 'Look, Rabbi, goddamn it, these old buildings are fire traps! They can go up in a second! I've seen it! I've seen people get trapped! We've got to get out, and get out now! What floor are we on?'

The rabbi looked oddly at him. 'The sixth.'

'Goddamn it, don't you know that there's not a piece of fire-fighting equipment on the Beach that can reach this high? We've got to get downstairs, and do it now!'

The ringing continued, filling the air around them with insistence. They could hear voices penetrating through the apartment walls and door, and muffled sounds of feet in the hallway outside. They all stopped and listened, all hearing several panicked screams as well.

'See! Damn it!' the young policeman shouted. 'Every-one else is getting the hell out! Come on, once a fire gets going in these old buildings, boom! They just go! There's just not that much time! We've got to get to the stairway now!'

Frieda Kroner sat down abruptly on a sofa. 'It is a trap, yes. But it is him that has set it.' She folded her arms. Her voice rattled, but she managed to force the words out: 'He is coming for us now.'

The rabbi sat next to her. 'Frieda is correct,' he said. 'We open that door and we will die.'

'We stay here, we're gonna get cooked!' the young policeman insisted. He stared at the old couple as if they were completely out of their minds.

'No,' Frieda Kroner said. 'I will not leave.'

'Nor I,' said the rabbi. 'It is how he caught so many of us once. Not this time.'

'You're out of your minds,' the policeman said. 'Look,' he pleaded. 'I'm right with you. Even if this crazy old fucker is out there, he's not going to try anything with me by your side. Come on, let's go!'

'No,' Frieda Kroner repeated.

The young policeman raised his eyes, imploring the heavens to force reason on the obstinate old people.

'We're gonna die!' he shouted. 'Miss Martinez, help me.'

But Espy Martinez just stared at the old couple.

'All right,' the policeman said unsteadily, after letting a short silence speak for them. 'Look, let's do this: I will go out and check it out. I'll see what's happening, and I'll come back for you as soon as I know the coast is clear. If I can, I'll bring a fireman. Got that? Okay? You sit tight, and I'll be back with help. Miss Martinez, you come with me, at least then you'll be safe and out, okay? Now, let's go!'

He hurried to the door, and Espy Martinez took a single

step behind him, then stopped.

'No, you go. I'll stay here with the rabbi and Frieda.'

The policeman turned around. 'Don't be crazy,' he said.

'Go!' she answered. 'I'm staying.'

The young policeman hesitated, then thrust open the door and disappeared down the now vacant corridor toward a nearby stairway.

At first the two men did not speak as the unmarked car, headlights flashing, siren wailing, hurtled through the diffuse city lights. Simon Winter gripped the door until his knuckles whitened with the strain. The city seemed to race past them, like a film in accelerated motion.

Walter Robinson steered the car with death in his heart.

As the engine surged and the wheels squealed in complaint, as the force of motion pinned him to his seat, he realized that he was in real trouble. Everything that meant anything to him seemed suddenly to be threatened by the Shadow Man: his love, his career, his future. This knowledge drove him to desperate fury. He threw the car down the street with an urgency beyond anything he'd ever known, gasping for air as the speed seemed to rob him of wind.

Winter spoke first, groaning as the car spun briefly out of control, then righted itself with an anguished machine complaint.

'Hurry,' he shouted.

'I am,' Robinson replied between gritted teeth. He shouted out an obscenity as some red-flash sports car started to pull out in front of them. There was a blaring of horns as they swept past.

'Two blocks, hurry,' Winter urged.

Walter Robinson could see the building looming ahead.

He saw the beat of the police and fire strobe lights twisting and turning in the night. He slammed both feet on the brake pedal, and the cruiser swerved to the curb.

The two men thrust themselves out of the vehicle. Robinson stood by the door, peering toward a melee of people in nightgowns, bathrobes, and pajamas, milling about in front of the apartment building, dodging out of the way as firemen started to string hoses to a nearby hydrant, while others lurched into air tanks and seized axes.

'Espy!' he shouted. 'Espy!' He turned to Winter. 'She's not there,' he yelled. 'I'm going up after them.'

'Go!' Winter replied. He waved the young detective forward with a sweep of his hand.

But in that second, as Robinson turned, Winter had another idea, a cold-steel thought that took no affection or devotion into its equation. He did not follow Robinson, as the frantic policeman dashed across the street and, ignoring the cries of protest and danger that suddenly rose from the fire department personnel, burst forward into the building. Instead, Winter slid slowly to the side of the street, stepping back into a shadow of his own, in the lee of a building, only a few feet away from where the Shadow Man had stood himself a short time earlier, although he did not know this. He searched out a vantage point from where he knew he could see almost everything. The panorama of firemen and trucks, policemen and rescue workers, spread out before him. But he kept his eyes on the clutch of people who'd emerged from the condominium and who were standing about nervously, frightened, pushed by the equipment and fear just off to the side of the building, wearing bathrobes and worry.

The ringing in the hallways continued. Espy Martinez

turned toward the old people. But Frieda Kroner rose.

'We must get ready,' she said.

But before she was able to move, the lights in the apartment abruptly quit, throwing the room into complete darkness.

Espy Martinez gasped, and both old people cried out.

'Stay calm!' the rabbi shouted. 'Where are you, Frieda?'

'I am here,' she said. 'Here, Rabbi, at your side.'

'Miss Martinez?'

'I'm here, Rabbi. Oh, my God, I hate it! Where are the lights?'

'All right,' the old man said evenly, 'this is what he will do. He is a man of darkness. We know that. He will be here any second. Frieda?'

'I'm ready, Rabbi.'

The three of them stayed in the center of the room, listening for sounds other than the ringing of the alarm bell. Then, after a few moments, penetrating behind that noise, they heard the distant wail of sirens heading toward them. But these were overcome by a pungent, frightening odor that began to seep around them like the fear they all felt.

'Smoke!' Espy Martinez choked.

'Stay calm!' the rabbi insisted.

'I am calm,' Frieda Kroner said. 'But we need to get ready.' Her voice seemed to trail across the room, and Espy Martinez heard her disappear into the kitchen. There was the sound of drawers opening and closing, and then steps as she returned. At almost the same time, the rabbi seemed to move about the living room, and Espy Martinez heard a desk drawer open and then slam shut.

'All right,' the rabbi said. 'Let's wait for the policeman to return.'

The smell of smoke, not strong, but still insistent, swirled around them.

'Patience,' the rabbi said.

'Strength,' Frieda Kroner replied.

Espy Martinez felt the darkness seep over her and through her, wrapping itself around her like some graveyard mist. She tried to tell herself to remain calm, but slowly she felt the tug and twist of panic searching around within her, seeking a handhold. She could hear her breath coming in short, sharp bursts, almost as if each intake of wind wasn't enough to fill her lungs, and like some drowning person, she wanted to thrash for the surface. She did not know, in that moment, what she feared the most: the night, the fire that lurked somewhere in the building, or the man the old people were certain was moving toward them steadily. All these things became tangled in Espy Martinez's imagination, along with ancient and unresolved fears, and she stood stock-still in the black room, feeling as though she was spinning in some terrible centrifuge.

She coughed and choked.

Then she heard another sound, muffled, close yet not too close, an urgent pounding.

'What's that?' she whispered. Her voice was cracked.

'I don't know,' the rabbi said. 'Listen!'

The pounding sound seemed to vibrate in the room. And then they heard a loud, demanding voice: 'Miami Beach Fire Department! Anyone in there!'

The pounding continued, and then the voice and the sound came closer. Espy Martinez realized instantly that it was a fireman, moving down the apartment corridor, knocking on every door, searching for anyone who might have stayed behind.

'It's a fireman,' she said loudly. 'He'll get us out! He's looking for us!'

And before either of the old people could react to this,

she jumped across the living room, half stumbling in the darkness over some wayward piece of furniture. She seized the door and pulled it open as behind her both the rabbi and Frieda Kroner shouted: 'No! Don't open up!'

She did not hear them, instead flinging the door wide and calling out: 'Here! Here! We need help!'

She heard a man's voice from close by in the darkness and could just make out a shape heading toward her.

'Who is it?' the voice asked.

'It's me,' she said, 'and the rabbi and—'

The blow caught her around the shoulder and across the jaw, knocking her almost senseless and spinning her around. She fell back into the apartment with a half scream and groan. She did not black out, though she could feel her grip on her consciousness loosened, and she was suddenly aware that she was on the floor and that there was a shape hovering over her. A shaft of light sliced across the room, and in her dizziness she saw the rabbi had a flashlight in his hand. She saw too that the figure looming above her had a knife and he was slashing down at her, just as the rabbi hit him in the face with the beam of light. The glare seemed to cause him to alter his swing, and she felt the blade carve through the air just above her.

The Shadow Man straightened up, lifting his arm as if to block the light that coursed from the rabbi's hand, and he did not see Frieda Kroner, who had jumped to where Espy Martinez lay on the floor and who was swinging an odd black shape toward him with a great grunt of exertion. The shape thudded fiercely into his arm with a dull, iron noise, and he screamed in unfamiliar pain.

The old woman was shouting then, in her native tongue: '*Nein! Nein! Nicht dieses Mal!*' Not this time! And she swung the weapon again, and again it found flesh.

The light in the rabbi's hand wavered, flashing about the

room as he too sprung toward the Shadow Man from the opposite side, so that the attacker was bracketed as he straddled the fallen young woman. In the rabbi's free hand he held a large brass menorah, which whistled as it cut the air. His first blow smashed the Shadow Man's shoulder, and the rabbi roared a deep wordless battle cry with his effort. The flashlight fell to the floor, and for just a second Espy Martinez saw the rabbi standing like a baseball batter in the hitter's box, readying a second swing. Her head pivoted dizzily and she tried to push herself up, only to be knocked down by the force of the Shadow Man's leg as it passed by her. His foot caught her chest, and for an instant she thought she'd been stabbed.

She wondered in that moment whether she'd been killed, then realized she hadn't. She pushed herself up again, straining to hear past the guttural cries coming from Frieda Kroner, until she heard the rabbi say, quietly, breathlessly, like a man who had won a hard race: 'He's gone!'

And she realized this was true.

She felt as if the world was suddenly quiet, although in reality the room around her was still being riveted by the continuing sounds of sirens and alarm bells.

She turned in the darkness to Frieda Kroner, who was speaking to her in German. '*Hören Sie mich? Sind Sie verletzt? Haben Sie Schmerzen?*' Are you all right? Are you hurt? Are you in pain?

And oddly, she thought she understood every word, and replied: 'No, no, I'm fine, Mrs Kroner. I'm fine. What did you hit him with?'

The old woman laughed suddenly. 'With the rabbi's iron teakettle.'

The rabbi picked up his flashlight and shone it into their faces. Espy Martinez thought they all must look pale, as if death standing so close to them had left a bit of his color behind, but Frieda Kroner, at least, had a wild, Valkyrie look of triumph in her eyes.

'He ran! The coward!' Then she stopped, and said in a much quieter voice: 'I suppose no one ever fought back before. . . .'

The rabbi, however, was direct: 'We must get him! Now! It is our chance!'

Espy Martinez gathered herself, nodding her head. She reached out and seized the flashlight. 'That's right, Rabbi. Follow me.'

And grabbing them both, she led them out into the corridor, like a pilot flying through a thick fog, pushing through the darkness for the stairwell.

Walter Robinson, battling an unfamiliar panic, unable to see, trying to feel his way in the blackness and run at the same time, raced up the emergency stairs, his feet making a drumroll of urgency against the concrete steps. He could hear his breathing, forced, harsh, punctuated by the distant sirens and the continual ringing of the alarm system.

He did not see the body until he tripped over it.

Like a blind-side block, it sent him spinning forward, pitched out of control, smashing his hands against the stairs as he fell. He shouted out in surprise and fought to regain his composure. He gathered himself and reached down, almost seized by some emotion beyond fear at the thought that his hand would find the wizened skin of either the rabbi or Frieda Kroner, or worse, the soft touch of Espy Martinez. When he felt the bulk of the body, he was initially confused. Then, as he groped in the darkness, he touched the policeman's badge. He drew his hand back sharply and realized that it was covered with blood.

He bellowed then, as loud as he could, 'Espy! I'm coming!' anything, he hoped, that might distract the man he was certain was ahead of him. Anything that might make him hesitate in his deadly task.

He still could see nothing, and anything he might have heard was obscured by the inner cacophony of fear. He seized hold of the stair railing and bounded ahead, racing again for the sixth floor.

He called out again: 'Espy!'

And then from within the darkness, he saw a shaft of light, and heard a reply: 'Walter!'

He cried a third time: 'Espy!'

And then he saw the three of them as they flashed the light toward him.

'Are you okay?' he called out.

'Yes, yes,' she shouted. 'But he's here!'

Walter Robinson reached out and grasped hold of Espy Martinez, who wrapped her arms around him, and whispered, 'Jesus, Walter, he was here! He was here and tried to kill me. The rabbi and Mrs Kroner, they saved me, and he ran. He ran away when she hit him. But he's here still, somewhere.'

Robinson pushed her back and looked at the old couple. 'Are you all right?' he asked.

'We must find him,' the rabbi replied.

The detective removed his weapon.

'He's here somewhere, right in this darkness,' the rabbi said. 'In the building somewhere.'

But Frieda Kroner shook her head. 'No, I think he ran. Maybe down the other stairwell, at the other end of the building. Quickly, quickly, we must go!'

Trying to hurry their pace, Espy Martinez clinging to Walter Robinson, and the rabbi and Frieda Kroner walking with the gingerness of age but the urgency of need, the

four of them began their retreat down the stairwell.
Robinson took the flashlight and led the way, pausing only
at the third floor to briefly examine the body of the
policeman. The old woman gasped when the flashlight's
beam caught the red stain of blood across the man's throat.
But what she said, was: 'Faster, faster, we cannot let him
get away!'

Simon Winter clung to his spot of darkness, watching the
scene in front of the apartment building. There is a
moment when one is fishing in shallow waters that one
spots just the slightest ripple of motion, as an unseen shape
beneath the surface pushes water in a direction different
from the wind and the currents and the tides, and one
recognizes the closeness of their quarry. It was that subtle
shift in the hurried movements outside the rabbi's home
that Winter searched for. He thought: there will be one
person here whose presence has nothing to do with fire
and alarm and being forced from the comfort of one's bed
in the early morning hours, and everything to do with
killing.

So he let his eyes scour the scene, looking for that small
push against the flow.

When he saw it, he straightened up sharply, dark
excitement filling his core.

What he saw was this: a thickset man, dressed in simple,
dark clothes. The man was hunched over slightly, emerging from the building, allowing himself to be directed by a
fireman who had better things to do, toward the knot of
displaced people gathered by the side of the street.

Simon Winter took a step or two parallel to the man.

He saw him disappear into the midst of the crowd,
picking his way from the front to the rear. The others were
all staring ahead, up toward their homes, searching for

smoke and flames, but seeing none, impatiently waiting some signal or information from the fire personnel who were hurrying in and out of the building.

But this one man seemed to have none of the same concerns.

Instead, he maneuvered slowly through the throng of anxious people, head down, obscuring his face, working steadily toward the back and the darkness of the street behind them.

Simon Winter picked up his pace.

He could not see the man's eyes, could not see his face, but he knew. For a moment he twisted about, trying to spot Walter Robinson or any other officer who might help him. But he could see none. He realized that he had stepped from the shadows himself, onto the sidewalk, and was caught in a shaft of light thrown by an illuminated store sign. Winter took a step into the street, just as the man looked up for one second and saw him, standing out, staring at him.

Both men froze, in recognition.

Then, suddenly, from behind them, in a sound that defeated sirens, alarms, and the noise of the fire-fighting machinery, Simon Winter heard a voice. It was raised high, but not a scream, more a sentry's great shout of alarm.

The words were in German and they fractured the night: '*Der Schattenmann! Der Schattenmann! Er ist hier! Er ist hier!*'

CHAPTER TWENTY-SEVEN
Morning

Simon Winter ran with a speed he'd not felt in years.

The street around him seemed a tangled maze of parked cars, shrubbery, garbage cans, and city debris. He swept forward with the energy of a man much younger, settling into a dogged, quick pace, thinking that this was not a sprint he was running, but a marathon. He could just make out the solid shape of the Shadow Man as the killer darted from darkness to murky gloom, dodging the shafts of light thrown by street lamps and the occasional store sign.

He had nearly a block-length lead on Winter at the start of the race, but by the time the Shadow Man emerged from the side street onto Ocean Drive, the old detective had cut a third of that away and left it behind him. He could hear the slapping sound that his basketball shoes made against the brick-red sidewalk, and he stretched his stride farther, so that his long legs rapaciously chewed up the distance.

The streets were empty in the predawn darkness.

The young people that were so prevalent everywhere on the Beach had slid away in assignation or frustration, leaving the nightspots quiet, lights dimmed. The usual thump of iron-hand music had evaporated into the night. No fast cars squealed their tires and accelerated in youthful posturing. No giggling, alcohol-smeared voices called out to each other. No crowds jammed the walkways searching for adventure. It was the dead time of the night, when fatigue even afflicts the young, just before night loses its grip on the city and daylight slowly fingers the horizon, searching for the morning.

Even the police and fire trucks that jammed the street outside the rabbi's apartment seemed suddenly to be nothing more than ancient memory to Simon Winter. If there were city sounds of sirens and urgency, they were distant, like childhood recollection.

He was alone as he ran, save for the specter ahead of him, dodging across the width of Ocean Drive, leaving behind the meager lights of the restaurants and bars that were only a short time earlier jammed with people.

Winter breathed in hard, and listened to the ocean.

It was off to his left, running parallel to his course as he pursued the Shadow Man. He could hear the waves beating their eternal tattoo against the shore.

He swept past the last of the night spots, slicing now next to high rises like so many huge monumental blocks that obscured the beach and ocean from the street. He could feel a stitch forming in his side, but he ignored it and ran on, letting the pounding of his feet fill him, keeping his eyes on the man ahead, who had settled now into a steady, fierce pace of his own.

I will run him into the ground, Winter told himself.

I will chase him until he turns gasping for air, exhausted.

And then I will have him, because I am stronger than he.

He bit down hard on his lip and then let air burst out from his lungs in a great gasp.

Other small pains tried to force themselves onto his

consciousness – a blister that erupted on his foot, a dull ache in his leg – but he ignored these, then negotiated with them. If you do not cramp up on me, calf muscle, then I will soak you for a long time in warm water, which you will enjoy and which will restore you. So I make this promise to you: give me this race and I will repay you tenfold, but just do not cramp up now. And as he said this to himself, the pain seemed to subside, and he picked up his pace slightly, wanting to laugh at the shape ahead of him.

He saw that the Shadow Man no longer dashed from darkness to shade, that he now ran straight ahead, arms pumping, an arrow seeking to simply outdistance his pursuit. This encouraged Winter, and gave him some new strength. He thought: now, perhaps finally, after all these years, you too know a little bit of the fear that arrives when someone relentless is on your heels. Now, perhaps, you know a little bit of what it was like for so many others. It's hard, isn't it, when you want to hide but you have no time, and the pursuit at your heels is striding closer with every yard?

Now, you've felt panic for the first time.

And I hope this feeling hurts.

He ran on, letting all the world around him slide away, until he saw only the Shadow Man's back as the killer fled, block after block, straight down the island toward the southernmost tip of Miami Beach.

Simon Winter saw the Shadow Man glance back once and then increase his speed, and he recognized this for what it was, the precursor to evasion; so when he suddenly shifted direction, like an athlete on a field of play, slicing off into a walkway that cut next to the end of a condominium building, Winter was ready, already sprinting hard, so that the change in direction wouldn't give his quarry even a moment to hide in some dark corner. The

Shadow Man must have felt the distance between them diminish, because he did not hesitate. Instead, he raced down the walkway and smoothly vaulted over a fence, heading toward the wide stretch of beach and the ocean beyond. Winter was prepared. The fence was chain link, about eight feet high, designed to keep people walking on the sand out of the condominium's property. He tried to take it in stride, grasping hold of the metal links and clambering over the top. He tossed a leg forward, but one of the sharpened wire links on the uppermost rim caught the cloth of his pants and he tumbled forward, momentarily losing his balance.

For a sickening instance he felt himself suspended in the air, and then he pitched out, falling hard to the solid packed sand beneath him.

Pain rose up and grabbed him.

Red hurt filled his eyes and he felt like a fighter who takes a blow to the chin, unsure whether he was still standing or had fallen to the canvas.

He lost his wind, and a momentary head-spinning dizziness wrapped around him. He had a taste of gritty sand in his mouth, and he forced himself to one knee, shaking his head to clear his thoughts.

He peered down the beach unsteadily. In the gloom of light thrown by the apartment building, he could just make out the shape of the Shadow Man running on the hard gravel and coral sand a dozen yards from the edge of the white-rimmed surf. His fall had lost him his advantage, and he pushed himself up, making a quick inventory of his body, searching for broken bones, and found none. Shaken, he stepped ahead unsteadily.

Simon Winter took a deep breath, gritted his teeth and started running again. First one hesitant stride, then another, squeezing speed past pain, recovering the pace that he hoped would shorten the distance between them. He could feel a trickle of blood at the corner of his lip and a contusion forming on his forehead and he thought he'd cut himself when he fell to the earth, and then, slotting these with the other stiffnesses and pains that were abruptly shouting for attention, he pushed on, ignoring them all.

The crash of waves against the beach was stronger now. He ran, keeping cadence with the rhythm of the ocean.

Night seemed to be loosening around him. He was suddenly aware of where he was: racing through the spot at the very tip of Miami Beach, where they'd come across poor Irving Silver's clothes, past the small, empty park across from Government Cut with its huge schools of tarpon, heading out the long rock jetty that reached far into the ocean.

As he ran, Winter thought: the Shadow Man has been here before and he is comfortable in this darkness. He thinks he owns it, but he does not know that I have been to this place as well, and so it is as much mine as it is his.

He clambered up onto the rocks and then to the wooden walkway that the fishermen used. You're here, he thought, somewhere straight ahead.

The old detective peered into the vaporous night. His eyes searched over the dark, hunched shapes of the black boulders that made up the jetty. And he thought: one of those figures breathes and waits.

From where the fishermen's platform ended, the jetty pushed more than a quarter mile farther into the sea. Winter stopped and reached slowly beneath his jacket, removing his old service revolver.

Then he stepped to the end of the fishing platform, still staring out at the haphazard jumble of jagged rocks. White spray slapped at the slick black shapes.

Did you know, he asked carefully, you were running to the end of the earth?

He nodded to himself. He ran to the darkness. He ran to where he knew there would be no light.

Simon Winter's hand rested on a wooden barrier constructed at the limit of the platform. I have fished here, he thought. It is time to fish again.

He knew a cautious man would simply wait there until light slid up over the horizon. He lifted his eyes and looked to the east and thought there might be just the smallest graying at the edge of the world. If he waited, he realized, soon enough a police car would come along, and soon enough dawn would mold shapes out of the blackness of night. But even as he thought of patience and delay, and recognizing that he'd pursued the Shadow Man into a corner, he clambered forward, over the wooden barrier, onto the glistening, wet jetty rocks. He continued searching for the man lurking in the remaining darkness, somewhere ahead of him. He thought: do not give him time to think. Do not give him time to catch his breath. Don't give him the time he needs to gather himself and prepare for you. Let the fear of the chase work hard for you. No one has ever growled at his heels the way you have this night. Take him now, when he is being hurt by this uncertainty. Although he did not say this to himself, it was almost as if Winter was afraid that by waiting for the morning half-light to show over the horizon, his quarry would somehow evaporate and disappear in the brightness of day.

This is our time, he thought. Now.

Moving slowly, trying not to lose his balance and slip on the wet rocks, he slowly worked his way toward the end of the jetty. He was alert, on edge, fighting to keep himself steady and knowing that somewhere, amidst the blackness, the Shadow Man had turned, hunkered down, and was waiting for him.

He said a small prayer, wishing that perhaps a stray light from the rich man's development on Fisher's Island would slap the jetty, just enough so that he could see the Shadow Man, in whatever crevasse he hid. This prayer, however, went unanswered. Muttering an obscenity, Winter pushed foward gingerly, trying to be certain of each step he took. The basketball shoes that had served him so well in the race down the street now threatened to betray him. They gave him little purchase on the satiny surface of the jetty rocks.

He felt his foot sliding, and he thumped down, catching himself before slipping into the sea waters. The edge of a rock creased his knee, sending a sharp pain through his leg. He cursed quietly, beneath his breath, and rose again, slightly unsteadily, pausing to search ahead, narrowing his eyes as he looked down the length of stone shapes.

But in that moment's hesitation, the Shadow Man surged from the darkness between two rocks, grunting with a great burst of force, driving his knife blade at the old detective.

Winter pivoted at the sound coming at him, lowering his shoulder to absorb the force of the assault. It was as if a piece of the night had risen up against him. He tried to bring his weapon to bear on the shape that thrust at him, but could not find the human shape in the grip of black that charged at him.

He shouted out, some crazed sound of fear, knowing that it was probably a knife slicing the night, hunting for his flesh. He grabbed out with his free hand to ward off the blow. For a second he felt a razor's breath jab through his palm, and he grabbed at the pain before it could find his chest, wrapping his fingers around the Shadow Man's wrist.

He realized that the same slippery dark world that had bedeviled him and had made his feet slide on the rocks had compromised the force of the Shadow Man's attack. Instead of striking out like some deadly feral snake intent on the kill, he had scrambled, slithering, losing some of his strength and forcing the knife slightly astray. Despite Winter's grip on the Shadow Man's arm, it bore down, slicing into the loose folds of his windbreaker, fraying his shirt, where, for an instant, it was caught like a fish in a net.

The momentum of the assault tumbled Winter backward. He felt himself falling, twisting like a drunk on the ice, slamming down hard against the rocks. He could feel the thickly muscled forearm still in his grip – he knew he could not let it loose and expect to live – and he dug his fingers into the man's flesh, holding the knife at bay, still struggling to bring his pistol around. The Shadow Man grabbed at him, and Simon Winter felt his own right wrist encased by a powerful hand.

Locked together, the two men thrashed on the rocks, strength against strength, trying to gain an advantage that they could turn into death. Winter pushed a knee forward, locking it against one boulder, and he used this to create leverage, jerking himself around, feeling a momentary weakness in his assailant. Both men groaned hard with exertion, saying nothing, but letting their grip try to speak for them.

The Shadow Man's breath was hard against him, and Winter bellowed in pain as the man's teeth tore into collarbone. The Shadow Man drew back and Winter smashed a shoulder toward the man's nose, hearing a thudding grunt as he connected. But the force of the thrust threw them both off balance. Like an old tree battling a hurricane wind, they swayed, then toppled hard. Still clasped together like a pair of murderous dancers, they rolled from the jetty, crashing once, then twice, against the sharp rock edges, and then tumbling into the thick, warm saltwater.

For an instant they plunged beneath the surface, still entwined together, still struggling. Then they burst upward, their heads breaking the ink-black surface simultaneously.

Winter gasped for air as the two men twirled amidst the waves. There was no longer anything beneath his feet, nothing to push against. They both dropped beneath the surface again, then rose, kicking, back into the air.

He could feel the Shadow Man pushing the knife inexorably toward his ribs, seeking to cut out his heart. Again he tried to bring the revolver, still locked in his grip, to bear, but the man's hand was too strong. The pistol wavered just inches away from where a bullet might do some damage, while all the time the point of the Shadow Man's knife sought to end the struggle.

A third time they slid beneath the dip and sway of the waves, the weight of water punching him like a fist. When they burst through the surface again, Winter realized they had thrashed their way farther from the beach and the jetty. For an instant, as they churned in the blackness that enveloped them, he could just make out the Shadow Man's eyes.

And what Simon Winter saw first, in the final darkness of this last night, was something both awful and simple. They were gripped in an odd stalemate of strength, and there was only one way to break it. He knew, right in that second what it was he had to do.

He understood: the only way to kill him is to let him kill me.

And so Simon Winter suddenly pulled the Shadow

Man's knife hand hard toward his side, letting the blade find the flesh above his hip, just beneath his ribs and away from his stomach, in what he hoped would not be a fatal stab. The sudden pain was sharp, a wet, horrific hurt as his body absorbed the blade.

The motion took the Shadow Man by surprise, throwing him off balance, and in that small time, he did not drive home the advantage that Winter had given him. His training and instincts, which should have caused him to raise the knife point up hard, killing the old detective, for the first time perhaps ever, failed.

As the knife hesitated in his body, Winter savagely reached across and grabbed his gun with both hands. Doubling his strength, he jerked the weapon up against the Shadow Man's chest, and shouting a great bellow of pain and rage that rose above the crash of the surf, he called on the old gun that he'd worn for so many years to answer for him one final time.

The water muffled the shots as he fired. But he felt the revolver buck in his hand and he knew that each bullet was smashing home.

He pulled the trigger five times.

A wavelet splashed in his face, and he felt the Shadow Man abruptly, almost gently, release his grip and slide back away from him. Winter gasped for air.

In the last darkness of night, Simon Winter saw a look of confused surprise on the killer's face. He felt the Shadow Man's hand drop from the knife, and then the blade fell away from his side, falling into the warm water. The old detective saw death just begin to seize hold of his adversary, but a final outrage soared within him, pushing past all the pain and shock. He reached across a wave, grasped hold of the Shadow Man's white hair and he pulled it toward him, jamming his revolver into the man's mouth open in the astonishment of dying. He whispered harshly, 'For Sophie, God damn you, and for all the others too.' He held the pistol steadily for just a half second to let his words crease the last moment of the Shadow Man's life, and then fired his final shot.

The sound echoed briefly across the waves, then was lost in the noise of the surf.

Walter Robinson drove the squad car slowly over the loose coral rock and sand of the access road adjacent to the ocean. In his left hand he held a powerful spotlight, which cut through the last of the night gloom like a rapier through loose folds of cloth. He swept the light in an arc across the expanse of empty beach, the beam dancing across the waves as they rolled toward land, following it with his eyes, searching for the old detective.

'Do you think he's here?' Espy Martinez asked quietly.

'Yes. No. Somewhere,' Robinson replied hesitantly. 'They both are.'

She did not respond to this, but continued to peer through the graying darkness. The rough stone of the road crunched beneath the tires of the policeman's car, and she cursed the noise it made. She tried to sort through all the sounds of the end of the night; the car engine, the tires against the road, Walter Robinson's harsh breathing so unlike the softer sounds he made when he slept by her side, the nearby rumble and slash of the surf against the shore. She thought if she could simply pigeonhole each sound, identify it, qualify it, assess it and discard it, then she would finally come across a single tone that was different, and that would be Simon Winter.

Or, she thought swiftly, the Shadow Man.

She had watched Walter Robinson plunge like a diver into the crowd of elderly people outside the rabbi's apartment, demanding, shouting questions at the gathering, a wild man, possessed. 'Did you see an old man? Did you see a man with a knife?' The rabbi and Frieda Kroner had accompanied him, rapidly speaking in several languages, like a pair of simultaneous translators. The people surrounding the detective had looked skittish, riveted by the suddenness of fear, unable to speak, until one ancient woman, clutching at the arm of an equally ancient man, had tremulously raised her hand.

'I saw,' she had said. 'I saw something.'

'What?' Robinson had demanded.

'A man. Not a man with a knife. But a tall man with white hair.'

'Yes, yes, where?'

'He ran,' the old woman said. She lifted her arm and Espy Martinez had seen a bony finger quiver in the air as if fighting a gust of wind, pointing to the ocean beach. 'He ran that way as if he were chasing after the Devil . . .'

She no longer knew how long they had been searching for the old detective. Ten minutes that seemed to be a thousand. A half-hour that was longer than any day she'd known. It seemed to her that each minute that slid past them laughed cruelly, mocking their hunt.

'He could be anywhere.' She cursed beneath her breath. 'We don't even know if they came this way . . .'

'I think they did,' Robinson replied, still swinging the flashlight's beam toward the beach and the waves beyond, his head halfway out the open window of the police cruiser. 'If he'd gone North, he would have been turning toward all the downtown lights. No, he would come this way. He'd run for the darkness.'

'And Simon?'

'Simon would chase after him.'

Espy Martinez took a deep breath. 'It will be daylight

soon,' she said. 'Maybe we'll spot him then.'

'That will be too late,' Walter Robinson replied. His hand clenched the steering wheel tightly. He wanted to gun the engine, surge forward, anything that would make him feel as if he were a part of the pursuit and not simply wandering about aimlessly.

Espy Martinez looked at the set of Robinson's jaw, saw the frustration tightening the muscles of his forearm. She felt helpless, like a physician standing at the bedside of some terminal patient. She turned away and continued sorting through the sounds again. A distant siren. A breaker finding the shoreline. Her own heartbeat in her ears.

And then, at that moment, something different. A single cracking sound, like someone far away stepping on a dry branch. A noise that rode the air directly to her like a lover's whisper.

'Stop the car!' she shouted.

'What? What? Did you see something?'

'Did you hear it?' she asked.

'What?' Robinson replied. 'Hear what?'

But Espy Martinez was already jumping from her seat, slamming the door on the still-rolling vehicle. As her feet hit the sandy road, she cried back over her shoulder, 'A shot, I heard a shot. . . .' Robinson jerked the gearshift into park and leapt after her.

Simon Winter rocked on the top of the waves like a child in a cradle. He could feel his life's blood slipping through the knife wound in his side and it seemed to him as if he was wrapped in an immense warmth.

He thought of Frieda Kroner and the rabbi, and he spoke out loud to them: 'You are safe now. I did what you asked.' In the same moment, he pictured his old neighbor and thought: Sophie Millstein, I have paid my debt.

He did not feel any pain and this surprised him. All the deaths he'd known over so many years had always seemed to him to be so many rippings and tearings, he had always assumed that violence was the bridegroom of pain. That he felt only a slight lightheaded dizziness intrigued him.

The weight in his free hand reminded him that he still held his empty revolver. He leaned back, as if reclining on the waves, and considered for an instant that he should simply let it slide from his fingers into the black water beneath him, but he could not bring himself to do this. Inwardly, he told the weapon: You did what I asked, and I am grateful. It was what I expected and you do not deserve to be abandoned and thrown away after such service, but I do not know if I have the strength to lift you up.

Still, he tried, failing the first time, then coughing back some sea water, and succeeding in slipping the weapon back into his shoulder harness, which gave him an immense sense of satisfaction.

Simon Winter took a deep breath. He clasped one hand over the bleeding wound, and with the other, he took a single, great overhand stroke, swimming for an instant.

He thought to himself that it would be nice to die on the beach, that when he slid away from life it would be good to have solid ground beneath his feet, so that when he had to face death alone, he could do so squarely. But the long stretch of sand was more than fifty yards distant, an impossible trek, and he could sense the tug of the tide, pulling him further from the shore. He swept through the water again with his free arm, but exhaustion abruptly filled him, and he told himself that choosing the site of one's own death was something of a luxury that few people could afford, and that he should pay this no mind, but accept what the next few minutes had in store for him. But, even with this thought ringing in his head, he found his arm pushing past the fatigue brought on by the chase, the fight and the wound, and he struggled again against the current.

This made him smile.

I have always been stubborn, he thought. I was a stubborn child, and I became a stubborn young man and years passed and I turned into a stubborn old man and that is what I am now and fighting is a good way to die.

He kicked hard with his feet, trying to swim with the last bit of strength that he had. He gasped for a breath of air, and saw something that astonished him, coming from the beach, piercing the gray hour. It was a shaft of light, and at first he thought it was death coming for him, and then he realized it was nothing so romantic; instead, it was something temporal searching for him, and he lifted his free arm above the waves as the beam probed the air about him, and finally fastened on his hand lifted high.

'There!' Espy Martinez shouted. 'Jesus, it's him! Simon!' She cried out to the old man. 'Simon! We're here!'

'Do you see ...' Walter Robinson began, but she finished, '... No, he's alone.'

He handed her the light as he started to strip off his jacket, his own weapon, socks and shoes. 'Hold the light on him,' Robinson insisted. 'Don't lose him.'

She nodded and stepped into the wash from the breakers, the tropical waters encircling her knees, trying to get closer to the old man. 'Go, Walter,' she said. 'Help him now!'

But she did not have to say this, as the detective was already thrusting himself headlong into the surf. He disappeared for an instant in a burst of white water, crashing through a breaker as it rolled onto the beach, emerging on the far side, his arms and legs stabbing furiously into the body of the ocean.

She kept the light riveted on the old man struggling far from shore. She could just barely make out Walter Robinson's dark form, darker even than the waters that gripped them both. She saw Winter's outstretched hand wobble and then dip out of sight, although she could still just see his shock of white hair like a whitecap on the waves. 'Go, Walter! Go!' she cried, although she didn't think her words would carry above the surf. Swim hard, she whispered to him. Swim fast, Walter.

He could feel the tidal pull helping him leave the shore in his wake, but he knew the fickleness of the ocean, for what was helping him this second, would turn on him treacherously when he reached the old detective. He kept his head down, rotating it only to grasp immense drafts of air and to check his bearings. His swim had none of the usual steady rhythm of exercise, but was filled with a fierce wrestling against the warm dark that encapsulated him.

Walter Robinson pierced the water rapidly. He was aware that the beam from the flashlight seemed to be dissipating, and realized that gray dawn was creeping across the horizon. He paid this no mind, but swam on, each pull with his arms straining his muscles. He called out once: 'I'm coming, Simon! Hang on!' but the effort to lift his head and shout disrupted the fury of his progress, and so he pushed his head into the waves silently, listening only to the splash of his hands and kick of his feet and the hoarse sound of his wind as he bit air from the last of the night.

Simon Winter put his head back, and glanced up once into

the sky, before he was smacked in the chin by a wavelet and he coughed out briny salt water. He tried to tread water with one arm while keeping his hand pressed to the wound in his side, but this was difficult, and he felt suddenly as if there were hands beneath the surface of the ocean pulling at him gently, coaxing him to relax and slide down under the surface. He kicked his feet again, keeping his head barely above water and thought for the first time that night, through the entirety of his pursuit and fight, that he was old, and that the years had left him with little except loose muscles and quick fatigue.

He breathed out slowly, and then he heard Walter Robinson cry to him. He tried to reply, but it seemed to him that the ocean surrounding him was filled with an insurmountable noise, and he could not. Still, he managed to raise his hand once and gesture, and he saw a flurry of explosions across the top of the waves as the young detective hurtled toward him.

'I'm here!' Simon Winter managed to say in what he thought was a shout, but was barely a whisper.

'Hang on!' he heard Robinson answer, and he did. He closed his eyes for an instant, thinking he was a little like an exhausted child fighting sleep, and then he was aware of the young man in the water beside him, and he felt Walter Robinson's furious grip on his arm.

'I've got you, Simon, just hang on!'

He opened his eyes and felt Robinson's arm encircling his chest.

'It's over, Walter,' he said quietly.

'Just take it easy, Simon. What the hell . . .'

'We fought, and I won,' Winter said. 'You make sure they know . . .'

'Are you hurt?'

'Yes. No.' Simon Winter wanted to say: How could a

man like that hurt me? But he did not have the strength.

'The Shadow Man?'

'Gone. I got him.'

'All right, Simon, you just lean back. I'll take you in. Just breathe easily and relax. You're gonna be okay. I promise. We'll go fishing tomorrow after all.'

'I'd like that,' Winter replied softly.

'It's gonna be okay,' Robinson continued. 'I'll save you.'

'I am saved,' Winter answered.

The old detective felt the young man's strength lifting him up to the top of the waves, and he leaned his head back and felt himself being carried forward, steadily, powerfully, toward the shore. He closed his eyes and let the rhythm of the swim rock him gently. He thought: I have become a tiny child again, cradled in my mother's arms.

Simon Winter sighed once, and opened his eyes. He looked back to the east and saw a vibrant red and gold band of light streaking urgently across the horizon.

'It's morning,' he said.

Robinson did not reply, but swam on, fighting the tide and the waves that slapped and pulled and insulted his every thrust, as he had so many times before. He was not precisely sure when the old man died, but he knew this was true as he staggered through the breakers, and felt Espy Martinez's hands reach for him, and gently lower them both to the beach, where, for an instant, the three of them all lay, side by side.

The sun rose hard, fast and insistent as if bored and impatient and eager to begin the day's work. It filled the beach with painful glare and an uncompromising heat that danced in waves above the chalky sand. The tropical sky was an iridescent blue, a Chamber of Commerce sky, marred only by an occasional puffed-out white cloud or

two that would meander lazily across the perfect palate li
an unwelcome visitor.

Walter Robinson and Espy Martinez sat shoulder-to-shoulder in the middle of the beach, their clothes drying stiffly on their skin. She had a blanket tossed over her shoulders, and she shivered once, though she wasn't cold and the air around her was building with the day's heat. Behind them a half-dozen police vehicles crowded the access road, and several uniformed officers were holding back a small crowd of the curious, gathering to watch the activity. A quarter mile off shore, a Coast Guard cutter and two Miami Beach police patrol boats wandered back and forth through the blue water. Martinez could see two divers readying equipment on the stern of one of the patrol boats.

'Do you think they'll find him?' she wondered out loud.

'I don't know,' Robinson replied. 'The tide was running out pretty fast.' He turned toward where a white-jacketed medical examiner was helping a pair of technicians enclose Simon Winter's body in a black vinyl bag. He caught one last sight of the old man's white basketball shoes as the zipper was sealed shut.

Robinson watched the medical examiner lurch across the sand. A light breeze ruffled the man's jacket, as he approached.

'The old guy didn't drown,' he said. 'There's a knife wound in his side. How'd he get that, detective?'

'He had a busy night,' Robinson replied.

The medical examiner huffed once, then moved off to supervise removing the body.

'Who was he?' Martinez asked quietly.

'The Shadow Man?' Robinson shook his head. 'I don't know. I doubt we'll ever know. He was someone once, but he probably changed names and identities so many times nce the war, that whoever he truly was was lost.'

She nodded.

'And now?'

'And now, nothing.'

She hesitated, then she placed her hand on his forearm. Walter Robinson picked her hand up and placed it to his forehead, as if it were ice that would cool his brow. Then he returned it to his own arm and smiled.

'Well, not exactly nothing,' he said.

In front of them, the technicians were lifting the body bag. Slowly, they started to struggle across the beach, their shoes digging down into the loose, chalky sand, as if the weight of the old man they carried had somehow grown and expanded and was almost greater than they could manage.

'Were you friends?' Espy Martinez asked.

'We were beginning to be,' Robinson replied. 'I thought he could teach me something.'

Martinez considered this statement for a moment, then said, 'I think he did.'

They sat quietly for another minute, until she heard her name called from the road behind them. They both turned and saw the rabbi and Frieda Kroner being restrained by a uniformed officer. The policeman turned toward the detective, and Robinson signaled him to let them pass.

'It's all over,' Robinson said, as they approached. 'You can thank Detective Winter for that. You won't have to worry about the Shadow Man again.'

'Poor Mr Winter,' Frieda Kroner said. She wiped at her eye. 'I shall thank him in a prayer and I will say one for all the others, as well.'

Rabbi Rubinstein nodded his head.

'One can never destroy every shadow, detective,' he said. 'Not from such a great darkness.' He reached over and grasped Frieda Kroner's arm in his and quietly added: 'But to destroy one, is a great enough achievement.'

Then the old pair of Survivors turned and, arm in arm, started back up the beach toward the city and their homes. For a moment, Walter Robinson and Espy Martinez watched them slowly pick their way across the beach as if memory itself were as loose and crumbling as the sand beneath their feet. Then he reached out and linked her arm in much the same way, and the two of them together followed.